THE KILLING GOD

THE KILLING GOD

GOD

BOOK THREE OF THE GREAT GOD'S WAR

STEPHEN R. DONALDSON

BERKLEY
NEW YORK

BERKLEY
An imprint of Penguin Random House LLC
penguinrandomhouse.com

Copyright © 2022 by Stephen R. Donaldson

Library of Congress Cataloging-in-Publication Data

Names: Donaldson, Stephen R., author.
Title: The killing god / Stephen R. Donaldson.
Description: New York: Berkley, 2022. | Series: The Great God's war; book 3
Identifiers: LCCN 2021057103 (print) | LCCN 2021057104 (ebook) |
ISBN 9780399586194 (hardcover) | ISBN 9780399586217 (ebook)
Subjects: GSAFD: Fantasy fiction.
Classification: LCC PS3554.O469 K55 2022 (print) |
LCC PS3554.O469 (ebook) | DDC 813/.54—dc23
LC record available at https://lccn.loc.gov/2021057103
LC ebook record available at https://lccn.loc.gov/2021057104

Printed in the United States of America
1st Printing

Book design by Kelly Lipovich
Title page art © Kirill Volkov / Shutterstock

To Ross Donaldson and Perryn Donaldson Pugh
FOR MAKING ME PROUD

TO Wyatt and Willa Pugh
FOR BRINGING JOY TO OUR FAMILY

AND TO Jennifer Dunstan
FOR EVERYTHING.

CONTENTS

THE KILLING GOD

PROLOGUE

OTHER INTENTIONS

Somewhere between life and death, or perhaps between wakefulness and slumber, Elgart floated. If time passed, he did not know it. If he had ever drawn breath, he could not remember it. But he did not feel the lack. He felt nothing except a lassitude that resembled a reprieve, a release from something unendurable. He had no desire to remember what it might have been. In this oblivious drifting, nothing could reach him. He would not be troubled by agony, or by the memory of suffering, or by the fear that pain may have drawn his secrets from him.

As he was, he did not have to choose his fate.

Nevertheless choices were made that changed his circumstances. They gathered the shreds of his mind. Fragments of memory emerged. At first, he felt nothing more than a vague sense that he did not want to sink lower. Somewhere below him lurked an excruciation that destroyed whatever it touched.

He wanted to rise. How else could he escape?

Perhaps he *was* rising; but the experience was not pleasant. As he drifted farther from the source of his agony, he remembered more of it. By increments, his tattered wits coalesced into a terrible shape.

Moving from agony to dismay, he recalled Archpriest Makh.

Yes, that was it: the source, the helplessness, the ordeal. The possibility that he had betrayed King Bifalt and Belleger.

Archpriest Makh.

Despite his swaddled drifting, Elgart felt a new pain. His memory of Makh had teeth. It bit like the jaws of a wolf. Involuntarily, he remembered that he had brought his ruin on himself.

Like a fool, a man who trusted himself too much, he had gone alone to the Church of the Great God Rile. There he had sat with the Archpriest and had tried to outwit his enemy. He had imagined that he could surprise or trick Makh into revealing the secrets of the Church. But he had been wrong.

The Archpriest wanted *his* secrets.

Makh's hands were like shovels, like cudgels. With impossible ease, he had made King Bifalt's spy helpless, unable to move any muscle that might have saved him. Then he had extended his power into Elgart's mind. Eagerly, he had commanded agony.

Obedient to the Archpriest's will, Elgart had felt exactly what his captor told him to feel, for as long as he was told to feel it. He remembered screaming.

The Archpriest had demanded Elgart's secrets. All of them. Any of them. But in particular, he had wanted locations. Warehouses. Hidden cellars. Abandoned storerooms.

Bullets.

It was probably a mistake that Belleger's kegs of gunpowder, dozens of them, were kept with the ammunition for the realm's many rifles. Crates of bullets by the scores would be destroyed if any of those kegs caught fire. Any single explosion among them would reduce an acre of the Open Hand to rubble and splinters. But where else could the gunpowder be kept? In Belleger's Fist? King Bifalt feared a blast among the old keep's foundations. More than the Fist would be destroyed. The realm's accumulated rifles were there. Belleger could survive the loss of a warehouse or two. The loss of its rifles would deprive it of its best weapon.

The Archpriest wanted to know where those kegs and crates were held. If the men and women he had seduced by sorcery could get at the bullets and gunpowder, Belleger would be crippled in the coming war.

As crippled as Makh had made Elgart.

But had Elgart given up that secret? Any of his secrets? He did not know. He remembered screaming. Oh, he remembered *that*. But he did not remember speaking. While he fought the impulse to confess himself, the horrors that Makh instructed him to feel had become his whole world.

Until—

—something.

Had the Archpriest been interrupted? Had there been sounds of violence? Elgart did not know. His head had been lifted. He had been given a drink of some kind, a rich wine like a kiss of sweetness. The taste had lingered in his mouth. It was still with him.

That taste should have been familiar. It had made his lassitude delicious. He wanted to remember his first taste of it.

Now he could recall every hurt that Makh had inflicted on him. Each detail was etched with acid. But the more distant past—Elgart's former life—had become as vague as mist. In pain, he had forgotten himself.

Still, choices he had not made continued to affect him. Slowly, he began to awaken.

As the hours or moments passed, he became aware of his body, his breathing, his appalling weakness. One muscle at a time, he realized that he was no longer sprawling on the Archpriest's table in the Church of the Great God Rile. He was not held flat, vulnerable, ready for torture and sacrifice. Rather, he seemed to sit half upright, propped on a hard surface that may have been stone. There was warmth on his face and brightness beyond his closed eyes. It made him think of sunlight.

He was not in the Church. Someone had moved him.

And while he pondered that mystery, he noticed that he could hear voices.

At first, they sounded as far off as his past life. When he concentrated on them, however, they became more distinct. Like the strange taste in his mouth, cloying and sweet, he should have been able to remember them.

One was crisp, authoritative: the voice of a woman accustomed to making decisions and acting on them. It said, "We must."

Another voice objected, "But we do not know his secret." It was softer. More seductive. "If we do not know how he does what he does, we cannot end it."

The first woman responded, "His death will end it."

"It will end *him*," countered the second. "It will not end what he can do. It will not prevent some other priest from wielding the same power. If we do not learn how his sorcery is exerted, we cannot protect ourselves. We cannot protect *anyone*."

"I understand you," snapped the first. "But we have no *time*. Pulling that cart costs days. It exhausts the horses. It may cost *many* days. I have hundreds of leagues to go. You must cross almost as many. Every day is precious."

Hells! thought Elgart. He *knew* that voice. If he could just remember—

The softer woman relented. "Then rouse him." She sounded frightened. "We must hope that he can be lured or coerced to betray himself."

Those women were as reckless as Elgart himself. Choosing to prod the hornet's nest— But he had always been that way. Surely they knew better?

Then a different voice said, "There is no need." A man's voice. Sleep or drugs blunted its edges. But something in it suggested a trickle of melting ice: a trickle that might become a torrent. "I will answer."

"Will you?" demanded the harsher woman.

Like a sigh, the man said, "It is why I have come so far. To answer."

Elgart made a subtle effort to open his eyes. Their lids were crusted with immeasurable hours or days of sleep. He managed only the thinnest slit. Through it, his sight was no more than a dull smear as if his eyes had forgotten how to focus.

Like the women's, the man's voice was familiar. Elgart had heard it more recently than theirs. He feared to recognize it.

"Then speak," said the crisp voice. "Tell us why you have come to Belleger. Tell us what your Great God wants here."

Here? wondered Elgart. He was still in Belleger? The notion gave him an obscure comfort. It was a foundation of sorts, the cornerstone of his life. It might help him remember.

Was the taste in his mouth a drug? A drug he had taken on some other occasion?

"I will," promised the man. The trickle of his voice was growing stronger. Its resemblance to flowing water increased. "If you will let me have my cross."

"Your cross?" asked the softer woman. "You surprise me. How can you need it now? It is only an object. It is not your mind."

"You do not understand." The man's tone suggested a shake of his head. "You took it from me, but you have it with you. I feel its nearness. It is not my mind. It is my knowledge of the Great God. Without it, my mind is empty."

That was the hint Elgart needed. He remembered the cross in the Church, the cross with the statue of a man behind it. He remembered sitting across a table from the Archpriest while Makh clutched like an old habit at his chest.

The cross—

"Explain," demanded the harsh woman.

"I will," promised the man again. "Only let me hold my cross. Only let me *see* it, if you will not give it to me. It will restore what you want."

The other woman said sadly, "Forgive our reluctance. You have given us cause to hesitate. Help us understand. Then we may be able to choose wisely. What part does your cross play in your knowledge of the Great God?"

With the sun on his face, Elgart felt air moving across his cheeks, a low breeze. He smelled grasses lush from the autumn rains, wildflowers mingled with the faint scents of meadow rue and mustard. Through the slits of his eyes, he recognized Makh on his right, no more than a pace away.

Repulsed by the sight—the memory—Elgart almost betrayed himself. He wanted to scramble away despite his weakness. For Belleger's sake, he remained still, feigning sleep.

The Archpriest sat as Elgart did, leaning on a boulder jutting from the grasses. Apparently, the old man had not been treated gently. His black robe hung open, exposing the bulk of a bare chest matted with hair and grime. His long hair and beard were a tangled mess, dirty where they had once been pure white. He had a look of confusion in his wide-set eyes. A deep bruise marred his cheek. His thick lips drooped.

Still, the jut of his nose promised certainty. His hands looked strong enough to fell an ox.

For a moment, he seemed to consider the sky overhead, asking it what he should say. Then he looked at the women.

With his eyes all but closed, Elgart regarded them. One of them was wrapped in a robe as white as new silk. The other wore a brown cloak over leather riding breeches. Something in his past made his heart beat faster.

Makh's voice held a note of turbulence as he answered. "The world you do not know is wide. It is full of strange sorceries. One of them allows the Great God Rile to store his thoughts and desires in an object like my cross. To store and express them. While I hold it, its contents are mine. When it is taken from me, they are gone. I cannot speak of them.

"If you will allow me to gaze at my cross, I can guess at its secrets. If you will allow me to hold it, I can answer you with assurance. Whatever you wish to know, I can tell you as if the Great God himself were speaking."

Instinctively, Elgart thought, No. Do not. Do *not*. He is too strong. He will torture me again.

"Very well," said the woman in white. "We will permit you to look at it."

Her companion seemed to question her. The harsher woman shook her head. While the brown-clad woman retreated to a saddlebag and opened it, the woman wearing white told Makh severely, "Do not imagine that we will put it in your hands. We suspect you of too much harm. We have no wish to hear your Great God speak. We will be content with your guesses."

"So be it," rumbled Makh. "I will attempt to satisfy you."

He sounded content.

Elgart knew what was coming. As he had done so often, he jumped to conclusions, and acted on them. Using every scrap of mind and determination that remained to him, he forced himself to stay still: a man too deeply asleep to move. But within his clothes, he began to tense his muscles and relax them, tense and relax them—one arm, the other, his chest, his abdomen—urging them to remember movement.

To remember specific movements.

The truest thing he knew about Makh was the way the old man rubbed at his chest as if he needed that touch to help him think. Or as if he needed to touch whatever his robe kept hidden.

From the saddlebag, the softer woman took out a wrapped bundle. Her manner betrayed her uncertainty as she handed it to her companion. In contrast, the woman in white did not hesitate. Discarding the wrapping, she held up the object it had concealed.

As she raised her arm, Elgart glimpsed a sheath strapped to her forearm. A throwing dagger.

Makh's cross was a smaller replica of the cross Elgart had seen in the Church. Smaller, but not small: it was as large as his hand with the fingers outstretched. It may have been made of bronze. In the sunlight, it shone like gold. And at its back, as in the Church, was a carving of a naked man with his arms draped over the crosspiece. Like the statue in the Church, the carving's eyes were rubies. They glittered redly at the Archpriest, promising power.

Trying to believe that he was ready, Elgart let the fingers of his right hand drift to his belt.

Makh sat forward. As cheerful as a rippling brook, he said, "I thank you. My Great God thanks you. I will answer you now.

"Give me my cross."

The woman in white tightened her grip on the metal. "I will not. A demand is not an answer."

In her tone, Elgart heard something he had never heard from any devotee of Spirit: a subtle tremor of strain.

"You will, Daughter," replied Makh. "You are the Great God's, as I am. You will obey his command. You cannot refuse.

"*Give* me my cross."

When the Archpriest reached out his hand, the devotee of Spirit took a step toward him. Tension showed in the knuckles of her grip. Her arm trembled.

"I *will* not," she repeated.

Grinning, Makh chuckled as if he had already beaten her. His hand looked strong enough to wrest the cross from a clasp of iron.

"Amandis," murmured the brown-clad woman. "Do not."

Elgart heard fright in her voice. Nevertheless he felt a rush of excitement. Amandis.

Amandis.

"I." The devotee moved another step closer. "Will." The determination in her eyes resembled fear. A rictus of effort stretched her lips back from her teeth. "Not."

"Fear nothing, Daughter," said the Archpriest gleefully. "One more step, and it will be done. Every question of your life will be answered.

"Give me my cross."

Elgart wanted to laugh himself. Suddenly, he was ready; sure of what he could do. He was no stronger than he had been while he slept. He felt stretched thin, as if he had gone too long without food—and far longer without water. Nevertheless he recognized Amandis and Flamora, the devotee of Spirit and the devotee of Flesh. He knew that they had saved him. He still had his last secret. And he had a debt to repay.

He was not going to fail. Not again.

"Amandis!" Flamora's voice rose. It hinted at panic. "Please!"

The devotee of Spirit's whole body was trembling. Elgart could imagine that she had never been beaten before; that her force of will had never cracked. As if she were quailing, she took one more step.

In triumph, the Archpriest stretched out his arm to snatch the cross from her—

—and Elgart struck.

In one motion, he whipped out the garrote from his belt, lashed it at Makh's grasp. The wire was as thin and strong as an artist of iron and the Decimate of fire could make it. It wrapped itself around the Archpriest's wrist; snagged there. When Elgart heaved with his whole body, his garrote ripped through Makh's flesh, through bone. It severed the old man's wrist.

Makh screamed. Blood spouted from the stump of his forearm. In red spray, his hand and his cross fell to the grass.

Elgart tried to move again. He meant to grab up the cross and batter it against the boulder, damage it on stone until it broke. If he accomplished nothing else, he meant to shatter the rubies. But he was too weak to rise.

Amandis was fast enough. While Elgart floundered on the grass, she hammered one of her daggers straight through the Archpriest's forehead into his brain. The Great God's servant was dead before his heart stopped beating.

"Destroy it," croaked Elgart. "Break the gems."

He wanted to say, It is the instrument of his sorcery. But Amandis did not hesitate. At once, she snatched up the cross and smashed its rubies against the boulder. Pain haunted the burnt umber of her eyes. Makh had taught her to doubt herself.

A heartbeat later, Flamora sprang at Elgart, flung her arms around his neck. They sprawled together on the grass while she kissed him. Her mouth lingered on his like the taste of drugged wine.

He gazed up at the clear sky, the brilliant sunshine. His eyes were too dry for tears. He understood nothing that had happened since he had confronted the Archpriest. But he was alive. That was enough.

PART ONE

ONE

QUEEN ESTIE ON THE ROAD

Queen Estie of Amika had told her husband that she would not return to her realm. Surely, he knew that she had meant Maloresse and Amika's Desire, her city and her castle-fortress. She had to go through Amika. Her road to the Last Repository crossed out of Belleger at Fivebridge. Past the Line River, it turned eastward toward the vast desert and the place where its newest stretches crossed the river's gorge. There, the theurgies of the Repository had built a bridge in the desert long ago, a crossing for caravans like Set Ungabwey's. Now it was sustained by a version of the same sorcery that kept the caravan-track through the desert clear.

In its way, the road was the crowning achievement of Estie's reign. It had cost her a number of years, the hard sweat of hundreds of workmen, and finally her father's direct opposition; but now it was complete: a comparatively direct link between Belleger, Amika, and the treasure-house of knowledge that was the Last Repository. Her road would take her to her goal with an ease and quickness that would have been inconceivable a decade ago.

Under better circumstances, she might have been proud of what she had accomplished. Now she had no time for pride. The Great God was coming. He might extinguish every life in Amika, Belleger, and the hidden library. When she thought about her road at all, she was grateful that it enabled her to travel swiftly. She had too little time.

Magister Facile had assured her that she, Estie, would learn the secret of her own nature in the library. There other Magisters would be able to identify the Queen of Amika's sleeping gift for theurgy. And when she knew what it was, she would also know whether she wanted it awakened. If she decided that she craved the use of her talent, those sorcerers would be able to deliver her true inheritance at last: the legacy that her father had concealed from her since the day she was born.

Before she and King Bifalt had parted, she had been honest with him. *I told myself that I was waiting for you. I waited for the day when you would choose to love me. But now I know the truth. I have been waiting to find out who I am.* Now she was eager to learn the truth.

For the same reason, she was also afraid. Her gift might prove to be a small one, useless in a time of war. And her husband loathed sorcery. He distrusted all sorcerers. Choosing to awaken her talent would mean turning her back on him. She could not forget the clenched anguish in his voice and face, in the blood on his mouth and the fire of his gaze, when he had protested, *I will never see you again.* Her eagerness seemed indistinguishable from dread.

Nevertheless she had other reasons for haste, better ones. While she was away, King Bifalt would be fighting battles that he could not hope to win. If she had not spent long years learning to compose herself, she would have been frantic to reach the Repository. She believed that the theurgists there had the power to save King Bifalt's realm—and his life.

She was riding in her personal carriage, a sturdy conveyance made for hard use and long trips rather than for the ostentation her dead father had preferred. Drawn by four dray-horses, it was large enough to seat six people with space to spare; it carried enough food and water for several days; and it had cabinets that could be opened to serve as bunks. Thanks to the care with which the stones of the roadbed had been fitted, the iron-shod wheels rolled smoothly, and springs on the axles softened the inevitable jolts. Even a weary old woman like Magister Facile could make her way to the Last Repository without discomfort.

There were twenty Amikan soldiers in the Queen's escort, men she had known long enough to trust. In particular, she had learned a fondness for their officer, Commander Crayn. With his sandstone eyes, his instinctive tact, and his willingness to question her decisions when they worried him, he suited her. He would keep her safe, care for her ordinary needs, and accompany her in silence when she wanted to be left alone.

Her fellow passengers were another matter. Oh, they were silent enough. But the character of their silence did not ease Estie's impulse to fret.

Magister Facile was a self-tightening knot of anger and anticipated bereavement. She sat in her corner of the carriage like a woman who had closed a curtain around herself. To some extent, Estie understood the old woman. Facile was angry at her circumstances; angry at herself for growing old while the man she loved remained young; angry at whoever had poisoned that man. But she had a more immediate grievance as well.

King Bifalt felt that she had betrayed him. She had concealed Estie's gift for sorcery from him while revealing it to Estie herself. Now he believed that Magister Facile had used his Queen-Consort for her own ends just as the Magisters of the library had used *him*. For that, Facile resented him. She had left her lover behind so that she could help him and Belleger prepare for the Repository's war. That should have been enough to earn the trust of Belleger's King.

But she did not say so. On the sole occasion when Queen Estie had questioned her, the sorceress had replied without unclosing her jaws, "I am cut off from Apprentice Travail." Travail had been her lover before she had left the Repository to serve King Bifalt. He was the only representative of her home who had been able to hear her across the many leagues between them. "Magister Avail speaks in my mind. He tells me Travail still lives. He is only failing, not dead. But he cannot hear me."

After that, Estie had given the old woman as much privacy as traveling together allowed.

The Queen's other companion, the monk of the Cult of the Many, maintained a different kind of stillness. The man known as Third Father sat with his head bowed. Apart from his breathing, he hardly

seemed to move. From time to time, he opened his eyes without looking around him. With his dun cassock cinched with white rope, his
head shaved into a tonsure, and his posture of humility, he could have
been an effigy of meditation.

Estie suspected that his stillness was a choice he had made long
ago. She had heard that he usually traveled on foot—and often for remarkable distances—despite his advancing years. When he sat for
hours without shifting or speaking, he seemed to be contemplating
thoughts that claimed his complete attention. What they might be,
Queen Estie could not guess. For all she knew, he had fixed his mind
on nothing more than silence.

But an hour or two before the carriage reached Fivebridge, he ventured to speak. Without raising his head or looking at Estie, he asked,
"Do you regret your choice of husbands, Queen?"

Startled, she replied at once, "No." Then she reconsidered. Third
Father's manner required the truth. "And yes. I regret that I have not
found my way through to him. We are separated by the iron of his
promises to me, and by his devotion to his people. I admire those qual-
ities in him. I do not regret that I married him. I regret that I am not
his equal."

If she were, Bifalt might learn to love her.

The monk shook his head gently. "You misjudge yourself, Queen.
You are not him. Why should you be? You have other strengths."

Firmly, Estie resisted her impulse to demand, Name one. Instead,
she said, "Yet I do not know myself. Help me if you can, Father. Do
you see a sorcerer waiting in me?"

He may have smiled. His posture and the shade inside the carriage
obscured most of his face. "No, Queen. I lack that gift. But sight has
other uses.

"I have studied the King. In the Last Repository, I saw that the
needs and desires of his younger self warred with each other. That truth
was unknown to him, yet it was plain to me. And I saw that his ignorance was both a weakness and a strength. His struggle enabled him to
surprise even himself. I thought then that he would serve Belleger well.
But I did not foresee how far his strength and weakness would carry

him. In the crisis which the librarian devised for him, he surprised me as well.

"When we spoke more recently, I saw that he has become the King that Belleger needs. He has been deeply wounded, and his hurts have made him bitter. But beneath his bitterness, his strength grows. He is not yet the man he needs himself to be. Nevertheless I believe he can become that man."

Abruptly, Magister Facile shifted in her seat. Sour with indignation, she snapped, "I disagree, monk. He dares to call Magister Marrow and the other servants of the Repository arrogant. He imputes the same arrogance to me. But who is more arrogant than the King himself? He speaks of his own people as *sheep*. I have heard him."

Taken aback, Queen Estie demanded, "As sheep? Why?"

The old sorceress muttered a curse under her breath. "For the obvious reason. He holds them in contempt. If they are frightened, they will scatter in all directions. Or they will follow anyone—or any *priest*—who offers to lead them. Like sheep."

For her own sake, Estie had caused Bifalt too much pain. Her desire to defend him now took the form of anger.

"Then find another word, Magister. They cannot both be arrogant, the librarian and King Bifalt. If his people are sheep, the King is their shepherd. They do not serve him. *He* serves *them*. Magister Marrow serves only his books. At the same time, he expects service from people who cannot refuse him. He does not care who is harmed by his demands."

In the obscurity, Magister Facile seemed to gather her outrage for a blistering retort. But then she caught herself—or the accuracy of Estie's response caught her. Sagging back against the cushions, she sighed, "Ah, Travail. What would you say if you heard me? I am an old woman, sick with age and ire. Others are able to care for you. I am not. And the librarian does not. He thinks only of his enemy."

Pulling the hood of her cloak over her head, she turned her face to the wall.

In an instant, Estie regretted her anger. Yes, Facile had manipulated her when she went to confront her father; but Estie had pardoned her long ago. Hoping that the woman would hear her, she said softly, "Forgive me, Magister. I should not have spoken as I did. You have earned more respect. The King takes too much on himself. If that is not arrogance, it is a kind of pride."

A kind that would not be satisfied until it killed him.

After a long pause, Third Father breathed, "There, Queen. That is one of your strengths. You have others." His tone quavered with age, not with pain. If he had been hurt as badly as anyone—as badly as King Bifalt and Queen Estie—as badly as Magister Facile—he had made his peace. "If he lives, the King will learn to prize them all. Then he will surpass himself yet again."

In the dusk of the unlit carriage, the monk resumed his meditative pose. So softly that Estie barely heard him, he murmured, "Thank you, Magister."

For a long moment, the Queen sat like a woman with her mouth full of questions which she had suddenly forgotten. Something had passed between her companions that she did not understand. Was Third Father grateful that the sorceress had charged Bifalt with arrogance? Were they pleased by her instant defense of her husband? Or did they want her to recognize that she too was arrogant, both like and unlike her husband?

She was Amika's Queen. She had brought about her own father's suicide rather than tolerate his threat to her realm. She had faced the massing Nuuri as if she could forestall an invasion by will alone. And she had imposed her road on both Amika and Belleger despite all the arguments King Bifalt and his counselors could array against her. How could she be so sure of herself without arrogance?

Yet she had accomplished none of that without help: without Magister Facile's power over her father, without the Devotee Lylin's defeat of the Nuuri Hearth-Keeper. Only the achievement of the road was hers.

What help did King Bifalt have? Elgart was gone. Magister Facile and Estie herself had forsaken him. He had only Klamath and Jaspid—and he shared none of his burdens with them.

She had assured him that she would never resemble the Reposito-

ry's librarian and the other Magisters there; but she did not fault him
for doubting her. She doubted herself.

The day before Estie had left Bifalt and the Open Hand, she had
sent a swift messenger to Amika. When she reached her own
lands at Fivebridge, she found Commander Soulcess and Chancellor
Sikthorn waiting for her, as she had instructed. And they had prepared
a heavy wagon laden with all the supplies she might need on her long
journey. In that way, they spared her the delay of a detour to Maloresse
and Amika's Desire.

Her plans would save her several days. Sadly, they would also cost
her a chance to visit her mother, Queen Rubia. The prospect of not
seeing her home and Amika's former Queen mother for perhaps the
last time made Estie ache. But she ignored that pang while she braced
herself to give Soulcess and Sikthorn, the stewards of her realm, her
last orders.

Both men knew that her road was finished. They had received those
tidings after sub-Commander Hellick had encountered Set Ungabwey's caravan. In addition, the Commander of her honor guard understood the necessity of keeping watch on the inlet of the Line's Cut:
an unlikely approach for the enemy, but worth guarding. He and the
Chancellor had already obeyed her command to imprison every priest
of the Great God Rile they could find. They had swallowed her decision to send all of her Magisters to King Bifalt. And Sikthorn had a
quick-minded man's grasp on the importance of making fleeing Bellegerins welcome in Amika. Bifalt intended to evacuate his entire realm
before the enemy struck. Now Queen Estie needed to entrust her stewards with forms of service that would disturb them more.

Walking, she led Soulcess and Sikthorn away from the garrison until she was sure that she would not be overheard. Glumly, she supposed
that giving them their orders privately could be considered a sign of arrogance. Whatever she said, she would not have to face the consternation
of her people when her intentions became known. By her own standards,
however, she was protecting the Commander and her Chancellor. She

was freeing them to ask their questions, raise their objections, and master their reactions without witnesses.

There was a chill in the air, a foretaste of winter. But the sun shone warmly out of a clear sky, touching Queen Estie's face with comfort. At this distance, the rush and twist of the Line River made a soothing murmur. Under other circumstances, the weather's kindness might have eased her task. Now it did not. There was too much at stake.

More out of respect for his years than for his wits, she addressed Thren Soulcess first.

"Thank you for obliging me, Commander," she said as if he could have done otherwise. "I am grateful for all that you and Chancellor Sikthorn have done for Amika. But our time is short. I will continue my journey in an hour. While I can, I must add to your duties."

Soulcess was a punctilious man, so clean and polished that he seemed to gleam in the sunlight. His reluctance as a fighting man might have disqualified him to lead the Queen of Amika's honor guard at a time like this, a time of war. But he had served under King Smegin, Estie's father. During that fraught time, his proven diligence, his manners, and his inability to draw his own conclusions had protected him from his monarch's cruelties. The Queen needed his diligence now.

"You are gracious, Majesty." He performed a fulsome bow. On occasion, he seemed unable to say anything without bowing first. "We have proven ourselves, I think." He may have meant that he had proven himself. "We can do more."

In contrast, Sikthorn looked more like an overworked scribe than a man who wielded his Queen's authority. But he knew when to be cautious and when to take risks. His diligence resembled the Commander's on a larger and more complex scale. Nothing that Estie required daunted him. And he had a rare gift: he could manage the Commander's shortcomings.

With a nod rather than a bow, the Chancellor remarked, "This will be an interesting time, Majesty." His voice sounded like a hinge that had not been tended for years. Still, he used it effectively. "No doubt, it will soon become more so."

Estie acknowledged him with a wry smile, but she kept her attention on Soulcess.

"I am sure you can, Commander. I will be clear. Any confusion now will cost lives." Before Soulcess could absorb that ominous statement, she said, "But first I must ask, where is sub-Commander Hellick?"

She had left him and his company of honor guardsmen patrolling the road ahead of her. At one time, she had planned to add him and his men to her escort. Since leaving King Bifalt, however, she had reconsidered.

Thren Soulcess had never been able to rule his expression. His sudden wince told the Queen that he expected her to disapprove of his answer.

"Majesty"—he swallowed hard—"I have recalled him."

Unable to stop himself, he bowed again.

Estie concealed her relief. Feigning displeasure, she demanded, "Against my instructions, sir?"

The Chancellor began to intervene. She stopped him with a small flick of one hand.

"Majesty," protested Soulcess, "I had only *thirty* men. Thirty to preserve order in Maloresse and keep watch on the whole of Amika. And our Magisters are gone. Hellick had *forty*." He looked to Sikthorn for support. "The Chancellor assured me that you would understand."

Queen Estie nodded. "Very well, sir." She made an effort to sound stern. "I do understand.

"Now I have new orders for Hellick *and* his forty men. Send them to the King in Belleger.

"I wish to be very clear, sir. War is upon us. King Bifalt needs those men more than you do."

The older man looked like he might turn away. Or, worse, he might bow again. But Estie did not give him time. Without pausing, she said, "Now I must ask what you have heard from sub-Commander Waysel. Has he finished delivering cannon to the Bay of Lights?"

On that subject, Soulcess was sure of his ground. He could answer with more confidence.

"He has, Majesty. Some days ago. As you instructed, he gave half of his men to the defense here. His return is imminent."

"Very good." Now the Queen shifted her attention to include Chancellor Sikthorn. Her next order would frighten the Commander, but its burden would fall on Sikthorn. "We have done what we can for the bay. Now we must attend to Amika.

"How many cannon remain to us?"

At once, Sikthorn showed his foresight. He had his answer ready. "Nine, Majesty, all siege-guns. We can forge more, but not quickly. We have exhausted our stores of iron."

Only nine? thought Estie. She had hoped for more.

Trying to keep up, Soulcess asserted, "They will suffice to defend the bridges, Majesty."

His statement elicited an honest frown from Estie. She did not want an argument. Nevertheless she was prepared for it.

"But that is not how we will use them, sir. I want them taken to the Last Repository. When Waysel and his men return, give that task to them. He has enough wagons. Tell him in my name to follow me as swiftly as he can. With the shot, chain, and gunpowder he will need."

Sikthorn simply nodded. He had expected this. But sudden alarm flushed the color from the Commander's face. He stared as if he had been stung.

"But—" he began, almost choking. "But, Majesty. The bridges! How will we defend them without cannon? If the enemy comes against us?"

Queen Estie gave her tone an edge to cut through the man's dismay. "You will *not* defend them, Commander. You will destroy them."

Soulcess gaped like a drowning man. He tried to protest and could not fill his lungs.

More gently, she told him, "The enemy will certainly come. When he has landed his army, he will strike first at the Open Hand. He must. It stands in his path. But when he has razed it, he will want my road. It will give him a direct approach to the Repository. Without it, he will be forced to pass through the whole of Belleger as well as the desert. *That* journey, he will fight to avoid.

"At any cost, he must be prevented from crossing into Amika. The

Line will block him at any other point. For the Repository's sake, he must not be permitted to use *any* bridge between the sea in the west and the desert in the east."

Again, the Chancellor nodded. "It will not be difficult, Majesty. If our stores of grenades and gunpowder do not suffice, we will manage with fire arrows and axes.

"The only question—"

"No, Majesty!" gasped the Commander. "With only thirty men? They are not enough! I will have to conscript—" There he ran out of air.

"I will help you, Commander," said Sikthorn while his companion struggled. "It will not be difficult, I assure you. And when the bridges are gone, we will be safe. The war will remain in Belleger. King Bifalt will fight it for us.

"The only question," he repeated to the Queen, "is *when*. The sooner we begin, the sooner we will finish."

"*That* will be difficult," admitted Estie. "I want you to save as many Bellegerin lives as you can. You must wait until the last moment. Until the enemy is almost upon you. Act then. Only then.

"Begin *here*." At Fivebridge, where her road would bring everyone fleeing from the Open Hand and central Belleger. "When that is done, destroy the other crossings at your best speed.

"Your task then, Chancellor, will be to feed and clothe and house and care for thousands of refugees. *Your* task, Commander, will be to preserve order, to assist the Chancellor, and to watch over Amika."

Soulcess wore his garbled comprehension and threatened pride like a rictus. He would think that she was turning her back on her realm. That she was fleeing to the sanctuary of the Repository. But she lacked the patience to comfort him. Sikthorn could explain her reasons when Soulcess was ready to hear them. She waited until the Chancellor said like scraping iron, "As you say, Majesty." Then she left him to deal with his companion's dismay.

She did not want another bow.

In one way, the Commander would be right about her. The responsibility for her people was hers, yet she had dropped it like a worn-out cloak. She was not proud of herself—and certainly not sure—as she returned to Commander Crayn, her escort, and her waiting carriage; but she could not have made a different choice. The implications of her decision to forsake her husband ruled her.

For the next three days, Queen Estie traveled smoothly among her guardsmen, trailing her wagon of supplies and three messengers she did not expect to need. The weather was kind despite the unspoken promise of winter in the east, cold enough at night to gild the grasses and gorse with frost, warm enough during the day to spare her the burden of heavier garments. In this region, the countryside was defined by gently swelling hills and shallow valleys clad in grasses or patches of bracken, and marked like signposts by small clusters of trees. Her road curved here and there to accommodate the counters of the terrain, but always it carried her eastward. And always it accompanied the course of the Line River, sometimes at a distance of a league or more, sometimes within arrow-shot of the hurtling waters.

As a kind of penance, she required herself to spend a few hours every day in her carriage, suffocating in Third Father's silence and in Magister Facile's woe. The rest of the time, she rode her horse in the company of her escort and Commander Crayn, taking advantage of the sunshine and crisp air. She could relax among the gruff observations, complaints, and jests of her guardsmen. And Crayn's casual conversation soothed her. He was not a fretting man. In his own way, he knew what she had asked of Soulcess and Sikthorn, and understood what she hoped to accomplish by leaving her realm in their hands. While she had nothing to do except follow her road, he attended to her physical needs, watched for signs of danger that she might not recognize, and talked with her about anything that came into his head.

As the days passed, Estie noticed more birds. In these less traveled stretches of Amika, they flourished. Alarmed by the carriage and riders, whole flocks swept up from the brush and scrub, swirled together overhead, then settled elsewhere as if by common consent. Smaller birds flitted here and there, or simply hopped away. And high in the sky, Vees beat their way southward, honking to each other like geese. Watching them, she felt a touch of regret, not because she envied their swift freedom, but because she knew so little about them. Ravens she could name, and robins, but no more than that. King Bifalt and the coming war had preoccupied her to the exclusion of almost everything else. She was ignorant of details that would have been obvious to any farmer or shepherd: details that she would have enjoyed knowing.

On the fourth day, she was still in her carriage, emulating the silence of her companions, when Commander Crayn called an unexpected halt. As the carriage slowed to a stop and settled on its springs, Queen Estie opened the door. At once, the breeze flicked her cheeks, tossed her hair. It was not blowing hard, but she sensed that it had claws. Winter was coming closer. Nevertheless she stood in the doorway while Crayn brought his mount closer.

"Majesty," he announced quietly, "you should see this."

She heard the hint of concern in his voice. Without waiting for her coachman to bring the step-stool that would have allowed her to make a dignified exit, she jumped down to the road.

The Commander dismounted with the ease of long practice, tossed his reins to one of his men. Touching Estie's arm, he nodded her off the road. When he had escorted her a few steps beyond the churned dirt left behind by the roadwork, he pointed her attention northward.

Beyond the dirt, she saw a slope covered with drying grasses and wilted wildflowers, a low rise, and—in the distance—a copse dense with shrubs and brush.

"Trees, Crayn?" asked the Queen, teasing him. "I have seen trees."

"The birds, Majesty," he replied. "Consider the birds."

She squinted in the cold for a moment. Then she saw them.

In small, scattered bunches, birds—she would have called them blackbirds—rose from the branches, pounding the air. Unlike the flocks she had seen earlier, swirling together, they seemed to fly in disarray. Some of them settled back down among the trees while others scrambled upward.

"Some movement disturbs them, Majesty," said Crayn. "Those that return to perch are at the fringes of the woods. Those that burst into flight mark the disturbance." He paused to be certain, then turned to face the Queen. "It comes toward us."

Instinctively, she followed his example. No longer staring at the copse, she asked, "What do you suspect?"

He shrugged. "A lost cow, perhaps, Majesty. Or a wild boar? Wolves in pursuit of a deer?"

Queen Estie was Amikan. "Or spies?"

"Or an ambush," suggested Crayn.

She frowned, thinking. An ambush was implausible. She could not be taken by surprise at this distance. But a spy? She had no idea who would spy on her road in this region, or why. But she did not need an explanation. The possibility was enough.

Over her shoulder, she glanced at her escort. The guardsmen were still mounted, waiting casually for orders. None of them paid any particular attention to the trees or the birds. But she saw several men loosen the shoulder straps of the rifles General Klamath had given them while they shared the training of his soldiers. Others checked their satchels of bullets. Like Estie, they were wary of spies.

She gauged the position of the sun, then made her decision.

"We will rest here, Commander. It is not too early for a meal. And while we are busy with ordinary activities, I want you to learn the truth of that copse. Take as many men as you choose."

"As you say, Majesty." Crayn's attempt to suppress a grin twisted his mouth. "We will enjoy capturing a spy or two. Any Amikan who cannot move more cautiously deserves to be caught."

Like a man with nothing on his mind, he returned to his guardsmen. Groaning in apparent relief when they heard his instructions, they began to dismount. Some of them turned to the chores of unpacking food and firewood. Others saw to the needs of the horses. But five remained in their saddles.

In no particular hurry, Commander Crayn stepped back onto his own mount. Gathering those five around him, he took them west, away from Estie's destination. First at a canter, then at a clattering gallop, they left like men with urgent messages to deliver to Maloresse, or to King Bifalt.

Queen Estie understood. As soon as Crayn's squad passed out of sight, they would leave the road and loop back around to the small woodland. When they entered the trees, they would approach from the north.

Then what?

Then anything.

Pretending that nothing had happened, she returned to her carriage and called through the open doorway, "Third Father. Magister Facile. We have paused to rest the horses and cook a meal. Please join us. If you are not hungry, you can stretch your legs."

The sorceress did not respond; but after a moment, the monk appeared. There he paused, eyes downcast, until the coachman remembered to bring the step-stool. Then he made his descent, an old man moving stiffly.

When he joined Estie, he murmured, "Thank you, Queen. No doubt you have cause for an early halt. I heard some of your men depart. If you have no need for me, I will help with the cooking." He appeared to smile. "The Cult of the Many teaches service."

Under her breath, she asked, "Then advise me, Father. Should I prod her? She needs sustenance."

The monk looked away. "She is herself, Queen. She will do what she must. Her desire to see Apprentice Travail once again will compel her."

Sighing, Estie accepted his counsel. She worried about Facile. But she had other concerns to distract her.

Overhead, thin clouds stretched their fingers westward. In the east, they looked thicker, but they did not promise a storm.

It was too soon to fear for Crayn and his comrades. They had not had time to reach the back of the copse. Nevertheless she caught herself listening for the sound of rifle-fire.

While Queen Estie ate, she studied the distant trees. Surely Crayn was among them now? Or perhaps now? The birds swirling above the woods continued their flurry of ascent and glide of return, but she could not interpret what they told her. The Commander and his men were Amikan: they understood stealth. Even encumbered by their mounts, they would do little to alarm the denizens of the copse.

Whatever they did, they apparently had no need for their guns. When Crayn emerged, he and three of his guardsmen were on foot. The other two followed behind them, leading all of the horses.

Estie did not need the muted exclamations of the men around her to inform her that the Commander had taken prisoners, three of them. Crayn had arranged his captives in a line among his comrades so that each of them had an Amikan hand on each arm.

Even at this distance, the Queen saw that two of the three were dressed in the garb of servants, loose brown shirts and breeches. They walked awkwardly; but they carried themselves with the straight backs and raised heads of men who were proud of what they did.

With one—servant?—on either side, the third shambled along as if he were embarrassed or craven. He wore the black robe of a priest.

A *priest?* Here?

She could not imagine what a spokesman for the Great God Rile was doing so close to her road. He should not have been free to wander anywhere in Amika. He should certainly not have been hidden in a place where he could watch for her.

Her enemies had used a Magister to prepare an ambush for her once. Could some traitor be relying on a priest now?

When Crayn had come halfway toward her, Estie realized that the steps of the captives were uncomfortable because their hands were tied behind their backs. Instinctively, she approved. She approved more when she saw that all three men were gagged.

The Commander had good reason for his precautions. He knew as much as his Queen did about the Great God's priests. From her—and from every rumor rampant in Belleger's Fist—he had learned that the Archpriest Makh had betrayed the realm. He had taken Elgart. In the process, he had caused one of Elgart's bodyguards to be murdered. In addition, Magister Facile had claimed that the priests were not sorcerers themselves. Nevertheless they *did* exert sorcery, theurgy which they drew from some unexplained source. And they wielded it with their voices.

Crayn had bound the hands of his captives so that they could not remove their gags.

Was that necessary? Estie did not know. After the Archpriest had vanished, the priests in the Open Hand had seemed lost or bewildered; deprived of their essential conviction. Had Makh been the source of their power to sway the Great God's followers by speaking?

If so, was he the *only* source?

The presence of a priest, any priest, in those woods was inherently disturbing. Queen Estie's honor guardsmen should have captured him some time ago. Certainly, he should not have been hiding where he could watch the road.

And he should not have had servants. That was an incongruous detail. In both Belleger and Amika, the priests were not known to require servants.

With a wave, the Queen redirected Crayn toward the small cook-fire near the carriage where her escort and Third Father waited, watching. Then she headed there herself.

If she had a sorcerer on her hands—or even a potential sorcerer—she was going to need Magister Facile.

As she neared her men, the monk stood to acknowledge her. "Queen," he murmured, gazing at the grasses around her feet, or perhaps at her riding boots, "this is unexpected." A slight shift of his head indicated Crayn's approach. "A priest of the Great God? Here?

"I see that your Commander is wary of him."

"He should be," returned Estie.

"Perhaps." The monk lifted his shoulders in a subtle shrug. "Will you hear my counsel, Queen?"

As Crayn brought the priest and the servants closer to face Amika's Queen, a screen of clouds slid like gauze over the sun. They cast a slight haze like hinted shadows over the carriage and the guardsmen, Esties, and the Commander's prisoners.

For a moment, she scrutinized the black-robed man. Behind his gag and his obvious consternation, he had a round face, a fleshy nose, and plump, beardless cheeks. Taken together, his features gave an impression of harmlessness. If he had smiled, he might have conveyed perfect sincerity. But his eyes contradicted the effect of his face. They were a sharp, almost startling blue that suggested both fright and cunning.

In contrast, the priest's men had no distinguishing features apart from a curious lack of deference—or perhaps of apprehension. Strong frames, muscular arms and legs. Common mouths and noses. Eyes of no particular hue. Untended beards. Estie had seen a hundred men like them in Belleger, or a thousand. They could have been Amikan, although their skin did not have the sallow hue of her people. But they stood erect on either side of their presumed master, looking straight ahead with an air of disinterest. Instead of fighting their gags, they gnawed the wads of cloth, as untroubled as cows chewing cuds.

Were they servants? Truly? Queen Estie doubted that. She would not have been astonished to learn that they were bodyguards. They may even have been the priest's captors.

With the priest and his men in front of her, she found it difficult to answer Third Father. She felt unaccountably alarmed. Strangers bound and gagged were no threat to her or her company. Nevertheless a nameless apprehension nagged at her.

Temporizing, she asked the Commander, "Did they resist, sir? Or try to flee?"

Crayn looked quizzical. "No, Majesty. We took them without difficulty. I am tempted to say they expected capture."

The priest watched Estie as if he were eager for an invitation to speak.

Unsure of herself, she answered the monk. "Of course, Father." She knew the worth of his counsel.

Third Father nodded another bow. "As you know, Queen," he said carefully, "the priests in Belleger appear to have lost their way. Perhaps this man has also. He may be harmless. In that event, he may be willing to explain his presence. By choice or by chance, he may shed some light on the doings of the Church. It might be wise to question him."

While Queen Estie considered her choices, she glanced around at her company. Her guardsmen were on their feet, watching the strangers warily. The teamsters were some distance away on the far side of the carriage with their heavy beasts. Estie hoped to see Magister Facile looking out from her seat in the carriage, but the window shades were closed.

Crayn and his comrades still held the priest and the servants. He seemed to know why Estie hesitated. With an obscure gesture, he sent one of the watching guardsmen away from the others. Moving casually, as if to perform some minor task, the man retreated behind the carriage. Then Crayn nodded to assure Estie that he was ready.

Steadying herself, Queen Estie made her decision. "I will do as you say, Father," she told the monk. Dishonestly, she added, "No priest of the Great God Rile intends harm." Then she said, "Please encourage Magister Facile to join us. I value her counsel as well."

The priest's air of gratification made her guts squirm.

"As you say, Queen." Third Father kept his head lowered. Reluctant to call attention to himself, he withdrew to the carriage.

Estie waited until he lifted the latch, opened the door. Then she faced Crayn again. With a command in her eyes, she nodded.

Under the comfortable clothes she wore for riding, sweat made her skin feel slick despite the air's coolness.

In response, Crayn and his comrades drew out their daggers. His men cut the bonds of the servants. He freed the priest himself.

Unseen by their captives, Crayn and his comrades did not sheathe their knives. A few of the other guardsmen shifted closer.

Neither servant moved until the priest reached up to pull the gag from his mouth. Quickly, they did the same.

The priest coughed once to clear his throat; drew several unobstructed breaths. Then he bowed deeply. When he looked up at Estie again, his smile was full of friendship.

His men remained upright, unsmiling. Neither of them gave any sign that they were aware of Amika's Queen, or of her escort.

From the carriage, Third Father's voice issued in low murmurs. Magister Facile's retorts sounded sharper, but the words were indistinct. She did not emerge.

"Majesty," said the priest, "I thank you." The subtle dimness shed by the clouds seemed to muffle his voice. "We are indeed harmless, I assure you. The Great God Rile desires only peace. He does not threaten."

Eager to appease her, he added, "I am Father Knout. I served the Great God in Belleger, in the Open Hand. There, your beauty and kindness are common knowledge. But common knowledge does not do you justice."

Estie swallowed an impulse to curse. Knout? That name was familiar, but too much had happened since she first heard it. For a moment, she could not remember. Then she knew.

Father Knout. The Beleaguered Eagle. Prince Lome.

Attempted treachery.

Knout was the priest who had paid for Lome's wine, ale, and grot—and had tried to learn where King Bifalt hid his stores of ammunition.

Now she understood Lome better. Even if he had kept his mind clear, he might have been taken in by the priest's easy manner; but she had never seen Lome when his thoughts were not blurred by drink. Sharply, she retorted, "Spare me your flattery, Knout. It is as common as what you have heard about me. I am not misled.

"I have questions. You will answer them. Here is the first.

"You served your Great God in the Open Hand. Why are you not there now?"

She meant, How did you escape General Klamath's men, or Elgart's remaining spies? How did they miss *you*?

Father Knout fluttered his hands. "Majesty," he exclaimed. "I do not understand your ire." His expression emphasized his innocence. "I am an obedient servant of my Church. The Archpriest Makh sent me to Amika. He charged me to warn our fellow priests that he feared King Bifalt. He anticipated murder or worse. I could hardly credit his concern. You sneer at common knowledge, but it is known everywhere that King Bifalt is not a bloody ruler. Still, I did as I was told. I left the Open Hand and Belleger, intending to reach the Church of the Great God in Maloresse."

He might have said more. Deliberately callous, Queen Estie interrupted him. "You say too much, priest, and tell me too little." If the

Archpriest was afraid, why had he asked so often to meet with King Bifalt? "You are not in Maloresse *now*."

As if he were looking for reassurance, Father Knout glanced up at the sun. Dulled by the clouds, its light cast a golden corona around it. When he faced the Queen again, he seemed chastened.

"Accept my regret, Majesty. It is as your monk said. I lost my way. The Great God's love enables us to be aware of each other. We are linked by his glory. When I lost my way—" He paused to swallow a pang. "You cannot imagine the hurt of that severance. But my faith did not waver. I did not go to Maloresse because I knew that my fellow servants were lost as well. They did not need the Archpriest's warning. They would know what to do. While I waited for the Great God Rile to show my path to me again, I chose to wander in your realm."

Abruptly, a subtle change came over Knout's companions. They did not turn their heads, not even to glance at the priest. They betrayed no interest in Queen Estie or her escort. They may not have understood what was being said. Nevertheless they now seemed to be paying attention.

Estie tightened her grip on herself. "I am not persuaded. Do you think I cannot imagine your hurt?" She was King Bifalt's lonely wife, untouched and unloved. "Perhaps not. But I can imagine what you might gain by misleading me.

"You were watching my road. You wanted to know who passed. Do you call that wandering? I call it scouting."

He must have seen Set Ungabwey's caravan. The library's enemy would know how to benefit from such tidings.

"No, Majesty." The priest began to sound frightened. "Do you think I am a spy? I am as lost as I say. I came here by chance. For safety, I took shelter in the woods, waiting for the Great God to reach out to me. When your men came, I did not resist. I have never harmed anyone. The Great God Rile desires peace. He does not countenance harm."

He wanted Estie to believe him: that was obvious. For that very reason, she distrusted him. Never harmed anyone? she thought. No one except Lome, who had no defense.

Still, his growing alarm gave her an advantage. She softened her manner, spoke more gently.

"Your plight must have been difficult, Father. You have lost your way. Your only path is to wander and wait, as you say, until your god reaches out to you. And you believe your fellow priests in Maloresse are lost as well. Yet they are not as lost as you. They still have purpose." He had just said so. "It seems a cruel thing, Father, that your god has singled you out for uncertainty while he gives them clear tasks to perform."

Knout tried to protest, "No, Majesty—" but she did not let him continue. Suddenly as harsh as her father, she demanded, "Be honest, sir. What use does your god have for his servants in my city? What instructions have they been given?"

Her challenge made the priest flinch. Apparently, she had found a question that he feared to answer. He avoided her glare. "Majesty—" he croaked. "Majesty, I—"

The bang of the carriage door as Magister Facile thrust it out of her way spared him from saying more.

The door shoved Third Father aside. He tried to recover so that he could help the sorceress down onto the step-stool, but he was old, and she was furious. She had reason to fear the Great God's priests, but her anger protected her. Pounding the treads with her cane, she descended to the ground. At once, she stamped across the grasses toward Queen Estie and her captives.

The monk came after Magister Facile, but he made no further attempt to intervene.

Estie flung a look at the old woman's knotted visage, then returned her attention to the black-clad priest.

While she was distracted, Father Knout's servants had taken hold of him, one by each arm. If she had expected him to be alarmed by the Magister's approach, she was mistaken. The support of his servants steadied him. In their grasp, he regained his composure.

The Queen had lost her advantage.

The light grew brighter as the cloud cover passed. The sun gave everything a keener edge, the carriage and the poised guardsmen, the sorceress, the priest and his men; the moment.

With Third Father behind her, Magister Facile reached Estie's side. She took another step closer to Father Knout, then stopped, bracing herself on her cane. For a moment, she peered at him as if she could discern his essence in his round face, his thick nose, his innocent cheeks. When she was satisfied, she drew back.

Over her shoulder, she told Estie curtly, "As I suspected. This man is no sorcerer. There is no scrap of theurgy in him. There is no power that he can wield. Not here."

To the priest, she rasped, "You are an empty robe. A nothing. It surpasses comprehension that anyone gives you credence. You preach against knowledge." She made a spitting sound. "Knowledge is all that saves us."

"Magister," answered the priest. He bowed to her as he had to Queen Estie. His smile was at its most sincere. It was not innocent at all. "I am grieved by your scorn. You misunderstand our teachings. Your knowledge is greater than mine. In your presence, I am indeed an empty robe, as you say. Yet I do not need saving. The Great God watches over me."

"Your *Great God* does?" demanded Magister Facile. "You lie, priest. You cannot mislead me now. He has forgotten you. If he ever knew your name, he has dismissed it from his mind.

"Your lackeys, however—" With an air of deliberation, like a woman following an unfamiliar scent, she moved to stand in front of the servant on her left. "They are another matter."

Several guardsmen gripped the hilts of their swords. Past Knout's shoulder, Crayn showed Estie the dagger in his fist.

Trembling with anger or apprehension, Magister Facile used her cane to prod the servant's chest. "Tell me your name, fellow."

The man accepted her poke as if it had no force and meant nothing. He did not react except to look at her and grin without parting his lips. In a distant voice like the cry of an unseen crow, he replied, "We serve the Great God Rile."

She nodded as if she had expected something of the sort. Driving her cane into the grass, she crossed in front of Father Knout to confront the other servant. Him she prodded as well.

"And you, fellow?" she insisted unsteadily. "What is *your* name?"

His reaction echoed his comrade's. His voice was the same. "The Great God's instructions are precise."

At that, the Magister stepped back, almost reeling. "Commander!" she called weakly. "Kill these men. The priest is nothing. *They* are dangerous."

At the same time, Father Knout stood straighter. He no longer needed the support of his servants. His whole face smiled. Even the glittering blue of his eyes seemed to smile.

"Magister." Estie rested a hand on Magister Facile's shoulder, offering support or comfort. "What do you see in them? How are they dangerous?"

Her men had swords and rifles. Crayn and his comrades were ready with their knives. Amika's Queen could not put helpless men to death. She was not her father.

The Magister did not so much as glance at Estie. Father Knout's servants demanded her concentration.

"I may have been mistaken, Majesty," she breathed in a husky whisper. "It may be that some god *does* watch over this priest. These servants may be *how* he watches.

"They also are not sorcerers. But there is a stink on them. Some vile theurgy has touched them. I cannot name it. I have never encountered a power like it." She seemed to mean, I cannot counter it. "Kill them now."

At Estie's back, Third Father said, "Ask your question again, Queen." He sounded strangely urgent. "How else will you know whether the priest is truly harmless?"

For an instant, Estie did not understand. Her attention was focused on the old woman who had once saved her life and sometimes been her friend. But then she grasped the monk's meaning. She had missed one opportunity. The priest's new confidence gave her another.

She did not look at Knout; did not let the peril of his servants—his guardians—distract her. Standing at Magister Facile's side and holding the woman's shoulder, she asked as if she knew the answer and only wanted confirmation, "Will you tell me now, priest? There can be no harm in it. What does the Archpriest require your god's servants in Maloresse to do when they are severed from him? What purpose did he give them?"

"Certainly, Majesty." Father Knout smiled more broadly. "As you say, there can be no harm in it. The Great God Rile desires only peace. His priests in Maloresse will—"

While Knout was speaking, Magister Facile gasped suddenly, "Majesty! It is an ambush!"

At that instant, both of Father Knout's servants moved.

Estie had seen Lylin fight. The devotee of Spirit was fast, too fast to seem human. The men with the priest were as fast.

Some vile theurgy has touched them.

With the speed of a bullet, the closer man attacked. His fist hit Magister Facile's sternum. Estie heard bones crumple: she may have heard shards shred arteries, lungs, viscera. The force of the blow flung the old woman backward. She fell hard, flopped like a doll among the grasses.

Estie's gaze—her whole heart—followed the Magister's fall. She did not see the other servant open a mouth full of teeth like fangs, sharp and pointed, made for ripping. She did not watch him take hold of the priest, sink his teeth into the priest's throat, tear out Father Knout's life in a spray of blood. She did not know that the last expression on Knout's face was one of utter astonishment.

Afterward, she remembered hearing the crack of a rifle. Too late, the guardsman Crayn had sent to hide behind the carriage had fired. His slug had pierced the head of Magister Facile's attacker. The man's head had burst like an egg struck by a rock.

Some time later, she learned that Crayn had slain Knout's killer. His blade had cut open the man's throat. From the wound, the killer's strength had gushed from him. He had fallen on top of Father Knout. Tangled together, they had lain in the spreading pool of their blood.

But moments passed before Estie was aware of anything except Magister Facile. When the Magister was hit, Estie followed the woman's collapse and sprawl as if she and the old woman had been tied together. She plunged to her knees and pulled the Magister's head into her lap before Facile's limbs stopped twitching.

Blood gasped from Magister Facile's mouth with every dying breath. She managed one word: a spatter of red. Then she was gone.

Her last word was, "Decimate."

Queen Estie did not know how long the shock held her; but eventually she began to recover.

She still clasped Magister Facile's head in her lap. The old woman looked shrunken somehow, diminished in death. Her eyes stared at nothing that did not horrify her.

Was this all that remained of the old woman who had saved Amika's Queen from her deranged father? This thin figure that had collapsed in on itself? This stain of blood? They were not enough to measure the meaning of Magister Facile's life.

When Commander Crayn came to claim his monarch, Third Father took her place. With a gentleness like reverence, he cupped the old woman's hand between his as if his touch might comfort her passing.

Holding Estie upright, Crayn murmured for her alone, "We must not linger here, Majesty. Where there are two such men, there must be more. There may be many more."

He was not trying to frighten her. It was his task to guard her. To take care of her. He did what he could.

Nevertheless his warning reached her. The killers cooling in death on the grass were only the first of their kind. There might be hundreds. Or thousands. An army of the Great God's men might already be in Amika, hidden to avoid the notice of spies and scouts.

"How—?" Estie had to swallow several times before she could make a sound. "How did they get here?"

"Across the lands of the Nuuri?" suggested Crayn. "I have no other answer, Majesty."

Still kneeling at Magister Facile's side, the monk said gently, "It can be done. If they traveled in small groups, or alone, and did nothing to molest the herds, the Nuuri might let them pass." After a pause, he added, "I have done it."

With a hand on her arm, the Commander directed Estie toward the carriage. "We must go, Majesty. We can protect you better when we are mounted and moving."

She nodded; but she stayed where she was. The suddenness of violence and blood numbed her. She could not simply walk away from Magister Facile's murder.

She felt sure that the priest was killed to silence him. She wanted to know what he might have told her. More lies and deflections? No. It would have been the truth.

Now she would never know. But she believed that nothing less than an attack on Amika and the bridges would justify his murder.

When Crayn's touch became a gentle tug, she forced herself to respond. "Yes, Commander. We must go."

"Leave these dead to the wolves." Queen Estie grimaced as she indicated Father Knout and his guards. Were there wolves in this region of Amika? She hoped so. "But I will not allow Magister Facile to become carrion. She has already given too much of herself. She will not give her flesh." As hungry as a vulture, sorrow beat its wings around Estie's head. "We will take her with us. Treat her gently. Wrap her well. We will build a cairn for her when we reach more rocky terrain."

Commander Crayn bowed. "As you say, Majesty." In a moment, he began shouting orders at his men.

As they scrambled to obey, the Queen added, "The messengers, Crayn. Send one to Maloresse. The others must reach King Bifalt and General Klamath. They need to know what has happened here. They need to know what we fear."

Again, the Commander promised, "As you say, Majesty."

With care that resembled tenderness, he helped her mount the step-stool into her carriage. Then he hurried away.

She was alone with the smell of blood on her hands and riding breeches until Third Father joined her. He had taken the time to wash his hands and splash water on his stained cassock. Saying only "Queen," he seated himself in a corner, bowed his head, and settled into his familiar silence.

She hardly noticed him. The beating of wings claimed her attention. It may have been the labor of her heart.

She believed that she had enough grief to occupy her. But when the carriage had been rolling eastward for an hour or two, guarded by her escort and trailed by the wagon of supplies, she learned that she was wrong. An unfamiliar voice spoke in her mind.

Where is Magister Facile? Is she dead? I cannot find her.

Its silent force jolted her. She had never heard it before, but she recognized it from her husband's description of his summons to the Repository long ago.

Magister Avail.

The monk must not have heard the same demand. Wrapped in his meditative stillness, he did not react to her sudden flinch, her instant tension.

You will try to answer, Queen, continued the voice. **Do not.** Each word was distinct, yet as soundless as her own thoughts. **I cannot hear you.**

If Magister Facile is unconscious—if drink or disease or violence have closed her mind—tell her when she wakes. Apprentice Travail lives. His death has been set aside. He will recover.

That was all. Magister Avail did not address her again. She could not call him back.

The old sorceress had accompanied the Queen on her journey in the hope that she would get one last chance to see her long-ago lover. If she had lived to hear them, Avail's tidings would have eased her bitterness. Speaking to Travail might have lifted some of her anger and resentment. Now he was alive and she was gone.

The cruelty of that mischance might have made another woman weep. Queen Estie did not. Long ago, her husband's father, King Abbator, had asked her to serve as a witness. Now there was nothing that she could do *except* witness. The Great God had done this. He would do more, and worse. The bloodshed he caused when he came would make what Magister Facile and Apprentice Travail had lost seem trivial.

That prospect did not soften Estie's eyes. It made them feel as hard as stones.

TWO

KING BIFALT IN HIS CITY

For days after the enemy's black ships broke open the reef that guarded the Bay of Lights, King Bifalt walked the streets, alleys, and lanes of the Open Hand. Alone apart from Malder and Jeck, Spliner and Boy—his bodyguards—and usually in the small hours before the early grey of dawn, the King went everywhere, studying his city and his people as if he were saying a protected farewell.

He was going to lose the Open Hand.

He had seen how the enemy's first probing had torn a passage through the reef. The fact that his cannon had sunk two of the black ships did not comfort him. The third had sailed away to report what it had learned. When the enemy came again, he would come in force—and he would come prepared.

Bifalt hoped that his guns and his men would exact a high price. But he believed in his bones that the enemy would prevail. Eventually, the defenses that he and his Queen-Consort had put in place with so much effort and blood would be destroyed. The King's forces would be driven out of the bay. Then they would be forced back from the bay's rim. Then—

Well. Then the defenders would retreat toward King Bifalt's city. Toward the Open Hand and Belleger's Fist.

Unfortunately, nothing would keep the enemy out of the Open Hand. Entirely unplanned, it had grown up around the King's keep on its hill during the generations of the old wars, Belleger against Amika.

As a result, it was an undifferentiated, indefensible sprawl. The Fist still had its old fortifications, its heavy walls and stout gate: the Hand had nothing. Cannon would have been useless in this maze. Entrenched riflemen might be able to hold back the enemy's first wave for a while. The Magisters of Belleger and Amika would do what they could. But mere guns and Decimates were no match for the enemy's sorceries. When they failed, the enemy would crash inward like a tsunami.

King Bifalt had spent years considering his responses.

Long ago, he had dismissed the idea of a running battle in the Open Hand, fighting house to house. He expected to face overwhelming numbers as well as fierce theurgy. Too many lives would be lost to no purpose. In the end, his city would be reduced to ash and rubble whatever he did.

He had also discarded the notion of evacuating the Hand fortnights ahead of the enemy. Too many Bellegerins still did not believe that they were in danger. He expected them to resist any order to leave their homes until the enemy was practically at their doors. If he compelled them to go, he would have to impose his will by force.

In addition, his people had nowhere to go except Amika. He and Queen Estie had planned for that—but only as a last resort. The early, apparently unnecessary arrival of Bellegerins by the hundreds and thousands would strain the resources of Queen Estie's realm to their limits. It might prove intolerable. Dispossessed Amikans and starving Bellegerins might go to war with each other again—in *Amika*. Both realms would be lost.

King Bifalt felt calamities crowding toward him wherever he walked: fire and sorceries, blades and arrows, helpless people slaughtered. *His* people. Nevertheless he had to accept that the Open Hand's destruction was inevitable. And he had to let his people remain where they were until the enemy's approach was obvious to everyone. What else could he do?

To his way of thinking, Belleger's Fist offered him his only possible advantage. If he could convince the enemy that he was prepared to sacrifice his city but not his keep—if he could convince his foes that he intended to make some kind of last stand in the Fist—

He had decided how to meet the challenge. His plans were fraught with dangers. Any mistake on his part, like any unexpected enemy tactic, would be fatal. But he was a man who did not hesitate to act on his own choices. He walked in the Open Hand again and again, reexamining every passage among the buildings for possibilities, searching his plans for flaws.

In its essence, what he hoped to accomplish was simple. He wanted to design and erect obstacles in the crucial streets, alleys, and intersections: barriers that would turn the enemy's forces toward Belleger's Fist. At the same time, those barricades would create open routes for the flight of his people. If he succeeded, the enemy would converge on his keep while his people ran for the northward road and Amika.

A simple plan. Its execution, however—

King Bifalt, Royal Surveyor Wheal, Land-Captain Erepos, and General Klamath had spent many days working on the answers to two questions. First, where should the barriers be placed to achieve both of their purposes? Second, how could a barricade be made strong enough to halt or at least deflect the hordes of the enemy? After all, it had to be either temporary or movable. Otherwise it would impede the city's many activities before it was needed.

Together, the King and Wheal had chosen locations for the obstacles. During his predawn walks, Bifalt had adjusted some of those positions in his mind. Others could not be improved. The design and construction of the barriers, he left to Erepos and Klamath. Both men had a resource that their King lacked: they could consult comfortably with Magisters.

Bifalt disliked sorcerers for their arrogance. More than that, he loathed sorcery itself. It gave gifted men and women power over ordinary people. They could wreak death from hiding and fear nothing, feel nothing. Their arrogance was the natural consequence of their abilities.

Nevertheless the King *needed* Magisters: a fact that never failed to gall him. He had no other defense against the enemy's sorceries.

During the early mornings that he had spent studying his city, the crisp weather of autumn had become an early winter. A chill drizzle fell. It was not cold enough to freeze—not yet—but it promised ice and storms. The dripping of the many eaves formed a damp background to his thoughts. Rainwater made gurgling rivulets in the gutters and sewers. Drops falling from the high roofs of the Fist hit hard enough to sting.

The wet and chill did not bother Bifalt. He liked edged weather. To keep the drizzle out of his eyes, he covered his head with the hood of his rain-cape. That was his only concession to ordinary comfort.

While the first signs of dawn crept over the eastern horizon, he expected either the Land-Captain or General Klamath to join him soon. He was running out of time. Now he wanted to know how they proposed to build the barricades he required.

Even this early, a few people were beginning to emerge from doorways along the street. Some of them merely emptied chamber pots into the sewer and went back inside. Others lingered at their doors enjoying a little soft rain before they faced the day's work.

In true Bellegerin fashion, this quarter of the Hand was called simply "Women." More than a decade ago, Land-Captain Erepos had suggested relocating all of the city's whorehouses to a single district. That way, he had argued, they could be defended more easily. After all, whores were the most vulnerable of the realm's women, at the mercy of their customers. They deserved the King's protection as much as anyone. They needed it more. And General Klamath's army in those days had been a bubbling stew of Bellegerin and Amikan resentment. He could not spare enough men to guard every house of comfort throughout the city.

When Erepos had succeeded at cajoling or coercing the whores to agree, primarily by offering them better accommodations at lower prices, other women soon found that they preferred to live nearby. Too many of them had lost their husbands and brothers, their fathers and sons, to the old wars. They valued the comparative safety of Women. Now the district flourished.

King Bifalt kept walking. As a man, he did not crave women. He desired only Estie. But she had left him: that was bad enough. She had left him so that she could become a Magister: that was worse. Worst of all, at least for him: when her gift was awakened, she would become a Magister of the Last Repository. Now the enemy was coming, and there was no one with whom he could share his darkest burdens.

He had tried opening his heart to Third Father, but the monk's response had only aggravated his overflowing bitterness. *You believe*, the old man had said, *that your abhorrence of sorcery is who you* are. *You are mistaken. It is a choice. Choices can be made. They can also be unmade.*

Choice is not a matter of truth and faith. It is a matter of truth and courage.

Kindly, relentlessly, Third Father had asked, *Can you tell yourself the truth, King? Do you have that much courage?*

The King knew that he did not. He walked in his city because he did not know what else to do. With Spliner and Boy ranging ahead of him, and Malder and Jeck trailing twenty or thirty paces behind, he continued tracing the lanes and hiding places of Women like a man wandering lost.

Along the way, he saw a woman sitting on the stoop of her small porch as if she had nothing to do and nowhere better to be. Rain dripped on her, but she ignored it. He could not make out her features or her age or what she wore. When she spoke, however, she betrayed that she had lost most of her teeth. An old woman, then—or one who had been badly abused.

As Bifalt drew near, she called like mockery, "Ho, fellow! What kind of man walks here at this hour? You will get no pleasure from me."

He trusted all of his bodyguards; but Spliner's devotion had a raw edge that Jeck and Malder did not understand. The former teamster might have slapped the woman for insulting Belleger's monarch. Fortunately, Boy, Spliner's son, was more amiable. The young man forestalled his father by ambling closer to the toothless woman.

"Greetings, Mother," he said easily. "It would please me to hear you are well. If we are out late, you are up early."

"Ha!" snorted the woman. "No one sleeps well at my age. What is your excuse? *I* am not your mother."

"I am a bodyguard." Boy's tone conveyed a smile. "My father still names me Boy. Hells, Mother, everyone does the same. But I must tell you. The man you called 'fellow' is King Bifalt. *Your* King, Mother. He is addressed as 'Majesty.'"

"Is he?" The woman seemed to peer at Bifalt. "*That* is Belleger's King? He is a sorry sight, *Boy*. If he is the King of Belleger, he is wed to the most desirable woman in the realm. But she has not given him heirs. He must be unable to get them.

"How can a King with no heirs be called 'Majesty'? There is nothing majestic about him."

In surprise, Boy stepped back. He had spent too much time in Belleger's Fist, where people guarded Bifalt's reputation jealously. He had not learned how to trade rudeness for rudeness.

King Bifalt saw no reason to remain silent. "Leave her, Boy," he commanded. "But mark that house. Fix it in your mind. Later, when you have a moment, tell the General or Erepos that I want that house given particular protection. The day is coming when we will all be in peril of our lives. Any woman who dares to slight her King at such a time has earned the right to speak her mind. If Erepos does not understand, Klamath will."

Muttering, "As you say, Majesty," Boy returned to his place across the street from Spliner.

As Bifalt walked on past her, the woman cackled a laugh. "Well said, fellow. Now I know you are not King Bifalt. *He* does not waste words on false kindness or empty generosity."

"Who knows, Mother?" replied the King. "First the times change. Then the times change men. Perhaps they will change me."

He was thinking of the hole that Estie had left in his heart. He threw whatever he could find into it. Statements she might have made. Thoughts she might have shared. But nothing filled the void of what he had lost. It weakened his foundations; made his other burdens harder to carry.

He did not believe that he would ever change. *Surpass* himself? No. Nevertheless he hoped the old woman could be protected. She could have been *anyone's* mother.

It was not his *wife's* fault that he had no heirs.

While he moved away, the woman sent another toothless laugh at his back. Now, however, she sounded less scornful—or perhaps less sure of herself.

King Bifalt knew how she felt.

A few streets later, Jeck came up behind the King. "Majesty." The bodyguard kept his voice low. "General Klamath has sent word. He will wait for you at the next intersection two streets over." With a gesture, he indicated King Bifalt's left.

No doubt, Klamath had sent one of his men—or perhaps his young aide Ulla—to locate the King's guards and whisper a message.

Bifalt nodded. With a quick word, he directed Spliner and Boy into the nearest alley on the left.

Following them, he strode down the alley, crossed a lane that might loosely be called a street, took a gap that was little more than a foot-path between a whorehouse and a tavern, and emerged near the inter-section Jeck had indicated.

In fact, it was a crucial intersection: one of the crossings where King Bifalt imagined setting up a barricade. The obstacle he had in mind would cut diagonally across the intersection to create two clear roads. If it succeeded, it would turn the enemy's forces entering the Open Hand from the south toward Belleger's Fist in the west. At the same time, it would allow streams of people to flee northward from the east. If the barrier could withstand the enemy's power—

Looking at the location again, King Bifalt swallowed hard. The risk he proposed threatened to choke him. He did not know how to design the barricade he needed. If Klamath and Wheal could not devise something strong enough to divert the enemy, Bifalt would have to sacrifice some of his sorcerers.

He dreaded that. At any distance, the Decimates were too indis-criminate. They would kill his people as well as their foes. Then the Magisters would be located and overcome.

He could not afford to lose any of them. They were too few.

But what else could he do? More of his people would die if he did not sacrifice his Magisters. Then his dishonor—his failure to be the King Belleger needed—would be complete.

He kept walking until he reached the intersection where General Klamath, First Captain Matt, and a few riflemen waited for him.

In silence, the General and his companions studied King Bifalt. When he joined them, the First Captain and his men bowed. "Majesty," said Matt politely. But Klamath dispensed with his usual courtesies.

Taking his King by the arm, he drew Bifalt away from the others until he could speak without being overheard.

Sunrise was near. Through the greying darkness, Bifalt could see the General's features clearly enough. Klamath had a peasant's face. When he scowled, he looked like a farmer fighting to plow stony ground.

He was scowling now.

"Majesty," he said close to King Bifalt's ear, "this is not like you. You have learned to slump. This posture does not inspire confidence. Have you reconsidered the Queen-Consort's message? Do you now fear an enemy in the north?"

Bifalt made an effort to straighten his shoulders. For a moment, he succeeded. But the change felt strangely unnatural. It made his neck and back ache. Somehow, without his notice, he had become a man who could not stand erect without strain. He let himself sag.

Irritated, he answered, "No. I have not. I do not. The killing of Magister Facile is grievous, but that loss is the library's, not ours. We lost her when she left with the Queen. For us here, one random priest and two men whose only weapons are fangs do not comprise an army. We can do nothing until we know more.

"I have larger concerns than *posture*." He snorted the word. "If you want me to improve it, give me a reason. Have you and Wheal devised a barricade for this crossing?"

Klamath knew his King too well. In his own way, he understood what Estie's departure for the Repository had cost Bifalt. A pang twisted the General's mouth. But it was not his place to probe the King's heart.

Klamath allowed his own shoulders to drop. "The Royal Surveyor will speak of that when he comes, Majesty. While we wait, there are other matters to report." With a nod, he indicated First Captain Matt and the riflemen. "I cannot say that they will lift your burdens, but you will want to hear them."

An involuntary grimace tightened King Bifalt's features. He forced it away. "Then I will hear them."

Ruling himself severely, he went with Klamath to rejoin the other men.

First Captain Matt was a modest man, but not a daunted one. He was taller than his General, and built like a stone watchtower. When King Bifalt asked him to speak, he answered with unassuming directness.

His report came from the relays of riders and signals that he had put in place to deliver messages from Set Ungabwey's men in the canyons of the Realm's Edge. Considering the distance, the caravan-master could communicate with remarkable speed.

According to Master Ungabwey, his mechanicians and their massive catapults, aided by the judicious use of gunpowder, had blocked the first of the three known passages through the range. An entire mountainside had been dropped into the canyon. Set Ungabwey's train was now moving to attack the second pass. He had encountered sporadic opposition from the foreigners who had been raiding across the south of Belleger, but his escort of riflemen had kept the wagons and men safe.

"Nevertheless," concluded the First Captain, "Master Ungabwey asks for more defenders. He expects greater opposition as he continues."

King Bifalt listened without giving Matt his full attention. The defense of the south belonged to Set Ungabwey. Whatever happened there, Belleger had neither the riflemen nor the Magisters to fight two armies at once. Bifalt had to believe that Ungabwey would succeed. His own battles were more imminent.

Brusquely, he thanked the First Captain. "If Set Ungabwey wants more men," he continued, "we have decisions to make." How much of his army could he afford to send south? "I leave them to you and General Klamath. I have other matters to arrange."

On that subject, Matt had more to say. "My home is in the south, Majesty. Raiders came near us. I knew some of their victims. I heard the tales. Those men are savage, but they have no weapons like ours. They may be shocked to learn how easily they can be shot before they are close enough to strike back."

He seemed to mean that he had already dispatched enough men to accompany the caravan.

General Klamath was not persuaded. "Or," he countered, "they may have sorcerers among them. They may strike back with the Decimates, or with sorceries we do not recognize."

King Bifalt had no answer. He did not trust anything that the Magisters of the Last Repository said or did. But he believed that they wanted to live—and to preserve their storehouse of knowledge. They had not risked a friend as valuable as Set Ungabwey on a whim. They knew what he could do.

To end the debate, Bifalt said, "The caravan's fate is your concern, First Captain. You and General Klamath will choose your response. I will not question it." Of Klamath, he asked, "Is there more, General?"

Glowering, Klamath relented. "As you say, Majesty. Matt and I will do what we can"—he glanced at the First Captain—"when we have given the matter further thought.

"I have little to add. As you know, the Queen-Consort has sent sub-Commander Hellick and forty of her honor guardsmen to join us. Second Captain Hegels has folded them into the army. And daily we receive pleas from Commander Soulcess. He believes that Amika is threatened. He wants reinforcements."

The King shrugged. He and Klamath had already discussed the honor guard Commander's appeals. They had agreed to ignore the possibility that Amika was in danger, at least for the present.

"Also"—General Klamath paused to brace himself for his King's reaction—"the Queen-Consort's Magisters have begun to arrive. Chancellor Sikthorn declares that they will all join us."

Hells! muttered the King to himself. *More* Magisters? This was not news. He and Queen Estie had agreed on it. But he did not *want* her Decimate-wielders. He hated relying on any theurgist. Through his teeth, he said, "They will be welcome." For Klamath's sake, he lifted his shoulders a bit. "What else did Sikthorn say?"

Estie had made a number of promises. Bifalt dreaded the possibility that she had neglected some of them. Or changed her mind.

Behind his scowl, the General relaxed. "He emphasized that Queen Estie is true to her word. Amika will accept our people, as many as necessary. They will be made welcome as if they were Amikan, fed, clothed, and housed. If they want work, they will have it."

King Bifalt swallowed a moment of relief. Estie had kept that promise. She would not forget more urgent commitments.

However, he masked his reactions. He knew how to hide behind his face. As if he had no personal interest in his wife's actions, he told Klamath, "When you reply to the Chancellor, General, give him my thanks. Then tell Land-Captain Erepos to prepare suitable accommodations for Amika's Magisters. Later, we will determine where and how to use their Decimates."

Klamath nodded a small bow. "As you say, Majesty." He and the King had already agreed that they could not make any firm decisions about the deployment of their forces until they knew more about the enemy's tactics. Then they would have to think and act quickly.

With an inward sigh, King Bifalt dismissed the General and the First Captain to their other duties. Accompanied by their riflemen, they left Bifalt alone with his bodyguards.

While Klamath faded into the lingering dusk and vague shadows, Bifalt continued to slump. But then, biting the inside of his cheek, he forced his back straight; raised his head until his chin seemed to jut at the buildings around him. He had spent a lifetime holding himself upright: he could relearn the habit. If Klamath saw him sagging again, his old friend would worry—and the General already had enough worries to discourage a pile of rocks.

It was enough that King Bifalt doubted himself. He did not want anyone else to doubt him.

When the Royal Surveyor approached the intersection a short time later, he had two Magisters with him.

King Bifalt groaned under his breath as he recognized Magister

Lambent. Slope-shouldered, nearsighted, and full of himself, Lambent valued himself highly despite his reputation as a coward. His Decimate was lightning: he was said to be powerful. In recent years, he had served Bifalt by inspecting and reporting on the progress of the fortifications in the Bay of Lights.

Even if the sorcerer had been Bellegerin, King Bifalt would not have chosen him for that task. Lambent's mind was as shortsighted as his eyes. But Queen Estie had insisted on him. With her sweetest smile—a smile that twisted her husband's heart whenever he remembered it—she had said, "You have better men for more important duties, my lord. And perhaps being required to perform a menial chore in your service will teach him a little humility. I will ensure that he does not disappoint you."

Bifalt had not detected any evidence of humility in the man. Lambent still treated him, Belleger's King, like a presumptuous upstart. And the sorcerer had nothing but contempt for what Commander Forguile, Captain Flisk, and their many laborers were trying to accomplish. Nevertheless Lambent's reports had been reliable despite his personal shortcomings.

No doubt, he accompanied Wheal now because he had put himself forward as Queen Estie's representative. Certainly, Wheal had not chosen him. Like the King, if for different reasons, the Royal Surveyor had no patience for Magister Lambent.

The other sorcerer was a young man as slender as wattle and bristling with eagerness. Dredging his memory, King found the Magister's name: Crawl. His Decimate was fire. Men like the General and Land-Captain Erepos considered him precocious.

In contrast, the Royal Surveyor gave the impression that he would have preferred to be anywhere else doing anything else. He came forward as if he were slogging through a quagmire: a small, earnest man with a head full of maps and little interest in anything else. If he had been required to plan and build a city, he would have been happy until the day he died. But now the library's war was imminent, and his mood had soured. He groaned to contemplate the destruction of the Open Hand. Unable to satisfy the King's requirements himself, he had turned to sorcery for help.

Magister Lambent acknowledged Belleger's monarch with a curt nod. No doubt, he considered that an adequate show of respect. In contrast, Magister Crawl's bow was tense with anticipation.

King Bifalt ignored both theurgists. "What do you have for me?" he asked the Royal Surveyor. "I do not know how much time remains. We must be ready."

Wheal sighed. "Majesty," he began, "we have—"

Magister Lambent interrupted him. "Lightning cannot do what you ask," he declared imperiously. "Wind. Drought. Pestilence. Earthquake. You will not use them here. They will only harm your city. They cannot match the enemy's power."

The Royal Surveyor coughed uncomfortably.

King Bifalt showed Lambent his most unforgiving visage. He held the Magister's gaze until he saw uncertainty creep into Lambent's gaze. Then he called, "Malder."

Malder was the biggest of Bifalt's bodyguards. A natural brawler, he could kill a man with a hug. A few strides brought him to the King's side. "Majesty?"

"This Magister"—Bifalt nodded at Lambent—"has forgotten common courtesy. Remind him for me."

Malder's grin showed a mouth full of broken teeth. Moving from King Bifalt's side to Magister Lambent's, he draped one heavy arm over the sorcerer's shoulders and began to squeeze.

A look of panic twisted the sorcerer's features.

Sternly, Malder said, "It is common courtesy, Magister, to address King Bifalt as 'Majesty.' It is also courtesy to remain silent until you are asked to speak.

"Do you understand?"

Magister Lambent swallowed convulsively. He nodded as well as he could in Malder's grasp. "Majesty," he croaked. "Pardon me."

Bifalt's smile was a private one. It did not show on his face. After a moment, he gave Malder permission to let the Magister go.

As the bodyguard stepped back, Lambent snatched a whooping breath as if he had been strangling.

Magister Crawl watched this display with fascination and a touch of anxiety. Wheal looked like a man who would have given anything for the freedom to walk away.

Keeping Malder where he was, King Bifalt said to Lambent, "I will pardon you, Magister, when you tell me why we cannot match the enemy's power. I know that it is great." He had never seen sorcery on that scale before. "But I do not understand why it exceeds our own. Is there some lack in our Magisters?"

"Lack, Majesty?" The sorcerer panted to regain his composure. "Yes. But the matter is not so simple."

"Then explain it," demanded the King.

Magister Lambent did his best to endure the King's uncompromising gaze. Briefly, he seemed to scramble inside himself, pulling his thoughts together. Then he recovered a measure of his familiar assurance.

"Consider, Majesty. There are three elements of power. They are control, duration, and reach. Control is the ability to place our theurgy where we wish—and *only* where we wish. *That* we lack. It may require training. Perhaps duration also is a question of training. We lack our foes' ability to *sustain* their efforts. None of our Magisters can wield their Decimates for more than a few heartbeats. Then they must rest to restore their strength. With training, their endurance might improve. But we do not train. Why should we when our gifts are not needed?"

As the sun showed its face over the buildings in the east, wiping away the last signs of dawn, more people emerged into the streets and lanes. From the whorehouses, soldiers scrambled, rushing to reach the training-fields in time for the day's muster. In less haste, workmen left the comforts of their beds. Wives and housekeepers began their chores while seamstresses, clothiers, shop-girls, and tavern servants made themselves ready. Accompanied by the groaning of oxen, carts trundled along the packed gravel of the roadways, carrying the city's traffic of goods and foodstuffs to the merchantries. Voices shouted greetings and insults. This early in the day, the intersection was not crowded. Later, it would be.

King Bifalt ignored the increasing activity. His concentration was fixed on Magister Lambent.

Perhaps because people were looking at him, the sorcerer tried to stand taller. "Where the enemy does *not* exceed us is in reach. Of that I am sure. He used the Decimate of lightning to break open the reef. Why was that necessary? What are your fortifications except an assemblage of iron and gunpowder? Iron draws lightning. It ignites gunpowder. One lightning-wielder could have destroyed a decade of your best defenses—if he could have cast his power so far. But that was not done.

"There must be an inherent limit to such sorceries. Or perhaps they are limited by the flesh that channels them. In either case, the enemy's reach is not greater than ours."

Satisfied with himself, Lambent waited for the King's approval.

King Bifalt made the Magister wait. He could think of another explanation for the enemy's forbearance. A direct attack on the cannon and gunpowder might well shatter the road leading down from the rim of the cliff to the strand of the sea. If so, it would destroy the enemy's access to Belleger.

"Very well, Magister," he said after a pause. "Your offense is forgotten. Answer one more question.

"We have been led to believe that any Decimate can counter the same force. A burning house can be quenched by the Decimate of fire. When a farmer's fields are parched, the Decimate of drought can bring rain. Is that true?"

"It is, Majesty." Magister Lambent's tone hinted at bluster. Yet he remained wary of Malder. "No lightning-wielder can harm me while I am aware of my peril. And there is more. Any Magister can sense the threat of any Decimate as it is summoned."

In that case, thought the King, he was going to need every wielder of lightning he had to protect his defenses in the Bay of Lights when the enemy attacked.

Not for the first time, he felt a harsh pang at Magister Facile's departure; her wasted death. She could have done more than counter any Decimate. She could have rendered men like Lambent powerless.

But he did not linger over what he had lost. He had kept the Royal Surveyor too long. Wheal had work to do. As did Crawl, apparently.

To Lambent, King Bifalt said, "Thank you, Magister. You may go."

Just for an instant, Magister Lambent stiffened. He had come without invitation and did not expect to be dismissed. But a quick glance at Malder changed his mind. With an awkward bow, he muttered, "As you say, Majesty," and turned away. Walking as quickly as his sense of his own dignity allowed, he left the intersection.

A crowd was growing around the King. People hurried or strolled past him. Some of them stopped to stare. Two or three carts slowed while their men regarded King Bifalt with plain curiosity. Unobtrusively, the bodyguards tightened their cordon around the King, Wheal, and Magister Crawl.

"Now, Wheal," said the King. He almost added, At last. "What do you have for me?"

"Majesty, I—" began the Surveyor. He glanced at Crawl. "That is to say, we. We have a proposal."

In a rush, he began.

"As you know, Majesty, we have considered iron. If the forges can make bars long enough. If the bars can be fixed to each other. Erepos assures me it is possible. But the difficulty, Majesty—" Wheal took a deep breath. "We have no means to secure them. The enemy will knock them down.

"There." He pointed to one end of the diagonal Bifalt wanted, a corner of the intersection. The large, squat structure there housed a prosperous ironmonger's store: so prosperous, in fact, that the whole merchantry was built of stone. "That can support an iron barricade. But across from it—" Wheal indicated the opposite corner, where a whorehouse rose to three levels. "That is wood. It cannot hold the iron we need."

Bifalt nodded. He and the Surveyor had discussed such problems often. When Wheal paused, the King said, "I understand. What do you suggest?"

With helplessness in his eyes, Wheal looked at Magister Crawl again.

The young man had been suppressing his enthusiasm. Now it rose up in him. "Fire, Majesty," he exclaimed at once. "Iron will not serve. We need the Decimate of fire."

The King raised an eyebrow. Rigid with patience, he countered,

"And burn down every building here? The Open Hand is tinder. Your fire will take the whole city."

"No, Majesty." Crawl almost laughed in his excitement. "Let me explain. We will dig a trench from corner to corner." An eager wave of his hand described a line from the ironmonger's to the whorehouse. "We will fill it with oil. Then we will pile wood over it to make a high barrier. Any wood. Planks. Timbers. Ordinary firewood. Furniture if we must.

"*That* stone will not burn." The ironmonger's store. "For safety, we can conceal a few men near it with barrels of water. I will hide myself *there*." The whorehouse. "When the enemy comes, I will fire the trench." He swung his arms over his head as if he could promise a blaze that filled the sky. "The result will be a storm of flame. Even the enemy's hordes will not try to break through it. They will search for another road."

Crawl's proposal had obvious flaws. "That will win us a few moments," conceded the King. Until the wood was consumed, or the oil under it. "Until your barrier falls to ash. Then the enemy will ignore it, and you will be forced to flee."

Magister Crawl's grin split his face. "I know the danger, Majesty. Magister Lambent has given us the answer. Until the enemy comes, I—" He caught himself. "We. Every wielder of fire who joins me. We will *train*.

"It will not be difficult to arrange. Piles of brush soaked in oil will suffice. With them, we can teach ourselves to raise small fires and let them burn, then quench them without allowing the flames to spread.

"In war, we have used our Decimates indiscriminately. But every Magister of fire is able to set his hearth alight without endangering his home. And we have nothing better to do until the enemy comes. We can train until we have enough control to fire the barricades and sustain the flames without causing a wider conflagration."

As an afterthought, he added, "Knowing our lives are at risk will inspire us."

King Bifalt was not convinced. He had never seen a Magister put himself in danger voluntarily. He did not know what to make of Crawl's eagerness.

While Bifalt studied the young man, Wheal said diffidently, "Taken together, Majesty, Belleger and Amika now have fifteen Magisters of fire. There may be more among the Queen-Consort's remaining sorcerers. But fifteen Magisters and a few squads of riflemen may be enough to turn the enemy toward the Fist.

"Diagonal barricades of fire should allow our people to flee on one side while the enemy advances on the other. I have nothing better to offer."

Biting the inside of his cheek, King Bifalt hesitated for a moment. He had a particular antipathy for Magisters whose Decimate was fire. Twenty years ago, his search for the Last Repository had been betrayed by a man named Slack who had that gift. Deprived of his power by the seventh Decimate, he had turned to treason. Then, much more recently, the traitors who had ambushed the Queen-Consort on her way to Amika and her father had relied on a fire-wielder. Such men were inclined to treachery.

Nevertheless Slack's declaration of his own convictions, then and now, struck Bifalt like a condemnation. *A man is not a man at all if he cannot enter and enjoy every chamber of himself.*

But if the Royal Surveyor had no other ideas, there was nothing better to be done. Of Crawl, the King asked, "What will you do if sorcerers of fire come to counter you?"

The young man winced, momentarily nonplussed. Then he brightened. "Perhaps they can be shot?"

With an inward sigh, the King announced, "Then I am persuaded.

"Magister Crawl, I leave the training of other Magisters to you. Command them in my name. If they are reluctant to share your peril, they will answer to me."

Almost bursting, the young sorcerer answered at once, "As you say, Majesty."

He may have wanted to say more, but King Bifalt had moved on. He gave the Royal Surveyor instructions that Wheal already understood. In Land-Captain Erepos' name, the King promised oil, wood, and labor for the work of making barricades. Then he thanked both men and dismissed them.

The young Magister left with a surge in his steps. Walking away in a different direction, back bent, head bowed, the Royal Surveyor resembled a mole burrowing through a mound of responsibilities and unhappiness.

When Crawl and Wheal were out of hearing, King Bifalt gestured his bodyguards closer. "Be wary of that Magister." His memories made his voice more hoarse than usual. "Have him watched when you cannot do so yourselves. You know what I fear. His eagerness troubles me." When Bifalt spoke to his Magisters in person, his commands were usually received with sighs or rolled eyes; suppressed impatience. "If he is true to his word, he may be the saving of many lives. If he is not—"

"Then refuse him, Majesty," suggested Jeck. More than his comrades, he occasionally presumed to advise his King. "You do not need him. You know his proposal. Some other Magister can take his place."

Without hesitation, Spliner promised gruffly, "If he is false, Majesty, he will be stopped."

"Do so," ordered King Bifalt. "But be sure of him first. If he *is* true, his excitement may prod other Magisters to match him."

If Crawl's attitude could persuade arrogant sorcerers to risk their lives. If the idea of *training* did not offend their tender sensibilities. If any of them wanted to increase their mastery. Or if they simply loved Belleger.

Hells! Bifalt did not *trust* those Magisters. But he needed them. He could not challenge the library's enemy without them.

As the bustle and busyness on the streets increased, King Bifalt walked on. Around him, his bodyguards kept watch without calling attention to themselves: a skill Elgart had taken pains to teach them. While they filtered through the crowd, they helped their King look for his next meeting.

For a time, he did not see the men he had asked to join him. However, he had not told them where he would be. And he had never expected the men he relied on to attend him instantly. They had other duties. Instead of growing impatient, he resumed studying the details of the Open Hand.

At the same time, he wandered among his memories of Elgart and Estie and treachery. Directly or indirectly, the priests of the Great God Rile had sought to destroy his stores of bullets and gunpowder. His own brother had conspired to break the alliance between Belleger and Amika by killing Amika's Queen. And his wife, loved and unacknowledged, was gone. Belleger needed its King to be a rock, as sure and unyielding as stone; and he had striven to be that man. But now he could feel his failure crowding close around him. The enemy was coming, and the defenses King Bifalt had prepared would not suffice. Such things burned like acid in his guts.

He had left Women behind, and was wandering the lanes of a quarter packed almost wall to wall with alehouses and inns, when the men he had summoned appeared. Ahead of him, Prince Jaspid stamped out onto the porch of an alehouse, dragging a smaller figure behind him.

Jaspid was using his left arm. The rest of his injuries had healed, but his right elbow had not recovered its full strength yet. He was about King Bifalt's height, and less obviously muscular than his brother. Nevertheless he could have beaten any six Bifalts in direct combat. He was the best fighter in Belleger, undefeated until the devotee of Spirit Lylin had almost killed him. And he was handsome, widely considered the most handsome man in the city; certainly better looking than his brother the King. Perhaps that was an effect of his gift for uncomplicated enjoyment, even delight. Even in his mock battles against five or ten of General Klamath's soldiers at once, he radiated something like happiness. Unlike Bifalt, Jaspid felt no bitterness toward Lylin. If anything, the Prince had fallen in love with her—or more deeply in love.

He was not happy now. His unguarded features were tight with indignation and disappointment. The man he was dragging out of the alehouse was his younger brother, the third of King Abbator's sons: Prince Lome.

Lome was a wastrel, a drunk; a man ruled by gall and sarcasm who felt slighted by his position as the youngest son, by his smaller stature and lesser gifts, and—if he ever told himself the truth—by his own refusal to take responsibility for who and what he was. Long ago, he had learned to shroud his aching desire for superiority in a fog of ale, wine, and a vile drink called grot. Recently, however, he had seemed to be changing. Estie had that effect on damaged men. As a result, Bifalt had allowed himself to hope. He needed Lome.

If Prince Jaspid had to haul his brother out of an alehouse by plain force, the King's hopes were misplaced.

Hells! Bifalt felt fire in his guts again. Lome was *necessary*. Even Land-Captain Erepos, who was trusted everywhere, could not claim as much authority as a Bellegerin prince.

Jaspid spotted King Bifalt at once. Pulling Lome to his side, the older Prince forced his brother to accompany him off the alehouse porch. Lome's steps betrayed a stagger as Jaspid brought him down the lane to face Bifalt.

Without a word, the King's bodyguards withdrew a few paces.

Instinctively, King Bifalt reached for the hilt of his saber. He wanted something solid to grip. But he had left Belleger's Fist to walk in the Open Hand unarmed.

He did not have it in him to believe he required protection in his own city. His bodyguards were a concession to General Klamath, the Land-Captain, and even the Queen-Consort. Over the years, however, he had grown accustomed to Jeck and Malder, Spliner and Boy. Their presence no longer felt like an intrusion—or a burden. As a result, he had learned the habit of going wherever he wished without his weapons.

Lacking his saber, King Bifalt locked his arms across his chest. As Prince Jaspid brought Prince Lome to him, the King said sourly, "An alehouse, Lome? At this hour?"

The younger Prince blinked to focus his eyes. In a blurred voice, Lome muttered, "I have lost the trick of sleeping. One hour is much like another." Then he made an effort to stand straighter. "Do you think I was drinking? I was not."

Jaspid always stood erect. It came naturally to him. Somehow, his stance made him look supple rather than stiff. But he sounded stiff enough.

"He had a tankard in front of him, Majesty. It was full."

Lome rolled his eyes like a man tired of insults. "I was *considering* it. Not *drinking* it. There is a difference."

"'Considering it'?" asked King Bifalt. "What was there to consider?"

For a moment, Lome seemed to contemplate a sarcastic retort. Then he let himself slouch until he was half leaning on Jaspid. "Hells, Brother. The hour is too early for questions. I had a decision to make. You have taught me to fret. That is why I do not sleep."

Bifalt tried to credit this protest, but he smelled ale on his brother's breath. "Did your decision concern a second flagon or a third? How much is enough?"

Instead of answering, Lome turned his head to Jaspid. After squinting for a moment, he looked down at Jaspid's grip on his arm. With his free hand, he tried to remove Jaspid's grasp.

Sighing, Jaspid let Lome succeed.

The younger Prince flexed his arm as if Jaspid's fingers had hurt him. He looked back at the alehouse. When he faced Bifalt again, he avoided the King's glare: a tacit confession.

"You did not send Jaspid," he slurred, "because you intend to castigate me, Brother. The hour is too early—and the time is too late. You missed your chance. The days when I might have heeded you ended when our father died.

"Since that woman you refuse to love convinced you to spare my life, I have done what you asked. I have attended your council meetings. And I have told you what I think, although you do not listen. What more do you expect from me?"

Bifalt remembered Prince Lome's opinion of the black ships that had attempted to broach the bay. *Your war is in* Belleger, *Brother. There is no other enemy.*

On one point, Lome was right. The King had not listened. He knew better.

As if he expected to be obeyed, King Bifalt said, "I have a task for you, Lome. It is a service no one else can perform. If you do it thoroughly, you will save a host of lives."

At that, Lome widened his eyes, exaggerating his surprise. "A service, Brother? Please tell me to examine all of our ale for taste and purity. Some of our tavern-keepers offer disgusting brews. They cause sloth and diseases. I am sure of it.

"Or perhaps it is wine that troubles you. I can—"

"Lome!" snapped Bifalt. "Stop this. I do not enjoy your version of wit. I am Belleger's King, and I am *in earnest*. Whatever else you think of me, believe *that*."

"Oh, I know, Brother." Lome smirked. "I *know*." Still, he avoided Bifalt's eyes. "You do not have a frivolous bone in your body. It is a curious lack. Perhaps it is like your lack of sorcery, an accident of birth. Or perhaps it resembles your refusal of your Queen-Consort's bed, a sign that you take yourself too seriously. I—"

"*Lome*," said the King again. Grimly, he swallowed an impulse to slap the younger Prince. He knew Lome's game, Lome's desire to provoke him. Instead of hitting his brother, he unfolded his arms to poke Lome's chest with one rigid finger. "*You*. I need *you*. You must save the folk of the Hand."

Prince Lome tried to continue. "I—" But now his surprise was not exaggerated. "You—?" He gulped several times. "Say that again. You *what*?"

"Lome." Bifalt made an effort to soften his tone. "Brother. *Listen* to me. You do not listen when I fault your drinking. In your place, I would do the same. But hear me now.

"You do not believe the enemy is coming. Perhaps you are right. If you are *wrong*, the peril is extreme. If the enemy *is* coming, he will break through our defenses in the Bay of Lights. When he has landed his army, he will march on the city. And *here* we have no defenses. He will raze the Open Hand.

"When he comes, our people must be evacuated. If they are not, they will die."

Gripping his courage in both hands, King Bifalt said, "I want you to command the evacuation."

In his own way, Prince Jaspid was as surprised as Lome. But his reaction was different. The light in his eyes was a warrior's eagerness. It resembled pride. "There, Lome," he said softly. "You crave a worthy place in the affairs of the realm. Your King offers it to you. Claim it while you can."

Shock kept Lome silent for a moment. Then he remembered the attitudes that had shaped his life. "Command?" he said unsteadily. "Nonsense, Brother. Who would obey *me*?"

"Who would not?" countered the King. "You are a prince of Belleger. A son of King Abbator. And I cannot ask Jaspid. I need him to fight. Also, he is not suited to command. It is not in his nature. You know that.

"You are my best choice."

He did not say, You are my only choice. Lome said it for him. "You mean that you have no one else." Protests seemed to rise in him like bubbles in boiling stew. "That, too, is nonsense. Give your 'service' to Erepos. Command *him* to command. The whole city knows him. Who could be better?"

Bifalt shook his head. "No, Brother. The whole city knows him, yes. But he does not give orders. He works by persuasion. He reasons with people, or cajoles them. At times, he bribes them." The district of Women was one example. "Everyone knows that he does *my* bidding. He does not tell them to do *his*. If he tries to command now, he will be met with arguments, or demands for favors, or pleas to be spared.

"He will help you, Lome. Think of him—"

The younger Prince interrupted by fluttering his hands as if he were scattering objections. "*Help* me? He does not even *like* me. *Nobody* likes me."

"Nobody *knows* you," put in Jaspid, still softly. "You keep to yourself. You always have. Even your drinking is private."

King Bifalt took a deep breath. Deliberately, he ignored Lome's denial. "Think of the Land-Captain," he insisted, "as your aide. He has other duties, certainly. But he will give you as much time as he can. He knows my plans for the evacuation. And he knows the people. He can introduce you to prominent men and women in every district. They can introduce you to others. With you beside him, Erepos can remind them of your authority. He can tell them why you have come to them.

"But the *commands*, Brother. The commands must be yours. Your authority is mine. Like mine, it comes to you from our father. *You* will not be met with arguments or demands or pleas. You will make it plain to our people that if they do not obey you they will be left to die."

The King expected more protests. He did not get them. Lome seemed to startle himself by asking, "You want us to flee? Where can we go?"

"To Amika," answered Bifalt at once. "Queen Estie expects this. Her realm will welcome you. Chancellor Sikthorn will provide for you and our people.

"Your best path is the Queen's road to Fivebridge. It is direct—and well supplied with inns. As for the rest of Belleger, even now Crickin"— the Captain of the Count—"travels everywhere, urging folk to leave their homes and make haste to the nearest bridge. Wherever they cross the Line, they will be made welcome."

For a moment, Lome simply gaped. Then, abruptly, he turned away.

The King's bodyguards edged closer in case the younger Prince tried to run. Jaspid put out a hand to dissuade him. But Lome stopped with his back to Bifalt; covered his face with his hands.

"Where?" he muttered to himself. "Where is it?"

Bifalt and Prince Jaspid exchanged confused glances. Neither of them understood.

Before the King could say anything, Lome exclaimed, "Ah!" and wheeled to confront him. "Now I see it. *There* is the flaw. You are not so perfect, Brother. There *had* to be a flaw.

"No doubt, your plans to flush your subjects out of the city are clever. No doubt, you will fight fiercely to protect our flight. And no doubt, Amika will welcome us, at least for a time.

"But the *bridges*, Brother. The road to the *library*. If that is our best road, it will serve the enemy as well. It will take him straight to his target. After he has overrun the Hand, he will strike at the library without the inconvenience of crossing Belleger and the desert. And while he does so, we will be no more safe in Amika than we are here."

"And you think I do not know the danger?" retorted King Bifalt. "I do. As does Queen Estie. She has made her own plans to counter it. Her guardsmen will be ready when you and our people cross into Amika. The enemy will not enter her realm while she has soldiers to defend it."

Scowling, Prince Lome studied King Bifalt. Bifalt saw doubts and desires squirm across his brother's features. He could almost name them. But he did not know where they would lead.

Then Lome let out a gusting sigh. "You astonish me, Bifalt. You almost make me believe what you ask is possible."

A moment later, however, his expression closed like a door. He glowered at the roadbed instead of the King.

"But no," he groaned. "I cannot do it." A kind of agony twisted in his voice, a dread that wracked him. "Your people know me by repute. They have nourished their scorn for decades. They will not obey me. They will only *laugh*.

"Hells, Brother!" he cried. "You are a monster. *I need a drink*."

Lome's distress made Bifalt *feel* like a monster. He had not chosen Lome's path in life—but he had also done nothing to redirect it. Still, he did not relent. That was his role here: here and everywhere. He did not relent.

He could not give his brother courage, or self-respect, or devotion to Belleger. But he could offer protection.

"Calm yourself, Brother," he said hoarsely. "No one will laugh at you. I will ensure it. I will give you—" He looked around at his body-guards. He could not do without Jeck. And Spliner and Boy were not veterans. They were not known as fighting men. "I will give you Malder.

"He will stand with you in his breastplate and helm. He will have his saber at his hip and his rifle on his shoulder. No one will laugh."

The big bodyguard had that effect.

If King Bifalt's unplanned announcement took Malder aback, he did not show it. His wits were as quick as Jeck's. Without hesitation, he approached Prince Lome.

In a voice like scattering gravel, he promised, "No one will laugh at you, Highness."

While Lome hesitated, caught between his fears and desires, King Bifalt considered what he knew about Lome's reasons for treachery and drinking. To Bifalt's way of thinking, they came down to outraged vanity. But he picked a version of them that would not offend his floundering brother.

"When you arranged to have Amika's Queen killed, you were trying to save Belleger. You believed that our alliance was our greatest threat. Now the threat is greater. Here is your chance to save Bellegerin lives— and to be *known* for saving them—without conniving or treachery."

At that, Lome flinched. Perhaps he did not expect Bifalt to know him so well. But then, slowly, he raised his head. His gaze climbed to meet Bifalt's.

Almost whimpering, he mumbled, "As you say, Majesty. I will do it."

A moment later, his old indignation came to his rescue. "But understand *this*." Imitating the King, he poked Bifalt's chest. "If even one of your 'prominent' men and women laughs at me—or if Erepos refuses any of my demands on his time—I will leave your precious Bellegerins to their doom."

Bifalt wanted to smack Lome. Instead, he mustered an uncharacteristic mildness. "As you say, Brother. No one will fault you for it."

"Ha!" cried Lome: a shout of triumph or a wail of grief. King Bifalt could not tell the difference. He doubted that Lome himself knew what he felt at that moment. But Bifalt had nothing more to say. He only watched as Lome turned, thrust his way between Malder and Spliner, and hurried away down the street.

Malder cocked his head at the King: a mute question. Speaking quickly, Bifalt answered, "Go with him. Keep my promise to him. If you have questions, we will talk later."

Nodding his acceptance, the brawler followed Lome.

Unlike King Bifalt, Prince Jaspid was laughing. He did not make a sound, but he shook with released tension, and his eyes were bright with mirth. When he could control his voice, he said, "Well struck,

Majesty." He had no scorn in him. He was simply pleased. "I would not have thought to turn his vanity against him. It is the only weapon he cannot deflect."

Until he lost sight of the younger Prince in the growing crowds, King Bifalt did not notice that his neck and shoulders ached as if he had taken a beating.

THREE

A VISIT TO THE BAY OF LIGHTS

As winter spread its hand over the western reaches of Beleger, Klamath son of Klimith rode out from the Open Hand with a dull dawn at his back and First Captain Matt at his side. Trailing a small company of twelve, they headed for the Bay of Lights, where the enemy would strike first.

Following the season of rains and drizzle, an unruly sheet of lead covered the region from horizon to horizon. Bruised and twisted clouds shrouded the landscape with gloom. The atmosphere had a heavy feel, an expectant hush, that promised snow. But the threat of storms did not trouble General Klamath. He could have found his way in any weather. For the First Captain, however, the beaten track was new. Until now, his duties had kept him in the vicinity of the Hand.

Without qualms, Klamath and Matt left the army to Second Captain Hegels. A former Amikan Commander, he was a humorless veteran with a literal mind. He demanded precision from himself and expected the same from his men. He would not waste time while the General and the First Captain were away.

The company they led were not soldiers. Eleven of them were youths, hardly more than boys, who had volunteered to join the bay's defense because they were fiercely interested in learning to fire cannon. No doubt, they sought adventure and a sense of manhood. To Klamath's eye, they had neither the strength nor the endurance to carry cannonballs or wrestle with the guns. On the other hand, he was confident that they could light fuses all day. In any case, Captain Flisk and Commander Forguile would find some use for them.

But the twelfth volunteer was a different matter. He was Father Skurn, a priest of the Great God Rile.

To Klamath's certain knowledge, Skurn was the last priest in the Open Hand. He may have been the last priest in Belleger. Father Knout was dead, and all of the others had been captured. Since then, they had accepted King Bifalt's offer to let them join Set Ungabwey's caravan. Perhaps they had been as lost as they seemed without their Archpriest.

Apparently, Father Skurn had made a different choice.

In his heart, Klamath believed that Elgart was dead. He considered Skurn a party to that crime. He had felt an instant fury when he recognized the priest. But he had not shown it. He had the soldier's gift for setting himself aside in the face of threats. He had seemed calm as he approached the priest.

Despite the heavy stillness, the air had teeth. Father Skurn had covered his black robe with an oiled rain-cape and wrapped a heavy shawl around his neck. Still, he suffered in the cold. His distress showed in the bursts of vapor from his mouth. The hood of his cape hid his features, but the jut of his beard betrayed that he was shivering.

Drawing his mount to the priest's side, General Klamath had said almost mildly, "You surprise me, priest. Your comrades have gone south. Why are you not with them?"

Skurn straightened his back, collected his breath. He appeared to remember that he had once been the Archpriest's right hand. After a moment, he countered as if he could not be cowed, "Truth?"

The General snorted. "Of course, truth. Nothing less will satisfy me."

He meant, I do not believe in gods. Or priests.

He also meant, You may not realize how easily your accidental death can be arranged.

In gouts of vapor, Father Skurn replied, "I want to see the ships that threaten you. And I hope to prove my honesty by serving where I can."

That was not the answer Klamath expected. "Why?" he demanded. "As I recall, you preach that there is no enemy. There will be no war.

King Bifalt has been misled by the library's Magisters. The only war is the one in every heart that does not put its faith in your 'Great God.'"

"It seems," rasped the priest, "I was mistaken." In a rush, he added, "Not about the war in every heart. *That* is truth. But about the library's Magisters. It seems they *do* have an enemy.

"Whoever he is, he does not serve the Great God Rile. Our God desires only peace. I want to see this enemy for myself. I want proof that he exists. I cannot understand why the Great God has not already overcome him. In his name, I will support your forces."

The General felt like spitting. He did not believe that the Great God desired only peace. But he saw no benefit in calling Skurn a liar. The priest would not be here now if he could be intimidated by anything less than a knife at his throat. His words were vapor, nothing more. His actions would reveal the truth. With a shrug, Klamath let the man join the boys.

Now the company of volunteers and the two commanders traveled together. At a steady canter, their trip would take less than half a day. While the boys chattered together, hardly able to contain their excitement, Klamath and Matt rode in silence. They each had their own reasons for visiting the Bay of Lights.

At first, Klamath had been reluctant to go. His duty called him to the bay, to the circumstances there and the final preparations for battle; but he fretted about his King. He did not like what he had seen of Bifalt's sagging shoulders, Bifalt's air of doubt. Belleger needed *King* Bifalt, not this slumped man who looked ready to stoop in defeat. But when Matt had requested leave to see the bay for himself, General Klamath had shaken off his reluctance. He knew why Matt wanted to go. And he had his own decisions to make.

Some time ago, sub-Commander Waysel had delivered the last of Amika's promised cannon. After years of effort and blood, the fortifications had been completed. But the cost had been high. Two hundred laborers had given their last strength. Too many of them had died on the terraces. And the plight of the survivors was little better. Their eyes were glazed with cold. A number of them had lost fingers and toes to frostbite, ears and cheeks. Working with stone in the bay's damp, bitter cold had left mangled hands, arms, legs. There were rotting sores and infections everywhere.

Since then, however, carts and wagons had carried them back to the Open Hand. Fresh workmen and servants had dismantled the bunkhouses, kitchens, and toolsheds from the fortifications; hauled boards, timbers, and stoves up the road. In the lee of a low hill near the cliff, the pieces of walls and ceilings had been reassembled to make housing for the cannoneers, riflemen, and Magisters who would fight the first battle against the invasion.

The gunners were all volunteers, but they were too few for the number of cannon. The riflemen were there to help them. An infirmary had been built, and physicians were already on their way. At present, however, the Magisters were still back in the Hand. King Bifalt and General Klamath had not yet decided which Decimates the bay's defense would need—and how many sorcerers the defense of Belleger could afford to risk. Klamath hoped that when he returned to Belleger's Fist, he would have clearer ideas to share with his King.

Matt's reasons for visiting the bay were entirely his own. The First Captain wanted to see his eldest son, Mattwil. The time that they had spent together among the training-fields outside the Open Hand had ended painfully.

During the past summer and autumn, Mattwil had been at work as a stonemason on Queen Estie's road. However, he had deserted his duty in order to warn Belleger that the road's Amikan overseers were using and torturing Nuuri slaves. That crime had been the doing of King Smegin, Queen Estie's father. The Queen had put a stop to it, but not before Mattwil had fled in the night. When he had delivered his report, he had worn his actions as if they covered him in Nuuri blood. He had not fought to defend them against Amikan cruelty: he had run away. Afterward, he had not known how to bear his shame. In his father's presence, and Klamath's, he had vowed that he would not fight in the coming war—and that he would never serve with Amikans again.

Matt would have given his heart's blood to cleanse his son's spirit; but Mattwil had refused his love. For that reason, and because he hoped that some good would come of it, General Klamath had sent the young man to Captain Flisk in the bay. The gun emplacements had a seemingly endless need for skilled stonemasons. And Heren Flisk was a kind man who understood shame. Klamath had trusted the Captain to provide the mixture of attention, neglect, and exhausting work that Mattwil needed. And he had hoped that the example set by Commander Forguile and the Amikan workmen would ease Mattwil's bitterness.

More than once since that day, Klamath had offered to recall Mattwil if Matt wished it; but Matt had declined. When the two old friends were alone, Matt had not troubled to hide his pain. "My son is a good man," he told Klamath. "Whatever he does, he has good reasons—although," admitted the First Captain ruefully, "he may not know what they are. He will find his way back to his family when he can."

Riding together toward the bay, the General set his own concerns aside at intervals to consider Matt's—and Mattwil's. But he said nothing. He had nothing new to add. Looking back, he wondered if he had been wrong to send the young man away at a time when Mattwil and his father needed each other. That was characteristic of him. He made decisions because he was King Bifalt's General and decisions were expected of him. Later, he doubted himself. Now he expected to learn whether his doubts were justified after Matt had spoken with his son.

He would not have been surprised to hear that Mattwil regarded him as the kind of man who sacrificed his own wounded after a battle.

Approaching the camp, the track curved around the dense woodland that rimmed the cliffs northward from the steep road down to the strand and the sea. Here General Klamath felt the fringes of the tormented winds battering themselves against the precipices and the wracked waves, whipping spray upward. Among the bare, black trees, a scout waved an acknowledgment to the General's company, then hurried away to forewarn Commander Forguile and Captain Flisk of Klamath's coming.

As the General passed the edge of the woods, he caught sight of the encampment. Interspersed with kitchens, the low bunkhouses formed a line away from the cliffs and the worst of the winds. Most of the bunkhouses were probably empty now. They would be filled as King Bifalt's Magisters and more riflemen came to join the gunners.

Ennis Forguile and Heren Flisk stood outside the nearest kitchen, waiting to greet the King's General. Behind them, a small crowd of riflemen, cannoneers, and servants gathered.

Winter had opened its hand over the Open Hand. In the Bay of Lights, it was already clenching its fist. Despite the shelter of the hill, the winds cut like serrated blades, and the cold was fierce. The conditions would be worse when the snows began.

A little distance from the Commander and the Captain, General Klamath halted his company. To Matt, he said in a soft growl, "When I have introduced you, take the boys and Father Skurn to the kitchen. Get them fed. And *watch* that priest. Soon you will be relieved. Then you spend as much time as you need with Mattwil. There is no hurry."

The First Captain nodded without meeting Klamath's gaze. He was scanning the bunkhouses and kitchens with a father's hunger, a father's apprehension.

Sighing privately, Klamath told his company to dismount.

As he and Matt walked closer, Commander Forguile sent servants to tend the horses. Some of the boys started to follow the General, but Father Skurn called them back. As if he had put himself in charge of them, the priest gathered them around him to wait for orders. He may have thought that young volunteers eager for the blaze and thunder of cannon would be easier to convert than grown men. Or he may have simply wished to demonstrate his desire to be of service.

Forguile and Flisk came forward. The Commander walked a little ahead of his comrade. He had always been more sure of himself than Flisk, and had done much to help King Bifalt forge an alliance with Amika, Forguile's homeland. But Klamath knew from their reports that they had become friends.

Both men wore rain-capes lined with layers of wool. Their garb, like their long exhaustion, made them indistinguishable from any of their laborers. Long ago, Ennis Forguile had been the first officer of

King Smegin's honor guard. Now he had set aside his orange headband and scabbard, and his trim goatee and moustache had become a ragged beard like any other man's. As for Flisk, he had lost his place in Belleger's army when an Amikan arrow had pierced his shoulder at the joint. That wound still hampered him. He looked weaker than Forguile; less capable. But the King thought highly of him. Naming him Captain, King Bifalt had sent him to serve with Commander Forguile overseeing the Bellegerins and Amikans constructing the bay's fortifications. Only the signal flags tucked under their belts marked them as officers.

Curtly, General Klamath introduced Flisk, Forguile, and the First Captain to each other. He took it upon himself to mention that Matt was Mattwil's father. Then he sent his old friend to the kitchen with the boys and the priest.

As soon as they were out of earshot, the General told the Captain and the Commander, "Be wary of that man." Gusts stung his cheeks, then scurried away. "He is Father Skurn, a priest of the Great God Rile. He claims that he has come merely to watch and serve, but he has crimes on his conscience. If he *has* a conscience. Put him to work like any other servant. Let him preach if he finds anyone to hear him. But do not let him anywhere near the guns, the gunpowder, or the fuses. *Do not.* I allowed him to come because I want to learn the truth about him."

Flisk flinched at these orders as if they were one worry too many. But Forguile met them with a reckless grin. Instead of answering Klamath, he summoned some of the nearby riflemen. To them, he repeated the General's instructions. Sure that he would be obeyed, he sounded both grim and cheerful.

That was enough for Klamath. He put the priest out of his mind.

"Now," he said more calmly. "Show me the fortifications. Tell me your concerns. We have decisions to make."

Forguile grinned again. Flisk straightened his back. Together, they took General Klamath up the slope to the crest of the hill, the rim of the cliff, and the steep road down to the jumble of boulders that blocked the surging seas.

Here the winds were ferocious. They tore against each other and rebounded as if they mirrored the waves below them, lashing at Klamath's eyes until he could barely see. Out *there*, he knew, beyond the reach of the long guns, stood the reef which had once sealed the whole bay. Now it had a gap among its teeth, a breach made by sorcery. The gap was only wide enough to admit one of the enemy's black ships at a time, but it proved that those ships had the power to enter the bay.

The reef was not the only obstacle that the enemy would have to clear away. Within the reef's wide curve, the whole floor of the bay was thick with massive boulders, mounds of stone, granite fangs. They ripped apart every heave and sigh of the sea's hunger for the strand, sent the waters piling against each other to form treacherous cross-currents, eddies, vicious whirlpools. The enemy would not be able to approach the shore until the whole bay had been made safe for ships.

When he had cleared his sight, Klamath looked downward.

In a distant age, some strange convulsion had broken open the former cliff-face. It was no longer sheer. Instead, it sloped away in five levels like nature's ramparts against the sea. During the past decade, those levels had been worked into walled terraces extending on both sides of the road. Then emplacements for Queen Estie's cannon had been set into the terraces. Only the road made them accessible from above or below.

Now there were forty emplacements, eight on each of the bay's five terraces, four on each side. The two highest levels held the long guns, the only cannon that could almost reach the inner wall of the reef. The next two terraces were armed with medium cannon. Eight heavy siege-guns defended the lowest. Each emplacement had its mortised housing clad in oilcloth to protect its supply of gunpowder. It also had its stone-walled trough filled with shot and chain. The guns in their trucks had been roped into the emplacements. And the cruel work of smoothing the terraces so that men could run along them was done.

That was the best that Belleger and Amika together could do. If those fortifications did not suffice to hold back the enemy, the invasion would begin in earnest.

General Klamath nodded his approval. Behind his mask of authority, he was in awe of what had been accomplished here. But he was also dismayed by the dangers of opposing an army of sorcerers with mere cannon. The gunners would be exposed to any Decimate that the enemy chose to throw at them.

"You have accomplished wonders," he told Flisk and Forguile, "and paid a high price. If I could, I would relieve you. But no one else knows your cannon and your cannoneers as well as you do. Now tell me. What are your immediate concerns? What do you need while we wait for the enemy?"

"The guns, General," replied the Commander promptly. "We have done what we can for them. They are wrapped tight in oilcloth. But that is not enough."

"The winds, sir," put in Captain Flisk. "They reach everywhere. And they carry rain. Or salt spray. Or snow when it comes. If the guns are not kept dry, they will fail."

"To be safe," added Forguile, "they should be cleaned every day. But our volunteers are too few. And too weak. Even your riflemen are near their limits."

"You need more men." Klamath spoke as if he did not expect to need every soldier he had. "And when the enemy comes? Do you have enough to work the guns?"

Hesitating, Flisk looked at his comrade. Forguile answered with assurance. "To fire and reload quickly, General, each cannon requires four. One to load and tamp down the gunpowder and wadding. One to carry the ball or chain. One to light the fuse. One to ready the next gunpowder and wadding so that the others can heave the gun back into position after it recoils." He shrugged. "We can make do with three. Four will be more effective."

The General made a mental calculation. Privately, he sighed. "I cannot spare as many as you need. I will send as many as I can. Keep any who volunteer as gunners. And enlist the servants if you must. Teach them tasks that do not require skill."

Carrying cannonballs was a question of strength, not of training.

Heren Flisk seemed to sag at the prospect of not having enough men. The Commander kept his mind on General Klamath's immediate question.

"Thank you, sir. We will do what we can. But we have another concern."

Klamath took a deep breath. "Name it."

"Ice," stated Forguile flatly. "In this cold, any water freezes on stone. Rain. Even spray. Snow when it comes. Ice makes every surface treacherous.

"We have run lines down both sides of the road." With a gesture, he indicated the ropes. "They are well anchored. But they are not enough. The road is too steep. Any man can slip." With an edge in his voice, he finished, "The ice will weaken us before the enemy comes."

The thought of men sliding downward until they crashed against the boulders of the strand made Klamath wince.

"The terraces are no better," put in Flisk as if he were arguing. "Already, ice sheets the lower levels. Soon it will be everywhere. Men running to the guns may break limbs." After a moment, he remembered to say, "Sir."

More for the Captain's sake than the Commander's, General Klamath mustered a tone of confidence. "That peril, at least, sirs, we can ease. You have a number of stoves. Use them all. If they do not produce enough ash, build bonfires. Ash will corrode the ice. Land-Captain Erepos will keep you supplied with firewood. No doubt, he will also deliver salt if he can, but ash will serve as well."

Trying to hide his relief, Heren Flisk sagged against his comrade. Forguile could stand the weight. He was not hampered by an old wound. Without calling attention to himself, he supported the Captain.

"Thank you, General," said the Amikan. "I had not thought of ash. As you say, it will serve."

Klamath gave the officers a moment. When he saw that Flisk had recovered his balance, and Forguile was waiting, he said, "So much for the present. Now we must consider our defense when the enemy comes. King Bifalt will send Magisters, but he needs to know which Decimates will be most useful." And how many Magisters he could afford to risk. "What are your thoughts?"

"Lightning," said the Commander at once. "It has range. It may be able to reach ships when they pass the reef."

Flisk shook his head. "But not fire, sir. The winds will scatter it."

"And not earthquake," put in Forguile. "Not unless the King wishes the road and the emplacements broken." All of his work and the Captain's wasted. "That may slow the enemy. It will not defeat him. He will be prepared to devise his own passage up the cliff."

General Klamath agreed. Nodding, he asked, "What of pestilence? What of wind and drought?"

"Pestilence has too little range." The Commander was sure. "When those Magisters are near enough to reach the enemy, his sorcerers will be able to strike at *them*. No Magister of wind can counter these gusts and gales. And drought will be useless here."

For a long moment, Klamath studied the bay: the froth and surge of the waters, the teeth of the rocks, the erratic scourge of the winds. He had his own ideas about the lesser Decimates, but he did not mention them. They were untried.

Finally, he thanked the Captain and the Commander. "You have done well, sirs. You will do more before the end. When I return to the Open Hand, I will send as many men as I can. Until the enemy comes, hold fast. And *rest*, both of you. Know that you are not alone. And that no one else can take your place."

Flisk looked clenched for endurance—and unsure of his ability to endure. Forguile's grin had a wild cast that promised extravagant efforts. Neither of them spoke again as they guided General Klamath back to the nearest kitchen and hot food.

When Klamath had eaten, he spent an hour among the bay's stubborn volunteers, offering praise and encouragement to anyone who seemed able to listen. Later, he went down to the terraces to inspect the emplacements for himself, and to watch how his riflemen worked with the cannoneers and the guns. When he was satisfied, he climbed back up the road to the rim of the cliff.

There he found the First Captain waiting.

Klamath was already breathing hard, tested by the steep ascent. The sight of his old friend seemed to seize the air in his chest.

Matt looked like a man who had taken a blow to the heart. In the afternoon sunlight, his eyes held a stifled pain that made him seem blind. He faced the General's arrival as if he had no idea who Klamath was. He was taller than Klamath, stronger; made for hard work and courage. Nevertheless he had been given a beating that he did not know how to bear.

Hells! thought Klamath. Mattwil.

At once rigid and unresisting, Matt went with Klamath as the General drew him back toward the buildings of the camp. He did not react as Klamath called for their horses. When servants and Captain Flisk brought the mounts, Matt went through the reflexive motions of checking the girth and tack, settling the saddle. Unaware of himself and Klamath, he stepped up into his seat.

Flisk held the reins while Klamath mounted. Looking up at Klamath, the Captain said like pleading, "I did not do enough for him, sir." He meant Mattwil. The General had sent Matt's son to him. "The work distracted me. And he pushed himself hard. But I imagined that he found a little peace. I did not expect—"

Klamath cut him off. "Enough, Captain," he said too harshly. "We must go. You did as much as Mattwil allowed. He is responsible for himself."

Kicking his mount, Klamath turned away.

After a moment of uncertainty, Matt joined him. Together, they left the camp, following the track on its winding way toward the Open Hand and duty.

The General kept his thoughts to himself until they put the afternoon sun squarely at their backs. As their shadows began to stretch in front of them, he finally broke into Matt's silence.

"Enough," he said again, still too harshly. "I am something worse than your commander, Matt. I am your friend. You cannot keep this to yourself, whatever it is. Tell me about Mattwil."

Then he listened, aching, while his old friend obeyed.

"Did you know?" Matt seemed to address the shadows. "He has a girl with him. A little thing. He could break her with one hand. But old enough to know abuse. Intense enough to value kindness. She clings to him.

"He does not cling to her. But he accepts her as if she has become necessary. He hardly spoke to me, except to tell me her name. She is Cloras. From Maloresse."

Go on, thought Klamath. Take your time. *Say* it.

Half groaning, Matt continued.

"He is battered, my son. Hands mangled. Nails broken. Bruises everywhere. His eyes reminded me of running sores. At first, I saw resentment in them. Then I thought that I was not real to him. A figment from someone else's past.

"Cloras spoke for him. She has a kind of timid boldness. She seemed to defend him. She asked if I knew you. 'Your General sent him here,' she said. 'That was cruel. Look at him.'

"I was looking. I could not look away.

"After a moment, he told her that he thought so at first. 'But I needed this work,' he said. 'Where else can I make amends?'

"I tried to engage him, but I did not know how. 'Will you return to the Open Hand now?' I asked. 'You and Cloras? I am the General's First Captain. I can take you with me, both of you. And I have news from your mother. She wrote to me, a letter carried by a man you know, a man and his family, neighbors leaving their home to escape the threat of war. Matta sends—'

"He stared at me until my throat closed. First, he said, 'Cloras has no family.' He seemed to reprimand me. Then he said, 'My place is here. I will not desert again.'"

With his head turned away, Matt asked like a cry, "What else could I do, Klamath? He is a man, not a boy. He has chosen his life. How can I tell him to make a different choice?"

Klamath felt his friend's anguish. In the cold, his tears stung his eyes. His voice was a growl of compassion.

"Blame the work, Matt. He has done more than he knows how to endure. It numbs him. But now it is done. He will remember your love when he regains his strength. And he will be safe while he recovers. No one will ask him to join the fighting. If he has lost his way, he will find it again."

The shape of the hills dimmed the afternoon light. A premature twilight spread around the riders. It seemed to reach far into a dark future.

As if he were confessing himself, Matt said to the gloom, "I fear that priest." He had become more and less than the man Klamath knew, harder and more bitter. "Do you remember, Klamath? Mattwil heard the same priest preach, or another like him. The Church—" The spurned father choked for a moment. "The Church gave my son another reason to accuse himself. He *believed* its teachings. They offered him their version of forgiveness, but even that he could not accept. If he accepts it now, he will be truly lost."

To that, Klamath had no answer. Instead of wasting words that would give no comfort, he nudged his horse closer to Matt's. With one hand, he reached out to grip Matt's shoulder for a moment. He had no other language for his share of his old friend's sorrow.

During the rest of their ride back to the Open Hand, they did not speak again.

FOUR

NEW USES FOR SORCERY

When General Klamath returned to the Bay of Lights several days later, he had a specific purpose. He was leading a company of untried Magisters. He and King Bifalt wanted to know whether their Decimates could serve the defense. If they could, the sorcerers would need to understand what was expected of them.

Before dawn in the bailey of Belleger's Fist, the General gathered the Magisters he had summoned. A heavy sky laden with winter had been dropping masses of snow for the past two days. More snow was falling now, and an aching cold covered the Open Hand. Along Belleger's coastal cliffs, the weather would be worse. Accordingly, all of the Decimate-wielders were so thickly bundled that they resembled sheep ready for shearing. In their wool and padding, several of them were too encumbered to mount their horses without help.

General Klamath had decided on eighteen of Belleger's and Amika's theurgists. Of them, three wielded the Decimate of drought. Klamath did not expect to use them in the bay. Their power could not reach the enemy. But he had a more immediate task for them. Snow was nothing more than frozen rain; and he had been told that every Decimate could counteract its own form of power. He wanted to see how drought fared in weather like this.

Among the others, eight were lightning-wielders: Magister Lambent and seven others. The General could have asked for more, but eight would be enough for his purpose. He wanted to test their range. And he had another test in mind for them as well.

To that number, Klamath had added seven Magisters of wind. He saw more possibilities in them than the King's other advisers did. He hoped to learn what the power of wind could do—especially in bad weather.

The snow was coming down as thick as a wall. Even the looming mass of the keep itself was barely visible. Inexperienced riders might lose their way without guidance. As a precaution, Klamath had assigned a rifleman to keep track of his charges.

He counted the Magisters again when they had mounted. He expected eighteen, but he found one more.

Squinting through the snow, he scanned his company until he identified the hedgehog shape of Magister Pillion.

Whose Decimate was earthquake.

Under other circumstances, Klamath would have questioned the man immediately. But the snow enclosed the riders like a shroud, and they had a long way to go. The distance would strain a vexed Magister like Lambent despite his past experience. It would seem cruel to people who had not spent countless hours on horseback. To spare them more waiting, he led them out of the bailey. He could speak with Magister Pillion along the way.

The General and his rifleman carried lanterns. Magister Trench had brought one. And a Bellegerin Magister of lightning, a woman named Visible, had done the same. Falling snow dulled their flames to the faintness of swamp-lights; but even that dim glow might keep the riders together.

Following Klamath, his company passed from Belleger's Fist through the fortifications of King Brigin's original city and out into the Open Hand. The riding was not difficult there despite the high drifts and packed sheets of snow. Winter slowed the busyness of the city, certainly, but did not stop it. The Hand held too many people with too much to do. Carts and horses, servants and workers plodding to and from their tasks, families needing food and water and wood, children at play: all had combined to pack distinct paths along the streets. Even

Magisters who rode poorly, like Pillion, and those with bad eyes, like Lambent, moved with comparative ease.

Beyond the fringes of the city, however, there was no road. Of course, riders traveled between the Hand and the bay every day: messengers, riflemen, servants, occasional recruits. Three of them had left ahead of the General, dispatched to warn Captain Flisk and Commander Forguile that he was coming. But snowfall had obliterated their tracks. Outside the Hand, Klamath and his company seemed alone in the world, muffled by dusk and cold. Flakes hissed on the glass of the lanterns.

Fortunately, there was no wind. The snow came straight down as if it had no limit. If any wind had whipped it into Klamath's face, he would not have been able to see his own mount's head. Even without that hindrance, he had to blink constantly to clear his sight.

Twisting in his saddle, he was able to make out a lantern behind him. But he could not identify the Magister holding it. The other lights might have ceased to exist, effaced by snow.

The General contained himself for a league. Then he halted; waited for his company to arrive around him. So far, he had not lost anyone.

To the group, he announced, "I need a Magister of drought."

"Why?" came the answer. He recognized the acid voice of Magister Whimper, a woman almost as arrogant—or perhaps as protective of her dignity—as Magister Lambent.

Calmly, Klamath answered, "Can you counter the snowfall directly above us?"

"Why not?" she retorted. "It is only frozen rain."

The General kept his tone mild. "Then do so. I want to see all of you."

"A waste of time," snorted Magister Lambent. "Foolish. This cold will kill me while we indulge your curiosity."

That was all the prodding Magister Whimper needed. Shedding clots of snow, she raised her arms.

Almost immediately, the snowfall over the company began to dwindle. Briefly, it spun like spume. Then it faded to a delicate scatter of flakes. Soon it stopped altogether.

It still fell thickly around the riders, blocking the vistas in every direction. But now they sat their mounts in a clear space like a ragged cylinder reaching for the clouds. While Klamath watched, the clouds themselves thinned overhead, letting a hint of the new day touch the company.

Hells! he thought. Amazing!

He had no words to describe his sensation of *openness* within the thick embrace of the snow. He had grown accustomed to its wet clasp. Its absence lifted his spirit like a small taste of victory.

In a world where such things were possible, *everything* was possible.

The effect was better than he had hoped. If it could be sustained—

But of course she could not sustain it. Klamath had time to count his company again; reassure himself that he had not lost anyone. They were all present, cloaked in inches of snow. Magister Pillion, in particular, looked like a child's snowman perched atop his little mare.

Then Magister Whimper sagged. At once, the snowfall resumed as if it had never stopped. The future became as blank as dark water.

Satisfied, General Klamath told his company, "You see that it can be done. The effort is draining, but it provides a respite. It will ease our journey.

"Magister Whimper, if you and your comrades in turn will give us as much relief as you can, we will all have reason to thank you."

In a blur of snow, Magister Trench slapped his thigh. "A kind thought, General," he declared, "especially for those of us who cannot tell west from indigestion." His jibe was directed at Lambent. "And well done, Magister Whimper. I will be grateful for whatever you can do."

"And while you talk," snarled Magister Lambent, "we are forced to wait again. Will you keep us here, General?" His use of Klamath's title did not express respect. "I need shelter and a stove, not more words."

With a shrug that shed weight from his shoulders, the General turned his horse to the west and led his company onward.

The snowfall was as heavy and blinding as before. It gave no sign that it would ever weaken. But it was less daunting. It could be interrupted. Klamath's companions had surprises in them. Even the weather acknowledged their power, if only for moments.

He intended to find a better use for them.

✳

For the rest of the journey, the riders were comforted by short intervals of clear air and better light. Those pauses came irregularly:
each drought-wielder needed a different amount of time to recover.
But they came by turns as General Klamath had requested. Although
their benefits were fleeting, they gave everyone something to look forward to.

During the fourth of these gaps, Magister Pillion brought his mare
floundering to Klamath's side. "May I ride with you, General?" he asked
meekly.

As the sorcery of drought faltered, and snow began to fall again,
Klamath replied, "Of course, Magister." He had questions to ask. "I will
be glad of your presence. Without a companion, I feel alone in the world."

"As do I," said Pillion. "And I need to speak." He hesitated for a moment. "But this snow blankets sound. I do not know if you will hear me."

The General swallowed a snort of amusement. "I hear you. An entire army could pass us, and I might not know it. Distant sounds do not
carry. But a rider beside me I can hear."

"Then let me speak."

"Of course, Magister," repeated Klamath. He wanted the small
man to feel at ease. "We all need something to occupy our minds while
we ride."

"Thank you, General." The small man sounded sincerely grateful. "You
know I have a wife and children," he said, then stopped himself. After a
moment, he confessed, "I do not know where to begin."

"Take your time." Klamath knew that the Magister had a family.
He had learned as much as he could about every sorcerer available for
the war, Bellegerin and Amikan. "We cannot hurry in these conditions."

Pillion tried again. "Then do you know that I called Elgart my
friend? He considered me *his* friend. Before we lost him."

Klamath's eyebrows went up. "No." Elgart's way with secrets had
been one of his most annoying traits. He had spoken of things that

Klamath would have preferred not to hear, and had kept private things that would have interested Klamath keenly. "*That* I did not know."

How had Elgart become friends with a minor Magister of earthquake? And why had Elgart chosen him?

Abruptly, Pillion changed his mind. "No, General. I must begin yet again. You have no interest in my family and friends. You want to know why I am here. Will you answer a question?"

For the third time, Klamath said, "Of course, Magister."

At once, his companion rushed to ask, "I have heard a rumor. There is a priest among the servants in the bay. Is it true?"

The General was surprised again—but not by the rumor. Teams of riflemen, servants, and messengers traveled to the bay and back in shifts. Rumors were inevitable. That Pillion had heard them, however, or that he cared enough to seek confirmation from General Klamath: that was a surprise.

Did Pillion worship in the Church? Had he come to consult with a servant of the Great God Rile?

Perhaps. Still, Klamath saw no harm in answering. "It is," he admitted. "He is Father Skurn. For reasons of his own, he volunteered to work as a servant in the bay."

Abruptly, the Magister's meekness left him. "I know him." Muffled by snow, his voice held a note of ferocity. "I must see him."

On his guard now, the General countered bluntly, "Why?"

"For Elgart!" cried Pillion.

Inside himself, Klamath took a step back. There was more at stake here than he had guessed: the man's vehemence made that obvious. He was outraged by what had happened to Elgart.

Magister Pillion had to be handled with care.

"Perhaps, Magister," said Klamath equably, "it would be well to start yet again. You and Elgart were friends. Do you believe Father Skurn had a hand in his disappearance? His death?"

"Yes!" snapped Pillion. Then, more quietly, he contradicted himself. "No. Perhaps. I do not know." After a pause, he added, "But I can imagine it. Those priests are *evil*."

Distantly, as if he were alone in the snow, he explained, "Elgart took me with him once when he went to the Church. He wanted to speak with the Archpriest. And he wanted to know whatever I could tell him about the sorcery of those priests.

"The Archpriest was elsewhere. Elgart met with Father Skurn. I was his witness. Now he is gone.

"There is no sorcery in Father Skurn. I am certain. Yet he can draw on it. I am certain of that as well. I felt its presence. And I saw him impose a kind of drowsiness on Elgart, a half-waking sleep.

"As for me—"

There was a blur of movement. In the faint reach of his lantern, Klamath saw Pillion flailing his arms as if the snowflakes were attacking him; as if he wanted to ward them off or punch his way through them.

"Father Skurn tried to *seduce* me. *That* is the theurgy he serves. He looked into me, and filled me with his hopes for me, and used them as lures. He wanted me to believe that I would become a mighty Magister— that I would be the mightiest of my kind—if I gave myself to his"— Pillion snarled the words—"*Great God.* And I would lose nothing.

"Nothing," he panted, "except my wife and children. My friendship with Elgart. My loyalty to King Bifalt and Belleger. They would all be chaff to a servant of the Great God Rile."

While Klamath listened, staring at his companion, Magister Pillion said, "General, the sorcery of the Church is *persuasion.* But it can be more, much more. It can also be *coercion.*"

That assertion fit with other things the General had heard, mostly from King Bifalt, who had heard them indirectly himself. Yet even Magister Facile had never ventured such a positive claim against the priests.

Thinking hard, Klamath probed Pillion for more. "I understand your dismay, Magister. But it does not tell me why you have come. I assume you intend to see Father Skurn again. What do you hope to gain?"

The small man had his answer ready.

"If he still has no sorcery—if he is truly as lost as the other priests appear to be—" Pillion shook himself. "Well. I will have nothing to say." Then he delivered his threat. "But if he can still draw upon his source of theurgy, he is too dangerous to live. In any battle, his power could be ruinous. I will urge you to kill him while you can."

The General blinked at his companion. "You braved this harsh ride simply so that you can look at Father Skurn? You mean to judge him?"

According to the people Klamath had consulted, Pillion preferred a quiet life in his home, surrounded by his children, cared for by his wife. King Bifalt had never asked the unassuming little man for anything else. The King would not ask anything, until war came to the Open Hand.

"For Elgart," replied Magister Pillion. "It is the least I can do to repay his friendship."

Klamath considered Pillion's revelation. The whole notion of a theurgy that *persuaded*—that could *coerce*—was foreign to him, as strange as the seventh Decimate itself, which could banish and re-awaken other forms of sorcery. Had the priest exerted a power that could be called upon from some distant source and used to bend minds? That was a terrifying prospect. It had terrifying implications.

Magister Pillion had done Belleger a great service by warning Klamath. But the meek earthquake-wielder had done more: he had taken upon himself the responsibility for determining how perilous Father Skurn's presence might be. The General had not expected so much courage from the small man.

Now, however, the responsibility was Klamath's. If Pillion saw a threat in the priest, Klamath had a decision to make. The Magister was right: the ability to seduce or even compel Belleger's defenders would make Skurn too dangerous to live.

But—

Hells!

Could General Klamath order the priest shot for no better reason than that he *might* do harm? Was there a man or woman breathing anywhere who might *not* do harm, given the right provocations? How was killing a man who might or might not intend treachery better than plain murder?

And there was another difficulty. If the Great God's sorcery could be used for *persuasion*, Klamath had to wonder whether Father Skurn himself had been *coerced*. How could a man whose choices had been taken away from him deserve death?

Such questions caused Klamath a kind of moral pain. They were beyond him. Despite his exalted rank, he was only himself. Some choices required a degree of certainty that he lacked.

He was not proud of his doubts; but at times like this, they defined him. Deciding who lived and who died was a burden for the King. Klamath had never wanted the authority to send men to their deaths. He was a good soldier: he could do what he was told. That was enough.

It had to be.

Eventually, the General's company reached the fringes of the bleak woodland spreading from the road and the encampment northward along the cliffs for two or three leagues. There two riflemen emerged through the snowfall: scouts sent to confirm that the General and his people had not lost their way.

When Klamath and the scouts had tallied the Magisters and found them all present, one rifleman left to report to their officers. The other settled his mount beside Klamath's.

The snow fell softly. Nevertheless it had the thickness of a deluge.

Riding with the ease of long experience, the soldier grinned at Klamath. "You had a pleasant journey, General?"

The General managed a wry grimace, nothing more. He had no room in his mind for jests.

As soon as he and his company reached the encampment, they left their horses to the servants and hurried into the nearest kitchen. Shedding snow in dense flurries, they shrugged off their cloaks and huddled around the stoves.

Soon, Captain Flisk and Commander Forguile came in. When they had greeted everyone, and had been ignored by all of the Magisters except Trench and two or three others, General Klamath took the officers aside to hear their report.

Forguile did most of the talking. Rubbing his shoulder, Flisk said almost nothing.

While the Commander spoke, Klamath glanced around at the riflemen, servants, and volunteers who had gathered in this kitchen; but he did not spot Father Skurn. After a moment, he realized that he had lost track of Magister Pillion.

Well, there were other kitchens, and the bunkhouses all had stoves. The priest was probably in one of them. He would not have been allowed to descend to the terraces and guns.

As for Magister Pillion, he had undoubtedly gone looking for Skurn. Klamath felt a moment of anxiety for the earthquake-wielder, then shrugged it off. Even if the priest *was* dangerous, he could not do any harm without revealing his secret—if he had one. General Klamath concentrated on his larger concerns.

The defense of the bay.

His company of Magisters.

While the General explained his intentions to Flisk and Forguile, his Magisters left the stoves and seated themselves at one of the kitchen's long tables. They stayed together, perhaps avoiding contact with lesser men and women.

Cannoneers and riflemen went forward to fill their bowls and plates at the steaming pots and platters the cooks had prepared. The Magisters did not. Clearly, they expected to be served where they sat. Fortunately, the servants required no prompting. Forguile or—more likely—Flisk must have spoken to them earlier. When they brought food to the Magisters, the kitchen was spared a display of sarcastic superiority.

General Klamath joined the Magisters without saying anything. He had not brought them here to correct their manners. Like Father Skurn's fate, that was King Bifalt's responsibility. Klamath only needed them to do what he asked. He did not need them to do it politely.

When they had all finished eating, the General rose from his seat. "Magisters," he announced abruptly, "it is time to show me what you can do."

Magister Lambent jerked up his head. "To what purpose?" he demanded. "I assumed that you were hoping for a break in the snowfall.

Our sorcery is wasted in this weather. Even lightning is useless here. We should remain in shelter until the weather shifts. Any half-wit would say the same."

Magister Trench responded with a laugh like a grenade exploding in his chest. Several of the other theurgists chuckled. Inadvertently, Lambent had suggested that he himself was a half-wit.

But the General was not amused. He would have enjoyed losing his temper. He was in that mood. However, he restrained himself. "You make a good point, Magister," he replied, "where the Decimate of drought is concerned. We will not need it until we return to the Open Hand.

"Magister Whimper, you and your comrades should rest while you can." He called them *comrades* deliberately, knowing that in fact they disliked each other. Theurgists who shared a Decimate tended to resent the reminder that they were not unique. "The rest of you will come with me.

"Captain Flisk and Commander Forguile have arranged an escort. Twenty riflemen, I believe?" Both officers nodded, Flisk with a solemn frown, Forguile grinning. "They will ensure that you come to no harm."

The Magisters stared at him. A Bellegerin sorcerer of wind named Gust started to protest. Perhaps he shared Lambent's attitude. General Klamath cut him off.

"We will leave now. Dress warmly."

At once, he turned away to reclaim his own heavy cloak.

After a moment, the Magisters scrambled to follow him. Lambent made a show of reluctance, then hurried to catch up.

Outside, the snowfall had eased slightly. It was still heavy enough for Klamath's purpose.

Beyond the kitchen door, there were trails like gullies where men and women had been forcing their way through the accumulated snow for days. On either side, the drifts reached Klamath's thighs. Against the walls of the buildings, they rose as high as his shoulders. Fresh snowfall already covered the marks of recent boots and hooves, but the gullies remained. They formed distinct paths among the buildings and from there to the road into the bay.

As the Magisters emerged from the kitchen, fifteen of them, they were surrounded by their escort. Led by Captain Flisk with a lantern, the company trudged up and over the hill toward the rim of the Bay of Lights.

The wavering light of Flisk's lantern guided the General and his charges to the steep road, the only access to the terraces and the ocean's bouldered shore. Elsewhere, the crude half-circle of the bay was protected by forbidding cliffs. Any slip on the road might be fatal. One step past the cliff-edge anywhere else would mean a killing fall.

There Captain Flisk faced the company. The bay's conflicting winds sent the snow skirling. His lantern seemed to flicker as he announced, "We are five steps from the head of the road, Magisters. You are safe enough. But keep your distance." Then he said more strongly, "General!" and made room for Klamath.

"And still I do not understand," snorted Magister Lambent. "This snow is blinding. How will we know a road we cannot *see*?"

Like the crack of a whip, a woman snapped, "Oh, be silent, Lambent." She was an Amikan sorceress of lightning named Brighten. "King Bifalt is too sparing with you. Queen Estie would put your feet to the fire. King Smegin would have put your feet *in* the fire. General Klamath will explain himself.

"Improve your manners. Have you forgotten the riflemen? Your Decimate cannot shield you from bullets."

Klamath could not distinguish Lambent among the sorcerers. Already, they wore new blankets of snow. But he suspected that Lambent was trembling with indignation.

The General maintained his mask of calm. "It is true," he said so that everyone would hear him. "You will never know a road you cannot see. Or a precipice. That is why we are here.

"We have no way to gauge the enemy's power. He has shown us that the outer reef will not stop him. With so much strength, he may strike at us in any weather. We cannot assume that he will only attempt a landing under a clear sky. We must be ready to defend the realm whenever he comes.

"In that defense, our greatest need is for the Decimate of lightning."

Klamath made a tossing gesture, throwing objections away. "I realize, Magisters, that your range is limited. Your bolts will not reach ships beyond the reef. But when the reef is broken, the ships will come closer. Then they will use the Decimate of lightning to strike at the cannon. Your purpose will be to dismiss that sorcery before it can cripple us.

"And to do *that*, Magisters," he stated more strongly, "you will have to position yourselves among the guns. Down on the terraces." Where they would be most vulnerable. "Which you can only reach by this road.

"Of course," he added, projecting a certainty he did not feel, "you will have help. Soldiers will support you when they can be spared. And there are ropes stretched down both sides of the road. Also, ash has been scattered on the ice. Captain Flisk and Commander Forguile have spread salt on the terraces. You will have better footing than you do at this moment.

"But I am not satisfied. You are necessary. Magister Lambent, Magister Brighten, all of your comrades, I will not risk you. You must defend the cannon. And you must do so in any weather.

"That is why I have brought Magisters of wind.

"There are seven of you," said Klamath to Trench and the other wind-wielders. "Two riflemen will watch over each of you." The chaos of winds past the cliff-edge had left bald patches in some places, ice and deep snowbanks in others. The woods stood farther back. "You will go north. When you have passed beyond the terraces, you will stand near the bay's rim.

"From that place, you will cast your Decimates south, between the terraces and the seas. You will attempt to clear away any snow or rain or spray that obstructs the sight of our gunners and lightning-wielders.

"Whether you exert your sorcery separately or together, I leave to you, Magister Trench. But understand what I hope to accomplish. I want to see if you suffice to push the snowfall here aside. When the enemy comes, even one clear glimpse will be useful. Half a dozen heartbeats of open air may save lives on the terraces."

Lives and guns.

The Magisters had questions. General Klamath did not pause to explain further. He was eager to learn what sorcerous winds could do against the bay's gales and this heavy snowfall.

"Go now," he commanded. "The sooner you begin, the sooner we can return to the stoves.

"Captain Flisk has his orders."

Nodding to the Captain, Klamath stepped aside.

Flisk obeyed at once. While he moved among the Magisters of wind, assigning the riflemen in pairs, the theurgists looked around anxiously; stamped their feet and blew on their hands; complained to each other. "This is folly," grumbled Lambent to Brighten. "The Decimate of wind is too weak. It can do nothing here." He would have gone on, but Brighten stopped him by turning her back.

Magister Gust protested more loudly. To Trench, he insisted, "We cannot do this. In this weather? Against the confusion of *these* winds? No. We must refuse. Tell the General. He will listen to you."

Trench responded with one of his explosive laughs. "Calm yourself, my friend. It is worth trying. We have never worked together. Who knows what will happen when we do something new?" Then he added with a softer laugh, "You will be safe. Your escorts will guard you."

Around the company, riflemen produced lanterns from under their cloaks. Flisk lit them all with his own flame. Soon, he was satisfied.

Instead of trying to command the reluctant sorcerers, Captain Flisk spoke only to Trench. "Will you follow me, Magister?"

In a tone like his laugh, Trench replied, "Certainly, Captain. I have trusted you before. And I am eager for the challenge."

Heren Flisk gave the man a bow like an act of private homage. Then he turned and walked away, heading north with the earned assurance of a man who knew every detail of the bay better than he knew himself.

At once, Magister Trench and his guardians left in the Captain's wake, tracing the furrow Flisk kicked through the snow. Flurries wrapped around them as they made his path wider.

Watching them, Klamath smiled to himself. Clearly, Flisk and Trench had some personal history; but the General did not know what it was.

After a moment of hesitation, Magister Gust followed. One at a time, the rest of the wind-wielders fell into line. Some of them probably did not want to face the General's disapproval alone. Others may have hoped for a chance to outdo their peers.

Within moments, they had vanished in a wild swirl of snow. One by one, the lights of the lanterns disappeared.

"Now we must wait." Magister Lambent tried for asperity, but his stiff lips and cold tongue hindered him. "Only a villager who has somehow become the King's General and *friend* would treat us with so much disregard. We are Mag—"

Someone Klamath did not see—a Magister or a rifleman—flung a handful of snow in Lambent's face.

Incoherent with outrage, Lambent could not find a retort. Instead, he sputtered obscenities and curses.

Of course, the man had a point. Klamath felt chilled himself. And the Magisters would suffer more than he did. They had not spent years training in every kind of weather. Without a lantern, they stood lost in the erratic winds and snows.

A view over the terraces was important. The potential of Decimates used together was more so. If Magister Trench and his company could work as one— If they were stronger that way—

The sorcerers aboard the black ships had forced a breach in the reef by combining their Decimates. Surely Bellegerin and Amikan Magisters could work together in the realm's defense.

The General bit down on his hopes, slapped his hands to keep his blood circulating, and waited.

Before long, he heard a muffled shout.

It was too soon. The Magisters of wind could not have gone far enough yet. Even halfway there, their voices would be lost in the wind and snow.

And the shout came from the wrong direction.

Wheeling, Klamath turned east to face it.

In moments, he spotted the snow-shuttered blink of a lantern. Then he made out the blurred shape of a horse moving toward him.

A horse and rider.

Ignoring the hazards of the packed trail, Commander Forguile hurried closer.

He had someone sitting between his arms. Someone small. And unconscious? Dead? The cloaked bundle flopped against Forguile's support, unable to sit upright.

"General!" shouted the Commander again.

Klamath surged to meet him. Who was that small? One of the boys, the volunteer gunners? No. They were not grown men, but he remembered sturdy frames, signs of strength. And an accident to any of them would not require his attention.

There was another possibility—

Swinging out of his saddle, Commander Forguile lifted down Magister Pillion.

Pillion seemed to have shrunk inside his many garments. Forguile was able to carry him with one arm, hold up the lantern with the other.

When Klamath recognized Elgart's friend, he felt something like terror. Suddenly, threats he had not imagined rode the winds and snow from all directions.

Pillion looked unconscious, lost in the last sleep of a freezing death. Snowmelt must have soaked through to his skin. By the veiled glow of Forguile's lantern, Klamath saw blue lips, cheeks the fatal pallor of ice, eyes that seemed snow-blind. Tears had frozen on the Magister's face. They caught the light like tiny gems. His whole body was shivering, wracked by a chill like a high fever.

Quickly, the Commander explained, "He was in one of the bunkhouses with three of your riflemen and that priest. He entered and stared. Then he cried out and ran. Your men went after him. But he turned the wrong way, deeper into the snow. One rifleman found him in a drift higher than his head. He dragged him out and brought him to me." Forguile paused for an instant. "I have not seen the other two. They must have searched elsewhere."

With his throat full of dread, Klamath demanded, "And you did not take him to the nearest stove?"

"He was conscious then. He needs to speak to you."

Klamath swore. "He cannot speak if he does not live. He could have told *you* what he needs to say."

Forguile winced. "He insisted, General." Hells, the Commander was older than Klamath, yet he was *embarrassed*. "He fought me. I feared he would harm himself. Whatever it is means more to him than his life. When he started weeping, I snagged a horse and brought him here."

General Klamath shrugged excuses aside. Harshly, he demanded, "Have you seen the priest?"

The Commander frowned. "Not since the dawn meal, General."

"What was he doing in that bunkhouse?"

"Preaching, I am told. Only that. He wanted a larger audience. Three were all who chose to hear him."

Cursing to himself, Klamath thought, Too late. It is already too late.

But too late for *what*, he had no idea.

Hurrying, he lifted Pillion out of Forguile's clasp. The small man's weight surprised him. Pillion's garments had absorbed too much water. Carefully, Klamath sank to his knees in the snow, then sat back on his heels, holding the Magister against him.

"Now give us space, Commander."

Forguile knew an order when he heard it. Magisters and riflemen had crowded closer. "Stand *back*!" he demanded. "And be still! Let General Klamath hear."

After an instant of confusion, the soldiers obeyed. Brusquely, they herded the reluctant Magisters away.

Bracing Pillion's head with one arm, Klamath rubbed the man's chest; tried to rouse him. That had no effect. Fearing that he had already waited too long, Klamath slapped the Magister's face lightly.

Again.

And again with more force.

Magister Pillion's eyelids fluttered. His eyes did not focus. Perhaps they could not. But his lips moved.

Scarcely audible, he asked, "General?"

Through his teeth, Klamath said, "I am here, Magister. Give me your report."

Pillion blinked as if he understood. Violent shivers ran through him. He hardly had the strength to form words. Klamath hardly had the courage to hear him.

"I saw!" croaked the Magister. "Here. I saw *him*." His shivering threatened to break him, but he clung to his dismay. "He was nothing. No sorcerer. No sorcery. I am certain.

"But he changed. I *saw* it, I tell you. Any sorcerer would see it. His power was restored. I saw it given back to him. And he saw *me*.

"I ran to warn you. Then I—" Pillion seemed to lose track of his thoughts. "There was snow everywhere," he breathed like groaning. "Too deep. I could not—"

The small, valiant man was done. His eyes rolled back in his head. Shivers scattered the shreds of his desperation. He slumped against Klamath's arm.

But Klamath had heard enough. Furious with himself, frantic for Pillion, he looked around for the nearest rifleman. "You!" he shouted. "Take the Commander's horse. Get this Magister to a stove! Warm him. Save him if you can."

"And send more men!" A heartbeat later, he added, "Mounted!"

Captain Flisk's company had to be warned. Klamath could not reach them fast enough on foot. He did not know the rims of the cliff. No yell would carry through the snowfall.

In a rush, the rifleman settled himself on Forguile's horse. At once, the Commander took Magister Pillion from Klamath, handed him up to the soldier. The horse wheeled away, goaded to risk a canter on the track to the kitchen.

The beast and its burdens seemed to dissolve in the snow. At the same time, Forguile arranged his remaining riflemen to shield the Magisters. Lambent and others shouted frightened questions. The Commander ignored them. He could not explain the threat. But he was a veteran: he could draw obvious conclusions.

Hells! thought Klamath. Oh, hells! How much time had passed since Pillion left the bunkhouse? Enough to almost kill him while he tried to fight his way out of a snowdrift. His warning came too late.

I have not seen the other two. They both had rifles.

There was nothing Klamath could do. He did not even have his own gun. He had left it behind as a sign that he was not taking the Magisters into danger. He wore only his saber and dagger.

But he was the General of King Bifalt's army. The challenge and the failure were his.

Painfully, he climbed to his feet. For no good reason except that he was afraid, he spent a moment brushing snow off his legs. Like the Commander, he ignored the Magisters. To Forguile, he said only, "Until we know more, we are safer where we are."

If he tried to take his charges back to the kitchen, they would spread out. The track was too narrow to keep the Magisters in a clump. And Klamath did not have enough men to surround them. Lambent, Brighten, and the others would be easy targets.

Privately, Commander Forguile urged, "Tell me what you can, General. What did he say that was worth his life?"

Klamath meant to answer, *The enemy is closer than we knew.* He practiced repeating the words in his mind. But he could not force them out.

He had not earned his place as King Bifalt's lead commander. Pretending that he deserved his rank was not enough.

His power was restored.

While Klamath tried to rise above himself, he heard a distant sound through the gabble of the Magisters. Nearby, it could have been the snapping of a twig. Far away, it could have been anything. A heavy bough cracking under its burden of snow. Ice breaking against itself as it shifted. A chunk of the cliff-edge shearing away.

Klamath had been a soldier for twenty years. He knew the specific *bang* of a gunshot.

It was followed almost immediately by a second shot.

Forguile recognized the sound as well. So did the riflemen. But falling snow masked directions. Did it come from the camp? The woods? Somewhere else?

Klamath knew. Only the worst explanation would be true.

With one part of his mind, he thought, Flisk. Fourteen riflemen. What are they *doing*?

With another part, he timed the motions of shooting. Pull back the bolt. Eject the spent casing. Push the bolt home to shove another cartridge into the chamber. Find a target. Squeeze the trigger without hesitation or tension, a movement as natural as a breath.

At that instant, he heard two more shots. They were almost simultaneous.

One quick breath later, they were answered by a fusillade. The rapid stutter of rifle fire seemed to come from all sides. Was it an ambush? A melee? It lasted longer than Klamath expected. Then, abruptly, it stopped.

No one fired again.

The consternation of the Magisters demanded his attention. "Calm yourselves!" he ordered them. "We are in no danger. Servants of the enemy have attacked Captain Flisk's company. He has fourteen riflemen. They have responded. If those servants were still alive, they would shoot again. Since they do not, they must be dead."

Dead, not fled. *I have not seen the other two.* They had been listening to Father Skurn when his sorcery was restored. Klamath did not believe that men *coerced* by the priest's strange theurgy would have run away.

"Are you sure, General?" croaked one of the Bellegerin Magisters.

Klamath grimaced bitterly. "Ask someone else. I am here, not there."

He meant, I sent those people to die.

Unwilling to meet the bafflement and fright of the theurgists, he gazed away westward. In clear weather, the encampment was an easy walk behind him. There the snow drifted down softly. But over the bay, fierce winds whipped and harried it. Beyond the cliff-edge, the clouds and their cold burdens writhed like a tormented sea.

He was not surprised at all to see an unsteady glare of silver in the distance. It flickered in the savage swirl of snow, reflected off the storm clouds in bursts like the urgent blinking of a signal-lantern. But he did not need to see it distinctly to recognize it for what it was. When Magister Brighten gasped, "Sorcery! The Decimate of lightning!" she only confirmed what he already knew.

Then he heard wind-muffled thunder. Distant and unmistakable, it sounded like the breaking of the bay's foundations.

The enemy had resumed his attack on the outer reef. His scouts had only made a breach large enough for one ship. Now he had arrived to renew his attack. The distant reef was only the first barrier. There were other obstacles. And the snowfall would hamper him. He was not close yet. His approach would take time. It might take a long time.

Nevertheless he had come.

For the first time, Klamath acknowledged that the enemy's name was Rile. Skurn had denied it. Now the truth was plain. Who else could have restored the priest's sorcery?

A kind of fever came over Klamath then. He was torn between haste and caution. King Bifalt needed him back in the Open Hand. The enemy had come sooner than anyone had expected. The army was not ready. That was the General's responsibility. But he was also needed where he was, at least for an hour or two. He had done too little to prepare Captain Flisk and Commander Forguile for the threat of Father Skurn's reawakened sorcery. And for all he knew, Flisk might be dead—in addition to several Magisters of wind. Before he left the bay, he had to deal with that cursed priest.

Klamath was an ordinary man with ordinary wits, ordinary courage, a soft heart, and no special gift of foresight; but he did what he could. Cursing himself, he summoned a messenger to carry his first report to King Bifalt. "And tell the King," he added, "I will return when I know more." Then he turned on Commander Forguile.

"Muster every rifleman here, sir," he demanded. "You will need them mounted. Find Captain Flisk's company. Bring him to me." If he still lives. "Attend to the Magisters with him.

"And begin a search for Father Skurn. He will not linger in the camp." He would be too easily found. "Scour the woods." They would be full of coverts. Most of the trees were bare, but they crowded close together, hiding their secrets. "And remember that he is *dangerous*."

The Commander stood at attention. Despite the snow and the gloom, his eyes showed an eager fury. He had spent ten years working on the fortifications, and Heren Flisk was his friend.

Bitterly, Klamath confessed, "The fault is mine. Magister Pillion warned me, but I did not share his fears. I should have had him guarded. I did not know the enemy is so close."

"The priest can draw on his Great God's sorcery. It spreads confusion. At its worst, it compels others to do his bidding. *Compels*, sir. *Make* them understand their peril. Skurn cannot be allowed to *claim* them."

Forguile nodded. "As you say, General. What of the guns? If the enemy is near?"

"Forget them," snapped Klamath. "They are useless in this weather. You will have time to ready them when you have found that priest."

At once, Commander Forguile wheeled away. His grin promised bloodshed as he ran toward the kitchens and the bunkhouses, the resting soldiers and the servants tending the horses.

General Klamath was in a hurry. "Follow me!" he barked at the Magisters of lightning. As quickly as he dared on the packed snow and ice, he led them back to the nearest kitchen.

When he entered the kitchen's shelter and heat, he felt a profound relief when he saw that Magister Pillion would live. The small man lay near one of the stoves, clearly unconscious; but now he was sleeping, not dying. A little life had returned to his cheeks. He still shivered in sudden spasms, but they were brief. Between them, he lay quietly.

If Klamath had been alone, he might have allowed himself to find comfort in Pillion's survival. But of course he was not alone. He had eight Magisters with him, all clamoring for explanations. He had hoped to show them the fortifications, the positions of the cannon; but that had become impossible. When Rile began his final approach, they would have to fight for their lives and their homelands without so much as a glance at the terrain of battle. Only Magister Lambent had seen it before.

Nevertheless the General ignored them. He had larger concerns. He belonged in the Open Hand with his army, or in Belleger's Fist with his King. But he could not leave until he knew what happened to Captain Flisk's Magisters—and to Flisk himself. King Bifalt would demand an answer. More than that, Klamath hoped to hear that Father Skurn had been captured or shot. Preferably shot. Alive, the priest might be capable of astonishing harm.

With his fists and his jaws clenched, General Klamath paced around the long tables and the stove, measuring the accumulation of his faults and fears while he waited for someone to tell him what he had to know.

The Magisters were not disposed to wait. For a time, the General's glare rebuffed them as they argued among themselves, trying to decide who would dare Klamath's ire. Then Magister Lambent put himself squarely in Klamath's path. Stretching himself to his full height, the lightning-wielder put on an imperious air: the mask of a man entitled by birth and power to make demands. Unfortunately for him, he could not conceal his alarm. His voice quivered as he spoke.

"Answer us, General. Explain the priest's power. It is like nothing we know. As we are, we are helpless. How can we defend ourselves if we do not understand what we face?"

Klamath had no patience for this. He faced Magister Lambent in silence until the man began to wilt. Then he said as if he were cursing, "You heard what I told Commander Forguile. That is all I know."

Pushing past the Magister, he continued pacing. While he walked, he watched the kitchen door, willing it to open.

Eventually, Captain Flisk came in from the snow. He had left with seven Magisters. He returned with four, and no one else. He must have sent his soldiers to join the search for Father Skurn.

Among the Magisters, only Trench had regained his composure. The others had the haunted aspect of people who had seen their own deaths, and could not stop seeing them. In the old wars, they had always killed from safety. They had never experienced violence directed at *them*. They hurried to the stove to warm themselves, and to share their dismay.

Heren Flisk looked worse than haunted. He looked shattered.

At once, General Klamath waved to one of the servants, called for flagons of hot cider. Then he seated himself at one of the tables and waited for Flisk to join him.

The younger man dropped onto a bench opposite the General, propped his elbows on the table, hid his face in his hands. His arms and shoulders trembled, but not from cold. When the servant set a steaming flagon in front of him, he did not glance at it.

With both hands, Klamath clasped his own flagon. He would have preferred to give Flisk kindness. The man had not been an active soldier since the time of Prince Bifalt's search for the library. During the intervening years, he had lost the habit of carrying his weapons. To protect the Magisters of wind, he had worn only his dagger. No one could hold him accountable for the people who had died.

But the Captain held himself accountable: that was obvious. At that moment, he did not need kindness. Like Klamath himself, he needed demands he could answer, duties he was able to perform.

"Report, sir," ordered the General softly. "I have been waiting too long. I need to know what happened."

Flisk flinched. He may have expected a stinging reproach. Nevertheless he had never lacked courage despite his self-doubt. He uncovered his face, raised his head.

"As you say, General."

Klamath sipped cider to steady himself as Heren Flisk began.

"We were nearing the place I had chosen for the Magisters to raise their Decimates. Beyond the reach of our lanterns, the snow veiled everything, and they did not reach far. An army could have crept up on us, and we would not have known it.

"The shots came from the woods. The first took Magister Shallow. The second killed Magister Scurry."

Two out of seven.

"You trained your men well, General. Before I could move—before I could *think*—they placed themselves between the Magisters and the line of fire. One of them died for his bravery. Another was grazed. I do not know their names. Many of your riflemen are new to me. But muzzle flashes exposed our attackers. Your men returned fire. Our enemies were killed.

"Now I am here. What more do you need, sir?"

What more do I need? thought Klamath. I need a hundred men like you. A thousand. And I need that priest dead. But he did not say so. "Did you look for bodies, Captain?"

Flisk nodded. "We did. We found two. They were—" His whole body shuddered. "They were your men, General. The riflemen can tell you their names."

"They were," admitted Klamath. He knew enough to be sure. "They were compelled by that priest." Then he pursued his questions. "Two Magisters were shot. You lost a third. How?"

Flisk seemed to wish that he could pound the table with his forehead. He needed a moment to master himself. Almost whispering, he said, "Magister Gust. I knew he was frightened, but I forgot him at the first shots. He must have panicked. As I turned to look for him, he went over the cliff."

Klamath winced. Magister Gust's death was a stupid waste. The man had done it to himself; but that did not lessen Klamath's responsibility.

Abruptly, he decided that he had pushed Heren Flisk hard enough. So that he would be overheard, he raised his voice.

"You did what you could, Captain. No one could have done better. The fault is mine. I was careless when I should have been watchful."

Flisk's shoulders sagged as if the General had removed a burden. At the same time, his expression pleaded. "Then tell me." He spoke in a hoarse whisper. "What happened? *How* did it happen? How did your men turn against us? And why did they come for *us*? Wind is a lesser Decimate. They could have done more harm killing Magisters of lightning."

"General, they were *your men.*"

Klamath sighed; but he did not look away.

"They turned against us, yes," he replied, "but they did not choose treachery. And they did us one service. Now we know that our enemy is the Great God Rile. Father Skurn is his servant.

"The priest was given a form of sorcery that sways minds. At its worst, it *binds* them. When he exerts it, even faithful men will do his bidding. He compelled your attackers to serve him.

"But they were not sent against *you*. Skurn did not know where you were or why you were there. How could he? He might have heard that I was coming. But no one would have told him I was bringing Magisters. Only you and Commander Forguile knew. And no one could have told him *why*. *I* told no one. Even you and the Commander did not know my intentions.

"No." Klamath sighed again. "I believe Skurn simply wanted to escape. He must have seen that Magister Pillion had recognized him for what he is. While he remains free, he can continue to serve his Great God. If he were captured, he would be shot. But to escape, he needed a distraction. He used my men to provide it.

"However, he could not allow them to kill near the camp. That would draw attention too close to him. Instead, he bound them to look for targets at some distance. They found *you* by the light of your lanterns."

For a moment, General Klamath glared around the kitchen, daring anyone to challenge or question his account. Then he found that he could no longer bear to remain where he was. He needed to talk to King Bifalt.

He surged to his feet. "Captain Flisk," he ordered as if he were sure of himself, "take command of our defense. While Commander Forguile searches for Father Skurn, prepare the guns and cannoneers for battle. I will return with reinforcements. And King Bifalt. For the present, keep these Magisters with you. Explain what you require of them. Protect them with riflemen."

Flisk's look of bafflement said plainly that he did not know what to do with Magisters of wind and drought. But General Klamath was in a hurry now.

He added, "Remind Commander Forguile. That priest's sorcery is fatal. We need him dead."

While Lambent howled protests and Trench shouted questions, the

General strode out of the kitchen, slammed the door, and called for his horse.

The snowfall was dwindling. Perhaps the storm would pass soon. When the fighting started, the bay's defenders might be able to see. Klamath told himself that would help. But he did not believe it. Rile's forces would be able to see as well.

FIVE

NEWS COMES TO BELLEGER'S FIST

Following two days of heavy snow, the sky over the Open Hand began to clear toward midafternoon. Winds from the east nudged the storm toward the sea. Finally, the sun shone on homes and merchantries and stables roofed with dazzling white; on the fortified walls that enclosed the old city; on bright icicles and small, poised avalanches hanging from the many eaves and sills of Belleger's Fist. The streets resembled clean satin where they had not been torn by the stubborn passage of men and horses, women and wagons, children and servants, all clinging to the demands of their daily lives. Where use and breezes had made drifts, snow covered stoops and porches, rose as high as windows. Large dogs intrepid enough to venture out disappeared entirely in the flurries of their own romping. For a few hours, sunshine gave even the most ramshackle, haphazard regions of the city an air of enchantment.

But the winds also delivered a ferocious cold. In the freezing air, icicles broke with a sound like rocks snapping. Loads of snow slipping from the canted slates of the keep's towers fell like grenades and burst on the lower roofs, the crenelated fortifications, the twisting lanes. The curses of people as they floundered along the streets echoed everywhere. The shrieks of giddy children resembled screams.

Between the window curtains of his private council room high in one of the Fist's towers, King Bifalt watched his city and shivered.

Ordinarily, he liked open air and cold. Now he kept the curtains closed and the hearth blazing. In fact, fires had been lit in several of his rooms. Nevertheless the cold found him wherever he went as if it had been sent to hunt him down.

Still, he stood at his windows and watched between the curtains. With as much patience as he could muster, he waited for Klamath's return. Until he knew the outcome of the General's experiments in the bay, he could not make his final arrangements to meet the enemy. In the meantime, he felt useless in his own realm. There was nothing he could do to improve his preparations, or to ease the decisions he would eventually have to make.

The light did not last long. As the sun sank behind the cloudbank sliding westward, shadows spread a premature dusk over the Open Hand. By increments, the King's city fell into gloom.

Again and again, Bifalt's gaze flicked to the gates of Belleger's Fist and the bailey almost directly below him. He was looking for riders.

It was too early to hope for Klamath's return. Encumbered by deep snow and burdened by Magisters, the General would be forced to spend at least one night in the encampment above the Bay of Lights. But he might send a messenger or two.

Bifalt would have preferred to wait alone. Unfortunately, he had a companion. His brother Prince Lome sprawled in a heavy chair as close to the hearth as he could get without singeing his garments. Knowing that the King kept only water in his chambers, Lome had brought a flagon of ale. So far, the Prince had not said why he had come.

King Bifalt did not care why. Not today. As long as Lome kept silent—

When a man on horseback came pounding along the streets, rushing through the keep's open gates, and skidding to a halt in the bailey, Bifalt felt a chill more acute than the cold outside his windows. Ice seemed to trickle in his veins. The rider could only be a messenger from the General.

Reports from elsewhere—from the training-fields, the scouts

around the city, or the relays that brought tidings from Set Ungabwey's caravan—would pass through First Captain Matt. If Matt had tidings to convey, he would send an aide. Or come himself.

Chewing the inside of his cheek, King Bifalt resisted the impulse to stride to the chamber door, open it, and listen for the sound of running boots. Instead, he turned to his brother.

Lome sat stretched out with his head back like a man napping. His flagon he held on his belly with both hands, but his grip was loose. However, he was not asleep. He looked up as Bifalt turned. His fingers tightened on the flagon.

Without preamble, he said, "Tell me again why you want me to command the evacuation." He often said such things when he was drunk, but now his voice did not slur. "I have no authority here. You know that, Brother. Tell me again why you think anyone will listen to me."

The King's mind was elsewhere, listening for boots outside his door, a sharp knock. "Tell me again," he responded reflexively, "why you conspired to have my wife murdered. You must know by now that we need Amika. We need *her*."

Lome waved a hand, dismissed his crime as if it were trivial. "Another good point on my side. I tried to arrange her death—and now you want me to lead your people to *her* realm? I will be killed at once. And if I am not, how do you suppose Amika will react when throngs of homeless Bellegerins arrive like beggars?

"Use your *mind*, Brother. Think clearly for once. You cannot expect *me* to save so many of Amika's ancient enemies simply because you do not know how to save them yourself."

King Bifalt ignored Lome's excuses. He had heard them all before. Absently, he said, "You have forgotten what you know of the Queen. Wait until you meet Commander Soulcess. Hells, Lome, wait until you meet Chancellor Sikthorn. If they do not sink to the level of your expectations, demand worse treatment. Describe your attempt on their sovereign's life. Perhaps *then* they will free you from the burden of being King Abbator's son.

"Until that time, Brother, your duty is clear. You will have to suffer the indignity of being a Bellegerin Prince."

Scowling, Lome lifted his flagon, then put it down without drinking. "How will you compel me?"

"Shame?" suggested Bifalt.

"Hells!" snorted the Prince. "I left shame behind so long ago, I no longer remember it."

King Bifalt heard the hard clap of boots from the hall outside his door. Boots running.

To silence Lome, King Bifalt snapped, "Events will remind you." His voice shook slightly.

As he turned to the door, it burst open. Prince Jaspid entered like the first blast of a gale.

Three strides from the King, he stopped. To have come so quickly, he must have run all the way from the bailey, yet he was hardly out of breath. Standing suddenly still, he looked ready for everything and nothing. Only the sharpness of his gaze betrayed his excitement.

Clearly, he had recovered from his wounds.

Well, he was the best warrior King Bifalt had. No Bellegerin or Amikan could match him. Still, Bifalt wished that his brother would occasionally show a little weakness. If Jaspid had ever looked daunted, the devotee of Spirit Lylin might not have felt compelled to beat him so badly.

The King found himself shivering. He could not control it.

From his place by the hearth, Lome lurched to his feet, came to Bifalt's side. For once, he was not staggering with drink.

Jaspid glanced at his younger brother, gave Lome a fragment of a smile, then faced the King. "That messenger is half-frozen, Majesty," he explained. "I sent him to the stables. It is warm there. He can recover while his horse is tended.

"He brought word from General Klamath. The reef is under attack. The enemy has come, the Great God Rile." After a slight pause, the older Prince added, "And there has been treachery. Captain Flisk and the Magisters of wind have been fired upon."

His announcement left a shocked silence in the air. Prince Lome stood with his mouth open. The fire in the hearth shed no heat. The flames hardly seemed to flicker.

The reef—

The enemy—

Treachery?

In that instant, Bifalt felt himself freeze. Chilled to the bone, he did not know how to move. His preparations in the bay were as ready as the weather permitted. He himself was not. Like Klamath and his other advisers, he had believed that the enemy was still distant. Estie's only message should have warned him that he was mistaken; but he had not drawn the right conclusions. He had simply taken Magister Facile's murder, like the Archpriest Makh's disappearance with Elgart, as a sign that his enemy was the Great God. Unable to bear thinking about the woman he loved, the woman who had abandoned him, he had not followed the implications of her warning.

Treachery.

Treachery that weakened the defenses in the bay when the cannoneers, Magisters, and riflemen there should have been preparing themselves to fight.

He needed to know how Rile had contrived a betrayal.

He needed to *stop shivering*.

Only a moment had passed. Jaspid might have said something more, but Lome spoke first. "In *this* weather?" he demanded. "Impossible! Klamath is mistaken." He sounded more indignant than appalled, outraged by this insult to his insistence that there would be no war.

That protest struck a spark in the ready tinder of Jaspid's nature. "*You* are mistaken, Brother," he snapped. "This is not a subject on which the General can be wrong. He is *there*. If the reef is under attack, he has witnessed it."

"It is still impossible!" cried Lome. "In this weather? The whole world has been blind for days!"

He must have realized that he could not escape now. He would have to command the evacuation of the Open Hand.

Bifalt was not listening. How? he asked himself. How had Rile done it? How had the Great God managed treachery in the Bay of Lights, of all places? Where everyone there served Commander Forguile and Captain Flisk, Amika and Belleger, Queen Estie and Bifalt himself?

As if his brothers had been waiting for him to speak, he asked, "How is it possible? Who betrayed us?"

At once, Jaspid turned away from Lome. "I know only what General Klamath told his messenger, Majesty. Shots were fired at Captain Flisk and the Magisters of wind. Only our soldiers have rifles."

Shrill with alarm, Lome demanded, "But who would do that? What sodden idiot gave rifles to men he could not trust?"

Abruptly, Bifalt remembered something that Klamath had told him. Several days ago, the General had taken a company of volunteers to the bay. One of them was Father Skurn. And Magister Pillion believed that Skurn's sorcery was *coercion*.

"Hells!" The King could not restrain himself. The cold seemed to shake his bones. "That *priest*!"

His brothers stared at him.

The frigid air from the window had claimed the King. It did not let him go. "Those priests," he said unsteadily. "They draw sorcery from their Great God. It makes them persuasive, but it can also *compel*. There is a priest among the bay's servants. He must have found a chance to compel riflemen."

And there was nothing that he, Bifalt, could do about it.

That was a bitter truth. Nevertheless he understood it now; accepted it. What choice did he have?

Grimly, he shook himself. To Lome's aghast gape and Jaspid's glare, he added, "But that is not our concern. We cannot answer it. General Klamath is not a fool. Ennis Forguile and Heren Flisk are not. They will put an end to that priest.

"Our concern is here."

For Lome's sake, he tried to sound soothing. "It is too soon to be afraid, Brother. The enemy is days away. Perhaps many days, if our cannon and the bay's obstacles hinder him. In any event, he is *my* challenge, not yours." It had been the concern of Bifalt's entire life since the day he had been summoned to the Last Repository. "You will have time to carry out your task."

Watching the rush of emotions across Lome's face, the stages of Lome's ragged effort to believe in himself, Bifalt stopped. He did not know what else to say.

Jaspid appeared to misunderstand the King's silence. Or perhaps he understood it too well. Carefully, he said, "You have received a blow, Majesty. You knew it would come, but you did not know when. You could not brace yourself. Allow yourself to recover. Whatever you do will have to be done at night. Now or an hour from now will change nothing for General Klamath."

King Bifalt grimaced. "The blow is nothing. It will pass. I will be myself again when I decide what to do."

"Then drink, Brother." Prince Lome made an attempt to sound commanding. "Ale is not grot, but it will warm you." He extended his flagon.

When Bifalt glanced at it, he saw that the flagon was still full. Lome had not been drinking.

That detail seemed to give Lome's gesture import. It resembled a sign of acquiescence.

Bifalt took the flagon, raised it to his mouth. At first, he sipped the ale. Then he drank it in long swallows. As far as he knew, it did nothing for him. But Lome's offer was enough.

When he returned the flagon to Lome, his shivering no longer ruled him.

"It is—" He cleared his throat, swallowed the sour taste of ale. "It is too soon to act," he told Prince Jaspid. "We do not know what is needed.

"Other messengers will come. Klamath will tell us more when he knows more. Until then, I must speak with the First Captain.

"Will you summon him, Brother?"

Jaspid's grin was a mixture of relief and satisfaction. "I have already done it, Majesty. He will come soon."

King Bifalt nodded. "In that case," he said, "I will wait by the hearth." Then he remembered to add, "Thank you, Jaspid."

He was grateful for both of his brothers.

First Captain Matt reached the council chamber long before King Bifalt expected him. He could not have ridden all the way from his post with the army in so short a time.

One glance told the King that Klamath's second-in-command had come for reasons of his own. The big man arrived with a storm on his open face. It made him look like a sheep-farmer who had found a third of his flock savaged by wolves. He must have been on his way before Prince Jaspid's call reached him.

Something terrible had happened.

Another blow.

The hearth's fire warmed Bifalt's skin and limbs, but it had not driven the shivering from his spirit. He was not ready to hear that Belleger's peril was worse than he had imagined.

Matt closed the door behind him, bowed to King Bifalt, scanned the Princes, then began, "Majesty, I—"

Bifalt stopped him with a harsh gesture. "In a moment, First Captain. Take a breath. Steady yourself. And drink." Moving with care, he went to the pitcher of water near his desk, filled a goblet, and offered it to the soldier. "I will hear you when it is empty."

Matt flung a look of consternation at Prince Jaspid. This was not the reception he had expected. Nevertheless he obeyed without hesitation.

When the First Captain was finished, King Bifalt took the goblet from him, set it down. Breathing deeply himself, he assumed the role he required himself to fill.

"Now, sir. Your face tells me your tidings are fearsome. I am ready to hear them."

He was not ready.

He had to be.

After his long climb through the keep, Matt was sweating. He wiped moisture from his brow. With his back straight and his chin up, he replied, "The signals, Majesty. The relay of signals. From the Realm's Edge."

Those signals were messages tied to the shafts of arrows and shot from man to man over the hills. At their best, they could deliver reports faster than any rider.

"Yes?" prompted the King.

Distinctly, the First Captain answered, "Master Ungabwey's caravan has been destroyed. Only the rearguard survived."

"What?" demanded Bifalt. "The whole caravan?"

This was worse than fearsome. It might prove ruinous.

"Majesty." Matt nodded. "The reports are fragments sent in haste. More signals will come. The rearguard will return as swiftly as possible. I do not expect the full tale before midnight. It may not reach us until the morrow. But what I know is this.

"Master Ungabwey found a narrows in the second pass." Unnecessarily, he explained, "The first, the eastern passage, he had already sealed. The second is the middle of the three. A league among the mountains, he came to a place where one great avalanche would close the way completely."

Unable to contain himself, Prince Jaspid asked, "Was he opposed, Matt?"

The First Captain answered without looking away from King Bifalt. "Not in the first pass, Highness. I know this from earlier reports. In the second, our men encountered scouts like the raiders who harried us last autumn. But those men fled when a few of them were shot. There was no concerted opposition."

"Then how?" insisted the King. "How was the caravan destroyed?"

Abruptly, Prince Lome went to the door, opened it partway. Through the gap, he told the servant outside to bring wine.

The other men ignored him.

The First Captain shrugged uncomfortably. "Master Ungabwey planned his avalanche, Majesty. His engines brought it down. The second pass has been closed as well. That much I know. But for the rest, I do not have details.

"There must have been some unforeseen crack in the mountainsides. Or some miscalculation by the mechanicians with their engines. The avalanche did not come down where it was intended. It fell on the caravan."

King Bifalt stared. The implications shook him. There were too many. And too many dead. The wagon-train included a large company of servants, mechanicians, and riflemen. It also included the last priests of the Church.

Half choking, he asked, "No one escaped? No one at all?"

He felt an oblique certainty. That must be why—

For an instant, he did not know *why* what. Then he did.

That was why Set Ungabwey had left his daughters in the library. He had not expected to live.

"I do not know, Majesty," sighed Matt. "The signals say only that the rearguard survived. I expect some of our men to search the wreckage. There will be more signals. And our men will return. They—"

Jaspid interrupted him. "What of the third pass, Matt?"

It was the westernmost road through the mountains.

The First Captain allowed himself to look away for a moment. "We have no defense there, Highness. We trusted Master Ungabwey's engines and skill."

With an inward wrench, King Bifalt put crushed men and women out of his mind. He had to consider Belleger. The loss of the caravan meant—

To steady himself while his heart shivered, he asked Matt, "What do you know of it, sir? The third pass?"

Squads of General Klamath's men had been following the tracks of the raiders since mid-autumn, studying the trails among the mountains. The King had heard their reports; but he wanted something more recent.

Now there was a hint of frenzy in the First Captain's eyes. He, too, was imagining the consequences of the calamity.

"Little enough, Majesty. Our men were ordered to avoid being seen. They could not trace the extent of the passage. But they believe that way is the enemy's best road. It is wide enough for a host of cavalry with its train of supplies.

"Master Ungabwey planned to attempt it last because it is farthest from the Last Repository."

Matt's gaze said what he did not. Farthest from the library—and closest to the Open Hand.

Gusts tossed the curtains. The air grew colder. At the door, Lome accepted a jug of wine. As if he were alone in the chamber, he took the wine to the hearth, sat back down in his chair, and began to drink from the jug's neck. Between swigs, he muttered to himself in disgust.

Prince Jaspid grimaced at his younger brother, but he stayed where he was, radiating impatience. At a word from his King, he might have left the Fist and rushed south to contest the enemy's passage alone.

For a long moment, King Bifalt said nothing. Rile's assault on the Bay of Lights had already begun. But no one knew how immense his forces might be. The people beyond the Realm's Edge were probably his allies. King Bifalt might find himself attacked on two fronts. He would be compelled to split his army.

And he did not have enough men. Or Magisters.

He believed that Rile would aim to destroy the Open Hand and much of Belleger before he turned his attention to the library. He would not leave an army at his back. From the bay, he would come at the city directly. And his allies from the south—surely, they were his allies?—would emerge from the mountains and drive north to join the attack on the city.

Bifalt understood the glint of frenzy in Matt's gaze. The First Captain had already asked himself the question that made the King wince. How could the combined forces of Belleger and Amika fight two foes at once?

But Bifalt knew that Klamath's friend had a more personal question as well. His family lived in the south of Belleger, in hilly, sheepherding country. If his wife and children had ignored the order to evacuate—

Deliberately, King Bifalt made Matt wait for an answer. He wanted the First Captain's full attention.

"Very well, sir. We have decisions to make. But first you must hear *our* tidings. You know that General Klamath has taken a company of Magisters to the Bay of Lights. Now we have received his first report.

"The attack on the bay has begun. The enemy is attempting to break open the reef."

Matt flinched at this news. The frenzy in his eyes became despair. Clearly, he understood that King Bifalt would have to confront the threat of invasion there. To prevent the enemy from forcing a landing on the strand. Or to keep his foes enclosed in the bay. If Rile's horde contrived to climb the road and reach easier terrain above the cliffs, it would crush the King's forces. The death of the realm would begin there.

To Matt, all of this meant that King Bifalt could not defend the remaining pass. An army of raiders would be free to enter Belleger. It might strike straight through Matt's farmstead.

King Bifalt understood.

Abruptly, he asked, "Do you trust Second Captain Hegels?"

The officer's eyes widened in confusion.

"I will be clear, sir," explained the King. "Do you trust Hegels to defend the Open Hand in my absence and General Klamath's? And yours?"

Matt scowled to control himself. "I do, Majesty. I cannot swear that he is loyal to Belleger. But his devotion to Queen Estie and Amika is absolute. He will give you his best until she recalls him."

King Bifalt's hands ached, but not from cold. He wanted to feel the heft of his saber in his grasp; craved the hard certainty of his gun against his shoulder. Lacking his weapons, he locked his arms across his chest.

"In that case, First Captain," he said grimly, "here are your orders. Do not concern yourself with the Bay of Lights. I will take four squads to support General Klamath."

Klamath had already committed riflemen to serve Flisk, Forguile, and the cannon. King Bifalt's reinforcements might be enough to help the cannoneers.

"Order Hegels," continued the King, "to prepare those men. Warn him to plan for the defense of the Open Hand. Then you, sir, will take the same number south. Depart as soon as you can muster your forces. If or when raiders emerge from the last pass, you will oppose them.

"I will allow you one Magister of earthquake. That Decimate may be useful among the mountains, if you do not make Set Ungabwey's mistake."

Then he added fiercely, "But understand me, sir. Do *not* sacrifice your men. Your task is to strike at the raiders until they give battle. Then you must retreat—and keep striking them. Do not allow them to disengage or turn aside.

"I want you to draw him *here.*"

Where the bulk of the King's army and most of his Magisters would be waiting.

If Matt could do that, he might save every town, village, and hamlet in the south of Belleger. He might save his family.

With as much confidence as he could summon, King Bifalt finished, "General Klamath and I will join you if we can. If we cannot, the Second Captain must be ready to lend his support."

As the King spoke, the burdens lifted from Matt's face. By the time Bifalt was done, the soldier Klamath had known during the old wars shone in Matt's eyes: the readiness for battle, and the knowledge that his assignment was vital.

"As you say, Majesty," he promised. "I will do it. I know the Magister I want. Her name is Astride. She is known for power—and good sense." A moment later, he added, "With your consent, I will also take sub-Commander Hellick. He is new to the army. He has a few rough edges I would like to smooth away."

Now King Bifalt found that he could hardly bear to look at the First Captain. He hated sending men into a doomed battle when he was not there to lead them. And he was *cold.* He felt a mad desire to retrieve his saber and hack at the chamber's furniture until his shivering stopped.

With a nod, he dismissed Matt. At once, the man strode away, taking his eagerness with him. When he closed the door behind him, the King was left alone with his brothers.

They gave him a moment of silence. Prince Jaspid spoke first. "What of me, Majesty?"

Bifalt had never known a man less inclined to self-pity than the older Prince. In fact, his beating at Lylin's hands had lifted his spirits. Nevertheless his tone held a hint of plaintiveness.

"You know me," he continued. "I live to fight. I was born for it." His fingers twitched. "Give me an enemy."

"And you know *me*," retorted the King without compunction or compassion. "I lack your skill, but I am as reckless as you. I need you with me. I need you to keep me alive."

Jaspid replied with a twisted smile. "Then you must be *very* reckless, Majesty. Otherwise, I will feel that I am wasted."

Give me time, thought Bifalt. Your chance will come. But he kept that promise to himself.

"And what of *me*?" protested Prince Lome from his chair. His chin was wet with wine. He had slopped some on his tunic. "Who will protect *me* while I try to satisfy your demands? Your man Malder does his best, but he will go with you to the bay. Who will enforce your authority?"

In the same harsh tone, King Bifalt answered, "Land-Captain Erepos. He is known everywhere. Use my name. Tell our people I have planned for their escape. Do not let their stubbornness discourage you. They may not heed you at first. When Rile comes closer, they will think differently. In better times, they will remember who saved their lives."

Lome muttered an obscenity; but he did not argue.

After that, the King sent his brothers away. He told Jaspid to help Matt and Hegels get ready. He had not given them much notice. And he suspected that Lome could use a chance to vent his dismay and drink in private, where no one would hear or judge him.

But Bifalt also wanted solitude for himself. He would ride for the bay with his squads soon enough. Until then, he did not know how to suffer feeling so *cold*. Not so long ago, he had enjoyed riding in every weather, in summer's baking sun and winter's biting winds. But that man, the King he had chosen to be, was gone. Rile's war had come to claim him. It would dominate his days until he died.

He would never see Estie again.

The monk Third Father had told him that he would have to surpass himself; but he did not know how that was possible.

He did not stop shivering until General Klamath returned from the Bay of Lights.

SIX

THE EFFECT OF CANNON

After General Klamath rode away, Captain Heren Flisk left the kitchen where they had spoken. Grimly, he went back out into the falling snow. Chilled despite his warm garb, he followed the trench from the encampment to the rim of the cliff and the head of the road. There was nothing he could do about what was coming: not in this weather, or at this distance. Nevertheless he felt compelled to watch the assault on the reef that shielded the Bay of Lights. The General had left him in command.

When the Great God Rile's ships passed the reef, Flisk would have to shout orders as if he knew what he was doing. As if he felt qualified to direct the first defense of Belleger.

Snow still fell thickly, but it had begun to diminish. Urged by a current of deeper cold from the east, the storm was drifting out to sea. Snow still masked the crest of the steep drop to the strand, but in an hour or two Flisk would be able to see more.

Within himself, he was alone, isolated by his fears. Commander Forguile and most of the riflemen were out on the hillsides or among the trees, searching for Rile's fatal priest. Flisk missed him. Ennis Forguile's presence would have comforted the Captain.

Despite his loneliness, however, Flisk was not alone. Half a dozen riflemen had accompanied him, men who had spent fortnights learning how to tend and fire the cannon. Apparently, they now considered themselves responsible for him. And other men had followed him as well, volunteers who had given seasons or years to the fortifications. They felt bound to the outcome of their labor. In addition, a few Magisters had left the heat and food of the kitchen. Not men like Magister Lambent, whose courage was as weak as his eyes, or women like Magister Whimper, whose Decimate of drought had no obvious use in the bay. But Magister Trench was there, joined by two lightning-wielders, Brighten and Visible, and a few others.

Falling snow still veiled the view. Even the nearest terrace with its cannon was veiled from sight. Nevertheless the attack on the reef was vivid in the distance. Its violence pierced the storm, an inconceivable barrage of sorcery burning and bludgeoning the hard coral. Blasts of silver left swollen afterimages like bruises on the scourged clouds. Mutters of breakage rode the twisted winds.

No one in Belleger or Amika had ever imagined that any one sorcerer—or any fifty sorcerers—could call down so much power, or aim it, or sustain it. But Captain Flisk knew what was happening. Like Magister Trench, he had witnessed the enemy's first probing strike, when impossible lightnings and appalling earthquakes had torn a gap in the barrier. Now he was watching a similar effort of destruction multiplied many times.

Flails of lightning cracked the obdurate substance of the reef. Then the Decimate of earthquake flung huge chunks of it aside. The shattering of the obstacle was muffled by the falling snow, the incessant crash of seas, the tumult of winds that harried the cliff's rim in all seasons. Still, Flisk could imagine it. At times, he seemed to feel the stone under him tremble like struck flesh as the bay's foundations were struck.

Half gasping, Magister Trench asked, "How can we save ourselves? What can be done against *that*?"

"Forget the Decimate of earthquake," snapped Magister Brighten. "The enemy needs the road. He will not risk breaking the cliff."

Captain Flisk agreed. But he did not say so. He had worse fears.

Cannon could sink ships, yes. And any ship that foundered would be utterly lost. The sea gave nothing back. The destruction of the reef would only make the thrashing of the waves fiercer, the sucking of the currents hungrier.

But destroying cannon would be child's play for any sorcerer with the Decimate of lightning. The power and the range.

Flisk reached out to grasp Magister Trench's arm. When he had the man's attention, he asked as quietly as he could, "I have heard that any sorcerer can sense the presence of sorcery before it strikes. Is that true?"

The Captain saw alarm stutter like reflected lightning in the sorcerer's eyes. But he also saw resolve as Trench concentrated on the question.

"A moment," answered the wind-wielder. "A brief warning. No more than a heartbeat or two. But yes. Sorcery announces itself. Its rising can be felt."

"Then tell me," returned Flisk. "Can you sense it now?"

He meant, Can the guns be protected? Can the gunpowder?

Trench jerked up his head, faced the distant blare and smash of theurgy. "At this distance? Through this storm?" His body tensed as if he were concentrating with every nerve. His arm resembled iron in the Captain's clasp. "No."

No? Flisk swallowed dismay.

But before he could respond, the Magister shifted his stance. As he had done at the Captain's request once before, he stretched out his Decimate to impose a space of comparative quiet on the howling, whining air.

Instantly, every sorcerer watching the bay stiffened. They looked around wildly for the source of theurgy.

Through his teeth, Magister Trench panted, "Yes. Now. Barely. It is less than a whisper. But yes."

Unaware of his own tension, Heren Flisk sagged. He did not know how to fight this enemy. The challenge surpassed him. But now he began to imagine that King Bifalt and Queen Estie's Magisters might be effective in the coming battle.

General Klamath had promised to bring more soldiers—and more sorcerers. Flisk trusted him. But he doubted that Klamath would be able to return before the next dawn.

The struggle in the bay might begin long before then. It might be over before the General arrived.

Slowly, the snowfall thinned, bringing with it a fanged cold. A clear, merciless sky showed in the east, shedding light as brittle as icicles. The sun remained hidden behind the westering cloudbank, but now Captain Flisk could see the terraces with their emplacements, the road stained with fresh wood ash and lined with frozen ropes for handholds, the strand piled with the debris of the convulsion which had shaped the cliff-face.

His first decision was clear. He sent a few soldiers to escort Magister Whimper and her fellow sorcerers of drought. After days of blinding weather, the cannon were buried in mounds of snow, useless despite the whipping confusion of the winds. The long guns on the two upper levels would be needed first. They had to be cleaned, dried; made ready to fire. Three drought-wielders were hardly enough. But their guards would help them. If they were quick—and if their stamina held—they might be able to retrieve the long guns from the drifts.

Flisk watched until Whimper and the others crept cautiously past the lip of the road and down the ropes. Then he let the Bay of Lights claim his attention.

For a time, most of the onlookers retreated to the heat of the stoves, leaving the Captain and his riflemen alone. But as daylight spread past the strand and out over the rock-bitten turbulence of the waters, more people came to estimate the Great God's progress.

The ships were visible now despite the distance. Men and women who understood what they saw gasped and swore. Relentless sorcery had reduced the wide jaw of the reef to a few solitary teeth. Gaps big enough to admit three or even five ships now gaped in the barrier, letting the full weight of the ocean's pounding rush inward. And inside the bay, out at the farthest reach of the long guns, were twelve—sixteen—no, twenty black vessels like the ones that had come before.

Their sails were furled. The winds would have torn the canvas to shreds, sunk the vessels. In pools of some unknown theurgy, the ships sat motionless, as still and stable as if they rested on iron platforms fixed to the bay's bottom. Sure of themselves despite the scouring seas, the raw power of waves that should have shattered them and swallowed the debris, those ships worked to clear the bay of its many obstacles: the jutting towers and plinths and fists of the coast's oldest stone; the boulders and scowling menhirs that would otherwise have made the approach to Belleger impassable despite the ruin of the reef.

Lurid with lightnings, and shivering at the force of the earthquakes unleashed from their decks, those ships were making the first stage of their Great God's invasion possible.

And beyond them, beyond where the reef had been, were more ships, too many to count. Despite the distance, and the dark shadow cast by the storm, it was clear that those vessels were larger than the ones in the bay. Far larger. They were not floating forts: they were castles made to ride the seas. Within them, they carried Rile's host. Heren Flisk would not have been surprised to learn that each of them held a thousand men.

If they achieved a landing—

If they could fight their way up the bottleneck of the road—

Captain Flisk did not believe that General Klamath would arrive in time.

Crunching through the hardened snow, Commander Forguile came to his comrade's side at last.

Flisk felt frozen inside his heavy garments, immobilized by cold and dread; hardly capable of thought. Nevertheless, suddenly, he was no longer alone in the watching crowd. The Amikan had that effect on him, his partner through all of his harsh years in the bay. Fighting the stiffness of his face, the crusts of ice at the corners of his mouth, the chilled awkwardness of his tongue, he said in a thin gust of vapor, "The guns." How had he neglected his duty so long? He should have dispatched the cannoneers to their posts an hour ago. "We must call the men."

Forguile did not answer him directly. For reasons of his own, the Commander rasped, "We did not find the priest. In this snow? He must have left a trail. We saw where he left the camp. But there are too many tracks." With a twitch of his head, he indicated the woods near the northward rim of the cliff, the dense stretch of trees that had sheltered two *coerced* riflemen earlier in the day. "The ground looks like fifty men have been swarming there for hours. Yet there *are* no men. I cannot imagine how it was done.

"That priest has eluded us."

Blinking, the Captain stared at his friend. His lids scraped his wind-abused eyes. After squinting out at the bay for so long, he could not focus on anything closer.

Forguile had lost Father Skurn.

A man who could do worse than cloud minds. A man who could compel treachery. Somehow, he had escaped. It should not have been possible.

Fifty men swarming everywhere? Who would do that?

Ennis Forguile had been exercising hard for hours. He was warmer than Flisk; better able to think and move. He took a moment to gauge the Captain's condition. Then he gave Flisk's shoulder a rough slap.

"We have time. Let those ships come a little nearer. Once we begin to fire, we may not get a second chance. We must do as much damage as we can quickly."

Forguile had hit Flisk's bad shoulder. The pain sent a jolt of alertness through him. He had not noticed Magister Brighten coming toward him. Seeing her at his friend's side startled him.

"You risk too much, Commander," she said urgently. "They are almost in *my* range. They may already be able to hit the cannon."

"But they will not," answered Forguile. "They cannot strike at us and clear their way at the same time. They will wait until we threaten them.

"Still, I understand you."

Briefly, he turned to bark an order at the nearest rifleman. "Summon the gunners to the long guns. Only them. We will not risk men on the other cannon until we have no choice."

While the soldier sprinted away, Commander Forguile faced Flisk again. "Go," he said sharply. "I will oversee the guns. You have a different task."

Captain Flisk understood. He had to move. He *would*—

"Magisters." He tried to shout, and could not. "All of you. With me."

Only Magister Brighten heard him. But she was enough. She summoned the other sorcerers.

Flisk paused long enough to tell Forguile, "Recall the drought-wielders." Then he lurched into motion, heading for the nearest kitchen. The Magisters watching the bay followed him.

As he left the onlookers, the Captain searched among them for some sign of Mattwil. But Matt's son and Cloras were not at the edge of the cliff.

Flisk chose to trust they were somewhere safe. Mattwil had sworn to General Klamath that he would not fight.

Hurrying in the opposite direction, the teams of cannoneers—four for each gun—went past him; but he had nothing to say to them. He knew them all. He refused to think that they were running to their deaths. Commander Forguile would manage them. Heren Flisk had to find the strength or the resolve or the sheer *worthiness* to make Magisters heed him.

The kitchen was a crude wooden structure large enough to seat fifty men while the cooks and servants fed them. It would have been bitterly cold without its oilcloth sheeting and its two hot stoves, one for cooking, the other for warmth. Most of the riflemen who had searched the woods with Commander Forguile were there. While they restored themselves, they waited for orders.

Standing close to a stove, Flisk began to shiver urgently. He had been exposed too long: the cold had soaked into his bones. He needed to speak. Time was precious now. But he could not master himself.

Then a servant put a mug of hot cider in his numb hands. As he sipped sweet warmth, he regained a measure of steadiness.

He had eight Magisters of lightning with him. Four of wind, the survivors of Father Skurn's *coerced* attack. They stood in a circle around Flisk and the stove. Magister Pillion was here as well. He sat at a table near one wall. He had recovered enough to attempt a bowl of stew. But he ate like a man who had difficulty finding his mouth with the spoon. He did not appear to be aware of anyone around him.

"Magisters," began Captain Flisk: a ragged croak. He faced the stove so that he would not have to see their alarm and skepticism. "You are needed. You do not require me to tell you cannon and gunpowder cannot withstand the Decimate of lightning."

There was a maelstrom of argent sorcery at work in the bay. Its bolts could destroy the emplacements at any time. When the cannon began to fire, Rile's sorcerers would strike back.

"What of it?" demanded Magister Lambent from somewhere at Flisk's back. "We can do nothing."

"You *can*." The Captain's voice shook. He used its tremors as if they were anger. "We will begin with the long guns. They are sixteen. You Magisters of lightning are eight. Riflemen will escort you down to the terraces. They will ensure that you come to no harm. Each of you will protect two cannon."

At once, Magister Lambent yelped, "We cannot! *I* cannot! We will be exposed!" As if his protest were irrefutable, he cried, "I cannot *see!*"

Heren Flisk did not turn. He had no strength to waste on Lambent's fears. Lives were at stake.

"We are *all* exposed," he snapped. "You will not be the first. The gunners have gone to their posts. They are doomed without you. If you die, you will not be the last."

With a snarl, Magister Trench added, "You do not have to *see*, you fool. You have to *feel*. And stop being such a coward."

Flisk had suffered Lambent's arrogance for years. He allowed himself to sneer. "For a Magister with your reputation, Lambent, the task will be simple enough. You will not attack. You will defend. You can sense sorcery as it rises. When it comes, you will *dismiss* it. I have been assured that any Magister can do as much against his own Decimate.

"While you shield the cannon, they will keep firing. They will hold the enemy back—if you do not fail.

"General Klamath will return with more Magisters. Until then, Belleger is in your hands."

Lambent tried again. "No! I *will* n—"

Abruptly, he gasped in pain. Captain Flisk glanced behind him in time to see the appalled Magister drop to his knees clutching his lower back.

Magister Brighten stepped away from Lambent. Grinning fiercely, she showed Flisk her braced thumb. She must have jabbed one of Lambent's kidneys. "I have wanted to do that for a long time," she said with satisfaction. "Your men will have to haul him into place, Captain. But once he is there, he will shield the cannon to save himself."

"What of us, Captain?" put in Magister Trench. "Do you have a use for the Decimate of wind?"

Flisk turned back to the stove. More cautiously, he replied, "I do, Magister. It is uncertain. You may find yourselves exposed for nothing. Or you may be crucial.

"I saw you exert your Decimate to extend the reach of your senses. Perhaps you can do the same for our lightning-wielders." To himself, Flisk cursed the loss of Shallow, Scurry, and Gust. "Our soldiers will guide two of you to each terrace." One sorcerer of wind for every four cannon. Flisk did not think they would be enough. "Do whatever you can there."

He was not conscious of listening for the first sounds of battle. He was too tired, too cold. But he was not surprised when he heard the start of a cannonade.

It resembled thunder rolling in the distance. The shrilling winds disguised it. The hillside and the trees muffled it. The cliff itself cast the hard bark of each gun out to sea. Still, Flisk recognized it at once.

Commander Forguile had decided that he could not wait for the Magisters any longer.

Sixteen long guns, each firing in turn: a series timed so that when the last cannon blared, the first would be ready to hurl another ball, another load of chain.

The waiting soldiers knew the sound as well as Flisk did. Their heads jerked up. They stiffened, braced their hands on the tables, poised themselves to leave their seats.

Flisk ignored the reactions of the sorcerers. Their fear and uncertainty and determination meant nothing to him now. Only the riflemen mattered. He had been one of them, once. He had to accept that he might be sending them to die.

"Do you understand your orders?" he asked them. "You have heard them often enough.

"Two of you will take each Magister. Do what you can to keep them alive." A moment of dread closed his throat. The riflemen would be as exposed as the Magisters; as the gunners. Swallowing hard, he finished, "General Klamath will bring more men. Until he comes, we must hold the bay."

The men were tired. They had been out searching in the cold for most of the afternoon. But nothing in the Bay of Lights had ever been easy. They were on their feet before Flisk mentioned the General's return. Efficiently, as if they had made their decisions long ago, they chose their partners and their Magisters. The two who were stuck with Magister Lambent had to lift him off his knees and drag him.

With a wry grimace, Brighten told Lambent's guardians, "Do not complain. He is a coward, yes—but he is also powerful. You will be safe with him."

Her manner added, As safe as possible.

Without speaking, the riflemen threw on their winter gear; helped the sorcerers put on cloaks and rain-capes. In moments, they were hustling their charges out the door.

Flisk did not know what to expect. If the cannonade took the enemy by surprise. If the first shots sank ships. If the sorcerers of lightning on those ships had no chance to strike back. If the long guns kept firing. Then the Magisters might reach their positions in time to make a difference.

Otherwise the Captain would hear heavy concussions as guns and stores of gunpowder exploded.

He needed to *be* there.

Nevertheless he took the time to retrieve his rifle, ammunition, and saber from his room in the nearest bunkhouse. He had paid too high a price for thinking that he did not need them.

When Captain Flisk returned to the head of the road, the light was failing as the sun set behind its veil of storm clouds. A deepening gloom covered the bay, the black ships, the furious thrash and throw of the waters. The more distant vessels, the transports, were concealed by the coming night.

Below Flisk's vantage, dusk made a vivid display of the battle. Out near where the former reef had bitten the seas, lightning still searched the bay for obstacles. Closer in, forked fingers of dazzling argent reached for the terraces, the cannon and gunpowder, the men. They left streaks across the Captain's vision, half blinded him. At first, he could not tell whether they struck, or where.

But he could still hear the hard shouts of the long guns. Every shot answered the lightning with spouts of flame. And he had been counting: all sixteen of them were still firing. Somehow, the fury of the enemy's sorcery had missed them. Or—

Blinking at the cold, the winds, the virulent extravagance of lightning, he forced his eyes to focus. Through the rapid stutter of theurgy and gunpowder, he looked down at the emplacements.

The teams of cannoneers performed their tasks with practiced skill: packing powder and wadding down the barrels; setting the fuses; lifting cannonballs or chain into the muzzles; putting flame to the fuseholes. As their guns blared, they jumped away from the recoil. When ropes as thick as cables stopped the recoil, the men rushed to roll the cannon back into place. Despite the bright peril arcing toward them, they maintained the rhythm they had been taught.

None of the gunners were the youths who had come from the Open Hand to fire cannon. Those boys had trained with the men; had practiced as much as anyone. But neither Flisk nor Forguile had felt inclined to risk them. They were a last resort.

As Captain Flisk's vision cleared, he saw that the wild bolts from the ships earlier had failed to hit the emplacements. They lacked the reach of the long guns. And now the Magisters of lightning were there, exerting their Decimates. Some of them whirled their arms as if they were flinging power. Others stood motionless, using only their minds and nerves; their desire to live. Whatever they did, they were succeeding. Hard shafts of silver seemed to evaporate over the waters, expending their force on nothing. The cannon were not harmed.

Whether or not the Magisters of wind were wielding their Decimates—whether or not their efforts served any purpose—Flisk had no idea. He had no sorcerous talent: he could not sense any of the theurgies contending in the bay.

After a moment, he spotted Commander Forguile below him. Braced on one of the ropes, Ennis Forguile stood between the first and second levels. The gloom was too dim for signal-flags: the effects of the lightning were too blinding. Instead, he bellowed instructions, yelled encouragement. His voice and his willingness to risk himself sustained the gunners' discipline. In sequence, sixteen cannon delivered a steady barrage.

The cannoneers were alive because Magisters protected them. And because they had already sunk the nearest ships. Earlier, Flisk had seen twenty vessels in the bay. Now he counted only fourteen. And he was sure of the number. The remaining ships were etched against the darkness by flagrant blasts of lightning.

Six ships down. With the little attention he could spare, Heren Flisk prayed that the corpses of those vessels would serve as fresh obstacles for Rile's approach.

Still, the battle looked impossible. He wanted to raise his rifle and fire, not hoping to hit anything but simply to express his defiance.

A moment later, a load of chain clipped a mast. For no apparent reason, the craft staggered as if it had struck an undetected boulder. Despite its unnatural stability, it heeled onto its side, exposed its flank.

One by one, cannonballs tore into it. Ravenous seas rushed inward, gripped the vessel. The men on the decks scrambled to save themselves. Inaudible in the winds and thunder, they may have screamed. But they had no chance. In moments, the waves tore them and their ship out of sight.

Flisk cheered without realizing that he had made a sound.

In an instant, the more distant craft reacted as if they had received a prearranged signal. Their sorcerers stopped hurling bolts into the waters. Instead, every Decimate of lightning was directed at the cliff, the terraces, the emplacements.

Those vessels were farther away. The Magisters had more time to react, an increment measured in fragments of a heartbeat. If they had been prepared for the change in tactics, or could have taken the moments they needed to rest—

Their stamina had limits. They were already near the edges of their strength. Captain Flisk knew that. Commander Forguile roared warnings. But the gunners ignored their peril.

Magister Visible was the first to fail. Giving her best, she protected the northern end of the second terrace. But she was not enough. During an instant of weakness, a crooked shaft of silver struck her as if it had been aimed straight at her heart. Flisk saw all of her bones outlined in fire. Then the gunpowder stored near her exploded. She and her guards burst into shreds.

Two teams of cannoneers died with her. Shattered by the blast, half a dozen paces of smoothed stone and fitted parapet became rubble. One gun was flung away, a crumpled wreck. Another toppled into the gap made by the explosion. Stained by blood and bodies, it twisted itself to scrap on the level below it.

That shock was enough. Without realizing it, Flisk and Forguile both howled, "WITHDRAW!" Their few sorcerers were too precious to lose.

The riflemen among the cannon knew their orders. They dragged at their charges. Trench and the Magisters of wind obeyed without urging. All of the teams on the north left their guns, running for the road. The Magisters there staggered after them.

But on the south—

Hells! Those cannoneers kept firing. Riflemen yelled at them. Commander Forguile shouted again. They ignored him. They resembled soldiers in one of the pitched battles between Belleger and Amika decades ago, transported by fury and fear into a state where only the guns mattered: the next target and the next shot. They could not disengage until their foes did or died.

Magister Brighten's guards manhandled her away to the road, hauled her by brute force up the ropes. The remaining Magisters stood with the gunners. Magister Lambent—*Magister Lambent*—shoved his guards away. He must have believed that he was safer where he was, protected by his own theurgy. The other sorcerers were like the gunners around them, lost in the madness of their struggle.

Forguile screamed at the soldiers, *"Bring* them! You must—!"

A second explosion cut him off. Another lightning-strike pierced the fading Decimates. It hit the cannon closest to him while the gunners rammed gunpowder and wadding down the barrel. Sorcery and lit gunpowder ripped the gun apart. The concussion knocked Forguile off his hold on the rope. In a spray of iron shards and splintered wood, he skidded downward.

Those gunners became mangled meat and bones.

Without hesitation, Flisk started toward his friend. From the crest of the road, he braced himself to slide downward through ash, snow, and patches of ice. Then he stopped. He was too far away to catch the Commander.

Somehow, the sorceress near the explosion still lived. It left her sprawling on the terrace: it did not kill her. One of her riflemen was lost. The other lifted her in his arms, staggered with her toward the road.

Three cannon kept firing. Two Magisters remained to shield them, Lambent and another Amikan, a man Flisk did not know.

When Flisk saw Forguile far below him reach out, catch the nearest rope with one hand, and wrench himself to a stop, the Captain understood that his friend was alive. Reeling inside himself, he howled at any soldiers who could hear him to get everyone else away from the long guns.

They tried to obey. Lambent's fellow Magister fled his post in a rush. To move the gunners, the riflemen had to clout a couple of stubborn heads. Then they forced that team to flee. But Lambent himself refused. And the gunners on either side supported him. One man from each team grappled with Magister Lambent's guards. The other three kept working.

Heren Flisk did not understand. He stared in astonishment as the only coward among the defenders went on shielding two of the long guns while the cannoneers continued firing. Lambent had surrendered himself to his theurgy. He had *become* his Decimate.

He was considered the most powerful of the lightning-wielders. The gunners he preserved may have believed that his strength would endure. Their exposure to instant death may have driven them insane. Or they may have thought that they would not survive leaving their cannon. The road was too far away. Because Lambent was so afraid, he had been positioned at the south end of the highest terrace, where his impulse to flee was obstructed by guns, gunners, and guards. Now he was all that kept his cannoneers alive. They stayed and fought.

His defiance could not last. Even terror would not sustain him much longer. But it was not enemy lightning that killed him.

Abruptly, Lambent clutched at his chest. His mouth fell open, gaping for air. He went rigid, locked in every muscle. For an instant, his eyes held pure panic.

Unable to make a sound, he toppled over the parapet.

That was the end. After his protection vanished, sorcery found the gunners, their cannon, their supply of gunpowder. It killed two more riflemen. The concussion dropped Flisk to his knees; deafened him. He could not hear the debris of the ruined terrace collapsing onto the next level, and the next. None of the long guns fired again.

Belleger and Amika had lost the first engagement.

But when the cannon were stilled, the black ships—thirteen of them—ceased their attack on the cliff. As if they had lost interest in their foes, they resumed their efforts to clear the bay for the larger vessels behind them.

Hardly able to hear himself gasping, Captain Flisk regained his feet. He had gone so long without his weapons that he had forgotten how they hindered his movements. But that was a trivial frustration. He had no attention to spare for it. He had lost too many Magisters, too many guns and gunners. And Ennis Forguile might be badly injured. He might need help. But Flisk could not go to him. He had to assess the damage and try to think.

Fortunately, the soldiers had their own under-captains, men without formal titles who could make decisions and take action. They had already sent six riflemen hurrying down the ropes to aid the Commander.

Flisk looked out at the sorcery stabbing like spears into the black waters of the bay. Through his boots, he felt the deep thud of earthquakes. For a moment, he watched the waves thrash as if they were in torment.

A throng had gathered around him. The Magisters of wind and drought were there. The survivors of the first engagement. Spectators from the encampment. Riflemen. Even the camp's physicians had come from their small infirmary. They had brought a stretcher for the stunned sorceress, Magister Glowing.

Flisk expected a gabble of fear, questions, demands; an onslaught he did not know how to answer. But the crowd was silent. People stared at him, trusting him to know how to defend the bay now. Relying on him to tell them.

The first voice he heard was Magister Brighten's. She stood apart from the crowd, peering down at the damaged terraces and swearing with soft fury. "You pile of droppings. You coward." After a moment, the Captain realized that she was cursing Magister Lambent. "Did you have to die? Were you too afraid to go on living? That is the most abject, pitiful, *arrogant*—"

She herself had tried to keep fighting. Her guards had forced her away. Perhaps Lambent's example had shamed her.

Flisk tried to swallow the residue of gunpowder, blood, and lightning that scorched his throat. When he found his voice, he croaked to the riflemen, "Who can give me a tally?"

One of the under-officers stepped forward. "It is not as bad as we feared, Captain. Still, it is bad. We have lost two Magisters. Five guns are gone, and five gun-crews." Hells, *twenty* men. Twenty trained, irreplaceable cannoneers. "And five of our comrades.

"If Commander Forguile is not too badly hurt—" The man's voice trailed away. He may have meant, The Commander will know what to do.

While Flisk fumbled for a reply, a hoarse call from the road snatched the attention of the crowd away.

Supported by two soldiers, with three more behind him, Ennis Forguile emerged from the bay.

In the east, the moon was rising, adding its pale silver to the argent ravaging the waters. It made the Commander's face and movements visible against the background of the enemy's barrage.

He had a bleeding gash over one ear, clots of snow and ash like contusions on his legs. He shifted his feet like a man who had endured a severe beating. With his right arm, he clutched his left side.

"That was exciting," he panted. Pain twisted his grin. "We did well, I think. But I may be hurt."

Roughly, Heren Flisk pushed his way through the crowd to meet the Commander. In his relief, he came close to flinging his arms around his friend. But Forguile's gaze warned him away.

"What is it?" he demanded unsteadily. "Hurt how?"

Forguile grimaced. "My ribs. They must be broken. I can feel bone." In a hoarse croak, he added, "Give me an hour. Then I will take teams to the medium cannon."

Heren Flisk shook his head. "No." His friend's presence made him stronger. Even Forguile's wounds had that effect. "Give *me* an hour. Then *I* will man those guns. *You* will go to the infirmary. You are bleeding, Ennis. Your ribs must be bound."

As if he outranked the Commander, Flisk told the soldiers nearby, "Take him. Watch him. Do not let him leave until the physicians release him."

Both men were Bellegerin riflemen. They hardly knew Captain Flisk and Forguile. But General Klamath and the First Captain had trained them well. They obeyed at once.

Ennis Forguile touched the cut over his ear; scowled at the smear of blood on his hand. It was an argument for which he had no answer.

Muttering protests like groans, he let his guardians draw him away from the cliff and the black ships, the virulent sorcery, and the distant fleet.

Briefly, Flisk watched his friend go. For a few moments, he studied the black ships until he was sure that their violence was still concentrated on the bay's obstructions. Then he returned to the camp to muster cannoneers for the medium guns.

Despite the loss of the long guns—despite the deaths of men and Magisters—he had one reason for gratitude. He still had enough experienced gunners to work all sixteen cannon—and enough riflemen to watch over them. He would not be forced to send boys down the terrace to die.

As for the Magisters, he had no intention of risking them again. When the ships came within reach of the medium cannon, they would be too close. Even a sorceress like Magister Brighten would not have time to sense a strike of lightning and counter it. The gunners would be completely exposed.

Chewing on his doubts, Flisk tried to believe that he would not lose them all. The enemy had never been fired on from the middle terraces. The ships might be unaware of those cannon. If so, the medium guns with their heavier balls would have a chance to wreak havoc before the Great God's sorcerers could react. And ships near enough to be hit by sixty pounds of shot or chain might be within range of theurgy from the cliff's rim. Then the bay's lightning-wielders would be able to counterattack.

Heren Flisk clung to those possibilities. Without them, he could not commit cannoneers and soldiers to the third and fourth terraces. He did not have it in him to send men to certain death.

SEVEN

TRUTH BY ANOTHER NAME

Mattwil and Cloras were resting in one of the bunkhouses when they heard the call for riflemen to help search for Father Skurn.

Their refuge stood at the eastern edge of the encampment. So far from the cliff and the bay, it was little used. It and others had been added to accommodate everyone whom King Bifalt would commit to the defense of the bay. But those forces had not arrived yet. The Open Hand was too distant.

However, Mattwil had not chosen this shelter for its privacy. He had led Cloras there to avoid the coming battle. He had vowed that he would not fight. He meant to keep his word.

A season ago, working on Queen Estie's road, he had failed to defend a band of abused Nuuri slaves. Instead, he had deserted. At the time, he had believed that he escaped to warn Belleger of Amikan evil. But now he knew the truth. He was a coward. He had fled to save himself.

Since that time, a shame that he called honesty had ruled him. In the Open Hand, he had heard Father Skurn preach. He remembered the priest's lesson.

Lie to me if you wish. Lie to each other if you must. But do not lie to yourselves. If you have no other courage, have the courage to tell the truth to yourselves.

He was honest enough to see his desertion for what it was. Still, the truth hurt him. He kept it to himself. Instead, he refused to take the risk that his actions would betray him. He stayed away from even the hint of combat so that he would not expose his cowardice.

That was crucial to him. He had already demonstrated that he could not keep his other vow. At one time, he had vowed to shun Amikans, the men who had tortured the Nuuri. Those men deserved worse than the condemnation he exacted from himself. But working with Amikans and Bellegerins alike in the bay had undermined his determination. Soon he could not tell them apart. People like Captain Flisk and Commander Forguile had won his respect.

And Cloras herself was Amikan.

She was with him now because she was always with him. She clung to his company. When she could, she clung to his arm. At those times when they were not too weary, she responded to him with a hunger that matched his. He did not understand it. To his way of thinking, she deserved better than the love of a deserter. Nevertheless he treasured her. Not many days ago, he had spurned his father's offer of reconciliation. He had not been able to bear the openheartedness of a man who could forgive his son's cowardice. Mattwil had enough courage to admit that he did not know how to forgive himself. He did not want forgiveness. He wanted to be left alone with his failures. For that reason, he had refused his father. Any other response would have been a lie.

But he could not spurn Cloras. She had become necessary. She did not know what he had done.

When he heard the call to search for the priest, he ignored it. In it, he sensed a challenge that might expose him. He owed the priest a degree of loyalty. He did not want to learn that he was wrong.

But Cloras was not like him. If she doubted herself, she did not show it. Despite her air of frailty and diffidence, she was certain—and unafraid to speak her mind. When the clamor of riflemen outside the building had faded away, she startled him by saying, "We must find him."

Mattwil regarded her with surprise. She sounded earnest. But that was her normal voice: she was always earnest. She had used the same tone when she had addressed Matt.

Your General sent him here. That was cruel.

To Mattwil's mute question, she said, "He summons us."

He could only stare. He did not know how to understand her. She seldom talked, and never about herself, or her desires, or what she wanted from him.

Frowning in vexation, she ducked her head. "I can feel him," she told the floorboards. "A tug in my mind. We must find him."

When the planks made no reply, she answered the questions he did not ask. "You heard him once. I heard the priests many times. In Maloresse, before I came here. I had no home. No family. No one who would spare a bed. Only a coin or two from men who used me. I went to the Church because it was warm. The priests made me welcome. They did not use me. Their voices entered my dreams while I slept.

"Now he needs us. We must not refuse."

Her appeal swayed Mattwil. He rose to put on his winter gear: his rain-cape with a heavy blanket draped over it, a pair of woolen socks that served as mittens. He would have gone out into the snow alone if Cloras had wished it; but she readied herself to accompany him. While she chose an extra layer of clothing, he asked, "Why does he summon us?"

She cocked her head, apparently listening. Then she answered, "He will tell us when we find him."

Mattwil started to ask again, Why? He meant, Why should we trust him? Do *you* believe in him?

The priest must have done something to offend Captain Flisk and Commander Forguile, who had been good to Mattwil.

But Cloras' earnestness stopped him. She had given herself to him and asked for nothing. He wanted to be worthy of her. He held the door for her, then followed her out into the cold.

The snow was fading. After days of heavy weather, the storm began drifting westward. Still, the falling snow was enough to blunt the outlines of the nearest buildings.

Reflexively, Mattwil started down one of the gullies that served as paths. But Cloras called him back. "This way." She pointed vaguely away from the camp across an expanse of undisturbed snow. When he joined her, she sent him ahead of her to force a way through the deep drifts. At his back, she dragged her extra garment over the snow to obscure their trail.

He shook his head in bewilderment. Still, he did not question her. If Father Skurn could summon her, he might also be giving her instructions.

Perhaps she had lost her mind. Mattwil did not think so. Her actions were strange: her manner had not changed. If she could lead him to the priest, he was willing. He had no questions for her. He had several for Father Skurn.

What had the priest done?

At the bottom of a hill, Cloras directed him northward. On lower ground, he had less difficulty forcing a path for her. They were below the woods along the rim of the bay. Interrupting the winds, the trees had caught the worst of the snowfall. He surged through snowbanks that came only to his knees, not his thighs.

Distant shouts reached him. Men called to each other, shouted questions and commands. Their mounts thrashed through the snow among the trees.

They were searching—

Of course. If Father Skurn had disappeared, where else would the riflemen look?

Mattwil did not know how far the trees extended. Working on the emplacements, no one had the energy to explore them. He could not guess how much time the men would need for their hunt.

If the soldiers failed to catch the priest where they expected him, they would range farther.

Cloras drew Mattwil to a halt. For a moment, she stood still, concentrating. Then she directed him eastward.

Among the hills below the woods, they came to a brief gully between steep slopes, almost a ravine. Along its near edge, someone had passed through the snow recently, leaving a trail.

A man on foot. And trying to hurry. Mattwil saw signs of falling.

Then he felt a tug. It pulled at his heart, but its message was unmistakable. *I am here.* Without a word, Cloras urged him to follow the trail. She came behind him, sweeping the hillside to obscure the signs.

Abruptly, a man rose to his feet ahead of them. He had fallen again—or, no, he had tried to bury himself, burrow under a snowbank. Layers of white cloaked him from head to foot. Mattwil knew him only by the sound of his voice, deep and resonant despite the cold, as he demanded, "Hide me."

Mattwil stopped. Cloras pushed him, but he stayed where he was. He had too many questions. The easiest to ask was, "Why?"

Father Skurn gestured, shedding clumps of snow. "Come closer, my son. I will make everything plain."

Mattwil squirmed. Suddenly, he did not trust the man. Nevertheless he obeyed. Cloras trusted *him*. With her urgent at his back, he approached the priest.

"Tell me why."

Instead of answering, Father Skurn stretched out his hand. Before Mattwil knew what was happening—before he thought to slap the hand away—the priest touched his forehead.

Saying nothing, the priest made everything plain. Mattwil's questions vanished. His distrust burst like a soap bubble and was gone. He knew how to obey. His bafflement remained, but it no longer mattered. Only hiding Father Skurn had any importance. Only keeping the priest alive—

Sure of himself at last, Mattwil dropped to his knees and began digging at the inadequate covert Father Skurn had tried to fashion, making it deeper; wider.

Big enough for three rather than one.

Fresh snow was easy to thrust aside. It weighed little more than feathers. But under the surface, the accumulation of days was heavier, colder. It formed an icy crust. Breaking into it hurt Mattwil's hands until they, too, began to freeze. Still, his purpose was clear. When he hit a patch that he could not break with his fingers, he used his elbows.

While Cloras continued sweeping away the marks of their pres-

ence, and Father Skurn stood watch, Mattwil dug a pit deep enough to
hide them all.

They did not need to speak. Everything was understood. In silence,
Cloras handed her spare cape to Mattwil. Pulling the priest after him,
Mattwil stretched out on his back in the pit, settled the priest beside
him; made sure that he had left room for Cloras. Then he covered himself and Skurn with the rain-cape. While she pushed snow over them
and packed it lightly, he propped up the cape so that there would be air
when the pit was filled. There he waited, half holding his breath, until
Cloras crawled in past their feet. As she settled herself beside him, they
shook their covering gently to scatter the snow over it; doing as much
as they dared to make the hillside look undisturbed.

"Lie still," murmured the priest. "I will know when we are safe. I
came to bring peace. With your help, I will succeed."

While the effects of Father Skurn's brief touch lingered, Mattwil
believed him.

Slowly, the warmth of their bodies melted the snow around them. As
it froze again, it formed a small cocoon. They were encased in cold,
numbed and protected by it. While they could draw air from the gap
Cloras had left by their feet, they would live, at least for a time.

Nevertheless a killing chill soaked through Mattwil's garb. It spread
from his limbs into his chest. At his side, violent shivers wracked Cloras.
She was too slight to withstand the cold. With what felt like his last
strength, he worked one arm under her, then rolled her—carefully,
carefully—onto him so that she could share his remaining heat. Her
breathing at his ear made beads of ice. They were going to deafen him.
But he did not try to shift her. The assurance that Father Skurn had
given him was gone, forgotten. Instead, he clung to the faint throb of
her heart. It gave him a reason to endure.

After a while, she stopped shivering.

An hour passed, or several. It felt longer. He sank into a stunned
cold that resembled sleep. He no longer knew who he was or what he

was doing when the priest announced abruptly, "We are safe." He did not sound like a man who had suffered.

With both hands, Father Skurn pushed at the rain-cape to lift its burden of ice and snow. For a moment, the cocoon resisted him. Then he broke through the crust. With the whoop of a man who had nothing to fear, he breathed fresh air.

Sitting up in the gap, the priest let daylight reach his companions. A clear sky covered the world where they lay frozen.

Mattwil tried to rouse Cloras. When he failed, he found that he still had a little strength. He was too weak and stiff to sit up with her slim weight on his chest; but he was able to roll over on top of her. With his arms around her, he braced himself on his knees. In that position, he held her close while he confronted the challenge of rising to his feet.

The task would have been easier if Skurn had helped him. But the priest stood aside. As if he imagined that his urging could overcome the cold, Father Skurn insisted, "Come. The sun is setting. Our time is now. *Come*, I say.

"I will not lose my only believers."

Mattwil recognized the empty hillside; the onset of evening. At first, the priest's voice and the winds were the only sounds. But then he seemed to hear a familiar booming in the distance: the blare of cannon firing in sequence. He heard or imagined the faint sizzle of lightning among the blasts.

Clasping Cloras to his chest, he surged upright.

"Yes, my son." Father Skurn's tone implied glee. "Cannon. The Decimate of lightning. The bloodshed has begun. I will end it. I have promised peace. Come and see how I achieve it."

The young man did not move. Cloras hung like death in his embrace. The pallor of her face mimicked the snow. She did not appear to breathe. The priest's desires could not reach him.

Shifting the girl who had chosen him, holding her with one arm, he slapped her cheek. Gently. A little harder.

She gave no sign that she lived.

"No," said Skurn. "You will both obey me."

One quick step brought the priest closer. Almost contemptuously, he brushed his hand across Cloras' forehead.

Her eyes snapped open. She took a gasp of air, and another. Her muscles tightened.

When she was able to focus her gaze on Mattwil's face, she gave a small sigh and relaxed against him.

Pieces of who he was began to return. He wanted to see her smile. He had never seen her features lift in that way. But her expression was always as earnest as her tone.

If Father Skurn had tried to touch his forehead again, Mattwil would have struck the priest's arm away.

Apparently, Skurn trusted Mattwil's obedience. "Now come," he said. "You will not have to carry her far. She will recover."

He seemed to know the secret of Mattwil's heart. The only question Matt's son could find was: "Where?"

"The woods," answered the priest. "You will guide me. We must reach the cliff north of the guns."

Mattwil only nodded. Holding Cloras with all his care, he began to slog upward toward the distant trees.

Father Skurn followed in the path Mattwil made for him.

As they ascended the slope, crested that hill, and approached the next, the sounds of battle reached them more clearly: the hard boom of cannon firing one after another, the hot burn of lightning. But there were no explosions. Apparently, bolts of sorcery had not hit the guns or the gunpowder.

Not yet.

He would have said that he was exhausted. Beyond this hillside, he would have to climb one more to reach the woods. But he continued forcing a weary trail through the snow. To save his life, he would not have put Cloras down.

However, Father Skurn was right about her. Soon she twisted in Mattwil's arms, met his gaze with more concentration. "I can walk," she murmured. "I can try."

He remembered more of himself. "Are you sure?" he asked.

"No," she admitted. "But I am sure you are tired."

With a rueful grimace, he lowered her to her feet.

She wavered for a moment, then found her balance without his help. When she staggered, she steadied herself by clutching at his rain-cape. Together, they started moving again.

"Good," said Father Skurn at her back. "Do not stop."

Mattwil obeyed while he tried to recall the questions that had troubled him earlier, in a different life: a time when he could not hear the priest's voice.

They were nearing the trees when they heard an explosion, a sound like a hole being torn in the face of the cliff. He could imagine it: the strike of lightning, the scale of the detonation, the shattered stonework. He had labored on the emplacements long enough to know what their destruction would look like.

Whatever had protected the guns earlier was failing.

"Good," repeated Father Skurn. "There will be carnage. Confusion. It will serve us."

The cannon kept firing. But now there was a stagger in the sequence. The gap between shots stretched. The men were leaving their guns—or they were dying. Mattwil counted as well as he could. Eight—? Only *eight*? There had been sixteen. Had that explosion taken out one whole terrace? More than one?

Abruptly, he found his voice. "How?"

Behind him, the priest mused, "How?"

Mattwil stumbled to a halt, turned to face the servant of the Church. "You talk about peace. You promised it. But men are dying." The cannon must have sunk ships. The enemy's forces were dying as well. "How will you bring peace?"

"Do not stop!" snapped Father Skurn. "I will make everything plain when we reach the cliff. You will *see* what I can do."

To Mattwil, he sounded like a man who would enjoy abusing Nuuri slaves.

While the young man hesitated, he heard another explosion. In an instant, more guns stopped firing.

"Mattwil!" panted Cloras. "We know those men. Some of them have been kind. If Father Skurn can save any of them—"

Hells! Oh, hells!

Trying to prove worthy, Mattwil attacked the hillside again.

Desperately, he floundered through the snow. The trees were not far now. He had almost reached them when a third blast shocked the air. He felt its power in the ground under him. It dropped him to his knees.

The guns did not fire again. As he struggled back to his feet, he knew that the defense of the bay had failed.

He wanted to believe that men dying with their guns was not his concern. He owed himself that much loyalty. Nevertheless he prayed for more shots. The medium cannon remained. As a last resort, there were the siege-guns. Surely, Captain Flisk had not surrendered. Commander Forguile had not. They would send gunners to the third and fourth terraces. To the lowest level if they had no choice. *Someone* had to resist the enemy.

Father Skurn could not prevent it.

"Guide me," demanded the priest as if he knew Mattwil's thoughts. "Watch what I do. You will see peace restored."

"Go, Mattwil," urged Cloras. She sounded faint; at the end of herself. But she did not falter. He had never known her to seem unsure. "We must help him. It is all we can do."

Groaning, Matt's son dragged his weakness toward the trees.

Evening was near. The sun cast an early dusk past the westering storm. Under the trees, the gloom was deeper. Yet Mattwil was able to move more easily. The ground must have been trampled earlier. His boots met only packed snow and patches of ice. Men had been here ahead of him, many of them.

At first, he assumed that the soldiers hunting for Father Skurn had disturbed the snow. But the evidence of running feet was everywhere. Had the riflemen searched *that* thoroughly? The whole woods?

Moving more quickly, Mattwil followed his instincts in the direction of the bay's edge. He was intimately familiar with the extent of the terraces, the positions of the emplacements. He did not know exactly where he would reach the cliff, but he trusted that he would emerge where Father Skurn wanted to be.

North of the guns.

With every step, he seemed to resemble himself more: a man who believed and doubted; a man who had given his oath and had no faith. He wanted to stop hurrying and demand answers. But Cloras had reminded him of a different truth. If Father Skurn could not end the fighting, everyone in the bay was doomed.

Leading his companion and the priest, he went on.

Slivers of silvery light began slanting through the snow-caked branches. The moon was rising. He had no other way to measure time. This day already felt interminable.

Ahead of him, a greater brightness filtered past the trees. It came in long flares and stutters, moments of hard whiteness among briefer instants of deep night. The Decimate of lightning. The enemy was still fighting. But no cannon answered the bolts. The soldiers and gunners were not fighting back.

As he crossed from the woods onto the bare rock that formed the rim of the cliff, he left the trodden snow behind. The incessant turmoil of winds there left only the uneven knuckles of ice. The ground's hands clenched the bay's edge like fists.

He was within twenty paces of the precipice.

Father Skurn caught up with him before he had gone half the distance. Cloras lagged behind, as weak as a shadow in the moonlight and the glare of sorcery.

Side by side, Mattwil and the priest looked out over the thrashing waters.

Skurn cheered at the sight, a shout of satisfaction. He clutched at his chest with one fist, brandished the other.

Mattwil needed a moment to understand that the encroaching ships were not attacking the emplacements and guns, the cliff, the defenders. Not now. As black as the waters where they sat, the vessels struck at the sea itself. Shafts of lightning as crooked as branches and yet as precise as knives flashed down to pierce the depths. Far below the surface, sorcery burned, destroying what it hit. He could not see

boulders shatter and scatter, juts of new reef fall apart, bulging fore-
heads of granite split: the seas obscured them. But he felt the violence
in his bones.

This was how those ships had broken through the outer reef. Now
they were clearing the way for the craft that carried the enemy's hosts.

By wan moonlight and dazzling theurgy, Mattwil glimpsed the
ruin of the first and second terraces; the debris of guns and stonework.
A few of the cannon remained in place. They may have been inaccessible. Worse, falling rocks had damaged some of the medium guns on
the third level. The unharmed cannon would be difficult to reach.

He could not see the crown of the road. The shape of the precipice
blocked his view in that direction. He wanted to believe that the defenders were massing to keep the enemy from attempting an ascent. Or
perhaps Captain Flisk and Commander Forguile intended to man the
medium guns somehow. Perhaps the officers hoped to hit the enemy
with a point-blank barrage. Mattwil wanted them to do *some*thing. He
had no hope for himself.

In the calamity of the defense, Father Skurn's exultation infuriated
Matt's son. While Cloras stumbled closer, he wheeled on the priest.
Skurn's power over him was gone.

"Now tell the truth," he snarled through the whine and cry of the
winds. "I do not *believe* you can end this. You have lied to us. You have
no interest in peace. Everything you say is a lie.

"You *serve* those ships."

There was no such thing as *faith*. Not in the way Father Skurn used
that word.

Grinning, the priest faced his only opponent.

"Inward peace is best," he sighed. "I would prefer it. I have done
what I can to teach it. But when the war within turns outward—" With
one hand, he gestured over the bay. "Ah, my son. There are times when
peace must be imposed. A greater strength must end the squabbling of
lesser forces. That time has come. I will show you what the Great God
Rile's strength can do."

"And *this* is the result?" cried Mattwil. "You rant of peace, but you
bring slaughter? It is madness! *You* are mad."

Father Skurn frowned. "You disappoint me, my son. But even now, it is not too late to teach you."

He was standing too close to Mattwil. He tapped the young man's forehead with one finger before Matt's son could protect himself.

The effect was eternity in an instant, an entire world's ages of strife and pain and learning compressed in a single brief touch. Without transition, Mattwil passed from fury into pride; into a version of Skurn's triumph. The priest was *here*, where the Great God intended him to be, and Mattwil had helped him. He had kept Father Skurn safe. He had guided the man to his destiny. His own accomplishment was greater than any act of faith.

Panting near him, Cloras gasped, "Mattwil."

Mattwil ignored her. She was nothing to him.

Grinning again, the priest turned to look out over the ships and the sorcery, the black waters. Avidly, he gripped some object under his garments near the center of his chest.

"You cannot imagine the glory of it," he proclaimed. "Already, whole continents bask in the Great God's peace. The lives of those people are relief and contentment and service. But he is not satisfied. He has endured the gods of folly too long, the brutish lust of the flesh, the overweening lust of the mind. He means to end them. When he has swept the false knowledge of pride and books from the world, he will teach all men and women to know their place in his peace.

"It begins here."

"Mattwil!" insisted Cloras. "Look!" She pointed urgently northward along the cliff, between the woods and the precipice. *"Look!"*

Her friend and lover did not even glance in that direction.

"Be silent, woman!" snapped Father Skurn over his shoulder. "You serve the lusts of the flesh. Their hold on you is too strong. I will silence you if I must."

"Mattwil," cried Cloras again, but softly, with tears and weariness in her voice.

Yet her earnestness remained, and her determination. From somewhere under her winter garb, she produced a thin blade more like a needle than a knife: a tool a seamstress might use to pick out stitches. With all of her remaining force, she jabbed it between the priest's ribs near his spine.

Then she mustered a shriek that pierced the winds and the sky, the frying shafts of lightning, the agony of the seas. Despite her weakness, her voice seemed to reach the whole bay.

Cursing, Father Skurn wheeled on her. With one heavy blow, he stretched her out on the stone. She flopped once and lay still, bleeding from her mouth, hardly breathing.

Mattwil did not look at her. He looked where she had pointed.

From the north, a mass of men came running toward him. A horde of them, too many to count.

They were not soldiers. They were not ordinary men. They ran without a sound, barefoot on the rough stone. Dark skin, dark clothing. Rags fluttered from their strong frames, the tattered remnants of peasant's garb. Moments of lightning exposed open mouths full of teeth filed for rending. They did not shout. If they panted for air, they did so in silence.

Mattwil understood. Cloras had stabbed the priest. She had shrieked a warning. Father Skurn had felled her with a blow. Between one heartbeat and the next, Mattwil's mind opened.

Skurn claimed that he would impose *peace* on the battle, but he meant *defeat*. These men were his means, his weapons. They would take Captain Flisk and Commander Forguile by surprise; kill every defender in their way. Because of them, the ships would be free to reach the strand unopposed.

And the timing could hardly have been better for the priest. True, the enemy had lost ships. But then the gunners on the first two terraces had been driven away or slain. Now the officers and their remaining soldiers were almost certainly mustering at the top of the road, readying themselves to repel the enemy. The men Father Skurn had summoned would rip them apart.

Mattwil had helped the enemy ships take the Bay of Lights.

And Skurn had hit Cloras. He may have killed her.

Matt's son sprang at the priest.

He had a stoneworker's hands, arms, legs. A stoneworker's instinctive grasp of leverage. Before the running men came close enough to stop him, he heaved Skurn into the air, held the man over his head. Strangling on anguish and shame, he croaked the only name that remained to him: *"Cloras!"*

Without thought or hesitation—without so much as a flicker of regret—he flung the Great God's servant over the precipice.

Then he watched the priest fall, screaming, as long as he could: no more than a moment. After that, the first of Father Skurn's men shoved him off the cliff.

Mattwil son of Matt and Matta had won a battle with himself, but he died too suddenly to know the truth.

Up on the cliff, Rile's men kept running. Some of them trampled on Cloras as they passed, but not deliberately. She was nothing to them. They had their orders, knew their purpose. Baring their teeth, they raced to fulfill Father Skurn's promise: to end the battle by slaughtering the Great God's foes.

EIGHT

THE LAST DEFENSE OF THE BAY

After Commander Forguile went to the camp's infirmary, Captain Flisk took his time. He had promised his friend an hour, although he knew that he did not have that much time.

Standing near the edge of the cliff and the road's crest, he had a good view of the black ships as they worked their way inward. With lightning and earthquakes, they made profound changes in the waters of the bay. Blocked by fewer obstructions, the seas ripped against each other less, surged more directly toward the strand. The spray of pounded boulders rose higher as the currents in and out again grew stronger. The ships were already in range for the guns on the third and fourth terraces.

Flisk suspected that they were in range for his few Magisters as well. Even rifle shots would reach them now, but the bullets would do no real damage. He could rally his forces *now*, if he chose. Any delay might prove disastrous.

Nevertheless he waited. He wanted to hit those ships with a shattering cannonade. For that, he needed them to come closer.

Perhaps he could afford to wait. The enemy's sorcerers had not attacked the remaining guns. They could have destroyed those cannon, those emplacements. Why did they hold back? Were they unaware of the medium cannon? The siege-guns? Or did they know something that Flisk and Forguile did not?

It was possible that the invaders had not spotted the rest of the guns. They could not see as well as Flisk could. Their relentless light-ning made them vivid to him: it must surely leave them half-blind. Light-struck, they might have difficulty distinguishing the details of their own decks. The light of the rising moon was too wan to help them.

The Captain hoped for that. He wanted to sink as many of those ships as he could before they finished clearing the way for Rile's fleet. To do that, he had to withhold his barrage until the last moment. If the guns fired too soon, they would not do enough damage. If he gave the signal too late, the enemy's counterattack would kill everyone down on the terraces.

How much time did he have? He had no way of knowing. Later might be better than sooner, but he could only rely on *now.*

With a private groan, he called a rifleman out of the tense crowd watching the bay. "Full teams for sixteen cannon," he told the soldier. "Trained men. No boys.

"Then muster your comrades." He believed that all of them had returned from the search for Father Skurn. "And every Magister we have. I mean to hit those ships *hard.*"

Even the sorcerers of wind might find a way to affect the battle.

The rifleman saluted as if Flisk were General Klamath; as if Flisk had ever done anything to earn so much respect. Shouting orders, he ran for the encampment.

Muttering to himself, the Captain gathered his courage to give orders that would get men killed.

From the edge of the precipice, he scanned the terraces. The moon had not risen high enough to lift them out of the cliff's shadow, but the flaring of the enemy's Decimate lit them in harsh flashes. On the third and fourth levels, debris from the explosions higher up had ru-ined two of the medium cannon. Rubble made two or three others all but inaccessible. In the confusion of broken stone lay parts of bodies: sepa-rated limbs, shredded torsos, fragments that might once have been heads.

Altogether, the defense had lost twenty gunners, five riflemen, five—no, seven—cannon, and two Magisters. One surviving sorceress of lightning might be too weak to fight again. Each of those losses was a heavy blow.

What Captain Flisk had in mind now would be worse. He meant to send sixteen teams of four to the medium guns. But he had only fourteen intact cannon. Only eleven if the barriers of rubble could not be cleared. Well, he would commit eleven teams to the working guns. The other cannoneers would have to tackle the debris. If they could free even one cannon with its stores of shot and gunpowder, that would help. If they could do more—

Under any circumstances, he had to assume that they would all be killed. Any enemy sorcerers who did not go down with the ships would have easy targets.

The prospect made Heren Flisk feel like a butcher. He arranged the rest of his plans to give those men at least a measure of cover.

Magister Brighten and her comrades would find the ships within reach of their Decimates. They might not have enough time to counter the enemy's lightning-wielders effectively, but they could at least try to distract those sorcerers by aiming for the men on the decks of the vessels.

For the riflemen, Captain Flisk had a different task in mind.

Around him, the winds shifted. He heard the crash of seas, the submerged crack of rocks broken by earthquakes. Then the clamor receded, leaving the more familiar whine and cry of air past the cliff's edges.

As the riflemen Flisk had summoned arrived, he gathered their informal leaders. "Tell your men," he instructed, trying not to let his voice shake, "to find cover along the cliff. I want them to watch the enemy without showing themselves. They may be able to spot men on those ships. If they do—and if you have marksmen who can hit a target at that distance—let them fire at will. Otherwise, do not shoot.

"I will take teams to the medium cannon. They will attempt a barrage, as heavy as they can manage. But they will be exposed, easy to kill. Unable to shield themselves."

He was explaining too much. The men around him probably had more experience than he did. They would know what to do. But he could not stop. If he did give these orders, he would not have the courage to condemn the cannoneers.

"When the barrage begins, I want every rifle firing. Tell your men to strike at the ships as fast as they can. I want a hailstorm of bullets." A threat to discourage the enemy's sorcerers. "It may do more to protect the gunners than our Magisters can."

The salute the soldiers gave him before hurrying to obey made him want to weep.

I will take teams— Could he do what Commander Forguile had done earlier? Forguile had been able to save himself. Flisk might not get that chance.

He had to take the risk. Better to fall with men he had sent to die than to stay where he was and watch their deaths.

Harried by Magister Brighten, the sorcerers straggled toward him. Lambent had been their self-appointed leader, but he was gone. With fury and shouting, Brighten took his place. Supported by Magister Trench with his sorcerers of wind, she made even the most reluctant lightning-wielders obey her despite their fatigue and the biting cold.

With her, she had the woman who had been struck down earlier, Magister Glowing. By moonlight and reflected theurgy, Glowing looked pale, unsteady on her feet, frightened. But she came.

The Magisters of drought were too few. Flisk hoped that they would do what they could.

To show his respect, he went to meet them all.

"Thank you, Magisters," he began. "You are needed."

"To do what?" demanded a burly man who had been one of the first to retreat from the upper terraces. "Those"—he seemed to search for an adequate insult—"hellish sorcerers have already beaten us. We are wasted against them."

Flisk made a placating gesture. "Calm yourself." He groped for the man's name and could not find it. "I will not ask you to go down the road again. You will use your Decimates as you did in the old wars, hidden where our enemies cannot target you."

His assurance drew a palpable relief from the Magisters. Even Trench gave a sigh of released tension.

But Magister Brighten was not eased. "Then what do you expect us to do?" Her outrage seemed to include everyone everywhere. "They are still too strong."

The Captain took a deep breath, tried to appear relaxed. The effort left him light-headed.

"Find your coverts," he answered. "Note the positions of the ships. At my signal, strike at them." He wished for the Decimate of fire, but no one here had that gift. "I do not expect you to sink them. I do not ask you to set them burning"—although he hoped for that. "I need you to draw the attention of the enemy's sorcerers. Make them counter you, or try to strike at you. While our gunners descend to the terraces and ready the cannon, they will be defenseless. They must have your attack to protect them."

"We understand, Captain," said Magister Trench. "But it will require a *sustained* attack. None of us can manage that. Perhaps Magister Brighten and her comrades should work in pairs. One pair to strike while the others rest, one after another by turns."

"Yes!" snapped Brighten. "Good." She was holding Magister Glowing's arm, supporting or compelling her, but she did not glance at the injured woman. "That we can do."

Flisk nodded approval. His heart lifted a little. Between them, Trench and Brighten gave him a measure of hope.

"And you can rest again," he added, "while the guns fire. It will compel the enemy's attention. If you sense sorcery aimed at the guns, try to deflect or dismiss it. If not, rest and wait. And be ready. The gunners will need your protection again when they are done."

"Yes," repeated Magister Brighten. Now her anger resembled eagerness. Like Lambent, she gave herself the right to issue orders. Keeping Glowing with her, she paired the other four Magisters of lightning quickly and commanded them to find their places. "Be sure of your targets. Watch for the Captain's signal. Now go."

After only a moment's hesitation, she was obeyed. The burly man in particular looked sheepish or crestfallen, unaccustomed to being told what to do; but he did not hang back.

While the Magisters of lightning spread out along the cliff to find their hiding places, Trench spoke for the Magisters of wind. "There is little we can do, Captain. The stability of those ships is unnatural. But perhaps we can unsettle them somewhat, if we combine our Decimates. An unexpected tilt may disturb those sorcerers."

That was more than Flisk had known to request. Not for the first time, he was grateful for Magister Trench's presence. But he had no words for what he felt. Instead, he gave the sturdy theurgist a salute.

With a grim grin, Trench led the other sorcerers of wind away toward the head of the road, where they would have a clear view of the whole bay.

Breathing against the clench in his stomach and the pain in his shoulder, Heren Flisk braced himself to take charge of the gunners.

They came from the encampment in a group as unruly as a mob. As Flisk had instructed, they left the boys behind. At least half of them had worked the long guns earlier. They knew the danger too well. The rest of the cannoneers were at the mercy of their imaginations. Grumbling and cursing, arguing with each other, muttering insults, they jostled and floundered along the beaten path. But they came.

Sixty-four men who had no reason to think that they would live through the next hour.

Grimacing until the muscles of his face ached, Captain Flisk prepared to say what he required of himself.

It will be bad, he imagined telling them. I cannot pretend otherwise. But you will sink ships. Our Magisters and riflemen will do what they can to cover you. And I will be there with you. You will not face a death that I do not face myself.

He meant to speak; but before he could begin, he heard a shriek.

It was faint with distance, little more than a hint in the cold. It could have been a bird, if there were any birds flying at night with so much sorcery in the air. Or perhaps a wounded animal, if any beasts remained in the woods after so many men had searched for Father Skurn. But there was such desolation in the cry, such urgency, that it pierced the winds.

That was a human shriek. Worse, it was a woman's.

There were only a few women among the bay's volunteers, all of them Amikan.

"Did you hear that?" He hardly made a sound. For no reason except instinct, panic clogged his throat. The gunners ignored him. They were too busy complaining; calling each other names.

Flisk pounded his chest. He coughed once to draw breath. "Did any of you," he shouted urgently, "*hear that cry?*"

Some of the spectators turned to stare at him: a Magister or two; a few soldiers. Half a dozen of them shook their heads, more in confusion than denial.

He tried again. "*Listen* to me! Did any of you hear that *cry?*"

Two riflemen stood near him, ready to carry orders. One of them said hesitantly, "I heard— Captain, I heard something. I *think* I did."

Flisk wheeled on him. "From *where?* I *heard* it, I tell you! A woman's shriek. Where did it come from?"

The soldier flinched. "Forgive me," he replied. "I am not sure what I heard."

Trench yelled Flisk's name. In a rush, the Magister left his fellows and the road, hurried closer. As he came, he called, "I did not hear it! But I know wind. I know how it carries sound. If you heard a cry, it came from the north."

Flailing one arm, he pointed along the cliff at the stretch of bare stone between the precipice and the woods.

Frantic with alarm, Heren Flisk flung his gaze northward.

He had good eyes. In full moonlight and flashes of lightning, he saw nothing except dark trees and dull grey rock and empty air.

He must have imagined the cry.

Instead of fading, his panic mounted. Earlier, he had asked himself if the enemy knew something that he and Forguile did not. Now he felt sure. Every nerve in his body squalled at dangers he could not see or understand.

Even as a young soldier before his only ride into hell, he had been troubled by a frightened streak, an inclination to see dangers everywhere. But when he had finally gone with Malder and Captain Swalish to fight the charging Amikans, he had forgotten his fears. He had no time for them. Only the Amikans had existed then, the battle—and his instincts.

Now he barely had time to bellow *"Riflemen!"* Then he saw that he was right.

Over a bulge in the uneven rim of the cliff, a dark mass of men came boiling. Without a sound, they ran past the crest like a sea breaking. Even by moonlight and lightning, Flisk could not estimate their numbers. But they filled the wide passage between the black trees and the killing plunge of the precipice. And they kept coming, more and more of them piling over the bulge behind their leaders.

At the worst possible time for the defense of the bay.

Beyond question, the enemy had known something that Flisk and Forguile did not.

With all the force in his lungs, Captain Flisk howled, *"We are attacked!"*

Then his instincts took over. He snatched at his rifle with both arms and fired.

He held the gun to his good shoulder. It took the recoil. Nevertheless the motions of raising, supporting, and aiming hurt his damaged joint like a fresh stab.

He ignored the pain.

At this distance, he could not pick a target. He did not know who or what he hit. But there were so *many* men— He could not have missed the entire surging mass. That was impossible.

Yet no one fell. No hesitation or stagger interrupted the swift, voiceless rush of the attackers.

Wincing, and unaware of it, Heren Flisk jerked back the bolt of his rifle, slammed a second cartridge into the chamber, fired again.

He wanted to shout orders, but the riflemen did not need them. They heard his shots, looked where he was shooting; saw their enemies. At once, half a dozen guns barked. A dozen more spat streaks of flame into the night. A moment later, all of the soldiers were firing.

Flisk endured a third shot, then paused to see the effect.

A few attackers dropped. Too few for so many bullets. The rest raced closer without faltering. They trampled their own fallen as if they did not know it.

They were driven by sorcery. Flisk had no other explanation. Some appalling, inhuman force compelled the charge, prevented the wounded from feeling or reacting to the fierce punch of lead.

He fired three more times, emptied his clip. He wrenched it out, discarded it, snatched another from his satchel of ammunition, slapped it into place.

From the rim of the cliff, the riflemen delivered a withering fusillade. The rapid staccato crack of shots rode the wind like iron-shod hooves on stone. As the strange attackers began to pass directly along the line of guns, the range was so close that the soldiers could hardly miss. And *still* too few of the strangers went down. Too many madmen trod on the bodies and kept running, careless of their own dead.

Inexplicably, they ignored the rifles. None of them turned aside to shove riflemen over the precipice. If they did not care about their fallen, they cared even less for their own hurts. The purpose that drove them was insane, as single-minded as lightning and earthquakes.

They rushed nearer. Aided by moonlight and sorcery, Flisk could take better aim. At one time, he had been an excellent shot. His muscles remembered his old skill despite the shrill pain in his shoulder. He shot one attacker in the stomach, then gaped as the man ran on as if the blood pumping from his belly cost him nothing.

Flisk swallowed his astonishment. Between one heartbeat and the next, he aimed again. This time, he shot the same man in the head.

Instantly, the attacker crumpled and was run over.

That was enough. Captain Heren Flisk did not waste the seconds he needed to learn whether other targets would kill. Pitching his voice to carry over the tumult of rifle-fire, he bawled, "The *head*! Aim for the *head*!"

Some of the soldiers must have heard him. More of the enemies dropped. None of the fallen regained their feet.

Flisk fired twice more before he realized that the dark sweep of men had begun to veer away from the cliff. Not away from the rifles: he was sure of that. The horde did not count its losses. The attackers were angling away from—

No! Not away *from*. Turning *toward*. They had spotted their prey, the men they had been sent to kill. They adjusted their silent race toward their intended victims.

The cluster of gunners.

Some of them were riflemen; but they had discarded their armor and weapons to free their movements.

In fear and fury, Captain Flisk understood. This insane force intended to slaughter the men who worked the cannon. To protect the black ships. Cannon were useless without cannoneers. Belleger's only effective defense in the bay would be lost.

And the gunners were too frightened or startled to move. If they had heard one threatening howl, they might have responded; but the silence of the charge gripped them.

Firing, Flisk moved to make his stand between his cannoneers and the charge. Two riflemen came with him with their rifles bucking in their hands.

They were only three. Against how many attackers? Flisk had no idea. Fifty? A hundred? More?

The strangers were within forty strides, or thirty.

The gunners should have fled. Instead, they stayed. They did not understand the threat. Or they did. They had come from the camp to fight and die.

Flisk emptied his clip, discarded and replaced it, kept firing. From all along the cliff, the soldiers shot furiously. Those who were farthest away, north and south, ran to close with the attackers. But they could not shoot accurately while they ran, and the madmen ignored any wound that was not mortal.

In moments, the assault would reach the cannoneers. Frantically, Flisk screamed for help.

Only Magister Brighten answered. She may have been the only lightning-wielder who grasped the peril—or was angry enough to endanger Flisk and the gunners—or trusted her control.

From the black depths of the heavens, she brought down fury.

Sorcery blazed among the attackers. A dozen of them seemed to burn from the inside out, incinerated by the fierce heat of their own bones. Two dozen. They fell in charred, smoking lumps of flesh.

Others dashed to fill the gaps left by the dead.

In the actinic flash of Brighten's Decimate, Flisk saw open mouths among the enemies, the living and the dead. He saw teeth like fangs, teeth filed to sharp points for rending.

He flicked a glance back at the bulge that had hidden the attack. There were no more men pouring down the slope. Rile had committed his whole force.

He had sent enough. While she sustained her Decimate, Magister Brighten savaged the attackers. The sheer quantity of bullets fired by trained riflemen killed and killed. Too many remained. Flisk could not estimate *how* many. But the knot in his guts told him that the gunners were still outnumbered.

The strangers kept coming, as incapable of fear as of pain.

Flisk had time to empty his clip and drop his rifle; pull his saber from its sheath. Then the surviving mass arrived like a tidal wave.

He felt the men behind him surge, bracing themselves for the onslaught. They may have been frightened, startled, confused. They were not cowards. And they were strong. They had to be: they had spent long hours wrestling with the massive weight of cannon, shot, and chain.

The Captain's men drew their sabers. Riflemen from all along the cliff sprinted closer, shooting as they ran or readying their blades. But Flisk had no attention to spare for them. A new kind of hell had come for him and the gunners with its fangs bared.

Simply to stop his first foe, avoid the nearest teeth, he wanted to thrust with his saber. But too many bullets had failed. He had no assurance that a piercing blade would succeed. Instead, he forced himself to aim a tight swing at the man's neck.

Blood sprayed from the cut. The man's head tilted unnaturally. He went down as if the strings of sorcery that kept him on his feet had been severed.

After that, Flisk concentrated on slashing. He cut at necks. Or at wrists. At knees. At anything that would keep his enemies from getting their hands and teeth on him.

One of his soldiers was already dead, throat torn open. Around and behind the Captain, gunners and madmen grappled with each other, struggled back and forth; killed or died. He heard screams of rage and fear from his men, cries of pain like sobs. The attackers fought in silence. Even their breathing made no sound.

Their fangs and jaws were strong enough to bite through wrists, tear forearms from elbows, rip chunks of flesh and muscle out of thighs. Any cannoneer who felt teeth on his neck never felt anything again.

Flisk fought wildly, swinging his saber with both hands, hacking at every enemy that tried to close with him. Blood splashed his face until he could barely see. If his shoulder hampered him, he did not notice the pain. But his enemies were too many. He could not keep all of them away.

Apart from the howls and groans, the frantic shrieks, he knew nothing about the struggle behind him. The bloodshed must have been atrocious, ordinary men and fanged assailants locked in killing. But if he turned to look, he would die. He had only moments left himself. His strength was failing. Soon he would swing too slowly, or with too little force, and those appalling fangs would—

At the same time, however, running soldiers crashed into the fray. Even Forguile was there, swinging the slight curve of his keen-edged Amikan sword as furiously as his broken, bound ribs allowed. The riflemen had dropped their guns. With their sabers, they hacked at the attackers.

Flisk saw heads spin from their bodies, mouths gaping. He thought he saw a clear space nearby. Then, unaccountably, he was on his knees in the red slush of snow and blood. Had the fight ended? Perhaps it had. Unable to rise, he would have pitched onto his face if Ennis Forguile had not caught him.

At Flisk's ear, Forguile said, "We were not ready." The Amikan seemed to believe that his friend could understand him. "We did not expect an attack. How could we? That pestilential priest's escape was our only warning. How could we imagine that he had so many men waiting to strike?"

Flisk hardly heard the Commander. He understood other things. "The ships?" he panted.

"Closer," answered Forguile grimly. "In perfect range. But their work is almost done."

For a moment, he appeared to choke. Then he said, "Our losses could have been worse. Many more of us might have died. We lost only half the gunners. You did well, my friend."

Captain Flisk understood that as well. Half the gunners were dead. He no longer had enough men for the medium cannon.

Briefly, he rested in his friend's support. Screams and wails echoed in his mind. They would fill Belleger when the ships finished their work and the fleet behind them forced a landing. The future of King Bifalt's realm streamed with blood.

But then he heard a soldier exclaim in surprise, "This one lives. Half his skull is gone, but he still breathes. His eyes watch me."

"Ask him," croaked Flisk. He tried to gain his feet. With Commander Forguile's help, he succeeded. "Ask him to tell us."

He meant, Ask him where he came from. Ask him how he *got* here. How many allies did Rile have?

The dying stranger lay among the corpses. He was barefoot; had no weapons except his fangs, his eerie strength, and his single-mindedness. His scant garments were a farmer's or a laborer's, vaguely Bellegerin in their cut, too thin for winter. Grey brain matter streaked with red showed on one side of his head. Gaping for air, he exposed his teeth. Without them, he could have passed for a poor and ordinary man anywhere.

Despite his wounds, he seemed to hear Flisk. Or sorcery still ruled him. His voice bubbled with blood. "The Great God's instructions are precise." He gasped for breath. "It is not his fault we failed." Another gasp. "Too many of us died coming."

"Died?" snapped Forguile. Abruptly, he released his friend; strode over bodies to the attacker. "Who killed them?" Crouching, he gripped the man's shoulders, shook him to get his attention. "Where were you landed? Did you cross Belleger to come at us? Belleger and *Amika?*

"How?"

Rile's servant coughed up a gout of blood and slumped. His head lolled loosely when the Commander shook him again; but he was already dead.

Hells! thought Flisk. All that way? Across Belleger and Amika? To attack us *here? Now?*

What kind of god *was* Rile?

"Gods and pestilence!" raged Forguile. "We are—!" But he could not find words for his ire and frustration.

Heren Flisk had other concerns. The *here* and the *now* compelled him: the purpose of the attack. The ships. He retched briefly to clear his throat, drew cold into his lungs. Still half choking, he asked, "Can anyone give me a tally?"

A rifleman nearby responded uncomfortably, "It is as the Commander said, Captain. Seven of our comrades are dead. One may die, if the stitchers cannot save him. Many of us are hurt, but we can still fight.

"We blame ourselves for the gunners. We count thirty-three crippled or dead. You do not want to look at them, sir. Those fangs— The damage is extreme."

Flisk groaned. Thirty-three cannoneers lost. Too few remained. In a crisis, each gun could be fired by a team of three—but not rapidly. Not rapidly enough to sink ships before lightning killed the men. He still had eleven medium cannon. He needed forty-four—

The burden was too great. He was not the right man to carry it. But his friend was hurt. There was no one else to bear it.

Of no one in particular, he asked, "How many gunners are hurt? Can they still work the cannon?"

"We can!" shouted a rough voice. "We will! For our comrades. Our friends. We will *punish* these monsters!"

Flisk swallowed a groan. They were not enough. They could only manage seven cannon—or eight, if one gun had a team of three.

Thirteen black ships remained in the bay, clearing the way. They were almost done.

Harshly, Commander Forguile declared, "We need the boys."

Heren Flisk flinched. He wanted to refuse. Those nine boys were youths at best, less than fully grown, overeager and barely trained. But they would not need strength and skill to light the fuses. And if he called on them—if he sent them to die—he would have full teams for ten cannon.

Forguile was right. The boys were necessary.

But before Flisk could force himself to give the order, the Commander added, "I will go with them." His tone defied argument. "My ribs are not so bad. I can handle a fuse." He had his numbers ready. "I make that forty-one. Send full teams to eight cannon. The others will make do with teams of three. All eleven will fire."

Forguile grinned fiercely. "There are only thirteen ships—and they are close. They will not be hard to sink."

Then he added, "But you will have to command us, my friend. I cannot light fuses and direct the attack at the same time."

He meant that he would not know when to recall the gunners.

Heren Flisk's private wounds ran deep. He did not believe that he could bear the responsibility for more losses. But there was no one else. And he had already given his instructions to the Magisters and riflemen. He could trust them to do as much as they could.

He answered the Commander with a broken grimace. "Bring the boys," he told a nearby soldier. "Do it quickly." At once, he turned to the cannoneers. "We will go when the boys come. Let them light fuses. Nothing more. They are not men.

"Follow Commander Forguile to the guns. But look to me for orders. I will tell you when to withdraw. Until then, I will advise your aim."

"We do not need advice, Captain," called the same man who had spoken earlier. "We see well enough." Lightning and moonlight would help. Then he admitted gruffly, "But we will welcome your order to retreat."

Flisk did not expect his orders to save any of them. He risked saying, "When King Bifalt hears the tale, he will be proud of his men." Then he walked away so that the gunners would not see his eyes weeping.

His tears made beads of ice on his cheeks. They seemed to take bits of skin with them when he scrubbed them off. But those little pains were trivial. His bad shoulder had gone numb. That, too, he ignored. He needed to gather himself. He had never imagined that his duties would require him to sacrifice *boys*.

At the head of the road, he located a servant among the spectators and asked the man for hot cider. At once, the servant ran for the nearest kitchen.

While Flisk waited, he sent the Magisters and riflemen back to their shelters along the cliff. They would be needed soon. As they dispersed, he huddled into his cloak and rain-cape, and tried to summon whatever it was that men called courage.

He did not understand his friend's recklessness.

The servant and Commander Forguile reached Flisk ahead of the boys and the gunners. Flisk took the mug, gulped cider, and was disappointed that it did not scald his mouth and tongue. He wanted warmth, but his drink had cooled in the sharp air.

Nevertheless he emptied the mug, returned it to the servant, and faced his friend.

Earlier, Forguile had fought wearing only a cloak over his strapped ribs. Now he was bundled in blankets, a cloak, and a rain-cape. His breathing steamed, yet he did not appear to feel the cold. Instead, he seemed unaccountably cheerful.

"Are they ready?" he asked as if the prospect of being incinerated by lightning or shredded by gunpowder pleased him. "The riflemen? The Magisters?"

Flisk managed a nod.

"Do they understand? I will not be amused if I die because some Magister or soldier neglects to defend me."

"They understand." The Captain shook his head. The Magisters in particular would be comforted by his orders. They were accustomed to striking from positions of safety. "They know why they are needed. They will do whatever they can."

Forguile nodded. He may have doubted his friend's assessment, but he did not have time to argue. The cannoneers were near.

They came in a tight bunch, almost clinging to each other. Like the Commander, they were bundled to the ears. Surrounded by strong men, the boys looked more eager than anxious. They had been drawn to volunteer by the imagined thrill of fighting for Belleger. With *cannon*.

Well, they were young. Flisk could not remember ever being so young, but he recognized the courage of ignorance when he saw it. They had not learned to believe in their own deaths.

In contrast, the gunners were grim, determined. They knew what they faced too well. Some of them had a different kind of eagerness in their eyes, a desire to deliver violence for revenge or blood-lust. Others did not hide their fear. They loved their families or their homes or their lives. They dreaded losing everything they considered precious. But they did not hang back.

If they could not stop the enemy here, all Belleger might share their fate. Then Amika would fall next.

None of the cannoneers saluted. Captain Flisk and Commander Forguile had never asked for that show of respect. All they had ever required was good work and endurance. The men simply stood ready; and the boys followed their example.

Without hesitation, the Commander stepped forward. "Thank you all." He sounded confident. "If we survive the next hour, I will thank each of you personally. Or Captain Flisk will, if I"—he gave the men a grin—"am indisposed.

"For the present, now is better than later. Those ships are perfectly placed to receive our welcome. It would be impolite to keep them waiting.

"Choose your teams and come."

Like a man who had never learned to doubt, Ennis Forguile turned and strode away toward the crest of the road.

Flisk had known for a long time that the Amikan Commander was

King Bifalt's friend; but he had never understood the bond between them better than he did at this moment. Belleger's King had the gift of making men like Ennis Forguile *believe*. Forguile knew how to make men share his beliefs.

In silence, the gunners followed him. Dragged along by his friend's example, Captain Flisk brought up the rear.

Closer to the bay's rim, the winds were stronger, colder. And now they carried the crashing, the repetitive thunder, of massive breakers on the strand: a strange sound to men who were accustomed to the cross-currents and immense boulders that had interrupted the direct surge of the seas earlier. On the terraces, the water's roar would be louder. Flisk would have trouble making any order heard, especially when the medium cannon began blaring. But he refused to think about what would be required of him.

It had to be done. Therefore he would do it.

With the cannoneers around him, Forguile paused to point out the usable guns. Then, without a glance back at Flisk—without any kind of farewell—he gripped a rope and began his descent.

In a tight line, the gunners followed him. One by one, they dropped out of sight as if they had vanished from the world.

The Captain's heart beat a fusillade in his chest. For an instant, he forgot his own responsibilities. But only for an instant. When it passed, he snatched cold into his lungs and yelled, "*Now*, Magisters! Start *now!*"

On the ships, there was no chance that anyone would hear him.

While his pulse threatened to choke him, nothing happened. But as he drew breath to shout again, sudden lightning answered him. Out of the cloudless night, two bright, branching bolts slashed downward.

Both blasts struck the same ship.

One made carnage on the deck. Men burned like torches. The other found the top of the tallest mast. Its sails were furled on its spars. They may have been too tightly wrapped to catch fire. But the Decimate ran down through the core of the tree. In an instant, the whole mast became kindling and ash. The spars fell, killing more men on the deck.

Loosened sails flung sheets of flame. When the blast expended itself, only a stump of the mast remained.

Flisk wanted to cheer. One or more of the slain might be sorcerers. It was possible.

But the enemy's assault on the bay's rocks did not waver. One black ship had been hurt. It may have been crippled. Twelve went on working.

As the last of the gunners hurried down the ropes, two more bolts joined the sorcery over the waters. Again, they both attacked a single target, a different ship this time. But they had less success. One tore down spars that scattered fragments of wood like shrapnel. The other hit the vessel's side, ripped a hole too far above the thrashing waters to do any fatal harm.

It was time for Heren Flisk to go. He had left his rifle in the slush behind him. Now he tossed his saber aside. It would only hamper him. Where he was going, weapons would be useless. At the last cannoneer's back, he left the crest of the road, lowering himself closer to the enemy's sorcery.

Below him, Commander Forguile and the first gunners were moving along the terraces to their cannon. Forguile had chosen the most dangerous post for himself: the fourth level, not the third—and the gun farthest from the road. Flisk swore aloud; but he was not surprised. Of *course* Forguile had claimed the most exposed position, the place where he was least likely to survive. No doubt he would have called it leading by example.

Flisk kept a grim hold on the rope. Despite the ash that had been scattered down the road, the hard freeze after the snowstorm formed fresh ice. He felt the threat of a slip with every step. The visceral tremor of submerged earthquakes shook him. Still, he spared enough attention to watch the enemy's sorcery, the sizzle and plunge of power into the depths. Brighter than any moonlight, and more acute than the sun, the lightning did its vicious work under the waters.

As Flisk passed the third terrace and crept down toward the fourth, two more bolts of force from his Magisters scorched the air. One caught the rear deck of a vessel, destroyed the men there as if it had pitched them into the heart of a furnace. But the other struck only waves and spume.

Magister Glowing, perhaps, still half-stunned by exploding gunpowder, too weak or too frightened to be sure of her target.

Abruptly, the enemy's lightnings ceased. While Flisk's Magisters continued to unleash their Decimates two at a time, doing as much damage as they could, Rile's theurgists changed their tactics. Instead of assailing the bay's floor—or the cliff—they used their sorcery to dismiss the power aimed at them. Blast after blast from the Magisters became silver mist in midair. Some of the bolts flared brightly as they dissipated. None of them touched the ships.

Now, my friend! thought Heren Flisk. Fire now! While you can! He finished his descent to the fourth terrace in a rush.

There he was alone. The last gunners were moving along the walled level toward their cannon. They were not ready yet. Forguile would wait until every gun was primed and loaded. But Flisk did not want that. His Magisters had too little stamina. When their force began to falter, the ships would be free to strike at the cannon.

Anchoring himself on the rope a little way below the fourth terrace, a position that allowed him to watch the cannoneers on one side and the enemy on the other, Flisk insisted, Now! Fire now! But he kept his plea to himself. The counterattack was in Ennis Forguile's hands. Where it belonged.

When it came, he did not hear the command. The first shout of cannon fire caught him by the throat.

Gun after gun spat fury across the waters. Under better circumstances, the first cannon would be ready to shoot again when the last had delivered its sixty pounds of iron. But the gunners had trained with sixteen guns, not eleven. Gaps in the barrage were inevitable.

Any delay might allow Rile's sorcerers to respond.

Eleven guns, one after another. They were loaded with chain, not balls. The heavy links stripped the lower spars on four ships, tore away structures that looked like housings, swept men from the decks. On a fifth vessel, the forward mast cracked and leaned. It toppled in a welter of splinters.

Then came a long moment of silence while the teams struggled to reload.

Flisk's Magisters could have used that opportunity to strike. It would distract the opposing sorcerers. But he had told Brighten and the others to rest. He was too far away to howl new orders. They would not hear him.

During that pause, there were no Decimates at work in the bay, no lightnings, no earthquakes.

Nevertheless the enemy had an answer. The damaged vessels sat where they were, waiting to sink. Before the cannon could fire again, the other ships moved.

Sliding eerily through the sharp swell and thrust of the waves, they rode some unnatural force as if they were coasting. With the swift delicacy of a dance, they shifted to place themselves behind the smitten ships, where the second barrage could not reach them.

That tactic was unexpected—and it happened too quickly. The cannoneers did not have time to correct their aim.

This time, they fired cannonballs. Mere wood could not withstand that weight of iron. Prows and sides exploded. Muffled by the incessant clamor of the seas, the balls seemed to wreak havoc in silence. Four of the damaged ships were broken. Borne down by their burdens, they dove for the bottom of the bay, seeking their graves. Unbalanced without its forward mast, the fifth vessel tilted over a gaping hole that sucked in the hunger of the seas. With terrible slowness, the black ship surrendered to the waves. Its men had time to watch death come for them.

There were still seven ships. They had lost their cover.

But now most of them sat beyond the reach of the medium cannon. The farthest vessels were well out of range.

This time, the delay was longer as the cannoneers scrambled to raise their aim.

Commander Forguile and his teams should have been ready sooner. But the sudden shift in the positions of the ships must have surprised them badly. They were not prepared for it.

Before the first of the medium cannon could fire, a flash of theurgy brought ruin.

During the brief instants of its blazing, lightning scoured the whole northward side of the third terrace.

In destructive fire, every grain of gunpowder there exploded. The shock was tremendous. It deafened the world. The cliff itself shook. Chunks of rock and twisted iron rode flames into the air. They seemed to hang in the brightness of the blast. Then they plunged down—

—onto the fourth level, crushing every man and gun below them.

The concussion almost tore Flisk off the rope. He did not hear himself screaming for retreat. If Forguile yelled the same command, his shout could not pierce the clamor.

All those men—! The *boys*—!

Staccato with urgency, interminable heartbeats passed.

Flisk barely glimpsed the second lightning-strike. It seemed to stop his pulse.

Forguile.

But the Commander was not hit. The terraces on the south were not. In the instant of its attack, the sorcery burst into bright mist. The winds blew it away.

Some lightning-wielder on the rim of the cliff must have seen what was happening; recognized the threat. A Decimate had dismissed the bolt.

There would be another. Or more than one. Even Magister Brighten could not banish every blast the black ships might hurl.

Flisk snatched a breath to scream again, then caught himself. None of the surviving gunners needed his orders. They were already running for the road and the ropes.

All of them except Commander Forguile in the south.

His team must have loaded his cannon even while theurgy ravaged the northern emplacements. Then he must have sent his men away. He was alone with his gun. As if he were calm, he adjusted the cannon's elevation, sighted along the barrel. Without hurry, he lit the fuse.

His gun roared. It slammed back against the ropes that stopped its recoil. Flisk did not see where the shot went.

Brighten or other Magisters shielded the southward terraces from a second bolt. They were not quick enough to stop a third. Directly behind Forguile, the third terrace went up in an appalling howl of lightning and gunpowder, flame and iron and wrecked stone.

The Commander seemed to vanish. The blast left Flisk blind as well as deaf. For long moments, he knew nothing. Then his senses began to recover, and he heard the rapid cracking of rifle-fire.

The nearest ships were still within reach of bullets. Every soldier atop the cliff was shooting as fast as he could. If Flisk had been able to focus his eyes, he might have seen slugs shredding the men on the decks, tearing the planks under them.

He might have seen gunners hauling themselves up the ropes to escape more lightning.

But there was no more lightning. It was not needed. If any of the siege guns on the fifth terrace remained intact, they were unmanned. The ships were free to resume clearing the bay's floor.

The Captain had foreseen none of this. Neither had King Bifalt. They had not known enough about Rile's power to imagine what his servants could do. Or how many sorcerers the enemy had.

Rubbing his eyes with his free hand, Flisk struggled to clear his sight.

After a moment, he managed to discern blurred shapes on the ropes. The cannoneers were little more than shadows in the moonlight and lightning, too dim to be counted, but some of them had reached the crest of the road. Others were close. The treacherous surface snatched at their feet. They gripped the ropes for their lives. Floundering, they struggled upward.

Flisk stayed where he was. He felt unaccountably exhausted. He had lost his friend. Without Ennis Forguile's encouragement, he could not move. The bay's defenses had failed.

Perhaps he could afford a little rest. He was not needed above the cliff. There was nothing that anyone could do until General Klamath brought reinforcements. The road was the safest place for him. Rile's sorcerers might scrub the whole cliff-top with lightning when the black ships came closer, but they would not strike at the road. The enemy needed it.

So did King Bifalt.

Heren Flisk closed his eyes, lowered his head. Briefly, he let himself imagine sleep.

A shout from above warned him. It was barely audible, but its consternation cut into him.

He jerked a look out across the dark waters and saw only what he expected to see. With their strange ease, the ships were gliding closer to resume the destruction of the bay's final obstacles. Nothing from the cliff threatened them.

Muttering under his breath, Flisk turned to peer at the road.

A small shape came sliding down its center. The outstretched arms of the last gunners on the ropes showed that they had tried to catch whatever it was; but it skidded past them out of reach.

Another shout demanded strength Flisk did not have.

The road was a treacherous mix of bare stone, ash-packed snow, and black ice. The sliding shape started to tumble, tripped by patches of bare rock and slickness. It became a man with his arms and legs flailing wildly.

The man had flung himself downward, trusting the ice. He may have meant to slide all the way. Instead, he was battered in every direction by the grip-and-release of stone, ash, and ice.

Groaning, Flisk tried to brace himself. *Some*one had to catch him, whoever he was. There was no one else. At that speed, the man would die when he hit the strand's boulders—if his tumbling had not already beaten him to death.

The Captain hauled at his rope, managed to draw out a little slack. He clenched it with his good hand, the hand supported by his undamaged shoulder. Spreading his legs, he crouched to stretch out his bad arm. He lacked the strength of the men above him; but unlike them, he was not taken by surprise. He could watch the desperate shape pitch closer.

Too soon or too late, he lunged.

Somehow, he caught a fistful of robe.

Earlier, his shoulder had seemed numb. Now he felt his arm

wrenched out of its socket. The whole joint became a shriek of agony. He may have shrieked himself, but he did not hear it. He could not hear *any*thing through the sharp hot Decimate of pain tearing his shoulder.

Nevertheless he did not let go.

The falling man's momentum swung him in an arc against the taut rope. As if inadvertently, one of his arms flopped over the lifeline. Some instinct for survival made him hold on.

Sobbing, and unaware of it, Flisk released the man's robe. His shoulder shrieked again. Then the limb dangled at his side, as useless as deadwood. Even if he could have borne the pain, he would not have been able to lift it.

He was still sobbing as he watched the small man struggle to plant his feet. But Flisk did not recognize him until the man turned painfully toward him.

Badly battered, bleeding all over his face, caked with ash and snow where his robe had not been ripped open: Magister Pillion.

Flisk's next sob stuck in his throat. His first thought was blank astonishment.

His second was, Oh, hells! No!

King Bifalt needed the road.

Pillion's Decimate was earthquake.

"Those whoresons," panted the Magister. Every word spattered blood. "Did they think they could *woo* me?"

Flisk had no idea what Pillion meant. An earthquake here might destroy the bay's last hope of defense, the last chance to oppose the enemy's ascent with rifle-fire. Pillion must have known that. He had thrown himself downward because every sane man on the cliff would have tried to stop him.

Flisk had no strength. He seemed to have no mind. He could not think of a way to prevent Pillion. Without his left arm—

Risking a fall, he let go of the rope; crept dangerously downward. When he could face the Magister directly, he gripped the man's robe again to demand his attention.

"They do not understand," spat Pillion. "I love my wife. I love my children. *I am not the man they want me to be.*"

Flisk heard Pillion, but the words explained nothing. "No," he countered. He was too weak to shout. "You must not. King Bifalt needs the road. It is a killing zone. When the enemy starts to climb, riflemen will—"

He intended to say, *Riflemen will slaughter them.* A sudden tilting under his boots interrupted him. The unexpected shift snatched his hand free, cast him aside. He fell until his back hit the opposite rope. Then he managed to grip the line.

Staggered by the ease with which Magister Pillion had dismissed him, Heren Flisk needed a moment to realize that King Bifalt was wrong. He himself was mistaken. There would be no killing zone. When Rile's forces were ready to climb the road, his sorcerers would do what they had done to the third terrace: they would wipe the rim of the cliff with lightning until every soldier able to aim a gun was reduced to charred meat.

Pillion faced the ships. "Do you want me to believe I can be mighty?" he panted. "The mightiest of my kind? I will show you what a lesser man who loves his family can do."

With a sweep of one arm, he summoned his Decimate.

At the last instant, Ennis Forguile scrambled up from the fifth terrace; got his hands on the rope.

A heartbeat later, the cliff itself shuddered. With a *crack* like the sundering of the world, the whole length of the lowest level broke away from those above it. A gap that could have swallowed Forguile ran from north to south along the shelf where he had been standing. The force of the rupture flung loose rocks like gravel into the air. Clouds of dust gusted along the winds.

For a moment, the cleft slope stayed where it was, unmooring the siege-guns from their emplacements. Then Magister Pillion shouted at it, and it leaned wider.

Flisk thought that the massive stretch of stone would simply lean until it fell, knocking itself apart on the boulders of the strand. But Pillion's Decimate did more. Another sweep of his arm brought up the bedrock base of the long section he had broken loose. Stone that had endured the unremitting violence of the seas for uncounted centuries was torn apart. From Flisk's horrified vantage, Magister Pillion appeared to raise the very foundations of the lower cliff and the strand.

Raise them and *heave*—

The shattering of that incomprehensible weight was louder than the wild waves, more full of anguish than the shrill winds. It extinguished every conscious scrap of Flisk's mind. Only his instincts saved him from letting go of the rope and sliding over the edge onto the bay's jagged new barricade.

When Commander Forguile came to shake his moaning shoulder, Heren Flisk lifted his head. Seeing his friend, the only question Flisk could manage was: "How?"

Forguile barely had enough strength to answer, "I jumped." He was using the last of his stubborn vitality to keep himself and Flisk from losing their hold on the lifeline.

There was no sign of Magister Pillion. Flisk could only assume that he had followed his gift onto the ruin he had made.

Later, while he and the Commander waited for help from the men far above them, Flisk chewed on his friend's answer until he understood it. When lightning had destroyed the third terrace, dropping rock and cannon and men onto the fourth, Forguile had saved himself by vaulting over the parapet to land on the fifth among the siege guns. How he had avoided being broken or killed by falling shards and rubble was less clear. Certainly, he had plenty of blood on his face, deep bruises and contusions. He had earned his utter weariness. Yet he seemed unaccountably cheerful.

That made no sense at all to Flisk.

Later still, after a few cannoneers and several riflemen had manhandled the Captain and Forguile back up the road to safety, Flisk heard that some of the servants had gone searching for Mattwil and Cloras. They had found the young woman. She was badly broken, unable to walk; but she managed to describe what Father Skurn had done—and how Mattwil had responded. Now she was in the over-worked infirmary, being cared for among the riflemen and gunners who had lost hands or eyes or the use of their limbs when the emplacements were destroyed.

The news that Mattwil was dead—that Flisk had failed in his charge to watch over Matt's son—was more than the Bellegerin officer could bear. He did not care who saw him weep. The secret of his damaged arm he kept to himself.

An hour or two before dawn, King Bifalt and General Klamath finally arrived with their reinforcements. They surveyed the defense for which Belleger and Amika had paid with effort, blood, and death. While Klamath, grieving, talked with the people who had located Cloras and learned of Mattwil's death, King Bifalt heard the reports of his officers and the bay's Magisters. He paid particular attention as Magister Trench and others confirmed that the attackers from the woods were not sorcerers themselves, but were instead driven by sorcery. But the King himself only listened. His shock and dismay were private.

Yet he spoke to Flisk. Resting a light touch on Flisk's torn shoulder, King Bifalt rasped, "You did well, Captain. You have no cause to blame yourself. If there is fault here, it is mine."

To Commander Forguile, the King said simply, "Thank you, my friend."

After that, he took General Klamath with him and began to gather firewood.

When riflemen, gunners, and then volunteers and servants grasped what the King and the General were doing, they, too, collected wood. With solemn care, they built a pyre for the dead.

The bodies they carried respectfully to the pile, closing the eyes and arranging the limbs of their lost comrades. After so much fighting, so much death, and a night without sleep, they were tottering on their legs. Yet they stood gravely at attention as King Bifalt prepared to light the pyre.

With a flaming brand in his fist, the King recited Belleger's traditional farewell to its fallen soldiers.

"Your blood for your comrades. Your blood for your people. Your blood for your King. No man can be asked to give more."

Then he added, "And our gratitude for Queen Estie, whose spirit is with you. Our deepest gratitude for her people, whose losses are as grievous as Belleger's, and whose support does not falter."

In the silence that followed, he tossed his brand among the dead and turned away.

By his command, the corpses of Rile's servants were consigned to the long slide down the broken road, where they came to rest on the wreckage that Magister Pillion had left to defend the bay. If any man among the Great God's forces cared, he might glimpse the fate that awaited him and tremble.

But Captain Flisk and Commander Forguile did not witness King Bifalt's actions. Forguile had been dragged back to the infirmary by a group of Amikan riflemen. And Flisk was asleep in the nearest bunkhouse. He had hoped to escape his sorrow in sleep; but loss haunted his dreams, and his heart was full of mourning.

PART
TWO

NINE

AN ENCOUNTER ON THE ROAD

Grieving over Magister Facile, Queen Estie traveled the distant reaches of her realm with only Third Father for company, and no answer for any of her sorrows.

Wrapped in his meditative silence, he did not speak to her, either to give comfort or to offer simple companionship. To ease her isolation, she could have ridden with Commander Crayn and his men. They would at least have talked to her. But winter had spread its grip across Amika. Storm clouds piled out of the east. For days at a time, they covered the land with gloom. Drizzles and cold rain gave way to falling snow. On occasion, the Queen positively required open air. Otherwise she stayed in the comparative comfort of her carriage.

Alone with her thoughts, she would have welcomed Magister Avail's silent voice. She hungered for news of what was happening in Belleger, or in the library, or anywhere. But he did not speak to her again.

The only tidings she received came from sub-Commander Waysel. He had sent a rider ahead to report that he was following her with a train of nine wagons carrying Amika's last cannon, all siege-guns. But the wagons were drawn by oxen. Despite their strength, they were not swift beasts. He did not expect to join her until days after her arrival at the Last Repository.

With that she tried to be content.

Yet she was not. While her carriage rolled endlessly eastward, she was useless.

When she reached the library, her straits would change. There she would see what a mere Queen could do to persuade the Repository's powerful Magisters that Belleger and Amika needed their immediate aid. And she would finally have a chance to learn what her slumbering talent for sorcery might entail. She had spent too many years wondering what she might have inherited from her father. Until she understood his legacy, she could not begin to consider who and what she wanted to become.

But the answers she needed were days away. In the meantime, she fretted. Despite the speed of her carriage, her journey seemed interminable.

Around her, the wintering grasses and spreading woodlands of eastern Amika began to fade. The hills remained, but now they were clenched into rocky knolls. Few of the shrubs were hardy enough to withstand the snow, and the patches of rough grass made poor forage. Without her wagon of supplies, both horses and men would have suffered. Fortunately, Chancellor Sikthorn had provided abundance for her journey. The worsening conditions did not slow her.

The terrain began to look crumpled as if some great force had pushed the hills aside. Fewer trees interrupted the dull white vistas. Then they were replaced by scrub oak and thorned brush. After too many days, Queen Estie came to the wide desert that marked the boundary of both Amika and Belleger.

She knew that the Wall Mountains rose along the distant edge of the desert, but she could not see them. The desert was said to be vast. Down a long slope, her road took her out of her realm and into a barren world of sand and dunes.

Soon it became obvious that no rain or snow ever fell here. The desert's winds, flowing out of the east in unpredictable gusts and hard blows, swirled the sands or lifted them like spume, reshaped the dunes; but they did not bring moisture. Instead, the clouds carried their burdens into the west. At dawn, the dunes were gilded with frost. In sunlight, they would have sparkled. But the sun did not shine, and the frost evaporated quickly.

Nevertheless the road remained clear. Queen Estie would have expected the winds to spread sand across the fitted stones. But the road seemed to be exempt. Like the caravan-track that crossed the desert north to south, the Queen's way was protected by unfamiliar sorceries.

And that was not the only use that the Magisters of the Last Repository had made of their strange powers. According to Set Ungabwey's interpreter, they had built and secured a bridge for caravans over the chasm of the Line River centuries ago. Master Ungabwey's own men had guided Estie's road-builders there.

Without the bridge, her road would have been useless.

She looked forward to seeing it. It would mean that most of her journey was behind her. But she still did not know how far she had to go. And what she could see from her windows—or from horseback when she elected to ride—soon became tedious. The contours of the dunes changed constantly, yet the dunes themselves never changed. They were simply sand, and more sand, and even more sand. Her carriage and wagon rolled along easily without seeming to make any real progress.

When Commander Crayn came to the side of the carriage in the middle of another featureless day and called, "Majesty!" Queen Estie almost gasped in surprise. She practically flung herself at the door, slammed it open.

"Commander?" A twist of wind stung her eyes with grit, but she ignored it. "Is there some difficulty?"

Powdered with sand as fine as dust, Crayn's face matched the sandstone hue of his eyes. His smile made the corners of his mouth and the crinkles around his eyes appear suddenly, as if they had been cut with a delicate tool.

"No, Majesty," he answered. "We all hate this desert, but we are making progress at last. My scouts have sighted the bridge."

Gripping the doorposts, Estie leaned as far out as she could to scan the horizon. "Where?"

With one hand, the Commander tried to wipe away his grin. "We cannot see it from here, Majesty. It stands beyond these dunes." He gestured ahead.

Queen Estie started to ask, How much farther? But Crayn had more to tell her.

"There is a rider on the bridge. Alone. Apparently waiting. And apparently a woman.

"You will know her, Majesty, if my scouts are not mistaken. She wears a hooded cloak of such whiteness that it mocks the sands."

Estie's heart beat faster. She had known only one woman who wore a cloak like that, a garment that shed blood as easily as it did rainwater and hard traveling. "Then take me to her." At once, she pulled herself back into the carriage and shut the door so that the Commander would not see her trembling.

Lylin, she thought. *Lylin.*

Despite his inward absorption, Third Father heard Crayn. "If she wears such a cloak," he remarked unexpectedly, "she is surely a most holy devotee of Spirit. But her raiment indicates her devotion, nothing more. She may not be known to you."

Queen Estie ignored him. Memories of Lylin heated her pulse. At one time, the devotee had served her well. More than once, Lylin had protected her from men who might have killed her. With only her hands, the assassin had prevented a war with the Nuuri. But she had also beaten Jaspid half to death. Estie could not forget that. It contradicted everything Lylin had done for her.

The Queen counted every sway of her carriage as her road curved among the dunes. Before long, she heard Crayn call to her coachman. At once, the carriage slowed. While she waited at the door, the coachman drew his horses to a gentle halt. As the carriage settled on its springs, she discarded decorum. Without waiting for a step-stool, she thrust open the door and jumped down to the road.

After sitting so long, her muscles were not prepared for the jolt of landing on hard stone. Awkward as a child, she fell to her hands and knees. But she staggered upright before Crayn could dismount to help her.

With his familiar discretion, the Commander did not ask if she was hurt. When he reached her side, he merely touched her arm to assure her of his support.

She *was* hurt. She had bruised her knees, scraped her hands. But those pains were too petty to distract her. Beyond her carriage, she saw the bridge at last.

For a moment, she could only stare. This close to the mountains where it began, the rift made by the Line River's swift turbulence was a true chasm: deeper than the Cut where the river split the rising ground toward the sea, but not as wide. Still, its width made the very idea of a bridge seem implausible. Estie could not have thrown a rock across the cleft.

Nevertheless the bridge was there, a high, graceful arch both broad and gradual enough to carry even the largest of Set Ungabwey's wagons comfortably, and footed on granite well away from each rim. When the Queen had commanded her people to devise a crossing, she had imagined a wooden construct secured by bands of iron. At her weakest, in her lonely bed at night, she had feared that her workmen would face an almost unsurmountable task, one that would require seasons or years to complete.

The theurgists who had made *this* bridge had worked with blocks of stone the size of her carriage. And along each side, they had devised a retaining wall to keep people, horses, and conveyances from plunging into the chasm. Such a span should have collapsed long ago, broken by its own appalling weight.

Power on that scale, enough to hold those blocks in place until they were all fitted snugly against each other, and then to seal them so that they would endure— The immensity of what had been accomplished here left Estie gaping.

As she scanned the arch, however, hardly able to absorb what she was seeing, her gaze was drawn to its crest.

A woman clad in white sat her horse there, watching Estie; waiting for the Queen to gather her scattered wits. The devotee sat her mount with the assurance of a woman who knew in her bones that no mere shudder of the earth would cause the bridge to fall.

The distance was considerable. And the woman's face was shaded by the hood of her cloak. Nevertheless Estie recognized her by her tall form, her easy grace, and the amused twist of her mouth.

Lylin. At last.

When Estie finally remembered to raise her hand in greeting, the assassin nodded once, then nudged her horse down the shallow slope. She made her descent at a smooth trot, then came along the road to meet with Amika's Queen. There, she dismounted.

Because courtesy demanded it, Queen Estie gave the devotee a formal Amikan bow. At Estie's side, Commander Crayn did the same. But Lylin stood upright. To the Commander, she offered her smile. Estie she acknowledged with a grave nod.

"Queen of Amika," she said in her familiar husky accent. "If my estimates are accurate, you have made good time."

The woman had saved Estie's life several times. But she had also abandoned the Queen without a word. She had almost killed Jaspid. And the devotees of Flesh had forsaken Belleger when Elgart had been taken or killed: when they were needed most. Estie's thoughts were like tinder, ready to take fire. Before she could stop to think, she demanded, "Where *were* you?"

Lylin did not answer. Her expression was unreadable.

At once, Estie caught herself. The woman was a most holy devotee of Spirit, not a subject of Amika.

More carefully, the Queen tried again. "Forgive my rudeness, Devotee. At one time, I considered you my friend. Now many things have changed. Will you tell me your tale?"

She meant, Why did you leave me? But she also meant, Why did you fight with Jaspid? What happened to Elgart? Where are the devotees of Flesh?

A flicker like a wry grin tightened the assassin's mouth. "A question for another time, Majesty. After coming so far, you will not wish to tarry. With your consent, I will ride with you for an hour." A tilt of her head indicated the carriage. "Then I will decide where my duty lies."

A nudge of Crayn's hand reminded Estie that she might prefer privacy. Certainly, Lylin might prefer it.

And Third Father was waiting in the coach.

With an effort, Estie assumed a more fitting air of calm. "Of course," she answered. "Please join us."

Her coachman was a diligent young man, proud of his place. During her brief exchange with Lylin, he had positioned her step-stool for her. She reentered the carriage with more dignity than she had shown leaving it.

The monk was little more than a vague shape in one corner. For days now, they had been traveling with the lamps unlit. The heavy twilight suited Estie's loneliness. But now she wanted to study her friend or enemy. She busied herself lighting the lamps while Lylin stepped into the compartment and closed the door.

Third Father rose to his feet as the devotee entered. With his usual humility, he bowed, keeping his eyes lowered. "Greetings, Devotee of Spirit," he murmured. "Your coming is timely. Queen Estie has need of you."

The assassin surprised Estie by bowing from the waist. "Does she? If a monk of the Cult of the Many cannot assuage her needs, there is little I can do."

Then she asked as if the question had no special meaning, "Do you stand surety for her, Father?"

The old monk shook his head. "I do not. I have been humbled. Like King Bifalt, Queen Estie has surpassed me." His lips hinted at a smile. "I can only hope that she will not be asked to stand surety for me."

His response elicited a grin from Lylin. "You jest, Father. Is that not also a form of pride?"

Was she *teasing* the monk?

The Queen's questions were imperative. She was spared the awkwardness of insisting on the devotee's attention by the slight lurch as her coach began to roll forward. She used that moment to sit and compose herself.

Briefly unsteady, Third Father remained on his feet. He seemed to be waiting for Lylin to sit. But Lylin stayed upright. The shift as the carriage moved did not affect her.

Queen Estie settled her back against the cushions. She was accustomed to keeping her seat while other people stood, even a monk of the

Cult of the Many and a most holy devotee of Spirit. Clearly, they knew each other. And clearly, Estie could not match either the monk's mild dignity or the devotee's prowess. But she was still Amika's Queen.

"Devotee," she said firmly, "the need Third Father mentions is for answers. Since I am in haste, as you say, perhaps you will begin with this. Why did you find it necessary to fight Prince Jaspid? You did him serious harm."

Instead of responding at once, Lylin seated herself with her familiar untroubled grace. As the monk followed her example more stiffly, she faced the Queen. Estie thought that she detected a hint of chagrin in the assassin's expression.

"You misunderstand the circumstances, Majesty." There was no apology in Lylin's tone. There may have been regret. "I did not intend to fight him. I urged him to turn back. He refused." Then she sighed. "His skill is great. As is his courage. But his wits are no match for them. When his ardor is roused, he does not *think*."

That reply told Estie nothing. "You may be right," she replied. "Still, you misjudge him. He would not have allowed himself to harm you." She did not add, I think he is in love with you. Instead, she asked, "Why did you want him to turn back?"

"That is not your concern, Majesty." If Lylin had felt any chagrin earlier, it was gone now. "I have been faithful to you, and to your people, and to Belleger. I am also faithful to the choices of *my* people. Where my encounter with Prince Jaspid is concerned, there was no conflict between my commitments."

"That is an answer," retorted Queen Estie, "not an explanation. I crave understanding."

"It is not mine to give," said Lylin without hesitation. A moment later, however, she added, "But I see your dilemma. In my own way, I share it. I must ask you to trust me.

"Your best course, Queen, is to tell me what you know. I have been away a long time. I have my own decisions to make, and what I have learned is too scant to guide me. To have come so far, you must have left the Open Hand before Master Ungabwey attempted the Realm's

Edge. What else can you impart? Has the war begun? Is there fighting in the Bay of Lights?"

Estie did not know how to respond. Her impatience was like flame: it threatened to set her on fire. She had been sitting in her carriage too long with nothing to think about except what she did not have. But she had spent enough time with Lylin to know that her frustration would have no effect. The devotee of Spirit would shed it the way her robe shed water and blood.

Did Lylin want news? She must have already talked to *some*one. How else could she know about Set Ungabwey's purpose?

When Queen Estie did not answer, Lylin asked a different question. "Or tell me of your journey. Has it been uneventful? Has anything happened that troubles you?"

Abruptly, the woman inquired, "What path has Magister Facile chosen? If she remains with Belleger's King, her Decimate will be precious."

That query stung Estie. It reopened her grief. The devotee and the Magister had seemed to be friends. Certainly, they had been familiar with each other. And Lylin was still a human woman despite the severity of her skills and devotions. Surely she had a right to know—

Instead of answering, Queen Estie turned to the monk.

"Will you advise me, Father?" The tightness in her throat betrayed her vexation. "She has done many things for me, but her other deeds baffle me. What should I tell her?"

"Advise you, Queen?" asked the old man, musing. "You do not need any counsel I can offer. The Cult of the Many does not judge. We are not wise enough. For that reason, it often appears that we do not choose.

"But we do choose. We would serve no purpose otherwise. An honest question deserves an honest answer. I will say this. We of the Cult serve in ways unlike those of the most holy devotees. Our choices do not resemble theirs. When I look at any devotee, however, I see fidelity."

His reply shamed Estie. She was too quick to judge. The assassin's treatment of Jaspid did not necessarily falsify what the same woman had done for Estie herself. Lylin had claimed that her loyalties did not conflict. That might be true: Estie had no way of knowing. But the devotee still had decisions to make. What she did might reveal more than what she said.

"Very well." Queen Estie faced Lylin again. "I will tell you what I can.

"But I must ask you," she insisted immediately, "to accept that King Bifalt and I have taken every precaution we can imagine to protect Amika and preserve Belleger's people. If you fault what we have done, I can do nothing now to improve our efforts."

The devotee nodded. "Of course, Majesty. I have no cause to doubt you. I can believe that whatever you and Belleger's King have done is good."

Good? thought Estie. She did not care if it was *good*. She wanted it to be *enough*.

At that moment, the carriage tilted back on its springs as it began to ascend the bridge. Queen Estie leaned a little harder against the padded back of her seat.

"Then I can say that we have had only one encounter on our journey. It was worse than troubling. It was—"

She wanted to say, It was *horrific*. But the word stuck in her throat. She had to swallow fresh sorrow and ire before she continued.

"Now Magister Facile is dead. Murdered."

She could still hear the crushing sound as the old woman's chest was shattered. She could smell the blood gushing from the Magister's mouth.

And the cruelest detail was that the old sorceress had never heard Magister Avail's message. She had died not knowing that the man she had once loved had survived his poisoning: the only man in the library who had been able to *hear* her for twenty years.

Lylin's only reactions were a lift of her eyebrows, a tightening of the muscles around her mouth. She said nothing. Nevertheless her posture as she listened implied vehemence.

Forcing herself, Estie told her tale.

"While we were still far from the desert, we saw signs that made us think of spies. Commander Crayn found three men. One was a priest of the Great God Rile, Father Knout. The other two had the look of servants."

In a few words, she described what she knew of Archpriest Makh's disappearance. To appease her doubts about Lylin, she did not mention Elgart. Instead, she remarked, "Without the head of their Church, the remaining priests seemed leaderless. Lost in some essential way. The priest we found said the same.

"He answered my questions with an air of willingness. He had left Belleger for Amika on instructions from the Archpriest. The priests in my realm had a task to perform for the Great God. When I asked what that task was, he may have meant to tell me. By chance, Magister Facile interrupted him.

"When she had examined him, she repeated her assertion that the Great God's priests are not sorcerers. Then she questioned the servants. Their replies betrayed that they were his guardians—or his captors.

"They alarmed her. Those men, she insisted, were *dangerous*. Some vile theurgy had touched them."

We serve the Great God Rile.

The Great God's instructions are precise.

"I tried to question the priest again. His guards or captors were too quick. One killed Magister Facile with a single blow. The other slew the priest.

"My guardsmen dealt with those creatures before they could do more harm. But Magister Facile was gone."

The assassin's attention did not waver. As if Facile's death was of secondary importance, she demanded, "Describe them, Queen."

Angered by her memories, Queen Estie held the woman's gaze. "I have seen you fight, Devotee. I know your speed. Those men were as fast. I did not see the second of them kill the priest. I clung to Magister Facile. But Crayn tells me his teeth were the fangs of a wolf. He ripped out the priest's throat with one bite."

As Estie spoke, an unusual frown twisted Lylin's mien. She studied the Queen a moment longer. Then she turned to the monk.

"You are a discerning man, Father. What can you add to the Queen's account?"

Without lifting his head, Third Father murmured, "You already know, Devotee, that the loss of Magister Facile is grievous. You may not know the extent of the loss. She has been the only means of communication with the Last Repository. Magisters there are able to observe events, but without her they cannot understand what has transpired."

Lylin ignored the implicit reprimand. She had one of her own. "At another time, Father," she countered, "perhaps you will tell me why she chose to forsake Belleger when so much hangs in the balance. For the present, I want to know what you saw in the priest and his killers."

Third Father grimaced at the floor, a small twist quickly wiped away. His tone had an uncharacteristic edge. "The priest was a timid man, Devotee. He depended on his bond with the Archpriest. His men were empty vessels. They had no thoughts or desires of their own. They were given a purpose. They carried it out. They could not have explained themselves. Without their Great God's commands, they would have been harmless."

The devotee of Spirit nodded as if the monk had confirmed a suspicion. As the carriage crested the bridge and began to tilt down the far slope, she faced Queen Estie again.

"Then my path is clear. I will ride ahead of you to the Last Repository. The librarian and his people must hear my tale."

Twisting her hands together, Estie tried to think of an appeal that would win what she needed from Lylin. The assassin had revealed *nothing*.

Before she could find the right words, however, Lylin gave her a grim frown. "But you have shed more light than you know, Majesty. I see now that your tale and mine explain each other."

The Queen held her tongue. She did not trust herself to speak.

"When we parted in Maloresse," began the devotee, "I rode to the lands of the Nuuri. You and Belleger's King need allies. I hoped to find them for you."

The *Nuuri*? Estie forced herself to breathe. Impossible. She could not imagine them as allies. Their animosity was too recent—and entirely justified.

"My progress was slow," said Lylin. "Each Hearth-Keeper holds her stable of men and her herd of zhecki far from the others. They need large tracts to feed their beasts on the rough grasses of the steppes. In addition, I had to earn the consent of each Hearth-Keeper to address her. Each in turn, they required me to defeat them in combat. Altogether, I bested seven of them. But when I had gained consent to speak, each Hearth-Keeper refused my appeal."

Mutely, Queen Estie nodded. After what her father had done, their refusal was inevitable.

"However," continued the assassin, "they did not refuse me entirely. Instead, they agreed to confer with each other. That is their custom in threatening times. One of them proposed a place and a day. The others accepted. I would be allowed a second chance to persuade them.

"All of this cost me the last fortnights of a long autumn. Winter had come to the steppes when the Hearth-Keepers met."

The assassin's sigh sounded bemused.

"Those Hearth-Keepers are strange women, Majesty. They greeted each other roaring insults and pounding on their chests. Some of them exchanged blows or grappled with each other. They mocked the stables of others and sneered at retorts. Then they seated themselves around a campfire and began to talk like friends or sisters after a long absence.

"When I heard them"—the devotee's tone hardened—"I knew they would refuse me. I knew why. But I had asked them to hear me. To honor their consent, I repeated my appeal." She shrugged delicately. "Then I accepted their answer when the Hearth-Keepers again refused to become your allies."

As Estie had expected. Again, she nodded without speaking. For her, the only surprise was that Lylin had put so much time and effort into a wasted quest.

The most holy devotee of Spirit did not raise her voice. Nevertheless it sounded like a clenched fist. "They refused because they are already at war."

Estie jerked up her head. Third Father covered his eyes.

"Strange men have invaded the steppes," explained Lylin. "Not as a great host. If that were the case, the Nuuri would have gone to war sooner. But the strangers come in widely scattered groups, some as large as a hundred or more, some smaller. And they do not seek conflict. Instead, they travel south, avoiding the Nuuri. Unwilling to risk their men, the Hearth-Keepers might have let the strangers pass.

"But the strangers are fools." Again, the devotee sighed. "They kill zhecki whenever they want meat. That is an offense the Nuuri do not tolerate."

With an effort, the Queen closed her mouth and concentrated. She knew too little about the Nuuri, but she had heard about them since childhood. She understood that their beasts were their lives. They protected the zhecki fiercely.

"As I say," continued Lylin, "the strangers do not seek conflict. But they do not shrink from it. When they are attacked, they fight. They are unnaturally strong. And unnaturally hardy. Only mortal wounds hamper them. Other hurts they ignore. Their bodies are their weapons. They do not need more. They fight with their fists, Majesty. And their fangs. Those teeth rend flesh. They bite through bone."

Gods! Estie flinched in shock. Men with fangs. Men like the ones who had killed Magister Facile and Father Knout.

Empty men ruled by the Great God.

"It is fortunate for the Nuuri," continued Lylin, "that the strangers have not come in a great host. The losses of Nuuri men and zhecki would have been extreme. And it is fortunate also that the strangers have no interest in their attackers. They defend themselves savagely, but they do not pursue. When the Nuuri withdraw, the strangers resume their trek southward as if nothing has happened to trouble them."

The devotee leaned closer to emphasize what she said. "Nevertheless, Majesty, the manner of the invasion has its own cunning. By coming in scattered groups, the strangers concealed the scale of their presence. As a result, the Nuuri were slow to recognize the truth. Each Hearth-Keeper believed that only her own herd was threatened.

"*Now* the Nuuri are united. They have sworn that no more strangers will be allowed to pass. That is alliance enough to content me."

Queen Estie resisted an impulse to turn away. Instead, she held Lylin's gaze. She could guess what the devotee would say next, and she did not want to hear it. She would have preferred to insist, No, do not tell *me*. Tell my *husband*.

He had prepared himself to fight in the west—and in the south if Set Ungabwey failed. He had done nothing to ready a defense against a force from the north.

But Lylin did not relent.

"Your tale, Majesty, proves that the strangers crossing the lands of the Nuuri serve the Great God, the power they name Rile. He rules them. I suspected it. Now I am certain.

"But it also proves another"—she took a deep breath as if even she needed to brace herself—"a more dangerous conclusion. Some or many of their kind have entered Amika.

"The Hearth-Keepers cannot know how many strangers have passed beyond their reach. They will kill as many as they can. But their distance from each other makes it impossible for them to know how many hundreds—or thousands—have escaped."

It was too much. Estie did not know how to bear it. A *third* enemy? And she could do nothing to warn Bifalt. She was helpless, as helpless as she had always been to breach the walls around his heart.

Abruptly, the devotee stood. "Now, Majesty," she announced, "I must ride to the Last Repository.

"I will not advise you to have no fear. But I urge you to fear as little as you can. I will be days ahead of you when I reach the Repository. As soon as I arrive, Magister Avail can make this new peril known to Belleger's King. He will do everything that can be done."

While the assassin called for her horse, a renewed pang snatched Estie to her feet. Lylin had told her too much—and not enough. This might be her last chance to get an answer.

As the devotee prepared to leave, the Queen asked once again, "Why did you fight Jaspid?"

Lylin paused. Over her shoulder, she said, "He demanded my best." For the first time, she sounded angry. "I could not give less. Not to him."

A moment later, she was gone.

She left Estie thinking that Jaspid may have achieved more than he realized.

Later, the Queen considered that perhaps the same could be said of her. She, too, had accomplished something more. She had swallowed her reluctance to trust the most holy devotee. The result was like opening a door. Lylin would warn the Magisters. Magister Avail would warn Bifalt. Estie's husband would not be taken by surprise.

Since the day of their first meeting, he had surprised her often. In fact, he had shaken her whole understanding of the world. Because of him, she had become more than she would have been otherwise, far more. When he knew what Magister Avail could tell him, he might be able to devise a surprise or two for this new enemy.

Estie hoped for that. The prospect eased her fretting as she settled herself to endure the last stages of her journey.

TEN

THE LAST REPOSITORY'S WELCOME

Queen Estie's journey from the bridge to the Last Repository took four days. During the first two, she traveled the road that caravans had used for generations or centuries. Crossing the desert at a distance from the mountains in the east, it made its way southward among the dunes.

Bitter winds tumbled down from the high peaks. Interrupted by patches of sunshine, heavy clouds rode west. The conditions would have been difficult, but the Queen's escort was well supplied against the weather. In the carriage, oil heaters kept out the worst of the cold.

Late in the afternoon of the second day, the company met a clear track leading eastward. Third Father confirmed that it led to the library.

"Is it the *only* road?" asked Estie.

His downcast manner suggested a shrug. "On foot, men can ascend the foothills wherever they wish. For horses, there are paths. But wagons and other conveyances must use this road."

Estie passed the monk's answers to Commander Crayn. The Commander called instructions to the coachman. For sub-Commander Waysel's sake, Crayn marked the place where the Queen's company turned off the main track. Followed by its burdened wagon, Estie's carriage finally left the desert behind and began to ascend the foothills of the Wall Mountains.

The end of the journey was near. The next morning, Queen Estie saw the Repository itself for the first time.

According to Third Father, it was still more than a day away. Here, however, the road crested a ridge that gave a view of the immense castle-fortress where it emerged from the cliffs of the Wall Mountains.

At the sight, Queen Estie's heart lifted. She jumped down from her carriage and hurried to the edge of the track to study the vista of the library.

It was *there* at last. Diminished by distance, it looked majestic nonetheless. Huge and indomitable.

Formed of white stone that seemed bright and pure despite the sky's glowering overcast, the enormous rounds of its tower rose against the snow-clad peaks. They stood in a tall stack, eighteen or twenty of them, each placed a little off-center to counterbalance the tower's imponderable height. And each of them contained *knowledge*: books of all kinds, papers, scrolls; maps in loose sheets or bound volumes; treatises on innumerable subjects; pamphlets of instructions and arguments. The Last Repository was a treasure-house of what could be known in the world.

Gazing across the rumpled rise of the foothills, Queen Estie did not wonder why the library's custodians wanted to preserve it. The wonder was how it had come to exist at all. It had to be ancient beyond imagining. It looked as precious as life.

She had spent too much of her journey fretting. Excited at last, she hurried back to her companions. Claiming her horse from Commander Crayn, she led her company forward at a brisk trot. She wanted to gallop, but she resisted the impulse.

Finally, at least some of her questions would be answered.

From a distance, the Last Repository had looked grand, wondrous, and yet somehow attainable: a place that could be reached and entered. Closer, the castle was too large for Queen Estie's eyes and mind to grasp. The road passed below it, heading south, then turned back to make its final approach. As she ascended the slope to the wide plateau that fronted the library, she felt herself diminished. The plateau itself was vast. She had no difficulty imagining Set Ungabwey's largest caravans settled there. Yet it seemed small below the height and whiteness of the library's base.

There the Repository's Magisters and its many other inhabitants lived. The massive block served as a foundation and defense for the tower of books that squatted like a fortress at the edge of the plateau. Its outer wall was featureless except for the high wooden gates of its only entrance. There were no other doors. But well above the gates stretched the crenelated balcony or rampart where its people could walk or watch—or fight.

Past that rampart, the rounds were only visible in glimpses. And behind them stood the sheer cliffs of the Wall as if the mountains themselves defended the fortress. In fact, the main keep extended deep into the nearest cliff. It was a place where hundreds or thousands of people could live in safety.

Despite her excitement, her anger, her need, Amika's Queen felt herself shrink at the sight. She was too small to find what she needed there.

She saw no one, either on the plateau or along the high rampart. Nevertheless her arrival had been noticed. As she and her immediate escort trotted onto the plateau, followed by her carriage, the wagon, and Commander Crayn's rearguard, they were greeted by the sound of mournful horns, a minor chord like an announcement of woe. And while the call echoed off the cliffs, the great gates eased open, noiseless on their massive hinges.

They resembled the doors of a crypt.

Instinctively, Estie halted. At her word, Crayn and his men settled their mounts into a line with her at its center. Their hands rested on their rifles, but they did not unsling the guns from their shoulders.

The gates parted only far enough to let two men emerge. They wore the grey robes of sorcerers. Apparently holding hands, they came toward the Queen at once. Almost at once, she realized that she knew who they were. Her husband had described them. To her, they seemed as portentous as living legends.

Magister Avail and Magister Rummage.

Magister Avail was a plump man as tall as Commander Crayn. His hair made an unruly tangle on his head. In contrast, his chin was beardless. Estie had no way of knowing whether he had aged in twenty years. Perhaps he had not aged at all. According to Magister Facile, sorcerers or physicians in the library could give such gifts. In any case, he walked with a lift in his steps.

And he was smiling broadly. Before he had come halfway toward Estie and her men, he called, "Hail, Queen of Amika! You are well come! We have high hopes of you—and for you!"

Bifalt had told her that the plump sorcerer and Magister Rummage were not actually holding hands. Rather, the dark hunchback, glowering and bitter despite his obvious strength, gripped his companion's hand so that he could tap words onto Avail's palm. Magister Avail was deaf. His companion was mute.

No doubt, the hunchback had already informed the plump man that Queen Estie had not answered his salutation.

To ease her sense of diminishment, she remained in her saddle. Sitting above them in silence, she watched the theurgists approach.

A few steps later, they stopped. Abruptly, Magister Avail seemed to see something that alarmed him. Worse, it struck him with sudden pain. His smile twisted into anguish. For no apparent reason, tears filled his eyes. Snatching his hand away from Magister Rummage, he clutched at his chest like a man suffering a crisis of the heart.

Without warning, he whirled away; hurried back toward the gates as if he were fleeing.

From somewhere far away, Estie heard him. He was apparently shouting at someone else, but his words reached her mind. She knew his mental voice. She had heard it once before.

No! I cannot. This is wrong.

Rushing, he reentered the Repository.

What has that vile man done to her?

The hunchback froze. Consternation and crueler emotions writhed across his visage. Then he recoiled from some blow that the Queen could not see or hear.

Hunching his powerful shoulders, he turned to follow his companion.

Too stunned for words, Estie stared at the suppressed fury of Magister Rummage's withdrawal and tried to breathe.

"Majesty?" whispered the Commander. "What was that? Have we offended them?"

She shook her head. To herself, she demanded, *What* vile man? My husband? *Bifalt?* Does that mad sorcerer call *him* vile?

Aloud, she countered, "How could we? We were expected."

Bifalt had not been greeted like this.

Instead of responding, Crayn nodded toward the gates. "Someone else comes, Majesty." Under his breath, he muttered, "Prepare for more rudeness."

Grimly, Estie nodded.

Another grey-clad figure had already left the Last Repository, a woman. Robe flapping, she approached in an undignified hurry, almost running. As she came closer, Queen Estie saw that she was about her own age. Auburn hair. Flushed cheeks. Dismay in her eyes. But this Magister had not been marked by Facile's tragedies or scarred by the hunchback's grievances. Under other circumstances, her expression might be naturally calm, even pleasant.

From a little distance, the woman panted, "Forgive us, Queen. You must forgive us. We did not know what to expect."

A few paces from the Queen's mount, she stopped with a slap of her sandals. After an instant's hesitation, she attempted a formal Amikan bow.

She must have read about that show of respect somewhere. Clearly, she had not practiced it enough to get it right.

With a gesture, Queen Estie instructed Commander Crayn and his men to remain mounted. Then she swung down from her horse. Disguising the protests of her overworked muscles, she faced the Magister. She had forgotten her sense that she was too small.

"Forgive me in turn, Magister," she said like a monarch. "*You* did not know what to expect? *I* did not expect the reception I have just received. I know those men by reputation. They were Magister Avail? And Magister Rummage?"

The woman nodded; but Estie did not wait for a reply. "What disturbs them, Magister? King Bifalt is not a *vile* man."

The Magister's eyes betrayed a flinch. She took a deep breath, held it to settle herself. Then she said carefully, "Again I ask your pardon, Queen. Magister Avail's distress is personal. It does not reflect our gladness that you have come. We admire Bifalt of Belleger, both as a man and as a King.

"I am Magister Oblique. I hope to offer you a better welcome."

Magister Avail's distress is personal? Estie had her doubts. Both his tears and his indignation conveyed a different message. But she needed the Repository's welcome. She had to accept it.

"Then I will thank you for it," she answered as calmly as she could. To steady herself, she offered the woman an Amikan bow with all of its florid details.

The Magister smiled tentatively. "I am relieved, Queen. You have had a long journey, and have suffered a loss. If your men will dismount, I will guide you and them into the Last Repository. There, servants will care for your horses. Your coach and wagon will be stored for you. And I"—now her smile seemed shy—"will answer as many of your questions as I can. They must be urgent."

The Queen refused to smile in return. "That is a gracious offer, Magister. I will take advantage of it.

"But I have one request. I assume that you will provide quarters for my guardsmen. I would like them near me."

Oblique showed Estie a perplexed frown. It seemed sincere. The sorceress may have wanted to ask, What do you fear? If so, she kept the question to herself. Instead, she nodded her assent.

"Of course, Queen. We have in mind a private suite with a number of connecting rooms. If they do not suit you, we will make arrangements more to your liking." Then she added, "You have not brought a maid or other servants. Our people will care for you."

Controlling herself, Estie accepted with a less formal bow. A nod to Crayn gave him her consent. While he and his men stepped down from their saddles, she looked to Magister Oblique again.

"One question I must ask at once, Magister. I fear a new enemy from the north. Has King Bifalt been warned?"

Oblique did not hesitate. "He has, Queen. The most holy devotee of Spirit Lylin has shared her tidings and your own. Magister Avail spoke to him at once. The news of Magister Facile's death has grieved us deeply. Nevertheless we trust that Belleger's King will contrive to meet this new threat."

To cover her relief, Queen Estie watched the Commander and his guardsmen gather to accompany her. Despite Lylin's assurance, Estie had not been confident that the library's Magisters would keep the devotee's promise. They had treated Prince Bifalt badly.

When her men were ready, the Queen asked Oblique a more challenging question. "My questions are urgent, as you say, Magister. When will I be allowed to speak with the librarian?"

The woman's smile seemed kindly. "You must be weary, Queen. Your journey has troubled you. And your prompt arrival suggests that you have not paused for a meal. You must be hungry as well.

"Magister Marrow and the custodians of the Repository are eager to speak with you. However, they are concerned for your well-being. As I am," she admitted. "If you will allow me to escort you to your quarters, you and your men can dine and rest until this evening. The librarian will meet with you then." The sorceress made a diffident gesture. "You may have a considerable audience, if that will not cause you discomfort."

A considerable audience— Under other circumstances, Estie might have felt a twinge of anxiety. However, she was still dealing with the effects of Magister Avail's greeting. Oblique's manner had a soothing effect, but it was not enough.

"How can I refuse?" replied the Queen. "You have offered answers. I hope you will not take it amiss when I challenge you. But my guardsmen and I are certainly tired and hungry. We will be glad to rest while I ready myself for the librarian."

Magister Oblique's smile showed more confidence. "Then come, Queen." Touching Estie's arm, she drew Estie toward the high gates.

Leading their horses, Commander Crayn and his men followed. Lurching into motion, the carriage and the wagon rolled forward behind them.

As she and Oblique walked, Queen Estie began her real task. "Perhaps, Magister, you will answer one question now."

"If I can, Queen."

"As you must know, I have crossed your bridge over the Line's chasm. To my eyes, it appears unimaginably ancient. It must have been raised by theurgy. Here is my question. If the library's Magisters can perform such feats, why do you fear *any* attack? Surely they can secure this"—she gestured up at the immense stone block—"this castle-keep against any assault."

Magister Oblique took the subject seriously. "And surely, Queen, Magister Facile must have informed you that there are many sorceries. They are not all Decimates, capable of both good and harm. Some do only good. Others only destroy. And some harm those who wield them.

"The gifts that fashioned the bridge ward it against time and weather. They cannot shield it from deliberate damage. With enough gunpowder, any ordinary man or woman could make it fall."

The sorceress spoke with an air of open friendliness; yet Estie felt suspicious. Bifalt believed that the library's sorcerers were skilled at seeming honest when they lied. Or at twisting the truth until it conveyed something else. Were there hints hidden in Oblique's words? Perhaps there were, although her manner dismissed the possibility. The Queen held onto her doubts, but she allowed herself to relax a little.

As she and her guide drew near, the gates opened wider. Without a sound, the heavy timbers and iron struts made way for her and her escort, her carriage and wagon. Gesturing a welcome, Magister Oblique led Estie into the library's mustering hall.

The space was enormous, large enough to hold the ceremonial hall in Maloresse several times over. Despite its size, however, it was well-lit by iron cressets that burned without fumes or smell. Their brightness revealed a number of stairways and doors of varying sizes around the walls.

Inside the gates, a crowd of servants waited, men and women. Estie missed a step when she realized that half of them were monks of the Cult of the Many. The others wore colored garments in different hues and styles; but the monks were easily identified by their robes belted with white ropes, their tonsured heads, and their self-effacing comportment.

Seeing them, she realized that she had forgotten Third Father. For reasons of his own, he had stayed in her carriage. Now he emerged. When he had nodded gravely to her and Magister Oblique, he went to join the servants.

Many of the others bowed to him or murmured greetings. The monks did not. Disregarding Third Father's years and his stature in the Cult, his people accepted his arrival as if it were a matter of course.

The Cult of the Many abided by strict notions of *service*.

As if Estie had expressed surprise, Magister Oblique said, "The monks of the Cult, Queen, are a treasure. We would not know what to do without them. We hire any who are willing to serve here, but the monks do so freely. It is a great gift."

While Queen Estie watched the monks, other servants bustled forward to take charge of her company's beasts. At the same time, they offered the Repository's welcome to her coachman.

With a bemused frown, Commander Crayn told his men to let their mounts go. Reflexively, they kept their hands resting on the hilts of their swords.

When Magister Oblique invited Estie to continue toward her quarters, the Queen complied distractedly. The image of Third Father toiling as a servant lingered in her mind. He may have waited in the carriage until he could join his people without calling attention to himself. But she suspected that his actions were also meant for her. As a demonstration of what service implied for him, perhaps? As a lesson about service itself?

She had too much to think about. Her mother had told her that she could learn many things from servants, if she chose to consult them.

She did not try to learn the route during her long passage up and down the stairs and through the chambers, lesser halls, and corridors of the keep. Commander Crayn would memorize the way for her. And she did not ask her guide any serious questions. She wanted time to secure her grip on herself.

When Magister Oblique opened an apparently unmarked door in a long hallway and ushered Estie inside, the Queen found that her quarters were more comfortable than she had expected. She had three rooms to herself: a bedroom, a spacious sitting room, and a bathing room with a privy. Rugs more sumptuous than anything her father had acquired covered the cold stone of the floor between the cushioned armchairs. To compensate for the absence of windows, tapestries softened the walls with lovingly rendered scenes of forests and meadows. In the hearth, a fire had already been lit: a necessary comfort this deep in the hard rock of the mountains. In the bathing room, the tub had been filled with steaming water. And on a low table against one wall, a damask cloth warmed a tray laden with food.

In addition, a doorway opposite the bedroom led to a series of connecting chambers. When the Commander and his men had investigated them, he could not suppress his grin. "Eight good rooms, Majesty," he reported. "More than enough. There is food waiting in each of them. Some have doors to the outer passage. All of them include bathing rooms, privies, and warm hearths. We will sleep in better comfort than we have known for days.

"It mystifies me, Majesty"—he tried to look grave—"how they contrive to vent those flues through all this stone. But the hearths do not leak smoke. It is a wonder."

Magister Oblique laughed softly. "Alas, Commander, that is a wonder I cannot explain. I have learned a great deal in my years here, but I still do not know how the hearths are vented. Or how the pipes deliver fresh water everywhere."

Crayn thanked her with something like gallantry. He had been won over. He might distrust every other sorcerer he met: he was prepared to trust Magister Oblique.

Estie felt the same way. Despite her suspicions, she liked her guide. Her husband had not prepared her to like anyone here.

"Now, Queen," announced the Magister when Crayn was done, "I will leave you for an hour. You and your men can sample our food, or bathe, or rest without my intrusion. When I return, I will answer as many of your questions as I can.

"Unless," she offered with nothing except kindness in her tone, "you prefer to begin now?"

Queen Estie did not hesitate. "Thank you, Magister. I will be glad to have a quiet hour. I can hardly remember my last hot bath. And I need a chance to arrange my thoughts."

Then she would need more time to harden her heart before her meeting with the librarian. Both Bifalt's curt descriptions and Elgart's more elaborate tales of their visit long ago had assured her that she would have to keep her wits and her distrust sharp.

"As you wish, Queen." The sorceress seemed pleased. "If you and your men put your soiled garments out in the hall, the servants will clean and mend them. Or new apparel can be made for you all. Simply ask any of the servants.

"In an hour." With a polite bow, Magister Oblique turned to the door. Pausing only long enough to show Estie that the door could be locked from the inside, she left the suite.

When Queen Estie faced the Commander again, he gave her a probing look. "Your thoughts, Majesty?"

"Are confused," she admitted. "I do not know what to make of our reception. If she is considered suitable to welcome us, why did Avail and Rummage approach us first? What am I that they did not expect? I want to trust her, but I have been warned to distrust everyone here."

Then she set aside her bafflement. "We will confront that concern when she returns. For the present, Commander, let your men rest. Rest yourself until I call. I will want you with me when I question her. Once we have heard her answers, we will decide how many guardsmen I should take to meet the librarian."

"As you say, Majesty." Clearly, Crayn believed that she was safe. Despite Magister Avail's reaction, she was still Amika's Queen. *That*, at least, the Repository must have expected. The people here might cause her distress, but they would not harm her.

With her consent, he crossed the sitting room to lock her door. Then he entered the connecting chambers and closed that door behind him.

Alone for the first time in more days than she wished to count, Queen Estie sighed. One thing at a time, she told herself. She could not answer her own questions. Uncovering the tray of food, she took a few swallows of a delicious ruby wine. Next she selected an unexpected bunch of ripe grapes. With fruit to ease her hunger, she passed into the bathing room to soak her sore muscles and heart in hot water, and to think.

Fortunately, Commander Crayn was accustomed to caring for her. She had forgotten her pack of spare apparel. He had not. It waited for her in her bedroom. She was dressed in her last clean garment, a simple gown she had kept aside for her meeting with the librarian, and was eating a slow meal, when a knock on her door announced Magister Oblique's return.

Softly, Estie summoned Crayn. In silence, she indicated her door. His slight frown was a sign of concentration, nothing more, as he unlocked the door and admitted the Magister.

Oblique entered with an air of uncertainty. "Have I come too soon, Queen?" However, the Commander's ready bow reassured her. Without waiting for a reply, she crossed the rugs to Estie.

In her bath, the Queen had resolved to be as polite as she had ever been in Belleger's Fist or Amika's Desire. Her father's example would do no good here. Masking her anxiety, she rose from her chair and repeated her formal bow.

"Not at all, Magister. Your timing is perfect. You must have many other duties. It is good of you to postpone them."

Magister Oblique offered another of her shy smiles. Instead of attempting a second Amikan bow, she replied, "You must not thank me, Queen. I should thank *you*. You are the most important of my duties, and the most desired.

"You have the look of a woman who has prepared herself. I hope that I can satisfy you. Your accomplishments are well known, and your reign in Amika has been admirable. It will please me if I can ease your mind.

"Shall we sit, Queen?"

Involuntarily, Estie stiffened. Flattery vexed her. She did not trust it. Still, she found it difficult to be suspicious of Oblique. If the sorceress was less sincere than she seemed, she had perfected the art of dissembling.

The Queen reseated herself, then offered Magister Oblique a chair.

While the sorceress moved an armchair closer to Estie's, Crayn stood beside the door to the connecting rooms. He had a gift for being unobtrusive. Magister Oblique gave him a brief glance, a small smile, before she turned her attention on Estie.

Queen Estie gathered herself. "You are a remarkable woman, Magister," she observed. "How have you heard of my doings? Amika is a small realm, and distant."

"Why, from Magister Facile, of course." Oblique answered without hesitation, but sadly. "While she lived, she spoke to Apprentice Travail. Until he fell ill—" She caught herself. "Magister Facile must have told you that he was poisoned. We still do not know who bears the blame for that crime." Then she resumed, "But until he was harmed, he had the gift of hearing her voice at any distance. She told him about you. He repeated her words to Magister Avail. Magister Avail replied, speaking directly to her mind.

"It was an unwieldy process, as you can imagine. But Apprentice Travail is skillful, and Magister Facile knew how to be concise. Their exchanges explained events that might have baffled us otherwise. We are all grieved by her loss. No one is more bereft than Travail."

In fact, Queen Estie did know how Magister Facile and the Repository had communicated with each other. But Oblique's answer gave her the opening she wanted. "Then I am confused, Magister," she admitted. "You imply that you can be aware of events in Belleger without Magister Facile's aid. How is that possible?"

During Prince Bifalt's search for the library, there had been occasions when the Magisters had responded instantly. Twice, they had intervened to save his life: feats which distance alone made unimaginable.

This was an easier topic for Magister Oblique. Her tone brightened. "We call them the Farsighted, Queen. Some are Magisters. Most are not. You will know them by their air of inattention. Other images fill their minds.

"Their theurgy enables them to observe places and actions elsewhere. If they know where to look, they can witness a crisis or calamity as it unfolds. At times, they can forewarn us. But first they must know where to look. And their gift is sight, not hearing. They can only interpret what they see by inference."

"And distance is no obstacle?" asked Estie.

"Queen." Oblique's manner suggested a mild reproach. "*Every* gift is limited. If it were not, the enemy would have discovered our location long ago, and the Repository would no longer exist. Our Farsighted can extend their reach across Amika and Belleger, but no farther."

Queen Estie was familiar with limits. Her own were acutely painful. Probing, she inquired, "What of Magister Avail?" She needed to understand his reaction to her. "Is he Farsighted?"

That query appeared to amuse Magister Oblique, but she answered it seriously. "He is not, Queen. His inward voice is his gift, and its cost is deafness. In other ways, he knows only what others are able to tell him by touch."

Estie raised her eyebrows. "He has no Decimate?"

"None." The sorceress shook her head. "Neither do I. Nor does Magister Marrow. Avail is a Magister because he is necessary. No one else can take his place."

Curious, the Queen asked, "And Magister Rummage? Is the same true of him? Was he crippled by his talent when it was awakened?"

Oblique sighed. "Alas, Queen, both his deformity and his muteness are accidents of birth. Like Magister Avail, he is necessary." She paused, then explained, "He understands violence, yes, but that is not theurgy. His gift is of another kind altogether. We have books that only he can read. Only he dares."

Only he—? Estie did not know what to make of that claim. She knew too little about the stranger forms of sorcery.

But she let the matter drop. The pressure of her real questions was rising in her. She needed to ask them.

"Thank you, Magister," she said. "I have distracted you from more important concerns. Now please tell me." She heard the note of urgency in her voice, but did not try to suppress it. "What do you know of the war? Has the Great God come? Has he attacked?"

She refused to ask, Is my husband safe?

She saw pain in Oblique's eyes before the Magister looked away.

"Yes, Queen. The Great God Rile has come. I will speak of him." She shook herself. "But first I must assure you that Amika has not been threatened. The strangers you encountered on your road, those that passed through the lands of the Nuuri— They have not struck at your people. Instead, they have crossed the Line River. We do not know how," she admitted. "Until the devotee of Spirit warned us, we did not know to watch for them."

Crossed the Line—? That should not have been possible. The bridges were guarded. But Estie could guess how it was done. If the fanged men had enough rope, and one man with the rope fought his way across the stiff current, any number of strangers would be able to follow him.

"*Now* the Farsighted watch," continued Magister Oblique. "The strangers have gathered in the north of Belleger, hundreds or thousands of them. But they do not advance. We surmise that they are waiting for instructions from their Great God."

Queen Estie allowed herself a moment of relief that her people had not been attacked. But only a moment. Almost at once, she asked, "And Belleger? The Bay of Lights? Have Rile's ships returned?" She knew about the Great God's scout-ships, nothing more. "Has the war begun?"

Oblique nodded grimly. "It has. Rile's hosts have entered the bay, a great fleet of ships. There must have been a battle. For a time, a heavy storm blocked the Farsighted, and then the sun set. But when it rose again, they saw that King Bifalt's forces had been defeated. His cannon had been destroyed. Many of his men were dead.

"Now the enemy has forced a landing. The King's soldiers and Magisters strive to defend the shore, but they cannot counter the sorcery at Rile's command. Lightning makes corpses too easily, and rifles have little effect. The Farsighted estimate that Rile's hosts will fight their way out of the bay soon, in another day or two at most."

Even from so many leagues away, the shock of that news reached Estie. Belleger and Amika had spent years of labor and many lives fortifying the bay. But all of that effort and blood had been wasted. Rile had brushed them aside.

How did Bifalt bear it?

She refused to believe that he might be among the dead. He had always seemed as unbreakable as Belleger's Fist. For him, death might be a kinder fate than living on while more and more of his people were slaughtered. But he would not sacrifice his life so soon. Not when the war had just begun. He would suffer the cost of it as long as he could.

She wanted to ask if the Farsighted had seen her husband, but she was reluctant to expose so much of herself. When she had mastered her first rush of alarm, she asked, "Do the Farsighted know Commander Forguile? Is he alive?"

"They know him by sight, Queen," answered Magister Oblique, "as they do King Bifalt. He and the King live. They have returned to the Open Hand. Now a man we do not recognize commands the defense as well as he can."

With her fingers, Estie rubbed her eyes to stop her sudden tears. Bifalt, she thought, aching.

He had hoped to win in the Bay of Lights, but he had expected to lose. Thinking ahead, he had planned for what would come next. Those preparations he expected to fail as well.

"My tidings are hard to hear," murmured Oblique. "I know it, Queen." She paused for a moment. "Sadly, I have more to relate. There have been other events. They may prove worse. Certainly, they are deeply felt here."

Queen Estie dropped her hand. Without it, she could only shield herself by glaring at the Magister.

"I will try to be brief." The woman's tone implied that the whole Repository had been shaken. "Master Ungabwey's caravan has been destroyed. An avalanche crushed it. His mission in the Realm's Edge has failed.

"Now men from the south ride into Belleger. Magister Marrow can speak of them if you wish. They are recorded in our books. *I* can tell you that they are allied with Rile.

"They issue in great numbers from the mountains. The King opposes them there. He may have imagined that a small force with rifles would hold against foes with javelins and blades. But the tactics of the invaders are strange. They avoid open battle. Instead, they appear to rely on an indirect form of theurgy. The Farsighted cannot interpret it. But they see the King's men fall. Some die. Many cannot ride or fight. The others retreat toward the Open Hand.

"The King has sent reinforcements," concluded Magister Oblique. "They are too few to halt the invaders."

Estie bowed her head to hide her face. Bifalt had hoped to defend Belleger against only the host from the bay, but he had braced himself for the possibility that he might have to fight on two fronts. He had not known that he had an enemy in the north until Magister Avail warned him.

What would he do? What *could* he do, except fail and die?

And Queen Estie could not help him. Coming here, she had made herself useless.

No, she thought grimly. *No.* Not yet.

Bifalt would fight until he died. She could not do less. There were many ways to fail. She was only useless if she did not make every attempt.

"So," she said abruptly. "The King is threatened on three sides—and he is alone. He needs aid." She felt as fierce as a snarl. "He must have the Repository's aid. The librarian must send Magisters to fight. He *must*. If he does not, he will answer for it.

"But Bifalt needs *me* as well. I am Amika's Queen, his ally in war and life. I am the question *you* must answer, Magister.

"What am I? What did you expect me to be? What am I that you did not expect?"

Tell me what I can *become*.

If she had glanced at Commander Crayn at that moment, she would have seen bright approval in his eyes.

Magister Oblique flinched. She must have anticipated Estie's demand, should have been ready for it; yet it stung her. For an instant, she started to rise as if she meant to leave.

Almost immediately, however, she calmed herself. One by one, she relaxed her muscles. Breathing deeply, she faced what Amika's monarch wanted from her.

"Forgive me, Queen." Her voice shook a little. "You startled me. I was not prepared to hear so grave a question so soon. I promised that I would answer your queries if I can. Some I cannot because they are not mine to answer. Others I must not because—" She hesitated, then rushed ahead. "Because you are not ready to know. You will not be ready until you have spoken with Magister Marrow. Then you will need to think long and hard before you ask such a question again."

"Ha!" snapped the Queen as if she were pouncing. "Is this your welcome, Magister? Your kindness? I *will have* an answer."

Oblique flinched; but she did not hesitate. "When you do, you will understand our qualms."

With that, she stood. "Now, Queen, I will leave you. Try to rest. When I return, I will take you to confer with the librarian."

Oblique's abruptness froze Estie. She needed a moment before she was able to retort, "I will be ready, Magister. If you wish, warn the librarian that I will make demands—and I will not be silenced."

As if she had not heard, the Magister went to the door. As she opened it, she paused.

"Please rest while you can, Queen." She had recovered her composure. "You have a few hours. Certainly, your reasons for coming to us are imperative. Nevertheless you must be weary. If you and your men would like more to eat, simply set your trays outside your doors. Fresh food and drink will be brought."

Then she left, closing the door with the firmness of another refusal.

Estie watched Commander Crayn lock the door. She wished that he could shut out the entire library, at least for a while; but that was impossible.

When he was done, he came to her. After a moment's hesitation, he cleared his throat uncomfortably. "Majesty—" he began. Then he shook his head. "It is not my concern."

He had led her personal escort for a long time. She knew him well. "Crayn," she suggested softly. "Tell me what troubles you. In this place, I trust you more than I trust myself."

A time might come when she would need her guardsmen.

He tried again. "Majesty." For a moment, his throat closed. Then he blurted, "Do you have a gift for sorcery?"

She held his gaze. "Why do you ask?"

"Magister Oblique assured you that Magister Avail's reaction to your arrival was personal, yet you continue to pursue it. I cannot think of another explanation."

Queen Estie grimaced ruefully. "And now you wonder how I can say that I trust you when I have kept a vital secret from you. You could be forgiven for wondering if I have ever trusted you. But the matter is not so simple.

"I knew nothing of this until Magister Facile told me. All of my life, *nothing*." She snarled that word. Her father had seen the truth when she was born, but he had kept the nature of her inheritance from her. "She surprised me out of my wits by saying I have a gift."

The memory made Estie wince.

"You could not see it for yourself," she went on, "because you are not a sorcerer. And no one told you—*I* did not—because it is dangerous." She had not spoken of it to anyone except her husband. "It is *dangerous*, Crayn."

She shrugged. "Or so I am assured. The nature of a sleeping gift is a mystery. It can only be recognized and awakened safely by a sorcerer who shares the same gift. No one else knows what will arise."

Magister Facile had feared *a holocaust. A power like the final Decimate.*

"That is why I have kept my secret." Except from the Last Repository. Here every Magister saw it. "I do not know what I might become. And I fear it. Even if my gift is not dangerous in itself, it frightens me. It is like an invisible grenade I carry wherever I go. I cannot defuse it or cast it away."

She had been told that her secret gave her power. Now she understood that it gave other people power over her.

Yet she needed it. It was part of her. And it might help her persuade the librarian.

Revealing herself made her squirm. It did not trouble the Commander. The sandstone hue of his eye seemed to flinch at nothing. When she fell silent, he gave her a moment. Then he said, "As you say, Majesty." One corner of his mouth twisted in a wry grin. "It is a dangerous secret. I will keep it."

Briefly, Estie could not find her voice. Conflicting emotions closed her throat. Crayn's affirmation reminded her that she had reason to be grateful. But the war had begun. Too soon, bloodshed would sweep across the whole of Belleger. It might claim Amika as well. And she would have given anything to see acceptance like the Commander's on her husband's face.

When she could speak again, she said hoarsely, "Thank you, Crayn. My life is in your hands. When Magister Oblique returns, I will want you with me. Until then, you should rest."

He stood straighter. "If you will do the same, Majesty."

She sighed. "If I can. My mind is ready to burst. But if I can settle my thoughts, I will rest. We have hours to wait."

"As you say, Majesty," he repeated. Unexpectedly, he bowed as if he were Commander Soulcess, full of his own dignity—or of hers. Then he went to his own quarters and closed the door behind him.

Again, Estie was alone. But now she was not unwashed, hungry, and short of time. She had hours ahead of her in which to chew over the bitter gristle of her father's legacy.

Her question was not: What am I that the library did not expect? It was: What am I that *I* did not expect?

Unfortunately, she could not answer herself. She needed someone else to tell her.

ELEVEN

OUTCOMES

Eventually, Queen Estie slept in her chair for a time. Later, she looked outside her door and found a fresh tray laden with more fruit, a different wine, new bread, and a steaming bowl of soup. She had no interest in food, but she ate as much as she could. And later still, Magister Oblique returned.

By then, Commander Crayn had already rejoined Estie. He looked refreshed in his cleanest garments, with his hair still damp from the bath and a good meal inside him. He even smelled clean. His rifle and satchel of ammunition he had left in his room. But he had kept his orange Amikan headband, his sword, and his dagger. His grin as he bowed to his Queen had a wolfish quality that she found oddly reassuring. She rose to her feet and watched while he unlocked the door to admit the Magister.

"Greetings again, Queen," said Oblique. Her manner had become more distant, perhaps more careful. "I hope you have rested well. Will you come with me now? The others are gathering. Many of our people are eager to see and hear Amika's Queen, but of course they will not all be present. Magister Marrow's workroom is too small to hold them. Still, it may be crowded by the time we arrive."

"Certainly, Magister," replied the Queen, assuming a mildness that had served her well as Bifalt's wife and Amika's Queen. "Commander Crayn and I are as eager as anyone."

The sorceress cocked an eyebrow at Crayn. She may have assumed that Estie would accompany her alone. But she did not object. With a nod, she stepped aside to let Estie and the Commander pass. Then she led them down the corridor and back into the complicated passages of the Last Repository.

As they walked, Magister Oblique said cautiously, "I must apologize, Queen. I hope you will forgive me. When you asked what you are that we did not expect, I was taken aback. It is a natural question. More than that, it must be crucial to you. But I was not prepared for it. I had imagined that you would broach it later, perhaps with the librarian.

"Thinking back on my response, I regret it. But truly, Queen—" She spread her hands as if to emphasize their emptiness. "I have nothing better to offer. We do not know you. Oh, I have heard the most holy devotee of Spirit's tales. She has assured us that you are courageous and resourceful. In addition, you do not compromise the integrity of your rule in Amika. But that is like hearing the contents of a book described. Only reading the book gives it substance.

"We hope to know you better, Queen. Until then, I have said all that I can without compromising my own integrity."

Magister Oblique sounded sincere. Beyond question, she had a gift for it. But Estie was determined to make her own decisions. Instead of acknowledging Oblique's apology, she asked her question in a different way.

Still mildly, she said, "Magister Facile assured me that there are theurgists or scholars here who can name my gift."

Startled, Oblique swallowed a laugh. "That is certainly true."

"And will I be allowed to speak with one of them?"

The Magister paused before replying. "It is not a question of *allowed*, Queen. The offer is not mine to make. First, you must hear Magister Marrow—and take time to think. Then, if you insist, you *will* be answered. I will see to it." Then she added, "But you must be sure of what you do. We will not impose our choices on you."

Queen Estie nodded. "Thank you, Magister." But still she was not swayed. The Magisters who had dealt with Prince Bifalt would probably claim they had not imposed their choices on him. Instead, they had mistreated and misled him until he made the choices they wanted.

To reach the level of the librarian's workroom, Magister Oblique led the Queen and Commander Crayn up one long stairway after another until Estie felt sure that she was high above the Repository's gates and perhaps even the outer balcony. Then they reached a hall with a doorless entryway halfway down one side. She heard the murmur of voices. The scattered sound of people talking grew louder as she approached.

"Our destination, Queen," said Oblique softly. "I will name some of the people there for you. But we will not spend time on formal introductions. Magister Marrow is always impatient. He says—" Her brief smile resembled a grimace. "He says that he has wasps buzzing in his head. His temper worsens by the day. We can exchange courtesies later."

Estie nodded without listening. From her first glimpse, she was studying the workroom.

As she entered, an instant silence fell.

It was a large space as long as the hall outside and half as wide. Opposite the entryway, high clerestory windows admitted the gloom of the cloud-studded sky. There were no cressets, lamps, or candles to provide illumination the blind librarian did not need. But she could see well enough by the light of other windows off to one side. She guessed that they faced west: otherwise, the view would have included mountains. Then a flash of sunlight low in the heavens confirmed her surmise. It was brief. Clouds in clumps passed across the sun like shutters opening and closing. But that first flash promised that sunset was an hour or two away.

The assembly did not fill the chamber. It could have held twice that number. But they were too many for Estie. She did not want an audience: she wanted the librarian's full attention.

The people were diverse. Perhaps half of them wore the grey robes of Magisters. Queen Estie recognized Magister Rummage glowering at her from under the clerestories. In the farthest corner, Magister Avail stood with both hands covering his face. A monk at his side touched his forearm to communicate whatever was said. In a corner opposite Avail's, Lylin's white robe was unmistakable. It seemed to gather all the light around her. She was accompanied by another monk, a young woman. Despite her humble posture, the monk and the devotee of Spirit conveyed the impression that they had been chatting like old friends.

The others were new to Estie. They turned to stare as Magister Oblique guided her into the center of the room. Some of them seemed to hold their breath. They ignored Commander Crayn.

Oblique indicated the monk with Lylin. "Fifth Daughter," she said privately. "When Third Father is absent, she gives counsel in his place."

Estie searched the room for some sign of Third Father, but did not find him. Instead, she noticed a dark brown man wearing nothing except a loincloth and several beaded necklaces. He had more beads knotted in his hair and beard, which had obviously not been washed for a long time. His lips moved as if he were muttering an incantation, but he said nothing aloud.

"A shaman," murmured Magister Oblique. "A healer. His name will mean nothing to you."

Beyond him were two tall individuals, a man and woman, wrapped in what appeared to be bedsheets. Both of them had the white skin and colorless hair of albinos. Estie identified them by their apparent inability to focus their eyes on anyone or anything nearby. They were Farsighted, watching people and events in distant places.

Near the entryway, two men stood apart from the gathering. Like Lylin's companion, one was a monk. The other was a youngish man dressed in a blue tunic and pantaloons, with tough boots on his feet. A mess of untended black hair hung like a cowl around his head, shrouding his eyes.

"Servants," explained Oblique. "I can ask them for lamps if you wish, Queen."

Estie shook her head. She hoped earnestly that this meeting would not last until sunset.

Another brief flash of sunshine struck a long trestle-table piled with books and scrolls under the clerestories near Magister Rummage. In a heavy armchair behind the table sat an old man with long hair and a thick beard, both so white that they almost matched Lylin's robe. He had a large volume open in front of him. Despite the gathering and Queen Estie's arrival, he was engrossed in his reading.

Crayn left Estie's side for a moment, returned with a tall stool. Since everyone else was standing, and she was the Queen of Amika, she decided to sit. From that lower vantage, she could see nothing of the man behind the table except the top of his head. Good, she thought. He could not see her either. If he wanted to speak with her, he would have to stand.

Finally, a woman near the table spoke. She was slight enough to be a girl. And small: her head would not have reached Estie's shoulder. Despite the assertive sweep of her stark midnight hair, she resembled a mouse, too unassuming or timid to break the silence. But she wore the grey robe of a Magister.

As if the effort of making herself heard embarrassed her, she announced, "Magister Marrow, the Queen of Amika is here."

The crown of white hair behind the piled books lifted. "Is she?" rasped a querulous voice. "I did not notice. I have been reading—"

Abruptly, the man surged upright. He was a tall figure, able to look out over every head in the workroom. But of course he could not *look*. He was obviously blind. The milky film covering his eyes made sight impossible.

"I have been reading," he repeated as if Amika's Queen were not present, "Hexin Marrow's *Eighth Decimate*. We have called it the Decimate of persuasion, but it is more powerful than we imagined. My ancestor's work has convinced me. The sorcery that inspired two seeming servants to murder Magister Facile was the eighth Decimate. The Decimate of *coercion*."

The old sorceress had tried to warn Estie. Her last word had been *Decimate*.

Now everyone stared at Magister Marrow: everyone except the Far-sighted. Searching their visions, they both turned, the man toward the northwest, the woman to the south. After a shocked pause, another Magister called out, "Across such a distance, librarian? Across an ocean, if not from another continent? How can the enemy cast his Decimate so far? Even for him, it should be impossible."

"Ah," rumbled the tall man, "yes." His manner hinted at a deeply suppressed fury. "The distance. Impossible, as you say. Rile must have invested his power in some instrument. A jewel, perhaps, or something similar, prepared to extend its master's Decimate. With such instruments, his servants can—"

The librarian pushed his fingers into his hair, tugged at it as if he were trying to pull his thoughts into order. "There was a priest with Magister Facile's killers." Both of the Farsighted nodded without shifting their attention. "Rile must have ruled the killers through him. Facile would have feared nothing less."

With enough force to pull out a few strands of hair, Magister Marrow wrenched down his hands. "This is more than speculation. Hexin Marrow's book suggests that the eighth Decimate—and perhaps only the eighth—can be used in this way. But it does not reveal the secret. The investment or preparation. The sending of theurgy to a distant instrument. Perhaps my ancestor did not know it. Or he did not live long enough to learn it."

At once, several people started talking simultaneously. Like the two servants, the devotee of Spirit and her companion listened intently. Magister Rummage looked like he wanted to howl. Magister Avail uncovered his face, gaped in dismay, then closed his eyes. The other theurgists could not contain their surprise and distress.

Only the small woman standing near the librarian's table betrayed no reaction. Her blankness no longer resembled timidity. It suggested tightly controlled fear.

Queen Estie felt the same apprehension. She had *permitted* those priests. Allowed them to establish themselves in Amika. Even encouraged King Bifalt to follow her example. Directly or indirectly, she had enabled their crimes.

Her husband had been wiser. He had been suspicious from the first.

Then the librarian cut through the mounting clamor. Harshly, he demanded, "Did you examine his body, Queen? The priest who was killed?"

His force silenced the assembly. It stunned Estie. At that instant, she could not have responded to save herself.

But Commander Crayn had sworn to protect his Queen. He did not hesitate.

"If you were capable of courtesy, Magister," he said like iron, "you would not ask that question of Amika's Queen. Her friend was murdered in front of her. Magister Facile died in her arms. *I* examined the body. Father Knout had only the clothes on his back. A small number of coins in his purse. And *this*."

From a pouch at his belt, he took out a small cross on its chain, a cross marked by one stark ruby. Like an act of defiance, he tossed it toward the blind man.

Following its flight with senses other than sight, Magister Marrow caught it. As soon as his fist closed on it, however, he gasped. In almost the same motion, he flung the cross and chain at Magister Rummage.

The hunchback snatched them out of the air. Without glancing at them, he put them away inside his robe.

Flexing his burned or stung fingers, the librarian croaked, "As I said. An instrument."

Estie had never been in a Church of the Great God Rile, but the tall cross there had been described to her: a heavy crucifix with a naked man sculpted on its back, his arms dangling over its crosspiece, his eyes like rubies staring out at his worshippers.

Each of Rile's priests must have worn a little replica of that cross.

A troubled quiet gripped the workroom. Men and women groped to comprehend this evidence of their peril. But Magister Oblique set her own reaction aside almost immediately. Resting one hand on Estie's shoulder, she declared unexpectedly, loudly, "Magister Sirjane Marrow, librarian and guardian of the Last Repository, I present Estie daughter of Rubia, Queen of Amika and Queen-Consort to King Bifalt of Belleger. Her reasons for coming to us are urgent. The time has come to hear them."

Estie jerked up her head, taken aback by Oblique's intervention.

But she was also grateful for it. As an untried girl, her father's favorite, Princess Estie had regarded her mother with disdain. Now she knew better. As Amika's monarch, she was proud to be recognized as Queen Rubia's daughter.

The librarian let out a sound like a strangled shout. "I *know* they are urgent, Oblique. I am only blind, not demented." Then he made an effort to compose himself. "The Queen of Amika," he said sourly. "The *admirable* Queen. Unheard-of in Amika." He shook his head like a man trying to clear it after a heavy blow. "I will hear you.

"But first I must introduce Magister Threnody." He gestured at the black-haired woman near him. "She will be my successor. Before I die, I will tell her everything that the sorcery of her transformation cannot provide. She will know what I have done, and why, and what must come next."

The small Magister's only reaction was a subtle wince. She bowed stiffly. Then she left the front of the room and went to efface herself in the nearest corner.

Before Sirjane Marrow could go on, Queen Estie replied. He had given her a chance to rally. Now she felt primed for confrontation, as ready as she had been to face her insane father.

Sweetly, she asked, "Do you expect to die, librarian?"

"Of course!" snorted the tall man. "So should you. Every life ends. And I am older than you know. But I will not end yet. Not until my work is done."

"Then, Magister," continued Estie as if she were offering him a cup of tea, "you must act while you can. Finish your work. Send aid to King Bifalt. I have heard Magister Oblique's tidings of the war. Belleger and Amika cannot stand against *three* hosts in Rile's service. You must send out your Magisters. You must send them *now*. Nothing less can save us.

"Nothing less can save the Repository."

"Send out—?" He gaped at her in mock surprise. "No! Who else will defend us when the war comes here?"

"You are the Last Repository." Queen Estie allowed herself a little sharpness. "The greatest storehouse of knowledge in the world we know. Surely, you have allies."

"Oh, we do." Marrow dismissed them. "We do. They are many. But they are also *distant*. That is the disadvantage of a *hidden* library. We have called on them. Some have refused. Others cannot come in time. If we do not keep our defenders close, we will be lost."

Estie was ready to argue. She wanted to ask, What about the devotees of Spirit? But Lylin was present: she could speak for her people. Instead, the Queen suggested, "Perhaps the people who guarded Set Ungabwey's caravan?" She fumbled for the name, found it. "The el-Algreb? You know them. They will answer your call."

The librarian sneered. "I *do* know them, Queen. *You* do not." Despite his blindness, his gaze was full of scorn. "They have already refused. We have nothing they want. They are a warlike people, fierce in battle. But they are content as they are. They have no use for us. Master Ungabwey rewarded them with solid coin. We cannot meet their price."

"No," insisted Estie. "They will fight when they understand the threat. You will have more allies than you are willing to admit. We have none."

Crayn nodded his approval. Magister Oblique gave the Queen's shoulder a gentle squeeze, then lowered her hand.

Magister Marrow replied with a bitter laugh. "Is that *my* doing, Queen? Is it *my* fault that Amika and Belleger have spent generations killing each other instead of reaching out to the wider world?"

He might have gone on in that vein, justifying himself. Instead, he changed his tone. "No, Queen." His effort to sound sympathetic was audible. He could not manage kindliness. "I understand your concern. I share it. But you approach it from the wrong direction. You ask me to take action now. You do not ask what actions I have already taken."

Queen Estie settled herself to appear receptive. "Then tell me, Magister."

"I will not," he began at once, "belabor the loss of Master Ungabwey. He was my *friend*, Queen. And he could have said that he had done enough. We are safe from the east because he sealed the passes through the Wall Mountains. But I wanted more. I sought his aid for Belleger and Amika.

"At my urging, he risked himself and his people and his wealth to shield your realm and your Bifalt's from the southern host. Now he is dead. It is not *my* fault that he failed. It is not *his*. His efforts *could* have succeeded. If they had, you would not reproach me. You would sit before me with gratitude in your heart."

At the edge of her vision, Estie saw the devotee of Spirit shaking her head. Disapproval? A warning? She could not interpret Lylin's reaction.

"However," continued Sirjane Marrow, "that is only the most recent action I have taken on your behalf." His suppressed fury began to leak past his composure as he spoke. "Who do you suppose secreted the papers that led Belleger to the invention of rifles? *Repeating* rifles, Queen? That knowledge was not left behind by some older, wiser generation. It was given to Belleger at my command."

Estie's face must have betrayed her surprise. "Being King Smegin's daughter," snarled the librarian, "you will want to know why I gave those papers to Belleger, not to Amika. The Amikan monarchs knew of our existence. Belleger did not. Why, then, did I give preference to your former foes? Being Queen Rubia's daughter, you will understand my answer."

A moment of brightness from the western windows streaked the workroom. The sun was close to setting. But Sirjane Marrow had no use for light. If his audience wanted lamps, no one said so. They were accustomed to his indifference, or they were not willing to interrupt him.

"Your father was a petty tyrant," he explained, "ambitious and cruel, like *his* father, and his father's father for generations. I did not *trust* such monarchs with rifles. They would have ravaged Belleger and done nothing to prepare for our defense.

"For the same reason, I gave Sylan Estervault's *Treatise* to your Bifalt. I wanted him to have cannon as well as rifles. With no guns and no sorcery, Amika would have been helpless. He would have been able to unite your realms by force. *Then* he would prepare for the real war.

"I have never been more astonished," he admitted, "than I was when your small-minded husband gave Estervault's book to Commander

Forguile." For an instant, he seemed chastened. "His way of uniting the realms was better than my intentions. Clearly, he is not always small-minded. For that, he merits my respect."

"I agree," put in Queen Estie sternly. She needed to say *something*. "My experience of him is not like yours. I can assure you that he is never small-minded."

Measured against the sheer number of lives that Bifalt had been fighting to save, her personal losses were trivial.

But Magister Marrow did not appear to hear her. He was still explaining himself.

"It will not surprise you, Queen, that I dislike your husband. His arrogance offends me. He has not earned the right to pass judgment. Still, I have learned to respect him. For his efforts and forethought, I respect him."

In some other place, a place where she had authority, Queen Estie would have stopped the librarian then. That is enough, sir. The words she wanted sprang to her mind, almost tumbling over each other for utterance. Do you accuse *him* of arrogance? King Bifalt of Belleger? You are its *epitome*. It has made you a tyrant.

Who else but a tyrant manipulates and sacrifices ordinary men and women to secure his own ends? Who else plans the ruin of people he has never met for no better reason than his belief that his needs outweigh theirs? You are the Great God Rile by another name, sir. What you call arrogance in the King of Belleger is his love for his people.

Bifalt's wife would have taken pride in flinging her accusations at the librarian. Queen Estie kept silent. This was not some other place. It was the Last Repository. Here, Magister Marrow ruled. Other issues were more important than her outrage.

She needed to hear whatever he would reveal. She knew by his manner that he was not done.

"But there is more, Queen." His underlying ire had the effect of bragging. "Rifles and cannon and restored sorcery were not the Repository's only attempts to aid Belleger. Long ago, my predecessors set plans for our defense in motion.

"Why do you suppose there is only *one* bay on Belleger's coast that offers passage past the cliffs? And why do you suppose the cliffs there fall away in terraces suitable for emplacements and cannon? That is not the work of natural forces. If your people had not spent generations on end killing each other"—his voice dripped scorn—"you would know of a convulsion that formed what is now the Bay of Lights. In fact, it was a precise sequence of convulsions. It was the Repository's doing, Queen.

"My predecessors sent Magisters of earthquake to work there secretly. They invited Rile's attack by offering him a more direct route to his goal than any other on this continent. And when my time came, I prepared the bay to repulse him. To be *defended*, Queen, with heavy iron and ordinary courage.

"In that, at least, I succeeded. Sadly, your King Bifalt has failed. Let him bear the blame, Queen. It is not mine.

"Now I have done what I can," he finished. "I cannot do more."

While the tall man regarded Estie with a kind of blind triumph, she trembled. In every part of herself—the woman, the wife, the Queen—she was appalled. She did not see Crayn shift closer to support her, or Lylin arrive at her side, or Fifth Daughter turn her face to the wall. Magister Rummage's glower and Magister Avail's strange distress meant nothing to her. Her limbs trembled as she rose from her stool to face the librarian standing. When she spoke, her voice rasped like a saw.

"And you did all this? The bay? Rifles and cannon? Taking away sorcery, then returning it? Contriving an alliance between Belleger and Amika? For *what*? To force King Bifalt to stand between you and your enemy?"

The last sunlight struck Sirjane Marrow's face. It made him look as complacent as a corpse after a peaceful death.

"What better purpose could there be? This is the world's last treasure-house of knowledge. There are books here, Queen, that no longer exist on any other continent. If we were not threatened—if we were not *always* threatened—our wealth could have filled this world with wonders."

Estie swore under her breath. She wanted to scald the old man's flesh. But she could not. To her cost, she understood that he was sincere despite his anger and sarcasm. He *believed* that knowledge was more important than lives.

Searching for self-control, she scanned the room.

Crayn's anger was plain on his face. The same ire flushed Magister Oblique's cheeks, tightened her breathing. Lylin's expression was unreadable. Magister Rummage had raised his head. He seemed to be sniffing the air. The shaman followed his example. Instinctively, Estie did as well. She smelled Crayn's cleanliness, and the devotee's. Other individuals nearby had not bathed recently. Two unfamiliar theurgists left the workroom in a flurry of disapproval. The servant in blue whispered something to his companion. When the other servant nodded, the youngish man left the room.

Perhaps unnecessarily, the librarian remarked, "Earlier, I asked Tak Biondi to bring wine. He will do so now. I knew that nothing would be accomplished here." His tone was as harsh as grot. "When he returns, Amika's monarch and I will drink to celebrate our disagreements."

That gibe was too much for Queen Estie. She had tried to regain command of her emotions. Suddenly, she did not care to restrain herself.

Still standing, still trembling, she asked with every ounce of her father's venom, "If you will not aid people who fight in your cause, sir, what do you expect them to do?"

"Do?" retorted Sirjane Marrow fiercely. "*Do?* I expect them to *die.* Let them pile their bodies against Rile's advance. What choice do they have?"

He was intolerable. His every sentence was more than Estie knew how to endure. At one time, she had confronted her father, who had ordered his own wounded killed after every battle. This was worse.

A scream gathered in her chest. She meant to release it. For Amika and Belleger and her husband, she wanted to unleash everything that was in her.

But she did not have time.

At that instant, the librarian's desk exploded. Terrible forces ripped the table apart, and him. The people near him were tossed aside. All of the workroom's windows shattered.

The last sound Queen Estie heard before the blast took her was Magister Threnody's shriek.

Seconds or hours later, Estie found that she could not breathe. Her hearing was gone as well. Silence formed a cocoon around her. But that was nothing. She needed air.

A heavy weight had fallen on her. It was crushing her to the floor. She did not have the strength to shift it.

Then it began to ease. When Lylin felt Estie trying to move, she nudged Crayn. With a groan, Crayn raised himself. Shrugging off timbers and rubble, he staggered to his feet. Lylin pushed herself off the Queen. At once, the devotee sank back on her knees and heels, letting Estie gasp for air.

Both of them had flung themselves over the Queen to shield her from the falling rain of glass and wood, the spray of blood, the rent organs and shards of bone, the wild storm of papers, the chunks of stone torn from the ceiling. The devotee of Spirit was simply faster than Crayn. She had landed on Estie a fraction of a heartbeat ahead of the Commander.

Retching, Estie fought for breath.

The air scraped her throat like gunpowder. But it was *air*. At least for a moment or two, it was enough.

Shaking with effort, she tried to lift her head.

Lylin assisted her. For a moment, Estie could not see. Dust and reeking fluids clogged her eyes. With the sleeve of her robe, Lylin wiped Estie's face. Blinking, Estie cleared her gaze.

Carried by breezes from the uncovered windows, shredded pages swirled everywhere. In clouds, they drifted down to settle like shrouds on half a dozen mangled bodies. The shaman was only stunned. Blood pulsed between ruptured ribs below his heart, but Estie saw his chest rise, fall, rise again. One of the Farsighted lay with her head at a sickening angle. The other knelt beside her, keening. Magister Avail's sorcerous voice was a howl, yelling soundlessly to every mind in the library for help. Magister Rummage lay on his side against the wall. One of the table's legs protruded from his lower belly. It looked as thick as an axletree. As far as Estie could tell, the monks in the room were still alive. She could not locate Magister Oblique.

Sirjane Marrow had become a horrid welter of shattered bones and gore. Clumps of white hair floated among the ruined papers.

Queen Estie of Amika pitched away from Lylin's support to vomit. Then the full effects of the explosion caught up with her, and she collapsed, unconscious.

TWELVE

STORMS ON THE HORIZON

While the great pyre for the dead of Belleger and Amika blazed, King Bifalt let the onlookers stand their vigil. Magisters and gunners, servants and soldiers watched the dance of flames with desolation in their eyes, sorrow and lost hopes. He did not have it in him to hurry them.

However, the King made two exceptions. In a tone that did not encourage argument, he sent General Klamath to the nearest bunkhouse. When Klamath had left Belleger's Fist with his company of Magisters the previous morning, he had intended nothing more ambitious than an experiment with sorcery. But since then, he had spent most of a day and night goading his horse through the snow. He needed rest.

More angrily, the King ordered Heren Flisk to the overworked infirmary. If the Captain's dislocated shoulder was not set soon, he might never regain the use of that arm. In any case, he looked like he was dying on his feet. His King had asked too much of him. Bifalt's anger was directed at himself.

For a while, the King stayed with the pyre and its mourners, watching wood and bodies burn like his heart. Then he and his bodyguards went to look out over the ruin of the bay's defenses.

Along the way, he dispatched a messenger with a summons for Second Captain Hegels. He wanted Hegels to take command of the opposition here. Perhaps riflemen could slow the enemy's ascent from the strand.

Four other people accompanied him. Commander Forguile was battered and bruised, obviously weary; but he wore his condition with a smile. Magister Trench's toughness was more mental than physical: he had hardly exerted himself during the battles. As if to prove himself, he came dragging Magister Whimper. Like her fellow drought-wielders, she had done nothing since her arrival except watch two of her comrades shot and lose another over the precipice. Despite her acid nature, she looked frightened out of her mind. And Magister Brighten followed the others, stumbling with exhaustion and grim-faced, but determined to have her say.

In shattering cold and bitter winds at the head of the road, King Bifalt studied what had become of his preparations for Rile's coming. The sight of the smashed cannon and wrecked emplacements made pain throb in his forehead, but he did not look away. He had expected something like this. Surely he had expected it? But not so soon, or at such cost.

He said nothing about the fierce strangers who had attacked the cannoneers. He believed that he understood what had happened. Queen Estie's only message had warned him about two similar men and the priest, Father Knout. Where there had been two, there could be twenty, or two hundred. He did not try to imagine how a large force had crossed the Line River to strike here. To his mind, the crucial point was the connection between the fanged strangers and Rile's priests. Magister Pillion had seen Father Skurn's power restored. Father Skurn must have summoned the attack. Now he was dead. There were no more priests in Belleger. King Bifalt felt sure that the strangers would not threaten the bay's defenders again.

Nailed to his duty, he spoke with his temporary advisers about other matters. He wanted to know what they thought sorcery and rifles might do against the Great God's forces here.

Many of the black ships that had opened the way for the enemy were gone. The rest had positioned themselves to stand guard as dozens of far larger vessels eased closer. Several of those heavy carriers now nudged the chaos of boulders and rubble that Magister Pillion had dropped onto the strand. Men swarmed on their decks, at huge open doors in their prows, and down among the rocks, preparing for a difficult ascent against rifle-fire and sorcery.

What could Bifalt's Magisters do to slow them? What good were rifles against so many foes?

So far, the enemy had used only lightnings and earthquakes. Perhaps those were Rile's only Decimates. "That changes nothing," said Brighten sourly. "They exceed us. And they are too close. We cannot sense their lightning in time to counter it. If we strike at them, they will incinerate us where we stand.

"As for earthquakes—" She shrugged. With Pillion gone, there were no Magisters of earthquake here.

King Bifalt allowed himself to rub his forehead. Working together, his earthquake-wielders could probably tear down a thousand paces of the cliff-edge. They might cripple the first ships. But the result of their efforts would be a slope, not a sheer wall. In the end, it might make the enemy's climb easier.

"Fire?" suggested Magister Trench. "Pestilence?"

The King shook his head. He needed the Decimate of fire in the Open Hand, and he had a different use in mind for the Decimate of pestilence.

"In that case, Majesty," said Trench, "we are left with wind and drought."

Rile's ships had already shown that wind could not hinder them. Drought would accomplish little in a bay full of water.

But Trench was not dissuaded. "I know wind," he insisted. "Another storm is coming. I feel it. With enough help, I can hasten it. And the Decimate of drought can do more than pause snow. It can spur the clouds to release a blinding snowfall.

"General Klamath had similar thoughts. He was not able to test them."

"No," protested Magister Whimper. "We are too few."

She seemed to mean that she was too afraid.

Forguile ignored her. "And while snow blinds the enemy, Majesty,

I can take snipers down into the ruins of the emplacements. When the storm passes, we can pick our targets. We will be near enough for that. If our men above the cliff keep firing, the enemy may not spot us."

"Yes," said King Bifalt after a moment. "But not you, Commander. You have done enough. Leave it to Hegels. You and Captain Flisk will return to the Open Hand with me."

The Commander's look of protest had a wry tinge. He smiled crookedly. "As you say, Majesty."

Without more discussion, the King sent another messenger to the Second Captain. His instructions were:

Bring only snipers. The riflemen here are enough. But gather every Magister of wind and drought. Bellegerin, Amikan, all of them. You will need them.

As the rider hurried away, Forguile asked, "Do you suppose, Majesty, that Rile's sorcerers wear distinctive garments? Will they resemble his priests?"

"We can hope," rasped Bifalt. Any distinguishing sign would help the marksmen choose their targets.

With that, he let the three Magisters and Commander Forguile return to the shelter of the kitchens. With his bodyguards, he went back to the pyre. There he told his people that the time had come to abandon the encampment. He had given the necessary orders before he left Belleger's Fist. A train of wagons would arrive soon to begin carrying away everyone who could be spared from the last defense. King Bifalt hated leaving *anyone* in the enemy's path, but he had to resist the invasion somehow.

When they dispersed to pack up their meager belongings, he went with them to offer any help they might need—and to make sure that they left nothing Rile's forces might find useful.

As soon as General Klamath emerged from the bunkhouse, however, Bifalt put him in charge of the evacuation. Rubbing his head, Bifalt ordered the Magisters of lightning to accompany him back to the Open Hand. No doubt the Second Captain's efforts would be weakened without them. But they were spent in any case; and he expected to need them later. The riflemen he had brought with him, he left to

Klamath. When Commander Forguile and Captain Flisk joined him, the King with his small company began the cold ride back to the Hand.

He had far too many lives on his conscience. They drove him like the pain in his skull. His failures were too expensive.

The halls of the Fist felt empty without Queen Estie. Forsaken, colder. Prince Jaspid was there, of course. Prince Lome. Land-Captain Erepos. Royal Surveyor Wheal fretting over King Bifalt's plans to defend the city. Purse-Holder Grippe with nothing to do except number the men he could not afford to pay. Only Captain of the Count Crickin was absent, harrying Bellegerins across the south of the realm to leave their homes. In his grim way, the King was glad to see them all. But they did not comfort him. None of them could take Estie's place.

Soon after her message, he had received a similar warning from Chancellor Sikthorn. Later, messages had begun to arrive from Commander Soulcess, increasingly frantic appeals for more men to defend Amika. King Bifalt had ignored most of them. But now, while the enemy remained in the bay, he felt that he could afford to heed Soulcess. He sent a rider to Maloresse with his promise that he would give Amika a hundred riflemen. They would depart in two days.

No doubt, Soulcess would object to that delay. But Bifalt wanted Amika's best-known officer, Ennis Forguile, to lead those riflemen, and Forguile was exhausted to the edge of his astonishing endurance. He needed at least a little rest.

When the King heard Magister Avail speak in his mind, he knew that he had done enough for Amika. Instead, he had a new problem. Rile's unnatural servants had crossed from Amika into Belleger, hundreds or thousands of them. Bifalt now had a *third* army to face, and he did not have enough men to meet even one of them.

According to Magister Avail, the fanged strangers had massed near Belleger's northern border, apparently waiting for new orders. That was fortunate. Bifalt would not have to contrive an immediate response. And the hundreds or thousands of invaders were far to the east. Perhaps they waited to support Rile's march on the library. Whatever their purpose, they would not endanger the evacuation of the Open Hand.

Rubbing his forehead, King Bifalt put the fanged horde out of his mind. He had more immediate concerns.

General Klamath had returned to the Open Hand a day after King Bifalt. On his ride to the city, Klamath had passed Second Captain Hegels and his collection of Magisters: nearly fifty wielders of wind and drought. The General and Hegels had spoken at length. When Klamath reached Belleger's Fist, he was able to assure Bifalt that Hegels understood his task.

After that, the King and General Klamath saw little of each other. The readiness and supply of the army, and the reports from First Captain Matt in the south, consumed Klamath's attention. To avoid a duty that daunted him, King Bifalt concentrated on the efforts to prepare the Open Hand for its defense and evacuation.

Some of those tasks belonged to the Land-Captain. Erepos was having wagons made as fast as the carpenters and wheelwrights could work. Bifalt intended to empty the city of food, leaving nothing that would serve the enemy. The more perishable provisions would go to Amika to help feed the sudden influx of Bellegerins. The staples along with mountains of winter gear would be sent eastward for the army on its way to the library.

When the King was satisfied with the Land-Captain's progress, he spent a while watching Prince Lome's beleaguered efforts to organize the flight of the city's inhabitants. Supported by Malder's armor, weapons, and weight of muscle, Lome was having some success despite his bitterness. Bifalt moved on.

In other districts of the Hand, he observed as Magister Crawl prepared the barricades that were intended to aid the evacuation by redirecting Rile's forces away from the main streets toward the walls of the old city. To Bifalt's surprise, he saw Crawl's fellow Magisters of fire helping with the construction of the barriers. Such men commonly disdained menial labor. And Crawl was the youngest among them, as slender as a sprig of wattle, and entirely unprepossessing in his manner.

Yet somehow he had persuaded a dozen Magisters of fire to sweat alongside carpenters and servants. They even fouled their robes digging trenches that would be filled with lamp oil so that the barricades would burn like bonfires, and keep burning.

The sight comforted Bifalt, but it did not ease the nagging pain in his head. He knew that he was procrastinating. Clearly, Erepos, Prince Lome, and Magister Crawl did not need him. He could no longer excuse his delay. He should have faced the responsibility that awaited him when he had first returned from the bay.

General Klamath would express his gratitude and respect to the families of his slain soldiers. Erepos would do the same for the relatives and loved ones of the cannoneers. As Belleger's King, Bifalt would only have to confront the same challenge once. But once was too often. He did not have it in him to express sorrow or offer consolation. He had never tried to console anyone in his life.

Still, he was more than Belleger's King. He was King Abbator's son. He did what his father would have done. Despite the pain pounding in his skull, he went to speak with Magister Pillion's widow.

King Bifalt did not associate with Magisters. He had only seen Pillion once or twice, and then from a distance. But he knew that the unassuming man had a wife. Therefore, presumably, children. That was the extent of the King's personal knowledge.

However, he knew precisely where Pillion's family lived. Long ago, he had given dwellings near the walls of the old city to Belleger's few earthquake-wielders. At the time, he had wanted those theurgists nearby in case the enemy used the same Decimate against the fortifications. Now he had other plans; but that detail was irrelevant to the bereavement of Pillion's family.

The homes he had provided were modest. In a city riddled with poverty, however, Pillion's house was comparatively spacious, comfortable, and sturdy. And—a rare luxury—it was graced by a plot of open ground large enough for a garden.

One glance told King Bifalt that Magister Pillion's garden was not a success. It was implausibly kempt and tidy; supplied with plenty of water; kept free of weeds and pests. Nevertheless its assortment of vegetables, herbs, and flowers were a discouraged lot. Clearly, the sorcerer had loved his garden—and just as clearly, he had no gift for growing things.

The King's headache pierced deeper. When he left Jeck, Spliner, and Boy at the garden gate, walked up to the dwelling's stoop, and knocked on the door as if he were announcing his own limitations, he had no idea what to expect.

Almost at once, the door was opened by a tumble of children. Instinctively, Bifalt stepped back. The two smallest ones fell at his feet. The older boys and girls stood in the doorway, staring with the solemn uncertainty of rabbits.

"Children—" Bifalt's voice caught. He rubbed his forehead; tried again. "Children, I am King Bifalt. I must speak with your mother."

Scrambling to his feet, one of the little ones retorted, "You are not Da. We want Da."

Bifalt opened his mouth. Closed it again.

Over her shoulder, the oldest girl called, "Ma! Ma! There is a man. He says he is the King." She clapped a hand over her mouth to cover a snicker. "He lies."

"Nonsense, child," answered a woman. "Being a stranger does not make him a liar." Behind the wall of her offspring, she appeared: a large figure with the shoulders of a drover, worried eyes, and a face that might have been lovely if she had smiled. "Perhaps he knows where your fa—"

The sight of King Bifalt on her stoop clenched her throat. For an instant, she looked as solemn and anxious as her brood. Then she croaked, "Majesty," and sank as if she had fallen to her knees. She may have been attempting a curtsy.

"Children." King Bifalt tried to soften his tone, but the effort only made him harsher. "Make way for your mother. I must speak to her." Gritting his teeth, he added, "About your father."

A little boy still sprawled where he had fallen. He glared up at the King. With unfettered indignation, he demanded, "Da! Bring *Da*!"

Hidden by her children, the woman chided them. "He *is* the King." She did not sound vexed. She sounded terrified. "That is not how we speak to the King."

Bifalt met the boy's glower. The world seemed to grow dark around him. Holding his breath, he bent down suddenly, awkwardly; lifted the child in his arms. The boy squirmed. Bifalt tried to hold him gently.

"My lady." The King's voice was louder than he intended. "I must speak with you."

The woman forced herself upright as if she lifted the weight of her whole family. For an instant, no more than that, she held Bifalt's gaze. Then she lowered her eyes.

"Children," she said softly, "go to your rooms. I will tell you what the King says when he is gone."

Bifalt did not hear a command in her voice. Clearly, her offspring did. Hurrying, they scattered into the recesses of the house, leaving only the boy in Bifalt's arms.

Without her children, the woman filled the doorway. At this time of day, there were no lamps lit inside. The gloom behind her empha-sized her broad frame, her thick arms. It did nothing to soften the alarm in her eyes or the tension around her mouth.

"Forgive us, Majesty," she said as if the words were as heavy as stones. "We did not expect you. How could we?"

While the King searched for a reply, she seemed to realize that he was holding one of her boys. Abruptly, she surged forward, took the child from his arms. Then she retreated to the doorway and stood there as if she needed the support of the doorposts. Or as if she wanted to prevent Bifalt from carrying his severity into her home.

Her mouth quivered as she said, "You came to tell me my husband is dead."

At once, Bifalt shook his head. "No, my lady." Finally, he managed to soften his tone. "I came to tell you that he died for your sake, and for your children."

She made one small sound like a swallowed sob. Tears filled her eyes. Her whole body seemed to wait for a blow that might kill her.

At that moment, Bifalt wanted nothing more than to turn away.

Instead, he straightened his spine, squared his shoulders. He was Belleger's King. He could have asked almost anyone to deliver this hurt for him. He had chosen to inflict it himself.

Long ago, the traitor Slack had told him, *A man is not a man at all if he cannot enter every chamber of himself.*

"I was not present," he said hoarsely, almost whispering, "but I have heard the tale. The men who witnessed his sacrifice speak of him with wonder.

"He opposed the enemy in your name. His power was extraordinary. Its effects killed him, but they were not wasted. With his Decimate, he did more than cannon and lightnings to slow the enemy's advance. His courage will never be surpassed."

Clutching her boy with his face nestled against her neck, Pillion's wife met Bifalt's gaze again. "Enough." Her voice trembled like her lips. Tears streaked her cheeks. "You have said enough. You can go. You cannot help us now."

King Bifalt felt that his forehead was splitting. He stayed where he was.

"No, my lady. I have not said enough. I did not command your husband to give his life. I would have forbidden him. I will command you in his place.

"You must take your children and depart. You cannot remain here. A new home will be provided for you in Maloresse. An escort will come for you when Land-Captain Erepos hears that you are ready. A great army means to destroy this city. I will not allow you to remain in its path. How else can I repay my debt to your husband?"

The woman stared at him. "You—?" Her youngest son clung to her. "*You* will not—?" For a moment, dismay gripped her. Then it became outrage. "Will you force us to leave our home?"

She stepped backward into the house.

"You will go," she told him. "We will not."

As if she were certain, she closed the door in King Bifalt's face.

He did not go. He did not leave the stoop until he heard her let out one long wail, a cry loud enough to shake the door in its frame. Then he turned and walked away. The pain was as specific as a needle in his mind. It was the price of being who he was.

Slack had not said, *enter every chamber.* He had said, *enter and enjoy.* But that was impossible.

Outside the garden gate, Bifalt rejoined his bodyguards and paused to think. He positively required Pillion's widow to leave her home and escape to Amika. But he could not simply order a squad of riflemen to compel her. For Magister Pillion's sake, if not for her own dignity, she deserved more respect.

Chewing on his cheek, he said hoarsely, "Flisk."

Jeck prompted him. "Captain Flisk, Majesty?"

The King nodded. To Boy, he said, "Find him. Bring him here." Heren Flisk had already been asked for too much, but he would not refuse this task. He had been with Pillion at the end. "Tell him that the widow will need help with her brood on the road. She does not mean to go, but he is kind. If that is not enough, his wounds may sway her." He had dislocated his shoulder trying to save her husband. "I cannot"—his throat closed for a moment—"can *not* allow the enemy to have her and her children."

Boy shared a glance with his father and Jeck, then replied with his usual confidence, "As you say, Majesty." At once, he walked away as if he knew exactly where he was going.

Bifalt valued Boy and all his bodyguards. But they were not enough. His pain was getting worse.

When circumstances allowed, reports reached the King from Second Captain Hegels in the west and First Captain Matt in the south. They did nothing to ease Bifalt's head, or his heart.

Defending the bay, Hegels tried the tactics Magister Trench and Commander Forguile had suggested. As the Decimate of wind hastened heavy weather, the Decimate of drought invoked snow to conceal snipers among the ruins of the emplacements. Covered by a fusillade from the cliff's rim, the Second Captain's best marksmen opened fire on soldiers emerging from the black ships.

As Hegels had expected, the enemy responded with flails of lightning. Nevertheless he considered the ploy a success. He intended to repeat it during the next snowfall.

The result was a disaster.

During the second storm, the ships had released dozens, no, hundreds of men onto the strand. They were small figures, carried no obvious weapons; but they were as agile as lemurs. When the skies cleared, they swept up over the rubble and the shattered terraces. Within moments, all of the snipers were dead, shredded by the clawed fingers and toes of their foes.

In the aftermath, Hegels sent his Magisters back to the Open Hand. His riflemen he kept. But they could do little more than watch as teams from the ships unloaded timbers, set pilings, and began constructing a wide ramp to replace the broken portions of the road. Before long, the ramp reached high enough to brace itself on undamaged stone. Then infantrymen shielded in iron came upward, ascending in ranks as if their numbers had no limit. They were difficult to kill.

The Second Captain saw no other choice. He ordered the final evacuation of the encampment. Using only his riflemen, he planned a fighting retreat while he waited for new orders from the King.

The King's response was simple.

Bring the enemy to the Hand. *Make* him follow you.

The news from Hegels was bad. In some ways, Matt's reports were worse.

The First Captain had intended to drive his men like a wedge into the army of raiders, hoping to reach the mountain pass that opened into Belleger. There, his earthquake-wielder, Magister Astride, could have attacked the pass itself. Any avalanche would hinder Rile's allies. Then the advantage of rifles might suffice to hold back the enemy.

But when Matt neared the Realm's Edge, the raiders already commanded the flanks of the mountains. Hundreds of them guarded the pass while more of their comrades arrived: men on horseback wearing loose garments of black-streaked white cloth open only at their faces, armed with javelins and long knives. Mounted, they had no defense against bullets except numbers. But their numbers were enough. Before Matt could reconsider his tactics, they rushed him.

Firing until his rifle barrel steamed in the cold, he found that even Magister Astride could not halt them. They vaulted their horses over her clefts in the earth and kept coming until her stamina failed. The First Captain was forced to withdraw.

For some reason, the raiders did not give chase. When he had put two leagues between his remaining riflemen and the enemy, he paused to examine his choices.

Of course, he signaled for reinforcements. But any soldiers that King Bifalt could spare would take days to arrive. In the meantime, Matt had his orders.

Sighing, he sent a dozen men back toward the growing host. They were to get within rifle-range, shoot until the enemy reacted, then run. How the raiders answered might tell him what to do next.

They answered by pulling back—but only until they were out of range. Clearly, they hoped to lure Matt's men closer. And just as clearly, they feared Belleger's rifles. They could not know how many soldiers the First Captain had hidden behind him.

Matt dispatched a few scouts to keep watch on the enemy. He set his sentries. Then he felt safe for the night.

He was mistaken. Hours after the sun's setting, his sentries reported a few small fires upwind of his camp. The men who set them must have carried their own wood. There was nothing to burn on these hills in winter.

With a handful of soldiers, Matt rode out to investigate. They were the first to smell the smoke. By the time they reached the fires, the flames had been abandoned—and Matt and his few companions were feeling sick. Reeling, they stamped out the fires and tried to ride back to their camp. Before they reached it, they pitched from their horses, vomiting up their guts. Their eyes burned. Matt's were bleeding.

Soon riflemen came to find them. But by then, a third of the First Captain's command had fallen ill.

The soldiers needed someone to lead them. Sub-Commander Hellick gave the order to flee. Matt and the sickest men had to be tied in their saddles while the whole company ran. Whenever they felt safe enough to rest, more small fires appeared upwind of them, and they fled again.

Fortunately, they were not pursued. Keeping a discreet distance, the raiders simply followed. If they were in a hurry to reach the Open Hand, they did not show it.

They may have been timing their approach to arrive when Rile's army struck.

When General Klamath brought the First Captain's tidings to the King, Bifalt did not waste his energy wondering how the raiders had devised a poisonous smoke. The fact of it was enough. Instead, he remembered a tale that Klamath had told him long ago. In the village of Klamath's birth, there had been a Magister of pestilence who had used his theurgy to heal diseases, infections, and tumors. Perhaps—

To the General's grim scowl, King Bifalt said, "Fifty riflemen, Klamath. I will not risk more. Instruct them to leave the enemy alone. They must aid the First Captain's men. And prevent more of those venomous fires.

"Send Magisters of pestilence as well. Do what you must to compel them." The Magisters Bifalt knew would not volunteer to leave their homes and risk death on an instant's notice. "I want them riding south in an hour."

After Klamath hurried to obey, King Bifalt paced around and around in his rooms, waiting for more reports. He refused to think about Matt's plight. That smoke was just one example of the horrors that sorcery could inflict on ordinary men. While he cursed to himself, he concentrated on reviewing his preparations for the coming siege.

They would not be enough.

During that time, Bifalt would have welcomed the intrusion of Magister Avail's voice in his mind. But from the Last Repository, he received only silence.

Early in the morning eight days after Matt had left the Open Hand, King Bifalt and General Klamath rode out to the same ridge from which they had watched Master Ungabwey's caravan depart, the high ground beyond the army's training-fields. Alerted by Hellick's signals, they went to meet the First Captain's return with his poisoned company.

King Bifalt would have preferred to face this duty alone. But the General belonged with him, and he could not refuse Jeck, Spliner, and Boy. For reasons of his own, Klamath brought his young aide Ulla with him on his horse.

Prince Jaspid had remained behind. In the absence of other officers, he had taken reluctant command of the army's training.

Bifalt was in no mood to wait, but he could spare the time. The host following Matt's company had slowed its advance. And in the Bay of Lights, Rile's army had not begun to march on the Hand. The chore of unloading so many ships was prodigious. An overwhelming force could not be landed, equipped, and provisioned without immense effort. Three days ago, Second Captain Hegels had believed that the enemy would be ready to move by now. Since then, he had extended his estimate. He did not expect the siege of the Open Hand to begin for four more days.

King Bifalt had time to treat men like Mattwil's father with the respect they deserved.

Nevertheless he dreaded this duty. Few things infuriated him more than seeing his people stricken, afflicted, or killed when he had not been there to fight beside them. The fact that Matt's company had been ravaged by sorcery only made him angrier. The riflemen struggling to return had earned sympathy from their King. They needed compassion and understanding. Bifalt knew that. But he had none to give. He should have been with them.

He missed Elgart. The former spy would have said something to ease the waiting.

Only an hour or two after dawn, the hills below and beyond the ridge still cast long shadows. There were no storms on the horizon, but unruly clouds scudded overhead, shedding patches of gloom. With so many sick soldiers, the First Captain's company would come along the valleys to make the riding as easy as possible. They were not in sight yet.

According to Matt's earlier signals, his men had managed to collect a few survivors from the destruction of Master Ungabwey's caravan.

King Bifalt assumed they were riflemen, the train's rearguard. The signals suggested other possibilities.

Perhaps the General had brought Ulla for his keen sight. Suddenly, the boy pointed at a line of deep shadows a bit west of south. "There, sir."

Klamath straightened in his saddle, squinted where Ulla indicated. Peering in that direction, King Bifalt saw movement.

The First Captain's company, his own soldiers and the men he had been sent to reinforce, made a deeper blot in the depths of the shadows. There should have been more, but the raiders and the smoke had killed too many. Without the Magisters of pestilence, many more would have died.

As the riders emerged into a swath of sunlight, Klamath released a long sigh. In a low voice, he asked, "Can you count them, Ulla?"

As if he feared a reprimand, the boy murmured, "Not yet, sir."

Ulla's tone caught King Bifalt's attention. For the first time, he looked at the boy closely. To save his own life, Klamath would not have reprimanded an honest boy. Whatever Ulla feared, it was not his General's disappointment. Yet he sat too stiffly behind Klamath. His face wore the twisted expression of a child who was trying not to cry.

The sight gave Bifalt an unexpected pang. There were already too many children with good reason to cry in Belleger and Amika. When Rile's armies came, there would be far more.

Chewing his cheek, he watched the company below him.

It came slowly. For the sake of men who had to be bound in their saddles, King Bifalt expected the riders to keep a gentle pace; but their caution seemed excessive.

Then he saw that they were dragging a travois.

His mind raced. A travois? The company had brought someone who could not be tied onto a horse. Not poisoned, then. Injured—but still alive.

The King could not wait longer. Sternly, he nodded at Klamath. Together, they nudged their mounts down the slope. The bodyguards followed.

They closed the distance at a hard canter. Along the way, Bifalt noticed Ulla again. The boy was not sitting stiffly now. He squirmed against Klamath's back as if he ached to drop to the ground and run.

As Matt's soldiers rounded a hill into sunlight, the King and General Klamath halted in front of them.

From his saddle, King Bifalt scanned the riders. Their losses had been severe. Among the survivors, at least a dozen men sprawled on their mounts' necks, kept in place with ropes. Several of the others were pallid and sweating, unsteady in their seats. The Magisters of pestilence, Bellegerin and Amikan, stayed near them.

The remnants of Master Ungabwey's caravan were soldiers, as Bifalt had assumed. They were easily identified. Their garments were torn, stained with sweat, and filthy. They must have worn themselves to shreds searching for survivors in the ruins of the caravan. Some of them had been hurt, no doubt by falling rocks, or by falling themselves. The King saw a broken arm here, a gashed forehead there; other wounds. In one way, however, they had fared better than the First Captain's riflemen and the soldiers Matt had been sent to reinforce. They did not look like men who had learned to fear the air they breathed.

Bunched together on their mounts in front of King Bifalt, Matt's command formed a frightened, flinching wall. He could not see the travois or its burden.

He expected General Klamath to address his returning soldiers at once. Instead, Klamath gave his first attention to Ulla. He pulled the boy around him, held him so that they sat face to face. "Hear me, Ulla," said Klamath as if he did not see the fear in the boy's face. "These will be my last commands. Find your father. He is secured on one of the horses. You will think that he is dead, but he lives. He *will* live.

"Tell him that you both have been released from Belleger's service. You have done enough. You will be given a place together in the Open Hand. Care will be provided. And when he is well enough for a journey, you will return home to Amika."

Ulla did not speak. He stared at Klamath briefly. Then he flung his arms around the General's neck, hugged him hard.

A moment later, the boy was gone, running among the horses to find his father.

Now King Bifalt understood. He had forgotten that Ulla was Amikan; and he could have guessed that Hellick was not the only Amikan Matt had taken with him. Klamath's consideration for his young aide, and for the boy's father, was typical of him. The dampness in his eyes as he sent Ulla away was typical. The King approved. He would have announced the same release and care for the stricken riflemen, but it was not his place to do so. They were General Klamath's to command or set free. Klamath would not forget.

Urging his mount forward, King Bifalt approached the man who had assumed Matt's command, sub-Commander Hellick. At once, the King demanded, "Where is the First Captain?"

Hellick pointed behind him. "There, Majesty."

A short distance away, several soldiers had dismounted to gather around a horse. Carefully, they were untying the ropes that kept Matt in his saddle. As the King approached, they lowered him to the cold ground, stretched him out on his back.

King Bifalt vaulted out of his saddle, strode closer.

He recognized the Magister watching over Matt, a Bellegerin called Solace. He was a tall man with a beard like a spade on his chest, a man worn thin by a hunger that food could not satisfy. His lined face and greying beard showed his years. He seemed to want to speak, but the King's attention was fixed on Matt.

Klamath's old friend lay like a dying man. Clearly, he had not been injured, not cut, broken, or pierced. His breastplate was unmarked. But his throat or his lungs had swollen shut, and the labor of his breathing rasped like agony. His eyes were open, staring at nothing. The dark red of burst blood vessels covered their pupils, their irises. His cheeks and forehead had a parched look that made Bifalt think of fever.

As Klamath arrived in a rush at his side, the King asked hoarsely, "First Captain? Can you hear me? Can you speak?"

Matt flinched weakly. His mouth only moved to gasp for breath.

Magister Solace cleared his throat. "It would be a kindness, Majesty," he said firmly, "to provide a stretcher. I have done what I can, but he was one of the first to breathe the smoke. The men with him then are all dead."

Bifalt wheeled away from Matt. "Spliner!" he snapped. "Boy! A stretcher for the First Captain. See to it!"

"And more for these other men," added the General sharply. "Those who cannot sit their mounts."

At once, both Boy and his father turned their horses; galloped away. Jeck stayed with the King.

The needle in Bifalt's forehead dug deeper. Through the pain, he asked Solace, "Will he live, Magister?"

Solace shrugged. "I cannot say, Majesty. He is strong. I will do more for him. If I can open his throat to swallow broth, he may endure until the poison leaves him. After that—" The Magister hesitated. Less steadily, he said, "But he will be blind. I did not reach him in time to save his eyes."

Bifalt snarled, "Hells!" There was nothing else he could say.

As if to himself, Klamath murmured, "He has a family. A wife and children. They were ordered to leave their home. If they are in the Hand, I will find them. He needs their care."

The Magister nodded. "As you say, General. My Decimate has many uses. Constant care is not among them."

Mentally, King Bifalt slapped himself, trying to restart his mind. He was Belleger's monarch. While he stood over Matt, he inadvertently kept all of the soldiers with him. Too many of them required beds and physicians. The others had earned rest.

He turned to bark orders; but General Klamath forestalled him. "Sub-Commander!" called Klamath. "Leave the rearguard with us"— the survivors of the avalanche. "Release the men who need stretchers. Let them rest here while they wait. The Magisters will watch over them. Take everyone else to the camp. See that they are given what they need."

Hellick's response was prompt. "As you say, General." To his men, he repeated Klamath's orders.

Groaning and muttering, the riflemen obeyed. Most of them shuffled their mounts through the crowd and moved away. Some who had not been exposed to the smoke lowered poisoned men to the earth. Then they, too, headed for the camp.

None of them saluted. Klamath had always discouraged that show of respect. But many of them met King Bifalt's gaze and nodded gravely as they passed. At one time, they may have doubted that the war would ever come. Now they knew the truth. And they had not known that the Decimate of pestilence could heal.

Before the sub-Commander turned away, he assured General Klamath, "I left scouts to watch the raiders. They will warn us if that army's pace increases. I estimate that it numbers close to two thousand men, armed and mounted. A long train of wagons follows them.

"When you decide your response, General, I suggest an attack on that train. The raiders have no other source of supplies."

Klamath took a moment to acknowledge Hellick's diligence. Then he dismissed the sub-Commander. In a short time, only the General, King Bifalt, and Jeck remained with the Magisters and the poisoned men. The remnant of the rearguard waited at a little distance, five riflemen who had walked all the way from the mountains so that their mounts could haul the travois.

Those men stayed where they were. Their exhaustion showed in their faces, their trembling arms and hands. The broken arm and gashed forehead Bifalt had noticed earlier were among them; but none of them were uninjured. They must have spent hours clambering over the debris of the avalanche, heaving stones aside, hoping to find survivors. To ease the strain of their exertions, they had all discarded their breastplates. Without that protection, they had suffered innumerable bruises and contusions. They looked like men who had been beaten by thugs.

King Bifalt still could not see who required a travois.

The Magisters attended their patients as the King and Klamath approached the makeshift carrier. By that sign, Bifalt knew that the travois bore someone injured, not poisoned.

In a moment, the King and Klamath passed Ulla kneeling beside a man stretched out on the dry stubble of the winter grasses. The boy clung to the man's hand. In a low voice, he babbled about everything and nothing: a child trying to reassure his father—or himself. The man's strained gaze never left Ulla's face, but he was too weak to reply.

Cursing privately, Bifalt walked past them.

As he drew near the rearguard, one of them ventured, "We did what we could, Majesty." He seemed to believe that an apology was necessary. "It was not enough. He was badly"—he coughed awkwardly—"well, you will see. I am astonished he still lives."

When the King saw the size of the travois' burden, he began to suspect—

"Jeck," he said under his breath, "we will need more men."

The bodyguard glanced at the travois. "As you say, Majesty." Turning away, he hurried for his horse. In moments, he was pounding up the ridge-side.

"How is it possible?" asked Klamath. "To survive an avalanche—?"

"We uncovered iron in the frame of his carriage," answered the rifleman. "And Tchwee— The interpreter, General. He was *strong*. He must have taken some of the weight. We found him crouched over the master. Mangled almost to pulp. But without him—" The man's voice trailed away.

A few more strides took King Bifalt to the side of the travois. He looked down at the ravaged form of Set Ungabwey.

At the best of times, the caravan-master could hardly stand. He never left his carriage because he could not walk without help. Now he lay as if he were being crushed by his own vast bulk. Both of his legs and one of his arms were badly broken. Shards of bone jutted through the skin. The blood pulsing weakly from his mouth spoke of splintered ribs, suggested pierced lungs or other organs. His heavy flesh slumped to both sides. If it had been softer, it might have dripped off him.

But there was still life in his eyes. Somehow— He needed only a moment to find and focus on King Bifalt.

Like a bubble of blood bursting, he breathed, "King."

Bifalt lowered himself to one knee, leaned over Master Ungabwey. He spoke in a choked whisper. "You tried to save us. You have paid too high a price."

Like a gasp, the fat man answered, "It is nothing." He managed a wet cough to clear his throat. "I expected death. I did not expect to fail."

Through his teeth, Bifalt rasped, "Be still, Master. Keep your strength. Men will come soon. They will bear you more gently. You will have the best care our physicians can give."

If nothing else, they would give him herbs to dull the pain while he died.

With his good arm, Set Ungabwey tried to clutch at King Bifalt, but he was too weak. "Hear me, King." The words came in a rush. "My daughters are safe. In the library. You must save them." Another cough racked his chest. "I am not done."

With that, he closed his eyes as if to seal a promise.

Not done? thought the King. Not *done*? *Look* at you.

He did not believe that the master would live to reach the army's physicians.

Nevertheless Set Ungabwey went on breathing. His heart kept forcing a thin beat of blood from his mouth.

Abruptly, King Bifalt stood. His knees were trembling. He felt unaccountably cold. His hard breathing made gusts in front of his face. Not *done*? Until this moment, he would have sworn that nothing the caravan-master suffered would distress him. His brief encounter with Set Ungabwey twenty years ago, like his exchanges with Tchwee before the caravan departed the Open Hand, had outraged him. Yet now Bifalt wanted to curse the library's Magisters for sending Set Ungabwey to die.

Was this what Third Father meant by *surpassing* himself?

No. Too many more people were going to die, and all of them had a higher claim on King Bifalt's heart than Master Ungabwey.

He had considered himself a hard man. He needed to be harder than *this*.

To Klamath, he rasped, "See to him, General. Tell the physicians to save him if they can. Is he not done? I want to know what else he thinks he can do.

"I must ride."

He meant, I am the King of Belleger. He had to turn his back on men who endured agony and would almost certainly perish because he had chosen to fight the Repository's war.

The General replied with a look of bafflement that quickly became comprehension. "As you say, Majesty." He had his own pains. He recognized them when he saw their signs in his King.

Striding past the rearguard and the Magisters—past men struggling for breath while they waited for stretchers—King Bifalt went to his horse. His bodyguards were gone. He was not encumbered by anyone who might insist on accompanying him. Or arguing with him. As soon as he gained the saddle, he urged his mount to run.

But he did not follow the company of riflemen on their weary trek back to the army camp. Riding the beat of his mount's hooves and the throbbing in his head, he angled eastward up the side of the ridge, heading for the highest crest he could see. From that vantage, he would see anyone who came looking for him. He wanted to be left alone while he tried to master himself.

He had not felt this fragile since Estie's departure—and before that, since the bitter hour when she had confessed her gift for sorcery. She had taught him to fear that he might break.

Not for the first time, he imagined making his last stand against the enemy in Belleger's Fist. He was the King: he belonged there. Let him die in the keep when Rile stormed it. Let the Magisters of the library face the consequences of their disregard. He would be able to say that he had done enough.

Unlike Set Ungabwey—

Bifalt was only considering the idea. He had not reached a decision. But while he rode upward, the notion of a last stand enticed him. It seemed positively luxurious. Especially if he could take hundreds of the Great God's men with him when he died. That was a trick he knew how to play.

Of course, Estie might never forgive him. But she already had a list of perfectly reasonable grievances for which she could refuse to forgive him, if she chose. One more would change nothing.

His people, on the other hand— They would feel betrayed. He was their King—and they would have to go on fighting without him. If he failed them, he would shame his father.

Riding to clear his mind, he looked up at the height he wanted to reach. There he could look down on his twisted fate and try to make peace with it.

Approaching from the opposite direction, a mounted figure reached the ridgecrest ahead of him.

The sun rising behind the figure made him unrecognizable, little more than a silhouette. And Bifalt was still half a league away. Still, something about the vague shape struck him as familiar.

The man on the rise turned his horse, apparently scanning the training-fields, the camp, the sprawl of the Open Hand. Soon his survey brought his gaze in the King's direction.

At once, the newcomer drew his mount to a halt. He seemed to peer downward. With a tentative air, as if he were unsure of his welcome, he lifted one arm and waved.

King Bifalt pushed his horse faster. With every racing stride, he considered possibilities and discarded them. No scout or messenger would arrive from that direction. An enemy? Waving? Nonsense. An emissary? Impossible. The east of Belleger held no one who might send a single rider here.

A random cloud covered the sun. Cold air gusting in Bifalt's face blurred his vision. Pain pounded in his skull. He wanted more speed, but the ascent slowed his mount.

As he closed the distance, the man waiting for him looked more and more familiar.

When he recognized the rider at last, his world veered into a new shape. Between one heartbeat and the next, every dimension and implication of his plight reeled.

The man was Elgart.

THIRTEEN

A MAN RETURNS

King Bifalt surged up onto the spine of the ridge and pounded along it toward the height where Elgart waited.

The man had changed. Bifalt discounted the grime and weariness of hard traveling, the dirt in the creases of the spy's visage, the ominous pallor of the scar that split his face. Elgart could not have arrived after so many days without a long road behind him. He was still the man who had been Bifalt's friend and spy, the man who had goaded Bifalt to surpass himself in the Last Repository.

But his mouth: that had changed. Countless times over the years, Bifalt had seen Elgart smile on one side while he grimaced on the other. Now his lips were a straight line, hard and sure despite his scar. They made him look like a man who had resolved his private conflicts. Whatever he had come for, and why he had come for it now, he was certain of it.

As King Bifalt approached, galloping, Elgart awaited him like a statue, as a man who could not be moved.

The King tested that impression. He did not slow his mount or offer a greeting. Instead, he sped alongside the other man's horse and punched Elgart out of his saddle.

Elgart landed on his back, hit the stony ground with enough force to knock the air out of his lungs. For a moment, he lay stunned. By the time he recovered from the first instant of shock and gasped a breath, King Bifalt was already standing over him.

"You witless son of a bastard!" yelled Bifalt. His fists were clenched as if he meant to beat Elgart senseless. "What *happened* to you? Where did you *go?*

"I thought you were dead!"

Elgart coughed for air. "Majesty." With one hand, he rubbed his chest where Bifalt had struck him. "That is your second blow. The first was harder. You have not been training."

Bifalt wanted to hit him again. To stop himself, he bit down on his fury. "Is that your answer?" he rasped. "After so long, you came back to tell me I have not been *training?*"

"No, Majesty." Elgart shook his head. "It was an observation, nothing more." Cautiously, he raised a hand to ward off a second blow if it came. Then, one muscle at a time, he climbed to his feet. Standing just beyond the King's reach, he lowered his hand. "I came to ask if you trust me."

He sounded as sure as his changed mouth; as uncompromising.

"Trust you?" retorted the King. "I do not *know* you. The Elgart I knew—"

The former spy interrupted him. "Then I will ask my question another way. Will you honor a promise I have made in your name?"

Bifalt could not swallow his ire and dismay. He let out an inarticulate howl. "How can I? I do not know where you went, or why you came back, or what happened to make you leave. I thought you were *dead.*

"Tell me, Elgart," he said, pleading now. "What happened to you? How did Makh take you and twist—?" No words were adequate for the horror of that possibility. *"Explain* yourself. Make sense if you can. I am not Magister Facile. I cannot dismiss sorcery from your mind. Tell me—"

Again, Elgart interrupted. "Majesty." Shadows drifted over the ridgecrest. "Bifalt." He came a step closer. "Listen to me. I beg you, *listen.* I will tell you everything, my whole tale. But first you must *listen.*

"You have no time. Do you hear me? *You have no time.* I must have your answer. They are ready to turn away. I cannot drag them farther with empty words. Do you trust me? Will you honor a promise I made in your name?"

Baffled beyond thought, Bifalt chewed the inside of his cheek and stared. If Elgart had asked about trust and promises before the Archpriest took him, the King would have answered without hesitation. But that Elgart was not this one. Too much had happened. Elgart had changed.

Yet surely the man's essential nature remained? His courage? His quick mind? His loyalty?

King Bifalt owed his friend a debt he could never repay. And his instinctive response was to meet every challenge, especially when he had not chosen it and did not understand what it entailed. Why else had he put aside his loathing for Magisters and Amika and lies by refusing to face Elgart in mortal combat long ago?

"Them?" he croaked.

"I cannot tell you." The King had never heard Elgart sound so earnest. "That condition was demanded of me. I had to convince them that I spoke for you absolutely. That you would honor any promise I made, even when you did not know who it was for or how it would be used."

Bifalt flinched. His world was still reeling. He had nowhere to stand except on Elgart's old friendship.

His voice shook as he asked, "What did you promise them?"

How could he honor any man's word when he did not know what had been offered in his name?

Elgart did not hesitate. "Rifles, Majesty. I promised five hundred. A thousand would be better."

That was a number King Bifalt could spare.

He took a deep breath; held it until he regained his balance. As he released it, he sighed, "Then yes. I will honor it."

An instant of brightness struck Elgart's face as clouds passed beyond the ridge. So quickly that Bifalt could not stop him, he surged closer, flung his arms around his King.

Just as quickly, he stepped back. "Then see, Majesty," he said, almost shouting. "See what I have gained in your name."

At once, he gave a piercing, two-toned whistle. It seemed to echo out over the ridge.

Almost immediately, a rider left the shelter of a lower hill. Cantering, he came straight up the slope.

More men on horseback followed him. Men and women. More and more of them. King Bifalt saw at least fifty. A moment later, fifty became a hundred. Then they were too many to estimate.

Lifting his face to the sky, Elgart yelled, "Allies! I have brought *allies!*"

Another cloud slid over the ridge. As it left, Bifalt realized that the riders were familiar.

They had turbans on their heads, bands of cloth draped with gauze to protect their faces from flies and dust. Their blouses above their scarlet sashes were loose to let their skin breathe. Below the sashes, they wore wide pantaloons tucked into dull black boots. For weapons, they had cutlasses at their hips, bandoliers of throwing knives across their shoulders. Some of them carried short bows, quivers of arrows. Most of the archers were women.

King Bifalt recognized their leader. The man had once been the chief scout of Set Ungabwey's caravan, younger then, but sure of himself despite his marginal grasp of Belleger's language. Twenty years had leathered his cheeks, given him deep squint-lines around his eyes. But the luster of his gaze belied his age. Since Bifalt had last seen him, he had acquired the predatory eagerness of a wolf.

"Hail, Suti al-Suri!" called Elgart. "Hail, horse-warriors of the el-Algreb! You have come because you were given a promise. King Bifalt of Belleger will honor it!"

The former chief scout drew rein ten paces from the King and Elgart. He had at least three hundred warriors with him, and more were coming.

From horseback, Suti al-Suri looked down at Bifalt. "I remember," he said like a man accustomed to being heeded. "Then *Prince* Bifalt. And dying. Now King. We are el-Algreb. We bow to no man." He bared his teeth in a thin smile. "But we meet honor with honor."

Bifalt needed to steady himself. He widened his stance, forced his shoulders back, lifted his chin. With an effort, he forced words past the tension in his throat.

"Elgart called you allies. Did you come to fight for us?"

"For you?" snorted Suti al-Suri. "No. We come for sticks with lead arrows. You call rifles. Elgart promised." This time, his smile was a grin of pure relish. "But you give, we fight where you ask, when you ask. El-Algreb *fight*."

With one fist, he punched the air. As one, the riders behind him gave a bloodthirsty howl.

The last of them had caught up with the others. Simply because Elgart had mentioned a number, Bifalt guessed that the spy had brought five hundred horse-warriors.

If he had brought fifteen hundred, they would still be no match for Rile's host. But they were far more than Belleger's King had dreamed of getting.

While the riders gathered, Elgart came casually to stand with his King, showing the el-Algreb where his loyalties lay.

"Then, Suti al-Suri—" began the King. But he stopped when he heard galloping hooves. Glancing over his shoulder, he watched General Klamath arrive.

At the last moment, Klamath flung himself out of his saddle and strode to King Bifalt's side. The look of joy he flung at Elgart was as vivid as a shout; but for the occasion, he swallowed his impulse to greet his old friend. "Your absence was noted, Majesty," he murmured. Then he addressed the former chief scout.

"Suti al-Suri, I am glad to see you." He showed his pleasure with a brisk bow. "You saved our lives twenty years ago. You may be able to save us again.

"Will you dismount? I am General Klamath. I command King Bifalt's soldiers. He must have offered you the best welcome we can manage, but I want to welcome you as well. Only tell me what you need, and I will find a way to provide it."

The King confirmed Elgart's promise. "They need a thousand rifles, General. With ammunition and training.

"Also, they must be ready in two days." Hegels believed that Rile's host would reach the Open Hand in four. If the raiders from the south quickened their pace, they could strike in three. "You will be busy."

Then he added for Klamath's sake, "But you will hear Elgart's account of himself when I have heard it." Half the people in the Fist would want to hear it. Howel, who had taken Elgart's place as the King's spy, would be delighted. "If he claims that he is tired of explaining himself, you can put him in chains until he satisfies you."

At the promise of a thousand guns, Suti al-Suri grinned again. Each of his warriors would have two in case one failed. He swung out of his saddle and dropped to the ground. Sure of himself, he came forward. His people stayed astride their mounts.

To the King, he said, "Elgart say call you 'Majesty.' Silly word. I call you 'Brother.'" To Klamath, he announced, "I call you 'Sister.'"

Without success, Elgart tried to stifle a laugh.

The General looked nonplussed. However, he was too good a soldier to falter. "And you, Suti al-Suri?" he countered. "What should I call you? Do you have a title among your people?"

"Title?" Over his shoulder, Suti al-Suri unleashed a spate of words in his own tongue, a rush of language like a tumbling stream. His people responded with a scattered guffaw, sharing a joke that King Bifalt missed. Facing Klamath again, the man answered, "I call Suti al-Suri. For convenience"—his sudden grin made him look almost boyish—"you call Suti al-Suri."

Reflexively, the King scowled. For convenience— The man must have learned that phrase from Tchwee.

General Klamath managed a smile. "Suti al-Suri, then." Under the circumstances, he could ignore incomprehensible jests at his expense. "If you will follow me, I will take you to the camp. While we get you settled—tents, beds, food, care for your horses, whatever you need—I will send men to gather rifles and bullets. That will take some time. But later this afternoon, this evening at the latest, my riflemen will be ready to teach you how to handle the guns. Tomorrow, you can start learning to shoot.

"It is a skill, Suti al-Suri. It takes practice. And shooting from horseback is a rare skill. You will *need* practice."

"Ha!" snorted the man proudly. "Brother says two days. El-Algreb master *rare* skill in one. Then we fight."

Klamath masked his skepticism with another bow. His face hid a jest of his own as he gathered his mount's reins and stepped up into the saddle.

King Bifalt agreed with his General. Firing a rifle was not as easy as Suti al-Suri imagined—especially from horseback. Bifalt himself had needed seasons to acquire his modest skills. But he said nothing. His world had changed, and his mind was racing. His whole view of the coming struggle took on new dimensions. It required different plans.

His dream of a last stand left him. The coming of the el-Algreb dismissed it. He had more to do.

Without haste, Suti al-Suri vaulted onto his horse. As the el-Algreb nudged their mounts to follow General Klamath, Bifalt said, "One question first, Suti al-Suri." Brother? Hells. "The Repository must have asked for your help." Those Magisters had known the el-Algreb for a long time. "Did you refuse them?"

He meant, Why? The warriors would not be here if they had not refused the library.

Suti al-Suri tossed his head disdainfully. "Those folk mighty," he sneered, "but they promise nothing el-Algreb want. We come for rifles."

Leading his people, he rode past the King and Elgart.

As the leader—the chief warrior?—passed, Elgart told King Bifalt softly, "His people have a word for him. Amandis translated it for me. It means, 'Foal of two mares.'"

"And *that* means?" asked Bifalt.

Elgart shrugged. "You can guess as well as I can, Majesty. Perhaps it means he loves a fight only as much as he loves his people."

To his surprise, King Bifalt found he was starting to like Suti al-Suri: another man with a divided nature. Bifalt wondered if the chief warrior's bravado masked an anguish to match his own.

Probably not. Suti al-Suri was too sure of himself.

King Bifalt let the question go. Changes and possibilities clamored for his attention. And Elgart had mentioned Amandis—

"Ride with me, Elgart," he said with something like his usual severity. "We can leave the el-Algreb to Klamath. Tomorrow we will see how quickly they learn." And by then, new reports would come from the west and the south, fresh estimates of the enemy's progress. "Now I want to hear your tale." He meant, *Right* now. "If we go slowly, you will have time to explain yourself."

Elgart replied with a wry grimace that made him look more like himself. "As you say, Majesty." When he had retrieved his mount, he added, "But I must warn you. Only the devotees can explain themselves. They left me no choice. I did nothing except give your word."

He sighed. "I was away too long. I hardly believed my own promises. If the el-Algreb had not been familiar with the devotees, I would have had no credibility at all."

King Bifalt kept his mouth shut until Elgart was seated in his saddle. Quickly, he mounted his own horse. After that, he was done waiting.

"Now, Elgart," he demanded. "Your tale. If I do not hear it soon, I will find a way to torture you."

Elgart cackled a short laugh. Then he began.

While King Bifalt and his former spy walked their mounts toward the Open Hand and Belleger's Fist, Elgart talked.

As Elgart told it, his tale was simple. The Archpriest had mastered his mind, rendering him helpless. Then Amandis and Flamora had intervened. They left the Open Hand with Elgart and Makh, imposing sleep on their captives with drugged wine. Days later, they allowed the former spy and the Archpriest to awaken. Amandis killed Makh. The cross that enabled him to draw on his Great God's sorcery was destroyed.

That power was a form of compulsion. Elgart had never experienced anything like it. Even the devotee of Spirit had failed to refuse it.

There King Bifalt wanted to interrupt. Why did they force you to sleep? You could have aided them. Muttering curses to himself, he allowed Elgart to continue.

When Elgart was able to ride, Amandis and Flamora separated. With all of the devotees of Flesh who had left the Open Hand, Flamora went her own way. Amandis took Elgart into the distant south beyond the Realm's Edge. There they met and argued with the el-Algreb. Elgart had made his promises. Enticed by the prospect of rifles, Suti al-Suri and his horse-warriors followed Elgart back to Belleger.

At that point, Elgart had said enough. He fell silent, waiting for King Bifalt's questions.

In the distance below the ridge, the training-fields were in turmoil. The passing clouds, light and shade, made the exercises Prince Jaspid devised look like chaos. But the soldiers responded quickly to Boy, Spliner, and sub-Commander Hellick. They scrambled for litters while the physicians gathered. With the Prince among them, riflemen and healers ran to aid the First Captain's wounded.

General Klamath's arrival with the el-Algreb was another matter, unexpected and unexplained. Descending the slope at an easy canter, they reached the open ground in front of the command tent soon after the company from the south. Their coming caused a rush of confusion. But the General had a voice that could reach the outskirts of the city, when he chose to use it. He did not tolerate hesitation. Within moments, riflemen were running to prepare accommodations and food for the el-Algreb. From Elgart's side, King Bifalt watched the General delegate half a dozen new duties, then gather a company and ride toward Belleger's Fist, where the rifles were stored.

"Do not misunderstand me, Elgart," said Bifalt roughly. "I am glad you were rescued." He did not mention what his friend's disappearance had cost him. "But you should not have needed to flee the city. Help me understand why Amandis and Flamora did not bring you to me when you were safe. I would have sent you to the el-Algreb at once. I would have honored any terms you chose to offer."

Elgart grimaced awkwardly. "At once, Majesty? The devotees did not think so. They did not know what harm Makh might have done to me. They did not know how long his power would hold. And when they had stunned and drugged him, they could not allow him to awaken. If he did, he would summon every priest in the Church against them.

In addition, they believed that your need for allies outweighed your desire to approve of their decisions. For Belleger's sake, they left the city in haste, and in secret."

Before long, a train of carts left the camp, following General Klamath. They would be needed to transport a thousand rifles from the storerooms among the foundations of the Fist. Later, they would be used to bring the crates of ammunition; but the bullets could wait. Simply having rifles in their hands would content Suti al-Suri and his horse-warriors, at least for a while.

"And there is this to consider," continued Elgart. "Amandis and Flamora did not know how the el-Algreb would respond. Those people had already refused the library. They might refuse me as well. Even the offer of rifles might not sway them.

"Your plight then would have been cruel, Majesty. You would have lived and made your plans and fought on false hopes until I returned. The devotees considered your ignorance a lesser evil."

King Bifalt suppressed an impulse to argue. He could not hold Elgart accountable for the reasoning of the devotees. Instead, he asked a harsher question.

"Do you know that Jaspid was on your trail? He might have caught up with you." The sight of Jaspid's injuries never left Bifalt. "But Lylin stopped him. She beat him almost to death. No one else could have survived her savagery."

Shock twisted Elgart's split visage. "I am sorry to hear it, Majesty." He needed a moment to compose himself. "I did not know. Amandis said nothing. She told me only that she feared any delay."

Fuming, the King looked away.

Below him, Set Ungabwey and the rearguard reached the camp at last. Spliner had taken eight strong riflemen to carry the fat man. Using the travois as a litter, they bore the caravan-master gently over the ridge and across the training-fields toward the physicians and the hospital. King Bifalt expected to see some sign that Master Ungabwey had died at last. But the frantic gestures of the carriers and physicians indicated that Set Ungabwey was still alive.

He might yet get his chance to show King Bifalt that he was *not done.* The King already had an idea about that. Despite his concentration on Elgart, his thoughts hurried in the background. New possibilities forced him to reconsider his plans.

He had one more question for his friend.

"The way you tell your tale," he said more calmly, "Amandis and Flamora managed your escape together. They were together when Makh revealed his power, and his instrument of sorcery was destroyed. But then Flamora and the devotees of Flesh rode away. Why did they leave us? Where did they go?"

He meant, We needed them. They had worked small miracles to keep the peace in the Open Hand.

To the King's surprise, Elgart laughed. "To make babies, Majesty," he said. Then he forced himself to answer seriously. "They know that Rile's war will not end with the library. It will go on until he has crushed all resistance. No homeland on this continent is safe, not even a land as distant and well defended as the home of the devotees and their men.

"The devotees of Flesh do not fight. They will do what they can for their people in another way. With children, Majesty. Rile's tyranny may take years to reach them. When he comes, the devotees believe that they will need more than their own abilities to preserve them as a people.

"If the library falls, that is their *only* hope. They are needed here, yes. But they have cause to fear the enemy's sorcery. I cannot begrudge any devotee her determination to preserve her own people if she can."

King Bifalt chewed on this explanation for a moment. Again, he wanted to argue. To his way of thinking, the devotees could do more for their people by supporting *him* now. However, they were not here to hear him.

Instead, he told his friend, "I accept what you say. If you can make your peace with their choices, I will try to do the same. But one thing I do not understand. Amandis and Flamora were traveling with Set Ungabwey's caravan. They left it suddenly—and just as suddenly, they reached the Church of the Great God in time to save you. How was *that* done? They are not known for sorcery. How could they have guessed that you would be in danger while they were days away from the Open Hand?"

"They did not, Majesty." Elgart's good humor took on a rueful cast. "Amandis lacks a forthcoming nature, but she answered that question while we traveled.

"When she and Flamora learned that the el-Algreb had refused Magister Marrow, they determined to intervene. They joined the caravan to reach Belleger's Fist and you. At that time, they hoped to persuade you to send me with Amandis to the el-Algreb.

"But on the road through Amika, they encountered a company of Queen Estie's honor guardsmen. From those men, they learned of her father's treachery, her father's use of Nuuri slaves. Then they knew that events were moving faster than they had supposed. They left the caravan to travel more swiftly.

"On the outskirts of the Open Hand, other devotees of Flesh shared what they knew of the Church and its doings. And soon Amandis and Flamora heard that I had gone to the Church alone. They came to my aid as quickly as they could."

Elgart sighed. "In the Last Repository twenty years ago, Majesty, they declared that they would stand surety for me. Now they have done so."

The King was not entirely convinced. The timing seemed unnaturally fortuitous. But he did not contest his friend's account. It was enough that Amandis and Flamora had found Elgart before the Archpriest broke him.

He had one last question.

"Then I confess I am in the most holy assassin's debt. Again." Long ago, Amandis had gone against Magister Marrow's wishes by telling Bifalt that the library had enemies. "Where is she now?"

Had she returned to the Repository? Would she be there for Estie?

"With her people," replied Elgart. "She trusted you to honor my word." He sounded sure. "Majesty, she believes in you. She does not say so. Her actions show it."

Well. To that, King Bifalt had no response. Tugging on his mount's reins, he turned his descent from the ridge to pass around the training-fields instead of heading into the camp.

"Come, Elgart. We will leave all those men to Klamath." He gestured at the crowds below him. "He will tell the horse-warriors whatever they wish to know. We cannot ask them to fight if they do not understand our straits.

"I must return to the Fist. If we take the long way around, I will have time to relieve *your* ignorance."

At that, Elgart grinned with his whole face. "That will please me, Majesty." He brought his horse to King Bifalt's side. "I am starved for tidings."

Belatedly, Bifalt noticed that his headache was gone. Somehow, Elgart's return had banished it. He found himself sitting straighter. His friend's attitude seemed to make him taller. That unconflicted grin was new, but the man's curiosity was familiar of old.

"Three armies, Elgart," he began. "Not one or two. We face *three*." Then he spent their ride around the fields into the city answering the questions that Elgart would have asked if he had known to ask them.

But the King said nothing about Estie.

Before long, they passed into the outer regions of the Hand. When the King had satisfied his friend's hunger for news and explanations, he halted his horse. He had exhausted his tolerance for rehearsing the past. Now Belleger's future called to him. His world had been altered. He needed time to consider it.

"I will leave you here, Elgart," he announced. "You are weary, I know. But before you find a bed, I must ask you to seek out Howel." The man had lost the woman he loved. "He has done what he can in your place, but he believes it is not enough. Your return will relieve him."

Elgart accepted the command with a nod. "And then, Majesty?"

"Then?"

"When I have rested. How can I serve you?" Wryly, he observed, "You no longer need spies. What else can I do?"

King Bifalt did not hesitate. "Help Prince Lome. I have asked him to command the evacuation of the Hand, but he does not trust himself. Or perhaps it is me he does not trust. Malder accompanies him, but his doubt remains. Your presence may stiffen his spine."

Familiar Elgart pulled up one eyebrow, dragged down the other. "Is he drinking, Majesty?"

"Yes," sighed the King. "But not as much as I expected." More firmly, he declared, "He can do this. Despite his fears, he remains our father's son. Still, I hope to reassure him."

Elgart nodded again. "Easy enough, Majesty. With my weapons, perhaps?" He allowed himself a wistful moment. "I have been naked without them too long." Then he grinned. "I am an amiable man, as you know, Majesty"—a characteristic jest—"but I can summon a look of ferocity for the Prince. Leave him to me."

The King started to thank his friend, but Elgart stopped him. "Does my return please you, Majesty? My pleasure is greater. Ask me to name another monarch who would trust his people to Prince Lome, and I will show you Amika's Queen. There is no one else."

Assuming a jaunty air, he turned his horse and trotted away. Despite his long absence, he probably knew exactly where to look for Howel.

Above the King, broken clouds still slid over the city, shedding their ambiguous omens of light and shade. But in the east, the shadows were darker under a thickening cloudbank. The touch of the breezes made him think of snow.

More snow might be good. His people knew the city. Rile's forces did not, despite what they had learned from those treacherous priests. A heavy snowfall would hamper them.

Prodding his horse into motion, King Bifalt headed for the old city and Belleger's Fist. He wanted to be alone in his rooms so that he could think.

When he reached his quarters, however, he found Prince Jaspid waiting for him.

Belleger's best fighter was in a state of high indignation. As soon as Bifalt entered, he demanded, "Elgart? With allies? Did you know of this, Bifalt? Why did you not tell me?"

A fire had been left burning in the chamber's hearth, but the air was still cold. Bifalt had left one window open. He had been warm enough earlier. Now he felt the chill. Clearly, the Prince did not.

The King was in no mood for accusations. He matched Jaspid's tone.

"You forget yourself, Brother. You know me better than that. Until Elgart returned, I believed that he was dead. For reasons of their own, Amandis and Flamora rescued him from the Archpriest." Jaspid would know those names. Bifalt had spoken of them often enough. "For reasons of their own, they took both him and Makh out of the city. For reasons of their own"—the idea still made him want to spit—"they did not condescend to let us know what they did, or why."

Deliberately, he thwarted Jaspid's ire. "It may interest you to know that Lylin aided them." Any mention of her took precedence in Jaspid's attention; but the King did not pause. "When she opposed your search for Elgart and the Archpriest, she did so to prevent you from hindering them. Your visit to the edges of death enabled their flight.

"They are like that, Brother. They did not concern themselves with the effects of Elgart's disappearance."

Jaspid stared as if he had been slapped. "But why—?" he began. He swallowed hard. "Why did she fight me? She could have stopped me with a word. An explanation."

"Could she?" countered Bifalt. "Would you have stopped? You have been in awe of her since you saw her fight. You have ached for someone to best you. A teacher? A test for your own skills? Did she half-kill you because you would not accept anything less?"

That was a new thought for the Prince. It silenced him. He was not inclined to question himself. He never hesitated. His certainty served him well in combat.

Bifalt knew the truth, if Jaspid did not. He had never seen Jaspid happier, or more at peace, than he had been lying in the army hospital, too badly broken to move.

Sighing, the King turned his back. Moving to the small table beside his desk, he filled a goblet with water from the flask there and drank it all. When he had refilled the goblet, he carried it with him to the nearest chair and sat down. While he waited for his brother to speak, he drank again until his goblet was empty. As he set it down, he gestured for Jaspid to sit.

For a moment, the Prince remained standing. Without meeting Bifalt's gaze, he admitted, "You ask a hard question, Brother. I cannot fault her. The fault must be mine." Abruptly, he shook himself, loosening his shoulders, flexing the tension out of his arms. When he had recovered his familiar relaxed poise, he faced Bifalt with a rueful grin. "I do not regret it. She gave me the best test of my life."

Still grinning, he took a seat.

"I have a hard question for you, Brother," he said at once. "But first I must ask what you know of these el-Algreb. It is good to have allies, but they are too few to discourage the enemy. Our three enemies," he amended. "How can they serve us?"

The King shrugged. "They are warriors—and they covet rifles. That is as much as I know." After a pause, he added, "At one time, their leader, Suti al-Suri, was the chief scout for Set Ungabwey's caravans. But my encounter with him was brief. I do not know him now."

"Then what will you ask him to do?"

"That is a hard question." The King had an answer, but he was reluctant to say it. It had too many flaws. For Jaspid's sake, however, he forced himself to reply.

"I hope to send him against the raiders, but his bravado troubles me. He believes that his warriors can learn the use of rifles in two days. That is nonsense. I might enjoy seeing them fail. To my cost, I need them to succeed. If they cannot use their guns well enough, they will not slow an army of at least two thousand men."

The Prince nodded slowly. "I have heard the Second Captain's reports. We cannot stand against the force that Rile has brought against us. If the raiders strike us at the same time—"

He let that idea hang. His frown emphasized the smolder in his eyes. "The el-Algreb are a hard question. I have a harder one.

"What do you want *me* to do?"

Before Bifalt could stop him, Jaspid went on, "I am wasted here, Brother. You know that. Let me fight. Send me with the el-Algreb. I can improve their skills with rifles while we ride. Or send me to Hegels. He will have a use for me. Or—"

The King interrupted him. "Enough, Jaspid." He raised his fists to show that he was serious. "I have a worse task for you."

At once, the Prince stilled himself. He looked as ready as a coiled snake.

Ah, hells. Bifalt did not want to say this. But it had to be done. Jaspid needed it.

"You will think me selfish," rasped King Bifalt. "I will be reckless with my life when Rile comes. I mean to be *very* reckless. But I cannot do what I must if you are not with me. I want you to keep me alive." He spoke softly, but his voice was hoarse with passion. "*I* will test you, Brother. No one else can do what I ask of you. Keep me alive."

The Prince had an open mien. His emotions showed in the muscles around his eyes, the line of his mouth, the clenching of his jaws. Bifalt saw his struggle. Jaspid burned to fling himself into the nearest melee. At the same time, he could not refuse his King's demand. His task as King Bifalt's guardian might call on his absolute best. Or it might require him to simply stand there while Bifalt gave the orders for battle. If he had been a man who trembled, his hands would have betrayed that weakness.

Again, he looked away. He did not reply until he had risen to his feet. Then he said as if he were speaking to the far wall, "You know that I will do what I can. You are Belleger's heart. It cannot withstand the enemy without you."

He had nothing more to say. Turning sharply, he went to the door and left.

Finally, King Bifalt was alone.

For a time, his brother's straits lingered, leaving him too restless to think. He trusted Jaspid's balance. The Prince would not falter when his King needed him. On one point, however, Jaspid did not know his brother. Bifalt might be Belleger's heart, but he had too little of his own. Estie had taken most of it with her.

Nevertheless brooding was an indulgence he could not afford. El-gart's return with the el-Algreb had altered his own straits. He needed new plans, or better ones, to take advantage of the gift that Amandis and Flamora had arranged for him.

There was no help for it. He would have to send the horse-warriors against the raiders from the south. Belleger's army could not fight two armies at once. Perhaps the el-Algreb would have some success even without the skills their new rifles required. And if they failed in the end, they might slow the raiders enough to give Bifalt or General Klamath the time they would need to adjust their own forces.

In the meantime, the King could imagine a way to improve his dream of a fatal last stand in Belleger's Fist. It did not *have* to be fatal— if he was clever enough, and could make the necessary preparations in time. That would force Rile to adjust his own plans for the destruction of the city. At the same time, it might give Bifalt a tactical advantage, one that he had not foreseen in his long discussions with Klamath.

King Bifalt had to review his decisions with General Klamath. He also had to talk with the chief horse-warrior. And, perhaps, with Set Ungabwey. He needed their help to evaluate the prospects that shimmered in his mind like miracles or mirages.

If Klamath could do his part, and the el-Algreb were as good as their opinion of themselves, and the caravan-master was truly *not done*, Bifalt of Belleger might be able to keep more of his people alive than he would have believed less than a day ago.

FOURTEEN

TWO CRIMES

Queen Estie floated as if she were drowning. She drifted deep within herself, resting in a place as comfortable as a womb. Gentle currents may have shifted her from side to side, but they had no purpose except to soothe and coddle her. Here she had no regrets, and all of her hurts were gone.

Gradually, however, she began to remember. Fragments of the past seemed to rise around her like bubbles. A few of them burst. They urged her to recognize them.

Had she received a blow? Were people dead?

Did she need to awaken?

The currents rocked her more firmly. She felt pressure on her shoulder.

A voice she knew well said, "Majesty." A voice she trusted. "You must awaken." It had the power to compel her. "You have slept enough. Now you are needed."

As she returned to herself, she gasped for breath.

But it was not air she needed. It was courage. The shock of recollection seemed to stop her heart.

Magister Marrow's workroom.

I expect them to die.

A blast that tore apart wood and stone and bodies. A weight crushing her to the floor.

The force of her memories jerked her into a sitting position. Suddenly, her eyes were open. But in the first instants, she saw nothing except

Commander Crayn crouching beside her bed, his hand on her shoulder. A lamp on a nightstand lit his face.

"Majesty," he murmured. "Do not be afraid. You are safe. And healed, if the physicians are not mistaken.

"Here."

Supporting her with one arm, he lifted a flagon of water toward her mouth.

As if by sorcery, the flagon evoked an instant thirst. Trembling, she took it in both hands and drank.

The water was bliss and agony. She had never been so thirsty. Water soothed her distress. Slowly, its freshness restored what she had forgotten. With every swallow, she recalled more pain.

The librarian was dead. One of the Farsighted. Others. She would have died under the rubble of the broken ceiling, but Lylin and then Crayn had covered her with their bodies. Crayn had taken damage that would have ended her.

"Good, Majesty," said the Commander. "Drink it all. I have more."

She did not know why she was so thirsty.

When the flagon was empty, she looked at Crayn. For the first time, she noticed that his eyes held a subtle tint of orange. Perhaps that was why they made her think of sandstone. Words came to her in a rush.

"How badly are you hurt?"

Frowning, he shifted a little away from her. He seemed to consider conflicting answers. Then he removed the support of his arm. With both hands, he opened his shirt.

It was not the fitted blouse he usually wore under his armor. It was looser, more a wrap than a shirt, secured on both sides by ties at the points of his hips. When he unclosed it, Estie saw that his whole torso was wrapped in bandages. They showed no sign of bleeding.

"Broken ribs, Majesty," he said ruefully. "Nothing worse." As he closed and tied his shirt, he added, "The physicians are remarkable. And the shamans. It will be a few days before I can swing a sword. But I can hold my rifle."

She put her hands on his shoulders, drew him closer. Fearing to cause him pain, she did not hug him. "Crayn." Memories and lost peace tightened her throat. "You saved me."

He looked away, cast half of his face into shadow. "The devotee reached you ahead of me. At first, I was ashamed that she took my place. Now I am glad. That weight of stone and timbers— You needed both of us."

"Here." He withdrew from her clasp to refill the flagon. "Drink again. You also were injured, Majesty. There was bleeding from your mouth. The healers feared some inward hurt. The shaman performed a strange ritual. The physician made you sleep. Now you must drink."

Estie lifted the flagon, took a few more swallows; accepted the pain that came with them. Soon she recognized her bedroom in the Last Repository. The door was shut.

"And you watched over me the whole time?"

She meant, When you needed care yourself?

The Commander smiled. "No, Majesty. My men stood shifts at your door while I was given care."

One by one, she put fragments together.

Why was she so *thirsty*?

Cautiously, she asked, "How long did I sleep?"

He looked away again. "Two days, Majesty. It is night again."

Queen Estie bit back her impulse to demand, Why did you allow it? His manner told her that he had more to say. Instead of challenging him, she confessed, "I would have slept longer." Then she asked, "Why did you wake me now?"

"I was commanded, Majesty."

"Commanded?" Who had dared?

Crayn sighed. "Strongly encouraged. They are alarmed, Majesty. They did not expect you to sleep so long. Now you are needed."

Needed? She felt a shiver of anxiety.

Although she had hardly moved, she ached in every joint. The force of the explosion lingered. Unsteadily, she murmured, "Thank you, Commander. I must have needed rest." With an effort, she calmed herself. "But I cannot imagine who here would say that I am needed."

"Magister Oblique, of course." With a touch on the flagon, Crayn encouraged Estie to drink again. "The woman who must now be the librarian, Magister Threnody. Another Magister whose name I do not know. Also, the monk who traveled with us, Third Father. And the devotee Lylin.

"Your sitting room grows crowded, Majesty." While Estie took another swallow or two, the Commander added, "Servants come and go. A few physicians. Magister Avail visited briefly. He came to assure you that his friend would live. He must have meant the hunchback, Magister Rummage. The rest intend to remain until you speak with them."

Gods! she muttered to herself. And she had slept for two days? *Anything* could have happened. There was treachery in the Repository. Magister Marrow might not be the only victim. Or the Farsighted may have seen something dire.

"Then I must go out to them." She pushed back her blankets, looked at herself. She was still wearing the gown she had chosen for her meeting with Magister Marrow. It was filthy now, clotted with dust, gunpowder residue, and blood that may have been hers or anyone's. "I need clothes, Crayn."

He nodded. "That is your only gown, Majesty. Your other garments are riding attire. But they are clean. While you empty that flagon"—he nodded to encourage her—"I will set out apparel. Then I will reassure your visitors while you dress."

With her consent, he crossed the room to a cabinet and opened it to select an outfit.

Cautiously, Estie swung her legs over the edge of the bed and stood.

Her joints were more than stiff. Every muscle felt crushed. The sudden jolt of pain left her light-headed. But as she forced herself to stretch, the sharpness receded to a more endurable ache. Drinking the last of the water cleared her head.

"I need to bathe," she told Crayn. She seemed to have grit and gunpowder ground into her skin. "Tell our visitors that I will be quick."

The Commander smiled. "As you say, Majesty." Moving a little stiffly himself, he left the bedroom and closed the door behind him.

The room was cold. Unattended, the fire in the hearth had gone to ash. Shivering, Estie hastened to wash off the worst of the grime and dress.

Magister Oblique had evaded direct questions about the Queen's hidden gift. Magister Marrow had expected her husband and everyone in Belleger to die. Now he was dead himself. There was at least one traitor in the Last Repository. And she was needed?

Gods! She hoped that she had wit enough to meet the challenge. She did not feel ready for it.

When she emerged into her sitting room, she found warmer air. Fire danced in the hearth, and a number of lamps shed their small heat as well as plenty of light.

The people Crayn had listed were all there. Magister Oblique, Lylin, and Third Father Estie knew. And she recognized the small, raven-haired woman, Magister Threnody, who had become the librarian. She felt a sting of dismay when she saw that Threnody was now blind. The woman's eyes resembled Magister Marrow's, milky white without pupil or iris. A consequence of the theurgy that made her intimate with the books and texts? That poor woman—

But Queen Estie shook off her reaction. She had other concerns. There was another individual waiting for her, a Magister she had not met. He was about her height, bald apart from a brush of hair above his forehead, and gaunt to the edge of emaciation. The look in his eyes reminded her of the Farsighted. His gaze seemed to be fixed somewhere else.

Exercising his talent for unobtrusiveness, Commander Crayn stood by the door to her escort's quarters as if he were part of the furniture.

The Queen's visitors had been sitting around the low table with its familiar laden tray; but they all stood as she entered. The devotee of Spirit smiled a greeting without speaking. If she had any worries in the world, she kept them to herself. Habitually humble, the monk watched the floor at Estie's feet instead of raising his eyes. In a soft voice, he said, "You are recovering, Queen. That is good."

"Queen," began Magister Oblique, apparently hurrying to obscure her concern. "I am relieved. We all are. We imagined that you would wake sooner. I wanted to send for a physician, but the librarian dissuaded me." Then she seemed to remember her manners. "You have not been introduced to Magister Marrow's successor, Magister Beatrix Threnody." She turned to the midnight-haired woman. "Librarian, here is Queen Estie of Amika."

Apparently, Magister Threnody did not need sight. Like the monk, she kept her eyes lowered; but the effect was different. Her gaze and her shrinking posture reinforced Estie's earlier impression of her. Her bold sweep of hair made a statement that her manner contradicted. She seemed almost desperately uncomfortable.

"Successor?" she murmured. "Hardly. I have only his awareness of the books. I cannot tell you what he has done, or why, or what must be done now." Briefly, her blind gaze regarded the Queen's face, then dropped again. "I did not choose this."

In a light tone, a singer's voice, the other Magister said, "None of us choose who we were born to be." He spoke as if he were continuing an earlier discussion. "I would have chosen a different gift myself." He made a brief humming sound. "Something less fraught."

"Forgive me, Queen," put in Oblique. "I must also introduce Magister Bleak. As one of the Farsighted, he speaks for them."

Estie nodded. At once, she found that she had many questions for the man. But she schooled herself to wait. Her own situation was fraught: she could not begin by demanding answers.

In a subtle effort to take command of the situation, she seated herself. From the tray, she took a cluster of grapes—and immediately realized that she was hungry. For the sake of her dignity, she forced herself to eat slowly.

With the exception of Magister Bleak, her visitors returned to their chairs. "Queen," he began at once, "I have no tidings for you. I came to express the regret of the Farsighted."

"We have failed the Last Repository." His tone resembled a lament. "If any of us had turned our attention closer, perhaps to the librarian's workroom, we might have seen who planned his death. Then we could have prevented it. But the need for that particular vigilance did not occur to us."

In an angrier tune, he explained, "We hope to make amends. For your sake, and the Repository's, we will attempt to stitch our separate visions into whole cloth. If we succeed, we will be able to relate the movements of the war as they occur. Ideally, all of them. You will know the fate of Belleger"—for an instant, his gaze focused on the Queen as if he recognized her questions—"and Amika. We will see the nature of the Great God's forces and estimate when they will strike.

"Now I will join my kind. When we have something to report, I will speak again."

He gave the librarian a curt bow. To Magister Oblique, he nodded. Ignoring Lylin and Third Father, he went to the door, jerked it open, and left before Estie could gather her thoughts.

Into whole cloth? The benefits were obvious. But she wanted answers *now*.

By the scent of the flask, she knew that it held wine, not water. A little wine might improve her composure. She poured herself a goblet of the ruby liquid, took a small sip, then forgot what she had in her hands.

"Well," she said to her visitors, "that was abrupt." She was only a guest here, but she was still Amika's Queen. Deliberately, she played the part. "He should not blame himself. Treachery is difficult to foresee. That is its nature."

Without pausing, she addressed Magister Oblique. "I am told that you need me. How can I serve you?"

Oblique glanced at Magister Threnody, mutely asking the librarian's consent to speak. When the small woman nodded, Magister Oblique answered Estie.

"You hope that we will send aid to Belleger. We understand. Who would not? King Bifalt fights for us. But Magister Marrow's death—his murder, Queen—raises a more imperative concern. The war is distant. We are threatened *here*. If we do not answer that threat, the Repository may be lost before the Great God can harm it. Your realm and King Bifalt's will perish in a wasted effort.

"We must find Magister Marrow's killer."

Estie raised her eyebrows. "And you believe that I can assist you?"

"If you cannot," countered Magister Oblique, "who can? We do not know how to proceed. Murder is unknown here. We have no experience with treachery. We are fortunate that Magister Rummage lives. He would be our first recourse. But his wound is grievous. He can do nothing until he heals. And he cannot advise us. Like us, he is baffled.

"The most holy devotee Lylin tells us that you have known treachery. We hope that you can guide our search for the culprit. We *must* answer this threat."

Surprised, Estie took a moment to think. Her first impulse was to bargain. Would the Magisters send aid to Bifalt if she helped them? Would they name her gift for her? Almost at once, however, she realized that bargaining would not strengthen her position. The Repository was in too much peril.

Forcing herself, she put her own needs aside.

While her visitors waited for a reply, she remembered the goblet in her hands, took another sip. Temporizing while she considered possible strategies, she said, "I know too little about the uses of sorcery. I have been told that it cannot read minds. Are there theurgists who distinguish between truth and falsehood?"

Magister Oblique spread her hands. "There are, Queen. But what is the use? *Multitudes* live here. How can we examine them all? The enemy will not allow us so much time."

"I see." The Queen nodded. "Then here is another thought.

"Magister Marrow must have spoken with Master Ungabwey. They must have reached some understanding. Why else would the caravanmaster attempt the passes through the Realm's Edge? And it was his custom, was it not, to rely on counselors? Were any of your people present when Magister Marrow spoke with him? They may have heard details that Magister Marrow did not share with you."

The new librarian winced. Both Magister Oblique and the devotee of Spirit looked to Third Father.

The monk cleared his throat. "Yes, Queen," he said carefully. "Master Ungabwey often desired counsel. I have served him in that way. And others—" For a moment, he appeared to lose the path of his thoughts. His gaze wandered the floor. Then he chose his answer. "The most holy devotees Flamora and Amandis were present on that occasion. They are absent now. And I was absent then." With a small sigh, he added, "Fifth Daughter attended Master Ungabwey."

After a pause, he said, "But she cannot aid you, Queen. I have spoken with her. She heard nothing that you do not already know. Only Master Ungabwey's insistence on safety for his daughters was unexpected."

When Third Father was done, silence filled the chamber. Lylin showed no reaction. Magister Oblique nodded as if the monk's reply confirmed her own conclusions. The librarian's eyes betrayed a hint of wildness despite their blindness. She may have been hoping—

Queen Estie drank another swallow of wine. "So," she announced. "We cannot look for help there. I have a better thought."

At once, everyone stared at her. Even Third Father raised his gaze.

"Tell me," said the Queen with an edge in her voice, "how it was done."

Oblique's mouth shaped the word, Done? Magister Threnody gaped like a woman in shock.

"I am familiar with gunpowder," explained Estie. "And I know the smell of fuses. But I cannot imagine how the gunpowder was put in place unobserved. And I truly cannot conceive how the fuse could have been timed and lit so that the explosion would occur when it did, without smoke or smell."

Despite her blindness, the librarian's attention had force. She seemed to think that Queen Estie was poised to produce an appalling revelation.

After a moment, Magister Oblique managed to admit, "Placing the gunpowder would not have been difficult. Magister Marrow was often away from his workroom. And the room has never been guarded. Anyone who observed his movements could have found an opportunity." Her voice faded.

"It is *here*," blurted Threnody. "All of the knowledge is here. In the books. The composition of gunpowder. The making of fuses. The making of fuses that do not smoke or smell." Her eyes flicked from place to place, searching her new memories. "Several texts discuss such subjects. A dozen? Perhaps one or two more." Then her regard snapped back to Estie. "But they are summarized in Estervault's *Methods for Devising and Using Bombs of Gunpowder*. It includes sections on timed fuses. And on ones that give no smell because they do not smoke."

Again, Magister Oblique protested. "But how does that help us? That knowledge is open to all. Only the books of sorcery are kept aside—not to preserve their secrets," she insisted, "but because they are useless to those who lack the necessary gifts. *Anyone* could have read—"

Estie cut her off. Concentrating on Magister Threnody, she inquired, "You know the books, librarian. Do you also know who reads them?"

"Who reads—?" That question struck the woman like a slap. She had inherited Magister Marrow's awareness too recently. "Who *reads*—?

"It is possible," she breathed as if the idea astonished her. It *should* be. If I can remember—" Abruptly, she jumped to her feet. "I must leave you." She smacked her forehead. "There is so *much*— I cannot sort it all. I must have quiet. And time."

Hurrying, she turned to the door.

Deliberately, Queen Estie put pity aside. In its place, she chose a tone of command. "Give me another moment, librarian. I have a second question."

Magister Threnody whirled back to her. "A second?"

"While you search your memories, look also for books of poison."

Oblique surged from her chair. *"Poison?"* she cried. Three steps took her to the librarian's side. She seemed to hover protectively near Threnody. "You ask too much, Queen. Magister Marrow was not *poisoned*."

Estie produced her kindest smile. "But the question may be crucial. It may lead us to Sirjane Marrow's killer."

"How?" demanded Magister Oblique.

"By the simplest means," answered Estie. "For us," she acknowledged, "if not for the librarian.

"Consider this. Magister Marrow's death is not the first attempt at murder in the Repository."

Beatrix Threnody looked like she wanted to weep. The devotee of Spirit smiled happily. Third Father watched the Queen as if he saw something in her that validated him. As if she had begun to surpass herself.

Groping for comprehension, Oblique asked, "Do you speak of Apprentice Travail? He was poisoned. But the shamans restored him. Do you know who poisoned him?"

"Of course not." Estie relaxed her smile. It took too much effort. "I have only"—she hesitated, unsure how to explain herself—"an Amikan way of thinking. What is the likelihood that two such crimes would be committed in so short a time? *After* you learned that Rile's armies are coming? Surely, it is plausible that one traitor attempted both murders?"

"But *why*?" demanded Magister Threnody. "Travail is only an Apprentice. He served us well, but he has no role in our defense. What would a traitor gain by his death?"

"Experience," declared Estie. Then she softened her tone. "Consider it, librarian. He—or she—" She hesitated again. "I will say 'he' for convenience. He desired Magister Marrow's death. He thought of poison. But he had to be sure that your healers could not undo his efforts. As a test, he chose a victim whose death would do harm, but who was not so necessary that the whole Repository would rally against his killer."

"I do not understand," murmured Magister Threnody.

"When his poison failed," concluded the Queen, "he settled on gunpowder."

Lylin nodded. She seemed to approve.

"But what do you want of *me*?" The librarian's voice betrayed her alarm. "Do you expect me to find the killer among Magister Marrow's memories?" She was panting as if the air had been sucked out of the room. "In his awareness of *books*?"

With an effort, Estie assumed her most demure, unthreatening demeanor. "No, librarian. The challenge is not so great. If you can recall who has studied poisons and gunpowder in the past season or two, you will narrow our search. Who has studied *both* poisons and Ester-vault's *Methods*?" She wanted to add, Who studied poisons first, then turned to gunpowder when Travail began to mend? But she hesitated to push Magister Threnody that far. "Among those men and women, you will find your traitor."

Despite his unobtrusive pose, Commander Crayn said distinctly, "Well done, Majesty. I would not have thought of it."

"Nor would I," admitted Magister Oblique. "If this is an Amikan way of thinking, it has much in its favor."

The monk had turned away from Queen Estie. Now he regarded the librarian, probing her with his singular insight.

"But I cannot do it!" said Threnody, almost wailing. "Are you all as blind as I am? So *much* has been forced into me! I can scarcely recall Magister Marrow's reading of *Eighth Decimate*. How do you expect me to—?"

"By calming yourself, librarian." Third Father spoke gently. "You have said it yourself. You need quiet and time. Quiet you can provide for yourself, and time you have. The Great God cannot come against you in an instant. Let Sirjane Marrow's knowledge reach you in its own way. It will come more readily if you calm yourself."

Slowly, Magister Threnody relaxed. For a long moment, she gazed blindly around the sitting room, studying details that Estie could not see. Then she took a deep breath and held it. As she let it out, she said, "Thank you, Father. You are wiser than I."

At once, the monk lowered his gaze.

Again, the librarian headed for the door. She could not see it, but she knew where it was. Before she reached it, however, she said over her shoulder, "The Queen I leave to you, Magister Oblique. Do what you think best."

Lylin rose like floating. "I will accompany you, librarian. I am con-tent with Queen Estie's recovery." She surprised Estie with a bow. "Majesty." Then she ushered Beatrix Threnody away.

The devotee's bow had the effect of validation. Estie could ask her own questions now. Magister Oblique might answer them.

When the door closed, Oblique returned to her chair. "You have shamed me, Queen," she confessed. "I did not see the connection. Two crimes, not one. It seems obvious now, but it eluded me."

Estie shrugged as if she were sure of herself. "It has been too long since you were threatened. The knowledge here is vast, but the Last Repository is a little world. And you are surrounded by people who share your beliefs. In effect, they diminish the *use* of your knowledge. Such wealth should not be hidden away."

Magister Oblique made a vexed gesture. "That is the Great God's doing, not ours. Tyrants drive us into hiding." As she spoke, she grew more heated. "You say we are not threatened. We are *always* threatened, Queen. Tyrants fear knowledge. It is the only true challenge to their rule. If you doubt me, think of your father. Think of what he denied you."

Queen Estie did not pursue the argument. She had gained the opportunity she sought. With her most queenly smile, Estie said, "Then tell me this, Magister. Who chose Beatrix Threnody? Who selected her to be Sirjane Marrow's successor?"

Tripped by the change of subject, Oblique stumbled. "Who chose—? I do not understand you. No one *chose* her. Her gift is an accident of birth, as Magister Bleak said. She has inherited the librarian's knowledge and duties because she was born with the ability to apprehend them."

The Queen smiled more broadly. "Magister Oblique, I begin to suspect that you misunderstand me deliberately. I will ask my question another way. Before he was killed, Magister Marrow knew that she would be his successor. He must have recognized his gift in her. But how did he *find* her? Did he examine everyone? Or was she put forward as his successor? Who knew what she was born to be before *she* did?"

Under pressure, Oblique did not see the trap. "*I* did," she retorted. "That is my gift, Queen. I told her so that she could prepare herself for what was coming. And I brought her to Magister Marrow so that he, too, could prepare her."

To steady herself, Queen Estie emptied her goblet in three quick gulps. With a thump, she set it down on the table.

"Then, Magister, you know the nature of *my* gift. But you have kept that secret from me.

"Will you tell me now? What am I that you did not expect?"

From his place by the inner door, Commander Crayn breathed audibly, "Yes."

Caught, Magister Oblique stared for a moment. Then she gave a short, sardonic laugh. But her brief bitterness was directed at herself, not at Estie. She braced herself on the back of the nearest chair for support.

"No, Queen," she answered. "I will not. But I understand you now. I will tell you what I can."

Estie held her breath.

The sorceress took a moment to compose herself. Then she sighed.

"First, I must ask you to understand *my* dilemma. I did not answer you at once because Magister Marrow forbade me. He believed that your ignorance would serve the Repository in some way. He did the same to Prince Bifalt twenty years ago, and was pleased by the outcome. But Beatrix Threnody is not Sirjane Marrow. When you have been among us longer, you will feel the difference. Already, you have seen that she doubts herself. And Magister Marrow did not teach her to follow his path.

"Now she has left you to me. I will not answer your question"—she tightened her grip on herself—"because the answer is not mine to give. You should hear who and what you are from someone who *knows*. My gift is mere insight. I have not *lived* with your gift. I cannot describe the power and the cost of what you will inherit."

Estie had to swallow hard to hold down her bitterness. She might have spat bile if Magister Facile had not told her something similar. A talent should be awakened by a sorcerer who shared the same gift. There were too many dangers to consider. On that point, the Queen could not accuse Oblique of dishonesty.

But her denied heart needed an outlet. Barely able to rule herself, she asked, "Will you tell me nothing?"

"Queen!" The Magister spoke as if she were flinching. "I have told you that you will not be denied. How have I failed to convince you? But the choice you demand is not easily made. And it is not *my* choice. It belongs to the Magister who shares your gift. I cannot say when you will be answered. I can only promise that you will not be kept in ignorance."

Estie did not know what to say. These refusals and delays seemed intolerable. She held the woman's gaze for a moment longer. Then she looked away. Choking down the congestion in her throat, she asked, "And until then? What must I do while I wait?"

Magister Oblique's sigh sounded like relief. "Of course, Queen, we still hope for your aid in the search for our traitor. But Magister Threnody may require hours or days to search her memories. While you wait, you have the freedom of the Repository. Go wherever you wish. If nothing occurs to you, let me suggest a visit to the library itself. Our books are the prize which the Great God seeks to destroy. It may ease you to know what is at stake."

Again, Queen Estie was expected to put herself aside. What choice did she have? Over her shoulder, she asked, "Commander?"

"I have slept for some time, Majesty," answered Crayn without hesitation. "Walking will do me good." His tone assured her that he was alert to the undercurrents in her query.

Estie nodded. "Thank you, Magister," she replied thinly. "Like my Commander, I have slept too long." And spent far too long waiting passively while crises mounted beyond her reach. "I will take your advice."

The sorceress mustered a smile. "Then, Queen, I will send someone to guide you." She rose from her chair. "With your consent, I will leave you now. *I*," she admitted, "have not slept enough."

"Of course, Magister," replied Estie. But before Magister Oblique reached the door, the Queen spoke again. "I will not wait long. My own need is imperative."

"I understand, Queen," said Oblique ruefully. "You have made that plain."

With that, Estie had to be satisfied.

When the sorceress was gone, Estie found herself trembling. She felt that she had suffered an ordeal and gained nothing. If she had not done so before, she was learning to understand her husband's anger now. The pressure of everything that she did not know, everything she feared, was making her fragile.

She needed to be stronger.

FIFTEEN

THE POWER AND THE COST

Thanks to Commander Forguile's descriptions, Queen Estie thought that she was prepared for the sight of the library itself. Yet when Magister Oblique's guide led her and Crayn onto the central floor of the great keep, she felt a rush of awe. She had entered a place of worship, a tower sanctified by its contents.

So long before dawn, there was no natural illumination. But lamps on the tables and cressets in the walls everywhere gave light. Level after level, the open rounds rose upward, fifteen, no, closer to twenty of them, each made like a balcony. The polished stone where Estie stood held a large number of trestle-tables without crowding—and without obstructing access to the many bookcases set around the walls. No doubt, each round above her held more bookcases. At this hour, none of the Repository's inhabitants were using the space. If there were people on the higher levels, she could not see them. She and Commander Crayn with her guide seemed to be alone in a hallowed space.

Here and above her were books, tomes, scrolls, folios of loose parchment; maps, commentaries, descriptions, primers; works of erudition like Hexin Marrow's sorcerous researches; texts of argument and counter-argument; histories, genealogies, legends, fables, myths. The knowledge of a world.

The Queen's guide was a bright-faced young apprentice named Truly. He was learning to be a scribe, an area of study that he addressed with gusto. Eager to please, he delighted in pointing out bookcases where Amika's Queen might find interesting volumes. The full history of Amika and Belleger, perhaps, including the tale of how they became separate realms? A discussion of the beliefs and customs of the most holy devotees? Or would she prefer the collected writings of the Cult of the Many? There were many. And, of course, texts on every conceivable form of warfare. Then, high on the upper rounds, the library held its vast understanding of sorcery.

There could be no greater task, declared Truly, than the work of the scribes, who labored to preserve the oldest and most decayed documents for the benefit of future generations.

Her guide spoke at length; but Estie ignored him. Instead, she stood where she was, gazing upward with her mouth open. She imagined that the answer to every desire and misery was *here*, available for the simple price of reading.

Truly may have been disappointed by his failure to spark her interest. He could not know that she was already aflame, if not in the ways he anticipated. She burned with possibilities. They were not for her—they might never be for her—but they were *here* nonetheless. If the library endured.

If her husband could save enough of his people, and hers.

If he could save himself.

Finally, Commander Crayn's voice drew her attention down from the riches of the rounds. "Am I permitted," he asked the Apprentice, "to examine a book? Any book that concerns the most holy devotees? I have a particular interest."

He had seen Lylin fight.

"Surely, surely," burbled Truly. "They do no good if they are not read. Will you choose a book yourself? Shall I select one for you?"

"May I take it with me?" pursued Crayn. "I mean to my quarters. I foresee an uncomfortable stretch of leisure. I would like to read in my room."

"Ah." That question stopped the young man. "Well. I—" He consulted the silence of the tower until an answer came to him. "With the librarian's permission, of course. You need only ask.

"The books are not allowed to wander. They are too precious. They are read here"—he gestured around at the tables—"and returned to their places. Only Magisters remove them for private study—and," he added quickly, "the librarian knows what they do." More calmly, he offered, "Shall I inquire for you? I do not suppose that the librarian will refuse."

Crayn patted the guide's arm kindly. "Do not trouble yourself. It was an idle request."

Queen Estie frowned, momentarily confused. Then she caught the Commander's hint. The books were not guarded. Only the librarian watched over them.

In fact, she had not seen any guards since her arrival.

"Truly," she asked, "do books ever disappear?" Texts on poisons, for example. Or on gunpowder and fuses? "Misplaced, perhaps? Or stolen?"

That notion shocked the Apprentice. "Never," he said promptly. "Men and women make mistakes. Even Magisters. But the librarian *knows* what we have—and where it is. That is her gift. A misplaced text can be found with ease. And any book that leaves the Repository can be recovered quickly. Magister Rummage does not hesitate when we are threatened with the loss of a book." After a pause, he admitted, "Or so I am told. I have never heard of that crime."

Estie mustered a smile. "Thank you, Truly. Your time and attention are a gift of another kind. Now, perhaps, you will guide us back to our rooms? We have seen enough for one night."

Her request startled Truly. He must have expected her to share his fascination. But he was too polite to object. Bowing, he ushered Queen Estie and Crayn out of the library.

In the complex of halls, chambers, and stairs which apparently filled the whole mountainside, Estie and the Commander lagged behind their escort. Privately, Crayn murmured, "You were right, Majesty. Peace teaches people to assume peace. This place has no defense against treachery."

Estie nodded. She had already done what she could to aid the search for Magister Marrow's killer. That burden was now the librarian's responsibility. And she, Estie, was still held by her first sight of the library. If Truly led her back to her quarters by a different route, she did not know it.

After a while, however, she realized that dawn must be near. She began to encounter occasional servants in the corridors or on the stairs. One and then another Magister passed her walking purposefully in the opposite direction. A blue-skinned woman clad entirely in feathers fluttered by, apparently oblivious to her own destination. From one chamber, Estie heard a distinct metallic clanking. It was brief, and she did not inquire about it.

Eventually, Crayn remarked, "Almost there, Majesty." With an effort, she looked around. She was in a hall one corner away from the corridor leading to her apartments.

A moment later, she heard a voice. Loud with indignation, a man declared, "This is *intolerable*."

With a flinch, Estie recognized Magister Avail's ire.

At once, the Commander left her side. Striding briskly, he moved ahead of Truly.

Behind her guide, Queen Estie turned the last corner and entered the passage.

It was a long, straight stretch marked by a number of doors, but she knew hers by the two guardsmen standing outside it. They were armed with their swords and daggers, but not their rifles. They may have regretted leaving their guns in their rooms. Estie saw at a glance that they felt threatened.

She understood their alarm. They were facing Magister Avail and Magister Rummage. Every sorcerer they had ever known could have destroyed them with a thought. Nevertheless they stood their ground, protecting the privacy of her rooms in her absence.

She doubted that they had done or said anything to provoke the two Magisters. Their refusal to stand aside was provocation enough.

Commander Crayn was already a dozen paces ahead of the Queen. He was unarmed himself, still wearing the wrapped shirt that covered his damaged chest, but he approached Avail and Rummage as if he had nothing to fear. In a crisp tone, a nice blend of authority and politeness, he asked, "Is there some difficulty, Magisters?"

While the hunchback tapped on the plump, rumpled Magister's forearm, Avail looked past Crayn, spotted Estie. Almost shouting, he called, "This is *intolerable*, Queen."

Crayn stopped directly in front of the deaf sorcerer. "*What* is intolerable, Magister?" he asked without raising his voice. "I ordered my men to guard Queen Estie's rooms until she returned. You cannot fault them for their faithfulness."

One of them give him a quick look of gratitude and relief.

Estie's guide had halted. He seemed confused. As she passed him, the Queen paused long enough to say, "Thank you, Truly. Your task is done. Now I must attend to my own duties." Then she walked on, leaving him to turn and scramble away.

Tightening her grip on herself, she approached the Magisters.

"Queen!" snapped Magister Avail.

She summoned one of her pleasant smiles. "Magister?" He seemed absurdly angry. Since he had stormed away outside the gates, none of his reactions had made sense. In Magister Marrow's workroom, he had given the impression that he was afraid to look at her. "How have I offended you? You cannot think that the diligence of my guards was meant to insult you."

Avail did not wait for Magister Rummage's translation. His voice rode over hers. "I was told to speak with you. I was *not* told that I would be forced to stand here when I could have been comfortable in your sitting room, numbing my pain with wine.

"Is it true? Did you demand my attendance? Then we should have been made welcome."

In the midst of his outburst, Queen Estie's heart staggered as if she had been hit as hard as Magister Facile. The air in the corridor turned grey. It was too thin to sustain her. She seemed to feel all of her blood slump toward the floor. She tried to brace herself on Crayn's shoulder. She lacked the strength to support herself.

Gods! she panted. Not *this*. Please!

Magister Oblique had kept her promise.

Surely there were other explanations? Avail may have brought news from the Farsighted. He had brought Magister Rummage to tell him what she said. Something had happened to Bifalt—

"Steady, Majesty," breathed Crayn in her ear. "Steady."

Her heart beat once. Its force shook her. She felt blood rush into her face. Her chest swelled. The pressure of her pulse made demands that she did not know how to meet.

Nevertheless she was Amika's Queen, daughter of Smegin and Rubia. Her father would have excoriated her for showing weakness. Her mother would have found a kinder way to help her. And she had made all of her choices long ago: all except this one. She had to face it.

Magister Avail had only come to speak with her. If she wanted more, he might refuse. If he offered more, *she* might refuse.

Deliberately, she took one breath, and another, until she was able to stand as straight as any queen.

"Forgive me, Magister." She was trembling, but every breath strengthened her. "A moment of faintness, nothing more." He was not blind. He must have noticed her reaction. "The power of that explosion— I am not entirely recovered."

To Crayn, she said, "Relieve your men, Commander. They have done well. Now I do not need them."

"As you say, Majesty." She heard the concern in his tone, but he did not let the Magisters see any flicker of uncertainty. Calmly, he dismissed the men guarding her door.

They tried to feign dignity as they opened her door, then retreated through her sitting room to their own quarters.

Holding up her head, Queen Estie faced the Magisters. Avail's ire grew, a grenade with a burning fuse. Rummage's black glower may have been meant as a threat, but she ignored it.

Trying for assurance, she said, "I regret my tardiness. I did not know that you would come so soon"—or why they would come. "You are welcome now. I believe there is wine. If you want more, we can summon it."

Followed closely by the Commander, she preceded her visitors into her sitting room.

She was as frightened as her guardsmen had been. She wanted to hasten into her bedroom, no, into her bathing chamber. There she could shut the door and take the time to compose herself. But Amika's Queen could not afford to show fear now. While Crayn moved to his place in the background, she seated herself in a chair facing the outer door. With a gesture, she invited the Magisters to share the remains of her meal and the flask of wine.

They did not enter. Magister Avail stood in the doorway, glaring at her as if the sight infuriated him. Magister Rummage held his deaf companion's hand.

"I saw your fear, Queen," Avail snarled. "You have your answer. If you want to know more—if you are such a fool—I will not come to you again. You must come to me."

He started to turn away. Then he whirled back as if he meant to fling himself at her. His fury filled the doorway.

"You do not know the pain you cause. You should not have brought your demands to me. Your father was a vile man. It was his place to prepare you, not mine. I have suffered enough. I do not deserve this burden.

"But the crime is his, not yours. I will say *this*. Turn your back on sorcery. It is not a *gift*. It is living death! To be so cut off from the world, every voice, every sound, isolated from even the simplest exchanges, unable to comprehend *anything* unless some kind friend shares it by touch—! That is terrible. Your doom will be worse. You will be cut off from *yourself*."

Abruptly, he stopped. Instead, he cried into the silence of Estie's mind, **It is a curse, Queen! Refuse it!**

An instant later, he was gone, taking Magister Rummage with him.

Out in the corridor, the first rush of shock had hit Estie physically. The second was emotional. Sitting in her chair, she filled a goblet with wine and drank it without noticing that her hands shook. She was not aware of herself. Her mind was an empty sheet of parchment marked only by the curse of her inheritance.

Her talent was Magister Avail's. Magister Oblique had sent him to tell her so. His deafness was the cost of his sorcery. He could speak to anyone anywhere, but he could not hear a person standing right in front of him.

She wanted to wail. At one time, she had wished for the ability to cast her voice into distant minds. Now she recognized the folly of that desire.

If she chose her gift, she would never hear Bifalt's voice again. If she refused it, she would have nothing to offer anyone.

Time may have passed. She was vaguely surprised to find Commander Crayn kneeling beside her chair. "Majesty," he said softly. "Estie. I understand as well as I can. It is not enough. Help me understand better."

Estie blinked. Her gaze wandered to her hands. Without realizing it, she had emptied her goblet. She did not know what she would say until she heard herself.

"I do not understand. My gift is a curse." It was worse than her worst fears. "That I understand. But how will deafness cut me off from myself?"

She meant, Can you help me?

Crayn had vowed to protect her. Abruptly, he rose to his feet and stood over her as if he were on guard. She expected him to be kind. Instead, he was stern.

"You are not Magister Avail. He is not Amika's Queen. You do not know who and what he was before he became a sorcerer. His power hurts him deeply. I cannot doubt that. If you accept it, yours will hurt you as well. But will your pain be like his? I do not think so. You are not him. You will not be cut off from yourself unless you allow it."

Estie did not believe him. But perhaps she did not need to believe. Perhaps it sufficed that he did.

Numb and empty, she sat where she was for a long time. The first time that Crayn went to answer the door, he returned with a fresh meal and a flask of water. The second time, he closed the door and turned to face her.

"Majesty," he said carefully, "you have a visitor."

She did not know how to respond. Eventually, she managed to ask, "Who?"

"I do not know him. A young man—well, younger than I am. His tale is written on his face. It is not a happy one. He did not give his name."

She tried to muster a little attention. "Did you ask him what he wants?"

Crayn hesitated, then said, "He hopes that he can ease you."

Estie's tone sharpened. "Did Oblique send him?"

"He did not say so."

She wanted to groan. She could not imagine anything that would blunt the teeth of her dilemma. Nevertheless she replied, "Invite him in." Her voice seemed to come from a distant room. "Let him explain himself."

The Commander gave her a hard look. As if what he saw satisfied him, he nodded. Rising to his feet, he addressed the man outside.

"We do not know you, sir, but you are welcome here. Please enter. Share our meal if you have not eaten. And tell us your name. Queen Estie will hear you."

Cautiously, the man came in. He did not presume to sit. Clearing his throat, he offered, "Queen." Awkwardly, he bowed. "Commander." He bowed again. "I am Apprentice Travail."

Estie needed a moment to recognize the name. Then she had it: Apprentice Travail, Magister Facile's lover before she had come to Belleger. He had been her only link to the Repository while she had aged and he had remained young. Until he had been poisoned—

That blow had broken the old sorceress. The prospect of never seeing him alive again had impelled her to abandon Belleger when King Bifalt needed her most. But Travail had survived. A different kind of blow had killed her.

Caught by what she knew about him, Queen Estie roused herself to look at the Apprentice more closely.

He wore a plain brown robe like the garb of the monks, but he did not resemble them in other ways. The physicians and shamans may have spared him the full weight of his years, but they had not shielded him from the costs of prolonged strain: the disciplined, desperate, endless effort to hear only one voice when thousands or tens of thousands clamored for his attention. While Magister Facile lived, his dedication must have kept him sane. But it had also worn galls as deep as cuts across his forehead, around his eyes, down both sides of his mouth. Now he looked like a man who had just left his sickbed. He made no attempt to conceal his trembling.

Estie saw a piercing woe in his soft eyes. But she also saw courage and kindness as well, the kind of love that would have transformed her if her husband had been capable of it.

Compelled by the debt she owed Magister Facile, Queen Estie rose from her chair. "Apprentice." She felt too weak to answer his bow. "Please be seated. We have food and water. Or wine." By increments, she began to remember who she was. "I grieve for your loss. I knew Magister Facile. On one occasion, she saved my life. At other times, she was my friend."

"Thank you, Majesty," murmured Travail. "You are gracious. But you have your own dismay to consider. I did not come to impose mine."

"Then sit, please," replied Estie. "Hear me a moment longer. Then I will hear you."

To encourage him, she seated herself.

Frowning, Travail nodded. Unsteadily, he moved to a chair across the low table from the Queen and lowered himself into it.

"Apprentice," began Estie, "Magister Facile was on her way to you when her end found her. She did not know that you would live. The thought that you might die without her was too much to bear.

"For her death, I have my own grief—and my own anger. The Great God Rile caused her death. If I had the power, he would answer for that crime."

He lowered his gaze. "Perhaps, Queen." He stilled his hands by clasping them together. "But I have no use for anger. I am content with sorrow."

Estie wanted to ask, Then why are you here? What can you offer that will ease me? But he deserved better courtesy.

"What you have endured humbles me," she said carefully. "I cannot imagine the extremity of your sorrow."

Sighing, he replied, "Facile made it possible. I clung to the one voice I loved most. Without it—" He shrugged as if something deep inside him had failed. "Other voices intrude. Even now, I find it hard to keep them out." He showed Estie a sad smile. "But Magister Avail comforts me. We were kinfolk of a kind, the three of us, the man who cannot hear, the man who hears too much, and the woman who could only speak. Without her—" He spread his hands. "His voice helps me sleep.

"It is not always a shout, Queen. It can be a caress. And it fills my mind until I am able to rest. Every night—"

He stopped as if he had said enough. After a moment, he explained, "I am here to speak of him, Queen. And for him."

Startled, Estie asked too sharply, "Of Magister Avail?" She had not forgotten his attempt to comfort Facile with news of Travail's recovery. "Then do so, Apprentice."

Travail met her gaze. "His manner is difficult. No one can say otherwise. It is a consequence of his deafness. His isolation galls him. How can he suffer his loneliness if he does not rail against it? But he knows himself. He knew he would botch—" Again, he smiled sadly. "I like that word. Botch. He knew that he would botch speaking with you. He told me as much.

"I came to say what he cannot."

Wondering, Estie inquired, "Which is?"

The Apprentice held her gaze.

"Magister Avail has a heart. Magister Marrow did not. He could not afford it. But Magister Avail does. Your plight appalls him. He is furious that you of all women, the Queen of Amika, are afflicted with his gift. His heart is speaking when he urges you to refuse it.

"Nevertheless he knows what he can do. He knows that what *you* can do may be needed before the end."

For a long moment, Queen Estie was silent, groping for a response. At this moment, the deaf man's capacity for thoughtfulness gave her no comfort. She did not know how to make the choice that her circumstances demanded.

Despite his weariness and woe, Travail said as if he were sure, "I can help you."

Her voice caught in her throat. Hoarsely, she asked, "How?"

He did not look away. "You know that Magister Rummage repeats what he hears for Magister Avail. I can teach you his code of finger-taps. You and your Commander. It may serve you. You can use it to measure the cost of your gift."

Estie froze. The Apprentice seemed to assume that she would claim her inheritance. His offer brought back her initial shock, her desire to protest. And yet—

While she remained stuck, Travail said, "It is as fluent as speech, Queen. It requires skill, nothing more. We relied on it, the three of us: my love, Magister Avail, and I. Magister Rummage brought it with him to the Repository. It is his, but others have learned it. Magister Oblique. Third Father. Several more. For those who cannot hear, deafness is not always isolation."

He hesitated briefly, then added, "I do not presume to know your heart, Queen. But I believe that knowing this code will ease you while you wrestle with your dilemma."

She felt unable to think. Travail's offer was too intimate. It asked her to set aside her fears. As if she were helpless, she turned to the Commander. "Crayn? What are your thoughts?"

She meant, Tell me what to do. But she could not expect him to carry that burden.

"For myself, Majesty," he replied, considering as he spoke, "I will be glad to learn this skill. I can imagine uses for it. It might benefit my men at times when they must be silent. It may benefit me when I wish to address you while others are talking."

That was enough for Estie. The code was valuable for its own sake. It did not imply a larger decision.

For the first time since she had been given the name of her gift, she managed a wan smile. "Then I will accept your offer, Apprentice. The Commander and I will be your students."

Travail rewarded her with a smile of his own, one that was not fraught with sorrow. "I am pleased, Queen," he admitted. "The task will be a gift. It will concentrate my mind."

At once, he added, "But I must be honest. I have never had a student. I must learn to teach. And you will not learn quickly. The code is complex. Much of it is condensed. There are many details to remember. No one masters it in an afternoon."

Estie did not say, That also will ease me. It would fill empty days. Instead, she said, "I am content. The Commander and I will learn it together. We can practice on each other between your lessons.

"But I do not want to ask too much of you." His trembling hands reminded her of his exhaustion, the strain of refusing voices that clamored for his attention. "You must respect your own needs. There is no hurry. The enemy is still distant. Fortnights may pass before I must choose my future."

For a moment, there were tears in Travail's eyes. Earlier, Estie might have misunderstood them. Now she knew that they were tears of relief. In his own way, his needs were as great as hers; but he had refrained from mentioning them until he had gained her consent. Without it, he would have kept them to himself.

It was no wonder that Magister Facile had loved him.

After the Apprentice left, Estie dismissed Crayn and spent some time alone, trying to gather her scattered emotions.

Her first question had been answered. She knew the name of her gift. Now she had to face a more searching dilemma. Did she want power like Magister Avail's? How much of herself could she bear to surrender?

Could a deaf woman still be Amika's Queen?

Would a deaf wife—a deaf sorceress—repulse her husband?

Travail's offer might enable her to examine the mystery of which Estie she would choose to be.

SIXTEEN

OUT OF TIME

The day after Elgart's return with the el-Algreb, King Bifalt rode out to the training-fields. The previous evening, the horse-warriors had been given their promised rifles. They had been taught the basics of handling and caring for their guns. This morning, Suti al-Suri's people would begin learning to shoot.

The King was more than glad to have allies. They were a gift he could not have expected. Nevertheless he looked forward to seeing the el-Algreb receive a lesson in humility. None of them had ever touched a gun before. Yet the chief warrior had declared that they would be ready to fight in two days. With rifles. From horseback.

Of course, any fool could fire a rifle. Accuracy required skill. Accuracy from the back of a galloping horse was a skill that commonly required seasons to acquire.

The el-Algreb would not be ready to challenge the raiders from the south in two days. Unfortunately, the King could not give them more time. Signals from the south and reports from the west indicated that both of Rile's armies would reach the Open Hand sometime on the fourth day.

By good fortune, the horse-warriors had other weapons: cutlasses, throwing knives, and a few archers. And they were excellent riders. They might be able to slow the raiders.

On a hillcrest at a safe distance, the King paused to watch the el-Algreb try their rifles for the first time.

The results were no better than he had expected. Harried by Suti al-Suri's shouts, and encouraged by the riflemen who served as their teachers, the horse-warriors sprayed bullets in the general direction of their targets. Some of them fell on their backs, kicked down by the recoil of their rifles. Others dropped their guns in astonishment or pain.

They needed more than practice. They needed instructors who spoke their language.

Behind them, General Klamath had the disgusted look of a man studying a disaster. Suti al-Suri waved his arms and yelled in his rapid tongue to no apparent purpose.

While the horse-warriors shouted laughter and jeers at each other, King Bifalt nudged his horse forward. Scowling, he cantered down the slope toward Klamath and Suti al-Suri. When he neared them, he vaulted out of his saddle. Stamping closer, he snapped, "This is not going to work. Those men are children with guns. We cannot teach them."

To Bifalt's surprise, Suti al-Suri was undaunted. He showed the King a look of excitement. "You mistaken, Brother," he declared. "Children, yes. Warriors also.

"Sister." He grinned at Klamath. "Tell teachers. No talk. Show. El-Algreb learn seeing. Tell teachers show."

"Majesty?" asked the General through his teeth.

King Bifalt shrugged. "Give them a demonstration, General. Tell your men to hit the targets a few times. Then have them act out every detail." How to stand. Where to put their hands. How to brace the stocks. "Suti al-Suri may be right."

He, too, did not believe the chief warrior. He himself had received torrents of instruction, seen hours of demonstrations; but ultimately he had only gained his own skill by the sensations in his body when he had managed a clean shot.

"As you say, Majesty." Glumly, General Klamath walked away among the el-Algreb to talk with his riflemen.

While he waited, King Bifalt asked Suti al-Suri, "Has the General explained what we want you to do? There is an army of raiders coming from the south. We hope you can slow them. There is another army in the west. We cannot let them both hit us at the same time."

Again, Suti al-Suri surprised the King. The chief warrior responded with amused outrage. "Slow?" he snorted. "No. *Stop*. Sending fleeing. El-Algreb do."

Glaring, Bifalt replied, "Has Klamath told you that the raiders number at least two thousand? And they can make a smoke that cripples or kills?"

"Two thousand? Four?" The warrior thumped his chest. "No matter. No fear smoke. El-Algreb whip like dogs.

"Hear Suti al-Suri, Brother. El-Algreb know raiders. Garb. Weapons. Manner. Call 'Cleckin.' Speech like chickens. Raid el-Algreb homeland. Try steal horses. Women." He thought for a moment, apparently working on a translation. "Also strong goat milk. Want much strong goat milk. Make heads spin.

"Cleckin come. El-Algreb laugh. Drive away. Know why?"

Mystified, King Bifalt shook his head.

Grinning like a boy, the chief warrior demanded, "Guess!"

"No." Hells! Bifalt wanted to spit. "I am not a child, Suti al-Suri. I do not play guessing games."

The man pretended to look chastened. "Forgive, Brother. Not game. Not in fight. I tell." He answered his own question. "Cleckin easy. They treat horses bad."

Unaccountably pleased with himself, Suti al-Suri turned to watch his people struggle with their guns.

His assurance invited Bifalt to trust him; but that was impossible. Bifalt trusted the el-Algreb as allies. Amandis would not have taken Elgart to them if they were not staunch. But he suspected that they had never faced overwhelming odds. They were going to learn that rifles were not enough.

Chewing his cheek, the King waited for Klamath to rejoin him.

The General approached in a fury. "It cannot be done, Majesty," he snapped. "They are not Prince Jaspid. It is not natural to them. They need *practice*. At least a hundred rounds today. And if they do that, they will not be able to lift their arms tomorrow."

Suti al-Suri raised his eyebrows, recrossed his arms. "Sister mistaken," he declared. "He not know el-Algreb."

Klamath turned on the chief warrior. "I am not your pestilential 'sister,' sir."

Bifalt understood. Like Elgart's return, the arrival of allies had lifted Klamath's heart. The General had begun to imagine at least one victory. Now he knew the truth. The el-Algreb were not ready. They were going to be slaughtered.

However, Suti al-Suri did not understand. His mien darkened. "I claim kinship," he retorted. "How offend?"

King Bifalt put a restraining hand on Klamath's arm. To the warrior, he said, "You do not offend. General Klamath is afraid." His long friendship with Klamath allowed him to say such things. "He fears what will happen to your people if they cannot master their guns."

"Then, *Sister*"—the chief warrior made the word into a sneer—"watch. Learn. El-Algreb *able*. El-Algreb *do*."

The King tugged Klamath's arm to prevent a response. "Shoulder pads, General," he said softly, harshly. "You must have more than enough." For years, the General had provided them to protect his new recruits. "They should help."

Klamath appeared poised to shout in his King's face. Bifalt's tug stopped him. Scowling, he swallowed his anger.

When he could reply without heat, he said, "As you say, Majesty. I will send for the pads."

At once, he strode away in the direction of his nearest aides. They would know where the leather pads were stored.

King Bifalt turned to the chief warrior. "Hear me, Suti al-Suri," he said sternly. "This is a serious matter. Careless men with guns can harm themselves while they learn. Fire your own rifle. Then you will understand. It has the kick of a mule.

"General Klamath will give you shoulder pads. Tell your people to *use* them."

The chief warrior opened his mouth; closed it again. After a moment, he managed to say, "I hear, Brother." He sounded almost meek. "Not trust pads. Make el-Algreb soft. But no shoulder, no warrior. I tell."

Then he recovered his confident grin. "Tell Sister no fear. El-Algreb *do*."

Unslinging one of his rifles, he went to test himself on a target. Along the way, he shouted a long tumble of words as swift as white water over rapids. King Bifalt prayed that Suti al-Suri was giving his people commands—or at least explanations.

But the King did not stay to watch. He had other duties.

With Land-Captain Erepos, Prince Jaspid had agreed to muster a team of men who had spent seasons or years laboring in the Bay of Lights. Now they needed work—and Jaspid ached for something useful to do.

When King Bifalt reached Belleger's Fist, he found the Prince and perhaps thirty laborers waiting for him. Some of them were too old: a few were too young. But most were hardy men who had been refused service in the army for one reason or another: a blinded eye in one case, in others the loss of fingers or entire hands. They glowered at the King like men with something to prove.

Among them, Jaspid wore an air of downcast dutifulness. He, too, had something to prove, if only to himself. But his mood lifted as King Bifalt led him and the workmen in a tour of the Fist's deepest level.

That space was large, as wide and deep as the keep itself. Earlier, the servants had hung a number of lanterns there. In the cold and damp, the light revealed a high, vaulted ceiling supported by massive pillars in an irregular scatter from wall to wall. Belleger's Fist was not a planned structure. Over the generations, Bifalt's ancestors had added walls, halls, chambers, battlements, and towers as they saw fit. And to carry the keep's growing bulk, they had raised more and more pillars. Passing through the foundations was like walking in a stand of mighty oaks.

In addition, the foundations held a few barred cells that passed for a dungeon, unsanitary rooms which Bifalt's predecessors had seldom used. Bifalt himself had only one prisoner: Postern, Queen Estie's deposed Chancellor. The King intended to release him tomorrow, or the next day. Even a traitor deserved a chance to flee for his life.

Other chambers were larger. King Bifalt had filled some of them with new rifles wrapped in oilcloth and packed in crates. After supplying the el-Algreb, less than fifty guns remained. No doubt, General Klamath would send soldiers to retrieve them soon.

Leading his brother and the workmen among the pillars, King Bifalt took them to the destination he had in mind.

It was a blank wall.

"Here," he explained, "we are facing northwest. As you know," although perhaps only Prince Jaspid did, "on this side Belleger's Fist merges with the fortifications of the old city. They share this wall. Beyond are a range of forested hills."

When the time came, General Klamath would hide supplies and horses for the King and his riflemen among the trees.

"I want a tunnel here"—Bifalt slapped the wall—"that opens near the trees. And I need it *soon*. The enemy is coming. I cannot give you more than three days. Two would be safer.

"Can you do it?"

Prince Jaspid raised his head. He was beginning to guess King Bifalt's intentions.

The workmen muttered to each other, peered at the wall. Studying the crude stones, one of them grated, "In winter, Majesty? Damp earth freezes. It will be like rock. And the wall is thick. Several paces at least."

The King waited.

After a moment, another laborer ventured, "Can we have more men?"

Sighing to himself, the King nodded. "Will twenty be enough?" The guards who had defended Belleger's Fist had all gone to join Klamath's army. His seneschal would have to cull the keep's servants.

The workmen shrugged dubiously, shuffled their feet. The first speaker said, "We can try, Majesty. We have made walls. We know how to tear them down."

Bifalt was in a hurry to start the work. Curtly, he told the men,

"Then go. Bring your tools." Picks, shovels, crowbars, wheelbarrows. "Begin at once. I will send help soon."

Apparently, the laborers trusted their King. Or perhaps they simply craved work. They strode away without complaint.

When he and Jaspid were alone, Bifalt faced the glitter in his brother's eyes. "I have a task for you as well, Brother."

Speculations passed across Jaspid's expression. He said nothing.

"Gather our stores of gunpowder." Belleger's alchemists had been mixing gunpowder furiously ever since Rile's first ships had approached the Bay of Lights. "Bring the kegs here. With fuses. You can decide where to place them."

As if Bifalt had struck a spark, Prince Jaspid seemed to catch fire. The glow of the lanterns echoed in his eyes like hints of fever.

"I can do it, Brother. I am faster than you."

He was not talking about the ordinary chore of collecting and placing kegs, setting fuses.

Grimly, King Bifalt summoned his full authority. "You *can*. But you *will* not. I need you with me. I need you *at your best*." Before Jaspid could argue, he said, "I have someone else in mind. He will be glad to do it."

To himself, he added, If he lives.

Jaspid's initial eagerness sagged. Clearly, he wanted to argue. After only a moment, however, he surrendered.

Waving a hand at the wall, he said sourly, "You should have started sooner. Then ten men could have done what you ask."

As if he were helpless, the King lifted his shoulders. "I did not think of it."

He meant, I was imagining a glorious death for myself. Until Elgart returned, I did not know that we had allies.

So that his brother would understand, King Bifalt took him to visit the man he expected to volunteer.

Master Ungabwey must have had uncommon reserves of stamina. Perhaps he needed them to support his bulk. Lying on several mattresses on the floor of the army hospital, he clung to life despite his broken bones, his lacerated organs. His physicians did not know how or why he endured. They were adamant that he could not be moved.

Of course, he would have to be. Otherwise he would be killed as soon as one of the Great God's armies arrived: a wasted death for a man who had come so far and given so much to protect his daughters.

Prince Jaspid stayed in the background while King Bifalt knelt beside the caravan-master. Since the King had last seen Set Ungabwey, the physicians had pierced the obese man's chest under his left collar-bone and inserted a hollow reed. "To help him breathe, Majesty," explained the hovering physician. From the end of the reed, blood bubbled whenever Ungabwey inhaled. "He would suffocate without it.

"Numbing herbs in wine seem to ease him. It is all he can swallow." After a pause, the physician added, "He is beyond us. We can cut into him to address his wounds, but we cannot manage the bleeding. We will hasten his death."

Yet somehow he had survived a long, rough trek by travois. His breathing was a wet, desperate wheeze. Pain dulled his gaze. Weighed down by his own flesh, he seemed too weak to lift even one of his arms. Nevertheless he noticed Bifalt's arrival at once. He watched as the King knelt beside him to speak.

Past the tightness in his throat, Bifalt asked, "Can you hear me, Master?"

The man blinked to signify a nod.

"Then tell me. Show me that you can answer. You assured me that you are not done. Does your resolve hold?"

Set Ungabwey's reply was a thin whisper. "It does."

"Can it hold for a few more days?"

The wounded man shuddered, but his gaze did not waver. "It can."

Ah, hells! King Bifalt bit the inside of his cheek. Then he met this challenge the way he had met so many others, with anger to mask his distress.

"If it holds, Master, I have a task for you. It will not spare the library. It will not save your daughters. But it will help. It will deliver a blow the enemy does not expect."

Briefly, he explained what he wanted Set Ungabwey to do.

"Impossible!" protested the physician at once. "He *cannot* be moved. It will kill him."

"We understand," rasped Prince Jaspid. "But the enemy will burn this camp to the ground. We want him to choose how he dies."

King Bifalt ignored both of them. All of his concentration was fixed on the caravan-master.

Between gasps, Set Ungabwey answered, "I will do. What you ask. For my daughters."

He may have been trying to smile.

"Thank you." The King's response was an involuntary croak. "While I live, I will be in your debt." From somewhere deep inside him, he mustered a grin that bared his teeth. "If you do not die too soon."

"Do you?" asked the master. "Have children?" Small spouts of blood came from the reed. "If you did. You would understand."

Apparently exhausted, he closed his eyes.

For a long moment, King Bifalt remained kneeling. Then he pushed himself to his feet. The effort forced out a soft groan. Elgart was right: he had not been training.

As he left the room, he took Jaspid's arm in an iron grip. "Do you see, Brother?" he rasped. "He is the perfect choice."

"But we must stay with him," murmured Jaspid. "Until the last moment."

The King nodded. "In case he fails."

In case the caravan-master's body could not keep his heart's promises.

By the time King Bifalt returned to Belleger's Fist, his seneschal was waiting for him.

This duty did not vex him. He valued any effort that might save a few more of his people. Briefly, he told the seneschal to dismiss the keep's servants.

"Give them as much coin as the Purse-Holder has left. Send them to Amika. Command them in my name if you must. But first choose twenty of the strongest. I want them to join the workmen in the foundations. Tell them to do whatever is asked of them." Some other ruler might have confessed that his own life depended on them. King Bifalt did not consider that detail worth mentioning. "The Prince and I will watch over them at the end."

With Elgart, he thought, if that self-willed man did not disappear again.

The seneschal knew his King better than to argue. Bowing unsteadily, he hurried away.

Somehow over the years, Bifalt had earned or been given the right to be obeyed without question. He was not sure how. But he was glad that he did not have to explain himself.

Late that evening, King Bifalt and Land-Captain Erepos met as they often did to discuss the progress of the day and the tasks of the morrow. But this time, Erepos did not come to the King's private council room alone. He had Elgart with him.

Bifalt kept one window open to the winter air. It reminded him of what his people endured on the road to Amika. But he had a fire blazing in the hearth. The Land-Captain stood near it, rubbing his hands in the heat. Elgart had found a flask of wine that Prince Lome had left behind. Holding a full goblet, he sprawled in one of the chairs to rest and drink.

Erepos was a short, thick man with a wide variety of smiles. Some were genial. Others threatened or warned, disarmed or cajoled, accepted or countered. At the moment, his smile was thoughtful. While he waited for Bifalt's questions, he watched the flames in the hearth as if they held Belleger's future.

The King considered Elgart for a moment, then began with the Land-Captain.

"How is Matt? What do the physicians say?"

Erepos gave the King a rueful look like an apology. "He is strong, Majesty. Remarkable, really. The physicians and Magister Solace agree. The poison has left him. He can be moved safely." The Land-Captain sighed. "But he will not regain his sight."

Bifalt scowled. Losing Matt grieved him. It would do worse to Klamath. But that did not explain the Land-Captain's air of apology.

"What of his family?" asked the King.

Erepos allowed himself a happier moment. "Fortunately, they left their sheep as soon as Crickin warned them. His wife. Two sons and a daughter." There had been three sons until Mattwil had sacrificed himself. "The woman, Matta, is furious at everyone. But she and her offspring give the First Captain better care than we could manage."

By increments, the Land-Captain's smile slipped. It became rueful again. "Because he is the First Captain, Majesty, and his family has lost a son, and for General Klamath's sake—" He hesitated, then said, "I sent them to Amika in your carriage."

"A good choice, Erepos." Apparently, Bifalt had forgotten how to laugh. Perhaps he had never known. The idea that he might have refused the use of his carriage was absurd. "I should have offered it at once."

"I am glad you approve, Majesty." Politely relieved, the Land-Captain proceeded to report on the condition of the el-Algreb after their first day with rifles. When he was done, he produced one of his more anxious smiles. "Magister Crawl is pleased with his preparations, Majesty." Now he did not hesitate. "But I am concerned for the evacuation."

"How so?"

"Your people are Bellegerin, Majesty." Erepos let his vexation show. "Stubborn as rocks. Some cannot shift their minds from one thought to another. And most of them have already left their homes once." They had been displaced by the privations of the old wars. "They resist.

"Prince Lome does what he can. He argues. He commands. He pleads. Elgart's presence helps him. But still—" He spread his hands helplessly. "Your people resist."

King Bifalt frowned. "How many?"

"Perhaps a third," admitted Erepos. "In the whole city"—his tone hardened—"too many insist that the war will not come here. They know of our defeat in the Bay of Lights, but they believe that the army will protect them."

None of this surprised the King. After a moment, he ventured his real question. "Is Prince Lome drinking?"

Erepos sighed again. "He is, Majesty. Sometimes he does not. At others, he drinks an astonishing amount." Then he added, "But drunk or sober, you cannot fault his diligence. He goes everywhere. He speaks to everyone. And even when he staggers with drink, he speaks clearly. He could sway a stone—if it were not Bellegerin."

"I have seen it, Majesty," remarked Elgart. "I would not have believed it otherwise. When he fails, it is not because he holds back from the attempt."

To himself, King Bifalt thought sourly that Lome kept trying because his failures fed his self-disgust. Like his treasonous attempt to arrange Estie's death, they justified his drinking.

At the same time, Bifalt felt strangely proud of his brother. Drunk or sober, the Prince was King Abbator's son.

As Belleger's King, Bifalt thanked the Land-Captain. As Lome's brother, he asked Erepos to stay with the Prince when the enemy arrived; to make sure that he and Lome left the Open Hand together. Then he turned to other matters.

"It is time, Land-Captain, to empty the Fist. I want nothing left behind that the enemy can use. Add the staples to the army's supply-wagons. Send everything else to Amika.

"When the army departs, I will keep two hundred men. Klamath has left supplies for us. We will not go hungry."

That startled Erepos. He must have expected Bifalt to go with the General. He showed the King his anxious smile. "If what I have heard is true, Majesty, two hundred is a paltry number. Do you mean to fight yourself? You will be overrun in an hour. The whole city—"

He left the rest of that sentence hanging.

King Bifalt's face tightened. "Cities can be rebuilt. The dead are gone forever." He had never discussed his plans for battle with the Land-Captain. Erepos already had enough burdens. "I must save as many of our people as I can. That is your task. Leave the Open Hand to me. If it burns, it burns. I will not waste my riflemen."

The Land-Captain wanted to protest. He had a smile for that as well. It resembled the one he had used while he argued with Chancellor Postern. But the King's tone kept him silent.

"Do I understand, Majesty," drawled Elgart, "that you mean to keep me with you?"

Bifalt nodded. "Yes."

"And Prince Jaspid?"

The King nodded again.

With a laugh, Elgart turned to the Land-Captain. "Then there is nothing to fear, Erepos. Save your alarm for folk who need it. The Prince is as good as an army. If I have nothing better to do, I can guard his back."

The Land-Captain was not reassured. He treated Elgart to a bitter stare. "Very good. The Hand will be defended by two hundred and *three* men. Oh, and I must not forget the King's bodyguards. Two hundred and *seven*. A fine number to fight for the only home we have ever known."

"Enough, Erepos." King Bifalt's voice was a rasp. "We have always known that we would lose the Hand. Rile's forces are more than we can withstand. But I do not mean to die here.

"A hundred of those riflemen will fight in the streets. They will attempt to convince Rile that the city *is* defended. Then they will rally around the Magisters of fire at the barricades.

"The other men and I will withdraw to the walls of the old city. Those fortifications will shield us. I will not engage the enemy unless I cannot avoid it."

The Land-Captain remained troubled, but he did not protest when his King used that tone. Instead, he asked stiffly, "Is there more, Majesty?"

Bifalt bowed. "No, Erepos. Help our people flee. That will be enough."

The man sighed. "Then I should return to Prince Lome. He pretends to dislike me, but he needs my guidance."

Returning King Bifalt's bow, he left.

When Erepos was gone, King Bifalt said drily, "You were not kind to the Land-Captain, Elgart. You have spent too much time with Suti al-Suri."

Prying his limbs out of his chair, Elgart went to refill his goblet. As he moved, he stretched his arms and back, loosened his neck. With more wine in his hands, he stood by the fire with his back to the King, contemplating his thoughts. Readying himself.

King Bifalt watched the former spy. He knew what was coming. He did not know what it would cost him.

Abruptly, Elgart stooped, picked up another log from the wood-box, tossed it on the fire. As much to the hearth as to Bifalt, he mused, "You welcomed me well, Majesty. If a hard fist can be called a welcome. It is enough that you kept my promise. Now I am rested. I begin to feel whole in my mind. And I have talked to a number of people in Prince Lome's company, learning what I can. In some ways, I am content. But there are one or two details that no one will share with me. Klamath will not, and he tends to blurt them. Hells, Majesty! Even Howel will not, and I confess that I badgered him.

"Majesty." He spoke more sharply. "Bifalt. I will not understand until I know. I will not understand *you*."

Bifalt tried to forestall his friend. "What is there to understand? I am what I am. I have no surprises in me."

Over his shoulder, Elgart glanced at Bifalt, cocked an amused eyebrow. "Do you mean no surprises like the time you refused mortal combat with me and instead gave the book on cannon to Commander Forguile? *That* astonished me. I imagined then that I knew you at last."

He turned his head back to the fire. "Now I know better. There is more." After a pause, he said, "You look like a man who has taken a beating. The bruises are deep. They do not heal."

Spinning on his heel, he confronted his King. "I call myself your friend. Tell me, Bifalt. I know that Magister Facile is gone. I have eyes. But where is Queen Estie?"

Bifalt looked away. He had expected Elgart to ask this, and still he did not want to face it.

"Please, Bifalt," breathed Elgart. "If you cannot tell *me*, who *can* you tell?"

Who? thought the King. Hells! No one. Everyone else already knew what they needed to know. He had told Klamath more than enough. In Klamath's place, Elgart might have guessed Bifalt's secret for himself. But everything was different now.

Elgart had been an effective spy. He probed when other men kept silent. He would know the truth when he heard it.

Another challenge. King Bifalt met it as he had so many others. "Do you think I have taken a beating?" To himself, he sounded like a cornered animal, fearful and fierce. "You have no conception."

Elgart waited. Half of his face smiled gently. The other side twisted in sorrow.

Snarling deep in his throat, Bifalt said, "Queen Estie has a gift for sorcery." That fact still hurt him like the thrust of a pike. "All of her life, it was nameless. Too dangerous to awaken. But visible to other sorcerers.

"Of course, Smegin saw it long ago. But he said nothing. She knew nothing until Magister Facile ambushed her with it.

"Now she has gone to the Last Repository. To become a sorceress." A woman he would be forced to loathe.

Watching closely while he listened, Elgart settled his expression. The cut halves of his face seemed to merge, making him one man where he had been two a moment ago. When he replied, he spoke cautiously, but without hesitation.

"At one time, Majesty, you despised Amikans. Now Commander Forguile is a friend. Even a sorceress may earn your regard in the same way. And leaving her realm while her people and yours are on the brink of war—" For an instant, he made his eyes wide. "That woman has courage. Whatever she becomes—and however you choose to think of her—you cannot deny—"

Bifalt felt close to breaking. "Have you heard *nothing*?" he interrupted, almost shouting. "Do you think I question her *courage*? I am not so *simple*. But she will become a woman who can work her will against people she cannot even *see*."

In response, Elgart showed a glint of anger. In his own way, he had been as loyal to Amika's Queen as to Belleger's King. "Do you imagine, Majesty, that Queen Estie of all people will suddenly become as careless and cruel as her father?"

That question shocked Bifalt. Elgart's query had the effect of an accusation. It wrenched the King's image of Estie into intolerable shapes. If he had been a different man, he might have wept.

"How can I know?" he confessed: a stifled cry. "Power is a snare. It seduces. There will be no hope for her if she surrenders to it."

Or for him.

"How can anyone know?" countered Elgart. Somehow, he contrived to sound like Third Father. "How could I suspect that you would give the book of cannon to Amika? None of us know anything. We can only do what we can with what we have." The King's friend paused to emphasize his point. "You have almost twenty years with your wife."

In some other life, Bifalt might have taken Elgart by the throat to silence him. In *this* life, he dropped his distress into a chair and covered his face with his hands.

Too early the next morning, King Bifalt received a blistering message from General Klamath. The el-Algreb were gone, heading south to confront the Cleckin. Klamath had written his tidings fiercely enough to tear the parchment. *Our beloved* sister *Suti al-Suri proclaims that his people are ready. His only concession to sanity*—several words had been violently crossed out—*is that they have taken the shoulder pads.*

In a second message delivered a short time later, the General wrote more calmly. He had sent sub-Commander Hellick to ride herd on the horse-warriors—if their recklessness allowed it. When they were beaten, Hellick would signal the disaster.

That should have been a heavy blow. Belleger would lose its only allies. But during the night, Bifalt had made himself numb. He had spent most of the time thinking about Estie.

He wanted to share Elgart's view of her. Instead, almost involuntarily, he found himself trying to imagine Estie as one of the theurgists he despised.

She was King Smegin's daughter. His example would work against her. Even so— How could she bear charring flesh and bone to ash with her father's Decimate? Bifalt struggled to imagine her killing in that way, but his efforts broke on the rock of his image of her.

Nevertheless he rallied when a messenger arrived from Second Captain Hegels. He had run out of time for his fears.

The man was one of the Second Captain's riflemen. He reported that Rile's host from the bay had quickened its pace. In response, Hegels had abandoned his efforts to slow the enemy. His losses were unacceptable: a dozen riflemen and two Magisters. At his best speed, he was on his way back to the city.

Retreating, Hegels had left scouts behind to watch the enemy. They were in no danger from the host itself, but they had to be wary of Rile's skirmishers. Those small, feral creatures—men?—ranged widely, and any rifleman they managed to catch was lost.

The messenger concluded with the Second Captain's most recent estimate of the Great God's forces. He judged that they numbered around thirteen thousand. Five thousand were heavy infantry clad in iron breastplates and armed with broadswords. Five thousand were light infantry wearing leather armor and carrying an assortment of sabers, scimitars, and cutlasses. After the foot soldiers came the many wagons of the enemy's supply-train accompanied by a multitude of servants. Among them rode a large force of men in the black garb of priests. And with *them* were Rile's cavalry, three thousand lightly armored men riding beasts that looked like deformed boars, long-backed enough to hold saddles, tusked for rending. The cavalrymen carried longswords. They guarded the supply-train and servants.

Despite Bifalt's years of preparation, the numbers shocked him. He had expected overwhelming force. He had not expected *thirteen thousand* foemen supported by priests.

Suddenly, he had too much to consider. Rile's host would reach the Open Hand too soon. Its attack might begin a full day sooner than he had anticipated. And General Klamath was not ready. Prince Lome and the Land-Captain were not. There were still too many people lagging in the city. The el-Algreb would not be enough to stop the Cleckin. Suti al-Suri's warriors were likely to be savaged.

As for the tunnel out of the Fist's foundations—

King Bifalt forced himself to think.

The Second Captain's messenger he sent to Klamath. Then he dis-

patched Prince Jaspid with Boy and Spliner to the army hospital. Set
Ungabwey would be needed in Belleger's Fist. He would require care,
and the King could not spare Jaspid. Next, he asked Jeck to rouse Elgart. Malder he ordered to wander the Hand with Prince Lome as long
as possible. There was nothing else that Bifalt could do for his struggling brother.

After that—

Fortunately, Crawl and his fellow Magisters of fire were in place,
waiting. They would be crucial. But the King had only one other advantage that he could see. An overwhelming force would expect an
easy victory. Its commanders might not stop to reconsider their tactics.

Perhaps. Bifalt's assumption might not be accurate. He had to act
on it anyway.

As soon as Jeck returned with Elgart, King Bifalt took both men
with him to speak with Klamath. Before the King received the Second
Captain's last report, he had hoped that Klamath might be able to
provide a measure of support for the surviving horse-warriors as they
fled toward the Hand. That was impossible now. The General would be
under intense pressure to decamp a day earlier than he had anticipated.
If he failed, he would not have the luxury of choosing the terrain for
his first engagement with the enemy.

King Bifalt's alliance with the el-Algreb had lasted for less than
two days.

PART
THREE

UNFAMILIAR TACTICS

While General Klamath hauled the combined army of Belleger and Amika into motion by force of will, sub-Commander Hellick followed the el-Algreb south.

He believed that he had proven himself by leading the First Captain's struggling company back to the Open Hand. His efforts had kept many of the smoke-stricken men alive. As a result, his assignment now had the effect of insult.

The bravado of the horse-warriors disgusted him. He had no patience for their extravagant assurance.

Worse, they were doomed.

They had reached the Hand after a long, wearisome journey. Then they had spent the previous day abusing their shoulders like children. They had no discipline. And they did not respect their foes, despite the fact that they were badly outnumbered. The raiders, the Cleckin, would shred them in a matter of hours.

Yet they were pestilentially sure of themselves. Riding out in the early dawn, they shouted raucously to each other and waved their guns, ignoring their own pain and ignorance. They seemed to imagine that their mere presence would rout their foes.

Under the circumstances, sub-Commander Hellick felt nothing but scorn for King Bifalt's so-called allies.

He was not alone. Riflemen answered the silly display of the el-Algreb with ripe insults or hoots of derision. From his command-post, General

Klamath paced back and forth, spitting a soldier's obscenities. His aides shook their heads.

Hellick waited until the el-Algreb passed out of sight. Then he followed the horse-warriors, cursing to himself.

At the crest of the ridge, he felt a sour relief when he saw that the el-Algreb had put away their rifles and settled into a more disciplined formation. Now they looked more like men with a serious task. If they could refrain from taunting the raiders before they engaged, they might manage an exchange or two before they were savaged.

The horse-warriors set a stiff pace, one that Hellick did not try to match. Being left behind did not trouble him. They deserved whatever happened to them. He had other duties.

Along his way, he stopped at every relay-post. First Captain Matt had established them to pass signals from the Realm's Edge quickly. Now they would do the same for the sub-Commander. He paused at each of them to explain why they were still necessary—and to warn the men that they would not be relieved. General Klamath needed all of his soldiers for harder tasks.

There were many such posts. Stopping often, Hellick did not catch up with the el-Algreb during the day.

Throughout the afternoon and into the evening, he traveled a region of tumbled hills. Like much of Belleger's south, this was sheep-grazing country. In kinder seasons, the hills were cloaked with the grasses sheep preferred. Draped in swaths of low shrubs and berry-bushes, the slopes were gentle enough for comfort. Scattered copses offered shade, and brief burns overgrown with trees supplied water. But now, deep in winter, the grasses were dried and brittle, the shrubs and thickets were stiff enough to scratch blood from the legs of unwary horses, and the copses everywhere had cast away their leaves. Under a cloudless sky, the stars at night seemed to cover the world with their freezing breath.

From time to time, Hellick passed hamlets and farmsteads, usually at a distance, all deserted. In one way, the threat of raids had done King

Bifalt a service. Bellegerins here had not resisted the command to forsake their homes and head north. As evening deepened around him, the sub-Commander could have stopped at any of the abandoned houses, barns, or stables for shelter and perhaps a small fire. But the thought of what the el-Algreb might do in his absence kept him going.

As the hours passed, he expected to come upon the horse-warriors at any moment. To rest their mounts if not themselves, they must have halted somewhere. Bitterly, he began to imagine that he would find them celebrating the prospect of an easy victory.

But he was wrong. He did not catch up with the el-Algreb until late that night. In fact, he did not know that he was near them until Suti al-Suri appeared at his side and stopped him with a hand on his reins.

The chief warrior seemed to arrive from nowhere, condensing out of the darkness like a figment. Startled, Hellick muttered a reflexive curse. At first, he did not understand how Suti al-Suri had contrived to take him by surprise. Then he realized that he had been expecting horses: the smell of their sweat, the munch of their jaws as they chewed fodder and grain, the soft snuffles and whickers of beasts resting. But the el-Algreb must have tethered their mounts somewhere else. Suti al-Suri was on foot.

Gesturing for silence, the chief warrior touched Hellick's arm, urged him to dismount. Mystified, the sub-Commander complied. A moment later, another warrior came to lead his horse away. Neither of the el-Algreb made a sound.

Too recently, Hellick had seen Matt's suffering. He had watched poisoned men die in brutal pain. He had to ask, "Fires?"

He meant, Smoke?

Suti al-Suri motioned for silence again. He stepped close, leaned his mouth to Hellick's ear. "Cleckin came," he breathed. "We killed. No fires. No smoke."

Brigin and pestilence! The raiders had to be nearby. Had they come so far since Hellick and his command had fled?

Worse, they clearly knew that the el-Algreb were here. Why else would they try to set their venomous fires?

Hellick forced himself to a choked whisper. "Where?"

The chief warrior waved a hand southward. "Camp there. Past hills. Wagons make slow. Two days from city." After a pause, he admitted, "Cleckin scouts see el-Algreb. Plan attack."

Even speaking more softly than the breeze, his tone conveyed assurance.

The sub-Commander wanted to ask, How can you fight them? Where are your *horses*?

What good were horse-warriors without mounts?

But Suti al-Suri was touching his arm again; gesturing. "Come," the man murmured. "You watch."

Drawing Hellick with him, he moved away.

Hellick pulled his arm free, unshouldered his rifle. He checked his sword in its scabbard. Then he tightened his cloak around him and nodded, pretending to understand.

Quiet as air, the chief warrior walked south along a shallow valley, then started up a hillside on his left. He moved like a man whose feet did not touch the ground, without any rustle of dried grasses or clink of shifting pebbles. Wincing at the noise of his own steps, Hellick followed.

The slope was not steep, but it stretched upward a long way. For a while, Hellick managed to cover his breathing. Then he began to pant openly. When Suti al-Suri brought him to the summit at last, he had to spend a few moments heaving for air before he considered his surroundings.

Clear skies gave the cold a whetted edge, but he was grateful for them nonetheless. They granted him moonlight.

On all sides, silver stroked the hills. Some of them were both distinct and elusive. Deformed by impenetrable shadows, the others seemed to crouch at obscure angles. All of them were lower than Hellick's vantage. When day came, he might be able to see farther. In darkness, he knew little more than what he could have deduced from horseback.

His guide indicated the south again. "Cleckin camp," whispered the warrior. Then he pointed at a vague gap between hills a bit to his right, a curving clot of thicker night. "Attack there."

He stepped aside, giving the sub-Commander a better view.

Squinting, Hellick discerned nothing that implied movement or foes. Moonlight and darkness defined the gap, that was all. Shadows closed it like shrouds.

"How do you know?" he asked softly. The Cleckin could come from any direction.

The chief warrior did not answer. He was already gone.

Brigin! thought General Klamath's witness. What was he supposed to see?

Shifting temperatures stirred the air over the hills. Low breezes sighed faintly in his ears. There was nothing to see.

He hugged his cloak tighter. He was going to freeze up here.

But soon he heard a sound so familiar that he had almost failed to notice it: a faint rattle. Muted by distance, it was barely audible. Still, he recognized it.

Hooves. Many hooves.

In the gap between those hills, the shadows seemed to seethe. At first, they squirmed vaguely. Then they boiled, spitting horsemen into the moonlight.

A long stream of horsemen. Hellick tried to estimate their numbers. He saw at least fifty—

In that instant, muzzle flashes split the night. The barking crash of a fusillade hit his ears. Long lines of rifles on both sides of the charging raiders fired.

And fired again. Again.

The el-Algreb on each side shot with the reckless abandon of wounded men. At that range, they could hardly miss.

Hellick could not pick out the shooting warriors. If they had been mounted, the moon would have exposed them. If they had been upright, their foes might have spotted them. They were prone, using the ground to brace their sore arms, their damaged shoulders.

Stuttering between light and shadow, bodies slammed to the ground.

They landed hard, blundered against each other. The clamor of gun-shots and screams mingled with the shrill shrieks of horses. In some ways, the mounts were better targets. During a charge, a fallen fighter was as useless as a dead one.

Somehow, Suti al-Suri's people had chosen the path of the attack. They had lured the Cleckin into an ambush.

The horse-warriors might act like children, but they knew what they were doing.

Beasts and riders fell, tripped the raiders behind them. Howls, cries, and curses filled the darkness. Hellick heard the sickening shat-ter of bones. The horses screamed in agony. The charge had already been broken, but the raiders following around the curves of the hills did not know that. They kept coming.

Hellick counted six volleys. Six bullets in each clip. He expected the el-Algreb to exchange clips and go on firing. They did not. Sud-denly, they were gone, melting into the shadows like bits of nightmare.

Their disappearance saved them. Prone, the warriors could not counter javelins and blades. They would have to rise. And Cleckin from the rear were flinging themselves off their mounts to attack on foot. But they could not locate their assailants.

As the sub-Commander raised his head to shout his approval, sur-prise closed his throat. Streaks of flame in the distance wrenched his attention away from the fighting below him. .

Fire-arrows!

Suti al-Suri's people had more than rifles, more than cutlasses and throwing knives. They had archers. And they were not content with ambushing the Cleckin. They had prepared a different attack as well.

Hellick could see the arching trails of flame clearly enough. He had no idea what they were intended to accomplish. A few of them fizzled out. But others hit where they were aimed and kept burning. They must have struck something flammable.

Something like dry oilcloth. The kind of canvas that would cover loaded wagon-beds in a supply-train.

More arrows left hot trails across the sub-Commander's sight. With burning oilcloth to guide them, the archers improved their aim.

Most of the second flight found the wagons. Already, four loads of supplies were on fire. Others were beginning to burn.

While the Cleckin were distracted by the ambush, the el-Algreb delivered a more serious wound.

Tiny in the distance, shouts of alarm rose from the enemy camp. Lit by the flames, figures as small as toys ran for the wagons. Some of them had wit enough to bring buckets of water.

Before the Cleckin could muster men to ride out and hunt for their attackers, the fire-arrows stopped. There were many wagons. Only a few of them were burning. But Suti al-Suri's people had no intention of risking themselves. They disappeared into the darkness.

Quickly, the raiders extinguished their damaged wagons. As the flames went out, the hills recovered their moonlit outlines. The cries, whimpers, and hushed commands among the fallen raiders faded as their comrades dragged them to safety beyond a hill. Soon only dead men and wrecked beasts remained.

In the aftermath, Hellick found that he was shivering. The el-Algreb had banished his disgust. Now he felt something that might have been awe. It was certainly relief.

As soundless as before, Suti al-Suri arrived beside the sub-Commander. "Stay wary," he advised in a normal voice. The danger that he would be heard had passed. "Cleckin scout good."

Moonlight made the chief warrior's smile look ghoulish.

A shudder of cold ran through Hellick. He took a deep breath to calm himself. As soon as he started to think, he had a throng of questions. But he did not know how to ask them. Or rather, he did not know how to phrase them so that he would be able to understand Suti al-Suri's broken answers.

"What—?" His voice shook. He was too chilled to speak steadily. "What was all that for?"

"Bait." The chief warrior indicated the ambush with a jerk of his chin. Then he pointed toward the burned wagons. "Also bait."

Bait? Hellick stared at the man. Then what was the trap?

Bait was useless without a trap.

Suti al-Suri studied General Klamath's observer for a moment, then shrugged. "Come," he said. He gestured off the hilltop. "You cold. El-Algreb make fire. Get warm. Much tell."

Hellick nodded. He wanted to understand.

Under an overhang of rock, the el-Algreb had built a comfortable fire. Its smoke curled up and away past the lip of the rock. During the day, it would have brought attention. At night in sharp cold, no one would notice it.

Half a dozen horse-warriors sat cross-legged around the flames with their leader and the sub-Commander. They gave Hellick a gourd of warmed water and strips of dried meat. Suti al-Suri and his companions looked relaxed, like men who were not in danger. Hellick suspected that they would look the same if they were in *immediate* danger.

Hunched close to the heat, he ate and drank until he stopped shivering. Then he began to ask his questions.

Where were the el-Algreb mounts? The chief warrior's answer was simple enough. They had been hidden in a small vale half a league away. Where the Cleckin had made their camp, they were effectively entrenched. Fighting them from horseback risked too many animals. Suti al-Suri's people had other ideas.

After that, however, Hellick had more difficulty making sense of the chief warrior's replies. Nevertheless the Amikan persisted. He repeated his questions, rephrased them, insisted on longer answers. After an hour that tested Suti al-Suri's patience, Hellick grasped what the el-Algreb had in mind.

They intended to cut the raiders to pieces with small snips. The idea of *bait* was crucial. As often as possible, in different ways and from several directions, they would lure their foes into striking back. Any Cleckin who responded would be ambushed. But baiting the raiders was only a ploy. Suti al-Suri's real purpose was to distract his foes from a greater danger.

His people intended to steal the raiders' horses.

"Not lose," he declared. "Cleckin not take bait, keep horses, not move. Or take bait, el-Algreb take horses, not move. Both way, Cleckin beaten. Go home."

That Hellick understood. The Cleckin wagons were drawn by horses, a use that Suti al-Suri called *bad*. As a result, the raiders had many more beasts than men. But the el-Algreb had snatched a chunk of the herd during the night. If the Cleckin lost too many animals, they would not be able to take their supplies with them. Their attack would fail. And if they stayed where they were to protect their mounts, the result would be the same.

The sub-Commander whistled through his teeth. The horse-warriors' tactics might succeed. They might actually win. He would not have believed it.

Nevertheless he remained skeptical until he climbed back to the height of his hilltop at daybreak. When the sun began to light the valleys below him, he could see the Cleckin camp.

They had chosen an attractive place to spend the night. It was a large basin, almost as level as a plain, and wide enough to hold the entire enemy force. On three sides, it was sheltered by shallow hillsides that good horses could ascend at a gallop. To the west lay a sharper bluff marked by bare rock and gorse. There an overgrown rift spilled fresh water into smaller streams wandering through the lowland. In almost every way, the basin was ideal—for an army that did not fear an attack.

For the el-Algreb, however, the camp was uniquely vulnerable.

For Hellick, one glance was enough to clarify Suti al-Suri's intentions. The Cleckin herd appeared to number more than three thousand head. Of course, the horse-warriors would not simply shoot the animals. But if they contrived to steal even a third of those beasts, they might force the raiders to reconsider their commitment to the Great God's war.

The Cleckin had an obvious counter. They could ignore the bait. Before their losses became severe, two thousand raiders massed and mounted could force their way out of the basin.

But that would require them to leave their supplies behind. They would have to ride north with no food and little water. And they had one other detail to consider: they could not know how many el-Algreb had come against them.

As Suti al-Suri had predicted, the raiders would lose this contest whatever they did.

The sub-Commander was satisfied. Sure of himself now, he sent his first signal to General Klamath. It said:

The el-Algreb can hold.

That was enough.

EIGHTEEN

"WHO AND WHAT YOU ARE"

Apprentice Travail's lessons saved Queen Estie from long days of chewing on her inability to make her most personal decision despite her uselessness in every other aspect of impending war. She studied the language of finger-taps with an indirect hunger that bordered on fever. Travail had suggested that learning Magister Rummage's code might help her make up her mind about her sleeping gift. She closed her mind to everything else whenever the Apprentice felt strong enough to teach. At other times, she practiced avidly with Commander Crayn. When other duties called him away, she sought out Magister Oblique.

Crayn was responsible for the honor guardsmen in Queen Estie's escort. They needed exercise and training. Guided by Magister Oblique, he led them with their horses and weapons out of the Repository and down a trail to an open expanse of stone below the keep. It lay midway between the library's immense plateau and the northward sweep of the road, and it provided more than enough space for mounted drills and combat exercises. The Commander spent his afternoons there, honing his men.

But he did not let that task preclude his service to his Queen. In the evenings, he and Estie worked on finger-taps until their hands ached and their concentration blurred.

Somehow, the days passed despite the prolonged silence of the

Farsighted. Without Apprentice Travail, Queen Estie might have lost control of herself.

Every day, she worried about him. And every day, she was relieved to see that his teaching met his needs as well as hers. He came to her like a dying man. Yet during each lesson, a bit of vitality leaked into his eyes. Whenever she mastered a particularly complex series of touches, a faint smile twisted his mouth. He did not mention his own condition unless she asked. Then he replied that he was learning to deafen himself. He may have been teasing her.

At all times, however, her private dilemma lingered in the background, nagging at her. Could she accept the power of her inheritance and its cruel cost? Should she? Why? Who would she be if she lost her essential connection to other people? To her whole world?

Magister Avail had called her gift a *curse*. He had urged her to refuse it. Now she could not explain why she hesitated to take his advice. What sane person would choose to follow his path?

Perhaps Avail himself was not sane. *He* had accepted the same gift.

Nevertheless the question haunted her like an ambiguous nightmare, a horror that held the secret of death and life.

How could she turn her back on the woman she was born to be and go limping into the gloom of a wasted future?

How could she not?

Fortunately, she was not pressed for a decision. She had time. Instead of forcing herself, she waited for news of Bifalt and the war. Failing that, she waited for Magister Threnody to compile a list of men and women who had learned how to poison Travail and murder Magister Marrow. Perhaps such things would help her answer her doubts.

But the Farsighted and Beatrix Threnody were silent. The only word that came to the Queen was from sub-Commander Waysel. He had sent a guardsman ahead to inform her that her cannon had reached the stone bridge in the desert. Seeing that the man was road-weary, Queen Estie asked him to join her escort. In his place, Commander Crayn dispatched one of his own guardsmen to meet Waysel's wagons and guide them to the Repository.

Thinking of the guns gave her a measure of relief, but it was brief.

Nine cannon were better than none, but they would not change the outcome of the war.

That depended on men like her husband and Klamath, men who were beyond her aid.

Without news, time no longer trudged. It crawled on its hands and knees. By increments, it frayed Queen Estie's concentration. One day, she found herself unable to focus her mind on Apprentice Travail's lessons. When Crayn sat with her that evening, they did not practice the tapping code. Instead, her thoughts slipped past every subject, trying to go in all directions at once.

When she had first arrived in the Last Repository, her rooms had felt cold, chilled by the imponderable mass of stone around them. The heat from her hearths had been barely adequate. But those fires had been burning for days. Now her sitting room seemed too warm. Perspiration made her gown cling to her skin. She pined for a window to let in a little fresh air.

What was happening in the Open Hand? In Belleger?

Were any of the people she had left behind still alive?

The sound of a knock on her door made her flinch.

At once, Crayn went to open the door. Then he stepped aside to admit Magister Oblique and Magister Bleak.

Queen Estie had not seen the man for days, but she knew him by his bald head with its solitary thatch of hair and his extreme thinness. The look of distance in his eyes had not changed.

She stood as if she had been jerked to her feet. Unsteadily, she gestured a welcome. "Forgive me, Magisters," she began. "I did not expect you. Can I offer something to refresh you? Commander Crayn will ask for whatever you desire."

Magister Oblique produced her best smile. "Thank you, no, Queen. We do not mean to linger."

As if Oblique had not spoken, Magister Bleak said, "Some ruby wine, yes. At their best, our efforts are thirsty work." He had a singer's voice which he used as if he were rehearsing a tune. "They are far from their best now. We struggle to weave our visions into a single tapestry. It is like trying to see with eyes that do not belong to us. At inconvenient times, even the strongest of us must eat or sleep. I need wine."

Without waiting for an invitation, he moved to the nearest chair, dropped into it, and covered his eyes with his hands.

An apology twisted Magister Oblique's smile.

Quietly, Crayn stepped out into the hallway. Estie heard him murmur a few words to a waiting servant. When he returned to his place, he left the door ajar.

The sorceress did not sit until Queen Estie, flustered, resumed her seat. Then Magister Oblique took a chair beside Magister Bleak.

While the Farsighted kept his eyes covered, Oblique explained, "I expected Magister Bleak to be brief, Queen. But he understands your plight. He will answer it in his own way.

"Forgive me if I repeat myself," she added. "I must remind you that the Farsighted *see*. They do not *hear*. That lack forces them to interpret events by inference.

"Master Set Ungabwey and the el-Algreb we know, of course. Commander Forguile spent a season or more among us. King Bifalt, Elgart, and General Klamath we have met, if only for a short time. Others Magister Facile described to us, primarily the King's brothers. In other cases, Magister Bleak cannot be specific."

"Of course, Magister," murmured the Queen. She had spent too much time contemplating the implications of deafness. The inability of the Farsighted to hear was of another kind than Magister Avail's, but some of its consequences were similar.

Magister Bleak lowered his hands. Humming to himself, he turned his head to peer at the door, obviously hoping for wine. Then he shifted to gaze past or through Queen Estie.

"We know Commander Forguile. Some time ago, he held the north bank of the Line River. With a company of riflemen. They were shooting at an army on the Bellegerin side. The fanged men. At first, those strangers stood where they were and died. Then they withdrew out of range. However, they remain too far east to join the Great God's forces. We turned our sight toward the Open Hand and Belleger's Fist."

Again, Magister Bleak seemed to forget words while he hummed.

Behind him, a servant appeared in the doorway, breathing hard. Crayn must have prodded her to hurry. On a tray, she carried four goblets and a flask of wine.

She did not enter until Queen Estie beckoned to her. Then she came forward and set her tray on the low table. Before Estie could thank her, she left, closing the door behind her.

Magister Bleak did not glance at the wine. He seemed to know it by its aroma. Still staring beyond Estie, he poured a goblet of dark wine for himself, drank it all. With a sigh of satisfaction, he refilled his goblet.

After a moment, he remembered his tune. Glancing at the Queen, he said, not unkindly, "I do not mean to increase your distress, Queen. I can only tell you what we have seen."

"That will be enough, Magister," answered Queen Estie. She knew Ennis Forguile well. His efforts to defend Amika without risking his men comforted her. "It will be more than I have now."

Bleak cleared his throat. His gaze drifted into the distance. With a lilt that resembled singing, he began.

"Magister Marrow spoke of Master Ungabwey's failure in the Realm's Edge. Now we know that he lives. He was borne from his ruin in the Realm's Edge to the army's camp outside the Open Hand. Since then, he has been moved. At first, our view of him was interrupted by buildings and crooked streets. But we glimpsed him as he was carried through the old city to Belleger's Fist."

The Farsighted emptied his goblet again, refilled it. Now he did not need prompting to continue.

"Days earlier, riflemen rode south while an army emerged from the Realm's Edge. Later, more men were sent to support them. Men and Magisters. The King's forces suffered significant losses. To our sight, it appeared that they had been stricken by some illness. They fled, dragging Master Ungabwey. Their dead they left behind. The wounded were tied in their saddles."

Magister Bleak paused to sip more wine and consider his description. His sketch of events made no sense to Estie, but she did not try to understand it. Instead, she concentrated on absorbing whatever the Farsighted could tell her.

When Bleak was satisfied, he continued.

"There is more. When the King's forces and Master Ungabwey reached the Open Hand, they were not the only arrivals. Elgart appeared as well."

Elgart! Hearing his half-sung name, Estie lost herself for a moment. After all this time? Like Bifalt, she had assumed that the former spy was dead, killed by the Archpriest.

Listening unnoticed, Crayn breathed a soft curse.

Their surprise seemed to please the Farsighted. "Magister Facile told us that Elgart disappeared and perhaps died. Yet he lives. And"—Bleak enjoyed the memory—"he did not return alone. He brought an army of the el-Algreb with him."

At once, Oblique demanded, "How? Magister Marrow offered them every inducement we possess. How did King Bifalt's spy win an alliance that eluded us?"

"We know only what we see." Bleak's melody sounded smug. "We saw the el-Algreb arrive. The next day, we saw them train with rifles. And early this morning, we saw them ride south. More than that is speculation."

Magister Oblique stared for a moment, thinking hard. Then she blurted, "King Bifalt offered them rifles." There was awe in her voice. "They have joined him—they have gone to oppose the raiders for him—because he offered them rifles."

More steadily, she added, "Whenever we imagine that we have King Bifalt's measure, he surpasses our expectations."

Again, Queen Estie did not try to understand. She did not know enough to speculate. For her, *early this morning* was the most important detail. The Repository's enemies were converging. The attack on the Open Hand would begin soon.

The Farsighted shrugged at Oblique's reaction. He did not turn aside from his tidings.

"There is more. After the el-Algreb rode away, General Klamath and his army also departed. But they headed east rather than south, leaving the Open Hand undefended. Perhaps they are preparing for a later battle. We have no other explanation. If they mean to forsake *us*, they would not ride east."

Some of that did not surprise Estie. Bifalt had always considered the Hand indefensible. But she did not know how he could bear abandoning his city. Her heart seemed to pause in her chest as she asked, "What of the King? Does he ride with General Klamath?"

Briefly, Magister Bleak focused on her again. "That is a curious detail." Then his gaze slipped away. "We saw him reenter the Open Hand when the army was gone. He had Elgart with him, and a number of riflemen. Some of them passed into the old city. Later, Prince Jaspid did the same with perhaps eight Magisters. That is all we know."

"Is that to be Master Ungabwey's fate?" protested Magister Oblique. "Will he die in Belleger's Fist alone while only a small portion of the army defends the city?"

No, thought Estie, not alone. She felt no concern for the caravan-master. She had never met him. But her pulse hammered and sweat soaked her gown because her husband had put himself in the same position. A vague number of riflemen were not enough to hold the walls, even with a few Magisters. Not against the strength that Rile had brought to Belleger. Trapped in the old city, or in the Fist, Bifalt and everyone with him would die.

Breathing hard to control herself, she asked, "Where is the enemy? When will Rile's army strike?"

How much time did Bifalt have?

Magister Bleak seemed baffled by her query—or perhaps her intensity. Cautiously, he answered, "It has been moving at the pace of infantry. There are cavalrymen as well, but they have not ridden ahead. The whole force has advanced slowly.

"Now, however, they have increased their pace. They will not reach the Open Hand later than tomorrow night."

Estie wanted to tear her hair. What did Bifalt hope to gain? What could he accomplish that would be worth the risk?

Oblique seemed to recognize Estie's alarm. "It appears," she said in a small voice, "that King Bifalt has snared himself. But he would not. He cannot mean to sacrifice himself. When his city is lost? That would be worse than folly. It would be madness.

"Will he leave Set Ungabwey to die?"

Abruptly, Queen Estie snatched up a goblet. Trembling, she poured it full. She had to hold it with both hands to gulp a few swallows of wine.

Through her teeth, she answered, "My husband has already surpassed your *measure* more than once." Magister Marrow's astonishment must have been extreme when Prince Bifalt forged an alliance with Amika. With King Smegin, who hated him. "He can do so again."

"To what purpose?" cried Magister Oblique softly.

The Queen did not reply. To herself, she admitted, If I knew that, I would not be so afraid.

Frowning, Bleak brought his gaze back into the room. Briefly, he regarded Estie; turned a mute question to Oblique. After a moment, he drank the last of his wine and rose.

"I have told you what I know." He sounded frustrated, as if Estie's exchange with Oblique had made him forget his tune. "We will see more tomorrow. Until then—"

The Queen stopped him. "One more question, Magister," she said as if she had the right to command him. "You may consider it a small matter. It has substance for me.

"What of Prince Lome?"

Magister Bleak cocked an eyebrow. "The lesser brother? Yes, in glimpses." He made it clear that he had no interest in Lome. "He wanders the outskirts of the Hand, accosting people in the street, or knocking on doors. Why? Who knows? Magister Facile informed us of his treachery."

Stung, Queen Estie looked away. "The lesser brother, as you say," she murmured. "But he, too, may surprise you."

She chose to believe that Lome was done with treason. He was a wastrel, yes, and often self-deluded. Nevertheless he was King Abbator's son. He would not turn his back on Bifalt or Belleger.

Unimpressed, Magister Bleak shrugged again. With a nod for Magister Oblique, he went to the door and departed.

The sorceress stood as well. She looked scattered, torn in several directions at once. "Forgive me, Queen," she said, hurrying. "I must go as well. Events have quickened. The librarian should not be left alone to manage their effects. I will return when I can."

Without waiting for an acknowledgment, she turned and left.

Commander Crayn followed her to the door, closed it after her. With an air of deliberation, he set the lock to ensure Estie's privacy. Then he turned his sandstone gaze on his Queen.

"Tomorrow, Majesty."

Feeling helpless, she nodded. "Tomorrow."

That one word conveyed too much dread.

The next morning, she dressed in her riding garments and winter cloak like a woman who had a long way to go. When Crayn and his men were ready, she went with them to collect her horse from the Repository's stables. Then she followed them out into the hard cold toward the open space where they trained.

To ease the way for caravans, the road down from the Repository's plateau headed south, then made a long, slow curve among the foothills toward its eventual intersection with the caravan-track. Within that curve, halfway between the keep and the northward reach of the road, lay a smaller version of the library's extensive porch. There the flat stone was broad enough for riding drills as well as exercises in combat and marksmanship.

Needing the distraction, Estie joined her guardsmen. For a while, she let them teach her some of their easier riding drills. Later, she rode around and around the training space, walking, trotting, cantering; working her muscles and her horse's until she felt that she had regained her former skill.

When she had returned to her quarters and changed into a fresh gown, she spent a few hours in the library itself, selecting books at random and reading them until they lost their hold on her attention. Too soon, however, her ability to concentrate dwindled. Feeling that she had learned nothing that might help her, she went back to her rooms.

As she had expected, she found Commander Crayn in her sitting room. He must have asked a servant for food: he had a meal ready for her. But he was not the only man there. Third Father awaited her as well.

The monk sat in one of the chairs, half-facing Queen Estie as she entered. In both hands, he held a goblet of water, apparently trying to still their trembling. His slumped posture and slack muscles conveyed the impression that he had aged years since she had last seen him.

Crayn stood at the door, holding it for Estie. In a low voice, he answered her mute question. "Only a short time, Majesty."

Holding her breath for no clear reason, Queen Estie moved around the low table, seated herself across from the monk. The food and drink she ignored. The lines of his face claimed her attention. There were more of them, or they were deeper. His features seemed to hang loosely on their bones, dragged down by fatigue. His eyes were barely open.

Without preamble, Estie said gently, "You are weary, Father. How can I ease you?"

He shook his head. "Weary, Queen? It is nothing. With my sons and daughters in the Cult, we have been everywhere in the Repository, watching—" His voice faded.

"Watching?" she asked.

Her query appeared to startle him. "Watching?" Then he admitted, sighing, "Yes. We see too little. But what we do see is sometimes clear. We watch for hints of more violence." He managed a sad smile. "Magister Rummage cannot be everywhere. His wound still hampers him."

Estie wanted to inquire, What can you hope to see? The Cult of the Many lacked the sorcery to separate truth from lies. But the monk's air of frailty stopped her. Instead, she repeated, "How can I ease you, Father?"

With an effort, Third Father lifted his head, gazed at her through a glaze of exhaustion. "You can forgive me, Queen. You came here to find the answer to a question. Now your question has found you. Your gift—" But he was too tired to face her. His head sank until his chin rested on his breast. "I came to say—" Again, he faded to silence.

The Queen looked at Crayn, hoping for a suggestion. He offered her a rueful frown, a small shrug.

Carefully, she urged the monk, "Have more water, Father. Let me raise the goblet for you."

He blinked a few times. Almost whispering, he breathed, "I may have neglected sleep. That is not true humility, to pretend that I am more than I am."

With exaggerated care, he lifted the goblet to his mouth and drank a few swallows. Some of the water spilled on his cassock.

Fearing that he would lose his grip, Estie stood quickly, stepped around the table to take the goblet. Setting it down, she seated herself on the table close to him and clasped his hands in hers.

"There is no hurry, Father. We can offer you a bed if you would prefer to rest."

His head came up a little. "Thank you, Queen. I came to say only that I have no counsel for you. Your question has found you. When you are ready, you will choose one path or the other. Both are perilous. Either will tell you who and what you are. Forgive me that I have nothing more to give."

Still standing by the door, Crayn remarked unexpectedly, "Avoiding the choice is also a choice."

Sighing again, Third Father murmured, "Yes." He sounded relieved. "Do you see, Queen? You have no use for my counsel. You have all you need."

His eyes closed as if he were content. Slowly, he sank away from her. His hands slipped out of her hold as he leaned back until he was slumped in his chair. For a moment, his fingers twitched, tapping a message for himself. Then he drifted to sleep. His mouth hung open like a sign of acceptance.

Quietly, trying not to disturb him, Queen Estie rose to her feet.

Both are perilous. *That* she knew.

She was disturbed by the monk's apology—but more by his determination to offer it. His vow in the Cult demanded too much of him.

Abruptly, Crayn gestured for her attention. A moment later, he opened the door to admit Magister Oblique.

The sorceress stood in the doorway with her lips parted, ready to speak. After a quick look into the chamber, however, she changed her mind.

Estie indicated Third Father with a tilt of her head. Silently, she shaped the word: asleep.

Oblique nodded. Rather than entering, she beckoned for the Queen to join her in the corridor.

Tidings—

Swallowing a sting of apprehension, Estie moved to the door. As she passed Crayn, she touched his forearm, commanding him to accompany her.

In the hall, Magister Oblique spoke urgently.

"Come, Queen. The Farsighted have done what they can. Many of them need rest. Magister Bleak and two or three others will attempt to describe their glimpses of the battle."

Sweeping Queen Estie and Commander Crayn with her, the sorceress strode down the corridor at a sharp pace.

Before Estie could ask a question, Oblique explained,

"You must understand, Queen. The Farsighted must have light to see. Darkness and deep shadows thwart them. Between us and the Open Hand, there is no terrain high enough to block their view. Nevertheless the setting sun half dazzles them. When night falls—which will be soon—they will see nothing except flames as the city burns."

Scrambling within herself, Estie said reflexively, "No."

"No?" demanded the Magister. She did not understand. How could she? The Repository had lost a vital resource when Magister Facile had left Bifalt's side.

"Rile will not fire the city," declared the Queen. "Not at once." She had been present for some of her husband's discussions with General Klamath. She knew their reasoning. "His army is huge, he has come a great distance with no supplies except what his ships carry, and he still has far to go. He hopes to scavenge in the Hand. He will not risk burning the city's stores.

"He has no priests to warn him. He cannot know that King Bifalt has emptied the city." That had been Bifalt's stated intention ever since Rile's ships had approached the Bay of Lights. "His own stores are gone."

After a moment, Magister Oblique breathed, "Extraordinary. I have said it before. Your King Bifalt exceeds our expectations."

Wait, thought Estie grimly. My husband is not done. He has more to show you.

She was proud of him—and terrified for him. She knew him well, but had no idea what he would do next. Whatever it was, it would be extreme.

Magister Oblique led the Queen and her Commander through the Repository by unexpected ways, but always upward. After the last stairway, they had climbed to a level below Magister Marrow's ruined workroom. Soon they entered a wide passage that seemed familiar. The former librarian's public chamber had opened on one side to allow free access. There, the windows on the narrow end of the workroom had faced west. They had looked down on the broad balcony and parapets above the library's gates. Here, the corridor led straight into Magister Oblique's destination: a rectangular space oriented with its long wall and tall windows to the west. As Estie approached the chamber, she saw a glory of sunset in the far distance, ruddy orange streaking through scraps of black clouds. It colored her destination the hue of flame, a sign that the world in the west was on fire.

That, she supposed, was the new librarian's workroom.

As she and Crayn followed their guide into the chamber, Estie noticed another difference between it and Magister Marrow's. Beatrix Threnody had chosen a place level with the outer balcony. Among the windows, doors allowed the librarian to step outside and watch the Last Repository's enemy arrive.

Despite her blindness, Magister Threnody was able to move like a woman perfectly aware of her surroundings. Estie had witnessed it.

The new librarian's singular talent must have gifted her with senses other than sight.

With Crayn at her shoulder, Queen Estie forced her attention away from the sun's dying and scanned the workroom.

A trestle-table like Magister Marrow's, but empty of books, occupied one narrow end of the chamber. There, tall stools had been scattered apparently at random; but none of the gathered people sat. Even Magister Threnody stood, overtopped by almost everyone. Estie located her by her wealth of stark raven hair. It commanded notice when she did not. No one present seemed less likely to be responsible for the library's knowledge and survival.

Queen Estie had imagined that every inhabitant of the Repository would want to hear the Farsighted, but she was mistaken. No more than twenty people had come to the workroom. And they were silent, apparently holding their collective breath.

Waiting—

Among them, Estie saw Magister Rummage with Magister Avail and—to her surprise—Apprentice Travail. The hunchback still wore a heavy bandage around his lower belly. Despite his strength, his skin had the pallor of convalescence. Travail stood beside the deaf Magister. One hand rested on Avail's forearm, ready to tap.

But there were no shamans or physicians present. No monks of the Cult of the Many, not even Fifth Daughter. No servants.

And none of the Farsighted.

None?

In the dying red of the sunset and the warmer glow of the chamber's lamps, Queen Estie studied the audience more closely. Apart from Travail, virtually everyone was a Magister. After a moment, however, she spotted a strange figure in a corner far from the librarian's desk. Except for her head, the woman seemed to be made of bright iron, metal polished to a sheen that caught the light. Then Estie realized that she was clad in armor from her shoulders to her feet. At every joint, the shaped metal plates made small clanking sounds whenever she adjusted her stance or shifted her grip on the hilt of her massive longsword. If her protection included a helm, she had not brought it with her.

Magister Oblique noticed Estie's staring. "She is a Knight of Ardor," whispered the sorceress. "She wears her armor at all times so that her strength will not fail in combat. I will introduce you later, if you wish. She is a—"

Abruptly, Oblique stopped herself as Magister Bleak led two companions into the chamber.

One the Queen recognized: a tall albino man with hair and eyelashes as white as the sheet he wore as a garment. She had last seen him kneeling beside his dead spouse, sister, or kinswoman, a victim of the explosion that had slain Magister Marrow. Now his grief was written on his features, as legible as his hard fury.

The other Farsighted was a short, round woman, hardly taller than Magister Threnody. Exertion flushed her cheeks as if she had been running to keep up with Magister Bleak. Consternation filled her eyes, the effects of what she had seen.

Like the albino, she was clad in a white sheet. The two of them were not considered Magisters.

Around Beatrix Threnody, the gathering parted. Magister Bleak strode straight for her, halted two paces in front of her. Without any word or bow of greeting, he announced, "We have seen what we can, librarian. Now there is nothing. The last glow of sunset lingers in the west, but the old city and Belleger's Fist cast their shadows over the Open Hand. Also, the moon has not risen yet. Without light, our gifts are useless."

"Not *nothing*," murmured the plump woman. But Magister Bleak ignored her.

"Then tell us," answered Threnody, "what has occurred there. We must know."

"Yes," said Bleak. "Well." He glanced at Estie. His tone implied a melody as he began.

"Late in the afternoon, the first of the Great God's armored infantrymen reached the city. We expected them to pause and gather while they prepared a formal siege. They did not. They marched into the Hand by the nearest street.

"Magister Rummage calls this the tactics of overwhelming force."

Estie could imagine the hunchback's vehemence as he tapped out his explanation. "They strike at once because they expect to sweep the King's forces aside with ease.

"As they entered the city, they began to fall, perhaps shot. Only a few, a paltry number. But those men did not rise again. Their fellows responded by attacking the buildings on both sides, rampaging through doors and walls where we could not see them. The riflemen there are surely dead."

The woman in iron interrupted him. "No." Her voice scraped like a blade sliding from its sheath. "Magister Rummage is correct. The enemy relies on overwhelming force. Belleger's King responds with the tactics of unequal warfare. He must. We call this form of combat 'sting and fly.' His men will not linger to be butchered. When they are countered, they will escape to another covert and strike again."

Magister Bleak scowled at the woman's presumption. Ungraciously, he admitted, "Perhaps.

"The pattern," he resumed, "continued for some distance. The attackers marched inward. Again and again, a few of them fell. Homes, stables, and merchantries were broken open. The infantrymen did not slow their advance.

"Then the light failed."

The albino cleared his throat. "At the last," he said in a high tenor, "we watched figures running over the rooftops. We could not see them clearly."

"After that," asserted Magister Bleak, "nothing."

"Not *nothing*," repeated the short Farsighted.

"What do you see now, Joyly?" asked Magister Threnody.

"Little enough, librarian," replied the woman anxiously. "There are small winks of light like flames. Less than stars. Gone in an instant. But they lie along the line of the enemy's march. They may show where rifles are firing."

Rifles, thought Queen Estie. Sting and fly. That sounded like Bifalt to her. He wanted to hurt Rile's forces, yes, but he would risk as few of his soldiers as possible.

"That line," she asked the Farsighted called Joyly. The muzzle flashes. "Where does it lead?"

The albino answered for his companion. "None of the city's streets are straight. But when we were able to see it, the march tends northward."

"Toward your road, Queen," hummed Magister Bleak sourly. "First into Amika. Then east. It is the quickest way."

"Keep watching," urged Estie. "King Bifalt will not allow Rile to take my road."

Surely there would be *something* to see. If Bifalt had not escaped the city. If he now led the opposition.

No. There was no *if* about it. She knew Bifalt too well. He was *there*. He would not hazard his men unless he shared their peril with them.

Her whole heart depended on his ability to surprise her.

The Magisters around her hardly seemed to breathe. Despite the wall of windows and the deepening cold of night, the chamber felt unnaturally warm. Apprentice Travail wiped sweat from his brow. Avail stood with his eyes closed, apparently concentrating on Travail's touch; waiting for news that he could relay to the rest of the Repository. Magister Rummage glowered at the Farsighted with his own fire in his eyes. Magister Oblique's attention was fixed on Bleak and his comrades. She might not have noticed if Estie had fainted.

Amika's Queen was not a woman who fainted.

She needed some reason to believe that Bifalt would survive.

"Joyly?" asked Magister Threnody.

"Nothing, librarian," murmured the woman. "Just those small winks. They are erratic, but they persist."

"Still tending northward," put in the albino.

Threnody turned to Estie. "Queen? What do you expect the Ki—?"

"There!" Magister Bleak's sharpness cut off the librarian's question. At the same instant, the other Farsighted flinched. "Fire! A *line* of fire! A *distinct* line. And it is intense. Wood and oil do not make such a blaze. Their flames would spread and diminish. This fire does not. It is fed by a Decimate."

"Yes!" snapped the albino. "At last! *Real* opposition."

"It sheds light." Excitement masked the tune in Bleak's voice. "We see its surroundings. It forms a diagonal across the enemy's march, blocking an intersection of streets. It does not harm the buildings. People flee there. The way north is open to them. The infantrymen must charge through fire to pursue."

"They will not," declared the stranger, the Knight. "Their armor is iron. The heat will roast them." With a touch of grim humor, she remarked, "It is not a pleasant death."

"They hesitate," said the albino. "Now they march again. But not through the barrier. They take a street westward." Bitterly, he concluded, "They will turn north at their next opportunity."

"Do you still see muzzle flashes?" asked Queen Estie.

Joyly answered without hesitation. "No, Queen. The fire is too bright. But infantrymen still fall." Clearly, she understood the point of Estie's question. "The King's men knew that this would happen. They are in position to shoot."

Estie forced herself to breathe. Sweat stung her eyes. Rather than wipe it away, she squeezed them shut. Ordinary sight was useless. She needed to *hear*.

And understand. And pray.

"*There.*" Magister Bleak clenched his fists. "They have found a way north. The whole march follows its leaders past the fire." With sudden satisfaction, he said, "And now they do not try to avenge their fallen. They stay in their ranks."

Nodding, the albino added, "Their pace quickens."

"They begin to grasp their peril," said the Knight. "They know now that the King is ready for them."

The idea thrilled Queen Estie. It appalled her.

"But their way north remains open," protested the albino.

Five heartbeats later, Bleak cried, "It does *not*! See?" He gestured as if his audience shared his gift. "Another line of flame! Again, it blocks the enemy's path. Again, it is diagonal—and as hot as the first. Wood, oil, and the Decimate of fire. The infantrymen are forced to the west again."

And in the west of the Open Hand, thought Estie, stood the old city on its hill. The old city and Belleger's Fist.

Bifalt was there. She felt sure of it. Every beat of her heart told her that he was there.

Magister Threnody turned to the Knight. "Sword Eradimnie, how do you interpret these tactics?"

The woman clanked her sword for emphasis. "The King means to deflect this enemy's attention, librarian. He has no other means to protect the north. A few deaths will not serve. But to succeed, he must give battle from a fortified place. Otherwise, he will be overrun with ease. These barriers restrict his foe's choices. They lure or compel the enemy to strike at him where he is strongest."

Behind the walls of the old city.

Magister Rummage nodded like a man in a rage.

Queen Estie opened her eyes, rubbed the sweat away. For a moment, she felt disoriented, unsure of where she stood among the Magisters. Then her vision cleared.

She moved to Joyly's side. Whispering, she asked, "Do people still flee north?"

"Yes, Queen," answered the woman. "A few."

Estie caught her breath, held it, then asked in a rush, "Can you recognize any of them?"

Joyly squinted into the distance. "One," she murmured carefully. "Perhaps two. The third son, Prince Lome? And is that—?" With a flick of her gaze, she referred her question to her companion.

"The Land-Captain," declared the albino. "Erepos."

The plump woman nodded. "They are the last, Queen. They shepherd others ahead of them. No one follows."

Queen Estie hugged herself to contain the clamor of her pulse, her nerves. She drew too many conclusions in an instant. Lome must have chosen to help Erepos evacuate the city. If so, he had put treachery behind him.

Lure or compel. Bifalt was in the old city. Offering himself as bait.

"Magister Bleak?" asked the librarian. Her innate uncertainty hampered her. "Has the enemy found another road north?"

"Yes, librarian." Bleak strained to see. Beyond the second line of fire, the vanguard passed out of the light's reach. "It may be a broad street. Foemen still fall. They do not—" He stopped himself, peering to pierce the darkness by force of will. Then he crowed, "Yes! A third line of fire like the others. The enemy must march through it or turn west."

"Belleger's King," remarked the Knight, "has foreseen the enemy's path. That man plans well."

"And the street west?" pursued Magister Threnody.

Magister Bleak understood her. "It leads toward the old city. The enemy is near enough to discern the fortifications."

"Then Rile's soldiers will forget the north and attack." Sword Eradimnie sounded confident. "They cannot leave a foe of unknown strength at their backs."

"The infantrymen do not turn aside," offered the albino. "They go where their leaders take them."

"The first fire fades," added Joyly. "The darkness there is too deep. I cannot see more."

Estie's gown clung to her limbs. Sweat made the fabric stick to her back. Why was the workroom so warm? Was there too much poised sorcery around her? Too much tension?

How many men had Bifalt kept with him in the Open Hand? Hundreds? But he must have scattered half of them through the Hand to shoot and flee, *sting and fly*—and to protect the burning barricades. Did he think that he could defend the old city with so few riflemen? Against the Great God's thousands?

Rile's spies, his priests, were gone. Without them, he might think that Belleger's entire army waited for him inside those walls. He had come this far guided by his strange link with his Church. Somehow, Elgart had ended that threat. Now the Great God was as blind as Magister Threnody. As blind as Estie herself.

Crayn touched her arm. "Are you well, Majesty?" he asked softly. "You are flushed. It makes me think of fever."

With an effort, Queen Estie turned to the Commander. He was not sweating. Excitement or apprehension heightened his color, that was all. Scanning the chamber quickly, Estie saw that only she and Apprentice Travail had moist faces, damp brows.

Fever? Poison?

She dismissed that possibility. She had too much at stake: more at this moment than anyone in the Last Repository.

Magister Bleak was complaining. "The vanguard has passed beyond the light. We are blind. We cannot tell if those men have turned back toward the Queen's road."

"The second line of fire begins to fail," reported the albino. "The march does not change."

"How will—?" croaked the Queen. She tried again. "How will we know what happens?"

No one answered her. No one spoke at all. The Knight's armor clinked softly in the corner. Twisted by the shape of his back, Magister Rummage's breathing was a raw wheeze. Magister Avail's lips moved without a sound, addressing minds elsewhere in the Repository. He kept his eyes closed.

Travail was watching Estie. When she noticed his gaze, she saw a new anguish written on his mien: a present pain, not an old one. His efforts to translate for Magister Avail wracked him—or something else did. Sweat ran down his cheeks like tears.

Then a sharp *"Yes!"* burst from Magister Bleak. *"That* is how!"

Joyly turned away in shock. The albino surged forward a step.

"Torches!" proclaimed Bleak. "The defenders have lit torches along the wall. Set below the parapets. They will not shine in the eyes of the riflemen. The men can see to aim."

"And the enemy?" prodded the librarian.

Without hesitation, the Farsighted Magister answered, "They gather in the open space before the gates, more and more of them. It appears that the Great God has given them no other task. When the fortifications fall, and the defenders are dead, his forces will do whatever they will to the Open Hand."

"Magister Bleak." Perhaps for Estie's sake, Threnody's tone held a hint of reproof. "Tell us more. Who holds the walls?"

He studied the scene. "We see riflemen, scores of them. But faces we know?" Scowling, he searched. "We—" Almost at once, he announced, "Yes! Elgart is there. He is plain enough. And Prince Jaspid. He stands on the ramparts like a man shouting defiance. But—?" He scanned far-ther. "Perhaps—? Yes, there. *That* is King Bifalt. We cannot be mistaken."

The heat was misery and helplessness. It was indecision. Estie felt a wild impulse to pull her gown down off her shoulders, let her skin breathe. She thought that her heart had stopped. As far as she knew, there was no way out of the old city except through the gates. Bifalt was trapped.

He was going to sacrifice himself.

After that, the Farsighted had difficulty describing the action clearly. Too many men were moving. The soundlessness of the scene must have been eerie. The growing multitude of Rile's infantry formed an uninterpretable turmoil. The position of the torches obscured the responses of King Bifalt's men.

Brief streaks of flame showed that those men were shooting, but the surrounding night concealed the effects of their fire. What could they do against foes in iron armor? Some infantrymen fell. Their numbers did not diminish the inrush of fresh forces.

One of Rile's officers must have bellowed a command, a shout no one in the Repository heard. Men ran at the gates, tried to break through with their shoulders. But the gates were strong. At one time, age had made the wood brittle. Over the years, however, King Bifalt had reinforced them. They held.

From somewhere, bowmen appeared in the throng of the enemy. They managed three or four flights of arrows. A few riflemen were struck. But the King's men had been training for years. Elgart was a superior marksman. And Prince Jaspid had no equal. When they were able to locate the archers in the seething mass of the enemy, they fired until there were no more arrows.

Bifalt could be seen in glimpses, moving along the wall to give instructions or advice, doing what he could for his few wounded. The fallen were hidden by the parapets.

Now Magisters appeared among the defenders, eight of them. Their robes did not identify their Decimates. And they did not unleash sorcery on the enemy. They stood together behind the riflemen while King Bifalt gave them their orders. Then they spread out to protect as much of the wall as they could.

They would not last long, thought Estie. She knew those fortifications better than anyone with her except Crayn. The scene that she fashioned in her mind stunned her. Whatever those Magisters did, they had too little stamina. They could not stand against an enemy who had broken into the Bay of Lights despite riflemen, Magisters, and cannon. An enemy whose sorcerers had powers she could not imagine.

She may have waited a long time for the outcome. Or the time may have been short. She could not measure it. Her husband's peril consumed her.

When Magister Bleak shouted, "Earthquake!" she might have fallen to her knees if Crayn had not caught her.

The infantrymen drew back from the walls. As they shifted away, the ground in front of the gates began to crack and heave. Chunks of dirt and stone were swallowed. Debris like scree spat upward. Ripples spread out along the base of the wall.

Estie could not see it. Fear and the Farsighted painted it for her. The enemy's Decimate grew stronger. In another moment, the gate's anchor-stones would start to split. Twisting forces would tear the gate itself apart. The men on the ramparts would be pitched to their deaths. Rile's solders would swarm—

"No!" gasped Bleak. "The King's Magisters—!"

While Bleak panted, the albino rasped, "Their Decimate is earthquake also. What one sorcerer can do, another can counter. They *dismiss* the enemy's attack. The ground settles."

Even this threat, Bifalt had foreseen.

Tension gripped the librarian's workroom. None of the Magisters moved a muscle. Commander Crayn stood as if he were made of stone.

"It is not enough!" cried Joyly. "Another wave—"

"The Great God's sorcerers," coughed Magister Bleak between gasps. "I did not know that they could be so strong."

"The ground rises again," snarled the other Farsighted. "Curse them! This heave is greater."

Working together, the King's Magisters fought back, all of them. They poured out as much of their talent as they had, like against like, striving to settle the earthquake as it shook the paving-stones, the walls, the gate. The riflemen fired and fired, trying to hit Rile's sorcerers. Even three or four losses among his earthquake-wielders might be enough.

"They can do it," panted Bleak. "They *can*."

But the Great God had already succeeded. The Farsighted had concentrated their attention on the area around the gates. Gripped by the struggle there, they had neglected the more distant stretches of the wall where the torches and Magisters were fewer.

All three Farsighted yelped as an eruption of stone and dirt snagged at one edge of their vision. They wheeled in time to see a wide section of the wall leap into the air and come crashing down, tremendous in its silence. The few riflemen there were flung into the rubble, caught by great blocks of stone and crushed. A Magister died with them. If they screamed, the Farsighted could not hear them.

A fatal gap had been opened. Rile's army surged toward it.

"Bifalt," moaned Queen Estie. She did not realize that she had said his name aloud. She had no idea that she was weeping. "Bifalt."

Magister Threnody stepped closer to Magister Bleak. She knotted her fists, clenched her courage in both hands.

"The King!" she demanded. "Do you see him? If his men still live? And his Magisters? What does he do?"

Bleak wiped his face. "Forgive me, librarian. The shock—" He jerked his head from side to side. "The King. The King."

Like a curse, the albino said, "Above the gates."

"Yes," agreed Magister Bleak. "There. With the Prince and Elgart. Other men. He waves his arms. He may be shouting. His riflemen and Magisters run. He must be ordering them off the wall. They are passing out of sight."

"And then?" asked the librarian weakly.

Bleak was too distressed for courtesy. "How can we know?" he practically shouted. "There is no *light*. Not behind the wall. Not in the whole of the old city. We cannot see without *light*."

From her corner, the Knight announced harshly, "He has lost his fortified place. He requires another. He and his people will withdraw to his citadel. His foes will pursue him."

Estie understood. The idea appalled her. There was no escape from the old city, not now, not through vast numbers of infantrymen. Where else could Bifalt go? Belleger's Fist was all he had left.

But from the Fist there was no possibility of escape. The heavy gates of the bailey, with the sturdy doors of the keep behind them, were the only way in or out.

Her husband had gone there to die, taking his riflemen and Magisters with him. Prince Jaspid and Elgart would be killed beside him.

Have mercy! she cried, as silent as the crisis of Belleger's Fist. Have mercy, Bifalt! On yourself, on your people, if not on me. We need you!

How long would the last defenders need to reach the Fist, running uphill through the old city to the Fist? She had no idea. She had passed that way countless times on horseback, or by carriage, but never on foot. And the Farsighted could not tell her. They had no light. Her husband would make his stand, first on the walls of the bailey, then at the doors of the keep, without witnesses. Without hope.

In the silence, Crayn nudged Oblique's arm. "Water for the Queen, Magister?" he whispered. "Is it permitted here?"

The sorceress shook herself like a woman waking from a trance. For perhaps the first time since the Farsighted had begun to speak, she looked at Estie. Her eyes widened in alarm. "Of course," she promised. "I will see to it."

At once, she left the chamber. In the outer hallway, she called softly for a servant. A moment later, she returned.

"What ails her, Commander? Is this another poisoning? Should I summon a shaman?"

"Ask Travail." Crayn's voice held a whetted edge. "He understands." The Apprentice was as flushed as Estie, as drenched in sweat. He would know if he was in danger.

Estie hardly heard Crayn and Magister Oblique speak. With all of her strength and will, her whole heart, she was trying not to imagine Bifalt's death, yet she could think of nothing else.

Before long, a servant entered the workroom. Keeping his head lowered, he gave a flask and goblet to Magister Oblique. Then he was gone.

Oblique filled the goblet, handed it to the Commander.

"Here, Majesty." He held up the goblet. "It is water. You must drink."

Estie blinked at him hard. He meant well. He was her friend. The heat was draining her. It felt as intense as the struggle she could not see. But she was not done.

She was *not*.

Lifting her hands as if she had never used them before, she took the goblet from Crayn, raised it to her lips, drank—and felt nothing. It was only water. It was not Bifalt's life.

Time passed until it stopped and there was light.

"Torches!" Magister Bleak's musical voice had become a guttural wheeze. "On the ramparts of the bailey. Over the doors of the Fist."

Frightened by what she saw, Joyly covered her face.

"None of the King's men are there. The King is not."

The white-skinned Farsighted bared his teeth, showing gums as red as blood. He knotted his fists in his hair, strained to pull it out in clumps.

"The gates are open," groaned Bleak. "And the doors."

"Can it be true?" whimpered Magister Threnody. "Where is the King? Where are his riflemen? His Magisters?"

"Wait," rasped the Knight.

Crayn cleared his throat. "They may be hidden in the city. If King Bifalt invites Rile's men to enter his keep, he may intend to seal them in. They will be trapped. In those halls and corridors, riflemen can kill them. His Magisters can, if they wield fire or lightning. Drought and pestilence will be too—"

A heavy thump sounded in the workroom. Another. Magister Rummage pounded the wall with his fist until a sorceress hurried to his side. Grabbing her forearm, the hunchback stabbed words into her flesh with such ferocity that she gasped.

"Magister Rummage says," she quoted, "do not be absurd. The foemen are too many. Suppose King Bifalt traps and kills hundreds of them. Thousands will remain. They will raze his city until he and his forces are dead. If that is his ploy, it gains nothing. He will be slain in the Fist."

The hunchback nodded bitterly, approving her translation.

"Wait," said Sword Eradimnie again.

"The infantrymen come." Magister Bleak seemed to be choking. "They see the gates are open. They pause. Several enter. They are not harmed. Others follow them. They fill the bailey. More crowd at their backs. They are—"

As one, Bleak and the albino gasped. "There!" coughed the pale Farsighted. "The King. On a balcony above the bailey. He is alone."

"This is madness!" croaked Bleak. "He appears to shout. He fires his rifle. He beckons as he turns away. Now he is gone."

The Knight clashed her forearms together to demand attention. "A taunt," she declared. "He goads the enemy into his citadel. I do not know why. From the first, he has aimed toward this result. But what does he gain? Until now, he has not fought like a man who means to die."

Over the Wall Mountains, the moon was rising. While Sword Eradimnie spoke, the Great God's officers organized the infantrymen. If they roared, no one in the Repository heard them. Dim and strange in the moon's silver, large companies ran across the bailey to the doors of the Fist. Dispatched by their officers, infantrymen sprang up the stairs in the bailey wall, hurried along the ramparts snatching up torches. When they descended, they carried the firelight with them. Over the Fist's doors, the flames remained, burning like an invitation.

Magister Bleak did his best to convey what was happening. Packed shoulder to shoulder, Rile's soldiers confronted the darkness inside the keep, brandishing their broadswords as they advanced. In a thick stream, a killing river, they entered Belleger's Fist with their few torches. Soon the waiting dark swallowed those lights. The fires above the doors lit the enemy as more and more and still more accepted the King's taunt. There was nothing else for the Farsighted to see. If the infantrymen met any opposition, it was invisible.

Estie's skin burned. With her whole body, she felt the pressure of a storm growing. Any spark might set her blazing.

Too quick and brief to reveal anything, a muzzle flash showed at one of the lower windows. And another, several rooms away. A short time later, torchlight gleamed at those windows. Swiftly, it moved on.

Moonlight showed more men marching like shadows into the bailey. They seemed endless. Torchlight glinted on their swords and their iron armor as they surged inward.

Belleger's Fist was small compared to the Repository, a minor pile of inhabitable stone. And it had been raised to endure a siege, not to be defended room-to-room. Nevertheless it was huge, hived with corridors and stairs, halls and chambers. Despite their hundreds and their constant inrush, the Great God's forces might need hours to search the whole keep. But they cut down everyone they found. Bifalt might contrive to stay alive a while longer. He had Jaspid and Elgart with him. His bodyguards. His surviving riflemen. He might last longer than Estie expected.

Tears ran down her cheeks, dripped from the line of her jaw. Sweat bled into her eyes. With every beat of her heart, she tried to give up hope, let it go. But she could not. She could not.

Surprise me, Bifalt, she begged. Please. Surpass yourself. I am not enough without you.

"We are done," wheezed Magister Bleak. "Without light?" The distance was gone from his gaze. He looked around him like a man who had never seen any of these people before. "We must rest. We will study whatever remains when the sun rises."

He turned to go.

The librarian put out a hand to stop him, then let it fall.

But the albino was angrier. His spouse or sister or friend had been killed. "Wait," he demanded. "There is more."

"More?" panted Joyly.

"The torches over the doors. They waver. Some wind has risen—" The albino caught himself. "No! *Look*, Magister. The doors crack. The whole front of the keep shudders. It is the Decimate of earthquake!"

Magister Bleak jerked up his head, squinted into the east. "What?" he asked. "The torches have gone out."

"*Now* they have!" shouted his comrade. "But there is moonlight. Can you not *see*? The walls crack. The cracks run upward. Windows shatter.

"That tower!" He pointed at something that only the Farsighted could see. "It *leans*. It will fall!"

"I see." Bleak seemed to be sobbing. "The stones are breaking. They cannot stand."

"It is the Decimate of earthquake!" repeated the albino. "The Fist crumbles. It will collapse on itself."

"But how?" Magister Threnody may have been trying to shout, but her voice was a whisper. "How did he persuade his Magisters to kill themselves? And him? And all his men?"

As if she had heard enough, the Knight of Ardor suddenly left her corner and stamped out of the workroom, clanking as she went.

More loudly, the librarian repeated, *"How?"*

"*Why?*" protested Magister Oblique. "*Why* would the King do such a thing? To himself? To his people?"

Again, the tall Farsighted wrenched at his hair. He tore strands from his scalp. "Ask the stars!" he yelled. "Ask the mountains! We cannot see his mind! We cannot see him at all!

"Belleger's Fist falls!"

"Everyone," panted Magister Break. "Crushed. Everyone there." Then he seemed to rally. "Hundreds of the Great God's men." He spoke more strongly. "Several hundreds. Perhaps the cost is not too high."

Queen Estie staggered. The whole keep? All of Belleger's Fist? Destroyed because King Bifalt commanded it?

The atrocity of it—

Deep inside her, down where her fears and passions twisted around each other, something broke. Her crisis became more than she could bear.

Snatching her arm away from Crayn, she strode across the chamber. He shouted after her, but she refused to hear him. She hardly saw the Magisters in her way.

As desperate as any madwoman, Queen Estie of Amika went to confront Magister Avail.

He still stood with Apprentice Travail's hand on his forearm. His eyes were open now, staring at Estie. The horror in his gaze had the force of a scream.

In silence, Travail wept. Nevertheless he regarded her as if he had known that she would come.

To the deaf sorcerer, she shouted, "Awaken me!"

Her distress was too flagrant to be misunderstood. He seemed to hear her without Travail's touch.

"*No*," he groaned. "Not like this. It is worse than folly." He appeared to wail, but he did not raise his voice. "You cannot make this choice now. The King's death— A terrible blow. You must choose calmly. You will hate what you have done if you do not choose calmly."

Estie surged closer. With both fists, she thumped the plump flesh of Magister Avail's chest. Fiercely, she insisted, "*Awaken* me. Do you think *you* have been cursed? *I* am cursed! My husband has made me a wasteland. I am left with nothing. Open your heart. *Awaken me.*"

Travail wrote the words like tears on Avail's forearm.

The Magister's features were a visage out of his own worst nightmares. He snatched his arm away. With both hands, he covered his face. "Queen," he moaned. "Oh, Queen. Is this what who you are requires?"

Then he seemed to shrink into himself, collapsing inward like Belleger's Fist. She had released an earthquake among his foundations. The prospect of losing him threatened to shatter her.

But he was not lost. He was searching himself for something. For courage, perhaps. Or cruelty.

Or compassion.

He did nothing that she could see, said nothing that she could hear. There were no gestures. No incantations.

Silence surrounded her. No one attempted to dissuade her. For her, everyone else had vanished, every emotion, every outcry. Only she and Magister Avail remained.

Only the two of them—and sorcery.

She no longer felt heated. She *was* heat. Without warning, her world reeled. There was no stone under her feet, no walls and windows and people around her, no sensations in her hands or her face or her skin, no air anywhere. Instead, there was *power*.

As soon as she felt it, she knew what she could do. She was not done. Not while she lived. The silence in the chamber had become absolute, but that blank quiet had no meaning. Nothing mattered except her awakened gift.

The voice of her mind. From her mind to other minds. To any mind she chose.

With all of her strength, she cried out: **BIFALT!!**

Then she surrendered. Until that moment, she had not realized that she was exhausted. The floor seemed like a good place to rest.

NINETEEN

AMONG THE FOUNDATIONS

As he left the balcony over the doors of Belleger's Fist, King Bifalt ran.

Not knowing whether the enemy would understand him, he had shouted, "I am here, you scum! Come for me if you dare! I will show you how the kings of Belleger defend their own!" But he had not stayed to watch the effect of his taunting. He had no doubt that the mass of infantrymen in the bailey would come after him.

True, they could not know how strong his forces were, or how many Magisters he had. Despite their devotion to their god, they were not witless. They would suspect some trick. Nevertheless the tactics of overwhelming force dictated their decisions. Bifalt had taunted them only to infuriate them. He wanted them to come after him at once.

He did not know how much longer Set Ungabwey would live.

Running, he went by the quickest ways down through the levels of the keep toward its foundations. Rather than fear, he felt a fierce eagerness. He was a soldier by nature and training. He could not win the war, but he knew how to win this battle.

If his preparations did not fail.

Prince Jaspid and Elgart accompanied him. Jeck led them. Malder watched their backs. Spliner and Boy were already in the depths, poised to do whatever they could to keep the caravan-master alive.

The King had lost a few riflemen to the enemy's archers, and more when the Decimate of earthquake had breached the walls. By now,

Magister Astride and her comrades should be waiting to escape through the tunnel when it was completed. His soldiers had other orders.

Many of them were the Fist's former guardsmen. They knew its passages. The King had instructed them to scatter and hide, shooting only when they caught the infantrymen by surprise. He wanted them to feign a desperate defense. "But," he had told them, "do not risk yourselves. Know your paths to the cellars. We cannot suffer more losses."

Skipping down stairs three at a time, Bifalt hoped that most of his men would rejoin him. Hells, he hoped for *all* of them. But he did not expect that they would be so fortunate.

"I can do it, Majesty," said Jaspid, not for the first time. He could have matched the King's pace for hours. And he hungered for grand gestures. He believed that only he could do what was necessary and live. "I am faster than you."

King Bifalt did not waste his breath answering.

He may have heard shots. He could not be sure. The slap of moccasins on stone obscured more distant sounds.

Three riflemen caught up with him. Then another five. He wished for more. But he had left the balcony while most of them were still spreading through the Fist. It was too soon to fear for them.

He and his companions slowed as they reached the only entrance into the Fist's foundations: an archway like a maw near the ceiling of the vaults. Two steps beyond the arch, the stairs clung to one wall, a hard turn to the left. Anyone foolish enough to rush through the opening would miss the turn and fall twenty feet to the floor.

Jeck and two riflemen hurried downward. King Bifalt paused with Elgart and Prince Jaspid to scan the forest of pillars that supported the whole of Belleger's Fist.

From the archway, those pillars prevented Bifalt from seeing his workmen and the mouth of the tunnel, but he knew where Set Ungabwey would be. The caravan-master had been placed half-reclining behind a column directly below the entrance and perhaps forty paces away. Alive or dead, he would be invisible to Rile's men when they reached the entrance and looked out at the vaults.

Alerted by footsteps and panting on the stair, Boy and Spliner stood beside Master Ungabwey to greet the King. They had the Magisters of earthquake with them. One had been lost when the wall of the old city fell. Now the remaining seven men and women waited anxiously, unsure of what to expect—or of what they might be asked to do. An earthquake here would kill them all.

Satisfied, Bifalt led Elgart, Jaspid, Malder, Jeck, and a growing number of riflemen down the stairs.

Boy and his father said nothing until the King neared them. Then Spliner cleared his throat.

"He lives, Majesty. I do not know how. We have feared—" He stopped, unable to find the words he needed.

Boy intervened. "For a day now, Majesty," he said, "we have feared that every breath would be his last. Every drop of blood he exhales seems to announce an end. Yet he is still with us. When he opens his eyes, his gaze is clear. He can make his needs plain."

King Bifalt nodded. "I will speak with him." A moment later, he told Boy, "Guide these Magisters to the tunnel. They must enter as soon as it opens. I do not mean to lose them."

He despised Magisters. He had always distrusted them. But none of these seven had shirked for an instant when he had risked them earlier. They had earned his respect.

"As you say, Majesty." Boy loosened his shoulders and rolled his head, making an effort to appear relaxed as he collected the theurgists. With him, they moved deeper among the pillars.

For reasons of his own, Spliner muttered, "A good son."

More riflemen hurried down the stairs, eight or ten of them. Bifalt considered his brother and Elgart. The Prince was like a burning fuse. If he did not keep busy, he might explode. Elgart was calmer. The scar that split his face gave his grin a wolfish cast, but he knew how to wait.

To Jaspid, the King said, "Organize the men as they come, Brother. Hide some behind the nearest pillars. Remind them that only a direct hit can hope to pierce that armor." The elevation of the arch would make shots from below glance off. "Place the others farther away to cover our retreat."

"As you say, Majesty." At once, the Prince went to intercept the men on the stairs.

While Bifalt considered a task for Elgart, one of the laborers came trotting from the back wall. He was a burly man caked in dirt, dust, and sweat. Too tired to bow, he announced bluntly, "We cannot do it, Majesty."

Bifalt had promised the workmen more time. He had not known then that Rile's army had quickened its pace.

His heart skipped a beat. Nothing showed on his face. "Cannot?"

"No." The man was breathing hard. Dismay showed through the grime on his face. "We are well under the wall. Twenty paces? But we have hit granite. It is like a shelf over our heads. We can chip at it, but it does not crack.

"It extends too far. We cannot dig past it."

Cannot? That was a heavy blow. Yet Bifalt accepted it like a soldier. When he misjudged his circumstances, he moved on without hesitation. Too many lives depended on him.

"Go to the Magisters," he commanded Elgart. "Take them into the tunnel. Tell them to deal with that granite."

Elgart paused long enough to ask, "Without collapsing the tunnel?" At once, he answered himself. "Perhaps. Magister Pillion used his Decimate like a shovel in his garden."

Grimacing for his dead friend, Elgart jogged away.

The workman took another moment to catch his breath. Then he followed the King's friend.

King Bifalt looked around, counted at least twenty riflemen listening to Jaspid's orders. More were on the stairs. They might not be the last, if the rest did not fall to Rile's men.

Leaving Jeck and Malder to keep watch, Bifalt went to see Set Ungabwey's condition for himself.

The caravan-master had lost much of his bulk. His wealth of flesh was melting off him by the hour. Perhaps that loss had sustained him somehow. He would not endure much longer.

In his crippled left hand, he held a knot of fuses. Any flame there would light them all. On the floor by his right hand waited a striker with an oil wick. When the time came, he would have to press the striker hard enough to make a spark. If the wick caught the spark and burned, his last task would be to lift the striker and touch fire to the fuses. Whatever happened then, he would be *done*.

From the knot in his hand, fuses snaked in all directions. Each of them led to kegs of gunpowder set against the base of a column. King Bifalt had selected twelve targets: more than enough, he judged, to accomplish his purpose. The timing of the fuses he had left to Prince Jaspid.

Once the fuses were lit, the enemy would see them burning, smoking. If they were too long, Rile's infantrymen might have time to stamp them out. For that reason, Jaspid had cut each fuse as short as possible. The result would be a staggered series of detonations. Their accumulating force might achieve as much as a single concussion. And if the enemy managed to extinguish one or more of the fuses, the others would still do their work. They might be enough.

The moment was near. King Bifalt could have wasted his time worrying it. Instead, he concentrated on Set Ungabwey.

In the flickering torchlight, the dying man looked like a figure carved in wax, an effigy of himself. Bifalt could not see him breathe. For a few heartbeats, the King scrambled to make new decisions. Send Jaspid to light the fuses? Do it himself? The last man to leave might be caught by the shock of the first blast—or by shattered stones flying like bullets.

Surely, that burden belonged to Belleger's King.

More riflemen were running down the stairs. Sure of himself, Prince Jaspid positioned them to protect the fuses as well as each other and Master Ungabwey.

Then a fresh bead of blood bubbled out of the tube in Set Ungabwey's chest that enabled him to breathe.

Bifalt dropped to his knees beside the caravan-master. Among the supplies that Boy had kept ready, he found a damp cloth. As carefully as he could, he dabbed the blood away. Next, he located a reed as thin as a needle. Easing it into the tube, he tried to clear out any dried blood that might block the flow of air.

A small flinch tightened parts of Set Ungabwey's slack face. He blinked, trying to open his eyes. After a moment, he looked up. His gaze was still clear.

With an effort that squeezed out more blood, he breathed, "Wine."

King Bifalt wiped away the blood, then picked up the flask of herbed wine that dulled the caravan-master's pain. Almost tenderly, he lifted it to Set Ungabwey's thick lips.

The man managed two small swallows. After that, wine dribbled down his chin.

Bifalt put down the flask. Bending over the man who had left him to die in the desert decades ago, he said, "The end is near, Master Ungabwey. The enemy fills Belleger's Fist. Soon they will find us. Then it will be time. When you strike the spark, lift the flame to the fuses. That will be enough."

The caravan-master studied Bifalt's face like a man waiting for the word that would give meaning to his long pain.

Bifalt was Belleger's King and Abbator's son. Harshly, he added, "You will not save your daughters, but you will strike a blow at the enemy. Whatever happens, he will feel that wound."

Set Ungabwey's sigh brought up more blood. He did not try to respond.

Riflemen continued to arrive. King Bifalt could not spare the attention to count them.

From the back of the cellars came a sharp *crack*, a sound like stone splitting.

Goaded by too many fears, the King demanded, "Do you understand?"

He meant, Can you do it?

The constant frown of the dying man's distress deepened. "It is," he wheezed. "Your realm. Your home."

The King swore to himself. "Do you doubt me?" he reported. "*Your* home was destroyed. You lost your people. You know what I feel. I will save as many of *my* people as I can."

With a wrenching effort, Set Ungabwey lifted the striker, braced it ready on his chest. Between ragged breaths, he asked, "How will? I know? The time?"

King Bifalt started to say, You will hear me. But that might not be enough. When the infantrymen arrived, a tumult of gunfire and iron armor would fill the high chamber. Set Ungabwey might not be able to hear—

Another *crack*, longer than the first.

Bifalt made another instant decision. "One of us will shout your name. We will shout until we see the spark."

Sighing, the caravan-master closed his eyes. He seemed to breathe a bit more easily.

Hurrying now, Bifalt glanced around until he spotted his brother. Without hesitation, he called, "Jaspid! Watch over Set Ungabwey. I must check on the tunnel. If I do not return in time, shout his name. Make him hear you."

"As you say, Majesty!" Torchlight glittered in Jaspid's eyes. He sounded suddenly eager, ready to take Master Ungabwey's place. But he did not stop ordering the riflemen.

He had set four men behind every pillar that offered a clear view of the archway and the stairs, two to shoot while their companions reloaded. Others he assigned to the columns farther back to cover their comrades and the fuses. The later arrivals, he sent to protect the Magisters, the workmen, the tunnel.

King Bifalt nodded. Cursing himself for his decisions and the Great God for whatever happened next, he led Jeck and Malder toward the tunnel.

He found Spliner and Boy, six Magisters, and a crowd of laborers hovering outside a wide hole in the foundation-wall. Among them, he recognized several of the Fist's servants, but Elgart was not there. On both sides, discarded earth and rock had been piled to extend the tunnel. As the King approached, two workmen backlit by lanterns rolled a heavy lump of granite to the opening. Panting, they let their companions shift the stone to the nearest pile.

More workmen appeared in the opening, lugging a granite slab between them. Behind them came others carrying ragged chunks. They all needed rest. Bracing their hands on their knees, they heaved for breath, retching on dust. At once, several of the laborers outside entered the hole to continue the work.

The King heard another distant *crack*.

As the men went in, Elgart squeezed past them. He paused briefly, choking on dust like the workmen, then came to King Bifalt. "That woman, Majesty," he gasped immediately. "Magister Astride." He was grinning like a madman. "I think I am in love. If I had not known Magister Pillion, I would not have believed that a Decimate could be used so precisely."

Gnawing on his cheek, the King waited.

"It would be easier," continued Elgart, "to *seal* the tunnel. But she puts her hands on that granite. She shudders with concentration. And the stone cracks. It *cracks*, Majesty. When she steps back, rocks fall at her feet like homage."

"But the way is not open?" demanded Bifalt. "We still have no escape?"

The former spy's face twisted. "Apart from her Decimate, Majesty, she is an ordinary woman. Weariness weakens her control. She will be forced to stop before she causes a collapse."

Behind King Bifalt, a shot echoed among the pillars. The first infantryman had arrived. The force of the slug spun him over the ledge. He pitched to the floor in a clang of iron.

Then half a dozen rifles barked. Metal rang, and rang again. An infantryman must have toppled down the stairs. His armor sang a song of broken limbs and blood.

Hells! To Elgart, Bifalt snapped, "We are out of time. Fetch out Astride. Drag her if you must. Then explain to the other Magisters. One of them must risk a true earthquake. We can only hold the entrance for a short time. Soon our foes will remember to *think*. They will bring shields to cover them.

"We will not last long when they reach the floor."

Set Ungabwey would have to light the fuses then or not at all.

Elgart nodded. "I understand, Majesty. As you say." At once, he whirled away to enter the tunnel.

Five or six gunshots. A pause. Five or six more. The chaos of falling iron rebounded from the walls, the pillars.

The King belonged in that fight. Belleger's Fist was his. He had made the decision to use it against the enemy. He needed to know what his Magisters would do, but he could not bear to wait while one of them obeyed him. Unslinging his rifle, he strode back toward the stairs leading down from the entrance.

Malder and Jeck stayed with him. Spliner and Boy watched over the Magisters.

Ahead of Bifalt, bullets ricocheted off stone, off iron, whining like angry hornets. Some of his riflemen were good shots. Others were simply calm enough to fire without rushing. The crash of falling bodies seemed to come from everywhere.

As he reached a column that allowed him to watch the archway, the shooting stopped. The infantrymen had pulled back.

The King did not believe for an instant that they had withdrawn. Of course, they *could*. They could keep him and his people trapped as long as they wished. When they had finished scavenging through the keep, Rile could send his own earthquake-wielders to tear the Fist apart. But Bifalt was sure. The Great God would not be content with a mere trap. The tactics of overwhelming force required a swift and fatal assault. The infantrymen had halted out of sight to regroup and think.

King Bifalt considered telling Set Ungabwey to light the fuses now. But the tunnel was still blocked. He moved one pillar closer to the stairs and forced himself to wait.

When Rile's soldiers reappeared in the archway, they had shields: breastplates which they must have claimed from men far behind them. Covering their vulnerable heads with iron, they pounded the stairs, a torrent with no apparent end.

At once, every rifleman who could see the stairs opened fire.

For a few instants, the breastplates deflected every shot. The first infantrymen reached the foot of the stairs. But then Prince Jaspid shot out an exposed knee up near the archway. Screaming, that man plunged against the soldier below him. Together, those two infantrymen knocked down the whole line. They crashed with a sound like falling anvils.

Yet the charge did not pause. Rile's men poured downward, as careless as spilled water. Even Jaspid could not hit a moving knee with every shot. And several of the toppled infantrymen began to rise from the floor. They still had their borrowed breastplates. Swinging their swords, they ran at the pillars, the riflemen. Perhaps they imagined that they were close to victory.

But they were not accustomed to fighting with shields: that was obvious. They no longer had the advantage of elevation. Holding their breastplates high, they left their torsos exposed.

A storm of lead greeted them. Fired at close range, slugs pierced the iron. Even glancing shots struck hard. Infantrymen were knocked off balance or flung backward. Instinctively, some of them lowered their shields: a fatal mistake. In moments, they were all down.

They were only the first to reach the floor. More followed them without hesitation. Many more.

Prince Jaspid concentrated his fire two steps below the archway. He missed once. Then he struck a man's hip. The bullet slammed through that man's leather skirt-armor. He staggered against the wall, started to pitch forward.

But he did not fall on the man below him. The infantrymen had already suffered one disastrous fall down the stairs. They were prepared to prevent another. The next man in line jumped lower, shoved his hip-shot comrade aside. Spraying blood, the infantryman toppled off the stairs. The charge rushed on.

Bifalt fired once. Again. Then he stopped. In the unsteady torch-light and the thick pall of gun-smoke, he could not be sure of his aim.

Between him and the stairs, bodies in a tangled pile gave their blood to the stone. Some of them still writhed, struggling to rise, or to live. But Rile's losses were too few. The nearest infantrymen kept coming. In a few more steps, their swords would reach the first of Bifalt's men.

Now? he asked himself. Was the time now?

At any moment, the attackers might notice the fuses. They might understand their peril.

Jaspid stood behind a column several strides away from the caravan-master, poised to take the dying man's place.

Deliberately, King Bifalt took his last risk.

"Now, Jaspid!" he yelled. "Set Ungabwey!"

His voice seemed to catch in his throat. He could hardly hear himself through the cacophony of screams, gunfire, ricochets, and clashing metal.

The Prince turned his head, met Bifalt's gaze, nodded.

As clear as a trumpet, Jaspid shouted, *"Set Ungabwey!"*

Then he began dodging among the pillars, moving to light the fuses if Master Ungabwey failed. If he had already lost his hold on life.

Through his teeth, Bifalt hissed, "You fool!" Now everything depended on the tunnel. Without it, he had nothing.

But he was out of time. To the nearest riflemen, he barked, "Back! Fall *back!*"

They had their orders. Trusting their comrades to cover them, they ran toward the far wall and the tunnel.

With his bodyguards, King Bifalt joined them. That was his duty. Set Ungabwey and his brother and the fuses were out of his hands. Moving more slowly than his soldiers, he bit the inside of his cheek until he drew blood. The taste steadied him.

As he passed them, the second line of riflemen took up the fight. After scant moments without gunfire, moments punctuated only by screams and running, rifles blazed defiance. The shouts of the guns and the whine of ricochets battered the air.

Hardly aware of himself, Bifalt slowed. Had Set Ungabwey succeeded? Would Jaspid? How long would the first burning fuse take to reach its gunpowder? How many of the fuses would the attackers spot? How many would they stamp out?

Bifalt's nerves shrilled with tension as he waited for hope—and still he was not braced for what came.

The first concussion hit him as if someone had slammed his back with a door. The blare of the detonation volleyed back and forth among the columns. Shards and splinters of rock shrieked through the air. The stone under his feet heaved like heavy flesh in pain. Trying to turn, trying to *see*, he missed his next step, sprawled on his face.

For an instant, he lay stunned. He thought that he had gone deaf. Then he wedged his arms under him, strained to rise.

Hands caught his shoulders, heaved him upright. As he regained his feet, he recognized Prince Jaspid.

Jaspid said something inaudible. Bifalt thumped his forehead with one hand, trying to clear his ears or his mind.

The Prince tried again. More loudly, he said, "He must have heard us." He seemed to whisper. "That old man." He shook his head. "He is tougher than any of us. He did it before I could reach him."

Jaspid had set the fuses. He knew them all. "The next blast," he added, "should come in three. Two. One."

That the King heard. With Malder and Jeck, he and his brother sprinted.

The second shock seemed to lift Bifalt and Jaspid off their feet. Or perhaps they were tossed by the stone under them. Cracks spread through the ceiling. Rocks rained behind them: small pieces, heavy blocks. Fresh screaming and the clang of struck iron filled the foundations.

The riflemen had been ordered to keep the enemy away from the fuses. They did what they could. Infantrymen crashed to the floor. But more raced down the stairs, a continuous stream. And they had seen the fuses, the burning and smoke. Some of them veered away to prevent more explosions. Others kept charging at Bifalt's men. Their broadswords cut through bronze breastplates and leather armor, hacked at limbs and necks. Bifalt saw three riflemen spurt blood and drop.

Four. Five.

There was nothing that he could do.

He did not know when to expect the next blast. Jaspid said nothing. Hurrying, they reached the back wall, the mouth of the tunnel.

Six of the Magisters were there. Spliner and Boy. All of the workmen. They were enclosed by a cordon of the King's soldiers. Were there as many as sixty riflemen? Bifalt had no time to count. Others were dying behind him.

From the mass of trapped people, Elgart emerged. As he approached, he shouted, "Magister Astride is here!" He pointed at a gasping woman propped against the wall, the only Magister coated in dust and sweat. "I had a hell's own difficulty getting her out, but you told me not to risk her."

The King shouted as well. He was not sure that he would ever hear clearly again. "Who went in?"

"They are *Magisters*, Majesty." Elgart gave him the benefit of a grin. "First, they had to *discuss*. Then they all volunteered. But one—" He paused to grimace. "Magister Bone. Not old, but in poor health. Coughing up his lungs. He said he could not survive the rigors of whatever comes next. He went."

Bifalt had time to think, If he is not too weak—

Then a third detonation shook the vaults. Thunder followed it as stones from the ceiling hammered down. That tumult covered the screams—if any of Rile's men were screaming. It sounded like ruin. The Magisters flinched or cowered. The laborers crouched like men who did not know which way to run. As if in unison, all of the riflemen staggered.

Grinding his teeth, the King told Elgart, "It must be now. We have no time."

From top to bottom, the nearby pillars spat stones and mortar. They would not stand much longer.

"Bone knows that, Majesty." Elgart's tone held a moment of sadness. "He will do what he can."

As the last few riflemen arrived, Prince Jaspid assembled them among their comrades. He knew the danger as well as Bifalt did. When the ceiling collapsed, it would bring all of Belleger's Fist down with it.

Bifalt ached for the next explosion. He wanted the Fist's destruction to take hundreds of Rile's men with it. He hoped for a thousand. But if the keep fell too soon—

Or if Magister Bone did not reach open air—

"A fuse has failed!" shouted the Prince. "The next blast is late!"

Abruptly, the floor jumped. It cracked like crazed glass. Breaks raced through the wall on both sides of the tunnel. The whole wall seemed to bow outward. Distance muffled the shrill cry of shattering granite. A sudden gale of dust and dirt spewed from the hole.

The Decimate of earthquake.

King Bifalt swallowed a mouthful of blood. That concussion might open the way—or it might block the tunnel completely.

He started to yell Elgart's name, but the former spy had already disappeared into the tunnel.

More gunpowder exploded. The blast shook the foundations from wall to wall. Its force blew out most of the torches. An accelerating avalanche of stones cut off the last of the light. Thick gloom and dust-clogged air swept outward. Bifalt could barely see. The only illumination came from the lanterns in the tunnel. Everywhere he looked, his people seemed to dissolve and become powder.

Behind him, a dozen infantrymen staggered out of the chaos. Prince Jaspid fired first. Jeck and Malder. A heartbeat later, more gunshots cut down Rile's men like a scythe of lead.

The King thought he heard Elgart call, "Come!" He may have been screaming. Bifalt heard only a whisper through the thunder and crashing of the Fist's end. He may have imagined it. But he had no choices left.

Choking on the dust in his lungs, he coughed, *"Go!"*

A few of the Magisters hesitated. Astride did not. Perhaps she thought that she might still be useful. Boy and Spliner took hold of the other Magisters, shoved them into the tunnel after Astride. At once, the workmen followed.

Bifalt watched with his heart as well as his eyes. If the passage was blocked, the rush of workmen would slow, then stop. But they moved on until they were out of sight. At Jaspid's command, the riflemen began swarming into the tunnel.

A wide slab of the ceiling crashed to the floor and burst apart fifteen paces behind Bifalt. Belleger's Fist was falling faster, harder. If he had thought about it, he could have measured his life in moments. But he had no attention to spare. Instead, he concentrated on the rush of his people. He could only see them past slivers of light from the lanterns. Then each of them passed into the darkness.

As long as they kept moving—

Another stash of gunpowder detonated. The explosion was little more than a groan amid the clamor of falling stone.

Abruptly, Bifalt felt Jaspid grab his arm. "*Now*, Majesty!" commanded the Prince. "I will keep three men to guard your back. You must go *now*!"

Bifalt felt unable to move. He stood where he was until Jaspid and Malder hauled him forward. Then he went, staggering, to join the last riflemen outside the tunnel.

Following Jaspid's example, they pushed their King ahead of them, did not let him linger or look back.

Scrambling in darkness, he fled the ruin of his home.

One after another, King Bifalt's people clambered over piles torn from the tunnel's roof. They came to Magister Bone's body. He lay dead, apparently unharmed. His heart or his lungs must have failed him.

The Magisters hurried past him, desperate for fresh air. They had lost only their weakest member. Perhaps they had expected to lose him. But the laborers were ordinary men. They recognized that Bone had given them a precious gift. One by one, they picked up chunks of rock and set them on his body before they went on, building a cairn for the fallen sorcerer.

The riflemen did the same. By the time King Bifalt reached the crude monument, only the Magister's face remained uncovered. Despite the choking pressure of dust in his throat and lungs, he paused to scoop up dirt in both hands, scatter it gently over Bone's slack visage. Jeck, Malder, and the men behind them added more rocks. Then they let their need for air drive them onward.

The outlet was a narrow split in the granite. Squirming through it, they came out on an open hillside behind what had once been the Fist's and the old city's northwest wall. At their backs, the keep was still falling in on itself, reducing the ancient seat of Belleger's kings to its own cairn.

Bifalt did not look back. Unsteadily, he ascended the slope until he stood in front of the people whom Elgart had gathered for him: six Magisters and perhaps seventy riflemen, a number of them wounded. To the east, the moon had risen above a sprawl of storm clouds. The crowd Bifalt faced looked as spectral as ghosts in the moon's silver. Beyond them in the northwest, fifty paces away, crouched the old forest clutching darkness in its bare limbs. Overhead, the stars glittered without pity or interest.

The King said nothing. No one broke the silence. The only sounds were the subsiding thunder and smash of Belleger's Fist and the wind keening through the trees. It was Bifalt's place to speak first, but he was waiting.

After a few moments, Jaspid and the last soldiers emerged. The Prince rested a hand briefly on his brother's shoulder as he and his companions went to join the other riflemen; but he made no effort to find words for what they had all lost.

Finally, the King cleared his throat. "You have done well," he said, hoarse with coughing. In the aftermath of the escape, he stood hunched like an old man. "You will do well again, when the time comes."

Then he told his people what they needed to know first.

"General Klamath has left horses for us in the forest. Food and bedding. Rain-capes. Warmer garments." A storm was coming. "A few tents. Water and fodder. Among the trees, we can make fires. We can rest there for a time."

And care for the wounded. That was essential. Bifalt had no stitchers or bonesetters with him.

To the workmen, he said, "I have no word for my gratitude. We will speak again when we have eaten and slept. It is my hope that now you are done with war."

He intended to say more. His people had a right to know what lay ahead of them. But he was struck dumb by the blare of a voice in his mind.

It shouted like all of the world's anguish: **BIFALT!!**

It dropped him to his knees. He knew that voice better than he knew his own. It was Estie's.

And he knew what it meant. She had learned who and what she was, and had made her choice. Now she was a sorceress. Like Magister Avail's, her voice could reach any mind at any distance, at the cost of total deafness for herself. Now there was no place for her anywhere, except in the library.

She had decided against her husband.

Stunned by the blow, he was gone before he fell on his face.

TWENTY

A GATHERING

Together, Jeck and Malder lifted their King from the scrub grass and freezing mud. Supported between them, he wobbled like an invalid or a drunkard, unable to stand, hardly able to see or hear. Estie's voice filled his world. It echoed back at him from the ground and the stars, from the darkness of the trees, from the destruction of Belleger's Fist.

Bifalt. Bifalt!

It was worse than sorcery. It was a choice. Estie had turned her back.

The Prince and Elgart reached him quickly. "Brother!" cried Jaspid. Elgart panted, "Majesty? Majesty?"

They could not know what Bifalt had lost.

Everything reeled. He was standing among the columns in the Fist's basement, or on the hillside, or in the sky. Blinking his eyes, he tried to focus. Somewhere inside him, there were words. He had something to say. Something to do. The war had only begun. But his world was dim with distance, too far away to compel him. Estie's shout had shattered him. Whatever Jaspid and Elgart needed to hear was lost in shock and loss.

Sharply, Jeck said, "Majesty!" He seemed to know his King better than Bifalt knew himself. Perhaps Malder knew him better as well. They had ridden into hell with him against Amikan cavalry and sorcerers.

"The enemy is not a fool. He will have scouts. We must reach the trees before we are seen."

Bifalt flinched. A whimper escaped between his teeth. He tried to call it back, but the effort was beyond him.

The enemy. The war. His people.

He needed words.

For the sake of his injured men, he found a few.

"Get everyone," he panted. "Into the forest. Help the wounded. Make fires."

The trees would shield fires from sight.

He could not say more. The truth shamed him. He was in too much pain to confess it.

Jeck glanced at Malder; at Jaspid and Elgart. At once, the Prince answered, "Elgart and I will protect him, Jeck."

Jaspid's skills were legendary. Elgart was well-known.

Jeck scowled. "As you say, Majesty." Reluctantly, he let Prince Jaspid take the King's arm. Malder allowed Elgart to replace him. The bodyguards strode away, calling commands to the riflemen and Magisters, to Boy and Spliner. Despite the lingering rumble of the Fist's ruin, their voices sounded too loud.

At Bifalt's ear, Jaspid whispered, "What hit you, Brother? All those stones. Are you hurt?"

Oh, yes, thought Bifalt. I am hurt. But those were not the words his wrecked heart demanded. He had to tell someone.

"It was Estie." The effort of speaking threatened to choke him. "In my mind."

Elgart flinched. He understood instantly.

The Prince did not. "In your mind?" he protested. "What do you mean? Was it that Magister who called you to search for the library?"

A small sound exposed Bifalt, a sob he could not suppress. He had never told his brother Estie's secret.

Suddenly fierce, Elgart snapped, "Leave it, Highness. This is not the time. We will speak of it later, you and I."

A true friend—

Elgart's retort was a slap in the face. Jaspid jerked up his head.

Anger flamed in his eyes. But he did not act on it. Restraining himself, he replied stiffly, "As you say, sir. We will speak."

Elgart nodded. Moonlight caught a glisten that may have been tears in his eyes. In silence, he and the Prince supported their King toward the trees.

Soon, Jeck and Malder returned. Gruffly, Malder said, "We will take him. Spliner and Boy have set up a tent. If he can sit and eat, there is a fire ready. If not, we will settle him in his bedding."

"He should not be seen like this," murmured Jeck. "His frailty will do more harm than his death."

Bifalt had made himself Belleger's cornerstone. If he was seen to crumble, his people might falter as well.

Elgart and Jaspid surrendered the King. Gently, Jeck and Malder bore him up the slope. The former spy and the Prince followed without speaking. Elgart could guess at Jaspid's thoughts, but he did not prod them. He had his own concerns.

Deep in the woods, Elgart and Prince Jaspid came to a clearing that would become a glade in springtime and turn lush during the summer. Now it was dirt and dead grasses exposed to the night air and the cold stars. But it was large enough to hold a camp for the survivors of the Fist's destruction.

Among the riflemen, some of the older veterans began stitching cuts and wrapping bandages for their wounded. Others distributed heavy sheepskin cloaks and oilcloth rain-capes, especially to the Magisters. Fires had been started to heat iron stewpots. But the King's people needed more than hot food. They ached for warmth to chase the fear from their bones.

Muttering to himself, Prince Jaspid went to take charge of the soldiers and post sentries. While he worked, Elgart scanned the camp.

The Magisters had one fire to themselves. They sat huddled around it like people who had no friends. Perhaps they did not want any. Elgart studied them until he located Magister Astride. Then he looked elsewhere.

At the other campfires, a few soldiers crouched over the flames to tend the stewpots. The workmen helped other riflemen pass out winter garments and raise tents. Beyond question, more fires were needed. For the moment, however, Elgart was satisfied. He looked for the King.

Near one edge of the clearing, the bodyguards stood near an isolated tent. No doubt they had put King Bifalt to bed there. So far from the fires, he would be cold despite his blankets. But he would not be seen until he was ready to emerge. Elgart approved.

For his own sake, he collected firewood from the pile that General Klamath had provided, took a brand from one of the other fires, and started a fire of his own a few paces from the King's tent. When he had it burning well, he settled down to warm his chilled bones and wait.

Almost at once, four soldiers joined him. He did not wave them off. But when three more came, he had to say something. In a pleasant voice, he advised them to leave room for the Prince.

Bitterly, one of them grumbled, "We will go when he comes."

Elgart shrugged to show that he did not object.

Before long, Prince Jaspid left what he had been doing. His hands and breastplate wore smears of blood, but he seemed unaware of them. At once, he went to the woodpile, filled his arms with logs and twigs, and built two more campfires. When they were alight, he approached Elgart.

Curtly, he told the riflemen, "I must speak with Elgart alone."

They looked around. Seeing the new fires, they struggled to their feet. Some of them bowed as they left.

When they were gone, Prince Jaspid stood for a moment, as upright as an icon, gazing around the camp. Then he sat down across the flames from Elgart.

Elgart had always enjoyed the openness of Jaspid's countenance. Everything that the Prince felt was reflected there: his angers, his frustrations, his enthusiasms. Elgart could almost read his thoughts.

Elgart reminded himself to be careful. The Prince had been hurt. That was obvious. But the scarred man could only guess at what it might be. The beating that Jaspid had received from Lylin? No. That kind of punishment was like a feast to a fighter with Prince Jaspid's skill and good nature. And there was this to consider. Jaspid's wits were sharp enough, but their horizons were narrow. Any man who dreamed of fighting alone against overwhelming numbers was not entirely sane.

Softly, Elgart asked, "How are our wounded?"

Jaspid grimaced. "Some will live. Two will not. Others need more care. For the moment, we have done what we can."

"And the sentries are in place, Highness?"

"They are," replied the Prince. Then he snorted, "Hells, Elgart. They should rest. We will not need them."

Elgart raised an eyebrow. "No?"

"I have reconsidered. The enemy has no reason to suppose that we still live." Jaspid began calmly, but his ire mounted as he continued. "And he has lost hundreds of men. He must be furious. Common caution will not relieve him. He will burn to strike *somewhere*, and strike *hard*.

"He will send his cavalry through the Hand to the Queen's road. If he can, he will enter Amika and exact retribution."

An obvious danger, thought Elgart. Under any circumstances, the Great God would aim to take advantage of that road. But the Prince had more to say. Elgart did not interrupt him.

Jaspid leaned closer, dangerously near the flames. Without preamble or forewarning, he demanded, "Bifalt said it was Estie. In his mind. But that is nonsense, sir. Destroying the Fist must have broken him. Tell me if I am wrong."

Elgart sighed. He was ready for this, but he did not like it. He did not have the right to betray any friend's secrets.

He also did not like Jaspid's tone. "You have not forgotten, Highness," he said mildly, "that my name is Elgart."

"I do not care if your name is the Great God," retorted the Prince. "I want an answer."

Elgart's face twisted, a grin on one side, a scowl on the other. "Briefly, then, Highness. The Queen-Consort has chosen sorcery. Her power is like Magister Avail's. Her mind can speak to any other mind. Distance is no obstacle."

Jaspid jerked back as if Elgart had swung a saber at him. He clutched at the first word he understood. "Chosen—? No one *chooses* sorcery. It is inborn, or it is not."

"Yes," countered Elgart, "it is a gift of birth. But it is nothing until it is awakened. *That* is the choice. Until we emerged from the Fist, King Bifalt did not know what she might become."

Watching Jaspid's dismay struggle across his mien, Elgart took pity on him. "Clearly, the Queen-Consort has reached the Last Repository." He insisted on her Bellegerin title, her bond with her husband. "She seeks aid for us, yes, but she has another reason as well. Some time ago, Magister Facile informed her that she has inherited a gift. While it slept, she was not aware of it. Magister Facile did not name it for her. She could not choose whether to awaken it or leave it sleeping.

"Now she has revealed her choice."

Nothing else could cause Bifalt so much pain.

Another man might have accepted that explanation and moved on. Jaspid's distress was more personal.

"Why did not Bifalt tell me?"

For that also, Elgart was prepared. To ease Jaspid's way, he replied as if he doubted himself. "Shame?"

"Shame?" The Prince winced. "What cause does my brother have to feel shame?"

Bifalt's friend made a placating gesture. "Consider it, Highness. In one way, the Queen-Consort's choice was between power and weakness. In another, it was between deafness and hearing. The cost of either choice was high. To you, or to me, our King's choice might seem trivial by comparison. On one side, he loathes sorcery and sorcerers. On the other, the Queen-Consort has been his devoted ally, and her love is his for the taking.

"Now he knows that he has spent many years choosing badly."

Jaspid opened his mouth, closed it again, struggling for comprehension. His gaze shied away. He had spent too long regarding his brother as the King, beyond question. He had never looked at Bifalt the way Elgart did.

Watching, Elgart tried to think of a way to help the Prince. After a moment, he offered a hint that a born fighter might understand.

"I spent days," he said, "with the most holy Amandis. She is more arrogant than anyone I know, man or woman, but she taught me a useful lesson. Anyone can be beaten. Anyone at all."

Reflexively, Jaspid protested, "Not Lylin."

Elgart allowed himself a soft laugh. "I did not say that Amandis was beaten in combat."

The Prince did not look up. Conflicted emotions fled across his visage. Briefly, he covered his face with both hands. When he lowered them, he was gazing not at Elgart, but up at the dark trees and the blind stars, searching them for answers. "*Not* in combat?" he asked as if he had forgotten Elgart. "Then how?"

The King's friend said nothing. He knew when to wait.

Abruptly, Jaspid shook himself. "She beat me too easily." Clearly, he meant Lylin. "That is the difficulty." With an effort, he met Elgart's gaze. "Perhaps Bifalt's dilemma is like mine. I do not know how to be her equal."

Elgart nodded to show that he understood.

The Prince made an effort to gather himself. He sat straighter, slapped his thighs. "Well," he announced. "I can only try. Bifalt must do the same. It may be enough in the end."

Unable to resist, Elgart replied, "Or perhaps those women will teach both of you."

Jaspid scowled at that suggestion, but he did not argue. When he rose to his feet, he had recovered his familiar oiled ease. "No doubt, you have more to say"—he knew Elgart that well—"but I have other duties. I must consider our wounded."

Moving like a man whose muscles never stiffened, he strode away.

With a sigh of relief, the scarred man turned his attention to his own concerns.

Elgart was bemused to find himself hesitating. He felt something that he wanted to pursue; yet now that his chance had come, he was strangely reluctant. The risk he had in mind was entirely unlike the ones that he had often faced.

There was no better time than this one, he insisted. There might never be another.

The cliché made him laugh. Such things had never reassured him. Only courage sufficed. Courage and clear wits.

Unable to match Prince Jaspid's example, he lurched to his feet. Long days in the saddle had not prepared him to run for his life. Every limb and joint protested as he left his post near the King and approached the campfire where the Magisters sat together as if they were alone in the night.

Summoning the insolence that had served him so well as a spy, he nudged a place for himself between two of the earthquake-wielders and sat down like a man who belonged there.

They all stared at him. Tightly wrapped in their winter cloaks and rain-capes, they looked like interrupted mourners, men and women who had gathered to grieve for their lost comrades. Elgart's intrusion did not please them. Nevertheless he smiled cheerfully and ignored them. He had come for Magister Astride.

He had chosen a seat opposite hers. Across the flames, he studied her for the first time. Until this evening, he had only known her by sight—and only at a distance. Now he regarded her openly.

She was a Bellegerin woman in her middle years. Despite her efforts earlier, the contrast between her prematurely silver hair and her unlined features made her seem almost young. Because it had once been his business to know such things, he knew that she was unmarried, childless. Now he wondered why. Her features were more than pleasant: they were pleasing. The brown of her eyes promised warmth under better circumstances.

The way the firelight moved across her features exposed her sadness as well as her fatigue. It also hinted at something more, something that resembled recrimination. Elgart guessed that she blamed herself for Bone's death. If her stamina had not failed—

Then he thought that perhaps she blamed *him*. After all, he had dragged her away when she might have succeeded.

With a mental shrug, he absolved himself. He had acted on the

King's orders. Losing Magister Bone was bad enough. Losing her would have been much worse.

When she noticed him staring at her, Magister Astride frowned; ducked her head into the shelter of her cloak's hood.

No better time—

"Magister Astride," he said, fulsome with appreciation, "I am in awe."

Her head jerked up. Surprise widened her eyes. She had not expected him to address her—and certainly not with awe.

Without a word, the other Magisters adjusted their seats, enabling their comrades beside Elgart to shift away from him. The one on his left, an older man, glared at him. The woman on his right kept her face turned away. In some sense, they must have known who he was. His scar was unmistakable, even by firelight. But they were both Amikan, unfamiliar with him. Their silence emphasized that he was not welcome.

He ignored them. Smiling, he concentrated his gaze on Astride.

Her mouth opened without a sound. She needed a moment to compose herself before she could ask, "In awe, sir?"

"Oh, yes, Magister," he replied at once. "Your control astonished me. To refine a power as vast as earthquake until it is little more than a chisel— 'Awe' is too small a word for it."

Someone in the circle muttered, "Horseshit."

Elgart smiled more broadly. "How did you learn such skill, Magister? It is scarcely credible. You must have spent seasons training." And causing considerable wreckage. "What inspired you to make the effort? You could not have known it would be needed."

The older man raised his voice. "Where is the King? Why does he permit this—?"

Astride silenced him with a small gesture. She had that much stature among her comrades, even with the Bellegerins.

Looking directly at Elgart seemed to cost her an act of will; but she met his gaze. Softly, she asked, "You are Elgart, sir?"

The sound of her voice tugged at his heart. For an instant or two, he almost lost his air of assurance. He forced a chuckle. "I am, my lady."

That *my lady* startled the other sorcerers. Magister Astride gave no sign that she had heard it.

"What is your title in King Bifalt's service, sir?"

Elgart grinned with half of his mouth. Different emotions twisted the other side of his face. "I have no title." Deliberately, he repeated, "My lady. At one time, I served the King in and around the Open Hand. Now I am simply a soldier."

She did not relent. "But you are also the man who brought those strangers to us? The el-Algreb?"

"I am."

"And you have no title?"

"None." To save his life, Elgart would not have confessed that he had spent the better part of twenty years as the King's Captain of Spies, ferreting out Amikan plots. Not at that moment. A nondescript Magister named Vault and another woman were the only Bellegerins in the circle; and even they did not know what he had been.

After a moment, Astride seemed to reach a decision. "If you have no title, I must call you by your name."

Unable to contain himself, Elgart laughed aloud. "That would please me, my lady."

She did not smile. He did not know whether she ever smiled. "And you must call me Astride. 'Magister' suggests distrust, and 'my lady' is too formal."

Elgart felt like dancing. Instead, he feigned gravity. "That, also, will please me." Distinctly, he added, "Astride.

"Forgive one last moment of formality. I must thank you. You saved our lives, and mine is precious to me. If I err occasionally, remember that I wish to honor you."

Astride shook her head, frowning somberly. "I do not want honor. I have a gift, nothing more."

The older man interrupted her. "You are the most gifted among us, Magister."

Another woman might have blushed, but her shyness took a different form. She ignored the compliment.

"You credit me with seasons of training, Elgart. I have done nothing of the kind. I was simply desperate. As we all were."

Her comrades looked startled. Clearly, they doubted her. *They* did not have her control.

"Hells, Astride," breathed Elgart. "Then you are even more remarkable than I supposed."

He did not know another Magister who could match her force of will. Even Magister Pillion's efforts in his garden were not so precise. Elgart's own resolve did not equal hers. The Archpriest had overcome him with little more than a word and a touch.

But he saw at once that he had vexed her. With a tinge of asperity, she replied, "I did what I did to save *myself*, sir. I was only desperate."

Elgart winced. Already, he had taken the wrong path toward her. Now she had withdrawn from him.

Before he could respond, Prince Jaspid's shout carried across the camp. "Elgart, I need you! This limb must come off. There are too many wounded. I am not enough!"

Elgart had fought his way through more hells than the Prince. He had more experience tending men cut and bleeding, men mangled by sorcery. He recognized the edge in Jaspid's voice.

Sighing, he forced himself to stand. Because he did not want to go, he risked saying, "I hope we will speak again, Astride."

As he turned away, she said, "Tell me quickly. How is it that you do not shy away from Magisters? Everyone else does."

A simple question. He had a simple answer. "Magister Pillion was my friend."

Wondering where he stood with her, Elgart went to help the Prince.

Sometime during the night, King Bifalt awoke with Estie's voice tolling in his ears. He wanted to shout at her, tell her that she had said enough. Long ago, he had assured her that she was free to make her own decisions. She had done so. She did not need to remind him that she was no longer his wife.

But when he tried to answer her, he could not make a sound. His mouth and throat felt like a fortnight in the desert. Hells, he was thirsty—

Where was he? He lay in a crypt of darkness. Instinctively, he tried to fling out his hands, block the blow that would finish him. One of his arms refused to move. It was bound somehow. The other struck a rough surface that shifted when he hit it.

Where *was* he?

Almost immediately, a wedge of unsteady yellow light opened beyond his feet. A figure stood in the gap, shutting out most of the light; but Bifalt saw enough to recognize that he was in a tent. He almost knew the silhouetted figure.

"Majesty?" asked Boy anxiously. "What do you need?"

Bifalt felt a moment of acute relief. A tent was not a crypt. It was not a prison. His bodyguards were with him.

Choking, he croaked, "Water."

"At once, Majesty." Boy disappeared. The tent-flap closed, restoring the darkness.

Bifalt's relief vanished as well. He was too weak to free his trapped arm from the tangle of his bedding, the weight of an extra cloak. Estie's cry had broken him.

He heard a scream in the distance, a cry of appalling pain.

The tent-flap opened again. Boy crawled into the tent, bringing firelight with him. He had a waterskin. When he reached Bifalt's head, he slipped one arm under the King's neck, raised him so that he could drink.

The scream came again. It receded into sobbing.

Bifalt drank because he had no choice. He feared that he was dying. That scream—

He swallowed quickly so that Boy would not take the waterskin away. Trembling with effort, he put his free hand on Boy's forearm. His grip was as frail as an old man's.

He managed to gasp, "That scream." Then he drank again.

Trying to give comfort, Boy said, "Take as much as you want, Majesty. We have enough."

He did not think that his King was dying.

When Bifalt was satisfied, Boy put the waterskin aside, lowered Bifalt back into his bedding. "We are in the forest, Majesty," he murmured. "Six Magisters. Prince Jaspid and Elgart. Most of the riflemen. We found General Klamath's horses and supplies. We are well.

"But some of your men were injured in the fighting. Cut or stabbed. Shredded by stones like shrapnel." Boy was indignant. "Those bastard infantrymen swing heavy blades. Two riflemen died. The Prince and Elgart tend the others.

"That scream? One man had a crushed leg. His comrades carried him here. The Prince was forced to sever the limb. Elgart burned the stump with a hot blade.

"The rest live, but they will not fight again."

The sound of screaming lingered in Bifalt's ears. The foundations of Belleger's Fist had been full of it. He had lost men. But Rile's soldiers had done most of the shrieking. Despite their Great God's power, they were still human enough to suffer and cry out as they died.

Bifalt clung to the memory of all that pain and death. It hurt him less than Estie's shout. He was a soldier, familiar with every possible howl and wail of agony. Those sounds were less appalling than the loss of his wife.

When Jeck opened the tent-flap, he let in the grey light of an early dawn.

"Majesty?" asked the bodyguard.

He said more, but Bifalt did not hear him. The King was still finding his way back to himself.

The war was upon him. Finally, he faced a challenge he understood. He knew what was required of him. He did not need to think of Estie.

With an effort, he struggled out of his bedding. He felt unconscionably weak, but he was growing stronger. When he freed himself, he saw that his bodyguards had put him to bed in his clothes. They had only removed his breastplate and weapons. His moccasins were still on his feet. He had not bothered to bring his helm.

The tent's gloom swirled around him as he sat up; but the moment was brief. Two deep breaths cleared his head.

"Majesty?" asked Jeck again.

Bifalt scanned the tent, found his rifle and satchel of bullets, his saber and dagger beside his bedroll. He coughed for a moment. There was smoke in the air.

Concentrating, he said, "Repeat that."

"Sub-Commander Hellick is here," said Jeck again. "You should hear his report." He hesitated, then added, "And the Open Hand is in flames."

Hellick? Bifalt was too frail to feel surprise. Instead, he put the subject aside. Somehow, the sub-Commander had reached him to report that the el-Algreb were lost. He would consider what had happened to them later.

The burning of his city he had expected. He knew what it meant. The Great God's forces were done scavenging. Now Rile took revenge on the Hand for killing hundreds of his men and leaving so little food or water.

Hells.

King Bifalt piled his weapons on his breastplate. Dragging it with him, he crawled to the tent's opening. Movement and old fury restored a bit of his strength. Still like a man worn down by too many years, too many deaths, he crept out of his tent into the edged cold.

Boy, Malder, and Spliner were there with Jeck. Malder helped the King to his feet. Taking their time, Jeck buckled him into his breastplate while Boy entered the tent to retrieve the heavy cloak. Malder secured the King's saber and dagger at his waist. A moment later, Boy draped the cloak over Bifalt's shoulders. In his thick arms, Spliner cradled his monarch's rifle, ready bullets, and rain-cape.

While his bodyguards prepared him, Bifalt looked around. His people were spread across a clearing deep in the forest. Campfires dotted the dirt and dead grass. Too many tents to bother counting were scattered here and there. Six at some distance from the others probably sheltered the Magisters. King Bifalt assumed that his surviving wounded occupied the cluster of tents near the western edge of the trees. Prince

Jaspid stood among them, head held high, chin jutting. Across the camp, he met Bifalt's gaze but gave no sign that he recognized his brother. Near the Prince, Elgart sat with his head in his bloody hands.

Alone at a separate fire, sub-Commander Hellick sat warming himself. When he saw the King, he rose to his feet, started to approach. Bifalt waved the Amikan back to the fire. He was not ready.

Pieces of his former self came back to him. The attention of his bodyguards reminded him of the man he was supposed to be. The wounded were his first responsibility.

Wavering, King Bifalt headed toward his brother. Step by step, his muscles remembered movement. He began to walk more steadily.

Along the way, Boy said, "A Magister wishes to speak with you, Majesty, an Amikan named Glower."

Conserving himself, the King said, "He can wait."

Ahead of him, Prince Jaspid had roused Elgart. Together, they came to meet him. In the grey dawn and the firelight, their hands and their breastplates looked wet, dripping with blood.

Despite his body's coiled ease, Jaspid radiated anger. At his side, Elgart looked simply exhausted.

"Are you recovered, Brother?" demanded the Prince.

King Bifalt spread his hands. "I am what you see." He had a demand of his own. "The wounded?"

Jaspid scowled. "We did what we could, Majesty. We have two dead. We may lose one more if Elgart did not seal his stump before he lost too much blood. Others died in the Fist. The rest are effectively crippled. We are left with sixty riflemen who can still ride and handle their weapons."

"We were fortunate, Majesty," sighed Elgart. "It is scarcely credible. Against all those infantrymen and the fall of the Fist? Sixty men who can ride and fight is an astonishing number."

The Prince stood rigid in front of Bifalt. "They are not enough. We have *ten* too badly hurt to fend for themselves. We cannot abandon them, Brother. If we do not leave riflemen to watch over them, they have no hope."

King Bifalt faced his brother like a man who could not be moved.

At this moment, that was his duty. His decisions had cost him forty soldiers and two Magisters. He had to outface his brother's outrage and helplessness—and his own shame.

"Do what you can," he said like a snarl. "I have decisions to make. I will speak to everyone when I have made them."

His plan to ride north and then strike east, searching for the horde of Rile's third army, seemed like a fool's dream. He had lost too many men.

Jaspid pulled back. Bitterly, he replied, "As you say, Majesty." His face showed every kind of distress.

For a moment, Bifalt hung on the edge of weeping. His people had done everything he asked of them, and their only reward would be a demand for more. He had to be better than this.

But he was starting to waver again. He was too weak to think. Over his shoulder, he told Boy, "Some stew, if you have it. Anything hot. I must eat." Then he turned back to Jaspid and Elgart.

"Clean yourselves. We should look like men who will do what they must when we hear Hellick's report."

He expected to learn that all of Suti al-Suri's warriors were dead.

"As you say, Majesty," answered Elgart. As if they could not bear to look at their King, he and the Prince walked away.

At once, Malder and Jeck took the King to a campfire at some distance from the tents of the wounded. As they seated him in the embrace of the heat, Boy arrived with a steaming bowl of stew and a fresh waterskin.

Bifalt did not care if he burned his mouth. At once, he began to eat.

Hunching over his stew, he did not notice the Magister until the man stood in front of him.

"Majesty?" asked the sorcerer brusquely. He was not accustomed to being kept waiting.

Bifalt raised his head, dredged up the man's name. He was Glower, one of Estie's Magisters. An older man—well, older than the King—with a round face, a grizzled beard badly trimmed, and a fringe of hair around his bald pate.

As a man, Bifalt detested him on sight. As the King, Bifalt could not ignore him. The Decimate of earthquake had saved his whole company, and the war had only begun.

"Magister Glower." King Bifalt did not stop eating. Between gulps of stew, he asked, "You have something to say?"

"If it does not offend you to hear me." Glower showed his impatience. "We have discussed our straits, Queen Estie's Magisters and yours. We will serve you. We can do no less. If you ask it, we will strive to match Magister Bone's example." After a pause, he added sourly, "Majesty."

The King had expected resistance. After all, he had not told the Magisters or his own riflemen what would follow when the wall of the old city was breached. He had imagined that the tunnel would be ready. Under the circumstances, his people had a right to feel misused.

He sat up to face Glower. Taking his time, he chewed the lump of meat in his mouth, swallowed it. Finally, he answered as distinctly as he could, "Thank you, Magister. Your promise speaks well of you. I will hold you to it.

"But know this." Thinking of his losses, he allowed himself a flash of anger. "I do not risk *anyone* lightly. I will not ask you or your comrades to hazard your lives unless I must."

At once, the King hunched again, sank down to concentrate on stew and water. He did not see Magister Glower's reaction. But he heard a small sigh, almost an apology, in Glower's tone as the man replied, "As you say, Majesty."

While the sorcerer walked away, Bifalt finished his meal, took a long drink. He did not feel equal to the challenges ahead of him. But standing to meet every demand was his duty. The remnants of his self-respect required it.

Swallowing a groan, he pushed his frailty upright.

Within a few moments, Prince Jaspid and Elgart joined him. In the firelight, King Bifalt saw that Elgart had washed his hands, but had not cleaned his breastplate. Streaks of dried blood marked it like protests. In contrast, Jaspid had made himself spotless. Only his expression showed his bitterness. He hated being responsible for other men.

Frowning, Bifalt ordered the Prince, "Tell the riflemen to keep their distance, Brother. And the Magisters if they approach. We should hear Hellick alone. I will speak to the men later."

He did not know what he would do without the el-Algreb.

Nodding, Prince Jaspid summoned the nearest soldier, made the man responsible for ensuring that the King was given privacy.

Elgart only shrugged.

Together, the three men went to join the sub-Commander. Bifalt's bodyguards stepped back when they saw him walking steadily. They would probably hear whatever Hellick said, but the King did not care. They had earned his trust long ago.

Sub-Commander Hellick stood at once. His face wore an uncomfortable mixture of irritation and relish.

Expecting the worst, King Bifalt demanded, "How did you get here, sub-Commander?"

The long line of Rile's marching soldiers lay between this forest and the south.

Hellick bowed with a degree of courtesy, then spread his hands. "Before we left, Majesty, First Captain Hegels told us that the Great God keeps his cavalry back to guard his supply-train. But suddenly—it was sudden to us—the cavalry left, racing toward the Open Hand. Their strange beasts are faster than horses. Then a portion of the light infantry slowed to wait for the wagons. They made a gap in the line. We slipped through it. The enemy did not respond. Perhaps we were not seen."

Bifalt stopped himself before he could ask, *We?* He had a dozen questions. One he thought he could answer. The rest Hellick might address if the King let him speak.

"Very good, sub-Commander. Now your report."

That was not the source of Hellick's irritation. "Majesty," he replied promptly, "the Cleckin have fled. Suti al-Suri's people routed them."

Prince Jaspid's eyes widened in surprise.

"Routed?" exclaimed Elgart. "How?"

Stunned, Bifalt lost a moment. He had not braced himself for good news. It seemed impossible, five hundred horse-warriors against two thousand raiders.

A grim smile tightened one corner of the Amikan's mouth. "The el-Algreb act like children, but they fight like men who dine on superior forces. The Cleckin did not know we were coming. They chose a convenient valley for their camp. The el-Algreb had the advantage of elevation. They knew how to use it. I will say more if you wish to hear it.

"But I must say this, Majesty. I could not imagine what they hoped to accomplish until Suti al-Suri explained it. Disguising their true objective with an elaborate series of feints, they contrived to steal the Cleckin horses.

"Without mounts, what could the raiders do?" Hellick sighed, enjoying the memory. "They fled south, back toward the Realm's Edge. They cannot threaten you now."

Prince Jaspid said nothing. His jaw worked, chewing expletives, but he kept them to himself.

Elgart was less reticent. "Amazing," he declared. "Amandis assured me that the el-Algreb are worthy allies. I believed her, of course. But I did not know how *much* to believe her."

King Bifalt braced himself on Elgart's shoulder. This gift was too great. He could hardly trust it. Needing reassurance, he asked harshly, "Is this true, sub-Commander?"

Hellick almost smiled. "It is my life as well as yours, Majesty. Amika's life as well as Belleger's. If my tidings were false, I would not be here to deliver them."

The smoke was getting thicker. It stung Bifalt's eyes. Leaning harder on Elgart, he rubbed his face with his free hand. Then a brief gust cleared the air. When he had mastered himself, he said, "Forgive me, Hellick." He stood a little straighter. "I do not question your honesty. But I did not expect this outcome. I would have been content if the el-Algreb had delayed the raiders. I did not dream of victory. Now I must think—"

When King Bifalt fell silent, Jaspid asked the obvious question. "Where are the horse-warriors now, sub-Commander?"

In an instant, Hellick's irritation returned. It resembled disgust. "That is a different tale, Highness. I have remained in contact with General Klamath by signal. When he learned that the Cleckin had fled, he ordered the el-Algreb to join him in the east. Suti al-Suri refused."

The Amikan turned to King Bifalt. "You know how he speaks, Majesty. I often struggle to understand him. But he seemed to say that his alliance is with you, not with the General." Embarrassed, Hellick added, "With his brother, not his sister."

"He intended to return to the Open Hand. He seemed to believe that you still live."

"And?" prompted Jaspid.

"His scouts found this clearing." Hellick's ire was fading, pushed aside by involuntary admiration. "You would not have seen them, Highness. They are better at stealth than any men I know. Suti al-Suri sent them to sweep this forest for threats. He may join you soon.

"The el-Algreb fear nothing except the Great God's skirmishers. Those men are swift, agile, and far too many. If they came upon you here, they might leave none of you alive."

Bifalt shook his head. He was chasing too many thoughts at once. Possibilities sprang on him suddenly or evaded him like rabbits. The skirmishers, he muttered to himself, trying to fix his attention on one subject. Of course. They would be a fatal foe among the trees. And among the horses. Despite their guns, Klamath's men would not fare much better.

That, thought the King, will be work for Magisters. Nothing less would suffice against the small, agile men.

While the sub-Commander waited for King Bifalt to speak, Elgart asked, "Does Suti al-Suri have any idea why Rile's cavalry raced ahead?" He coughed at the smoke. "Any idea at all?"

Bifalt surprised himself with an answer. "I can guess."

Prince Jaspid nodded, but said nothing.

Hellick frowned. "Majesty?"

"Rile is arrogant," declared Bifalt, rushing to keep up with his mind. "His tactics betray him. He did not imagine that we would leave the Open Hand practically undefended. The notion that we might destroy Belleger's Fist ourselves never occurred to him. When it fell, he must have realized that we are not children to be killed with one stroke.

"He sent his cavalry to secure the Queen's road. He intends to hold it so that his army can follow unopposed."

Again, Jaspid nodded. "Commander Forguile is there," he assured Hellick. "He has a company of riflemen. And both Commander Soulcess and Chancellor Sikthorn have been forewarned. Rile will be met in ways that surprise him."

Perhaps Bifalt should have taken that opportunity to explain Estie's intentions, but his thoughts had wandered. He needed to reconsider his own intentions. Rile's cavalry was already on the road. Bifalt could not cross it to challenge the horde of fanged strangers in the north. He would have to oppose the enemy in some other way.

And he now had the el-Algreb to consider. Their unforeseen support made his forces stronger, but he was not prepared to risk them against Rile's cavalry. According to Hegels, those men rode beasts too ferocious to confront on horseback.

Carefully, Elgart asked, "What will we do, Majesty? The men are waiting. And the Magisters. They know we must go. We are useless where we are."

Yes, thought the King without responding. Over the years, he and Klamath had debated the advantages and perils of dividing their forces. They had rejected the idea. It would weaken the army. But now Suti al-Suri had answered that argument for him.

He dropped his hand from Elgart's shoulder, straightened his back, raised his head. "Of course," he said like the man he had once been. "We have rested enough.

"Sub-Commander, find your way to the el-Algreb. Inform Suti al-Suri that we will ride south." Toward Rile's light infantry and supply-train. "Jaspid, ready the riflemen. They must take only what they can carry. We will leave the tents and everything else for our wounded. I will ask the workmen to care for them. They will be as safe here as anywhere."

Some of the bitterness lifted from Prince Jaspid's face. King Bifalt was glad to see it, but he did not pause.

"Gather the Magisters, Elgart. Ready them to ride. Tell them that we go to inflict another surprise on the Great God."

The King's haste infected the men around him. They took only a moment to absorb his instructions. Then Hellick hurried away. Prince Jaspid bowed to his brother before he left. Spliner and Boy rushed to pack the King's bedroll, rain-cape, and winter gear. Jeck and Malder busied themselves examining Bifalt's weapons.

Elgart lingered briefly. He had questions, but he did not ask them. After a moment, he shrugged and turned away, calling for Astride as he strode toward the tents of the Magisters.

In the light of the rising sun, a broad swath of smoke plumed across the eastern sky. Bifalt was grateful that he could not see the Hand itself through the trees. He had chosen to surrender it; but watching his city in flames would have wrung his heart.

Instead, he concentrated on what he could do with his riflemen, the horse-warriors, and six earthquake-wielders. They were too few to change the course of the war, but they might be able to slow Rile's advance. They might even infuriate him.

King Bifalt hoped for that. Enraged foes were reckless.

TWENTY-ONE

———

LONG SLOUGH

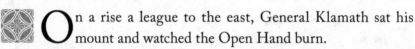On a rise a league to the east, General Klamath sat his mount and watched the Open Hand burn.

Flames leapt into the dawn with an audible roar. Sparks drifted upward like dying stars. Here and there, the fire found abandoned jars of oil or volatile mixtures in an alchemist's shop and blew up like grenades, spraying ruin. Everywhere, structures howled and crumpled: shacks, homes, old mansions, merchantries; stables and barns; smithies, woodpiles, sheds. The conflagration took everything it touched.

The sight sickened Klamath. The Hand had been his home ever since he had joined Belleger's army, back in the days of King Abbator's reign. Long ago, he had ridden into hell several times. He had survived arrows, blades, colliding horses, and indiscriminate sorcery. He had carried bleeding comrades out of the carnage until he felt that he had used up all the strength he would ever have and could not stop weeping. But the inferno of the Great God's cruelty afflicted him with a different kind of pain. It was like a sword to the stomach, a cut too deep for tears.

From that wound, Belleger might never recover.

The sun had begun to rise only a short time ago, climbing above the storm clouds in the east. He could see the flames with frightful clarity. Despite the distance, he seemed to feel their heat on his face. Nevertheless he did not turn away. He was waiting for news.

Earlier, he had learned that the el-Algreb had beaten the Cleckin:

an unexpected relief. But then he had received word that Suti al-Suri had refused to join him. Under other circumstances, Klamath would have been furious. However, a second signal from sub-Commander Hellick had reported that the horse-warriors had returned toward the Open Hand to search for King Bifalt. After that, the General had put the el-Algreb out of his mind. They had gone beyond his reach. He was left hoping that they would find the King alive.

Now Klamath had riflemen scouting everywhere, some of them hidden along the line of the enemy's march from the Bay of Lights, others dangerously close to the city and Rile's forces. They contacted him whenever they could. During the night, one of them had reached him. The man had described the almost unimaginable death of the tall stone keep where Belleger's kings had ruled for generations. He had delivered those tidings with horror.

Before dawn, other reports spoke of the fierce rush of the Great God's cavalry pounding north along the Queen's road. A thousand men? More? Rile must have sent them to secure the river crossing at Fivebridge.

Klamath wished them joy in the attempt. If Amika's defenders had obeyed their Queen, the cavalrymen would find the bridge broken, cast into the turbulence of the River. Their frustration would be answered with rifle-fire and grenades.

Yet Rile still had his infantry. The rest of the cavalry. Those feral skirmishers. And innumerable sorcerers clad like priests. Losing the men who had died in Belleger's Fist might infuriate the Great God. Their sacrifice would not hamper him.

Klamath's First Captain watched with him. Hegels needed his chance to see how the enemy repaid opposition. Captain Rowt was there as well. He had earned his place by bringing his riflemen and sorcerers out of the city safely. In addition, the General had ordered five Magisters to join him, one to represent each of the Decimates among his forces. They sat their mounts with dismay in their eyes like reflections of flames.

The rest of the army was a league farther east on lower ground, and still moving.

Klamath trusted certain of his Magisters. Trench and Brighten had proven themselves with wind and lightning. Crawl's leadership at the barricades of fire deserved respect. And Magister Solace had earned the General's regard by keeping his friend Matt alive.

But he worried about Magister Whimper, the drought-wielder. Despite her haughty manner, she was a fearful woman, easily intimidated. She might have refused his commands if she had dared. Nevertheless he had a particular need for her Decimate.

Beyond the reach of the city's flames, Rile's infantrymen were arranging themselves in columns. Klamath saw hundreds of the iron-armored men with their heavy broadswords. Hundreds more wore hardened leather and carried an assortment of weapons. Among them moved Rile's priests holding staffs of black iron. And the skirmishers—

Those men—if they were men—did not join the ranks of the infantry. Instead, they ranged more widely in all directions, searching for scouts or traps.

Speaking to himself, Captain Rowt murmured, "I thought they would make camp." He seemed to need the reassurance of hearing his own voice. "They must need rest and food. They have been marching for days."

Hegels answered him. "Perhaps, Captain, they eat while they march and sleep on their feet. Perhaps they are sustained by sorcery. Or perhaps they await their Great God's coming. Who knows?"

Klamath shook his head. "They will come for us. Rile is angry now. He needs resupply. He will want to punish us for leaving the city empty." The General looked over his shoulder. "And that storm is drawing closer." He smelled moisture on the wind. "We will have snow before nightfall. If he does not advance now, he will lose time. He may lose us."

Klamath's army would certainly have to make camp. But he had ordered them to go at least three leagues beyond the place where he proposed to surprise the enemy. In that clash, he intended to risk as few of his people as possible.

"If they come," remarked Hegels, "we will need an answer for those skirmishers. They are too many, and too fast. If they catch us while we are camped, we will have carnage on our hands."

Speaking so that the others could hear him, General Klamath

replied, "We may have an answer, sir. You do not know the terrain." Hegels was Amikan, unfamiliar with Belleger. "Two leagues to the east, there is a lowland called Long Slough. In springtime, when the snows in the Realm's Edge melt, it is a river. But when the runoff passes, it leaves behind a stretch of marsh and bog. Men and horses can cross it, but they cannot cross quickly. That mud *sucks*. It can drag off a man's boots, or break the legs of a galloping horse. The skirmishers may founder.

"It is called *Long* Slough because it extends more than a league from south to north."

"You will rely on sorcery," put in Magister Trench abruptly. "The enemy cannot march so far before nightfall. They will reach this Slough after dark. And there will be snow. The conditions will be against us. Rifles may be useless. You will need the Decimates."

"Yes," admitted Klamath. "I need sorcery. But I will rely most on you, Magister Whimper. And on you, Magister Crawl. And on you, Magister Brighten."

As he said Whimper's name, she flinched. She might have turned away, but Brighten gripped her arm. The lightning-wielder resembled a fuse burning toward an explosion. In contrast, excitement lit Crawl's face like flames.

General Klamath sighed. In his heart, he was not a man who told Magisters what to do. Until recently, he had assumed that they would be commanded by King Bifalt, not by an ordinary man like Klamath.

The gift for sorcery was rare everywhere; but for reasons that no one understood, Belleger and Amika gave birth to more drought and fire than any other Decimate. Despite her fears, Magister Whimper represented thirty of her peers, Bellegerin and Amikan. Magister Crawl led twenty-two fire-wielders. After the deaths in the Bay of Lights, Brighten spoke for only nine other Magisters. Solace was one of twelve whose gift was pestilence. Trench had no more than fourteen men and women like him.

Klamath hoped that they would be enough. What else could he do? In the end, this war was always going to be a slaughter.

Already, leprous splotches were appearing around the city as the flames ran out of fuel. In an hour or two, there would be nothing left of the Open Hand except ash and charcoal. Within the old city's damaged fortifications, only the outer wall of Belleger's Fist would remain, cracked and torn by the death of King Bifalt's reign.

Klamath needed to go, but he was reluctant to leave. The dying fires demanded that he remain to bear witness.

"All this?" murmured Rowt. "For what? To destroy books? What does the enemy fear from them? How can they threaten a Great God?"

"Nonsense!" snapped Magister Brighten. "He is Rile, nothing more. Men who call themselves gods are jumped-up sorcerers. They delude themselves to mask their fear."

Trench watched her closely. "Then tell us, Magister. Answer the Captain. What does Rile fear from books?"

"Knowledge," she retorted. "The library. Any man or woman who knows whatever he does not. He may not fear any army. He may not fear *us*. Knowledge may be the *only* threat. But it is enough. A self-proclaimed god must stamp it out."

In a scraping tone, Magister Solace said, "I concur. Any Decimate is a two-edged blade. The same must be true of Rile's sorcery. If his great strength is his power to coerce, then his great weakness must be that his hold can be broken. Any knowledge that he does not possess may render him powerless. He fears it because it may undo him."

Trench regarded Solace quizzically. "I did not take you for a scholar, Magister."

The pestilence-wielder shrugged. "I think. It is worth the effort."

Klamath drew a deep breath, released it slowly. He understood Brighten's point, and Solace's. Privately, he may have believed it. But it changed nothing. His concern—his *only* concern—was the first battle. It would come during the night, in a snowstorm; or perhaps tomorrow morning. He had to be ready.

Turning his back on the Open Hand's ashes, he gave his officers their orders.

"Return to the army, First Captain. Take the Magisters with you.

Find suitable terrain at a safe distance. Establish our camp. Then choose two hundred men. They must be ready"—he glanced at the sky—"no later than midday. I have heavy work for them."

Hegels scowled, but he did not hesitate. "As you say, General." Klamath's manner did not invite questions.

"Captain Rowt," continued the General, "you are now my aide."

At one time, the young man had saved Queen Estie's life.

Rowt snapped to attention while Klamath commanded, "Assist the First Captain. Later, I will make other demands." Because he was an ordinary man, no better than Rowt, he added, "If you wish to refuse my service, do so then."

Beneath the ruddiness of cold, the Captain's face betrayed a deeper flush. He seemed shocked by the idea that he might refuse his General.

Moving on, Klamath instructed the Magisters to accompany Hegels. "When he makes camp, you must eat and rest. Sleep if you can. And tell your comrades to do the same. I will need you at your best."

Only Magister Crawl replied, "As you say, General." But the others turned with him when he pulled his mount's head to the east. Following the First Captain, the company cantered away down the side of the rise.

General Klamath studied the sky and scented the air to assure himself that the storm would not come too soon. When he was satisfied, he allowed himself to mutter, "Where *are* you, Bifalt? Are you even alive?"

Then he rode east. He had no time for fear.

As the first flakes of snow began to fall early that evening, the General rested in his saddle on the vantage he had chosen for himself. He had already positioned the Magisters of drought, fire, and lightning where he wanted them. Only pestilence and wind waited near him. The men who had worked all afternoon on the slope below him had returned to the camp. Commanded by Captain Rowt, eighty fresh riflemen were spread out on both sides of the General. The soldiers had left their horses in a hollow behind them. They would shoot more accurately on solid ground.

As dull as the last twilight, the waters and muck where the army had crossed Long Slough lay directly below Klamath. Here, the ridge where he waited rose higher than the hills opposite him, but its slope was as gradual as theirs.

However, he was not relying on the ascent to slow the enemy. He had other plans. Here and for most of its length, the wetland was eighty or a hundred paces wide. That was enough.

By increments, the snow fell more thickly, imposing a premature dusk. A lifetime's experience assured Klamath that the storm would soon wall out the rest of the world, but would not become a blizzard. It brought too little wind. But whatever happened, Rile's forces would not stop for it. The Great God was surely angry. And he had a long way to go.

No doubt, Rile's skirmishers could track General Klamath's army despite the snow. They would lead the Great God's forces to the place where that army had crossed Long Slough. But they might not sense the danger, not with snow and darkness in their eyes, their noses. If they carried lanterns or torches, so much the better for Klamath's purposes. Their lights would reflect off the snowfall, foreshorten their sight.

From the General's vantage, Long Slough looked unchanged: a thin sheet of dark water flowing sluggishly, interrupted here and there by straggling marsh-grasses and signs of bog. But its level was rising. It would rise more. In the distance, safely upstream, twenty Magisters of drought were at work, wielding their Decimates to draw down snow from the storm, water from other sources. As the stream deepened, it would conceal more of its dangers, its hungry muck and bogs, its lurking quicksand.

That was only the first of General Klamath's gambits.

Earlier, riflemen had dug two long trenches in the slope below Klamath. One was perhaps fifteen feet above the Slough. The other was about that far down from the crest of the ridge. Both of them were deep. Klamath's Magisters could stand in them without being seen.

To make those trenches, the riflemen had simply shoveled dirt and rocks into Long Slough. The debris would complicate the currents and add to the mire.

Now Magister Whimper and her remaining Magisters of drought were in the lower trench, heavily bundled against the cold and wet, waiting miserably. A few of them were at work increasing the snowfall, hastening the full weight of the storm. The rest would take their turns at the first sign of the enemy.

Magister Crawl and his fire-wielders occupied the upper trench with Brighten and her Magisters of lightning. For the present, they had nothing to do except keep themselves warm. Their task would be to provide cover if or when the Magisters of drought were threatened. Until then, they had been ordered to hold their Decimates in reserve. Fire and lightning would be needed if the riflemen and other Magisters were not enough.

Trench and the Magisters of wind had been told to wait for further orders. For the Magisters of pestilence, Klamath had a different task. He wanted them to strike as soon as their power could reach the skirmishers.

With no pretense of courtesy, Magister Solace had rasped, "Sorcerers sense sorcery. If Rile sends sorcerers, they will recognize us. He may hold back."

Klamath thought not. Like the snow, the threat of drought and pestilence would not temper Rile's anger. But such things might distract his forces from the hazards of Long Slough.

While darkness and snowfall tightened their grip, General Klamath tried not to fret. This pause was like the interminable waiting before battle during the old wars. That had been a time of dread and loose bowels. It had not ended until the men were swept into the horrific clash of arrows and blades, of rampant sorcery. This interval was no different. It had to be endured.

Perhaps two hours later, Klamath seemed to glimpse a wink of pure white through the falling snow.

He refused to concentrate on it. He may have imagined it. Instead, he forced himself to gaze elsewhere, straining to pierce a veil of snow that he could only feel, not see.

The snow came down heavily. Over his winter garments, he wore a cloak two inches thick. The men and women nearby were nothing more than lumped shapes like suggestions.

Then he saw the light again. This time, it did not disappear. Sure of itself, it shone through the storm like a distant star. It was sorcery, it had to be: a kind of sorcery that he had never encountered before. And it was not alone. Soon he made out half a dozen white beams. More. They formed a line across the west. A long line.

How many infantrymen were on that line? Or cavalrymen?

It was unlikely that Rile had dispatched all of his cavalry to take Fivebridge.

More lights cast their brilliance. By their movement, Klamath could gauge their progress. That line was still some distance away. The skirmishers would be closer, a deadly throng of them. They would reach the Slough first.

Good, thought the General. Long Slough offered him his best chance to answer those feral men. It might be his only chance.

"Now!" he called down to the Magisters of drought. "Give me more snow. As much as you can."

He had no gift for sorcery. He could not sense it. But he felt the weight of snow on his shoulders increase. The level of the Slough would continue to rise.

Exposed by the lights, the skirmishers seethed eagerly.

They had halted their advance. Rile's sorcerers must have felt the Decimate of drought. They paused to assess the peril.

The brightness of their lights was astonishing. It shone from globes the size of fists attached to the tops of iron staffs. The staffs were as tall as their wielders, men clad in black like priests. Etched in radiance despite the night and snow, those men stood with the assurance of commanders.

They held their staffs in gaps between columns of Rile's forces. The light limned the hulking shapes of tusked beasts, their eyes as black as ebony.

The Great God had sent his cavalry.

Klamath cursed to himself. In this place, he could have fought in-fantry almost indefinitely. But cavalry? The weight of those mounts might sink them—or they might be powerful enough to force their way through the muck. On open ground, they were certainly fast enough to outrun the General's horses.

Four of the fuming beasts waited in the spaces between the priests. Scanning quickly, Klamath counted fourteen priests, fourteen bright staffs, one anchoring each end of the front. They lit the way for col-umns of cavalry. In that light, the tusks of the mounts were slashes of ivory. Steam gusted like fury from their nostrils. They ripped at the ground with hooves like claws, or tossed their heads impatiently, eager to kill.

The tactics of overwhelming force. They had been thwarted in the Open Hand, and against Belleger's Fist. Apparently, Rile had not learned from the experience.

Klamath had told his Magisters of fire and lightning to do nothing until Whimper and the other drought-wielders were in danger. He re-peated that order. Turning to Captain Rowt, he said past cold-stiff lips, "Those butchers will charge." They believed that they could stamp out Belleger's resistance here. "Tell your men to hold fire until then. I want your best marksmen shooting at those priests." Distance and snow would hinder ordinary accuracy, but the bright globes would make good targets. "The rest must fire at those beasts." The massive animals would be in range when they hit the waters. "If their mounts fall, the men will be helpless."

"As you say, General." Captain Rowt hurried away.

Abruptly, Klamath heard a wet noise, a faint splashing. The in-creasing snowfall muffled it, but he knew what it meant. A wave of skirmishers had entered Long Slough. The splashes were the thrashing of small men in deep water and clinging mire.

"Magister Solace," he commanded. "Begin now. Cast your Deci-mate into the Slough."

The dour man did not answer, but his arms and shoulders shed clots of snow as he gestured, directing his sorcery. His comrades did the same. In moments, the waters were thick with disease.

The current would carry the pestilence downstream, but while it persisted it would sicken every skirmisher it touched.

The splashing worsened. Klamath heard thin squeals. He did not know what to expect from the feral men. If they tried to rescue their struggling kindred, the Decimate of pestilence would claim them.

The priests would detect more theurgy, but they would not know where their foes were hidden. Not in this storm.

The General beckoned for Magister Trench, drew the wind-wielder closer. "Hold," he ordered. "Hold until they charge. Wait until the first beasts hit the Slough. Then raise your Decimate. Drive snow into their faces."

Harried by sudden blasts, the cavalrymen might lose sight of their peril.

Instead of responding, Trench pointed at the enemy.

Klamath turned in time to see the priests dip their staffs in unison. They misunderstood the cries of struggling and fear from the bog, or they did not care.

As one, the whole front surged forward. Crouched over their mounts' necks, the warriors gripped their longswords and clung to the beasts' harnesses.

The best of the riflemen began firing: small popping sounds in so much snow. Their shots had no effect.

Only moments now. Hells, those beasts were *fast*. Klamath could measure the time in heartbeats.

The priests had dismounted. They did not lead the charge. As the columns pounded past them, they strode closer, holding their staffs with the confidence of too much power.

Below them, they would see an easy slope. A dark stretch of water that seemed to swallow the sorcerous light. Another gradual rise to higher ground. General Klamath's army had passed this way. Therefore it was safe. The priests must have expected their cavalry to sweep down the hillside, plow through the water, and hammer their way up the slope on the far side. Belleger's army must be waiting just beyond the ridge-crest. Why else did the enemy rely on sorcery to slow Rile's forces?

Nothing could slow those beasts.

Ignoring rifle-fire and the Decimate of drought, the cavalrymen crashed like an avalanche into the treachery of Long Slough.

From higher ground, the globes of the priests did not give Klamath enough light. He imagined the hooves of the beasts crushing skirmishers into the muck. He could not *see* it.

Then he could.

Magister Brighten's need to strike was too much for her. With the other lightning-wielders, she brought down killing bolts. Their Decimates stuttered like shutters opening and closing as individual Magisters paused. Still, their lightning lit the turmoil in the waters.

Below Klamath, a doomed swarm of the small men or creatures floundered, sick and drowning, trying to swim. The cavalrymen ignored them. The great beasts fell on the skirmishers, drove them deeper into the water and mud.

In any case, the beasts could not stop, not when so many more came behind them, crowding at their backs.

Still, skirmishers remained on the far hillside. They did not add their deaths to the frantic turbulence of the Slough. The priests must have halted them.

Somehow, Magister Crawl and his comrades resisted the temptation to attack prematurely.

The speed of the charge was its undoing. Muck sucked at the legs of the beasts. Flailing skirmishers hindered them, tripped them. Cavalrymen fell as their mounts collided. Mire and pestilence took them. Their rush became chaos, a tumult of floundering and hoarse cries.

In response, the priests gestured with their staffs. At once, the ranks of cavalry on the trampled slope slowed. Slewing on snow and mud, they stopped.

Nevertheless the priests could not save the beasts and men still plunging downward, carried by their own momentum. There were hundreds of them, too many to count.

"Now, Captain!" yelled the General. "Now!"

At once, gunfire blazed along the ridgecrest. Bullets slammed into the exposed men, the mired beasts. Then the riflemen raised their sights. Their fusillade marched up the opposite hillside like the front of a hailstorm.

Watching the fury of lead hit, Klamath felt a pang of alarm like an omen, the first hint of disaster. Bullets tore cavalrymen from their mounts all along the enemy's line. Blood sprayed from their wounds. They fell and died as easily as other men, swallowed by the Slough. But the beasts—

Hells! Down in the water and mud, the animals brunted ahead, fighting the cling of mire and weeds. With or without their riders, their great strength carried them forward. Hooves driven too deep into the muck snapped legs, toppling beasts onto their sides until the waters devoured their screams. Many of them were lost. Many more were not. They seemed to shrug off bullets like raindrops, like snowflakes. They endured the Decimate of pestilence. Some of them staggered in their tracks. Rearing, they trumpeted pain. Yet they righted themselves. The staccato glare of lightning in their eyes gave them a look of madness as they surged out of the Slough and pounded upward.

In bursts, Brighten and her comrades defended the slope. Sorcery scoured the beasts until they were clad in agony.

At that moment, Crawl and his Magisters of fire struck.

A holocaust of flame charred beasts, killed men, made the waters boil. Like the lightning, it came in irregular spasms as the Magisters unleased their Decimates, paused to gather themselves, attacked again. But their fire was savage. In moments, Magister Crawl and the others had covered the whole surface of Long Slough with flame. Then they worked their way up the opposite slope. Like the incessant punch of bullets, sorcerous fire stalked the priests.

For a few heartbeats, General Klamath imagined the taste of success. Then its flavor turned to gall in his mouth.

Flames did not touch the priests. Bullets and lightning did not. Some power shielded the men in black.

Then one of them swung his staff in a throwing motion. As bright as lightning, its globe arced upward, untouched by the snow. It sailed closer. While Klamath watched, it came down into the upper trench, among the Magisters of fire and lightning.

When it struck, it exploded like a keg of gunpowder.

The detonation shook the ridgecrest where Klamath sat his mount. Bodies were tossed away like scraps of cloth or ruined dolls, Magisters of fire, Magisters of lightning, half a dozen of them, more. Sheets of dirt and chunks of stone rained down into the lower trench, stunning or scattering Magisters of drought.

Through a haze of shock, Klamath heard Captain Rowt yell, "Our fault, General! We did not know what to expect!"

Klamath ignored him. To hit one of those globes while it was in the air would require supreme marksmanship. He did not believe it could be done.

Desperately, he howled, *"Retreat!"*

He had the appalling sensation that the priests were laughing at him.

The surviving Magisters from the upper trench did not need his command. They were already scrambling up the slope, clawing the ground for speed. They had lost at least a quarter of their number, but Klamath could not tell who still lived.

Behind them, the drought-wielders from the lower trench began to flee. Frantic with haste, they crawled or staggered, helped each other, pushed each other backward. They were exposed on the ridgeside—

Another priest swung his staff, hurled his bright globe.

Stricken, the General watched the shining ball arch high enough to plunge down on him. Instinctively, he kicked his feet from the stirrups, started to vault out of the saddle. But the globe did not reach him. Instead, it seemed to falter. An instant later, it dropped toward the Slough.

Magister Trench had intercepted it with a slap of wind.

Too shaken for chagrin, Klamath swung back into his saddle.

Without fire and lightning, darkness closed over the ridge, the Slough, the opposite hillside. Still, the theurgy of the priests shone like fallen stars. Three more lights sailed. A rush of gunfire answered. One globe detonated in midair. The other two arced closer—

Hells and gods!

—and turned away, driven backward by Trench and his Magisters of wind.

Klamath prayed for explosions among the enemy.

He was disappointed. By some unknown act of sorcery, the priests caught the globes with their staffs.

Another omen.

The priests glanced at each other. As one, they dipped their staffs again: the command to charge.

Rile's cavalry obeyed without hesitation; without thought. The beasts sprang into motion, an explosion of a different kind. Some of them had already lost their riders, but they had their own savagery to goad them.

And behind them came rank after rank of fresh cavalry, men and mounts in appalling numbers.

Now General Klamath understood that Rile did not care about his losses. He could afford them.

As Magister Crawl stumbled onto the ridgecrest, Klamath reached down, grabbed him by the shoulder. The young sorcerer was bleeding from a scalp wound. The blast in his trench must have hit him with a rock. Ignoring Crawl's stunned look, Klamath shouted, "Gather the Magisters! All of them!" He did not ask how many men and women Crawl had lost. Crawl probably did not know. "Get them to the horses! Run!"

Magister Crawl managed a dull nod. Without a word, he shambled away.

Below Klamath, the second charge slammed into the wetland. The beasts struggled. Oh, they struggled! But only with their footing. Now their hooves did not drive down into the muck. The weeds did not tangle their legs. They seemed to plow the surface of the waters. They slowed but did not stop.

Klamath wanted to weep.

The beasts were forcing their way over the bodies of fallen skirmishers, men, other creatures. Their own dead made a ford across the bog.

Most of the Magisters from the lower trench were still scrabbling up the ridgeside. Soon those beasts would be able to overtake the drought-wielders.

Voice cracking, Klamath cried over the thrashing of the charge, "Solace! Rowt! Protect Whimper's people!" Then he wheeled his mount to face Magister Trench. "Go!"

Trench scowled in protest. "Those globes—" he began.

"Are you blind?" yelled Klamath. "The priests will not waste their power! Their cavalry will finish us!"

An instant of incomprehension froze Magister Trench. Then he grasped that this battle was lost.

Shouting at his fellow wind-wielders, he led them at a run down the back of the ridge toward the horses.

Solace and his Magisters were as relentless as their stamina allowed, but their power was indiscriminate. To avoid the Magisters of drought, they had to fling pestilence at the riders and beasts still in Long Slough.

Gunfire was more accurate. The riflemen concentrated on the front of the charge as it surged out of the waters.

Suddenly calm, Klamath stepped down from his mount, unslung his rifle, lowered himself into the slush and snow to steady his arms, and joined the fight to save his last drought-wielders.

The task seemed impossible. He needed an entire clip to drop the nearest creature. Fortunately, a number of the beasts were already wounded. Some were dying with every stride, stricken by pestilence and bullets.

Yet they kept coming. They were almost near enough to catch the weakest Magisters. Klamath and the riflemen fired, fired, until their gun barrels steamed in the cold and their hands were scorched when they slapped in fresh clips. Beasts stumbled onto their sides, squalling as they knocked down mounts and riders below them.

One creature at a time, the charge stalled.

In small clusters, Magisters reached the ridgecrest. Klamath did not waste time counting them. He did not know how many had been broken or buried by the first explosion. Ignoring his burned fingers, he went on firing.

Without orders, Magister Solace took command of Whimper and her panicked comrades. In his dour fashion, he herded them downhill toward the horses.

When they were gone, General Klamath surged to his feet.

"Go!" he roared. *"Now!"* Then he ran to help Rowt with the wounded.

He did not start to weep until all of his survivors were mounted and fleeing eastward through the storm.

TWENTY-TWO

IN STORMS

For two full days, a snowstorm covered Belleger from the Wall Mountains in the east to the crashing seas in the west.

In the Last Repository, the Farsighted were blinded, unable to penetrate the heavy clouds, the veils of snow. Even the boundaries between day and night were scarcely distinguishable. Twilight faded into deep darkness and back again with nothing to mark its passage.

As a result, no one in the Repository knew whether King Bifalt had survived the destruction of Belleger's Fist. No one knew the fate of the el-Algreb in the south or the movements of Rile's fanged horde in the north.

And no one knew that the combined armies of Belleger and Amika were fleeing for their lives ahead of the Great God's cavalry. General Klamath's desperation was hidden from them.

Led through the snowfall by a depleted throng of skirmishers, Rile's cavalrymen gave chase. Commanded by priests riding tusked beasts, they ran hard, seeking slaughter.

The General's forces began with a substantial lead. Hours before the first Magisters returned from the ridgecrest, First Captain Hegels had broken camp. At the first sign of Klamath's defeat, he had harried the army into motion. When General Klamath caught up with him, they had time to organize their flight.

Without pausing, Klamath put Hegels in the lead with a squad of Bellegerins, men who had once lived in this region and knew the terrain. Then he arrayed his riflemen in a long stream wrapped around his remaining Magisters of fire, lightning, wind, and drought. The first exploding globe had killed seven drought-wielders, six Magisters of fire, and two of Brighten's comrades. The General could not afford to risk those that remained.

Taking the rear, he kept Captain Rowt, six riflemen, all twelve Magisters of pestilence, and Magister Crawl with him. He did not expect the skirmishers to match his pace. Instead, he told the soldiers to watch for Rile's cavalry. The pestilence-wielders he instructed to cast their sorcery behind them whenever a rifleman shouted a warning. Above everything, he had to hinder those infernal beasts. Mere horses could not flee fast enough or long enough to stay ahead of the enemy. First the mounts would die, their hearts and strength broken. Then the whole army would fall. For the next hours, nothing except sorcery could answer Rile's skirmishers or slow his cavalry.

Sooner than Klamath had hoped, the Magisters began unleashing their Decimates. After that, the night became a frantic blur. Following his army, the General goaded his horse through night and snowfall.

By turns, Solace and the other Magisters slumped in their saddles; rested along the necks of their mounts. If they had any effect, it did not show. The cavalrymen kept coming. When Klamath looked back, he glimpsed their blurred shapes through the snow.

One after another, the pestilence-wielders drew on their dwindling reserves. Behind them, beasts stumbled. Riders fell. The General's forces gained ground.

In response, the pursuit slowed. The priests could sense sorcery. They gave up their attempt to simply overrun Klamath's forces. Instead, they matched his pace at a distance, waiting for his horses to fail.

That moment might come soon. And the stamina of the Magisters would not last much longer.

Despite the snow, the brilliant white of the priests' globes exposed them. They stayed behind the leading cavalry. Nevertheless Klamath feared that they were near enough to hurl their explosions or unveil some other form of attack.

Abruptly, a priest confirmed the General's concern. A shining ball came arching through the snow.

Warned by a shout, Magister Crawl dismissed the globe with a sweep of flame.

Later, Hegels took the army toward a line of shale bluffs that Klamath recognized. There some ancient upheaval had lifted up a wall against the west. The bluffs did not extend far on either side, but they blocked passage except through a narrow defile. Long ago, a river must have run along it. Now the cut was dry.

As General Klamath entered the defile, the Decimate of fire erupted from the rims of the bluffs.

Advised by his Bellegerins, the First Captain had sent Crawl's comrades racing up the shallow slopes on the eastern side. When Klamath was safe in the defile, the fire-wielders struck.

Their first blast was a massed attack. While the riders farther back skidded to a halt, the whole front of the enemy's rush was caught in an incinerating wash. Staggered waves of flame followed, taking every living thing that they could reach.

Klamath found himself panting in time to his mount's urgent gasps. He needed only moments to pass between the bluffs. As he emerged, he saw that Magister Brighten and her comrades had accompanied the fire-wielders. At once, they attacked the sides of the defile. Their bolts tore through the shale, sending it down in jagged sheets. Rubble clogged the cut. Even beasts like Rile's would snap their legs if they tried to run there.

The General risked a brief halt. His soldiers scrambled to water the horses, snatch a few bites of food for themselves. The Magisters sat their mounts to eat. Too soon, Klamath ordered his people to resume their flight.

A dawn that he could barely discern found them laboring eastward through the snow.

So it went all that day, and the next. Without sleep or rest, almost without food, they forced their exhausted mounts into the blinding snow and cold. They were able to endure only because the enemy had learned caution. The priests held the cavalrymen back to avoid the Decimate of pestilence and the surprises of the landscape. But they were always there, always coming.

Testing the enemy, General Klamath slowed his army. The struggling mass of riders had gained enough ground to pass around waterskins and packets of food. At rare intervals, they paused at streams while their horses drank. Between halts, they survived by relying on the shapes and possibilities of the terrain.

On one occasion, the First Captain's guides took the army into a forest. The woodland covered a few square leagues, no more, but it was thickly overgrown, as dense as a jungle. The only paths were the trails of deer, the tracks of woodcutters. Bellegerins who knew the region led the riders along snow-clogged ways while the cavalrymen crashed among the trees, forcing their own paths by brute strength. When Klamath finally left the forest, the Magisters of fire and lightning were ready. They transformed the woodland into an inferno. The Magisters of wind fanned the flames. The Magisters of drought sucked away the snow.

That trick won a temporary respite. It gave General Klamath's people a little rest, kept the horses from foundering. But it did not last long. Shielded somehow, the cavalrymen began emerging from the flames. Klamath's army fled again.

As the leagues passed, his opportunities to slow the enemy dwindled. Twice his people reached brisk rivers that could only be forded by men who knew their secrets. The complex currents and rapids probably cost the enemy a few lives, a degree of inconvenience; but those gains were small. Beyond the rivers, Belleger became a land of knotted hills marked only by wintering shrubs and occasional trees, useless to Klamath's army.

He was exhausted himself; and he had already pushed his people past their limits. Hampered by heavy snows and strain that did not slow the enemy, he had nothing left except desperation.

Trembling with an entirely personal shame, he sent Captain Rowt ahead to relay new orders.

On command, Hegels slowed the army to a walk, deliberately encouraging the enemy to close the gap. At the same time, he dispatched two dozen riflemen back along the army's track. They were told to hide themselves as well as they could and wait for clear shots at the priests.

General Klamath did not hope for much success. For those riflemen, he had no hope at all. Exposed by their firing, they would be hunted down. But their deaths might increase the enemy's wariness. The priests could not know how many men Klamath was willing to sacrifice. In his place, they would have no scruples.

As Klamath rode on, he heard the distant bark of rifles: single shots followed by rapid fire as his soldiers emptied their clips. To him, they sounded like cries of pain. At once, clusters of beasts scattered. The clamor of trampling hooves and rending tusks came almost immediately.

Still, the General's ploy had an effect. When the riflemen were dead, the cavalry advanced more slowly. He had purchased a few more hours of survival.

The cost felt too cruel for tears. Nevertheless it was his duty. He did not allow himself to flinch from it. After nightfall of the second day, he demanded another sacrifice. He left two Magisters of pestilence behind, hidden to ambush the enemy. The priests would sense their sorcery, but the cavalrymen would not know where to look for its source. Given time, pestilence was as fatal as fire or lightning.

Whatever those Magisters did, Klamath could not hear it. The only sign that they had not wasted their lives was a sudden, brief flurry of gestures among the shining globes. Even that brightness barely pierced the snow.

But the enemy came no closer. Exhaustion reduced the army's mounts to a ragged stumble—and still the enemy came no closer. Eventually, even the pinprick lights of the priests faded.

During the night, the snowfall dwindled. The worst of the storm had passed. The sun might show itself at dawn. Then the enemy would charge. Klamath believed that. His army had reached the end of itself. The priests would seize their chance. One swift rush would bring this long chase to a close.

He tried to think, and could not. In darkness, this stretch of Belleger offered him nothing, not even a pile of boulders or a stand of trees for cover.

Conserving its last strength, he halted his poor mount and turned to face the enemy. When the time came, he would be the first to die. If he accomplished nothing else, he could choose the terms of his end. His people could make their own choices.

He had been right all along. King Bifalt should have chosen someone else to be his General.

He would know it when the enemy charged. Those hells-cursed globes would tell him. He tried to imagine how he would unsling his rifle, where he would find the resolve to take aim and fire.

Captain Rowt came to his side, and Magister Solace. Neither of them spoke.

Klamath was glad for their company. He did not want to die alone.

He expected to hear shouts like battle cries, the sudden white glare of sorcery. There was nothing. The charge that did not come. A long time seemed to pass before he began to wonder if it would come at all.

Without orders, Captain Rowt goaded his horse toward the enemy. In moments, he disappeared in darkness.

Klamath clung to his saddle-horn. The deep silence of snow covered him. He should have heard something when Rowt died. Surely, he should have heard something? A shot or two?

He heard nothing.

When Rowt reappeared, he sat slumped in his saddle like a man with a mortal wound. Tears made streaks of ice on his cheeks.

"They—" He seemed to be dying, but he was only exhausted. "They are gone, General. I found trampled snow, a field of it. I saw small flickers of sorcery, but they faded.

"General," he said like a sob. "We beat them."

Klamath did not try to understand. He had no use for explanations.

Carried out of himself by a tide of relief, he relaxed until he was lying on his back in the snow.

During these days, Queen Estie knew nothing of the war. She remained in her quarters. Occasionally, she had visitors that she refused to see. She had no courage to spare for them. None of them were deaf.

Since the awakening of her gift, she had been imprisoned in an absolute silence. Every sound had been taken from her.

At one time, she had believed that she knew what to expect. She had been warned often enough. She had imagined that she was prepared to bear the cost of her talent. Now she knew the truth. No warning could have readied her. Her loss was as vast as her world, and as intimate as her heart's blood.

After her awakening, Crayn had supported her back to her rooms. She had been too weak to walk so far on her own. But in those first moments, she had not known how badly she needed his help. Seeing his mouth move, she understood that he was trying to reach her. The soundlessness of his efforts was no surprise. Other shocks were worse. When she realized that she could not hear the gasp of her own breathing, or the faint impact of her sandals on the stone floor, something inside her snapped.

Her noiseless passage through the corridors and halls of the Last Repository insisted that she had ceased to exist in some fundamental way. Cut off from other people, she had lost herself. Despite his support, Crayn was severed from her.

In every way that mattered, her deafness left her effectively dead.

When she reached her chambers, he seated her in the sitting room. Because he offered it, she swallowed a little wine. In the same way, she ate a few pieces of fruit. Telling him that she wanted her bed, she seemed to make no sound.

He helped her into her bedroom, set out a soft robe in the warmth of the fire. After that, as silent as a figment, he had slipped out of the room and closed the door, leaving Queen Estie of Amika terrified.

Without his presence, his touch, she felt that she herself had become the figment. When she put herself to bed, the touch of her blankets was mute. The pressure of the pillow on her head had no meaning. Even dying animals could be comforted. Another wild cry rose in her, a wail that the whole Repository would hear. Her own frenzy stopped her. Her heart made no sound, but the force of her pulse was tangible. It insisted that she had not lost *every* connection. She remained bound to her fears.

Then the toll of the past few hours washed over her. As the labor of her heart slowed, it carried her to sleep.

Sometime later, a voice touched her mind.

Queen? I must speak with you.

Startled upright in her bed, she asked, "Avail?" Or perhaps she did not. She heard nothing.

Yet she must have made some noise. Almost immediately, Crayn opened her door and hurried to her bedside. His mouth moved dumbly. Like hers, his voice was a dead thing.

Grimacing at his mistake, he reached for her hand.

She jerked it away, a gesture that refused him. With her thoughts, she called, **Avail?**

Queen, replied the Magister, **speak more softly.** He sounded vexed. **There is no need to shout. Your last cry was heard everywhere. It burst Apprentice Travail's eardrums. Many others bled from their ears. Magisters and scullery-maids felt a force like an explosion.**

Only form the words in your mind and think of me. I will hear you.

Instinctively, Estie recoiled. "Gods!" she gasped. "Travail—?" He had tried so hard to help her—and she had hurt him? "Will he recover? Can he be healed?"

Her chamber remained as soundless as a tomb.

Crayn grabbed her hand, held it when she tried to pull away. Laboriously, he tapped words onto her forearm.

—Calm yourself, Majesty. I hear you.

With an effort, the Queen met his troubled gaze. Unsure of her control over her human voice, she enunciated carefully, "Not now, Commander. Wait."

Perplexed and anxious, Crayn let her withdraw her hand.

She turned her head away. Closed her eyes. Concentrated.

Magister Avail?

That is better, Queen, he answered. **It will become easier. I do not mean to distress you. I know you are afraid. The price you have paid is a horror. You will pay it for the rest of your life. I know. I pay it every hour of every day.**

I disturbed you because I must tell you two things.

Estie sat back against her pillows. She wanted to shout, No! Not now! It is too much! She meant, I have lost more than my life. I have lost my husband. But the surge and pause of her pulse steadied her. To that extent, she was still alive.

Scowling until her forehead seemed to split, she asked, **Do you have word of King Bifalt, Magister?**

No, Queen, he sighed. **That is the first thing I must tell you. We have no news of the war. Since the fall of Belleger's Fist, a snowstorm has covered the whole of the west. The Farsighted cannot pierce it. We are as ignorant as you.**

An inaudible sob slipped past her self-control. The dampness on her cheeks told her that she was weeping. On his knees beside her, Crayn looked like he wanted to weep as well; but she ignored him. She needed all of her resolve to frame another question.

And the second thing, Magister Avail?

It is this, Queen. You are not alone. He sounded strangely gentle now, almost caressing. **Nor am I. For the first time in bitter decades, I am not alone. We can speak to each other, Queen, you and I. We can tell each other that which no one else should hear. Your sacrifice grieves me, but I am also grateful. Do you hear me, Queen? I am** *grateful.* **If I can ease your suffering in any way, you need only ask.**

Estie needed a long moment before she could reply, **I hear you.**

She wanted to tell him that his gratitude was wasted. His voice was an intrusion that she had no power to refuse. And he did not know if Bifalt still lived. He had nothing to offer except despair.

But she retained enough self-command to say nothing. Travail had told her that Magister Avail had a heart. Long days ago, Avail's concern for Magister Facile had demonstrated it. His recognition of her gift had shaken him badly. And the Apprentice was a wounded man who had set aside his long sorrow to teach her. He had earned her credence.

Fortunately, the Magister seemed to understand some of what she felt. He left her mind alone.

For Crayn's mute anguish, she had no answer.

When he was gone, she slept again until a dream of mad things screaming without a sound woke her. Her terror lingered, but she clung to the throb of her heart until she was able to move. Despite her weakness, she found her way out of her blankets, forced herself to stand. Did she need hearing to keep her balance? Perhaps she did. Her bedroom spent long moments sliding past her before it decided to stay in one place. With an effort, she tightened her robe and went out the door.

Strangely shy, as if she were naked and had no right to intrude, she opened the door to see who was there.

Apart from the Commander and two of his guardsmen, the sitting room was empty.

At once, Crayn jumped out of his chair. One of his men he dismissed to the guardsmen's quarters. The other he sent to the outer door, apparently to deliver a message. While the man stepped outside and closed the door, Crayn strode to Estie's side and took her arm. With his fingers, he offered her the word he knew best.

—Majesty? Majesty?

The red rims of his eyes and the pinched muscles around his mouth told her that he had not slept. He had stayed on guard, waiting to help her.

She felt a pang of concern for him. "Crayn," she blurted, "you should rest. Your men can care for me."

He managed a rueful grin.

—I will, Majesty. When you have eaten.

He gestured at the low table among the armchairs. A tray there held a large meal, flasks of wine and water, goblets. Then he added:

—I have asked for Magister Oblique. My tapping is weak.

Estie nodded. She should have smiled for his sake, but she did not have it in her. Seating herself, she reached for a flask.

The table tilted. The walls skidded past her. She was going to drop the flask.

The Commander seemed to understand. With one hand, he took the flask. The other he rested on her shoulder. After a moment, her surroundings settled.

From the flask, he poured the Repository's ruby wine into a goblet. By touch, he told her to drink.

Unable to trust herself, or the table, or the whole room, Queen Estie lifted the goblet with both hands. The first taste seemed to restore her balance. She drank more deeply.

"Thank you," she said, if she said anything at all. Carefully, she began to eat. Every piece of fruit, every tender sliver of roasted chicken, every bite of fresh bread assured her that the table would remain level.

Soon the guardsman outside opened the outer door. Bowing, he ushered Magister Oblique into the chamber, then retreated to stand outside.

Oblique seemed short of breath. Her cheeks were flushed, and her hair had been tossed into a tangle. She must have run to arrive so soon after she was summoned. As the door closed, she paused to compose herself. Then she sketched an Amikan bow for Commander Crayn. But she did not bow to Estie. Instead, she came to the table and seated herself beside the Queen.

Smiling to mask her alarm and sadness, the Magister extended her hand. An invitation.

Inside Estie lived a small girl who had been her father's favorite. That child was wailing.

Unsure of her ability to contain her emotions, she gave her forearm to the sorceress.

Oblique's eyes were luminous with tears. She wrote more quickly than Crayn, but also more distinctly.

—Queen of Amika, I am glad to see you. I have been concerned for you. We all have. You have suffered a cruel blow. I hoped that you would sleep longer. How else can you bear the first rush of pain? But now I find that I was wrong. You have other needs.

The sorceress paused, then tapped:

—You have reserves, Queen. You keep them hidden, but they will serve you well.

As if in response to a threat, Estie's balance faltered. The lines of Oblique's face blurred. The walls leaned their tapestries at impossible angles.

The Magister nodded.

—It will pass, Queen. Your life has taught you to rely on sound. But your ears have not been damaged. You will feel stronger as you grow accustomed to silence.

Estie breathed deeply until her dizziness faded. Seeking reassurance, she asked the first question that occurred to her.

"How is Travail?"

The Magister frowned unhappily.

—Your shout was powerful, Queen. It was heard everywhere. For some, it was too loud to be endured. It damaged his eardrums.

At once, she added:

—They will heal. The shamans know how to care for him.

Oblique's expression said, Do not blame yourself.

At some cost to himself, the Apprentice had given Estie a necessary gift. She hated to think that she had hurt him. But the Magister had not answered her underlying question.

She tried again.

"Before that. He was sweating. He may have been weeping. He looked sick."

Had he been poisoned a second time?

Oblique nodded as she replied.

—As did you, Queen. Travail is not a Magister, but he *is* a sorcerer.

He feels the presence of sorcery. It filled the librarian's workroom. And Magister Avail had asked the Apprentice to translate for him. Travail is too brave to refuse, despite his weakness.

"But why?" protested Estie. "Why was *I* affected? My gift was still asleep. How could *any* sorcery affect me like a fever?"

Oblique's mouth formed an *Ah* of comprehension. At once, she tapped her answer.

—I have seen that effect before. What you felt, Queen, was the struggle of your talent to awaken *itself*. It is a part of you, an essential part. It wanted to express itself.

—In some form, every talent yearns for use. This is as true for an impulse to carve wood as it is for any sorcerous gift. Men and women feel compelled to pursue their gifts. If their gifts are not awakened, they themselves are never fully awake.

Without warning, Queen Estie was angry. Fear gave her the force of fury. Deliberately, she used her other voice.

Then why were you so reluctant to rouse me? Why did you twist and squirm when you could have helped me? Did you consider me unworthy of my gift? Did you *fear* me?

Stung, Magister Oblique sprang from her chair, strode away to the far side of the room.

At once, Crayn went after her, barking silent demands. For an instant, she twisted as if she meant to slap his face. Then she mastered herself. Whatever she said seemed to ease him. He returned to his post by the door to his quarters.

With a shudder, Oblique brought herself back to Estie. She had ire in her eyes, and frustration, as she held out her hand, asking for Estie's forearm.

Shaken by her own vehemence, Estie could not refuse.

The Magister's touch was tense. It felt like anguish.

—Perhaps I appeared false to you. If I squirmed, as you call it, I had good cause.

—I do not understand Magister Facile's conduct. She should not have spoken of your gift, not when she did not know what it is and could not prepare you for the burden. It is yours, not hers, yours to desire or refuse. No one else should be allowed to determine who and what you are. Since your arrival, I have tried to avoid compounding her fault.

As suddenly as it arose, Estie's anger failed. A desire to weep threatened to overcome her.

Hoping that her unheard voice would suffice, she answered, "Magister Facile spoke to prepare me for my father. She wanted me to recognize who and what *he* was. I do not fault her."

After a moment, Magister Oblique produced a tentative smile. Like an act of kindness, she wrote:

—Yet you are afraid. You have *been* afraid. How could you trust a woman who appeared to hold the secret you feared?

—Sadly, I cannot relieve you now. Perhaps Magister Avail will know what to say. If not, only plain courage will serve.

Estie shook her head. She could not expose her heart to Magister Avail. His moods were too extreme, and his losses did not resemble hers.

Concentrating so that only Oblique would hear her, she reverted to her gift.

I do not find courage in myself, Magister. The cost is too high. I am cut off. The silence is a knife. Without sound, I *bleed*. I cannot leave my rooms. There is too much silence everywhere.

Magister Avail cannot heal me.

To her surprise, Oblique had a reply ready.

—Then let others come to you, Queen. There are people here who fear for you, or who simply mean well. Let them visit you. One at a time, at your own pace. Accept what they offer. Let them show you that you are not entirely cut off.

Then she added:

—With your consent, I will stay to translate for you. Your Commander is an admirable man, but he is not fluent. For the present, I have no duties that I cannot fulfill whenever you choose to rest. Let me help you.

Estie hesitated. **Can you understand me when I speak aloud? Do I speak clearly?**

Oblique's smile became a beam.

—I can, Queen. You are clear. Your lips and tongue will not forget the habit of speech. In time, you will remember that you are strong.

Instinctively, Estie wanted to refuse. She was reluctant to rely on the sorceress so intimately. But what else could she do?

Instead of answering the Magister directly, she turned to Crayn.

"We have been unkind to you, Commander. You cannot know what Magister Oblique has said. She urges me to accept an occasional visitor. Later, I may wish to do so. Please inform your men that my needs are changing. Then you must rest." More softly, she said, "You are essential to me, Crayn."

Embarrassment complicated his anxiety for her. He paused long enough to mask his concern. Then he bowed and left her, heading for his quarters.

He seemed to take the last remnants of her former life with her. Her chair tilted under her again, and the walls leaned in like threats. They took a long time to recover their balance.

TWENTY-THREE

KILLERS

In silence, Queen Estie finished her meal. Perhaps because she could not hear any of the small sounds she made, she appreciated Magister Oblique's presence. The sorceress demanded nothing, made no attempt to communicate. She seemed content to sit where she was indefinitely, wearing her gentle smile.

Finally, the Queen said, "Thank you, Magister. I must sleep."

Oblique touched Estie's forearm long enough to reply:

—I will remain a while.

Then she sat back in her chair, watching Estie's efforts to stand and remain steady. Her calm and her smile expressed an assurance that the Queen did not feel.

Estie had imagined taking a bath. She wanted to soak the stains of fear and strain off her skin. They smelled like dried blood. But she found that she could not refuse her bed. Climbing into her blankets, she settled her pillows and tried to believe that she would be able to relax.

As soon as she closed her eyes, her world disappeared. Even her fears uncoiled themselves like serpents and slid away.

When she returned, bathed and dressed, to her sitting room, she found fresh food and drink on the low table, a replenished fire burning warmly in the hearth, and Magister Oblique waiting with Commander Crayn.

Estie stifled a flinch. She had prepared herself to feign composure. After years as Amika's Queen and Bifalt's wife, she knew how to conceal herself behind a pleasant demeanor.

The Magister greeted Estie with a gentle smile. Crayn nodded his approval as he stood to take his place by the inner door.

Almost steadily, Estie walked to the table and poured a goblet of water for herself. The table remained in its place. The tapestries on the walls hung straight. She held the goblet with both hands as she drank. When she felt ready, she took a chair beside Oblique.

Testing her courage, she cleared her throat. "You spoke of visitors, Magister."

The sorceress extended her hand. Her tapping was steadier than Estie's heartbeat.

—There could be many, Queen. Shall I list them for you? The choice is yours.

Estie stopped her. "First, I must ask you to repeat what you say aloud. I do not wish to exclude my Commander."

She meant, I need him.

A touch of embarrassment crossed Oblique's face as she turned to Crayn. She appeared to speak. He appeared to reply.

Meeting Estie's gaze again, Magister Oblique wrote:

—He thanks you, Queen. I will remember to include him.

Estie managed a smile. Striving for queenliness, she replied, "Accept my gratitude. And forgive my earlier distrust. A visitor or two may do me good." One at a time, at her own pace. "I would like to see Lylin."

The devotee's self-assurance made her an uncomfortable presence. For that very reason, she might remind Estie that Amika's Queen knew how to rule.

Magister Oblique's features slipped into a frown.

—The most holy devotee of Spirit has left the Last Repository.

Left? While Rile was on his way? The idea startled Estie. It did not fit her image of Lylin.

To Estie's stare, Oblique explained, repeating what she said to Crayn as she tapped.

—As you know, Queen, the most holy devotees do not justify themselves. However, I am sure of one thing. They are a vulnerable people. They know that if the Great God is able to destroy the Repository, he will not stop there. The most holy devotee must have gone to defend her people.

Reflexively, Estie objected. "Surely, they can do more good here? They can save their people by saving the Repository."

The Magister's answer was a shrug.

—What can I say, Queen? They make their own choices. We do not choose for them.

After a moment, she added:

—They have always done so. When the most holy devotees Amandis and Flamora selected Elgart for their teaching, they did not explain themselves. Yet they chose well. Through him, they transformed the Prince.

Yes, thought Estie. She knew how Elgart had changed her husband. Nevertheless Magister Marrow's manipulations had exacted a price. They had been worse than cruel. They had made Bifalt a man who could not love her.

Oblique's inadvertent reminder twisted Estie's heart. She needed a moment to recover her masque of calm.

Like a woman grasping at a mirage, she sighed, "Well. It seems that I must have a visitor." Anything to distract her from the way her heart ached. "Do you have a suggestion, Magister?"

The sorceress shook herself. Carefully, she wrote:

—My list is long, Queen. But perhaps it would be well to begin with a more familiar face. Your sub-Commander Waysel is here. The snow slowed him. He did not arrive until this morning.

As she repeated this to Crayn, he came closer. Standing in front of Estie, he nodded vigorously. His mouth shaped a *Yes*.

As a matter of course, Queen Estie knew Waysel well. She liked him for his genial style of command. But his coming represented the war. He would want orders that might get him and his men killed.

While Estie hesitated, Magister Oblique tapped:

—There is one thing that you must understand, Queen. He knows of your sacrifice. He heard your shout. That was inevitable. We could not refuse him an explanation.

—He and his guardsmen have rooms nearby. If I call for him, he will come at once.

Estie took a deep breath. She drank more water. When the goblet was empty, she set it on the rug beside her chair. Her hands were trembling.

"Then I must see him." She answered the Magister, but she was looking at Crayn. He understood her well enough to tell Waysel whatever she could not. "I am ready."

She was not.

Her Commander nodded again. He and Oblique exchanged words that seemed soundless. He gave the Magister a small bow, then strode to the door and passed his instructions to the guardsman outside.

Estie was still trembling when Waysel appeared.

He was a pudgy man, habitually pleasant, but his composure had deserted him. He had heard too many tales of a guardsman's life under King Smegin's rule. He entered the sitting room as if he feared for his life.

Apparently vexed on his Queen's behalf, Crayn barked silent commands. Obeying, Waysel forced his reluctance into a chair. But he sat on its edge, poised to run. The warmth of the hearth drew sweat from his brow.

His demeanor confirmed Estie's fears. If this was how one of her officers reacted, Bifalt's response would be worse. Hoping to reassure the sub-Commander, she explained Magister Oblique's role at her side. Then she asked for his report.

He may have been deaf to everything else, but he knew how to deliver a report. Through Oblique, he told Estie that the cannon had arrived safely. The guns had been placed where the hunchback wanted them, oiled and tightly covered in canvas. The kegs of gunpowder waited near the doors of the Repository. His men had survived the snows without mishap.

While he spoke, he avoided Estie's gaze. His attention was fixed on Oblique's tapping hand, plainly suspicious of her translation. As soon as he was done, he clamped his mouth shut.

This was not how Estie had encouraged her officers and men to converse with her. Aching, she tried to regain his trust.

With her other voice, she said, **Hear me, sub-Commander,** thinking that she had spoken mildly.

Waysel reacted as if she had stung him. He jumped from his chair, retreated to the nearest wall. His eyes stared, white with unreasoning fright.

Magister Oblique started to rise. Estie stopped her with a gesture.

Hear me, Waysel. How could he refuse? **You know my voice. I can speak in your mind. But your mind does not speak to *me*. I cannot know your thoughts. Do not fear that I know your thoughts.**

This is a shock to both of us, but I am still your Queen. If we survive this war, I will return to Amika and reclaim my throne. Do you *hear* me, Waysel? No sorcery can change who or what I am.

I am not my father.

For a moment, the sub-Commander seemed stunned. Nevertheless he was an honor guardsman, an officer. Panting, he rallied.

Through Oblique, he said:

—Majesty. Majesty. I was told, but I did not understand. I could not believe— You are deaf? Stone-deaf? And yet you have sorcery? Forgive me, Majesty. You have gone beyond me.

Queen Estie did not reply. Instead, she urged Magister Oblique to approach Waysel.

At once, Oblique hastened to the sub-Commander's side.

She stood close to him, touched his tense arm gently, offered him her concerned smile and soft voice. At first, his responses were frightened. As she answered them, they became angry. Then, gradually, he began to resemble the man he had once been.

Estie heard nothing. The chamber was as empty of words as a waiting coffin. But she watched Waysel's progress. When she saw that he had regained his composure, she told him to go back to his men.

Taking a grip on himself, the sub-Commander presented her with the full formality of an Amikan bow. Then he withdrew.

The Queen sighed. To Magister Oblique, she said, "You see what I fear. That was a small example. Others will be worse."

Certainly, her husband's would be. If she ever saw him again.

Oblique faced her sadly. When she returned to Estie's side, she put her hand on Estie's forearm without sitting.

—I understand, Queen. It is harsh. When Magister Avail was awakened, there was no one who could speak to him. But none of our people feared him. In that way, your plight is more cruel.

As Estie nodded, the sorceress wrote more.

—Forget my list, Queen. You have done enough. I will leave you now. Rest as well as you can. But I must insist on one more visitor. When I come again, I will bring the librarian. She needs to speak with you.

"Perhaps," murmured Estie, keeping the depth of her reluctance to herself. "If I can." She yearned to be alone.

To her surprise, Magister Oblique bent down and hugged her briefly. Then the sorceress left.

Queen Estie's hands shook as she tried to eat a little fruit. Her encounter with Waysel had drawn blood. She did not feel ready to lose more.

She spent an hour drinking wine. When she had achieved a comfortable state of numbness, she asked, **Magister Avail?**

She did not know the time of day. He might be asleep. But his answer came at once. **I hear you, Queen.** He may have been waiting for her voice. **What troubles you? I would like to see your face while we talk. May I come to you?**

No! she protested. Then, more quietly: **No. I am not ready.**

She sensed a sigh. **I am a Magister of the Last Repository, Queen. I am not accustomed to pleading for permission.** Sadness leaked through his asperity. **But the librarian insists. I will abide by your wishes.**

How can I help you?

Carefully, Estie asked, **Will you answer a question, Magister?**

If I can, he snapped.

If you cannot, she mused, no one can. **Does this become easier? This silence? This.** *Complete.* **Isolation?**

No, he retorted. After a pause, he added, **And yes.**

At first, no. Nothing can prepare you for it. It is unnatural. The people around you may think that they understand. They do not. The loss of sound never fades. Nothing can draw the fangs of that snake.

But later— He paused again. **In my case, Queen, Magister Rummage taught me the language of touch. After the horror of my awakening, that was my first taste of connection. Of being** *included.*

Here, Queen, I am surrounded by people who wish to speak with me. They do not suffice. Taken together, however, they are enough. My loss is softened by my service. I am *needed,* **Queen, needed in a good cause. No one doubts my worth.**

Estie wanted to ask, Will that be true for me? I have nothing to offer. I am only the Queen of Amika. How can I bear my loss if no one needs me?

But she could not say that to Magister Avail. It sounded too much like self-pity. Of course, he would understand. He had never stopped pitying himself. But she did not want bitterness. She wanted an *answer.*

Hours later, or perhaps the next day, Queen Estie received Magister Oblique and Magister Threnody in her sitting room.

Estie wanted to believe that she was ready. She had eaten and slept, and the time that she had spent alone with Commander Crayn had steadied her. Her hands no longer trembled. But those signs of recovered strength were superficial. Her heart seemed to shudder at every breath. She greeted Oblique and Beatrix Threnody from behind a façade of calm.

Magister Oblique's manner was earnest. She seemed hopeful, almost expectant, as she ushered the librarian to a seat opposite the Queen. After an inaudible exchange with Crayn, she took a chair beside Estie. Her smile hinted at an emotion that might have been eagerness. On Estie's forearm, she tapped:

—Be calm, Queen. I am only here to reassure you.

Estie nodded vaguely. Her attention was fixed on the librarian.

At first, Magister Threnody looked unchanged. She sat with her head bowed so that the fall of her black hair could mask her timidity. A closer study, however, discerned the signs of a deep fatigue around her eyes and mouth. Past her hair, her gaze glittered with a concentration that resembled fever. She gave the impression that she had come trailing a long escort of demands.

Queen Estie went through the motions of offering food and water or wine. Her guests replied with perfunctory thanks. They had not come to be refreshed.

Pretending that she ruled here if nowhere else, the Queen gave her guests their opening. "I see, Magisters, that you are here for some purpose. Perhaps you will speak of it now. I ask only that you share with my Commander whatever he does not hear. I will not have him excluded."

Beatrix Threnody turned to Oblique. They exchanged a few sentences. When the librarian was satisfied, she nodded behind her raven veil. In response, Magister Oblique wrote on Estie's skin:

—The librarian is pleased by your willingness to see her, Queen.

Estie shook her head. "It is nothing, Magisters, a small gesture to repay your consideration."

Magister Threnody looked to Oblique. Her expression suggested that she was asking her companion to speak for her. But Oblique shook her head.

The librarian appeared to clear her throat. Then she began. As she spoke, Magister Oblique translated for her.

—I insisted on seeing you, Queen, for two reasons. The first is this. I must assure you that Magister Avail is your ally. He will be your friend, if you allow it. He hopes to serve you in some way.

—To prove himself, he has undertaken a task for you. It is something that you could do for yourself, but it has not occurred to you. We expect the skies to clear this morning. When they do, he will call out to King Bifalt. He will tell the King to find high ground and face east so the Farsighted can see him. If he complies, we will know that he still lives.

Suddenly confounded, Estie blurted, "Why?" What was the use of trying to reach him? She had already put her whole heart into one cry. What was the good of speaking to him if no one could hear his reply? And if he was dead—

For Beatrix Threnody, Oblique answered simply:

—We need him as much as you do, Queen.

For herself, Magister Oblique added:

—We need him *more*. Thousands of lives and half of the world's knowledge are threatened. Who else can save us? No one else will make the attempt.

The Queen in Estie recognized the truth of Oblique's assertion. The woman in her, the forlorn wife, felt the kind of pain that she would have expected from a knife in her chest. Oblique's bald statement seemed to redouble the force of her grief. She had tried *so hard* to give up hope for Bifalt.

She might have responded with enough force to drive the women from her rooms; but Commander Crayn was already kneeling in front of her. He had heard the librarian. In an instant, he had shoved the table aside to reach her. Resting his hands on her thighs, he wrote:

—Majesty? Majesty! What they say is kindly meant. It does not lessen you.

Startled, Beatrix Threnody flinched. She did not know what she had done to alarm the Commander. Briefly, Magister Oblique's hand clenched. Then her touch eased to a caress.

Estie ignored them. Crayn had all of her attention.

His open concern was a gift. It was his form of sorcery. She could accept it from him, if not from either of the Magisters.

With an effort, she swallowed her distress and became Amika's Queen again.

"They made me think of Bifalt," she told Crayn. "I did not expect it. The pain will pass."

At once, Beatrix Threnody shrank back in her chair. Clearly, she had not expected to distress Estie. Magister Oblique seemed to hold her breath.

After a moment, the Commander nodded. One touch at a time, he tapped on her thighs:

—I am here, Majesty. Speak in my mind, and I will send these women away.

Then he rose to his feet and returned to his post against the wall.

For his sake, Estie said, "Thank you, Commander." Bracing herself on his presence, she addressed her guests.

"Forgive me, Magisters. Commander Crayn is alert to my moods." Without pausing, she said, "You mentioned two reasons, librarian. Please give Magister Avail my thanks. I am ready to hear the second now."

Magister Oblique released a sigh.

—Forgive *us*, Queen. We have been thoughtless. We can only imagine the difficulties you endure.

Queen Estie shook her head to dismiss apologies. Clinging to her self-control, she put them aside.

"You came to say two things, librarian," she replied. "What is the second?"

Magister Threnody winced as her companion referred the question to her. She said something inaudible. Magister Oblique nodded. Gathering herself, she resumed tapping.

—I will speak for the librarian now. The words I write will be hers.

Dishonestly, Estie promised, "I am ready."

While Beatrix Threnody began, Oblique's touch acquired a new intensity.

—You suggested a way to discover Magister Marrow's killer. You asked me to search Sirjane Marrow's memories for anyone who has read certain books. I have done so. I found three names.

For an instant, Estie froze. Then her heart thudded. Lost in herself, she had forgotten—

Magister Oblique said a word to the librarian. Magister Threnody frowned uncomfortably, but she gave her consent. Oblique repeated it for the Queen.

—Four.

The librarian sighed. Her companion repeated:

—Yes, four. But one I dismiss. He is Tak Biondi. He became Magister Marrow's personal servant. Magister Rummage disapproved. He considers Tak Biondi impertinent. But the librarian enjoyed the young man's manners. For many reasons, they spent hours together. I cannot believe that Tak Biondi contrived Magister Marrow's death.

Tak Biondi? Estie had heard that name before, but she did not try to recall where or when. Without warning, new possibilities changed her world. While Magister Threnody spoke and Magister Oblique tapped, Estie's inner doors shifted, opening abruptly, or opening on new rooms.

Here, she thought. Here was her chance to be of use.

As if she were shouting, she said, "Tell me. When did he join your service?"

Oblique repeated Beatrix Threnody's reply.

—A year ago? Perhaps a little less.

Queen Estie nodded, putting that detail in its place.

"And the others?"

The librarian answered with more confidence.

—One is a student. He wishes to be an apprentice of warfare. While Magister Rummage is consumed by other concerns, he seeks to educate himself.

—Another is a scullion. His only explanation is that he has an appetite for knowledge. He has read books of every description, from shipbuilding to the language of flowers.

—The last I am inclined to dismiss also. She is an old woman, Harlinea, who came to us as a girl. She married here, had children here. Her family works for us as well. She began as a servant. Now she is a teacher of servants. If she wished to make poisons or gunpowder, she could gather what she needed easily. But I cannot imagine any cause that would tempt her to murder.

—Still, I am left with the scullion and the student of warfare.

Queen Estie suppressed her impulse to ask what *other* books these four had read. The librarian might need days to find an answer among Magister Marrow's memories. Instead, she inquired, "You have truthseekers among your people. Have they examined your suspects? *All* of them?"

Magister Threnody nodded.

—Yes, Queen. One apprentice studies the sorcery of sound. Her gift exceeds her teachers. She knows both truth and lies when she hears them.

"And what does *she* say?"

The librarian sighed again.

—She reports that all four are honest. She heard no lies.

That surprised Queen Estie a little. She had expected more. But she had already imagined an explanation. If the sorcery of sound could recognize truth, in another form it might also disguise falsehood.

For the first time in days, she felt ready for what was coming.

"Your Apprentice has a gift for sorcery. Surely, then, she is sensitive to sorcery in others. Did she find any hint of it in her search?"

The librarian betrayed a flash of irritation as Magister Oblique repeated her answer.

—No! I would have said so at the start. We would not ignore a hint of that kind.

Queen Estie was pleased to find that she could produce a disarming smile. "As you say, librarian. I am merely exploring possibilities. That one I can discard." At once, she continued, "Did Magister Rummage accompany your Apprentice?"

Now Beatrix Threnody was shocked.

—Certainly not. He is a clenched fist. I did not wish to frighten innocent folk.

Estie nodded as if that explanation sufficed. "If my questions seemed intemperate, librarian, please forgive them. They are an Amikan way of thinking, nothing more.

"How does Harlinea account for her reading?"

A brief clench of vexation tightened Magister Threnody's expression. Vexation or fear. She doubted herself too much to face Queen Estie's questions calmly.

—She is dying, Queen. She has an illness, and does not wish to alarm her family until she is sure of it. Rather than consult our healers, she sought a cure for herself. Poisons that kill can also heal, and the making of gunpowder requires substances that may counter sickness. Sadly, she did not find a cure.

Oblique's writing turned brusque.

—Now, Queen, we have sent healers to her. Our servants care for us. We care for them.

Queen Estie responded with the smile that she used to charm unsuspecting men. "And Tak Biondi?" she inquired. "How does he account for his reading?"

The librarian seemed to fold in on herself, hiding behind her hair. Magister Oblique gave Estie a look of exasperation.

—Now I do not speak for the librarian, Queen. I speak for myself.

—Tak Biondi read what Magister Marrow instructed him to read. Fearing treachery, Magister Marrow told him to educate himself on the subject. A precaution. And later, when the extent of King Bifalt's reliance on gunpowder became clear, Magister Marrow sent his servant to read more widely. I can only assume that Magister Marrow wanted Tak Biondi to educate *him*. He had no time for study himself.

"Ah," breathed Estie. "Thank you, Magister. I see your dilemma, and the librarian's. You have four possible culprits. Each of them has an explanation. Each of them has been examined. Now you do not know how to pursue your search.

"How may I serve you?" As if she did not already know what Beatrix Threnody wanted, she added, "Deaf as I am?"

Commander Crayn had an answer. He stepped forward to offer it. With a gesture, Estie stopped him. In a situation that might threaten her, he would not hesitate to inflict pain.

The librarian shook her hair aside. Her eyes seemed to search the chamber for a reply, not to Estie's question, but to her own uncertainty. Her lips moved, forming words that Estie could not hear.

The Queen pitied her briefly. In some ways, Beatrix Threnody's talent was as cruel as Estie's. Her lack of self-assurance was not a flaw in her. Her gift was an unfortunate accident of birth. As Estie's was.

But Amika's Queen was in no mood for hesitation. She forced herself to speak softly.

"Would you like me to pursue the matter?"

Chewing her lips, Magister Oblique spoke for the librarian.

—You have known treachery, Queen. Without your guidance, we would not have known how to begin looking for our own traitor. We cannot proceed without your help.

Queen Estie was as ready as she could be with only her pulse and her breathing to reassure her. "Very well," she promised. "I will do what I can.

"But I must have two companions. First, Third Father, if he is able to join me. Otherwise—"

Oblique interrupted her, protesting:

—How can he assist you? He has no sorcery, and the Cult of the Many does not judge. I can translate for you.

Estie's smile felt sour, but she did not soften it. "Second, I will need Magister Rummage."

If Third Father did not know the language of touch, the hunchback certainly did.

Abruptly, Magister Threnody faced Queen Estie again. Her wide stare expressed a profound shock.

Hurrying, Oblique translated the librarian's protest.

—Do you doubt our Apprentice?

"Librarian," replied Estie, "I doubt everything. I doubt myself. But different minds often ask different questions. Different ears hear different answers. Third Father is perceptive in his own way. His insights have value.

"As for Magister Rummage—" She sighed. "Fear can be useful at times. The threat of harm puts any inquiry on a new footing." She was Amikan: her father had taught her this. "It can be more effective than harm itself."

When she had confronted Prince Lome's treason, he believed that she had the power to command his execution.

With an air of desperation, Threnody asked through Oblique:

—You will threaten *Harlinea*?

At that moment, Estie had no intention of explaining herself. Did these women want her help? This was the price.

"If I must."

Beatrix Threnody sprang to her feet, whirled away. She did her uncertain best to storm out. Estie expected her to slam the door. At the last instant, she closed it softly.

Magister Oblique also rose, but with more dignity. Resting her hand on Estie's shoulder, she wrote:

—Do what you must, Queen. Magister Rummage is healing well. I will ask him and Third Father to join you. It is a dark day for us when we are reduced to threats. But our days will be darker still if you cannot prevent another murder.

Without waiting for a reply, she followed Threnody.

Alone with her Commander, Estie faced his protests. He bristled with them. They turned the sandy hue of his eyes a dangerous brown.

Even now, she was sure. A sorcery that masked lies might be capable of anything. She was not willing to risk him.

"Understand me, Crayn. It is not your place to accompany me now. Whether they know it or not, these Magisters created their own dilemma. Or Magister Marrow did. One of them must answer it. Magister Rummage is the obvious choice.

"Third Father will counter his recklessness. And if I am threatened—" She shrugged. "I will be safe enough. His response will be extreme. Then the outcome will be his responsibility. It must not be yours."

Crayn betrayed a subtle flinch. He straightened his back, stood like iron. But he did not reply. She would not have heard him. Instead, he bowed stiffly and returned to his quarters.

Queen Estie felt a pang on his behalf, but she did not linger over it. She had been given a gift, a purpose. She refused to waste it.

During her absences, servants had provided the Queen with new apparel. She selected a soft brown shirt that looked like leather and felt like silk, with trousers to match. Until she put them on, she did not notice that they were the exact hue her husband had worn for their wedding.

That suited her. Nodding to herself, she added a pair of supple sandals for her feet. Then she returned to her sitting room to wait.

Two hours later, she was deep in unfamiliar regions of the keep. Third Father walked on one side of her, Magister Rummage on the other, holding her hands. By touch, they guided her.

The monk still looked too old for his years. He moved with a loose shuffle, like a man who had become accustomed to losing his balance. Nevertheless he seemed less frail than he had been. The way he held her hand, with his fingers curled in her palm, conveyed a slight tremor, but his touch confirmed that he knew the code of taps.

In contrast, Magister Rummage strode like compressed rage despite the severity of his recent wound. Silent snarls bared his teeth, and every cramped breath resembled a curse. Yet his grip on Estie's hand was gentle, even considerate. His friendship with Magister Avail must have taught him to withhold his strength.

Queen Estie was the first to speak. She asked, "You know where we are going?"

Magister Rummage answered without hesitation:

—To search for Magister Marrow's killer.

As if in response, Third Father wrote:

—You will not threaten the innocent, Queen. You do not have that in you. You believe that you know the killer.

Estie replied aloud. Both men needed to hear her, and she did not have the skill to write with both hands simultaneously. As if she had no doubt, she said, "Tak Biondi."

Magister Rummage's glare grew bright. He demanded:

—Why?

Estie did not say, Because Magister Marrow trusted him too much. Instead, the Queen answered, "Because he is impertinent. Because his coming was timely for the Great God. And because he will not suffer for it if I am mistaken."

The monk nodded to himself. Magister Rummage quickened his strides, drawing her and Third Father with him.

This far down in the mountain, the air was always cold. Despite the chill, however, the wide corridors were well-lit and dry. At the hunchback's pace, Queen Estie felt warm enough. After a while, Magister Rummage brought her to a broad stairway. At its foot, lighted passages branched away in all directions. Here, Rummage told her, the servants had their homes. The hallway he entered stretched into the distance.

At intervals on both sides were wooden doors strutted with iron. To Queen Estie's question, the Magister replied that the doors had been made strong in case the mountain shifted in its long sleep.

The monk added:

—This is not a dungeon, Queen. The Repository has none. These are comfortable quarters.

As they walked, Magister Rummage informed Estie that the four suspects had been instructed to remain in their rooms until they were summoned. Whatever they thought of their orders, they could all use the rest.

Before long, the hunchback brought her and Third Father to the door he wanted. Still holding Estie's hand, he faced her. The light of a nearby cresset gleamed like eagerness on his knotted features.

—You are ready, Queen?

She hesitated. She had not felt ready for anything since her gift had come to life. She feared that the silence would drive her mad. But she knew how to do what the librarian had asked of her. What was the worst that could happen? She would hurt the sensibilities of a man she did not know. In any other outcome, the mute Magister's presence would protect her.

She tightened her grip on herself and nodded.

Grinning, he released her hand and knocked on the door. His heavy fist rattled the door on its hinges. Finding it unlocked, he opened it and entered without waiting for an invitation.

Third Father raised an eyebrow at the Magister's rudeness, but he did not comment. Together, he and Queen Estie followed Magister Rummage into Tak Biondi's quarters.

The chamber was well-lit. In each corner, lamps rested on tall stands. Two lanterns shone on the mantelpiece. The fire in the hearth added its own brightness. Rows of candles burned on the end of the table that Tak Biondi apparently used as a desk. The books lying open there suggested that he had no reason to discontinue his studies.

The room itself was only a little smaller than her sitting room. It had two inner doors, one presumably for the bedroom, the other for the bathing room. Both were closed. But there were no chairs. When Tak Biondi read, he used the only stool.

In other ways, the space was entirely unfurnished. Its occupant had done nothing to make it comfortable or home-like. In its severity, it reminded Estie of her father's private study, a place that did not tolerate weakness.

Like a man expecting visitors, Tak Biondi half sat on the near edge of his table. At first glance, he seemed young; but his face had a middle-aged look of wear, of hard use. He wore a blue tunic and pantaloons, tough boots. They may have been his only garments. If so, he kept them scrupulously clean, but had not mended their frayed cuffs or repaired the cracked leather of the boots. Over his forehead, his black hair hung in an unkempt mess. It resembled Magister Threnody's, but it did not gleam in the light like hers.

He was smiling, a twist of the lips that made him look habitually sardonic.

Entering, Magister Rummage went at once to stand in the nearest corner. Just for an instant, Queen Estie missed his presence at her side. Then she realized that his post gave him a direct line toward Tak Biondi.

Holding Third Father's hand, she assumed her most regal posture. For different reasons, she offered her suspect a pleasant smile.

"You are Tak Biondi?"

In response, his mouth moved, saying nothing that she could hear. However, the monk's translation came promptly.

—And you are Queen Estie of Amika. I saw you the night of Magister Marrow's death. The whole Repository is aware of you.

After a slight pause, he added:

—Do you know, Queen? Magister Marrow chose me. I thought of him as a friend, almost a father. But I never heard him speak my name until the night of his death. Does that surprise you?

What, never? For an instant, Estie lost track of her intentions. Was it possible that the former librarian had only called his personal servant by name once? Or was Tak Biondi simply toying with her?

With an effort, she collected herself. "It is strange, certainly," she admitted. "But Magister Marrow was a strange man. He did many things that I would like to understand."

Through Third Father, Tak Biondi responded:

—For example, Queen? Perhaps I can help you.

"For example," replied Estie, "I am told that you spent many hours with him. What did you find to talk about?"

This time, her suspect had more to say. The twist of his mouth did not waver. He kept his eyes hidden.

—We spoke of warfare, Queen. He was the *librarian*, not a soldier. He had read a variety of texts, but he needed more, and he had no time. On his instructions, I read for him. We spent our hours discussing the Repository's peril. I was—how shall I put this?—a mirror for him. I reflected what he knew. In that way, I showed him what he did *not* know.

—For example, he had not considered that the Great God might strike by treachery. In addition, he did not know how to prepare for a siege. And he had no more than a sketch of the many ways that gunpowder can be used. I read to educate him.

Queen Estie already knew that Tak Biondi had studied poisons. She wanted to ask him *when*. Was it before or after Apprentice Travail had been stricken? But that approach was too blatant.

In any case, the servant was still speaking.

—The books are open to all, Queen. But no one is permitted to remove them from the library proper. Yet I have done so.

He gestured at his table.

—Magister Marrow trusted me.

With one hand, he rubbed his sternum. Tossing his hair aside, he gave Estie a glimpse of the confidence in his gaze.

She let the silence hang for a moment. While she considered her next question, she made a point of looking at Magister Rummage to remind the servant that he was in danger.

Tak Biondi was not troubled. If he had anything to fear, he did not show it. Instead, he asked a question.

Third Father continued to translate for her.

—Given time and the librarian's trust, I read a great deal. Do you know, Queen, there is a book that you might find useful? It is an old tome, dusty with disuse, but perfectly legible. Long ago, a scholar named Lamit Karsolsky wrote on many arcane subjects. The book I mean is called *A Complete System of Gestures for Speech with the Deaf and Dumb*.

His smile sharpened.

—The words are demonstrated in diagrams.

Queen Estie knew what he was doing, but he caught her nevertheless. Gestures for speech? she thought. A whole system? The benefits were obvious. With gestures, people could address her without touching her. And gestures might be easier to learn than the intricate code of taps. Crayn might master it more readily. And her husband—

Gods! If Bifalt had that book—

Still, she recognized Tak Biondi's ploy. She had used it herself. And he was not done. Rubbing his chest again, he added:

—I am surprised, Queen, that the librarian has not already offered you Karsolsky's book. And I am utterly astonished that Magister Marrow did not share *A Complete System* with Magister Avail. I cannot imagine his reasons. Magister Avail should not have been made to suffer.

The hunchback was mute, not deaf. He seemed to take the servant's gambit as a personal insult. *He* had not made his friend suffer. Glowering, he took a step closer.

But he stopped when Tak Biondi responded with a look like a taunt. It was too soon for threats. After a moment, Magister Rummage drew back into his corner, biding his time.

Queen Estie felt a strange tingling in her nerves. It was too faint to recognize, too brief.

In Amika or Belleger, that would have been enough for her. Magister Facile had warned her. But here she needed more.

To the monk, she tapped quickly:

—Watch him, Father.

Then she smiled for Tak Biondi.

"Naturally, I am interested in Karsolsky's book. But I am intrigued by your discussions with Magister Marrow. I wonder, did you ever consider what would happen to Amika and Belleger if the Last Repository falls?"

Tak Biondi held one hand to his chest like a promise that he spoke from the heart. The other he spread to show Estie that it was empty, helpless. As fast as the monk could write, he said:

—Now *you* surprise me, Queen. Yes, we did. He believed that the outcome would be ruinous. For my part, I have no opinion.

He grinned acidly.

—How can I know such things? I am only a servant.

The light in the room seemed to grow brighter. It frayed Estie's reasoning. She wanted to squint.

"But if you were to speculate, Tak Biondi?"

He frowned.

—Speculate, Queen? Do you mean *guess*?

"I mean *imagine*." She found it harder to speak pleasantly. Her smile cost her an effort. "You have been here for some time. You have read many books. You knew Magister Marrow's mind. What do you imagine would happen to Amika and Belleger?" She tried to seem as confident as Tak Biondi. "Purely as a matter of casual interest?"

If Magister Rummage could have made a sound, he might have snarled.

Rubbing his chest, Tak Biondi erased his frown. His sardonic air took on a keener edge.

—You are serious, Queen?

Without raising his eyes, Third Father wrote:

—Be wary, Queen.

Estie shook her head. The increasing light blurred her concentration. "I am. My people are at risk, Tak Biondi. I must consider every outcome. Even the most fanciful."

The servant grinned.

—Very well. Purely as a matter of casual interest. Saying nothing of my own opinions or desires.

—It occurs to me, Queen, that the Great God may bring peace.

As if she were choking, Estie managed to demand, "Explain."

Tak Biondi nodded.

—I will.

—In my time here, I have observed as much as I can. And it appears to me—this is merely an observation—that knowledge breeds discontent. It breeds exclusion and arrogance. Over time, it breeds fear. And fear breeds strife. Discontent is the direct cause, but it is superficial. Knowledge breeds war.

Still half sitting on the table, Queen Estie's opponent slowly closed his hand on the fabric of his shirt. The brightness around her became more intense. His garment assumed a startling shade of blue. Disquiet scraped along Estie's nerves. She felt Third Father's translation through a haze like a mirage.

—This is speculation, Queen. But consider yourself. Why have you come here, if you were not discontented? You craved more. And now that you have more, are you not still discontented? Knowledge gained is peace lost.

His manner grew more animated. His smile became predatory.

—In your case, surely, the pain of that loss is extreme. In your darkest hours, you must feel that your former life was preferable to your present distress.

—And if that is true, it must be true for others as well. While you are discontented, and Amika, and Belleger, and, yes, even the Last Repository, you will never have peace until it is given to you.

For a moment, the Queen lost her place in Tak Biondi's answer, or in Third Father's rendition. Yet there was one word that insisted on her attention. Groping, she found it.

He had said *until*, not *unless*.

That was a mistake.

She was Queen Estie of Amika, her father's daughter as much as her mother's. Resisting her confusion, she glanced at Magister Rummage.

He appeared to tremble in the grip of a crisis. His eyes caught the light like a madman's.

With as much care as she could muster, she said, "You fascinate me, Tak Biondi." Her voice shook. "Please continue. When the Great God has given us peace, what will life be like for the people of Amika and Belleger?"

He must have known that she was cornering him. He shrugged without moving his hand from his chest. His smile slipped to one side. Black hair hid his gaze.

—It will be quiet, Queen. It will be simple. When there is no discontent, your people will taste true peace for the first time. Afterward, they will desire nothing less.

On the heels of his translation, Third Father told her:

—There is sorcery here. It is not his, yet it increases.

The swelling of the candles and lamps had become unendurable. Estie ducked her head.

"You speak like a man who has experienced it, Tak Biondi. You have known the Great God's peace."

His voice gave her nothing but silence. She could not hear it. He hid behind his hair. But he shifted to stand upright. She saw his mouth tighten and stretch as Third Father repeated his response.

—What? Me? Nonsense. You asked for speculation. That is what I have given you. My discontent is as great as yours.

As the monk tapped, she felt a heavy thump. It was a sensation, not a sound: it came to her through the air or the walls as if the mute stone of the Repository had spoken.

It made her look at Magister Rummage again.

She turned in time to see him slam the back of his head against the wall: a second thump. Fury knotted the powerful muscles of his arms and shoulders, strained them to the tearing point. But he did not move, except to strike the uncaring stone with his head again.

Her father had beaten his head against a wall when he was rendered helpless.

She faced Tak Biondi again. Defying her weakness, she demanded, "Show me what you have under your shirt."

His hand at his chest knotted into a fist. It gripped tightly. The cloth of his shirt seemed to blaze. A gap in his hair let her see the flash of vehemence in his eyes.

—It is nothing, Queen. A trinket. It has no meaning.

Urgently, Third Father added:

—Beware!

Like a conjuror's trick, a knife appeared in Tak Biondi's free hand, a long dagger. All the light in the room seemed to concentrate on its edges. With absurd ease, as if he were floating, he came at Estie.

She tried to move. None of her limbs obeyed her. She had no defense against power like this. She braced herself to die.

At that instant, Third Father released her hand, left her side. Frail and weary, worn down by his years, he stumbled toward Tak Biondi. Almost falling, he grappled for the blade.

In surprise or self-defense, Tak Biondi let go of his shirt. He needed both hands to prevent the monk from taking his knife.

Their struggle took less time than Estie's heart needed to beat once, but it was enough to free Magister Rummage. Roaring in silence, the hunchback launched himself like a blacksmith's hammer at the anvil of Tak Biondi's head.

Estie did not understand how the servant could react so fast. She only knew that Magister Rummage jerked to a halt in an instant, a sliver of an instant, before he struck Magister Marrow's killer. Tak Biondi had already wrenched the monk aside. Now he stood behind Third Father with one arm wrapped across the monk's chest. The other held his knife at Third Father's throat.

Tak Biondi was shouting. Estie heard nothing.

Despite his rage, Magister Rummage did not attack. Instead, he turned his fury on himself. With both fists, he punched his own head. Then he whirled away.

Breathing hard, he came to the Queen's side. At once, he grasped her forearm and wrote fiercely:

—That whoreson says that your death would crown his service, but he will be content with a hostage. A revered monk is ideal. He will deliver a fatal blow before we kill him. If you wish to save the monk, you will surrender yourself.

Queen Estie found that her mind had cleared. The light no longer hurt her eyes. When he was not touching whatever was hidden under his shirt, Tak Biondi could not confuse her with borrowed sorcery.

To herself, she promised, I will not.

She did not waste time speaking aloud. Deliberately, she focused her mental voice on Tak Biondi. As if she had earned the right, she commanded, **Let him go.**

The man jerked as if he had received a blow. Wildness filled his eyes. He shouted again, spewing threats that did not reach Estie. His blade drew a line of blood across the monk's throat.

She was more than Amika's Queen. She was a sorceress. She summoned all of herself.

I said, Let him GO!

Tak Biondi's head seemed to explode. Blood burst from his eyes, his ears, his mouth. The skin of his brow split as the bones holding it twisted. His whole body spasmed, flinging the knife away, throwing him back against the table. While Third Father stumbled free, Tak Biondi flopped to the floor.

A moment of darkness came to the Queen. Tak Biondi was not the first man that she had killed. After her father had arranged an ambush for her—after she had slain one of her attackers and faced the outcome— her guts had rebelled. Fearing that she would vomit again, she retreated blindly to the wall, lowered herself down it, sat hugging her knees on the cold stone.

When the darkness passed, she saw Third Father on his hands and knees. His head hung down, almost touched the floor. Blood dripped from his cut, but he ignored it.

Behind the monk, Magister Rummage flipped Tak Biondi's corpse onto its back. Roughly, he reached into the man's shirt, found a chain around the neck, jerked it loose. Holding it in front of him, he showed it to Estie.

Lit brightly on all sides, a small golden cross hung from the chain. On each end of the crosspiece, a tiny ruby glittered.

She gave it a glance, nothing more. Third Father was crawling toward her. When he reached her feet, he pushed himself up onto his knees. His blood demanded her attention. When she forced herself to face him, he met her gaze as if he had never seen her before. He looked as plaintive as a child.

With his hands on her knees, he asked:

—Have I surpassed myself at last, Majesty?

To answer him, she wrapped her arms around him, hugged his head to her shoulder. Softly, she breathed, "Rest, Father. You have done enough."

She did not know how the Cult of the Many judged such things. She could not say whether he had gone beyond his own expectations. But for the first time, he had called her *Majesty*. That sufficed.

TWENTY-FOUR

ANOTHER SURPRISE

On a bed of dead, damp leaves, King Bifalt crouched at the crown of a hill, looking down at the beaten track that ran from the Bay of Lights to the smoking ruin of the Open Hand. He had brought only his officers to this place: Prince Jaspid and Elgart, Suti al-Suri and sub-Commander Hellick. He wanted them to understand his intentions.

After one short night sheltered by the forest, he had led his forces south. Along this edge of the forest, the trees and brush crowded close to the hill's rim. The drop below him was not sheer, but it was steep enough for his purposes, high enough. It would prevent Rile's infantry from striking at his position. Of the skirmishers that Hegels had described, Bifalt saw no sign. Their Great God must have taken them east.

Opposite the King, a lower range of treeless hills left more than enough space for Rile's army to march past, but the supply-train would not be able to escape on that side. The slopes were too rugged for wagons.

On the track, more wagons than Bifalt had ever seen lumbered along, drawn by oxen and dray-horses. To the west, it stretched out of sight in the early daylight, coming as if it had no end. To the east, the line wandered away among the hills.

Wherever they could find room, a host of men crowded the trail. Unarmed but warmly dressed, they had to be the army's servants or slaves, men who would do the hard work of caring for the army. If the First Captain's estimate was accurate—thirteen thousand soldiers—Rile would need a multitude of serving-men.

Among them, infantrymen guarded the wagons. According to Suti al-Suri's scouts, perhaps half of Rile's light infantry had dropped back to protect the supply-train while the cavalry raced ahead, presumably to secure Queen Estie's road. Those soldiers looked alert despite their long trek. But to protect a train of that length, they were spread thin. They did not pose a serious threat in any one place.

To Bifalt's way of thinking, Rile had made several mistakes. First, he had not sent his cavalry toward the Queen's road sooner. Instead, he had allowed his heavy infantry to waste time among the snares of the Open Hand. Then he had not prevented those soldiers from entering Belleger's Fist. By such misjudgments, he had lost hundreds of men. He had let the last Bellegerins escape the city. And he had given Queen Estie's Commanders their opportunity to destroy the bridges. Now he was trapped in Belleger.

He was probably furious. If he had learned the lesson of his mistakes, Rile would have provided better protection for his supply-train. His recklessness now showed that he did not count his losses. Instead, he had turned his rage elsewhere.

Toward General Klamath's army.

He either did not know or did not care that he would have to fight his war without the aid of the Cleckin.

As King Bifalt studied the train, however, he saw that his enemy was not as heedless as he had hoped. Among the servants and infantrymen were Rile's black priests, priests mounted on the tusked beasts of the cavalry and holding tall staffs that looked like iron. Beyond question, they wielded sorcery. Each staff was crowned by a shining globe of such brightness that it stung Bifalt's eyes.

The sight of their power filled his mind with curses.

Chewing the inside of his cheek, he said nothing until Elgart murmured, "Those priests will harm us. What do you think, Majesty? Our guns can reach them, but the range will hinder accuracy."

With a wrench, Bifalt put himself aside. To his brother, he said harshly, "Elgart is right. We must rely on gunfire. Arrange our men along these hillcrests"—he gestured eastward—"out of sight. When the signal comes, they must drop as many priests as they can."

Jaspid's nod promised that he understood. Every dead priest would be one less weapon in Rile's arsenal.

Grimly, King Bifalt turned to the chief warrior of the el-Algreb. "Can I trust you, Suti al-Suri?"

Bifalt often made the mistake of thinking that the chief warrior was a young man; but his impression was an effect of Suti al-Suri's manner and fragmented speech. He was probably older than the King. When he chose, he could restrain himself. Instead of reaching for his weapons, he demanded, "Why ask? I el-Algreb. I call you Brother. Why insult?"

King Bifalt held his gaze. "General Klamath asked for your help." Against Rile's cavalry, Klamath would need help desperately. "You turned your back."

"Ah." Suti al-Suri snorted his scorn. "*That.* Sister not ask. He *tell.* Make mistake. Give bad order. Help *you* help *him.* You will see."

The King needed a heartbeat or two to sort his way through the man's reply. Then he grasped Suti al-Suri's point. The chief warrior understood Klamath's circumstances. The General needed allies who could ride to his aid when he was desperate.

"Good," answered Bifalt. "Now I see what you see.

"But understand this. My men will come last. I need your warriors to break through that line"—he pointed toward the enemy's advance—"and hold it open so that we can follow.

"We may be some distance behind you."

The man's grin was like Jaspid's nod: a promise. "El-Algreb do."

"Good," said King Bifalt again.

At once, he turned to Elgart. He was in a hurry now. Every delay put him farther behind Klamath. "You have the Magisters," he told his old friend. "When the el-Algreb are ready, I want Astride and the others to use their Decimates. But remember the priests. They can sense sorcery. Whatever happens, keep the Magisters safe. Get the men you need from Jaspid."

Earlier, he had wondered how any of them would last without supplies. But Hellick had informed him that the el-Algreb had taken more than enough from the abandoned Cleckin camp. The horse-warriors were more than clever. They were capable of foresight as well.

Gathering himself, the King gave his last orders. His officers knew what he expected of them, but they would need time to reach their positions. Only Hellick saluted as they left.

Bifalt should have left as well. He still had to choose a hilltop for himself, a vantage that would give a view of the enemy's line in both directions. Nevertheless he lingered for a few moments, watching the priests while he ground down his emotions for the alchemy that transmuted pain and shame into cold, calculating fury.

An hour later, he waited with Jeck, Malder, and Boy in the shelter of the last trees near the crown of a lower hill. Behind them, Spliner held their horses.

Here the edge of the forest rose to a crest roughly midway between his former place in the west and the shallow vale to the east where the el-Algreb would gather. He was only four paces below the hilltop. He planned to stand there while his forces took the fight to the enemy.

He refused to think that his surprise might fail. Instead, he tried to count what it might cost. He did not know what those priests could do. If too many of his people died, success would be as ruinous as failure.

In full daylight, he watched a storm advancing from the east at its own slow pace. Its first wisps mingled with the smoke rising from his city's death. By the taste of the air, he knew that the coming clouds were thick with snow. Already, the twigs and branches around him clicked against each other like heralds as the breeze stiffened. Still, he judged that the storm would not reach him before midafternoon, perhaps not before evening. His attack would not be hampered by gloom and snow.

With him, Malder stood like a plinth, untouched by the cold or the prospect of battle. Jeck shifted his feet restlessly, flexed his arms again and again to keep himself limber. Only Boy was shivering, but not because he felt chilled. He had the task of riding away to set the el-Algreb in motion. It was essential that Suti al-Suri's warriors did not charge prematurely. They had to hold back until Boy reached them. Until the confusion on the trail had mounted into frenzy.

In his heart, the King trembled. He told himself that he was eager. That was true enough. But it masked a deeper truth. He feared for the people who would risk their lives at his command.

Sooner than he expected, a small movement ran like a gust through the dead leaves. It lifted them in a little swirl, then let them drop. He might not have noticed it, but it seemed to push against the flow of air carrying the storm.

Every muscle in his body pulled taut.

Another gust came, stronger than the first. Leaves drifted among the tree-trunks. A sensation like a distant rumble of thunder reached him through the soles of his moccasins.

Jeck snapped to attention. Malder shifted one foot to widen his stance. "Majesty?" whispered Boy tensely.

Another rumble, heavier, more distinct. It set the leaves dancing. The horses felt it. Snorting, they tugged against Spliner's grip.

"Wait, Boy." The King's command was a hoarse croak. "This is only the beginning. They may be testing themselves"—probing the rock for fault-lines, points of weakness.

The next tremor sounded like a groan in the earth.

With his bodyguards, King Bifalt moved to the crest of the hill and looked west.

With the force of a dozen hammers, a long *crack* like a string of granite bones breaking shook the trees, tossed the leaves upward. It made Bifalt stagger.

A moment later, the whole face of the bluff he had chosen leaned away from its moorings.

Trees toppled behind him. One fell so nearby that he felt its breath on his face.

For an impossible moment, four or five heartbeats, the wide stretch of stone simply stood there, motionless, as if it could not make up its mind. Then its weight overcame it.

Screaming rock against rock, the wall slid down toward the supply-train, the servants, the sparse infantrymen. The priests.

As it dropped, it broke apart, became boulders the size of houses, slabs broad enough to block the trail. The fragments hurtled downward. The hill under the King's feet lurched. Below the rock-fall, scores of servants and a few priests must have screamed while they could. He did not hear them. The guttural howl of shattered stone, smashed wagons, and crushed men covered every other sound.

To Boy, Bifalt shouted, "Go!"

Boy sprinted. Snatching the reins of his frantic horse from his father, he flung himself up and into the saddle as his mount ran like panic among the unsteady trees.

A moment later, Bifalt heard the insistent barking of rifles through the shrill wails of Rile's people. The Magisters were done. Now the attack depended on guns.

From the rims of the hills, bullets struck.

The King tried to watch. At first, he could not focus his eyes. There was too much to see. Furious at his weakness, he blinked and blinked until his sight cleared.

Aftershocks ran through the hills. Distance and turmoil hindered accuracy. Bifalt saw half a dozen priests knocked from their mounts; saw servants and infantrymen cut down. But other men in black leapt to the ground, crouched behind their beasts. They began to defend themselves. The shining of their globes intensified as they summoned their sorcery.

The fusillade stuttered. It did not falter. The riflemen had to recock their guns for every shot. They had to snatch out spent clips, slap loaded ones into place. But Prince Jaspid had fifty men, all that Elgart had not taken to guard the Magisters. Their bullets cut like scythes through clusters of panicking servants, running infantrymen. And Jaspid was a supreme marksman. Taking his time, he picked his targets. Every shot killed a priest.

The globes became blinding. It made the priests harder to hit. Most of them wheeled their staffs around their heads. Squinting, King Bifalt saw the effect.

No shot hit any of those men. Several of Jaspid's soldiers must have been concentrating their fire on each priest. The sorcerers should have died. Yet none of them fell. None of them tried to flee. The whirling of their staffs and the glare of their globes seemed to banish bullets.

Other priests hid behind boulders or thick slabs, behind piles of rock and crushed bodies. They did not spin their staffs. Instead, they swung the iron instruments in throwing motions.

Their globes were flung away. The bright balls arced higher and higher, impossibly high. Most of them sailed toward the riflemen. In the west, one threatened the position of Bifalt's Magisters. Plunging down, it fell short. Instead of striking its target, it hit the raw hillside below the crest. There it exploded like a keg of gunpowder.

The King had never seen sorcery like that. It surpassed his nightmares.

The blast ripped another wound in the bluff. Dirt and rocks rained down on the shattered wagons. Bifalt watched for shreds of grey cloth, limbs and broken bodies, splashes of blood.

There were none. Elgart had withdrawn the earthquake-wielders in time.

Other explosions followed. From both directions, more priests arrived, forcing their mounts through the turmoil of servants, the useless shouting of infantrymen. More globes scorched the air. Their detonations shredded the hilltops where Jaspid had placed his riflemen.

At once, the fusillade stopped. Only the repeated bark of a single gun still opposed the priests. As the bright assault arched higher, a rifle fired six shots in quick succession. One by one, six globes exploded, wasting their force.

"*That,*" muttered Jeck, "is Prince Jaspid."

If he said more, it was covered by the eruption and ravage of increased strikes.

Malder gripped Bifalt's arm. "Majesty! We must go!"

The King nodded. He wanted to shout at his brother, Run! But no cry of his would be heard through the shock of detonations, the down-pour of rubble. Run *now*!

Jaspid might keep fighting. This was his dream, to stand alone against impossible odds.

But his display of marksmanship had fixed his position for the priests. A dozen globes came for him.

His rifle did not speak again.

The blasts transformed that hillcrest into a crater. Rocks spouted from the concussions. Uprooted trees toppled downward.

The shocks knocked the air out of Bifalt's lungs. He did not try to shout or pray. Instead, he wheeled away, sprinting for Spliner and the horses. Jaspid dreamed a fool's dreams, but he was not fool enough to wait for death.

With Jeck, Malder, and then Spliner behind him, King Bifalt rode in a spray of leaves through the forest, heading for the vale where he had told the el-Algreb to gather. He had used the Decimate of earth-quake as a diversion, an attempt to draw the supply-train's defenders away: a tactic that Suti al-Suri knew well. By now, the chief warrior's army should be opening a way through the enemy's disrupted line.

If Prince Jaspid and any of his men still lived, they would reach the vale ahead of the King and his bodyguards. As would Elgart and the Magisters. King Bifalt goaded his mount at a madman's pace, rushing to count his losses.

Half a league south of the trail and the enemy, the King called a halt. They were sheltered behind a hill, hidden from Rile's priests and infantrymen, and well beyond the priests' sorcery. At last, he could afford the time to measure the cost of what he had done.

Thanks to Elgart, the Magisters were safe. For the el-Algreb, the diversion had been a success. It had drawn the attention of the priests and infantrymen, allowing the horse-warriors to break through the enemy's line and hold the gap open with few losses. But Prince Jaspid and the riflemen had not fared so well. They had been too close to the detonations.

Cursing, Jaspid covered the contusions that marred his face. He had always hated the burdens of command. There was a haunted look in his eyes as he confessed that exploding sorcery had taken ten of his men.

"The fault is mine, Majesty," he growled. "I did not expect"—his throat closed as if he were choking—"those globes. I left our retreat too late."

"Hells, Brother!" Bifalt matched his voice to Jaspid's. Ten men lost, when he could not afford to lose one. "None of us *expected* those globes. How could we?"

To ease his brother, the King promised, "The time will come when you must fight as you have always wished, blade to blade against un-countable numbers. On that day, you will get your chance to repay what this war has taken from you."

"Blood," declared Suti al-Suri unexpectedly. "We tend."

In the fluid tongue of his people, he called orders. At once, several of his warriors hurried toward the riflemen. Many of them had been hit by flung stone and broken branches.

Grimacing, the sub-Commander explained, "They are too proud of being warriors, Majesty." A cut on his cheek wept red. "If they could not treat wounds, none of them would survive."

King Bifalt studied his brother until he saw some of the tightness leave Jaspid's face. Then the brothers and Elgart went with Suti al-Suri and Hellick to watch how the el-Algreb cared for the cuts and bruises among the soldiers.

On the ride to the place where the el-Algreb had left their stolen supplies, King Bifalt chewed his cheek and raged to himself. He had entered Belleger's Fist with a hundred riflemen. Only fifty re-mained, Jaspid's surviving forty and the ten who had guarded the Magisters. He had hoped to escape with an effective fighting force. Even with the el-Algreb and the Magisters, fifty riflemen were too few.

Going slowly so that the wounded could rest, the King's diminished army did not reach their immediate destination until after midday.

There on a broad plain the el-Algreb had left their wagons of supplies. While the warriors and the men guarding the wagons greeted each other with eager shouts and good-natured taunts, King Bifalt took in the unexpected bounty.

The Cleckin had left a treasure-trove of stores. Suti al-Suri had brought four wagons loaded with fodder, grain, bedding, tents, food-stuffs, and barrels of water. Grinning, the chief warrior added that his people had also retrieved casks of fermented goat's milk. If any of the riflemen or Magisters needed relief, they could get drunk.

King Bifalt scowled at the suggestion. The storm front was coming closer. The first snows might begin to fall in an hour or two. General Klamath's army had left the Open Hand a full day ago, riding east. He was probably deep in the storm by now—and well ahead of both the King and Rile. That was good for the moment. Still, Bifalt was anxious to gain on Klamath: a difficult task in heavy snow. He could not afford the indulgence of strong drink.

"Do not unload the wagons," he told Suti al-Suri. "We will rest here until the men are fed. Then we must go."

The man raised his eyebrows. "For why, Brother?"

"You know why," answered the King drily. "It was your idea." Then he shrugged. "We will talk while we eat." Thinking, he added, "But we need scouts to watch the enemy. Hellick says that your warriors are good at that. Will you—?"

"Done," interrupted Suti al-Suri. His expression conveyed an ami-able disdain. "The el-Algreb wise. Fight many battles. Not need orders. Scouts there." He jerked his head in the direction of the Open Hand. "With"—the word he wanted eluded him for an instant—"relays. Send reports."

King Bifalt stared. He considered himself a war-like man. The el-Algreb had war in their bones.

He gave the chief warrior an honest bow. "Accept my thanks, Suti al-Suri. You knew it when General Klamath made a mistake. *Tell* me when I make one."

The man's answering bow mocked Bifalt's, but his laughter was genuine. "You wise also, Brother. Wise different. We"—he touched his chest, then tapped the King's breastplate—"beat any foe."

Still chuckling, Suti al-Suri walked away.

Apparently, King Bifalt had more to learn about being humbled.

Before he ate, Bifalt called Elgart and Prince Jaspid to join him. Together, they walked a short distance away. There they honored the men they had lost.

Gruff with loss, Jaspid named all of the fallen one by one, the soldiers who had died in Belleger's Fist as well as those slain by thrown sorcery. Elgart expressed gratitude and sorrow in his own way. Last, King Bifalt recited the old Bellegerin salute for the dead. Some of the fallen had been Amikan, but Bifalt did not think that they would refuse Belleger's respect.

"Your blood for your people. Your blood for your comrades. Your blood for your King. No man can be asked to give more."

Jaspid added, "When we have won this war, we will acknowledge you better."

Bifalt hugged his brother and his old friend. That was unlike him; but he did not expect to get another chance. He gave them a moment to recover from their surprise. Then he sent them back to the others.

King Bifalt took a moment to clear his mind. When he felt ready, he went to share a meal with the people he relied on most: his bodyguards, the Prince and Elgart, Hellick, Suti al-Suri, and Magister Astride.

While they ate sitting on the hard ground, the first relay of el-Algreb scouts returned. They spoke to the chief warrior at length. With Elgart's help, and Hellick's, King Bifalt understood Suti al-Suri's version of their news.

No doubt in response to what the King's Magisters and riflemen had done, Rile had dispatched some of his cavalrymen west to defend the damaged supply-train. Others were returning toward the Open Hand, turned away by their failure to enter Amika. The rest were in pursuit of General Klamath's forces: more than a thousand men mounted on their fearsome beasts. That was bad enough. The tusked creatures were faster than horses, stronger. Even in heavy snow, they would chase down Klamath in a matter of hours. Worse was the horde of skirmishers keeping pace with the cavalry. And worse still were the priests mounted on their own heavy beasts, carrying their bright globes.

With Rile himself, the foot soldiers followed the trail of the cavalry at their own iron pace.

Hells, thought Bifalt. Hells. Klamath was in trouble. He could not hope to survive without help.

The King had no more time for doubts—or for lessons in humility. Briskly, he gave his orders. His small army would head east as fast as possible on a line that paralleled Klamath's retreat. Bifalt aimed to gain ground until he could strike at the enemy's rearguard. To accomplish that, he would have to drive his forces into the heart of the coming storm.

When he had explained his intentions, he faced the chief warrior. "But understand this, Suti al-Suri," he said roughly. "Your scouts must not expose themselves. No doubt, they will be tempted to shoot a few soldiers or skirmishers, or even priests." Against overwhelming numbers, the el-Algreb preferred to strike and run, strike and run. They relished that form of war. "They *must not*. If they do, they will expose themselves. The enemy will know that we have left the west. He will be ready for us. We cannot help General Klamath if the enemy expects us."

Suti al-Suri listened with an angry scowl. "I—" he began, wrestling with his instincts. But then he mastered himself. "Tell scouts," he snarled. "Give order." The way he said the word betrayed his disgust. "Brother wise. El-Algreb do."

At once, he surged to his feet and hurried away, shouting as he went.

Sighing, King Bifalt gave one more order. In a tone that did not encourage debate, he put Spliner and Boy in command of the wagons. They were experienced teamsters: the el-Algreb were not.

Boy objected. He seemed to feel that he was being demoted. But his father accepted the task with a curt nod. Long ago, Spliner had killed to save Prince Bifalt's search for the library. He did not need to prove himself again. Ignoring his son's arguments, he took Boy to the wagons.

Satisfied, the King rose. Without a word, Prince Jaspid and then Elgart stood as well. Around them, the el-Algreb had finished tending the horses. Grimacing, Bifalt gave in to his impatience.

"That storm will be on us soon!" he called. "We must go!"

When his people were ready, he turned his face to the east. At a hard canter, he led them into the heart of the storm.

PART FOUR

TWENTY-FIVE

ALTERED NEEDS

Shaken by violence, Queen Estie sat with her back against the wall in Tak Biondi's chamber. Blood still pulsed from the traitor's eyes and ears, his split forehead, but it was dwindling. The many lights made the pool around his head look black. It stained the stone floor like an accusation.

Third Father remained kneeling in front of Estie with his hands braced on her knees. His arms were all that supported him. Without them, he might have fallen on his side. The cut along his neck was a thin line like the stroke of a quill. It looked shallow. Nevertheless it dripped blood as if it would never stop.

Crouching over Estie, Magister Rummage gripped her shoulder. His fingers dug in as he commanded:

—Rouse yourself, Queen. The blade may have been poisoned.

Poisoned? The thought shook her. Her whole body flinched. The monk had saved her life. She could not bear to lose him.

The hunchback's grasp was a demand.

—Use your voice!

For a heartbeat or two, she stared at Third Father's wound. She could not look away. Then her head jerked back, smacked the wall. Her *voice*.

Still, she needed a moment to compose herself. Magister Avail had warned her against shouting. She had just seen what the full force of her power could do. She had to be sure of her control before she spoke.

Spreading her sorcery as widely as she could, she said, **Third Father is hurt. The blade may be poisoned. Send help.** Was that enough? No. Unsteadily, she added, **We are in Tak Biondi's quarters.**

Glowering, Magister Rummage told her:

—Good. Shamans will come at once. And physicians.

She started to say, We have to stop the bleeding. But then she realized that his blood might carry some of the poison away. He was in no immediate danger from the cut itself. It was not deep. It would have been trivial if clotting had sealed the wound.

Softly, she pleaded, "Third Father? Can you hear me?"

With an effort, the monk nodded.

His face was growing pale. So that he would not fall, Queen Estie put her arms around him again; hugged him as if her embrace might keep him alive.

Soon she would have to think about what she had done to Tak Biondi.

She feared that her strength would fail, that she would lose Third Father before the Repository responded. Within moments, however, two shamans burst into the chamber. She hardly noticed the grime of their bare skins and loincloths, the beads and feathers woven into their hair and beards, the rattles and pouches in their hands. Instead, she watched their gruff care as they took Third Father from her and stretched him out on the floor.

One shaman squatted beside the monk, lifted one of his arms and let it fall, pulled up an eyelid, prodded his abdomen. The other retrieved Tak Biondi's dagger. Cautiously, the shaman sniffed the blade, then touched it with the tip of his tongue and spat.

The two men appeared to growl a few words at Magister Rummage. He must have understood them. As soon as he nodded, they went to work. One of them stamped a foot on the floor and shook his rattles while the other opened three pouches.

From one, he dusted Third Father's wound with a yellow powder that smelled like a latrine. Using a dirty cloth, he covered the cut. Prying open the monk's mouth, he scattered colorless granules from a second pouch onto Third Father's tongue. The third pouch held a thick liquid which he poured onto the granules. At once, he pushed the monk's mouth shut and began stroking his throat to encourage swallowing.

Estie's guts squirmed at the sight. The actions of the shamans looked like mummery, a performance designed to mystify the credulous. But she sensed their theurgy, a subtle tang that felt benign.

Abruptly, Magister Rummage pulled her to her feet. As if he were taking pity on her, he clasped her hand and tapped:

—He has been poisoned, but he will not die. It is the same poison that whoreson gave Travail. They know how to treat it now.

Estie said nothing. She could not look away from the shamans and Third Father. She felt hollowed out, as if something essential had been taken from her.

For a moment, the hunchback hesitated. Then he made a decision. Glaring, he thrust her out of the room. When he had shut the door, he forced her back the way they had come. Despite his air of suppressed fury, he did not handle her roughly.

Empty of something that mattered to her, something vital, Estie let the Magister take her wherever he wished.

Gradually, however, the effort of moving her feet brought back a shock that she did not want to feel. She began to tremble. Without the hunchback's grip on her arm, she might have stopped. She wanted to cover her face.

She had killed a man. And not with a blade. With her mind.

With sorcery.

She stumbled as if she had been shoved.

Tak Biondi was not the first man she had killed. Once, she had punched a blade into an attacker's throat. Surely that was the same thing? Twice, men had tried to end her life. Twice, she had killed them defending herself.

But it was not the same thing at all.

The first man had intended simple murder. Tak Biondi had done far more harm. He had probably revealed the Repository's location to his Great God. He had certainly tried to kill Apprentice Travail. With Magister Marrow, he had succeeded. Given the chance, he would have committed more crimes.

He had to die.

And yet—

She realized now that she had been in no real danger. Or rather: she would not have been in danger if she had known what she could do. She had not killed Tak Biondi blade to blade. *That* her husband would have called honorable. She had slain him with her mental voice.

The truth seemed to shake her bones. Her power resembled a Decimate. Like drought, fire, and the others, it could be used to do good and cause harm. Why had Bifalt always loathed theurgy? Why had he been so quick to dismiss its benefits? Now she understood him. Any Decimate could do what she had done. It could kill men and women who were helpless to defend themselves.

If she had known enough about her power—if she had let Magister Avail teach her—she could have ended Tak Biondi as soon as he produced his dagger. She might have been able to stop him without killing him.

Had she learned *nothing* from her husband?

This was the result, this shame. If Magister Rummage had not kept her on her feet, she might have dropped to her knees. Killing Tak Biondi, she had lost something essential. But it had not been taken from her: she had given it away. She did not know what to call it. It felt like a kind of purity.

Somehow, she had to make amends. For her own sake. And perhaps to vindicate the years of trust that Bifalt had given her.

It was fortunate that Rummage remained hidden behind his black scowl. She had no idea what was in his mind. She only knew that he was in a hurry because he refused to let her lag. She ignored the stairs they climbed, the passages they followed, the people they passed. Her need to confront herself required too much strength.

She was still trembling as the hunchback compelled her down the corridor that led into Magister Threnody's workroom.

Through the doorless entryway, she saw sunlight. It shone on the pure white drifts that covered the balcony beyond the librarian's windows. Reflected light cast dazzles like instances of lightning into her eyes. They seemed to promise that she was already lost. That she would not be able to answer her shame.

As she entered the chamber, everyone there turned to stare at her: Beatrix Threnody, Oblique, Avail, other Magisters, Fifth Daughter in one corner. Even Magister Bleak looked away from his private visions. Sword Eradimnie's armor caught a quick flash of sunlight as she faced the Queen.

They must all have heard Estie's call for help.

Several of them began talking at once, asking questions Estie could not hear. She ignored them to concentrate on the librarian. Magister Threnody had dismay written all over her face. Her mouth made shapes like cries.

Magister Rummage translated the librarian's plea:

—Is it him? Tak Biondi? A man I trusted?

Queen Estie replied so that everyone would hear. **It is.** She did not want to say the words aloud. **He held a poisoned blade to Third Father's neck. He would have killed me. He carried a small talisman.**

The hunchback held up the cross, golden and gemmed.

It is like the one that Magister Facile's killer wore.

She shocked the room. Beatrix Threnody shrank into herself. At once, Oblique hurried to her side. From her place against the wall, Fifth Daughter clamped a hand over her mouth and ran out. Magister Bleak flinched. The Knight of Ardor thumped her chest, a soundless clash of iron on iron.

Then Magister Avail asked, **Is he dead, Queen?**

Estie did not want to answer. The truth shamed her. It infuriated her. But the deaf man's naked chagrin compelled her.

He is. I burst his brain with a shout. Hoping to excuse herself, she added, **He had already cut Third Father.**

But there was no excuse. She had refused to let Avail teach her. Without knowing it, she had chosen to be a woman who killed.

Uselessly, Avail said something aloud. At Estie's side, Magister

Rummage was breathing hard. A fury of his own bared his teeth. If he had possessed any voice, he would have snarled. His fingers told her:

—Magister Avail is my only friend. He says the fault is his.

As if she had been accused, Queen Estie jerked up her head. Now she focused her voice exclusively on the deaf sorcerer.

I killed him. *You* did not. The fault is mine.

The deaf man spread his hands. **I should have insisted. I could have warned you. You do not know your own power.**

There was too much in the room, too many people, too many needs. The librarian's whole body seemed to plead for something that Magister Oblique could not give, some form of reassurance or comfort only Amika's Queen possessed.

But Magister Rummage reacted with fury. He could not have heard her. He may have heard his friend. His fingers jabbed her forearm hard enough to raise bruises.

—Ask her!

Astonished out of herself, Estie turned to the hunchback.

"Ask who? Ask what?"

His teeth bit chunks out of the air.

—The *librarian*! Ask her about the *book*!

Magister Oblique shouted at Rummage. She could not have seen what he wrote, but his ferocity must have been obvious.

Estie understood him too well. Nevertheless she was out of her depth. His vehemence implied questions that she did not know how to answer. Lives seemed to be at stake. When Tak Biondi had described Lamit Karsolsky's book, she had recognized its value at once. But she had also assumed that he was simply trying to distract her. Until this moment, this instant, she had not realized that he had spoken to do the Repository more harm.

What he had told her might be as explosive as gunpowder.

She did not want to aggravate Beatrix Threnody's distress. Yet she could not refuse Magister Rummage. She was full of stresses like lightning, and the hunchback had tried with all his strength to protect her. It was not weakness that had kept him from Tak Biondi: it was the sorcery of coercion.

Bracing herself on his shoulder, she faced Magister Oblique and the librarian.

"Magister Threnody." Her voice shivered. "I have a question."

Everyone except Magister Avail could hear her. Perhaps she should have asked for a private audience. But she was too overwrought to pause. The throbbing of her forearm demanded an outlet. She had to speak *now*. If this was atonement, it was necessary.

At once, Rummage left her. In a rush, he went to Avail and assumed his familiar position holding his friend's hand.

Without his support, Queen Estie tottered. But she did not fall.

Magister Threnody shifted away from Oblique. Her fragile sense of herself had taken a blow. She avoided Estie's gaze. Under other circumstances, she might have fled. Her mouth made a shape that may have been, Yes?

Estie's power was too close to the surface. She did not trust herself to use it. Instead, she replied aloud.

"While I questioned him, Tak Biondi tried to distract me." She could not pretend to speak calmly. "He spoke of a book. The author's name was Lamit Karsolsky. The book is called *A Complete System of Gestures for Speech with the Deaf and Dumb*.

"Do you know it?"

Grinding his teeth, Magister Rummage translated. His tapping turned the deaf man's rumpled face pale.

In contrast, the librarian's first reaction was relief. She had been asked a question that she understood. Without hesitation, she turned in the direction of the library proper. Her eyes shifted from place to place, scanning the shelves in Magister Marrow's memories.

Estie wanted Crayn. Leaving him behind had been a mistake.

Sensitive to the Queen's dilemma, Magister Oblique came to her side. With her fingers, she gave Estie's bruises a light caress. But she wrote nothing while the librarian searched.

Soon, Magister Threnody nodded. At least for a moment, she was sure of herself. Lowering her gaze, she faced Estie. As she spoke, Oblique tapped:

—Yes, Queen. The book is there. It is very old. Why do you ask?

Magister Avail's chest heaved, panting heavily. The blood was gone from his face. He looked like his heart might fail.

"Then tell me," demanded Amika's Queen. "Why has this book been kept from Magister Avail? From Magister Rummage? From the whole Repository?" She felt like shouting. "Why have those poor men been condemned to silence?"

Comprehension struck Beatrix Threnody in an instant. Like Magister Avail, she blanched. Like him, she gasped for air. Her response was a cry.

—I do not know! I did not know the book *existed*! My memories are too recent! I have spent my efforts on poisons and gunpowder!

—That decision must have been Magister Marrow's!

Avail's power rose to a strangled howl.

AH!

It drew Estie away from the librarian. Stricken, she watched an overweight, unkempt, and lonely man break. He crumpled to his knees as if every bone that held him upright had snapped.

Magister Rummage dropped with him, holding his only friend in a fierce hug. Tears streamed down Avail's face. Silent sobs wrenched the hunchback's chest.

Rummage was stronger. He had been mute from birth. He had not been made deaf by sorcery.

But both of them had trusted Sirjane Marrow.

Suddenly, Queen Estie's needs seemed unimportant. They were nothing compared to what those two men had suffered.

Shouts and confusion filled the workroom. Magister Oblique repeated them as well as she could.

—What? How? What is happening? How are they hurt?

And over and over again:

—Why would Magister Marrow *do* such a thing?

Estie ignored everything else. Controlling herself, she faced the librarian. Pitching her voice to carry over the tumult, she said, "I did not know Magister Marrow. I cannot know his mind. But I know that he *needed* these two men"—the sorcerer of communication and the man of violence. "Perhaps he believed that they needed each other.

Perhaps he believed that their isolation would bond them. He was arrogant enough to make his decisions without consulting the people they affected.

"You see the outcome."

Intentional or not, that bond was obvious now.

Beatrix Threnody's distress was obvious as well. For her doubts, Estie had no answer. But Threnody's pleading took a different form. Oblique translated it.

—What can I do, Queen? I am not Magister Marrow. Tell me what to do.

Estie did not hesitate. "Make copies of Karsolsky's book. *Many* copies. Share them everywhere."

If enough people learned Karsolsky's *System*, it might ease the deaf man's isolation, and the mute's.

It might make hers easier to bear. It might count as amends.

The librarian promised:

—We will. We will begin at once.

Their exchange silenced the workroom. Estie saw the change. Magister Bleak seemed to hold his breath. Sword Eradimnie stood motionless. The Queen was able to continue more quietly.

"Where Tak Biondi is concerned, librarian, no one is at fault." She meant, You are not. "His sorcery concealed his lies. There is nothing that anyone could have done to expose him. He revealed himself to me only because I distracted him.

"*Now*," she concluded before anyone could interrupt her, "summon a healer." She gave orders as if she had the right. "If there is nothing else we can do for them today, a healer will help them sleep."

Even an ungifted Amikan physician could provide herbs that imposed slumber.

With a gesture, Magister Threnody sent a Magister to obey. She tried to summon a smile for Estie, but it was a twisted thing, distorted by remorse and uncertainty.

The Queen might have felt sorry for her; but her heart was elsewhere. With as much care as she could muster, she focused her voice on Rummage and Avail.

You are not alone. I did not understand before. Now I do. I will do whatever I can.

Then she sagged against Oblique. Drained by shock and turmoil, she was suddenly tired. If Crayn had been with her, she would have asked him to take her to her quarters. Instead, she allowed herself to rely on Magister Oblique's support.

Eventually, she would have to come to terms with Tak Biondi's death. She would have to face the dread that had caused her to reject Magister Avail's help. If she could, she would do something to relieve him and Magister Rummage.

But not now. She had reached the limit of what she could endure.

Magister Bleak was the only Farsighted in the workroom. Humming to himself, he ignored most of what he heard after Queen Estie's arrival. He knew that he was surrounded by pain. Perhaps he should have attended to it. But as the days passed and the Last Repository's doom came closer, he found it harder and harder to refuse the call of distances. That was his gift, the gift of the Farsighted, that intimate lure. Whenever the sun shone, the vividness of places and people far away made those nearby seem as vague as shadows.

Now, for the first time in days, the skies were clearing. Sunshine already covered the foothills and the desert and a portion of Belleger. Reluctant to do anything else, Magister Bleak watched. Old habits that passed for consideration kept him from speaking until men had come with stretchers, and Avail and Rummage had been induced to drink healing potions. He held his tongue while the heart-sore men were borne away to their chambers. Musing over his personal music, he kept silent until even the shaken librarian and the overwrought Queen were looking at him. Then he told them what he saw.

Etched by sunlight against a background of deep snow, General Klamath's whole army lay like scattered corpses.

Of course, the people around Bleak reacted. They had questions. They wanted explanations or reassurance. But he had none to give. Instead, he described the scene in his mind.

After a few moments, he spotted signs that at least some of the General's men were not dead. While he watched, a few soldiers struggled like cripples to their feet. One of them may have been Klamath.

To see without hearing was cruel. Magister Bleak did not know whether the General had stood to rouse his men, or to regard what he had lost before he died himself.

But then another man climbed out of a snowdrift. Under his white, wet burden, he wore a heavy cloak. Nothing marked him as a sorcerer except the flames in his hands, the Decimate of fire. Unsteadily, he warmed himself. When he could walk, he went among the litter of bodies, heating other men until they could stand.

Magister Bleak spoke in a voice congested with melodies like laments. Uncharacteristically, he felt like weeping.

The distant figure who might be Klamath dragged men to their feet. When he had enough soldiers on their feet, he sent them to tend the surviving horses. He may have been shouting. He looked too weak to raise his voice.

Then other Magisters of fire showed themselves. They started foraging for something to burn, anything that they could use to make fires. They had no wood. They were on an open plain, wide and treeless. Snow covered everything. But the sorcerers scavenged unused rain-capes, loose sheets of oilcloth, wasted tents, coils of rope, even scraps of worn leather. They started fires that needed constant attention to stay alight.

Apparently, those fires cast good heat. Shedding clumps of ice and snow, riflemen crowded close to them. Moments later, looking stronger, they left to make room for other men.

With the help of the fires and two men the Farsighted did not recognize, the man who was surely the General seemed to haul his army out of its collapse by sheer force of will.

As the end of the storm drifted westward, Bleak saw farther. The trampled length of the army's back trail shocked him. It stretched to the edge of the sun's light and beyond.

Hoarsely, he declared, "They have come an astonishing distance. They must have been hotly pursued by some force. Whatever it was, it is gone now.

"They will not move again."

There were tears in the librarian's eyes. Queen Estie listened like a woman whose heart threatened to burst.

Magister Bleak clung to the music of his gift.

He could not imagine how the General's men would survive without better fires—and without food. From their packs, some of the riflemen and Magisters unloaded a bit of grain for the mounts, perhaps something for the men. It would not be enough. The Open Hand had sent heavy wagons east ahead of the General, but a fleeing army could not stop for resupply.

Bleak felt a hand on his arm. His vision swam out of the distance to focus on Queen Estie.

"Thank you, Magister." Aftereffects darkened her gaze. "I have heard enough." She swallowed an obstruction in her throat. "Please send word if you see any sign of King Bifalt."

Moving carefully, she turned away, hiding her face from the sunlit windows.

An unfamiliar emotion tightened Magister Bleak's chest as the librarian sent Magister Oblique to accompany the Queen. Estie of Amika tugged at him strangely. In his own way, he understood her straits. But he had no attention to spare for her. The music of his gift drew him back to General Klamath's army.

K lamath son of Klimith remembered his father.

As a younger man, Klimith had been strong and hardy, capable of seemingly unlimited exertions. During those years, Klamath had dreamed of becoming a man like his father. But time had not been kind to Klimith. As he aged, he became increasingly feeble. Too soon, he lost his strength, and then his balance, and then his continence. Toward the end, he was helpless to care for himself. At the same time, he could not forget what the years had taken from him. Nothing remained for him except to clench his teeth so that he would not inflict his bitterness on his family.

Now Klamath knew how his father had felt. The ice in his garments cracked at every movement. His moccasins were frozen to his feet. He stood with his legs spread because he expected to fall on his face at any moment.

King Bifalt had done well in many things, but he had made a mistake when he had made Klamath his General. Klimith's son would have served his King better as an ordinary rifleman, a man who could do what he was told because he was not expected to give those commands himself.

Fortunately, First Captain Hegels was younger. He had a lean man's resilient toughness and the severity to demand obedience. And Captain Rowt was younger still. His endurance reminded Klamath of the man Klimith had once been.

"This is bad enough." Klamath wanted to sound like a General. Instead, he spoke in an unsteady whisper. "It will get worse."

Hegels and Rowt said nothing. Decisions were the General's burden, not theirs.

"Tell the men," croaked Klamath. "And the Magisters. Eat everything they have. Get warm." He could smell the stench of burning oilcloth and leather. "Then put them to work."

The First Captain chewed his silence. After a moment, Captain Rowt asked hesitantly, "Work, sir? What can they do?"

A few soldiers had already given the army's remaining grain and fodder to the horses. Hegels had seen to that.

Klamath wavered on his feet. He needed time to find a thought in his head. He had to remember that all of these people were in his care.

Finally, he managed to say, "Horses. The dead ones." He had no idea how many mounts he had lost. Or how many men. "And the ones that need to be put down. Drag them closer." He gestured vaguely around him. "They will burn." If the Decimate of fire could not set them alight, the Decimate of lightning might succeed. "For heat. And meat."

If dead horses could be made to burn, muscle, bone, and organs, the flames would be visible for leagues. When the sun set, Klamath would have to send out sentries. But not now. Caution could wait a while.

"Then ask Solace." For a while, Klamath's mind wandered among his memories of his father. Of visiting Matt and Matta on their sheep farm in the south of Belleger. Of the Bay of Lights. Then he remembered watching the Open Hand die and came back to himself. "Can pestilence treat frostbite?"

Frostbite was not an illness. But it killed healthy flesh. Dead flesh leaked poisons. *That* was an illness. Perhaps pestilence would save a few lives.

Perhaps the Decimates would be enough.

Trembling in every muscle, Klamath shambled to the nearest fire. When he had absorbed enough heat to warm his breastplate and restore a little sensation to his hands and face, he ate snow to ease his thirst. Then he joined the men who had started trying to drag frozen horses closer.

Together, Magisters of fire and lightning made dead mounts into fires that burned hot and long. Among his people, General Klamath ate charred horseflesh and tried to suck heat in through every patch of skin. When he could feel his fingertips and began to think that he might not lose his toes, he stood to address his army.

As if there could be no doubt, he said, "That hells-cursed cavalry has been recalled. The enemy needs it elsewhere. From now on, his forces will come on foot.

"I do not fear them. We are days ahead. Because we must, we will keep watch in short shifts tonight. But our real foe is the cold. These fires will burn down. They may not save you.

"Do what you must to stay alive. This is not a time to prove your strength. If you cannot stop shivering, approach Magister Crawl or another Magister of fire. If you fear for your fingers and toes"—your noses, your cheeks—"consult the Magisters of pestilence. The enemy will come. I need you alive."

Hegels gave stricter orders, but Klamath did not listen to them. Setting an example, he retrieved his miserable mount, brought it to the nearest fire's heat, and rubbed it down with part of his cloak. Then he urged it to the ground. When it had settled itself, he stretched out against it. Sharing his cloak and its body heat, he prayed that there would be no wind. The cold was enough.

That night was as bad as Klamath expected. It was not worse. His cloak and his horse kept him from freezing. He managed a little sleep.

A shout from one of the sentries woke him. Jerking up his head, he scanned his people with cold-blurred eyes. A few of the riflemen were already up, stumbling around to check on their comrades. Most of the soldiers still lay with their horses, sleeping or dead. Enough oilcloth had been set aside to make crude coverings for the Magisters. None of them had emerged yet.

General Klamath took his time. In the fading grey of dawn, he struggled to his feet. When he had broken enough of the ice in his clothing to stand, he urged his poor horse to rise. It lurched drunkenly up onto its legs, shivering and dull-eyed in the cutting air. But it would live, if he could feed it.

Rubbing the crust from his face left his skin raw. Blinking his eyes to clear them made them sting. Nevertheless he looked around for the man who had shouted.

The sentry stood a hundred paces away to the east, but he was pointing south. "General!" he called again, a cry that scraped his throat. "There!"

Shifting his feet like a crippled man, Klamath turned.

There was a rise on that side of the plain. He had not noticed it the previous day. It sat alone on the horizon, more like a tor than a hill, the ancient remains of a volcano. Boulders knuckled its sides. Its crown stood high above the plain. The sun had already touched there, lifting the crest out of the surrounding gloom.

As solitary as the tor, a man stood there. Instead of looking down at the wreckage of Klamath's army, he faced the east. Sunlight shone on his bronze breastplate.

A rifleman, then. Alone? And unaware of the General's people?

No. After a moment, the man turned. With one arm, he waved a greeting. Then he disappeared down the far side of the tor.

Beckoning to the First Captain, Klamath asked, "Did you see that man? Did you recognize him?"

"The distance, sir." The Amikan was reluctant to commit himself. He took a breath. "He looked like King Bifalt."

To his surprise, Klamath found himself sitting in the snow. The King? Tears made ice on his sore cheeks. He felt unable to hold up his head. The King?

He hardly heard himself ask, "Can any of the men ride, Hegels?" Were any of the horses strong enough? "I want to be sure. There must be men behind that rise."

King Bifalt had not come alone. That was impossible.

Gruffly, Hegels answered, "There is no need. Look."

Klamath braced his hands in the snow to straighten his back. With an effort, he forced up his head.

Through the sting in his eyes, he saw riders canter past the slope of the tor. Soon, they were touched by the sun, and he could count them. The light defined them against the white background. The legs of their mounts kicked up plumes of snow. They were seven.

One was King Bifalt. He had Prince Jaspid with him. Elgart. Jeck and Malder. Sub-Commander Hellick.

And Suti al-Suri.

Waving, the chief warrior shouted proudly, "Sister! El-Algreb bring bounty!"

Moments later, the King and his companions slowed their mounts. In a rush, Bifalt vaulted out of his saddle, hurried toward his old friend. Then he stopped, waiting for the General to rise. The other men waited on their horses.

Klamath did not feel able to climb as far as his feet. He could not prevent his eyes from bleeding tears.

Peering up at his King, he asked, as petulant as a child, "What took you so long?" Then he was ashamed of himself. Groaning, "Majesty," he held out his hand, mutely asking for the First Captain's help.

As if the General weighed nothing, Hegels lifted him. At once, Klamath staggered toward King Bifalt and hugged him.

Bifalt had become a different man. Instead of refusing Klamath's embrace, or tolerating it, he flung his arms around Klamath and held him fiercely.

Klamath clung, trying to make the moment last.

It did not last long. Too soon, the King stepped back. His eyes were full of pain as he studied his friend's face, his friend's condition.

Without looking away, King Bifalt addressed Hegels.

"First Captain. Tell the men that help is coming. We have supplies, more than enough. Suti al-Suri's doing, not mine. They are half a day behind us, but Spliner and Boy will bring them."

Hegels bowed. "As you say, Majesty." Like a man who did not feel the cold, he strode away.

With a gesture, the King summoned his companions to dismount. He gave Klamath time to hug first Elgart, then Jaspid. He did not begin to issue orders until they were satisfied.

"Jaspid." Now he sounded more like himself. "Sub-Commander. Go among the men. Help them if they cannot stand. Urge them to move. Tend their horses. Reassure them.

"Check on the Magisters, Elgart. I want to know their state. Their losses. I will hear whatever they wish to say.

"Jeck. Malder. Forgive an unpleasant task. The General and I need a count of the dead. He suffered losses while he fled, and the night was cruel. I need to know our numbers."

Nodding, the Prince, Elgart, and Hellick left. When Jeck and Malder started to obey, however, Klamath stopped them.

"That duty is mine, Majesty. I will do it. The First Captain will help me." He glanced around. "And Captain Rowt. You entrusted your men to me. I will bear the burden."

He meant, Do you see now? You should not have made me your General.

Bifalt grimaced. "Nonsense, Klamath. Count the dead? I doubt that you can count your own fingers." More gently, he said, "I know what you have done. It is more than any King could have asked. Your losses are Rile's doing, not yours.

"By your standard, we have had an easy ride. Jeck and Malder are not worn out, frozen, or heart-sick. Let them bear this one burden for you."

Klamath could not stop his tears. If he had not been so weak, he might have embarrassed himself by sobbing.

With a flick of his hand, King Bifalt sent his bodyguards away. Then he took Klamath's arm. "Walk with me, General," he commanded. "You are frozen. A little exertion will warm you. We can talk when you stop shivering."

Aside to Suti al-Suri, he suggested, "Perhaps you will join the Prince and sub-Commander Hellick. Describe your exploits to the men. You may lift their spirits."

Unable to protest, Klamath let the King's firm grip draw him away.

Their breathing came in gusts of vapor. The cold rasped at their lungs. Deep snow dragged their steps. But they were in sunlight now. Even this early, the sun's touch felt like kindness.

Trying to do his duty, the General began, "My report, Majesty—"

In a comradely way unlike his usual demeanor, King Bifalt bumped Klamath's shoulder. "I do not need your report. The el-Algreb are remarkable scouts. They watched you. They admired your efforts in Long Slough. Afterward, they followed your flight. The forest you burned shook even their bravado. You will not believe it, Klamath, but Suti al-Suri speaks of your tactics with reverence."

Klamath scrubbed at his face until his skin seemed to bleed. He could hardly see where he put his feet. "We were done, Majesty," he said. "Worse than done. If Rile's cavalry had not turned back, we would have been slaughtered."

"Then," declared the King, "it appears that we aided you, although I did not know it. From the woods behind the Open Hand, we contrived an attack on Rile's supply-train. The Magisters did considerable damage. The riflemen and the horse-warriors fought well. If there had been fewer priests, we would have done more. That fool of a god had sent too much of his cavalry to the Queen's road. His train had no defense except sorcery.

"Now I believe that our assault caused him to recall his cavalry. And I believe—" King Bifalt caught himself. "No, I *hope* that he thinks we are still in the west, threatening his supplies. If so, he needs his cavalry there."

"And we killed many," said General Klamath. "Many."

"Yes, you did." King Bifalt sounded almost gentle. He was not the man Klamath remembered.

A moment later, the King stopped to face his General. The sun was in Bifalt's eyes, but he did not shade them. Instead, he let his old friend consider the wounds that loss and anger and restraint had cut in his features.

"There is something that I must tell you, Klamath," he said carefully. "It is hard for me to say, but you will understand."

Forcing himself, he explained, "Queen Estie has a gift for sorcery. She went to the Repository to discover her talent. Now she has claimed it. She is lost to us."

His tone said plainly, She is lost to me.

"She can speak in our minds. She cannot hear us. Her gift has made her deaf."

Klamath stared. He wanted to ask, Are you sure? But he could see the answer in Bifalt's expression. The King had always loathed sorcery and sorcerers. He would not have looked so bereft if she had refused her power.

Under better circumstances, the son of Klimith might have wept for Amika's Queen. He did not care that she could speak. That she could no longer hear was inexpressibly cruel.

Perhaps later, he would ask how Bifalt knew what Queen Estie had done. For the present, he had no idea what to say. Elgart might have found something to offer the King. Klamath had nothing. Bifalt had shared his deepest pain. It had changed him. But where Estie was concerned, he was still himself. The only voice that he would hear was the voice of his grief.

In his own way, General Klamath did his duty. He called the King's thoughts away from his wife. Swallowing the tightness in his throat, he asked, "Why did you climb that tor?" And climb it alone? "It was not to look for us. Suti al-Suri's scouts must have told you that we are here."

"I was commanded," answered Bifalt hoarsely. "Magister Avail spoke in my mind. He told me to find high ground and face east. So that the Repository could see me, if you can believe it."

Then he shrugged. "I heard him as the storm cleared. I did not find high ground until this morning."

"And this troubles you, Majesty?" asked Klamath. "Did you wish to remain hidden from the Repository?"

From your wife?

Bifalt made a growling sound in the back of his throat. "I do not know why they care where I am."

Now Klamath had to suppress a smile. That growl reassured him. It was more than familiar: it was characteristic. He spread his hands. "How could they not, Majesty? You are their only defender. You do not wish to be, but you are. *They* are merely sorcerers. What can they do? The Great God is a sorcerer as well, and he is *ready* for them. Whether we live or die, you are all that they have ever had."

Why else had the library's Magisters worked so hard to make Bifalt the King they needed him to be?

King Bifalt squinted against the sun for a moment. Without his accustomed rancor, he drawled, "No doubt, they would say that they exist to preserve knowledge, not to fight for it. I call that slippery reasoning."

After a moment, he added, "You are a good friend, Klamath. You do not defend Queen Estie. She has enough defenders"—he tapped his chest—"here."

Then he took the General's arm again. Together, they resumed walking.

When the King had composed himself, he said, "Now our circumstances have changed. We must speak of what we will do."

Klamath allowed himself a moment of relief. He felt that he and his King had passed a crisis. Now they could reassume roles that he understood, the roles that warfare demanded.

While Bifalt explained his orders, Klamath said nothing. The King's intentions were extreme, but Klamath accepted them. What else did he expect? When the wagons arrived, his forces would be able to eat and rest. That was enough. He was only the General. Bifalt was Belleger's King.

Harried by images of Tak Biondi's death, Magister Avail's distress, and Klamath's desperation, Queen Estie floundered until the Repository's scribes delivered their first copy of Lamit Karsolsky's *System*. Crayn had tried and failed to ease her. Holding the tome in her hands steadied her. It felt like hope.

When Magister Marrow's killer had mentioned it, its possibilities had distracted her. Now she knew that her first impression was accurate. The benefits of speaking with gestures and signs instead of finger-taps were obvious. Thanks to its many illustrations, *A Complete System* was easier to learn, and it could be seen from across the room. With it, Estie would not need an interpreter always at her side.

Frustrated by his difficulties with Magister Rummage's code, the Commander was as avid as his Queen. Together, they pored over the book for hours, studying its methods and teaching each other. It seemed to keep her sane.

But when Joyly arrived the next morning, practically dragging Magister Oblique with her, Karsolsky's work was forgotten. The eagerness of the Farsighted made it clear that she had come with news. She had brought Oblique to translate for her.

The suddenness of their coming startled Estie. For a moment, she froze, unable to express her hunger for news.

Without waiting for an invitation, Oblique took her familiar place sitting beside Estie. The Farsighted would have preferred to stand. She might have preferred to dance. She had to force herself to accept a chair.

Queen Estie shook herself. When she had recovered a measure of feigned calm, she managed to say, "You have something to tell me."

She meant, Tell me *now*.

Joyly glanced at Magister Oblique. Oblique rested her hand on Estie's forearm, then nodded.

Excitement flushed the short, plump woman's face. Burbling silently, she spoke through Oblique's touch.

—I wanted to be the first to tell you, Queen. We have seen King Bifalt.

For an instant, Estie seemed to lose her place in the world. Her husband was still alive. In spite of everything— The chamber tilted. By some sorcery of its own, it became King Smegin's ceremonial hall in Amika's Desire. She sat beside her father on a dais as Commander Forguile brought Prince Bifalt forward. King Abbator's inheriting son approached like a man who had shed every fear. The heat in his eyes promised that he had come to change her whole life.

But then Oblique's grip tightened on Estie's forearm, and the sitting room settled. Almost choking, Estie pleaded, "Go on."

Overflowing, Joyly complied.

—Magister Avail asked him to find high ground so that we could see him. But that was yesterday, when the skies began to clear. Apparently, he was not able to respond until an hour ago. We saw him clearly, Queen, lit by sunrise. Now he is with General Klamath. With Prince Jaspid and Elgart. And the el-Algreb.

While Queen Estie held her breath, the woman continued.

—Yesterday, we feared that some or all of the General's men were dead. But they made fires. With flames and lightning, they set their dead mounts burning. That kept them alive. This morning, most of them arose.

She hesitated.

—Perhaps not all.

There the Farsighted fell silent. She may have believed that she had said enough. But Magister Oblique had more. For Crayn's sake, she repeated herself as she wrote.

—The Farsighted have also scanned Amika. They have seen no sign of the enemy. All of your bridges are gone. Commander Forguile guards Fivebridge with a company of riflemen—and with a man we take to be Prince Lome. While he has guns and grenades, the Commander can hold the Line River.

Estie said nothing. She could not think about anything except Bifalt.

Briefly, Oblique stroked the Queen's forearm, wiping other words away so that she could resume her own tidings.

—Also, there is this, Queen. It is speculation, but we lack certain knowledge. To come so far in so short a time, General Klamath must have been pursued by the Great God's cavalry. But then the cavalry withdrew. Why, we cannot imagine. The fact remains. Those men and beasts have returned toward the Open Hand.

—His infantry march toward us. Their numbers are immense, but they are not swift. Only their sorcerers are mounted. Time will pass before they can threaten the General again.

Queen Estie shook her head. She should have been grieved by what Klamath and his army had suffered—and relieved that he had survived. Instead, she received Magister Oblique's news without attending to it. The shock of learning that Bifalt lived shook her foundations.

The pressure pulled her to her feet. She needed to anchor herself until she recovered her balance.

Then she remembered the sense of purpose that had taken her to face Tak Biondi, and had sustained her past his death to her confrontation in the librarian's workroom.

Trembling, she asked, "How is Magister Avail?"

Magister Oblique rose from her seat, clasped Estie's forearm. Quickly, she tapped:

—He is in his quarters with Magister Rummage. They have locked the door. They refuse healers. They refuse servants with food. They have turned the librarian away. Their distress must be extreme.

As if she were not staggering, Queen Estie faced the Magister. "Will you take me to them?"

Oblique looked helpless.

—You do not understand, Queen. They—

Estie was a monarch who had forsaken her people, abandoned her husband—and for what? So that she could become deaf? She had no patience in her. Politeness was impossible.

She interrupted Oblique sharply. "I understand well enough. I expected dishonesty from Magister Marrow. But *they* trusted him"—Avail and Rummage. "To them, he was worse than dishonest. He disregarded their well-being."

Unable to bear the delay of an argument, she turned to Joyly. "Will *you* take me?"

The Farsighted may not have understood the Magister's reluctance. She nodded vigorously.

Feverishly, Oblique wrote:

—They will admit no one.

Queen Estie snatched her arm away. "They will admit *me*." She picked up the book. "I will give them Karsolsky's *System*."

If they accepted it, it might lessen their isolation.

At once, Crayn came to her side. He may not have understood her intentions, but he knew what he saw in her. His firm grip held her arm so that she would not stumble.

Without waiting for Magister Oblique's approval, the Farsighted rose from her chair. Trembling for reasons of her own, she led Queen Estie and Crayn to the door.

In a rush, Estie left her rooms, hurrying so that she would not hurt anyone by shouting. Bifalt was alive. She had work to do.

TWENTY-SIX

CHARGING IN

Standing outside the door of Magister Avail's quarters, Queen Estie demanded entrance. She did not waste her time on polite knocking or timid requests. Instead, she used sorcery to insist, forcing both the deaf man and the hunchback to hear her.

As she arrived, she had sent her guide, Joyly, to summon food and drink for the grieved, bitter Magisters. Commander Crayn she kept with her. He carried the book for her. She did not let her demand leak into his mind. It was not for him.

When she had repeated herself twice, Magister Avail retorted, **Go away, Queen. There is nothing here for you.**

Grinning like King Bifalt when he was determined to have his way, she insisted again.

Let me in. I know what you suffer. I have been betrayed. My father tried to have me killed. Then he tried to kill me himself. Let me in.

Abruptly, the door was snatched open. Magister Rummage confronted her with his teeth as if he wanted to take a bite out of her face. On both sides of his mouth, long-dried tears had left streaks in the grime of his visage. His hair looked torn. Small bald patches of his skull showed red.

Crayn shifted closer, held the book so that the hunchback could see it.

Magister Rummage flicked a glance at it. The angles of his scowl changed. His eyes betrayed a wince.

He could have slammed the door. But he had been with her in Tak Biondi's room. His attitude toward her had changed. And her manner defied resistance. After a moment, he stepped back to let her enter.

With her Commander, she walked into Magister Avail's rooms.

They were much like hers: higher in the carved stone of the Repository, closer to the librarian's workroom, but similarly furnished and windowless. The first chamber was the sitting room. Only Magister Rummage was present.

The room had two inner doors, both shut. No doubt, one led to Magister Avail's bedroom and bathing room. The other may have connected to the hunchback's quarters. She did not care which was which.

So that both Magisters would hear her, she asked, **Where is Magister Avail?**

In my bed, Avail snapped immediately. **Where I belong.**

With a lift of one eyebrow, the Queen referred her question to Magister Rummage.

Glowering, the voiceless man led her to a door, opened it for her.

Propped up by pillows, Magister Avail lay on his bed. It rested against one wall with its head in the corner. Perhaps he felt safer with stone on two sides of him. Rather than his Magister's robe, he wore a long, rumpled nightshirt which did nothing to disguise the fact that he had not done anything to care for himself. The sour smell of sweat and unwashed flesh hung in the air. His hair resembled a nest for untidy birds.

This place is *mine*, he rasped at Estie. **You are not welcome here.**

She puffed her cheeks in a silent snort. As she approached the bed, she took Lamit Karsolsky's book from Crayn and dropped it on the blankets. Aloud, she asked Crayn to bring her a chair.

Radiating vexation, Magister Rummage went with Crayn. They each brought a chair from the sitting room.

Queen Estie placed hers facing away from Magister Avail. With a gesture, she asked the hunchback to sit in front of her. Glaring, he seated himself close enough to tap on her thighs. When he was settled, she began to do what she could for Magister Avail by the simple expedient of ignoring him.

"Tell me," she commanded Magister Rummage, "how you will defend the Repository."

He bared his teeth. His heavy fingers wrote a demand:

—Why?

She had come too far to hesitate. "Because my people are dying for you. King Bifalt's are dying."

The hunchback closed his mouth over his teeth. One after another, frowns and grimaces chased his thoughts. When he reached a conclusion, his expression settled in a scowl.

—We are not made for war. The Repository itself defends us. Its walls were fashioned to endure. If it cannot protect us, nothing will.

"But you have Magisters of all kinds," she protested. "Many of them are mighty. Will they do nothing?"

Magister Rummage appeared to sigh.

—They will do what they can. When the Great God comes, our people will oppose him from the battlements. But we cannot match him. We have never aspired to warfare.

His touch dug deeper.

—Sirjane Marrow had cruelty in him. You know that. But in one thing, he saw us clearly. We are not enough. We have never been enough. We need your King Bifalt.

Carefully, the Queen countered, "I find that difficult to believe. You have vast abilities. Distance is no obstacle to the seventh Decimate—or to the Farsighted. Surely, other sorceries have the same reach.

"Before Prince Bifalt came to you, he could have died twice." Once when a bolt of lightning should have killed him, once when he had absorbed the explosion of a grenade. "You must have saved him then. Why are such feats impossible now?"

That question startled Rummage. He seemed to search his memory for the occasions she meant. Finally, he answered:

—Yes, Queen. That was done. Some among us are called Shields.

They wield a power that deflects force at the last instant. Lightning. Gunpowder. But few are born with the gift, and it has no range. It must be used near where it is needed.

His writing became more urgent.

—Understand me, Queen. That was twenty years ago. The Great God's coming was a distant fear. Only your war with Belleger endangered the Prince. And the Farsighted were watching. We knew well in advance when Belleger would fight again. We sent Shields to hide themselves and ward the Prince.

—King Smegin's ambush of his quest was more perilous. Again, we knew of the danger. But we did not have much time. Our Shields could not be sure when and where the Prince might be threatened. And then night fell. The Farsighted were blinded. Only the sounds of fighting enabled one Shield to find and protect him.

—Now the Great God has overrun the west of Belleger. What can we ask of our Shields? We cannot simply hope that they will serve some purpose. They will die for nothing.

Impatiently, Queen Estie glanced at Magister Avail. He had picked up the book, but had not opened it. Instead, he studied it the way she would have studied a coiled snake.

She faced the hunchback again. "Then you will do nothing to help the people who die for you? Nothing at all?"

He winced.

—Not yet. We dare not. But the desert is *our* realm. We know the sands. There, the King's armies will find resupply. And we will send guides to show them the secret ways among the dunes. Between its western edge and the caravan-track, the Great God will struggle for every step. The sands themselves will defend us.

—Once he discovers the track, however—

Rummage looked away to hide the darkness in his eyes.

—It will serve the Great God well.

With a twitch of one arm, Crayn caught Estie's attention. His eyes directed her to Magister Avail.

A quick look showed her that the deaf man had opened the book.

She considered speaking to him then, but she was not done with Magister Rummage.

"Yet we are not your only allies, Magister," she said more harshly. "The el-Algreb are not. You have others.

"Tell me about the Knights of Ardor."

Magister Rummage bared his teeth in a bitter, soundless laugh.

—They did not come to fight for us. They are on a quest.

—In their homeland far across the seas, they are mercenaries, Queen. War is their trade. They barter their services. They seek to improve. When they heard the rumor that one great library still exists, Sword Eradimnie and her comrades were sent to find us if they could. To learn.

—The Great God's coming has taken them by surprise. They could escape. They have time. But they refuse. They have learned too much here. They will not forsake the Repository.

—Queen, they are only five. What can they do?

Estie wanted to ask, They have no sorcery? Their iron would not protect them from lightning and fire. But Magister Avail interrupted her.

I will not do it, he snarled so that everyone could hear him. **Your demand offends me. Magister Rummage is my friend. I will not learn to live without him.**

The hunchback had his own dilemma, his conflicting loyalties to Avail and the Repository. The look he flung at the deaf man resembled pleading.

Then you are a child, Magister Avail, retorted the Queen. Like him, she let everyone hear her. **You think only of yourself. When the war comes *here*, it will separate you and your friend.** Whatever happened, Rummage would command the fighting. The battle was his responsibility. **That will harm him. It will not harm you. *You* can address him whenever you wish. *He* will be forced to use messengers— if he has any.**

You said once that I am not alone. Nor are you, Magister. You are only deaf. Your friend has no voice.

Sudden gratitude spread across the mute's face. It made Estie's eyes sting. After a moment, he wrote firmly:

—Leave him to me, Queen.

He showed her his teeth.

—I will raise such bruises on his hands and arms that he will fear my touch. Then he will know why we must master this book.

Queen Estie blinked to hold back her tears. She had been sure of herself, feverish and strong. Now the risk that she had just taken caught up with her. In its aftermath, she felt strangely lost.

"Can you command more copies?" she asked unsteadily. "You will need them."

Magister Rummage shrugged.

—Anyone can ask, Queen. Only the librarian can command.

As if she trusted her balance, Estie surged to her feet. "Then *I* will command her."

With Crayn at her side, she headed for the bedroom door. She had no idea what she would have done if Magister Avail had shouted at her. Fortunately, he remained silent.

As she and Crayn crossed the sitting room, the outer door opened, and Fifth Daughter came in carrying a heavy tray of food and drink. Nodding a bow, the monk hurried into Avail's bedroom.

Estie leaned more heavily on the Commander's support. In a voice, she said, "Thank you, Crayn. For everything. While we walk, I will tell you how Magister Rummage answered me."

By touch, Crayn remarked:

—You were harsh, Majesty. Perhaps that was necessary.

Estie blinked away a few more tears. "Can you find the librarian's workroom from here?"

His firm nod assured her that he could.

Trusting his hand on her arm, the Queen braced herself to make demands of Beatrix Threnody.

For several days, the skies were clear. The cold had no remorse, but the sun gave its warmth. During the day, the top layers of snow melted, and reflected glare left burns like scars on exposed faces. At night, the snow froze into sheets like brittle bone.

During that time, Queen Estie dedicated most of her hours to Lamit Karsolsky's *A Complete System of Gestures for Speech with the Deaf and Dumb*, learning it herself and teaching it to her guardsmen. If anyone had asked her why she wanted to master a second mute language, she would have said that she needed something to do. That was true enough. Nevertheless it masked a deeper purpose. Her studies were a gift for her husband. She would never hear the distinctive intensity of his voice again; but he would still be able to speak with her—if he chose to make the effort.

Whenever Magister Avail addressed her, however, she interrupted what she was doing and gave him her full attention.

He must have received what he needed most from his friend. Resuming his duties, he was often with one or another of the Farsighted. He shared what they told him.

In that way, Estie heard that King Bifalt and the el-Algreb had not stayed with General Klamath. From somewhere, they had produced wagons of food and supplies. Then they had ridden away, taking only two Magisters and a single wagon with them, heading north.

One other Farsighted watched Rile's horde of fanged strangers. Apparently, those nameless men had waited, passive and directionless, for the storm to pass. But now a number of mounted priests had joined them. They were on the move, plowing through the drifts on a line that would join the Great God's infantry before they reached the desert.

Clearly, King Bifalt aimed to intercept the fanged men.

This news gave Queen Estie a pang, but she could not say that it surprised her. Bifalt was only being himself. A man who had survived the fall of Belleger's Fist would not hesitate to risk his life against the far greater numbers of the horde. And he was not alone. As well as the el-Algreb and two Magisters, he had a company of riflemen and his bodyguards. Prince Jaspid and Elgart were surely with him. They might be enough.

For a day and a half after the King's departure, General Klamath had stayed where he was, giving his men and Magisters time to recover their strength and care for their horses. At the first sign of Rile's infantry, however, he broke camp and began to withdraw, drawing the infantrymen after him.

But he did not allow the enemy to advance unopposed. Occasional squads of riflemen rode near enough to fire a few shots, then galloped away. At unexpected intervals, bolts of lightning struck from the cloudless sky, killing infantrymen indiscriminately. From time to time, Klamath's men paused to dig trenches in the snow. The infantrymen stepped over them easily; but when several ranks had passed, the trenches erupted in flames. They must have been filled with oil and lit by a Magister of fire.

As a result, Rile's forces made no attempt to close on the General's army.

Before much longer, the Farsighted spotted the Great God for the first time. Magister Avail sounded alarmed as he described what they saw.

Accompanied by two of his priests, Rile rode on a long platform apparently strapped to the backs of four tusked beasts, beasts he managed without reins or teamsters. He was a tall man, unnaturally so, hairless and entirely nude. Even at that distance, he looked more like a statue fashioned of bronze than a living being. Yet his perfect form seemed to glow with gold sorcery. He traveled through a nimbus of vapor as his emanations melted the snow around him.

Only his eyes were not golden. They blazed with the red of burning rubies. In one hand, he gripped a staff, a tall shaft forged in the shape of a cross. On the end of each crosspiece, and atop the staff, were gems the color of his eyes. Like his eyes, they shone with scorn and power.

The image made Queen Estie's guts squirm. She had never seen the cross and the naked statue in the Great God's Church, but she had heard about them. Vaguely, she had supposed that Rile might resemble his emblems. Still, she was not prepared for the *fact* of his appearance. Anyone who looked at him would quail.

That night, she spoke briefly with Avail. From her bed, she asked, **Is he alive? Could that figure be a statue? Could his priests give a statue the appearance of life?**

No, retorted the deaf sorcerer. **What purpose would it serve?** His fright had become irritation. **It is a distressing sight, yes. But if it were a lifeless thing, its effect would fade.**

Then he sighed. **The Great God must command his forces from** *somewhere*. **If he is too distant, his control might falter.**

Remembering how she had reprimanded Avail in his quarters, Estie said quietly, **I understand, Magister. Thank you. I am grateful for what you share with me.**

After a moment, he replied, **You said it yourself, Queen. We are not alone.**

Then he was done.

For the next few days, Queen Estie continued her teaching. When Magister Avail addressed her, she marked Klamath's progress on her vague mental map of Belleger. More anxiously, she measured her husband's distance from Rile's horde. They would confront each other soon.

But then came a day when the deaf man said nothing. After a few hours, his silence eroded her concentration. The gestures of *A Complete System* began to seem like empty hand-waving. Defeated, she dismissed her guardsmen. Pacing around her sitting room, she tried for patience while she waited for Magister Avail to speak.

She did not hear his voice until late that afternoon. When he spoke, he sounded too shaken to provide details.

I am sorry, Queen. King Bifalt has been routed.

Queen Estie did not hesitate. She took Commander Crayn and left her quarters, hurrying to find someone, anyone, who would tell her more.

When Suti al-Suri's scouts reported that the horde was half a day away, King Bifalt called a halt.

His small army could have ridden farther. He had not been pushing the pace, and their wagon carried plenty of food and fodder. But sunset was coming, and the King needed time to talk and plan. Captain Flisk and Commander Forguile had described those fanged strangers. They were formidable despite their lack of weapons. Indiscriminate gunfire would not kill them. Hells, it might not slow them. Worse, they were supported by priests with shining globes. Any rash assault would fail.

The riflemen and the el-Algreb started campfires for food and warmth. In the waning daylight, Bifalt called his advisers together. Sitting in a ring around one of the fires, they discussed their intentions.

Suti al-Suri spoke for the horse-warriors. Prince Jaspid and Elgart were there, as were the King's bodyguards. Sub-Commander Hellick was not. King Bifalt had released him to General Klamath along with the Magisters of earthquake. The King's path took him across a region of open plains like the steppes of the Nuuri, a rumpled stretch of land that appeared almost flat. Earthquakes would be of more use among the sands of the desert. To replace Astride and the others, Bifalt had claimed Magisters Brighten and Crawl. They sat waiting with his counselors.

King Bifalt's first question was for the chief warrior. "What do your scouts say?"

Suti al-Suri studied the fire, avoiding the King's gaze. He seemed chastened—or perhaps daunted.

"Bad foes, Brother," he muttered. "Bad for horses. Fast like skirmishers, but big. Long fangs." His hands clutched reflexively at his bandolier of daggers. "Kill horses easy as men. More easy."

Bifalt nodded. "Then we will have to fight at a distance."

He imagined streams of horse-warriors riding along the edges of the horde, doing as much damage as possible and wheeling away before the enemy responded. The Magisters could punish any counterattack.

The chief warrior flicked a glance at King Bifalt, lowered his eyes again. "How fight distant? Rifles not good." He may have meant that his warriors lacked accuracy with their guns. "Need hills."

"We have none," remarked Prince Jaspid. "And no cover." His tone was carefully neutral. "The terrain will not help us."

Suti al-Suri was not done. "And black men," he added bitterly. "Sorcerers. Long staffs. Shining balls. Explosions. Too many." Abruptly, he glared at Bifalt. "Ride tusked beasts. Faster than horses."

Too many? wondered King Bifalt. A sudden thought knotted his guts. Only a lifetime of severity masked his alarm. Those priests had not been sent to command the horde. Rather, the horde had been gathered to protect Rile's sorcerers.

The strangers were cruel foes. They could savage any ordinary army. But they would be useless against the hard stone of the Last Repository. The gates were the keep's only point of weakness, and they could withstand the fanged men. For any other attack, Rile would have to rely on sorcery.

The Great God had not brought so many men and beasts merely to destroy Belleger and Amika. His underlying purpose was to provide cover for his sorcerers until he reached the library.

Chewing his cheek, King Bifalt sat silent while his preconceptions crumbled.

Elgart may have sensed the change in his King. Or he may have been occupied by his own emotions. Grinning with half his face, he drawled morosely, "This begins to sound impossible, Majesty. The priests will let nothing stand in their way."

King Bifalt tightened his grip on himself. He had to make Suti al-Suri understand. He kept his attention on the chief warrior. "It is worse than it sounds." He needed the el-Algreb. "My men have fought those strangers before. They are difficult to kill. They shrug off their wounds and keep coming." He remembered Flisk's horror. "A bullet in the brain stops them. Or a cut through the neck. A shot to the heart may not be enough.

"Can your warriors hit a target as small as a head, Suti al-Suri? From horseback? At a distance?"

The chief warrior cleared his throat, spat into the fire. "You mock us, Brother. We not do. Rifles still strange."

The King ignored Magister Brighten's scowl of fury, Magister Crawl's open dismay. They knew the dangers too well. Still speaking to Suti al-Suri as if only the chief warrior's reaction mattered, King Bifalt replied, "That is not mockery. It is a fact. I want you all to understand it." His old outrage was a lump of ice in his heart. It held him steady. "We cannot fight the horde the way you defeated the Cleckin.

"We have to risk a direct assault."

That startled Prince Jaspid. Elgart's eyes widened in surprise. Magister Crawl started to protest. But Suti al-Suri spoke first.

Straight at the King, he snapped, "No! Why? Fanged men slaughter. El-Algreb die. Horses die. Fangs terrible."

In the distant west, the sun was setting. The fading sky showed a few stars. Already, the air felt colder.

Bifalt hunched closer to the fire. His voice was a low growl. "You will not die if you keep your distance. My men and I will bear the brunt." His riflemen and the Magisters. "I want you behind us."

Jaspid sat up straighter. As he considered his brother's intentions, he seemed to grow sharper, whetted by a born fighter's eagerness. Elgart scowled skeptically, but he did not object.

Suti al-Suri was openly appalled. "Brother want el-Algreb *safe*?"

"No," admitted Bifalt. "I want you to guard our backs. But the choice is yours. There will be other battles."

For a moment, he let his long anger speak. "Those men are slaves, Suti al-Suri. I do not care how many of them we kill. I do not care if we kill *any* of them. I want the priests.

"I am going to drive straight at them until we are close enough to shoot them. While we do that, I hope that you can keep their slaves from surrounding us."

The chief warrior muttered to himself for a moment. Then he rose to his feet. Fiercely, he answered, "You want save el-Algreb. You insult. We fearless. We *ally*."

Whirling away, he went to rejoin his people.

At once, Magister Brighten demanded, "What of *us*, Majesty? What do you expect Crawl and me to do?"

King Bifalt grimaced. Even when his only desire was to kill sorcerers, he needed sorcery on his side. He took a moment to compose himself. Then he replied brusquely, "Ride with me, Magister. You may be more effective than we are.

"As for you," he told Magister Crawl, "stay back. Use your Decimate. Protect us from those globes."

If even one of the exploding balls hit the riflemen or the el-Algreb—

Magister Brighten's eyes burned. She looked ready to fry any number of priests. And Magister Crawl summoned a measure of confidence.

"Can it be done?" Elgart sounded rueful, as if he were letting go of something precious. "We have too many foes."

King Bifalt ground his teeth until his jaws ached. "We can only do what we can do. If we fail, no one can fault us."

Elgart released a musing breath. "You forget, Majesty. I have seen you do more than you can. I was there when you took your first step toward an alliance with Amika."

At that time, Amika was Belleger's only enemy.

Bifalt spread his hands: a gesture of helplessness. He had no answer.

"In any event"—Prince Jaspid stood like a blade swept out of its scabbard—"we will do more than Rile believes we can." He sketched a bow to his brother. "I must speak with the men, Majesty. They will need their orders."

Despite his well-known reluctance for the task, he had become a commander.

At once, Elgart rose. "The Prince will make it sound like a glorious death." He chuckled sourly. "Someone should remind them to clean their guns."

When Jaspid walked away, Elgart followed him.

King Bifalt remained where he was, alone apart from his bodyguards and the Magisters.

Jeck and the others had been silent since they sat down. Now Jeck cleared his throat. "Elgart is right, Majesty," he said carefully. "We have too many foes. You should let Prince Jaspid lead the charge. We cannot lose you."

Bifalt swore to himself. Estie had already turned her back. What reason did he have to fear dying?

"That is why I have you," he answered. A moment later, he added, "My brother does not need to lead. He will do more than any of us."

Jeck glanced over at Malder. The big man shrugged. Spliner and Boy said nothing.

L ater, King Bifalt lay in his bedroll under the open sky, watching the careless stars burn. On this night, their indifference had the effect of an omen. They may have been suns themselves, but they gave too little light.

He hoped that his people would get the rest they needed. Their lives were his to sacrifice or preserve. *He* could not sleep.

He was still watching the heavens when Suti al-Suri came to him.

"Brother." The chief warrior made no attempt to speak softly. Silhouetted against the dying embers of a campfire, he looked threatening, as fatal as a curse. "Enemy comes. Found scout tracks." Even the el-Algreb could not move without marking the ice and snow. "They run. Come soon."

Hells! Those whoreson priests! King Bifalt flung himself out of his bedding, snatched up his breastplate and cloak, his weapons. "How much time do we have?"

Suti al-Suri consulted the stars. "Soon. Too soon."

The King did not pause for thought. His voice had never lost its hoarseness, but he could make himself heard.

"Up!" he blared. "Everybody up! The horde is coming! We need daylight to fight!"

Jeck and Malder were already with him. He grabbed Malder's arm. "Tell Spliner and Boy," he snapped. "They have to save the wagon"— the supplies. "Tell them to go as fast as they dare. We will catch up with them when we get the chance."

At once, the brawler seemed to disappear among the sprawl of bedrolls and tents.

A moment later, Prince Jaspid started yelling. Elgart joined him. Suti al-Suri's fluid language ran through the shouts like a stream in spate.

Heaving themselves into motion, King Bifalt's forces fled back the way they had come.

The King's army was fortunate. Even running hard, the horde could not outrace his horses. In effect, the fanged men held back the priests. His people were able to keep their distance.

They were still moving at a hard canter as the sun began to rise over the eastern mountains. Slowly, the landscape around them took light.

Gnawing his cheek, King Bifalt scanned the plain. He needed hills, escarpments, piles of boulders, even a copse or two. There were none. He would have to fight in the open.

He had expected that, but he did not like it.

When he felt the sun's first warmth on his face, he called a halt. He was still an hour or more ahead of the horde. The riflemen and Magisters needed that time to eat, rest, care for their mounts.

Swinging out of his saddle, Bifalt went to find Suti al-Suri. He had only one thing to say to the chief warrior.

"I trust you, Suti al-Suri. But be cautious. This battle is just the beginning. Rile has many more men. Klamath will have to face them without us. You must live long enough to tell him what happens here."

Despite his air of youthfulness, Suti al-Suri seemed stern and sure. In one hand, he held his rifle across his chest. "Ally, yes," he said. "Keep promise. Kill priests. Kill fanged men." He reached out to tap the King's breastplate. "Not die, Brother." He almost smiled. "Ally die shame el-Algreb."

Bifalt turned away to cover his grimace. The chief warrior's promise did not comfort him. It only meant that more people were going to die.

Harried along by Prince Jaspid and Elgart, the riflemen were getting ready. Jeck and Malder had a cold meal waiting for the King. Jeck made no attempt to hide his concern. Malder kept his to himself.

Magister Crawl wandered aimlessly among the soldiers, working his fingers as if he were practicing arcane gestures. Magister Brighten's mood had improved, lifted by the prospect of unleashing her Decimate. She resembled a whetted blade.

Scanning his forces, King Bifalt nodded. What he meant to do might be a mistake. That would not surprise him. He was often wrong.

Nevertheless he trusted his people to make even this misjudgment look like a victory.

Like Suti al-Suri's promise, that assurance gave him no comfort.

When one of the scouts brought word that the horde was less than a league away, Bifalt loosened his saber in its scabbard, checked the action of his rifle, slapped a full clip into place. Together, he and his bodyguards went to their horses. Trotting side by side, they joined the Prince and Elgart.

Suti al-Suri's warriors took positions behind and to the sides of King Bifalt's soldiers. Some of them brandished their rifles to demonstrate their eagerness. Others gentled their horses with calm faces and mild voices. Anxious and determined, Magister Crawl kept watch for flung globes.

The riflemen made a wedge with King Bifalt and his bodyguards at its tip, Prince Jaspid and Elgart a pace back on either side. Magister Brighten took the center of the formation, guarded on all sides. Bifalt believed that the priests would stay deep in the horde, heavily warded. He meant to force his way into the enemy's onrush until Brighten's Decimate could reach the priests. His men might be able to open a gap with gunfire. Once they pierced the horde's front, however, they would be swarmed. Their rifles would be useless. They would have to rely on their sabers—and on the covering fire of the el-Algreb.

Like the destruction of Belleger's Fist, this charge was a desperate tactic. And like that ploy, it depended on the resolve of King Bifalt's people. It was his responsibility, yet he could do little to determine its outcome.

He had always needed help. Even his one great achievement, his alliance with Amika, would have been impossible if Commander Forguile had not faced King Smegin with him. In the end, it was always the people he had sworn to serve who paid the price.

Glaring, he waited for the enemy.

His sight was not as good as it had once been. Even in full sunlight, he could not see far enough. Most of the snowfield was as flat as the plain, but where his army had passed, disturbed clumps of snow and ice caught reflections that hurt his eyes.

Finally, Jaspid stood in his stirrups, peered into the north. As he resumed his seat, he nodded to King Bifalt.

"It is time, Brother." The Prince spoke softly, but his voice had the clarion timbre of a tantara.

As if he had never faltered and did not know how, King Bifalt told his company, "At a canter, men. We will not charge until we can be sure of our targets."

With his heels, he nudged his horse forward.

In formation, his riflemen matched his pace.

The way ahead was comparatively easy. His passage an hour ago had broken up the icy crust, beaten down the underlying snow and slush. Even at a gallop, he would not need to worry about his mount's footing.

Now he could see a blur in the distance ahead, a seethe of running men. Behind them, the sorcerous shining of globes marked the priests. He did not try to count them. Whatever their number, they were more than enough.

Flicking his reins, he began to move faster.

Then the gap between him and the horde seemed to close with astonishing swiftness. The blur became a throng of individual men running shoulder to shoulder with their mouths gaping to bite and their breaths gusting. Their fangs resembled curved daggers shaped and sharpened to rend.

The el-Algreb advanced in support. Holding their guns ready, they stayed far enough back to avoid crowding the riflemen and risking their own horses.

Bifalt did not need to shout. He had no orders left to give. Careless of his aim, he snatched his rifle to his shoulder and fired once into the mass of the enemy. Then he kicked his mount into a controlled gallop.

A heartbeat later, his men fired as well, those who had clear shots: Jeck and Malder, Jaspid and Elgart, the riflemen along the outer edges of the wedge. Led by the heavy punching of bullets, King Bifalt and his company rushed at the horde.

Without transition, astonishing speed became an etched sequence of details. Prince Jaspid killed with casual ease. Elgart was a fine marksman. Jeck was good enough: his preferred weapon was his saber. Malder was merely competent. He fought better with his fists.

Beyond the wings of the wedge, the el-Algreb began shooting furiously. Against ordinary men, their fire would have been lethal. But the strangers shrugged off hits to their limbs and bellies, even to their chests. Lashed by lead like sleet, they kept coming.

Then they slowed. With their fellows piling behind them, their whole front lurched to a halt.

They were not hurt. They did not fear gunfire.

They stopped to feed.

With the frenzy of hornets, they swarmed their fallen. Fingernails like claws gripped the dead as they ripped out great chunks of flesh with their fangs, gulped down muscles and viscera. Spattered with gore, one stranger slurped intestines like noodles. Another broke open a skull with one bite, devoured the brain and most of the face.

Faster than King Bifalt could count the dead, they were gone.

Shocked by the sight, the riflemen and horse-warriors lost momentum. Gunfire staggered into silence. Men too stunned to think hauled on their reins. Even the King—

Hells! Rile's slaves were *starving*. That was the goad the priests used to drive them. They were rabid with hunger. They would eat any man that fell, comrade or enemy.

Screaming, King Bifalt kicked his horse forward. As fast as he could, he emptied his clip, wrenched it out and discarded it, slapped a new one into place.

Behind him, his soldiers and the el-Algreb resumed firing. Stung by horror, they blazed at the horde.

Only Prince Jaspid had not paused or slowed. Instead, he had surged ahead, shooting as he went. With Jeck and Malder, Bifalt followed. Elgart joined them. Every gun in the King's small army spat lead.

But now none of their bullets struck.

A swirl between Bifalt and the horde distorted his vision, a smear like a mirage, like incipient blindness. Strange theurgy veiled the massed enemy, dismissing gunfire as if the slugs had simply melted out of existence. It had the effect of a solid wall—and it was coming closer. It pushed air ahead of it, a blast so sudden and incomprehensible that it nearly unhorsed the King. Jeck and Malder crowded close to keep him in his saddle. Even Jaspid was staggered.

Through the smudge of sorcery, Bifalt saw priests drawing closer. Their beasts shouldered men aside, trampled some of them. Other men pounced on the fallen to eat, but the priests ignored them. Matching each other, the sorcerers aimed their staffs at the riflemen. Bifalt had no gift for theurgy, yet he felt power pouring toward him, twisting the air, stopping bullets. The globes at the ends of the staffs shone like bits of lightning.

Oh, *hells*!

The King wheeled his mount, tried to think. Jaspid had stopped shooting. So had Elgart. The riflemen had wrenched their mounts to a halt. Behind them, the el-Algreb stared, stupefied.

One heartbeat later, Magister Brighten answered. Her first bolt struck the migraine smear.

It did not pierce the power of the priests. Instead, it spread out like cracks in glass and evaporated.

Her second slammed out of the sky beyond the barrier. It lit a priest. He burned like phosphorous. His globe exploded. The concussion flattened men, wrenched beasts aside.

Somehow, the other priests kept their balance. Their sorcery did not waver.

Brighten's third strike ripped through the horde like a scourge, shredding slaves.

In response, the priests aimed their staffs higher, lifting their power to cover them. The Magister's next lightning-bolt hit like the first, left a crazed web of white fire across the wall and accomplished nothing.

At that instant, three flung globes sailed up from the horde. Like balls of concentrated sunlight, they arced over the smear of distortion or passed through it. Carrying high over King Bifalt's head, they plunged down toward the el-Algreb.

Magister Crawl was ready. With gouts of flame, he detonated two of the globes in midair. But they were falling too fast. He missed the third.

Its explosion ripped through warriors and horses. Blood sprayed from the blast, limbs and shredded torsos, great hunks of horseflesh. Too many of the el-Algreb died.

Bifalt's mind had gone blank. Too much was happening.

But then the screams of his allies reached him. Their shrill agony brought him back to himself.

He saw fanged men sprinting *through* the wall of sorcery. The shimmering blocked bullets and lightnings from his side: it let men and globes pass from the other.

"Retreat!" he howled. "Go! *Run!"*

His riflemen obeyed. Frantically, they spun their mounts and scrambled away, dragging Magister Brighten with them.

Over her shoulder, she hurled lightning that incinerated the nearest strangers. Then the urgent jostling of her guardians forced her to grip her saddlehorn while she fled.

Elgart stayed with the King. Jeck and Malder crowded close to him. Only Prince Jaspid stood his ground.

Alone against the enemy, Jaspid fired and fired. He had a wild light in his eyes. His hands were blurs of speed as he emptied his clips, replaced them, kept shooting.

Every man he killed slowed the horde's rush for a heartbeat or two. Others fell on the dead to feed. Their frenzy blocked those behind them.

Resisting his bodyguards, Bifalt surged forward to grab his brother's arm.

"Jaspid, *no!* I *need* you!"

His grip stopped the Prince. Jaspid seemed to hear his King for the first time. Slowly, he turned his head, focused his attention on Bifalt. The light faded from his eyes.

Then he snatched his horse around to follow the fleeing riflemen.

Bifalt turned like his brother, took his bodyguards by surprise. He collided with Malder, bounced off Jeck, and kicked his mount for speed.

He had delayed too long. Behind him, more of the horde raced through the migraine veil, slavering for food. The nearest slave sprang for Bifalt's horse, dug his claws into the steed's hindquarters. As it screamed, the man bit through its spine near Bifalt's seat.

His mount pitched to the ground. Instinctively, Bifalt tucked into a roll, avoided the thrashing horse. But he landed awkwardly. The impact knocked the air out of his lungs. A bone in his off-hand snapped.

Elgart was right. Bifalt had not been training. Long ago, however, he had trained hard. Ingrained reflexes saved him. In one motion, ignoring his need to breathe and the sharp pain in his hand, he drew his legs under him while he swept out his saber. His first slash cut deep into the neck of a fanged man.

Then Jeck and Malder were on the ground with him, fighting desperately. Jaspid spun among the slaves like a whirlwind. Every swing of his blade flung blood. An instant later, Elgart joined them. He was not like Jeck, an artist with his saber, or like Jaspid, who did everything easily; but he fought with the cold calculation of a born killer.

They were not enough. They could not stand against the horde's numbers. Only the hunger of their foes spared them. The nearest attackers sprang on their dead and dying fellows instead of tearing Bifalt and his defenders apart.

But rifles were firing again. Their sharp retorts were getting louder. Bullets staggered the slaves. Wounds bloomed on their arms, their hips, their chests. Some of them fell and became food.

Grinning, Prince Jaspid committed slaughter.

Overhead, two more globes sailed above the fighting. Flame answered them. Bolts of lightning stalked among the men around Bifalt and his defenders.

Covered by Decimates, Suti al-Suri appeared with several of his warriors. They swept Bifalt off his feet. Malder, Jeck, and Elgart. Even Jaspid. Galloping madly, they carried the King and his comrades away.

The King had lost his rifle. His hand hurt as if it had been bitten. He struggled to breathe. But his grip on his saber was iron. He clenched it like a man who would never let go.

One, he thought bitterly. *One* priest. That was all. None of the others had been touched.

Later, while his surviving forces ran southward, he would not have said that he had been routed. He would have called his flight a strategic retreat, an attempt to preserve his forces while he searched for terrain that he could use.

But in his heart, he felt routed.

TWENTY-SEVEN

BAD WEATHER

When Queen Estie had learned what the Farsighted could tell her about King Bifalt's encounter with the horde, she sank to the floor and sat there, absorbing the news. She did not know where she was. The chamber where Crayn had found Magister Bleak and the others was unfamiliar. But she did not care. She needed to gather herself until she felt steady enough to stand.

Somehow, implausibly, her husband had survived. Again. Jaspid and Elgart were still with him. He had his bodyguards. Whatever happened next, he would not have to face the catastrophe of his attack on the horde alone.

Apparently, he had chosen well when he had picked his two Magisters. They had kept him and many of his people alive. He had lost only a handful of riflemen. The losses among the el-Algreb were worse, but hundreds of them remained.

Still, the image of helpless men blown apart by sorcery troubled her deeply. She turned from it to other concerns.

Magister Rummage had described Shields to her, but he could not have prepared her for the power of that particular theurgy in the priests' hands. Working together, they had raised a barrier that protected Rile's slaves from bullets and lightning. And yet the fanged men had been able to pass through it. She had not known that such feats were possible.

When she trusted herself to speak, she addressed that query to Magister Avail.

His reply sounded bitter. **We have all the knowledge in the library, Queen. We do not have all the knowledge in the *world*. The Great God has secrets that remain hidden from us.**

Gradually, she became aware that the Farsighted and her Commander were still standing, waiting for her. Their presence made the simple indignity of sitting on the floor among them uncomfortable. Raising one hand, she let Crayn lift her to her feet.

Magister Bleak seemed to study her. His humming held notes of sympathy, but he did not speak. The other Farsighted turned away as if to avoid embarrassing her.

With a tremor in her voice, Queen Estie thanked them. Then she followed Crayn back to her quarters.

She relied on her Commander. If she had unburdened all of her turmoil for him, he would have borne it. Now she wanted something more from him.

She wanted him to think and speak as a soldier.

In her sitting room, she insisted that he take a chair and a goblet of wine. She poured wine for herself. Sitting opposite him, she told him what was on her mind.

She spoke aloud. He used gestures and hand-signs. His grasp on Karsolsky's *System* was incomplete, but he was becoming fluent.

She began by giving him her version of King Bifalt's reasons for charging the horde. "Yes," she admitted uncomfortably, "he hates sorcery and sorcerers. But that does not make him insane. It did not drive him to charge. He saw a danger that we have not considered."

She held Crayn's sandstone gaze. "Help me understand him, Commander. What did he see in priests with exploding globes and Shields? What could be worth his life?"

Crayn took a long moment to consider the question. He drew a deep breath, let it out. Frowning, he suggested carefully:

—You know the King, Majesty. I do not doubt what you say of him. My first thought is this. If the Farsighted are not mistaken in what they saw, then—

He hesitated, unsure of himself—or disturbed by his own reasoning. "Then?" prompted Estie.

—Then the Magisters here have mistaken their defenses. They are more exposed than they imagine.

This was what Queen Estie wanted from him. "How so?"

—They believe that the desert is their realm. They expect the sands to protect them. But have they considered how the power of Shields might be used among the dunes?

—Sand is only sand, Majesty. Together, Rile's Shields may be able to thrust even the highest dunes aside. They may be able to force a path through the desert.

The Queen flinched, but she did not interrupt him.

He spread his hands.

—Then ask yourself this, Majesty. What does Rile gain? An easy passage through the desert, yes. But then what? His cavalry and infantry and the horde together cannot breach the Repository's walls. Can the sorcery of Shields? I do not think so. This stone is iron, not sand. And it is *thick*. His priests can raise as many Shields and fling as many globes as they wish. They will accomplish nothing. And while they attack, the Magisters here will rain slaughter with their Decimates.

—If the priests are the true threat, Majesty, their Great God has wasted a long journey.

Scrambling to keep up, Estie thought, Then the *true* threat must be— Before Crayn could say more, she panted, "A moment. Give me a moment."

Then she caught up with herself.

"If the priests are not the true threat, Rile must have brought them to protect something else."

Rile himself might be the true threat. Or he might possess some other secret, a form of sorcery about which she, and perhaps the Repository, knew nothing.

At once, she jumped to her feet. "Come, Commander. We must speak with Magister Rummage again. He may need to reconsider the Repository's defense."

Crayn surged upright. "As you say, Majesty." She was in a hurry, but he was fast enough to reach the door ahead of her, open it for her. Together, they left the sitting room.

On her way to the quarters that Magister Rummage shared with Magister Avail, the deaf man summoned her. He sounded almost polite.

When she knocked on his door, he opened it immediately. He still resembled an invalid recovering from a long illness. His eyes had a yellow tinge, and the flesh of his face sagged on its bones. But he had bathed. He wore his traditional grey robe. He may have tried to force a comb through his unruly hair.

Nodding, he ushered the Queen and Crayn into his sitting room.

The hunchback was there, bent over in a chair with his elbows braced on his knees. His posture emphasized his deformity. He carried the bulge of his back as if its weight threatened to break him. It made him look more like a cripple, less like the strong and violent man that the Repository needed.

He and Magister Avail were not alone. Sword Eradimnie stood to one side. Apart from her helm, she wore the full armor of the Knights of Ardor. She was only a handspan or two taller than Estie, but her broad frame and burnished iron seemed to dominate the room as if it were too small to contain her.

Estie had been raised within the walls of Amika's Desire, a glowering edifice that was more a fortress than a castle. And in Belleger's Fist as well, she had spent her days mostly enclosed by stone. She was accustomed to living deep in places like the massive bulk of the Repository. But now she felt cramped, unable to draw a full breath.

The Knight's presence had that effect. She had the worn features of a woman in her middle years. An ingrained squint suggested that she had spent most of her life outside in all weather, training or fighting.

The pale blue of her eyes and the uncompromising set of her mouth promised that she knew how to look death in the face.

Without waiting for Estie, Magister Avail seated himself beside his friend. At once, the hunchback took the deaf man's hand. For a moment, they both studied Amika's Queen. Then Avail said, **Be seated, Queen. Sword Eradimnie has given us her counsel. Now she waits for your response.**

Queen Estie took a deep breath, shook herself into a semblance of calm. Deliberately graceful, she selected an armchair opposite the Magisters. Behind her, Commander Crayn turned to the Knight and offered a formal Amikan bow. With a twist that may have been a smile at the corner of her mouth, Sword Eradimnie acknowledged him by clashing her mailed fist on her breastplate. Swallowing whatever he felt, he joined her near the wall.

His mask was good. Only Estie, who knew him well, could see that he felt diminished beside the Knight.

Feigning unconcern, Queen Estie smoothed out the rumples in her apparel. "My response to what?" she asked.

Magister Avail frowned. **Use your voice, Queen. Let us all hear you. I will speak for Magister Rummage.**

Estie reached for her gift. **Very well. You say that Sword Eradimnie waits for my response. My response to what?**

The hunchback tapped swiftly on his friend's hand. Almost simultaneously, Avail announced, **Magister Rummage says this. He did not foresee the power of the Great God's priests. He hoped for an easier defense. Now he knows that we must rely on you. Sword Eradimnie wishes to know whether you will do what is needed.**

Startled, Estie held her breath. She had come to warn the Magisters. She had not expected to be met with a demand. Suddenly, she had too many questions.

But she kept them to herself. Her father had taught her to hold back until she knew what was at stake. When she could breathe again, she replied, **Then tell me. What can I do that all of your sorceries cannot?**

The hunchback's fingers moved like vehemence. Magister Avail repeated the words as fast as his friend wrote them.

Those whoreson priests will master the desert. The Great God will come against us whatever General Klamath and King Bifalt do. But he will not come *here*. Avail indicated the whole library with a gesture. **If he does, he will be within our reach. He cannot be certain that he will escape harm. He will strike from a distance.**

Our dilemma is simple, Queen. I must stand on the battlements to direct our defenses. The fury of Rummage's tapping began to look like terror. **My friend must be there to convey my orders. But from that vantage—even from the highest point of the library—I cannot watch the Great God's approach from the caravan-track. Even when his forces attempt the foothills, they will be beyond my sight. I will not see what they *do* until they reach the road below the lower plateau.**

The Great God will want that clear space for himself. Our strongest Magisters cannot cast their Decimates so far. He will be safe there.

Unable to remain silent longer, Estie put in, **I understand, Magister. But you have not explained why you require *me*.**

Magister Rummage turned his head, bared his teeth at her. Now even his glaring resembled fear.

I require your *voice*, Queen. And your *eyes*. When the Great God comes, you must be near him.

At that, Commander Crayn signaled for Estie's attention. But she could not tear her thoughts away from Avail and Rummage.

For his friend, the deaf Magister said, **I require you to watch him. There will be fighting until all of our defenders fall. If you do not watch what he does and tell me, I will not know how to respond.**

Sword Eradimnie said something to Crayn. She may have been trying to reassure him. But he ignored her. Leaving her side, he strode across the room to stand in front of his Queen. With his hands, he shouted:

—*No*, Majesty! These men are *insane*. It is too dangerous!

She understood. His gestures were simple. Nevertheless the hunchback's demand held her.

How had he become a Magister if he had no sorcery? What qualified him to command the Repository's defense? Beatrix Threnody knew every book. Avail could speak to everyone anywhere. What could Magister Rummage *do*?

Estie only knew what Oblique had told her. He was able to read books that no one else understood. Why was that obscure gift considered a necessary power?

Yet she was already half persuaded. How could she refuse when everyone she had left behind was likely to die?

She knew how to set her own fear aside. She had been practicing that form of self-discipline for a long time.

As if he were answering Crayn, Magister Avail cut in. **We are not madmen, Queen.** He had recovered his familiar vexation. **What we ask is dangerous. But the risk is not as great as you suppose. We have prepared a place of concealment. You will be well hidden.**

More sadly, he added, **We will do what we can without you if we must. But if you accept, you may prove to be the pivot on which the battle turns.**

Crayn insisted:

—*No*, Majesty.

As he studied her, however, his shoulders slumped. He knew her too well. Glowering, he returned to his place beside the Knight.

Again, Sword Eradimnie said something to him. It must have made sense. He answered with a curt nod.

Prodded by Magister Rummage, the deaf man continued.

Whether or not you will be threatened depends on you. The Great God's attention will be fixed elsewhere. *That* we can ensure, if we accomplish little else. If you do not expose yourself, you will not be seen.

Abruptly, Queen Estie had heard enough. She had other questions, but they could wait. Gathering herself, she rose from her chair.

For Crayn's sake, she said, **I will consider it. I am inclined to do what you ask. But first I must see this place of concealment.**

Magister Avail hid his face by bowing his head. For no clear reason,

Estie suspected that he was frightened. For her? Perhaps. For his friend? Certainly.

Tomorrow then, Queen. Magister Rummage will guide you.

Estie did not hear what the armored woman said. She had to wait for the mute's tapping and the deaf man's translation.

Sword Eradimnie thanks you, Queen. She and her Knights will honor their promise.

At once, the Sword turned to the door. The silence of her iron seemed unnatural as she left.

With nothing more to say, Queen Estie assured the room, **Tomorrow, Magisters.** Then she and Commander Crayn followed Sword Eradimnie out.

She did not start to doubt herself until she had walked halfway back to her own quarters. More than ever, she wanted to know the name of the hunchback's talent.

In her rooms, Queen Estie ate a small meal and tried to relax. But she was too restless to settle herself. Instead, she gnawed anxiously on the Repository's defense. She had missed her chance to find out what the Knights of Ardor had promised—or what contribution Magister Rummage might make.

To one question, however, she could obtain an answer. She asked Crayn to summon sub-Commander Waysel.

Waysel had surprised her by mastering *A Complete System* with almost insolent ease. And he had proven himself to be a good teacher. Gratefully, she had assigned him to share his skills with her guardsmen. After a while, his proficiency had relieved his earlier chagrin in her presence. He knew how to address her now.

He arrived promptly, ready for whatever his Queen required.

When Estie explained what she wanted, Waysel's manner changed. An almost boyish eagerness thrust his deference aside as he replied:

—The cannon, Majesty? I should have offered days ago. Forgive my lapse.

Queen Estie reassured him with a touch on his shoulder. Then, bundled in cloaks against the cold, she and her officers left the Repository to stand on the keep's stone porch.

That plateau was huge, broad enough to hold any number of wagons, carriages, and other conveyances without crowding. To the north, it thinned until it became a passage leading around the Repository and upward into the mountains. On the south, the stone opened for the only road from the caravan-track. Beyond the sheer front of the keep, the roadway began a long, gradual curve back northward as it descended, then wandered away among the foothills.

From the edge of the porch, Queen Estie had a clear view of the smaller plateau that served as Crayn's training-field. Jutting like a shelf among the hills, it lay at a considerable distance, yet well above the road's northward line.

Hugging her cloak around her, she looked for the place of concealment that she had been promised. The slopes were littered with boulders and outcroppings, all cloaked in snow. Any or none of them might suffice to hide her.

Along the outer rim of the training-field, Amika's siege-guns on their trucks were visible only as mounds of snow and ice: four off to Estie's right, five arrayed directly below her. Pointing, Waysel signed:

—Magister Rummage's orders, Majesty, conveyed by a man I do not know. We aimed them before we wrapped them in oilcloth. With enough warning, we can have them ready to fire in an hour. The shot and chain are there. The wadding, gunpowder, and fuses are stored in the Repository.

—Those four cover the road. We have been told to expect cavalry. The infantry are more likely to come from the west. Those five can fire at men ascending the foothills.

—But, Majesty—

The sub-Commander faltered, suddenly unsure of himself.

"But what, Waysel?" asked Estie. "I need to know."

Waysel took a deep breath.

—I wonder, Majesty, whether Magister Rummage understands siege-guns. They are heavy and powerful, but their loads do not carry far. Aimed as they are, they can pound the road into rubble. But their trucks do not allow us to lower their muzzles. Their balls and chain will pass over any foemen who gain the road. They may do serious damage lower down. They will not prevent a more immediate assault.

—And there is this, Majesty.

He scrubbed his hands over his face, trying to wipe away his doubts.

—We have been forbidden to fire on the cavalry. We must let any number of them pass unharmed until we receive some signal. Magister Rummage seemed uncertain. It may be fighting when the cavalrymen reach the gates. Or it may be a shout in our minds.

—I do not understand, Majesty. What will the Repository gain by allowing the cavalry to pass?

Controlling himself, the sub-Commander gazed out over the west; but he watched Queen Estie sidelong, waiting for her response.

She dismissed his question. She had no experience to guide her opinions. Instead, she concentrated on other concerns.

"You do not have enough men, sub-Commander." Each siege-gun needed four men. He had only twenty. "I have no use for my full escort. Commander Crayn can spare his guardsmen."

Crayn nodded, but she was not done. "Magister Rummage's tactics are beyond me. You will face a more pressing threat. You may be aware that Rile has many sorcerers, his priests. They fling globes that explode like gunpowder. From the road, they may be able to reach the guns."

The sub-Commander winced.

—What can we do, Majesty? We are not riflemen.

She gave him a smile, hoping to comfort him. "If Magister Rummage does not think of it, I will ask the librarian to send Magisters of fire. They can protect you."

Briefly, Waysel muttered to himself, or to Crayn. Then he replied:

—Thank you, Majesty. We will do what we can.

To that extent, Queen Estie was content.

The next day, the weather changed. The open skies and bitter cold were replaced by broken clouds heavy with rain, sleet, hail, and bouts of thick snow. Storms came tumbling over the Wall Mountains and boiled westward, dimming the world. Without better light, the Farsighted could discern little and be sure of less.

While the heavens blustered and spat, Magister Rummage arrived at Queen Estie's quarters.

She had been warned about the weather. Expecting wet and cold, she wore her warmest garments under her cloak. When the hunchback knocked on her door, she was as ready as she could be.

Commander Crayn opened the door promptly, but the Magister beckoned for Estie without entering. The fear that she had sensed in him earlier smoldered behind his familiar glower.

With Crayn, the Queen left her rooms to accompany the mute Magister.

He took her along an unfamiliar route. At first, he seemed to guide her into the depths where the servants lived. At the top of the last stairway, however, he turned to an unmarked door. It admitted the Queen and Crayn to a long corridor indistinguishable from many others. They passed a series of doors until Magister Rummage selected one apparently at random and pushed it open. Beyond it stretched a featureless passage full of gloom.

At its end, it became a small balcony at the head of a steep stairway.

Here there were torches in cressets. From the balcony, the stair led down to a round chamber about the size of Estie's bedroom. At first glance, it appeared to have no exit. But then she noticed a gap on one side cut at a sharp angle away from the stairs.

As Magister Rummage started downward, he took Estie's hand. For reasons of his own, he tapped:

—A choke-point.

The air was getting colder. Her breathing left gusts of vapor. Trails of moisture streaked the walls. Ice puddled on the floor.

At the foot of the stairway, she found a passage barely wide enough for three people to walk together. It was dim, lit by only three torches set far apart. It ran through the rock for several hundred paces, then ended in darkness.

With Magister Rummage holding her hand and Commander

Crayn at her back, Queen Estie walked shivering along the passage until she came to a heavy door. It was made of thick timbers bound with iron and secured by three bolts.

The hunchback paused to write:

—This is your escape, Queen. The enemy cannot know that it is here. If you find yourself threatened, you can retreat here and bolt the door. It will hold while you summon help and flee.

Without waiting for a reply, he turned to the door.

It looked too heavy to move, but when he shot the bolts and pushed, it opened easily.

At once, a blast of cold air and sleet struck her. She shielded her eyes while Magister Rummage tugged her outside.

Erratic winds brought spurts of rain, stinging bursts of sleet. Small hailstones bit at her face, her shaded eyes. For a moment, she saw nothing except the dirt under her boots. Then she looked up.

She was in a place like a niche, a little patch among standing boulders. At first, she thought that she was completely enclosed by rock. But then she saw a sliver of space that she could have slipped through on her left, the southwest. The boulder there leaned slightly away from the raw hillside.

Fighting sleet, hail, and rain like flung pebbles, she examined her covert.

Blank stone rose at her back, too high to allow her any glimpse of the Repository or its porch. In front of her, three boulders formed a crude wall. However, the stones had fallen naturally, or had been placed, to leave gaps between them, little windows. The one on the right faced the plateau where her cannon waited. Through gusts of rain mixed with spitting snow, she could make out the whole expanse of the plateau, but nothing beyond it.

A larger gap opened westward, allowing her to see the slopes of the foothills on this side. When the veils of rain and sleet parted, and the flurries of snow passed, she glimpsed the road. It seemed far away.

Firmly, Magister Rummage tapped:

—Here, Queen, you will see much that Magister Avail and I cannot. What you tell us will determine our choices.

He did not appear to feel the cold, the wet. Estie did. Shivers like shuddering ran through her in waves until he drew her back into the passage and shut the door. Until she tried to speak.

While she hugged herself for warmth, the hunchback and Crayn stood waiting, watching her. In Crayn's gaze, she saw an alarmed resignation. He knew what she would say. Magister Rummage's scowl betrayed nothing.

Finally, she managed to say, "I understand now, Magister. I will do it."

If this weather held, she would need warmer apparel.

Just for an instant, Crayn's features twisted. Then his expression became blank. "As you say, Majesty."

The mute Magister bared his teeth at her. He may have been attempting a smile. If so, the effort failed.

On their way back to the Queen's rooms, the Commander tried to reassure her.

—The enemy will need a battering-ram to get through that door, Majesty. And riflemen or Magisters on that balcony at the top of the stairs can hold the passage indefinitely.

—If I believe that you are threatened, I will drag you away. My oath of service requires it.

Estie acknowledged his gestures without attending to them. She kept shivering, and her mind was elsewhere. Somehow, looking out from the niche made the Great God's arrival seem imminent. The fighting might begin soon. Too soon. She might be called to witness the final battle before she was ready.

She would never be ready.

But she was mistaken about Rile's coming. The storms lingered. Days passed before the skies over the Wall Mountains and eastern Belleger opened, and the Farsighted could see again. Even then, however, they had nothing urgent to convey. They knew only that General

Klamath had contrived to stay ahead of the enemy despite the pummeling weather. They could not explain how Klamath's success had been achieved.

Between the spurts and blows of the weather, the General's scouts reported that Rile's cavalry now advanced beside the marching infantrymen. Hearing that, Klamath felt his heart tighten in his chest. His army was too near the enemy to escape if the cavalrymen charged.

Fortunately, the wide plain where he and his people had rested had given way to a region of rumpled hills, rocky outcroppings, and valleys like ravines. He did not know this stretch of Belleger, but he welcomed it. On terrain like this, a retreating army had one advantage over a vastly superior force: it could surprise the enemy. Grinding his teeth, General Klamath used the cover of the hills and the constriction of the valleys to do as much harm as possible.

Even at this distance, the Decimates of fire and lightning discouraged Rile's cavalry. Hidden riflemen punished the reduced throng of skirmishers whenever the small men probed closer. In the narrower ravines, the Decimate of earthquake dropped rock-slides. Yet Magister Solace and his pestilence-wielders proved to be Klamath's best defense. The priests could block bullets. They could disperse bolts of lightning and deflect whips of fire. For some reason, however, their power had less effect on the Decimate of pestilence. Magister Solace's comrades left pools of disease behind them, pools that lingered until the Great God's soldiers marched or rode through them. Then both men and beasts sickened. Many of them died.

Apparently, these tactics taught Rile a measure of caution. He protected his forces by keeping his distance.

When the weather permitted the Farsighted to watch again, the General's army was no more than a day west of the desert.

From the rise where he sat his horse, Klamath was able to see the teeth of the Wall Mountains rising along the eastern horizon. Clad in ice and snow, they caught the early sunlight and shone. By that sign, he knew that the desert was near.

In his grim, weary fashion, he was looking forward to it. He imagined that his Magisters would make the dunes deadly to the enemy.

Nevertheless he was a man who worried, and he had a new concern. Concealed by bad weather, an increasing number of priests had joined the vanguard of Rile's army. The brilliance of their globes made them easy to spot. Klamath had no idea why the enemy needed so much sorcery, but the possibilities alarmed him.

He clung to his hopes, and urged his forces, and kept moving.

When Queen Estie spoke in his mind, the shock almost knocked him out of his saddle.

Klamath. She spoke softly, but her voice was unmistakable. **My friend. I must warn you.**

He listened like a man transfixed, unaware of Captain Rowt at his side, afraid to miss a word.

You are near the desert. If you hope to oppose Rile there, you will fail. The theurgy of his priests thrusts obstacles aside. If it shifts entire dunes, they can clear a path for themselves.

Clear a path? thought Klamath. Can they *do* that?

It is a frightening prospect, Klamath. But you will have help. There will be supplies waiting at the desert's edge. And guides who know the secrets of the dunes. They will lead you to the caravan-track.

"General Klamath?" asked Captain Rowt for the third or fourth time. "What troubles you?"

Klamath demanded silence with a glare. The Queen had more to say.

I will not urge you to be brave, Klamath. You are already that. But I must test your courage.

King Bifalt has met the horde. He was beaten back.

As if she could imagine the effect of her news, Queen Estie allowed the General a moment to master himself.

Klamath did not try to think. Holding his breath, he waited.

He was repulsed by sorcery. There are priests among the horde, many of them. King Bifalt could not penetrate their power.

Since then, he has been in retreat. He may have attempted to draw the horde away from you. If so, he failed. The el-Algreb still harry the horde. His Magisters strike at the priests. They fare poorly.

Klamath heard Queen Estie sigh. **This is frustrating for me, my friend. It must be maddening for you. King Bifalt cannot tell us what is in his mind. We do not know what he will do. As matters stand, the horde will join Rile's army soon after you reach the desert.**

Pressure welled in Klamath's chest. He ached to question her, but she would not hear him. Nevertheless she was Estie of Amika, the Queen-Consort he had known for decades. She knew what some of his questions would be.

We believe that King Bifalt is unharmed. Elgart and Prince Jaspid remain with him. His Magisters and riflemen give him their best.

Again, Queen Estie paused. After a moment, she admitted, **I fear for him, Klamath. He is who he is. Only extreme actions will content him. He is distant now, but he may try to join you.**

The General agreed. King Bifalt was that kind of man. And for his own part, Klamath refused to imagine facing the last battle without his King. He had already done as much as he could. He could not do more without King Bifalt.

Protect him if you can, my friend. He heard tears in Estie's voice. **We all need him. I cannot bear to lose him.**

Then her voice was gone. It left an empty space like a sob in Klamath's mind.

The change must have shown on his face. Almost immediately, Captain Rowt asked again, "General, what is it?"

Klamath resisted an impulse to slap himself. He needed a jolt of some kind to break the Queen's grip on him.

"Hells, Rowt!" he snapped as if he were furious at his aide, not himself. "*Give* me a moment." Then he commanded, "Gather Hegels and Hellick. The leaders of each Decimate. We have new orders. I will only explain them once."

The young man flinched in surprise, but he obeyed without hesitation. Digging in his heels, he galloped away.

Rubbing his face with both hands, General Klamath began to change his plans.

Keeping Rile's forces in sight was no longer important. Neither was setting traps. And he could not afford to be slowed by King Bifalt's wagons. He had to reach the Repository's supplies and guides in time to benefit from them before the enemy caught up with him. After that, his work would be done, at least until someone like Queen Estie told him what to do next.

The next day, Queen Estie sat with Magister Oblique while the Farsighted watched. Their reports came promptly.

The Repository's commanders kept their word. When General Klamath's army reached the stretch of barren hardpan that marked the edge of the desert, loaded supply-wagons were waiting, tended by a number of servants and guides with a small herd of fresh horses and plenty of feed. By then, the General had increased his lead on the enemy. His riflemen and Magisters had time to eat a good meal and rest for an hour before the guides led them eastward among the dunes.

Magister Oblique remarked:

—Without prior knowledge, Queen, those paths are difficult to find. And the servants will follow, erasing signs of the General's passage. He will reach the caravan-track safely.

More carefully, Oblique added:

—Then Magister Avail will speak to him for Magister Rummage. He will give the General his orders.

Estie assumed that Rummage wanted Klamath to hold the track if he could and contest it if he could not. But she did not ask. The Farsighted had news of King Bifalt.

The King had sent the el-Algreb ahead of him. Following them among the twisted hills of eastern Belleger, he raced away from the horde. If he did not turn aside, he would come up against the unbroken line of the Great God's infantry, cavalry, and wagons.

Magister Oblique estimated that the horde would join the Great God's main army in a few hours.

Estie shuddered to guess at her husband's intentions. At the same time, she felt a form of relief. He was still fighting, still risking himself. He would not shy away from one battle until he found another, more dangerous struggle.

He had known what he was doing when he destroyed Belleger's Fist. She had to trust that he was sure of himself now.

TWENTY-EIGHT

FEARS

Although Queen Estie did not know it, she was right about Magister Rummage. He was afraid. He believed that he was going to die.

The prospect of an ordinary end, in battle or in his bed, did not trouble him. That fate claimed everyone. What he feared was worse. It required him to do more than choose death. It would eradicate him from the world.

He had three gifts. The first had been given to him by his parents, who loved him enough to devise the code of taps to ease the burden of his deafness and deformity. It had served him well. The second was an instinct for swift violence. On occasion, it had served the Repository well. But the third—

Ah, the third. It was an obscure ability to read texts that meant nothing to other sorcerers and scholars. For that reason, it was fatal.

He could not explain it. Those books were written in plain language. And in themselves, their secrets were only knowledge, neither a blessing nor a curse. Nevertheless he understood *why* those particular volumes resisted comprehension. They enabled a form of sorcery that made any Decimate look like a child's toy.

Under better circumstances, Magister Rummage might have enjoyed his gift. He liked power. Now it horrified him. He was always angry because he was always afraid.

His gift required the deliberate surrender of his reasons for living.

Again and again, he asked himself one question. How could a man loved by his parents, a man respected throughout the Repository, a man with one friend as dear as a brother: how could such a man kill himself?

He had no answer.

Instead, he had striven to forestall that choice. Of course, he had studied what he grimly called the *arts* of warfare. But he had concentrated more on the library's long history, reading about those occasions across the millennia when it had been attacked and forced to flee. Although those assaults had failed, each of them had exposed more of the Repository's powers. And that exposure had invited subsequent attacks, efforts predicated on what the previous failures had revealed.

The Great God must have studied those histories as well, or other versions of them. He would seek to know how or why earlier tyrants had failed. To understand their mistakes so that he would not repeat them. He would take a new approach.

Some of the differences were already apparent. He had brought a larger army. He had far more sorcerers. He had expended more effort on spies to learn the weaknesses of the people who stood in his way. But his most threatening innovation was his use of the eighth Decimate. Through his instruments, and by his own power, he had perfected and extended the sorcery of coercion. His control over the horde demonstrated his strength. No tyrant before him could have done so much.

For himself, Magister Rummage did not fear the Great God's Decimate. He did not fear it for the librarian and his other comrades. They had been forewarned. But it had other uses. And it might not be the Great God's only innovation.

What then? To defend the Last Repository, Magister Rummage had nothing more than an inexperienced assortment of Decimate-wielders, the Knights of Ardor, and King Bifalt's failing forces.

Then? Ah, then. Through his teeth, Rummage snarled silent curses.

Wrestling with his dread, he wandered among the restricted books shelved on the upper rounds of the library. He took down books that he had read before, scanned them to confirm their contents, then put them back. The dangerous texts were scattered here and there on the highest levels, apparently at random to disguise their presence. To reach them, Rummage stormed up and down the stairs between the rounds like a man who knew what he wanted but could not find it. In truth, however, he was simply passing time. Waiting. Lost.

And listening.

Magister Avail was with the librarian and the Farsighted. Magister Oblique was there to translate for him. Avail repeated what he learned to everyone who needed to hear it. The mute sorcerer listened closely.

Several days ago, General Klamath's forces had paused at the edge of the desert for an hour of food and rest. Then they had followed the Repository's guides among the dunes. By that time, the horde had joined the Great God's army. King Bifalt with his riflemen and the el-Algreb had confronted the continuing stream of infantry and cavalry, wagons and priests.

The Great God drove his forces hard. Without the eighth Decimate and the hunger of the horde, his host could not have sustained the pace he set. Clearly, he did not care how many men he worked to death. As he advanced, soldiers failed and fell. Whether or not they still lived, the horde tore them apart.

Perhaps for that reason, the infantry kept marching.

In contrast, General Klamath and his men had recovered some of their strength. After two days of steady plodding, they had reached the caravan-track. This time, they did not pause. The enemy's vanguard was not far behind them. The priests had cleared their god's way with frightening ease. Already, the enemy was less than a day from the track.

Instructed by Magister Avail, General Klamath and his riflemen followed their guides higher into the desert. The guides led them toward terrain that they might be able to defend effectively: the foothills above the road.

Now, while Magister Rummage perused texts that meant nothing to him, he heard that the Great God's host had gained the caravan-track.

At once, the god sent his cavalrymen north along the track, hundreds of them, then thousands, racing at the full stretch of their beasts toward the road leading up to the Repository.

They had only a few priests with them.

That startled Rummage. He had assumed that the cavalry would come to take and hold the road. But without adequate support from the priests, the cavalrymen would be vulnerable to sub-Commander Waysel's cannon.

Why would the Great God waste them?

Magister Rummage had to think. He was missing something.

Meanwhile, the god's infantry crossed the track and continued upward. Ahead of them, sorcery parted the sands. The men marched as if they were beating their way over open ground.

At that pace, they might gain the road below the lower plateau in two days. The cavalry had much farther to go, but the speed of those beasts was astonishing. Those men might arrive well ahead of the infantry.

From the foothills above the road, General Klamath's riflemen would oppose the infantry. If King Bifalt struck at the enemy's rear with the el-Algreb, he might do significant damage.

But still—

Rummage could not procrastinate any longer. This war had been coming for a long time. Now it was almost here. He had decisions to make.

As irate as a whirlwind, he rushed to the round where the book he dreaded was shelved. Despite his fear and fury, he lifted down the book gently, cradled it like a loved infant in his hands for a moment. Then he tucked it safely inside his robe and swept away to rejoin Magister Avail and the librarian.

He needed his friend's voice and Magister Threnody's authority to help him swallow his dread.

Reentering the desert at the rear of his army, Klamath lost sight of the caravan-track. The twisting of the secret paths blocked his horizons. He could not measure Rile's progress—or his own. He had no idea how long this stage of his unforgiving trek would last.

When the sands under his mount's hooves finally faded into bare dirt, he found himself facing a steeper ascent among the boulders and outcroppings of the lowest foothills. There, however, his guides took him along trails intended for horses. Soon he could look back out over the desert that had nearly killed Prince Bifalt, Elgart, and him twenty years ago. From his vantage, it seemed to stretch forever into the west.

After so much time among the dunes, the air seemed almost unnaturally clear. Behind him, the enemy's position was unmistakable. It was fixed by plumes of sand and dust cast upward with sorcery, or by immense, unstable mounds shifting in response. Rile's forces were coming closer, but they were still behind the General. That gap would increase as the infantrymen scrambled among the contorted slopes of the foothills.

When the Great God caught up with Klamath, the last battle would begin in earnest.

The General wished that he could ascend the winding trail faster. Fortunately, he was not forced to wish for long. Sooner than he expected, he arrived on the road.

He had been here once before, but he did not remember it. He had traveled in a drugged sleep. And when he had left the Repository, he had been given a map that took him almost directly to western Belleger. The road was new to him.

Nevertheless he knew approximately where he was. To his left, the road followed the contours of the foothills northward, descending slowly toward its junction with the caravan-track. To his right, it ran well past the Repository before beginning its long curve back up to the keep's vast porch.

Studying the hills, he saw a rim of rock a considerable distance above him, an outcropping of some kind. It jutted out from the slopes in a way that implied a level space behind it. And high above it rose the Repository itself, thrusting its rounds of books and papers skyward. The white stone held the sunlight like a promise. Set against the cloak of snow draped over the Wall Mountains, that white threatened to dazzle him.

After uncounted leagues, he was near his goal at last: the cause and prize of the Great God's war.

General Klamath would have preferred to send his army south toward the Repository by the easiest route. But Magister Avail had been speaking in his mind, and he knew his duty. Leaving Prince Jaspid and Elgart to watch over the riflemen and Magisters, he called for First Captain Hegels, sub-Commander Hellick, and Captain Rowt.

He had orders to give and expected protests. For privacy, so that they could express themselves without being overheard, he led them a short distance away. There they dismounted. Standing stiffly on legs that had forgotten everything except riding, they faced each other.

None of them looked as worn down as Klamath felt. Hegels kept everything hidden behind his humorless mien. Hellick had not been part of the General's desperate flight ahead of Rile's cavalry. And Rowt was young.

"Here it is, sirs." The General's voice was hoarse with weariness. "We have new orders." He tapped his forehead. His officers knew what that meant. "We are told to make our stand there." He gestured up at the foothills. "We must do what we can to prevent the enemy from climbing higher."

His men turned to study the slopes. In many ways, that terrain was ideal for riflemen opposing a superior force. The ground was a chaotic litter of boulders and scree, stony soil, narrow gullies like gulches, dead or wintering brush clinging to patches of dirt. More men than Klamath had could have hidden all over those hillsides and fought without exposing themselves.

Captain Rowt was the first to ask a question. "What of our Magisters, sir? Those hills suit us. They will not suit them."

Klamath sighed. "I will send them along the road to the Repository. They will return, or they will not, as they choose. For the present, they can rest in better comfort. With us or without us, they will defend the Repository."

He missed Crawl and Brighten. He had learned to trust them, as he had Trench and—more surprisingly—Solace. But he felt sure that King Bifalt's need for fire and lightning was extreme.

Sub-Commander Hellick spent a moment longer scanning the hills. Then he gave a growl of approval. "Good, sir. Excellent. There we can hold off the infantry—and perhaps the cavalry as well—while our bullets last. Then we can withdraw under cover."

Klamath sighed. Hellick's view of the situation was too simple.

"Defend the Repository," muttered the First Captain. His tone was thick with scorn.

Klamath turned his attention to Hegels. "Say it, First Captain. Tell us what is in your mind."

Hegels glanced back up at the hillsides, then faced Klamath again. "Hellick is right," he sneered. "There we can oppose the Great God's infantry, and perhaps his cavalry. *Until*"—he snapped the word—"shining globes rain down on us. Then we will perish."

Passions that the First Captain had kept to himself broke through his restraint. "If *that*"—he pointed at the foothills—"is the Repository's idea of defense, it is nothing. Those Magisters intend to sacrifice us.

"What have they ever done to earn our blood? I say it is enough. We have crossed the whole of Belleger and the desert, exhausting our-selves, fighting and dying, for the Repository's sake—and now they order us to give more? We have done enough."

In his heart, Klamath agreed. The war had been like this from the start. Its cost was too high, and its necessity was an abstraction. The lives of his men could not be measured in books.

But the war would not end here. It would take everyone eventually.

He could have stopped Hegels then. He did not. The man had contained himself too long. If he did not release what he felt, it might break him.

Klamath rubbed his face, calmed himself. Carefully, he asked, "What do you suggest, First Captain?"

Without hesitation, Hegels declared, "We are wasted here. If we must give our lives, we should do so in a better cause."

Hellick stared at his fellow Amikan. Rowt stood in shock. General Klamath ignored them.

"Then name it, sir."

Hegels had his answer ready. "*Amika.* It has not been threatened yet. It will be." He gathered force as he spoke. "It is poorly defended. It needs us. We should ride to the caravan bridge and take the Queen's road south. Instead of dying for what we cannot save, we should fight for what remains. The future of Queen Estie's realm."

"She will not thank us for abandoning her people."

Klamath could have wept then. He knew the First Captain's pain. In his own way, he shared it. He had watched the Open Hand die. But what Hegels wanted was impossible.

Softly, the General said, "Forgive me, sir. I do not mean to shame you. But I know more than I have told you." He had heard it from Magister Avail. "Rile's infantry will come here. His cavalry has gone to claim *this* road. It will be his before we can reach the caravan-track and the last bridge.

"We cannot help Amika." Or ourselves.

Aching, he watched Hegels' certainty crumble. Behind its weather-beaten surface, the First Captain's face lost blood. His posture sagged as his passion drained away.

Rowt and Hellick said nothing. What could anyone say?

After a moment, Hegels turned away. As he went to his horse, he stumbled. But he was too weak to reach the saddle. Leading his mount by the reins, he walked unsteadily back to the men he was supposed to command.

"He will rally, sir." Hellick did not sound sure.

Klamath hoped so. When his riflemen had taken their positions scattered over the foothills, he could not be everywhere. He needed Hegels.

Later, Klamath watched the First Captain gather the Magisters for their ride to the Repository. Hegels had resumed his duties despite his chagrin. That gave the General a measure of reassurance.

Then Captain Rowt called for his attention. The young officer was peering up at the foothills as if he had caught a glimpse of movement.

At first, Klamath saw nothing. His eyes were no longer young. "Captain?" he inquired.

Studying the slope, Rowt murmured, "General, sir. I thought I saw a man. Up on that rim." He drew a sudden breath, a quick gasp of air. "*Several* men." A beat later, he added, "They may be Amikan."

They stood at the lip of the outcropping. Klamath could see them now. They appeared to be waving. And cheering?

Beyond question, they were Amikan. And soldiers. Sunlight made exclamations of their orange headbands. They must have come with Queen Estie.

Klamath turned away so that Rowt would not see his tears.

He was still wrestling with his unruly heart when the Queen spoke to him again.

Forgive another intrusion, Klamath, she said. **I lack the means to ask your permission.**

She had it whether she knew it or not.

The Magisters here assure me that you are on the road below the Repository. You have had a terrible journey. You and your men must have many needs. Prepare a list and send it to me. They will be met.

After a moment, she added, **In what comes, your mounts will be a hindrance. Servants will come for them. The Repository will keep them safe.**

She paused once more, apparently collecting her own thoughts. When she resumed, her voice had a sharper edge.

We are not sure when the enemy will arrive, but it will be soon. I must ask you to prepare now. You know what to do. Ensure that your men are well hidden. The enemy must not see you.

And Klamath? Heed me in this. When the cavalry comes, let it pass. Do not strike until the cannon fire. That will be your signal.

Fight while you have bullets. Then retreat. There is a plateau above you. You can gather there.

The Queen seemed to sigh. **I hold your life in my heart, Klamath. I will help you as much as I can.**

For a moment after she was done, fresh tears blurred Klamath's vision. They stung his cheeks in the cold air. How had King Bifalt ever refused her love?

As she had promised, she had brought cannon to the Last Repository. The coming battle might not be as fatal as General Klamath feared.

When he had mastered himself, he gave Hegels the task of composing the list Queen Estie wanted and dispatching it to her. He spent an hour resting to conserve his strength. Then he walked for a while among his riflemen, reassuring them—or hoping that they would reassure him. The wagons loaded with the supplies he had been promised lifted his spirits.

As the sun began its slow slide toward evening, he summoned all of his officers and their under-captains to explain Queen Estie's orders. She had not said so, but he expected Rile's infantry to come uphill in a straight line toward the Repository. He divided his men into two companies, one for each side of that line. The force that would position itself on the south, he gave to First Captain Hegels. He took the north side for himself.

Fretting, he watched the riflemen scramble up into the foothills, searching for suitable coverts. While they settled themselves, he walked up and down a stretch of the road, convincing himself that they were well hidden. Finally, he went to find his own place.

He chose a mound of boulders and smaller stones high enough to hide him. There he was well below the rim of rock where he had seen Amikan soldiers. When the sun rose again behind the Wall, the shadow of the keep's tall white tower would cover him. But first he would have to endure a cold, lonely night.

Since her visit to the cannon with sub-Commander Waysel, Queen Estie had returned every morning. Rising well before dawn, she had walked out onto the Repository's porch. There she had studied the west while the sun rose.

She was not Farsighted. Even in full daylight, she could not see past the bulges and hollows of the foothills. Still, she kept her vigil. When the sun rose high enough, she was able to watch plumes of sand rise into the air like sun-gilt feathers, heaved aside by the illimitable power of Rile's priests. They came closer every day. And every day, they seemed closer than they should have been.

They frightened her. Nevertheless she stood outside for an hour every dawn, scanning the west with Crayn as silent and grim as rock at her side. She did not need to tell him that she was hoping for some sign of her husband.

Day after day, she watched. But she did not linger. She would be told if the Farsighted had anything to report. Shivering in the cold, she went back inside.

During that time, the Repository learned that the Great God's supply-train was gaining on his infantry. Now beasts like those the cavalry rode hauled the wagons. The need for food and water among Rile's forces must have become acute. What other explanation could there be?

Queen Estie supposed that this was good news. It implied that the Great God's strength did not transcend the ordinary needs of his men. But she was not comforted.

Her routine did not change until she learned that General Klamath's army had reached the road below the cannon. After that, she was too busy for vigils—and too anxious. A new sense of urgency compelled her.

She spoke to Klamath willingly enough, although the experience left her feeling lost. Without the sight of his face and the sound of his voice, she could not gauge his reaction. It was like addressing a blank wall.

Less awkwardly, she welcomed the General's Magisters to the Repository. More of them had survived than she expected. They were weary and drooping, stained with every kind of grime and fouler fluids. Some of them wore wounds inadequately tended. But they bowed to her uncertainly. The Amikans attempted formal homage, yet they also seemed uncertain. At first, she suspected that her presence discomfited them. They did not know how to regard Amika's Queen as a deaf sorceress. Studying them, however, she realized that they were not troubled by her. Their clenched faces and flinching eyes betrayed a strange reluctance. For some reason that they could not explain to a deaf woman, they did not want to accept the comforts and care of the Repository.

Baffled, Queen Estie left them no choice. Hanging their heads and dragging their feet, they followed the keep's servants.

The arrival of a rifleman bearing General Klamath's list of needs was easier to bear. At another time, the tale of his army's privations might have shaken her. Under the circumstances, she was simply glad to have it. She knew what to do with it.

With Commander Crayn always at her side, she took the list to the librarian.

Beatrix Threnody greeted her with a distracted, half-frightened air. She appeared to have shrunk in recent days, worn down by her sudden inheritance of knowledge and authority. Estie might not have picked her out of a crowd of Magisters to lead the Repository. But her self-doubt seemed to increase her sympathy for more ordinary needs; or perhaps they did not threaten her. She accepted General Klamath's list and promised to act on it at once.

Returning to her quarters, Estie planned to rest. The war was almost here. When it arrived, her task would require all of her stamina and concentration. But then, finally, Fifth Daughter came to her with news that she was anxious to hear.

Despite her downcast gaze and humble demeanor, the monk looked excited. She betrayed a shy smile. Through Crayn, she told Estie:

—Third Father is recovering, Queen. The shamans have done well. He still needs help to stand, but he can sit up and feed himself.

Beaming her relief, Queen Estie said, "*Thank* you." At once, she asked, "May I see him?"

The young monk took a breath.

—I believe so. It is not my place to say, Queen, but I think that he will welcome a visitor.

If Fifth Daughter had not been a monk, Estie might have hugged her. Instead, the Queen put her hand on Crayn's shoulder: a brief assurance that she wanted his company.

"Then, please. Lead us."

Covering her mouth to hide another smile, Fifth Daughter showed Queen Estie and Commander Crayn the way.

The monks of the Cult of the Many occupied rooms among the keep's foundations where the servants lived, but they had several corridors to themselves. Third Father's quarters were at the end of a long hall marked by dozens of doors. Thinking of his condition, poisoned by Tak Biondi's knife, Estie felt dismay that he had to walk so far to go anywhere. For a man of his years, every destination was a pilgrimage.

As Fifth Daughter reached the last door and knocked, Estie bit her lip against the chagrin of her memories. That the old monk had been bedridden for days was her doing.

If her guide was invited in, Estie did not hear it. Fifth Daughter opened the door a little, peered inside. Whatever she saw reassured her. Beckoning for the Queen and Crayn, she entered.

From the doorway, Estie saw a chamber only slightly larger than a cell in her father's dungeon. It was certainly as austere as a cell. Apart from the old man sitting up in his bed, the only sign that the room had an occupant was a clean cassock and belt-rope hanging from a hook on one wall. The single stool looked lonely, an unwanted luxury. Glancing around in the light of the lamp over the bed, Estie was relieved to see another door at the back of the cell. It suggested that Third Father's severity did not require him to live without a bathing room.

Contrary to his usual practice, the old monk raised his eyes to Estie's face. As if he had forgotten her deafness, he spoke.

Quickly, Crayn gestured:

—He says, You have come, Queen. That is good. Will you enter? Will you sit?

Shaking off a flustered moment, Estie took the stool, moved it to the side of the bed, and seated herself. It was low: she had to look up to meet his gaze. That suited her. He would not be able to avoid her eyes without turning away. She did not want him to hide himself from her—and she did not mean to hide from him.

Fifth Daughter stood behind the Queen. Commander Crayn remained in the doorway.

The lamp above and behind the old man left shadows on his face. His cheeks looked hollowed out by age and illness. His eyes seemed sunken in their sockets. Yet he did not evade her concern. Taking her hand, he wrote:

—You did not come seeking my counsel, Queen. That, also, is good. I have none. You have gone beyond me.

She had no idea what he saw in her. Carefully, she replied, "I cannot say how deeply I value your life, Father. I came because I want to see you." She paused to swallow. "And because I need to express my regret."

He managed a frail shrug.

—You have no fault to regret. I tried to stop Tak Biondi. The cost is mine to bear.

Shaking her head, Estie replied, "Not that, Father. Of course, I am sorry that you were hurt. But what I regret is—" Even now, she found the truth difficult to confess. "I regret my ignorance. Magister Avail offered to teach me. I refused.

"I was afraid, Father. I feared the harm that I had already done." She had seen Apprentice Travail's ears bleeding. "I feared that the King—" No. She had to face this. "That my husband misunderstood my cry. And my deafness, Father. I took it as a kind of death. I was not brave enough to learn more.

"Your wound is the result. And Tak Biondi's death. My ignorance killed him, Father. He might have told us more of Rile's plans. That loss is my doing.

"I regret my cowardice, Father."

Still, the old monk held her gaze. He remained upright until she was done. Then, trembling under his blankets, he sank back onto his pillows. His fingers tapped like a whisper.

—Truth, Queen. I thank you. The Cult of the Many values it.

He closed his eyes. Estie worried that she had exhausted him. But he had more to say.

—You astonish me. Weak as I am, you astonish me. Now I find that I do have counsel for you. If you will hear it?

Estie did not hesitate. "Of course, Father. Anything."

His chest lifted, let out a sigh.

—Speak more truth. To your husband, perhaps? If you choose. Or to these Magisters. Some of them have forgotten that the ungifted deserve respect as much as they do.

More? thought Estie. She bowed her head to spare herself the sight of the old monk's ravaged features. Did she need to confess more? Even to Bifalt?

Perhaps she could.

TWENTY-NINE

THE GREAT GOD'S CAVALRY

Late that night, General Klamath located Hellick among his widely scattered riflemen. Together, he and the sub-Commander made their way up the knuckled slope of the foothills.

It was not an easy climb. With only starlight and the moon's silver to show the way, they had to feel their way. Jagged boulders reared against them like threats. Loose dirt slipped under their feet, their reaching hands. They went carefully until they reached the rim of the outcropping where they had seen Amikan soldiers.

They found sub-Commander Waysel waiting with a shaded lantern in one hand. A handful of guardsmen stood around the plateau, keeping watch.

Klamath had never met the man. Hellick knew him well.

When they had been introduced, Waysel said quietly, "I am honored to meet you, General." In the dim glow of his lantern, his round face looked hollow. "I know a little of what you have endured. I expected you to bring your men here. They could rest better, and you could watch our cannon at work."

"We have other orders, sir." Klamath did not know how much time he had. He might need to be back in his covert soon. "Show us the cannon. Tell us what you hope to accomplish."

Waysel shrugged. "As you say, General."

Leading the way, he took Klamath to the four north-facing siege-guns. "When we are told to fire, these will shatter the road. We may need to adjust their aim a little, but they will succeed." Then he went to the five pointing down at the foothills. "With these, we can punish the Great God's men as they climb. Their balls and chain will pass over the road." He sounded embarrassed. "We cannot aim them lower. Their trucks will not permit it. But we will do what we can."

Klamath said nothing. He would have preferred more siege-guns. Nine would have to suffice.

For a moment, the three men stood in silence, gazing out over the benighted west. In the distance, the glow of sorcerous globes marked the enemy's location. By their sheer numbers, they made a stark black horizon of the foothills. But they were moving. Apparently, the priests had begun their ascent some time ago.

Their shining held a hint of gold, a vague tinge that marred or enhanced the power of the priests. Klamath thought that he knew what it was.

Too tense to watch for long, he turned to Waysel.

"We were told to hold fire, sir, until we hear a signal. I assume that your cannon will give it. What are your orders?"

Waysel seemed flustered. "We were told, General— That is, sir—" With an effort, he steadied himself. "Magister Rummage commands the defense here. He instructed us to hold fire until hundreds of cavalrymen have passed below us.

"He did not explain himself. Perhaps we will understand when the enemy comes."

General Klamath nodded. "Thank you, sir. We expect Rile's infantry to come straight uphill. But they will arrive after the cavalry. For the present, obey Magister Rummage. My riflemen and I will do the same.

"If you see Queen Estie, give her my thanks."

Without another word, he turned away, taking Hellick with him.

When they were gone, sub-Commander Waysel spent a little while chewing over his uncertainties. Then he sent one of his guardsmen to the Repository to summon the rest of his men and Commander Crayn's. He needed them to prepare and work the guns.

Fearing the priests, he prayed that either his Queen or the librarian would not neglect to give him Magisters of fire.

An hour before dawn, Queen Estie and Commander Crayn reached her post.

Crayn had brought his weapons. In addition, he carried a large pack of provisions and bedding. Estie hoped that she would have opportunities for rest and relief, but she suspected that she might need to eat and sleep in the passage.

Leaving his pack in the hall and the heavy door open, Crayn followed her out into the open shelter of her covert.

The air felt frigid, poised for disastrous changes. It stung Estie's cheeks, made her vision blur. Moments passed before she could pick out a few stars directly overhead. They seemed lonely against the fading black of the sky.

With signs and gestures, Crayn said:

—I fear a storm, Majesty.

She winced. What could the defenders do then? Bad weather might not hamper the priests. Even if it did, their Shields would protect them from rifle-fire. And if it did not, they could batter the hillsides with globes until all the riflemen were dead.

From the gap between boulders on her right, she watched Waysel's command preparing the cannon. He had enough guardsmen, all of his and most of Crayn's. They would be ready to fire soon.

Down the slope below her, the road was invisible. Night and the shadows of the Wall covered it. Klamath and his men were well concealed. Nothing in the darkness suggested movement.

But the globes of the priests made their presence vivid. They were still below the road. Their sorcery cast white light at the deep heavens; etched the outlines of the lower foothills like acid. Gods, they were many! And theirs was not the only power. Through their shining ran delicate tendrils of gold, as vague as mist, and as complex as a spider's web.

The Great God was coming closer.

Would a storm slow him? Estie did not think so.

More to the south, night still held the hills. There was nothing to see. There might be nothing until the sun rose. Rile's cavalry would arrive from the north.

The cold drew shivers from the marrow of Estie's bones. The night felt as expectant as an indrawn breath. The pause before the pounce.

Waysel had cannon for both the cavalry and the infantry. But he did not have enough. And the Magisters he needed had not come. Despite Estie's urgent demands— Without them, the priests might sweep the guns aside like toys. They might shatter the whole plateau.

Crayn gestured:

—Dawn is near, Majesty.

The hush over the hills demanded quiet. Even the men at the cannon worked in silence. Waysel's few commands were muted.

—There is sunlight on the mountaintops.

Only the highest peaks could be seen from the Queen's vantage, but their ice and snow caught the sun like premonitions.

The skies were still clear.

She hugged her cloak around her and waited.

As the darkness faded to dusk, Magister Avail addressed her. She heard something shrill in his voice, an edge of alarm.

Queen, he said, **the Farsighted have enough light. The Great God's supply-train has reached the edge of the desert. His servants unload the first wagons. The horde follows the priests upward. The infantrymen lag behind.**

The cavalry will come soon.

Wrestling with herself, Estie asked, **What of King Bifalt? Or the el-Algreb? What do the Farsighted see?**

Nothing, snapped Avail. Then he made an effort to calm himself. **The Farsighted have other concerns. What does the Great God need from his wagons? What does he think that the horde can accomplish against cannon? Can his priests stop cannonballs? The Farsighted have no answers.**

Estie swallowed a lump of dread. No, she commanded herself. Stop. Let Bifalt go. She had to trust that he had not been lost.

With an effort, she turned her attention to the cannon.

The siege-guns were hers, forged in Amika. Fired downhill, their shots would carry over the road. They might reach farther than Magister Rummage expected. If the priests hurried, Waysel's barrage might miss them entirely. If the hunchback waited too long, even the horde might escape.

Why did he intend to let the cavalry pass unharmed?

Why had he refused to give Waysel Magisters?

Her Commander knew no more than she did. Nevertheless she breathed, "Reassure me, Crayn. What does Rummage hope to accomplish?"

Crayn did not reply directly. Cocking his head, he signed:

—Wait, Majesty.

A knot in her guts coiled tighter. "Why?" She tried to imagine what had caught his notice, but she felt only the slow sigh of air past the boulders, the flow of winter. "What is it?"

He hesitated.

—Hooves.

Then he shook his head.

—Now it is gone. Some trick of the hills must have brought it for a moment.

She bit her lip. She was beginning to understand the impulse that made Bifalt chew the inside of his cheek until he drew blood.

Below her, the enemy rose toward the road. The deeper twilight of the Repository's shadow still shrouded the priests, but their globes lit their way, bobbing and threshing as they hastened. They aimed to join the rush of the cavalry. Or they would gather and pause at the edge of the road, ready to surge upward when the cavalry passed.

Gods! she thought. Where are Waysel's Magisters?

Faint with distance came the low tremor of massive hooves striking smooth stone. She felt it.

Crayn snapped upright, cupped his ear to the gap.

The trembling sensation vanished. Then it came again more strongly. He reported:

—They are near, Majesty. We will see them when they round the next turn.

Reading her mind, he stepped aside, let her stand where she could watch what came.

She held her breath to concentrate. Waysel's men were poised around their cannon, crouching to conceal themselves from below. Prone at the shelf's rim, Waysel watched the road.

The priests were still climbing, running with the horde at their backs.

There. North of the plateau, Rile's cavalry appeared past a bulge in the hillside.

She had been warned, but still the sight stung her. She had never seen such beasts. They were larger than the zhecki of the Nuuri, larger even than the illirim Set Ungabwey had used. They made their armed riders look like dolls. Their tusks gleamed through the froth on their muzzles. They had been galloping since they had reached the caravan-track, yet they came at a furious pace. The impact of their hooves made Estie's covert quiver.

They were some distance north of the cannon, half a league or more; but at that speed, they would be within range in moments.

Waysel had been forbidden to fire. Not until he received a signal from the Repository.

That was madness. The line of cavalry stretched out of sight. It seemed to stretch to the limits of the world. Those beasts had to be stopped *now*. Only the siege-guns could do it.

Waysel's guardsmen did not move.

Below the lip of the road, the white blare of sorcery scrambled higher.

The cavalrymen reached the perfect place to be hit. Their leaders hammered onward. More beasts and their riders rushed into sight, hundreds of them, thousands. For all Estie knew, the Great God had brought every able man he possessed to fight this war.

The cavalry hurtled three abreast below her. At that pace, the riders would not need long to reach the porch of the keep. Behind them, more mounted beasts kept coming.

Crayn tugged her arm to get her attention. He echoed her thoughts.

—This is all madness, Majesty. Rile and Magister Rummage are insane, both of them. What can Rile gain? From the battlements, Magisters will rain down Decimates until every man and beast is dead. But the Magisters also gain nothing. While they exhaust their sorcery, they cannot strike elsewhere. Whatever happens, the way will be open for the rest of Rile's army.

Apparently, Magister Rummage relied on General Klamath. If so, he was mistaken. The horde alone was enough to overwhelm Klamath's men. The Shields of the priests stopped bullets—and the riflemen did not have endless ammunition.

Estie did not know what to do.

She should have argued with Magister Rummage. Demanded an explanation. Even now, she could shout at him. But she was too late. He did not have time to change his mind.

Her alternative was to countermand him. Tell Waysel to fire *now* with all his guns. Why else had she been placed where she could watch what was happening?

But she did not know enough. She did not even know what form of power Rummage wielded. If she overruled him, his plans might fail, plans that would have succeeded otherwise. He had spent decades getting ready. How likely was it that she saw the danger more clearly than he did?

Below her, the first priests neared the road. Through the glare of their globes, she saw their theurgy shimmering. It formed a vague smear across her vision, an insidious distortion that made her eyes hurt. Nevertheless it did not block sight.

Behind the priests, the starving mass of the horde rose like rabid animals.

She bit her lip until the pain became too sharp to endure. Then she steadied herself with her hands. Gripping Crayn's forearm with one, bracing the other on a boulder, she set her face to the downhill gap and watched the swift torrent of the cavalry, the clambering haste of the priests and the fanged men.

The thunder of hooves made no sound that she could hear, but she felt it like the approach of an earthquake. Here and there among the beasts rode priests, but they were few. Apparently, the cavalrymen did not require coercion. They served Rile willingly.

When Crayn jerked her arm, she gave a startled gasp. He was pointing back up at the Repository.

—The gates, Majesty! They have opened the gates.

There was nothing to see. The shape of the upper slopes hid the whole Repository.

"Tell me, Crayn!" she panted. "*Tell* me."

Concentrating, he answered:

—I do not understand. I heard the gates. Now I hear hooves. *Other* hooves. Iron-shod. Their clang cuts through the thunder.

Then he exclaimed:

—No horse is that heavy.

The gates had been opened? How would that help the Repository?

From his post on the balcony outside the librarian's workroom, Magister Rummage studied the racing cavalry.

From the outer wall of the balcony with its crenellations and its sheltered vantage points, he could see the whole extent of the road. With approval, he noted the discipline of sub-Commander Waysel and General Klamath as they waited for his signal. More bitterly, he marked the progress of the priests leading the horde.

They were coming faster than he had anticipated. More and more of the fanged strangers crowded behind the priests. The others spread out on both sides, panting and ravenous.

Still, they were not an immediate threat. Arriving when they did, they would be forced to pause while the cavalry passed. Until their way was clear, there was little that they could do except expend their globes on an apparently empty hillside. In any event, they were General Klamath's problem. Magister Rummage faced a more pressing danger.

Despite his fury and desperation, he held Magister Avail's hand loosely. He had the strength to break his friend's fingers, but he had taught himself not to do so.

He was useless without Avail's voice.

As the leading cavalrymen rounded the curve to his left and pounded upward, Rummage told his friend to give the first signal. The enemy was in position. The road there ran along the rim of a dangerous drop-off on one side and the steep rise of the foothills on the other. The cavalry had nowhere to go except up the road.

At Magister Avail's command, sudden force slammed open the Repository's gates. At once, the Knights of Ardor clattered out of the mustering hall onto the upper plateau.

This was their choice, not the hunchback's. They were only five. By now, hundreds of cavalrymen were on the final ascent. But the Knights were warriors by trade, and they valued the Last Repository. They had insisted on their right to fight for it.

Magister Rummage had to admit that they were needed. The gates were made of heavy timbers and bound with iron, but they were not granite. They had to be defended somehow—and Rile had too many priests. Rummage could not afford to exhaust his Magisters against cavalrymen.

Led by Sword Eradimnie, they emerged on their black steeds, heavy destriers bred for battle, and more powerful than the horses Magister Rummage knew. They had to be to carry the weight of all that bright iron. The Knights were armored head to foot, from helms and visors to stirrups. They carried swords keen enough to cut a man in half. And they bore lances, long shafts of ironwood with blunted tips to punch rather than pierce.

They came out, not into sunlight, but into the dense gloom of the Repository's shadow. Nevertheless their armor seemed to shine with its own radiance as if they were incarnations of strength. Their air of pride as they gathered showed an absolute readiness, the assurance of long training and many victories.

With Sword Eradimnie at their point, they formed a tight wedge. Cantering at first, then stretching into a full gallop, they descended the gradual slope to meet the Great God's cavalry. The hooves of their mounts and the flexing of their armor made a sound like swords beating on shields.

The shock as they met the cavalry was appalling. For Magister Rummage, it was also wonderful. The beasts of the enemy were larger, heavier, presumably stronger. They could do cruel harm with their tusks. But they had not been trained like the destriers. Sword Eradimnie drove among them like iron lightning, parting them on both sides. And on both sides, her comrades struck. In an instant, the front of the cavalry became chaos.

Beasts were forced, screaming, over the rim of the road. They pitched their riders headlong down the rock-clenched slope. On the other side, they tried to scramble upward; but their footing betrayed them, and they toppled. Cavalrymen fell and were trampled by squalling beasts and battle-bred steeds.

Following her spear, Sword Eradimnie forced her way down the throat of the cavalry. Her comrades thrust aside or cut down every beast and rider that avoided her. Still, the sheer numbers of her foes slowed her. In turn, they slowed the other Knights.

An unlucky hit broke Eradimnie's lance. It burst into splinters in her hand. Without pausing, she snatched out her longsword. Nevertheless the loss of her lance slowed her more. Without it, she had to hack at her foes one by one. Despite her speed and strength, she could not continue her charge.

Another lance snapped. Drawing their blades, the Knights followed at their leader's back.

A beast gored the belly of a destrier. Squealing, the horse stumbled away, tossed its rider. The Knight went over the drop. Bouncing from boulder to boulder, his armor rang like a load of anvils.

Beasts and cavalrymen fell with him, dragged off the road by his plunge. Their bodies made a mass of blood and iron, tusks and blades.

An icy gust kicked at Magister Rummage's face, colder than the air around him. He tasted moisture, a promise of snow. Strong sunlight still poured past the high peaks, but a storm was coming. He felt it in his bones.

"A storm?" croaked Magister Avail. *"Now?"*

Cursing mutely, the hunchback turned away from the Knights and cavalrymen. He had seen enough. With a tap on Avail's hand, he sent his second signal.

From the height of the balcony, neither sorcerer heard Waysel shouting. His men did. In a rush, they sprang to their cannon.

The guns had been primed, loaded. Their fuses needed no more than three heartbeats to burn. Then their booming echoed off the face of the keep. Their harsh reports crashed against the mountainsides.

Four siege-guns covered the road where Rile's cavalry still sped from the north. Half of them had been loaded with chain. The thick iron links cut through riders and beasts like scythes. Blood splashed in all directions, a thick gush that masked the carnage. Dozens of men and mounts were swept away. Bits of limbs and entrails sprayed everywhere.

The other guns fired cannonballs. They did less damage to the enemy, but they tore chunks out of the road. After one volley, its surface was broken, littered with treacherous holes and gouges.

The priests among the cavalry must have been screaming, but they could not halt the momentum of the charge in an instant. For the soldiers and beasts, the second blast of chain was almost as ruinous as the first. More cannonballs struck the road. Slabs of rock broke loose, slid and tumbled down the hillside. Cracks gaped in the smooth stone.

Magister Rummage turned away. Those guns would keep firing until the road became a death-trap. Until they cut in half the long serpent of the Great God's cavalry. And General Klamath's soldiers were already at work, pacing their shots to be sure of their aim and conserve bullets.

With his heart thudding in his throat, Rummage looked down at the other cannon.

Their shots passed over the growing mass of priests, the deep throng of the horde. The contortions of the slope hid the effects of the balls and chain. He hoped for slaughter at the rear of the horde, among the infantry, but he could not be sure. The guns might be wasting their fire on empty ground.

That was his fault, that failure of foresight, but he did not waste time regretting it. The sight of skirmishers among the priests arriving at the edge of the road distracted him.

In the mute Magister's dreams, General Klamath had already contrived to kill all of those small, feral men. A useless wish. Many of the skirmishers had died. Enough still lived.

Amika's Queen had argued that the Great God's priests would attack the cannon with exploding globes. She had insisted on sending Magisters to protect Waysel's men. To appease her, Rummage had agreed. But he had not complied. He believed that he knew what was coming.

The Great God wanted that plateau. From there, he intended to stage his final assault. To preserve it intact, he had committed his cavalry to engage the Repository's defenders, not to defeat them, but to demand their best efforts so that he could ascend to the plateau unopposed. When he was ready, his priests would not throw their globes. They would send the skirmishers to clear the way.

Those small men were fast and agile, difficult for riflemen to hit. In any case, Waysel's men would be busy with their guns—and General Klamath's soldiers were widely scattered below the outcropping. If fire and lightning could not stop the skirmishers, they would almost certainly reach the plateau. And if the storm came quickly, the General's riflemen would be blinded. Waysel's men and cannon would be lost. The Great God would take the plateau.

The doom that Magister Rummage dreaded was coming closer.

He wrote demands on Magister Avail's hand.

—Warn Waysel! Watch for the skirmishers! Be ready to flee!

That was the best he could do. It was likely that the sub-Commander and Queen Estie had never seen those feral men before. They did not know the danger.

Nothing they did would make any difference.

To the south, the remaining Knights of Ardor had taken the brunt of the enemy's charge. Farther back, the few mounted priests had succeeded in halting the rush of beasts. The cavalry no longer piled into the rear of the fight. The men engaging the Knights had more room to move.

Still, the Knights held. The fighting around Sword Eradimnie and her last comrades had become a melee. A second warrior had been lost when her stallion was gored. With its guts ripped open, the horse had stumbled off the road's rim. The woman had gone down the hillside like a boulder until she ended in a pile of broken iron.

But Sword Eradimnie had lost comrades before. So had the Knights with her. They fought on. Possessed by a cold, calculating fury, she swung her longsword with the speed of a whirlwind and the force of an executioner's axe. Her comrades did the same. They drove their foes back, and back, as if they believed that they could defeat all of Rile's cavalry.

Cannon shouted in the distance. Eradimnie heard the barking of rifles, the cries of wounded men and beasts. The fight was not hopeless.

When her opponents broke off, she imagined for an instant that they might turn and run. She was mistaken.

Losing ground, the cavalrymen changed their tactics. They seemed to realize that their mounts were a hindrance. The beasts were less agile than the destriers, less disciplined, slower to obey. Almost as one, the cavalrymen dismounted. With their broadswords, they drove their beasts aside; sent many of them plunging off the road to break their legs or necks and die.

On foot, they had an advantage. The Knights could only hack down at them. One good thrust to a barrel or cut to a leg could take down a steed. And while the horse fell, its rider would be momentarily defenseless.

But the Knights of Ardor had trained for this as well. Their mounts were weapons of war, as expendable as lances or warriors. When Sword Eradimnie saw a cavalryman shove his blade into the chest of her steed, she reacted without hesitation.

Vaulting out of her saddle and over the destrier's neck, she landed feetfirst on that man before he could draw back his weapon. While the impact crumpled him, she swung her sword, severed a head on one side, chopped halfway through a torso on the other. Then she stood braced and ready, reaping blood.

Her speed and power cleared a space around her, allowed her a moment to choose her next attack. But only a moment. In desperation, three cavalrymen rushed her together. Wrapping their arms around her, they forced her off the road.

She took them with her as she fell.

The first boulder she hit snapped her back. The second crushed her helm. Her life was over before she finished her long tumble.

In her covert of stones, Queen Estie had no idea what was happening above her until she saw one of the Knights roll past her, a smashed ball of armor. Then she began to understand what Crayn was telling her.

Unable to see the Repository or any part of the road's final ascent, she had fixed her attention on Waysel and the cannon. Gouts of flame from the muzzles and subtle tremors in the ground told her when the siege-guns fired. But the extent of their position prevented her from seeing where the shots struck.

Nevertheless she trusted Waysel's determination to obey his orders. She assumed that cavalrymen and beasts were dying. That the road was being shattered. That the long charge of Rile's cavalry would be cut off.

She turned to scan the growing mass of priests at the edge of the road, the rising tide of the horde. From the priests, she sensed only the sorcery of their Shields.

Waysel's balls and chain carried over the priests and fanged men, hit somewhere farther down the slope. But the priests did not use that opportunity to advance. Instead, they waited while the cavalry streamed past them. Behind and beside them, the fanged men crouched, slavering.

The riders were still coming, but with every stride their charge slowed. When Queen Estie saw the first Knight fall past her, she began to make sense of Crayn's urgent gestures. Magister Rummage had sent the Knights of Ardor to meet the charge. Sword Eradimnie's promise— Sick at heart, Estie watched cavalrymen skid or topple down the hillside, dozens of them. And beasts, some already wounded, some snapping their legs on the confusion of scree and rock, some dying as they struck boulders.

What the Knights were doing seemed impossible, but its effects were unmistakable. Estie saw them in the welter of falling bodies, and in the slowing approach of riders farther down the road. Sword Eradimnie and her comrades were mighty—

Then another Knight crashed and died. Suddenly, something above Estie changed. Men and beasts had been tumbling past her. Now most of the fallen were beasts.

Shouting with his hands and arms, Crayn told her:

—The cavalrymen dismount! They sacrifice their beasts to fight on foot!

Estie watched until she saw another iron-clad body crash downward. She thought it might be Eradimnie herself.

Groaning, she turned away.

Downhill from her, General Klamath's men were firing. She could not hear the shots, but in the dusk of the Repository's shadow, she saw quick streaks of flame. Blood spurted from cavalrymen and beasts. Riders and mounts dropped away.

Despite the sun's rising, the air grew darker. Breezes curled around through Estie's shelter, bringing a deeper cold.

On the road, confused cavalrymen halted their beasts. They wheeled in circles, milling as if they had lost their minds; searching for ways to escape. She expected the priests to issue commands, impose some kind of order. Instead, the few sorcerers among the cavalry abandoned their own mounts. Scrambling off the road, they hurried to join the throng of priests.

Bullets took more riders, more beasts. The cavalrymen had been cut off behind and blocked in front. They had nowhere to go—and no orders. Rifle-fire covered that whole stretch of the road. Queen Estie could almost identify the moment when the cavalrymen realized that their position was hopeless.

Some of them hauled their beasts plunging down the foothills. Perhaps a few of them survived the treacherous descent. Others simply dismounted and ran, diving for the shelter of the rocks. The rest surged up the slopes, hunting for Klamath's men.

While Estie watched, the cavalry that had once come within hours of slaughtering General Klamath's army was routed.

A premature twilight spread over the foothills. The air seemed to be marred with ash, more and more of it, a low, drifting fall. The breezes were gone. The new cold tightened its grip.

Crayn touched her arm. Mutely, he pointed at the heavens.

A black storm came sliding past the peaks. It must be riding a steady wind, but no wind reached her. The air over the whole region felt slain, as still and chill as death.

That was not ash in the air. It was snow.

It fell straight down, as delicate as tossed feathers, and as deceptively gentle, but thicker by the moment. Already, bits of wet white clung to the tops of boulders, the sheets of scree. The globes cast a ghostly illumination through the gloom. Past the gaps in Estie's shelter, she watched the vista slowly fade behind veils of flakes.

Crayn wanted her to withdraw. In the keep, he could bolt the door against the cold and wet. Every part of her was shivering, but she resisted. The priests were ready to attack.

She expected them to surge across the road and begin flinging their globes, using the snow to cover them while they destroyed Waysel and her cannon. But they did not move.

Instead, they released the horde.

As if they were howling, the fanged strangers rushed onto the road, racing to feed. Rabid with hunger, they attacked the dead and the dying, beasts and cavalrymen. Tearing bodies apart, they devoured flesh and muscle, tendons and bones, faces, whole skulls, entrails. But they were not satisfied by the feast in front of them. They were too many. To ease their starvation, they spread out in both directions, north and south. Even men and mounts unscathed by rifle-fire were torn down and eaten. Only their armor spared the dead Knights from being consumed.

Stunned by horror, Estie surrendered to Crayn's urging. Her last sight as he drew her away was of a pack of small men crossing the road. They were no more than half the size of the fanged strangers. Like the horde, they carried no weapons. But they climbed the slopes with the speed of nightmares.

In moments, they outran the lights and disappeared in the snow. Still, they lingered in her mind like images of ruin.

The Great God's cavalry was gone. Nevertheless he was winning.

THIRTY

TO MAKE AMENDS

From his hiding place above the road, General Klamath watched the horde feed.

The sight made him sick. It also infuriated him. The Great God's casual willingness to sacrifice his own men revealed a depth of cruelty that the son of Klimith could not have imagined. The cavalrymen had been discarded like rubbish.

During the old wars, the Amikan monarchs had put their own wounded to death. That had shocked Klamath then. This was worse.

What purpose had the cavalry served? Klamath had only one explanation: to clear the way. The Repository's Magisters could have shattered these foothills, wrecked the lower plateau and the road, blocked every approach with rubble. Then Rile's forces could not have reached their target without an arduous and vulnerable scramble. But instead, the cavalry had forced the keep's defenders to concentrate on a different threat. Now Rile could ascend with ease. Only Klamath's soldiers and Waysel's cannon stood in his path.

The thickening snowfall hindered the riflemen. It did not appear to hamper the skirmishers. As the small men scampered across the road and started upward, Klamath felt a fist close around his heart.

Their numbers had been cut down in Long Slough, but those that remained might be enough for Rile's purpose. Blinding snows covered the foothills. Storm clouds sealed the world. Soon Klamath would not be able to see even one of the feral men until it sprang on him.

His people knew what to expect from the skirmishers. Only Hellick had not encountered them. Nevertheless the General passed his orders from man to man.

Sabers and daggers. No guns. A muzzle flash would betray the shooter's position.

He set aside his own rifle, his satchel of ready clips. In silence, he drew his saber, loosened his dagger in its sheath.

He had been instructed to retreat to the plateau when the priests and the horde advanced. After speaking with sub-Commander Waysel, the King's General had decided to disobey. Anyone on the flat outcropping would be exposed, defenseless against the Shields and globes of the priests. Klamath meant to stay where he was.

But Waysel and his guardsmen were already exposed. Klamath hoped that they had withdrawn to the Repository.

Hope was not enough. He needed to be sure.

A low call summoned Captain Rowt. When his aide joined him, General Klamath left his shelter and began to climb.

By his reckoning, he was well below the northern edge of the outcropping. With snow in their eyes, hardly able to be sure where they put their hands and feet, he and Rowt worked their way upward. Klamath listened for explosions, but he heard nothing except his own hoarse breathing.

The climb seemed long. Before he was ready, a sound reached him, an iron scraping like metal on stone. Instinctively, he shoved the Captain away and jumped aside.

With a muffled clangor, a siege-gun fell near them. Too heavy to roll, it stayed where it landed.

Hells! The skirmishers.

Climbing more urgently, Klamath found the wall of the plateau. He and Rowt hurried around it to a manageable slope and went upward.

On the plateau, they found too many bodies, guardsmen and skirmishers. As gentle as kindness, the snow covered the fallen in mounds like cairns. Waysel's men must have fought hard. No more than five feral creatures remained to do their god's bidding.

Struggling to shove cannon off the plateau, the last skirmishers did not notice General Klamath and Captain Rowt.

Klamath clenched his jaws against his anger and dismay. As soundless as the snow, he and his aide struck. The skirmishers were quick. They were not quick enough. In moments, they were dead.

Afterward, Klamath spent a while wiping snow off the faces of the guardsmen until he found sub-Commander Waysel. Waysel's throat had been torn open. The slashes looked like the work of claws.

Swearing privately, Klamath paused to recite the Bellegerin affirmation of honor for the dead. But he did not linger. Watching over each other, he and Rowt went back down the slope to their coverts.

Waiting again, cold, wet, and furious, Klamath surprised himself by cursing Bifalt's name. The King should have been here. This should have been his battle. It did not belong to the son of Klimith.

Two days earlier, King Bifalt felt lost. He knew where he was, but he had no time. He was moving too slowly.

From the first, he had trusted that the desert would hinder the enemy. He had even imagined that the sands might stop Rile entirely. For that reason, he had refused Suti al-Suri's urging to chase after the foot soldiers and strike at the enemy's rear. An attack like that would hurt Rile's infantry. The god himself would not care. He had men to spare. And it would delay Bifalt. The last battle might end before he arrived to take part.

That possibility was too much for him. He could not endure it. He felt an imperative need to catch up with Klamath, to stand with his friend and his riflemen in the final struggle.

Instead of harassing Rile's infantry, King Bifalt looked for a way south.

He believed that he would find Klamath on that side of the enemy's march. If the General reached the Repository's road there rather than in the north, he would have a shorter approach to the temporary safety of the keep.

Riding through the hills of western Belleger during days of dirty weather, King Bifalt took his diminished army south, seeking a way to cross the enemy's line.

On the edge of the hardpan bordering the desert, he found his chance. For reasons that he did not try to understand, the leading wagons of Rile's train stopped there. Guarded by more than a dozen priests, the servants were at work setting the oxen free and replacing them with tusked beasts. That delay left a gap between the supply-train and the rear of the infantry.

Covered by bouts of sleet, thrashing rain, and snow, King Bifalt's men and the el-Algreb crossed the hardpan unopposed.

Then, however, they had to face the desert.

Bifalt wanted haste, but that was impossible.

His people had to scramble over sands that shifted under every hoof, and to contend with new, inexplicable sand-slides that loosened the surfaces. They were forced to abandon their supply-wagon and use its horses as pack-animals. Soon, Suti al-Suri's scouts lost the enemy's track. Their last report informed the King that the sorcerous shimmering of the priests seemed to command the dunes, clearing the Great God's passage.

Bifalt would have been worse than lost without the el-Algreb.

Their scouts were valuable. Their familiarity with deserts was even more precious. Suti al-Suri and some of the other horse-warriors had spent many years crossing regions like this for Set Ungabwey's caravans. They had a feel for the shapes of dunes, the stretches of stable sand. When the chief warrior took the lead, the army made better progress.

Of necessity, however, his path wandered. He kept to the hollows and valleys between dunes, the lower trails where the sands were less likely to shift. Bifalt's forces moved more quickly with less effort, but they did not always go east.

The storms had passed. Now the air was as dry as the dust kicked up by the horses. The cold cut at everyone's lungs. Between patches of sunlight, the shadows of the dunes were everywhere, spreading their chill shade. The riflemen, Magisters, and even the mounts coughed without clearing their lungs. The el-Algreb protected themselves with cloths over their faces. The King's men did what they could.

King Bifalt coughed as much as anyone, but he had a soldier's disdain for mere discomfort. The sand scorned his desire for haste. Despite his hunger to join Klamath and fight, he could not quicken his pace.

He would have given his damaged hand to hear something useful from the Repository, but there was nothing.

Vexed to the verge of howling, he rode in the vanguard of his forces as if he could drag them faster by brute will. But the el-Algreb scouts were always out of sight among the dunes ahead of him, choosing his way with their characteristic mixture of caution and recklessness. The King required himself to trust them.

After hours that felt interminable, a shout carried back to him from the scouts. As he listened, the chief warrior's voice lifted.

"Rider," he explained. "Good."

Bifalt jerked up his head. A *rider*? More than that: a rider the el-Algreb apparently knew? What in all the hells was a rider like that doing here?

"Who?" he demanded.

He meant, Who and why?

Suti al-Suri grinned. Like a taunt, he answered, "Wait."

Bifalt wanted to hit the man. Instead, he urged his horse to trot a little faster.

Before long, he spotted her past a curving slope of sand. Escorted by one of the scouts, she sat her mount in a wide hollow between dunes. At first glance, he recognized her by her flowing white robe, a white so pure that it seemed to shed sand and dust like water from a rain-cape. Then he found her name.

Amandis. A devotee of Spirit.

No, he thought. Impossible.

Elgart had told him that they had all gone to serve the survival of their own people. But he knew her too well to be mistaken. Twenty years ago, she had taken Elgart from him when he had first entered the

Repository. Later, she had warned him that the library had an enemy. And more recently, she had snatched Elgart from Archpriest Makh to save Belleger. Without her intervention—her interference—King Bifalt would never have received the gift of an alliance with the el-Algreb.

Bifalt rode straight to her, dismounted in a flurry of sand. After long hours in the saddle, his legs threatened to drop him. Ignoring his unsteadiness, he peered up at her.

Despite the long years since he had last seen her, she looked as lithe and ready as ever. At first, she seemed unchanged, untouched by time. Then he saw the new lines at the corners of her eyes and mouth, the slight toughening of her skin. Her gaze had acquired shadows that suggested uncertainty.

Coughing to clear his lungs, he said hoarsely, "Greetings, Devotee."

The riflemen nearby stared. The el-Algreb knew her. The King's men had never seen a woman like her.

Bifalt saw amusement in her eyes, or perhaps scorn. Effortlessly, she dropped to the sand and faced him.

"Greetings, King of Belleger," she began. "You have made good progress. I expected to find you farther west."

"Suti al-Suri's doing," replied Bifalt. "Not mine."

She was not a woman who smiled readily, but the corner of her mouth twitched. Turning to the chief warrior, she said, "Greetings, Suti al-Suri. You have done well. I was wiser than I knew when I asked your people to be the King's allies."

He replied with an el-Algreb bow, a gesture that he had never given Bifalt. "High praise, most holy," he murmured. "It humble el-Algreb."

Behind the King, several of his people sat their mounts with the bodyguards, Elgart and Prince Jaspid. Elgart had the air of a man who wanted to cheer. Jaspid looked disappointed. He may have hoped to greet Lylin rather than Amandis. More riflemen were arriving. Bifalt ignored them all.

He felt strangely daunted in the devotee's presence. Her sudden coming seemed to demand more of him than he knew how to give.

With an effort, he asked, "What are you doing here?"

She had taken Elgart from him without regard for the effect of his friend's disappearance.

Amandis faced him again. "A wasted question, King. I am here. That is enough."

Abruptly, Elgart dismounted, drawing Prince Jaspid with him. Together, they joined Bifalt.

"Perhaps the point of the question, Devotee," said Elgart mildly, "is to let you show your respect for the man who asks it."

She frowned at him. "Have you forgotten who I am, Elgart?"

Bifalt remembered her inhuman quickness. For her, the decision to act and the completion of the movement were immediate. Long before he could react, she had taken one of her daggers from her sleeve, closed the distance, and aimed her blade at Elgart's throat.

Yet she did not reach her target. Jaspid caught her wrist. Showing his teeth, he kept her dagger from Elgart's neck.

"I have not forgotten you, Devotee." Elgart's voice had an unfamiliar edge. "But I have learned that arrogance is a game of two players. If one does not play, the other cannot. And I know something that may surprise you. Prince Jaspid has been schooled by your sister in Spirit Lylin."

Whatever Amandis felt, she kept to herself. Briefly, she considered Jaspid's grasp. Then a slight movement of her shoulders suggested a shrug. When she stepped back, the Prince let her go.

"Very well," she said, not to Elgart, but to Bifalt. "I will answer. But do not mistake earned assurance for arrogance. The distinction has weight.

"I have come to help you, King. Is that not obvious? Perhaps you should ask why I am here *now*. I have other duties."

Bifalt swallowed his tension. He made an effort to seem calm. "Very well, most holy," he replied. "I accept your reprimand. I wasted my first question. Here is another. If you will, tell me why you have come now."

Amandis regarded him as if she saw signs of change. "The Repository's need is also obvious. But Elgart reminds me that it would have no hope at all without you. I will answer to show my respect."

With Bifalt's bodyguards, Crawl and Brighten moved closer. Riflemen edged near. Only Suti al-Suri kept his distance.

"It was not the intention of my people," said the devotee, "to participate in this war. If we mean to survive it, we must care for our own. But Magister Avail has been speaking to me. I heard his desperation.

"From him, I know that Sirjane Marrow is dead. The new librarian means well, but she is timid. The burden of the war falls to Magister Rummage, and he holds back his sorcerers for the last defense. Only your General Klamath stands against the enemy.

"If Magister Avail had said nothing else, I would not have heeded him. My people are at risk, King. Their need for the devotees of Spirit is extreme. But he also assured me that *you* may have forsaken the Repository. You are lost in the desert, or you have turned away, or you are dead.

"That I did not expect. Even the young upstart I first met would not have done so, and you have become more. Now I can see for myself that you have kept Elgart's promise to the el-Algreb, and that you strive to join the fight. These are not the actions of a monarch who turns his back.

"I came to do what I can. I am too old for children."

Bifalt hid his shock behind a severe frown. Amandis seemed to be saying that she *believed* in him. A most holy devotee of Spirit? He might have challenged her, but he felt too shaken to take the risk.

Under the circumstances, Magister Marrow's death meant nothing to him. He had chosen his path despite the former librarian's manipulations and dishonesty. He saw no reason to step aside now.

Sternly, he said, "You have not come too soon, Devotee. How will you help us?"

That question she answered without prodding.

"The el-Algreb serve you better than you know, King. They will lead you to the caravan-track. Beyond it, I will guide you. I know paths that the enemy does not. You will travel more swiftly."

At once, Bifalt asked, "Will we catch up with Rile before he attacks the library?"

She snorted. "Another wasted question. I have no sorcery. I see only what you see." Then she appeared to relent. "Suti al-Suri's scouts will know more when we reach the foothills."

The King had more questions. Some of them might not be wasted. But while he tried to choose one, Elgart intervened.

"Will you share a meal with us while we rest, Devotee? We have enough."

The King expected a brusque refusal. Instead, Amandis studied the former spy. "A game of two players?" she mused. "An interesting notion. If you had mentioned it while we rode together, we might have done it justice.

"This is not the time," she said more firmly. "Rest if you must. It would be better to ride on. We require haste."

King Bifalt took the hint. "Prince?" he asked his brother. "Can your men wait to rest? We should go."

Jaspid did not hesitate. He lacked the instincts of a commander. His responsibility for the riflemen hung over his head like a personal storm. But his brief success seemed to restore his spirits. He almost smiled as he replied, "As you say, Majesty." Together, he and Suti al-Suri began calling orders.

Most of the King's soldiers had dismounted. The horse-warriors had not. While the riflemen swung up into their saddles and resumed their formation, Bifalt examined himself. To his surprise, he found that he no longer felt lost.

Amandis knew quicker paths. If the chief warrior did not, neither did Rile. And the foothills of the Wall Mountains were not the desert. Their obstructions could not be swept aside like dunes. They would slow the enemy.

There was still a chance that King Bifalt would arrive in time for the last battle. An hour ago, he would not have believed it. Now he was able to hope.

For the rest of the day, the King's forces followed Suti al-Suri's scouts through the desert. During the night, they stopped for a few hours of rest. By the flickering light of their campfires, they fed themselves and cared for their mounts. Then they sprawled on the cold sand to sleep under a broad sweep of stars and a fragment of moonlight.

For reasons of her own, the devotee of Spirit took King Bifalt aside.

She was little more than a shape in the night. It covered her features like shadows. But her robe seemed to gather the starlight, transforming her to a faint shimmer among the dunes.

Behind them, only the sentries stirred. Too frustrated to rest, Prince Jaspid watched over them. Everyone else had fallen like stones into pools of sleep. There were no sounds from the camp apart from the snuffling of the horses, the soft hiss of sand under the mounts' hooves, the cracking of embers.

Bifalt expected Amandis to ask for the tale of the war. He was ready with a blunt, foreshortened version. The direction of her thoughts surprised him.

She stood half facing him, gazing away across the camp at the opposite dune. Her voice was a whisper in the night.

"This is difficult for me, King, but I must endure it. You have earned more respect than I once gave you. Now I am troubled by questions of arrogance. I will tell you a thing that only Elgart knows.

"I have never been beaten, not once in my life. But the Archpriest overcame me." Seen from the side, her eyes reflected a hint of flames. "Much as I struggled to refuse him, I was not enough. If Elgart had not saved me, I would have sacrificed"—she made a helpless gesture—"everything.

"I am here to make amends."

Bifalt resisted an impulse to hold his breath. By Elgart's account, his role in Makh's defeat had been trivial. The most holy devotee saw it differently.

But she was not done. While he absorbed that revelation, she offered another.

"I have seen my sister in Spirit Lylin."

Involuntarily, he flinched. He could not hear that name without reacting. Yes, Lylin had saved Estie's life more than once. But she had also beaten Jaspid almost to death.

"She came to our homeland from the Last Repository while I was there. Her tale is her own. I will not share it. But I will tell you a thing that Elgart does not know.

"She has refused our men. That is uncommon. Our men are more than desirable. Like our children, they are precious. Many approached her. She refused them all. When I left our homeland, she did the same by a different path." Amandis shrugged. "She did not say why. I did not ask. But now I begin to suspect that she also seeks to make amends."

Listening, Bifalt knotted his fists, gnawed the inside of his cheek. To anyone else, he would have retorted, Make amends? Hells, she *should*. But he could not vent his indignation to Amandis.

Trying to control himself, he asked the question that mattered most to him.

"Did Magister Avail say anything about Queen Estie? Did Lylin?" Were the devotee's revelations difficult for her? This was difficult for him. "I fear for her."

He meant, How badly have I hurt her?

Amandis may have considered that another wasted question. Nevertheless she gave him the courtesy of an answer.

"Magister Avail said nothing, King. His thoughts are fixed on the Repository's defense. Your Queen does not affect his demand for aid. Lylin said only that she is well."

"She took cannon with her," returned Bifalt as if that detail were relevant in some way. "Her men know how to fire them."

For the first time that night, Amandis turned to him. "That is good," she said distinctly. "The Magisters will not disregard her. They need her guns."

Turning away, she left Bifalt alone in the dark.

He watched her go until the wan glow of her garb faded from sight. Then he covered his face with his hands.

He had heard too much. The devotee's confessions baffled him. If he could have talked about them with Estie, she would have helped him understand them. But he might never get the chance to speak with her again. Hells, he might never see her—

How had she become so necessary to him? He had desired her

from the first, her and no other woman. Yet desire alone did not ex-plain the emptiness that his separation from her left in his heart.

He gave his people another hour while he wrestled with himself. Then he roused them to resume their trek in the desert.

Well before dawn, he learned that Rile was still ahead of him. Suti al-Suri's scouts delivered fresh news.

The devotee spoke the el-Algreb tongue. Translating for King Bi-falt, she declared, "The enemy is on the caravan-track. A host of men on tusked beasts are racing north. No doubt, they will take the road through the foothills to the Repository.

"The men that Suti al-Suri calls the horde lead the enemy's advance. They follow a great many priests through the dunes. The foot soldiers trail behind."

"Why?" demanded Bifalt. "Why send his cavalry that way? What can they do against the Repository?"

Amandis countered, "How else can they reach the enemy's target? Have you forgotten the foothills? They are too rugged for beasts or horses that do not know the hidden paths."

The chief warrior nodded. "Cross track soon, Brother. Most holy lead. Easy paths. Gain ground."

That was enough for Bifalt. He remembered the caravan-track, the bare iron-rutted road formed to ease the journey for the wagons that supplied the Repository, but he had only the vaguest memory of how he had survived after Set Ungabwey had abandoned him there. At the time, he had been half dead with thirst and hunger. The ride had felt long to him. Perhaps it would seem shorter now. All he cared about was gaining on the Great God.

Among the foothills at last, sheltered from sight by buttresses of raw stone and ancient spills of shale, the devotee of Spirit halted the army. A pale statue in the waning night, she sat her horse until the King joined her with his comrades. Speaking quietly, she announced, "We are now less than a league below the road. It passes southward above us before its last curve up to the Repository.

"We must be cautious now, King. It will be fatal if the enemy's mounted force catches us crossing the road. Strung out as we are, we cannot defend ourselves."

Privately, King Bifalt groaned. Every instinct in him cried out for haste. But those instincts had betrayed him against the horde. They had cost the el-Algreb too many horse-warriors. His damaged hand was badly swollen now, throbbing constantly, almost useless.

Defying himself, he asked Amandis, "What do you suggest?"

She was sure of her answer. "Suti al-Suri's scouts can watch the road for us. We should walk now. When we are near enough to gauge the danger, we can decide whether to attempt a crossing."

Hells! thought the King. But he did not object. Instead, he replied as if the word did not wring his heart, "Good."

He did not need to consult Suti al-Suri. The chief warrior was already whistling to his relay of scouts.

Grinding his teeth, Bifalt told Jaspid to pass the word. "We walk now. If nothing else, the horses will be grateful." Then he added, "Urge the men to eat and drink while they can. They will need their strength."

Despite his own yearning to forge ahead, the Prince muttered, "As you say, Majesty."

On his orders, the army dismounted. Dragging their reluctant mounts, they began to ascend on foot.

A stone's throw below the road, they stopped.

From their position, they could not see the Repository or the high peaks of the Wall. Storm clouds piled over the mountains, casting their own gloom. But there was enough light to reveal the army's surroundings, the rocks and dead brush, the shale and boulders, the occasional patches of scrub oak. Over his own harsh breathing and the panting of his people, Bifalt heard the clatter of hooves.

Lying flat on dirt and pebbles below the road's edge, he watched Rile's cavalry sweep past, charging like thunder.

At a word from the devotee, Suti al-Suri spread out his horse-warriors on both sides. Sending their mounts farther down, the el-Algreb hid to avoid being seen. Prince Jaspid arranged the riflemen behind the King in case some cavalryman or priest chanced to notice him.

None of the riders glanced downward. They goaded their beasts like men avid for bloodshed.

Time passed. The sun rose above the coming storm. Bifalt's hand stung him with every beat of his pulse. And still Rile's cavalry ran past, an immeasurable torrent. For reasons of his own, he must have committed his entire mounted force.

Through the unrelenting clamor of hooves, Suti al-Suri heard the whistling of his scouts. He reported that a mass of priests was gathering below the road. They had brought the horde with them, and the small skirmishers. There they waited to let the cavalry go by.

Then Bifalt heard the sounds of distant fighting, the unmistakable clash and ring of iron. Without thinking, he crept higher until he could see the upper stretch of the road. Squinting between boulders, he saw cavalrymen and beasts sprawl downward in swaths of blood. Their opponents were few, but the Repository's defenders rode huge black steeds, wore full armor.

One by one, they fell as well. When they went down, they clanged on the rocks and boulders like huge bells shattering.

Yet they stopped the charge. The following cavalrymen were forced to slow, then halt. Perhaps warned by their priests, all of the riders above King Bifalt restrained their mounts.

A moment later, the characteristic booming of siege-guns echoed off the mountainsides. From somewhere above the road, the cannon sent their balls and loads of chain over the heads of the massed priests, the horde. If their shots did any damage lower down, Bifalt could not see it. But other siege-guns must have been aimed at the northward reach of the road. They must have torn the road apart. Abruptly, the rush of cavalry was cut off.

Above him, the charge collapsed in confusion. Riders wheeled their beasts, waiting for orders or looking for ways to escape. At least for the moment, they had nowhere to go.

Through the storm's gloom, muzzle flashes suddenly appeared. Their cracking reached Bifalt an instant later. From positions scattered all over the hillsides, hundreds of rifles shredded the milling cavalry.

Klamath! The General had chosen his battleground well.

Panting with relief and excitement, Bifalt scrambled from place to place, searching for a better vantage. He found only glimpses of the dying cavalrymen and beasts, but that was enough. The ones who tried to save themselves by plunging downward were met by the blades of the el-Algreb. Those that surged up the slopes gave Klamath's riflemen better targets. Rile's cavalry had no escape.

For long moments, the King believed that Rile had suffered a vicious defeat. He did not see his mistake until the horde emerged to feed. Rushing up and down the road, they sank their fangs into every cavalryman, the living as well as the dead, and gorged themselves.

The sight horrified Bifalt. In an instant, he realized that Rile had planned for this. Hells! He had even planned for Estie's cannon. He had kept himself and his infantry at a distance so that they would not be struck by cannonballs and chain. Then he had released the horde to clear away the litter of bodies.

Meanwhile, his cavalrymen had accomplished their true purpose. They had lured Klamath's men to reveal themselves. Spread out as they were, the riflemen now had no effective defense against the horde and the skirmishers, or the sorcery of the priests.

When the storm broke over the mountains, and snow began to fall, even the weather seemed to serve the Great God.

THIRTY-ONE

IT BEGINS

For two days, the snow fell, as gentle as dust, and as thick as a deluge. During that time, there was nothing to do because there was nothing to see. Even the globes of the Great God's multitudinous priests were dimmed, visible only as occasional blurs of light. Of his other forces, the Farsighted glimpsed no sign. King Bifalt and the el-Algreb might as well have ceased to exist. General Klamath and his army were concealed. Queen Estie had told Klamath to retreat to the lower plateau. After the charge of the cavalry and its slaughter by the horde, he had made a different decision.

Apparently, sub-Commander Waysel had done the same. With Estie's consent, Commander Crayn crept down through the storm to the lower plateau before Rile's men could reach it. He returned to report that Waysel and the Queen's honor guardsmen were dead. Immured in snow, Waysel's command lay surrounded by a number of smaller bodies. Three of the siege-guns had been pushed off the rim of the plateau. Without cannoneers, the others were useless as well.

During those days, Queen Estie carried a burden of grief for her slain men. For her husband, she refused to grieve. She could not imagine what had happened to him, but she declined to believe that he had been lost. He was somewhere doing something necessary. Anything less would have been too much to bear.

Around her, a feeling of loneliness gripped the massive keep, a sense of isolation draped like dread over the world. The loss of the Knights of Ardor filled the air like the smoke of wildfires. People scurried everywhere furtively, or huddled in their quarters, as if the Repository were already under siege. Students and teachers forgot each other. The servants still had their tasks, but they flinched while they worked. Scribes left their desks to wander the halls, as aimless as ghosts.

The silence of the snowfall seemed to demand quiet. When groups or individuals spoke to each other, they talked in whispers as if they feared being overheard. The people most responsible for the library—Magisters Threnody, Rummage, Avail, and Bleak—kept watch together in silence, dismayed by what the storm concealed—and by what its passing might reveal.

Shaken by the horde's feasting, many of the Repository's people withdrew to their homes. For decades, they had feared what was coming without knowing exactly *what* they feared, apart from the ruin of their treasured books. And even that fear had a quality of abstraction. It surpassed imagining. But now they did not need to imagine it. They had seen it in its rawest form as fangs tore through flesh and viscera and bone, devouring the living and the dead alike. Even the bravest of them were shocked to the core by the Great God's viciousness. When they could speak of it, their whispers trembled, and the blood drained from their faces.

But for Magister Rummage, it was the loss of the Knights that left him rigid with rage and shame. He had allowed them to waste their lives.

For some time, he had believed that the enemy's first goal would be to take and secure the lower plateau. From there, the Great God would launch his assault on the Repository itself. But when Rummage heard that the enemy's cavalry was on the road, he had considered other possibilities. True, there were only a few sorcerers among the cavalrymen. As the riders approached, however, they would pass directly in front of the thronging priests. Magister Rummage expected those priests to join the charge. They would rise to the Repository's porch and attack the gates. What other purpose could the cavalry serve?

To his shame, the mute man had condoned Sword Eradimnie's promise. Now he knew that he had misjudged the Repository's enemy.

The priests had not accompanied the charge. Without them, the cavalry had posed no serious threat. Neither the riders nor their beasts could have survived the gale of Decimates with which the Repository's Magisters would have greeted them. Cut off from any possible retreat by Waysel's cannon, they would have been decimated.

The Knights of Ardor could have joined the defense of the lower plateau. Instead, they had died for nothing.

Scourging himself, Magister Rummage clutched his book to his chest and prayed that he would be brave enough to use it.

During this time, Queen Estie also wandered the halls. Occasionally, she walked with Third Father, but he was still too weak to stay on his feet for long. More often, she accompanied Magister Oblique while the sorceress pursued her own duties.

Oblique went everywhere, pausing to talk with everyone she found, spreading news and solace. To the students and scribes, the cooks and scullions and chambermaids, the healers and apprentices, she listened patiently. In return, she offered them whatever they seemed to need: simple explanations, broader assurances, reasons for hope.

This was a side of Magister Oblique that Estie had not seen before. She spent long hours at the woman's side, hoping that her mute presence would aid Oblique's efforts. For herself, she had only one pertinent question. She asked it early.

What of the seventh Decimate, the power to render sorcerers impotent over astonishing distances? Could it be turned against Rile himself? If not, could it be used to counter the Shields of the priests? Then they would be vulnerable to bullets and blades and blunt fists, more vulnerable than infantrymen. Losing their support might cripple the Great God.

Still unfamiliar with Lamit Karsolsky's *System*, Magister Oblique tapped her answer on the Queen's forearm.

—Every Decimate has its own limits. To affect any individual sorcerer, or any small group, the wielder of the seventh Decimate must stand near its target. Spread farther, the Decimate effaces *all* sorcery. And it endures until it is dismissed. It may be able to overcome the Great God's coercion, but it will render us powerless.

—If the struggle is reduced to mundane violence, we are lost. The walls will hold. The gates will fail. Without our Decimates, we cannot withstand the Great God.

Thinking of Klamath's peril and Waysel's forlorn death, the Queen asked, "Will Magister Rummage commit any of your sorcerers to help the General? The Magisters he brought with him are now in the Repository."

The sorceress looked abashed.

—Forgive me, Queen. I thought that you were informed. I believed that they acted at your command.

—They have gone out into the snow, all of them. A servant led them. They intended to reach the lower plateau ahead of the enemy. From there, they planned to disperse across the foothills. They mean to fight for the General when the time comes.

—It is brave and foolish of them. But they are Bellegerin and Amikan. They refuse to forsake their own people.

An unexpected wave of relief and pride washed over Estie. She rubbed her eyes to hide their burning. "Then they have done well. When I can, I will honor them."

Magister Oblique replied:

—They deserve no less. All of your people, and King Bifalt's as well.

Wearing the twisted expression of a woman who felt too many conflicting emotions, she continued on her way.

For a few moments, the Queen was silent. She had wasted too much hope on the seventh Decimate. Now she had to pin all of her yearning on trail-worn men and women who had fought their way across the whole of Belleger and yet refused to accept the Repository's sanctuary.

Magister Oblique had neglected to speak aloud for Crayn's benefit.

When Estie had mastered herself, she told him what she had said. He bore the disappointment more staunchly than she did.

During the nights and days of the storm, his heavy cloak and almost enough food enabled General Klamath to endure the cold. Shivering occasionally, and working his arms to make his blood flow, he watched the ascent of the enemy.

The snow fell as soft as down, but so thickly that he could hardly see past the reach of his arm. Nevertheless the shining of the priests' sorcery marked their passage. Through the windless shroud of snow, he witnessed the first of them finding their way upward, leading the dark mass of the horde. Behind them came more priests with the heavy infantry. And a day later, the Great God himself followed, striding powerfully in a golden glow tainted by the crimson of his eyes and gems. With him, he brought a number of servants carrying obscure burdens. At his back, the light infantry crossed the road guided by still more priests.

On the General's strict orders, his men waited, keeping themselves hidden. During the cavalry charge earlier, they had exposed themselves. Now they were left alone, protected by the storm, and perhaps by Rile's scorn for his foes. If they opened fire now, none of them would survive the horde's response.

Perhaps King Bifalt would have acted in some other way. The son of Klimith no longer cared.

Long hours of day and night passed, and still Klamath waited.

Perhaps he had spent too much time immersed in his King's distrust of sorcery and sorcerers. He assumed that his Magisters would choose to fight as they had done during the old wars, from a place of safety. When Captain Rowt found him during the second night to report that they had returned, all of the gifted men and women who had come from the Open Hand, Klamath was speechless. Now they had come back to him? In this storm? Of their own volition?

"General, sir," prodded Rowt. "Where do you want them?"

For a while, Klamath had no answer. His thoughts whirled. Suddenly, he had more than riflemen. He had *Magisters*, a wealth of them. More than twenty drought-wielders. Perhaps fifteen Magisters of fire. Eight, no, seven with the Decimate of lightning. Magister Solace and eleven other pestilence-wielders. And a full fifteen Magisters of wind led by Magister Trench.

Was that all? No. King Bifalt had given him six earthquake-wielders, Magister Astride and five others.

What could he do with such largesse?

Unfortunately, it was all on his side of the enemy's ascent. He could not ask anyone to attempt a crossing through the priests and the horde and the heavy infantry. Hegels would have to be content with bullets and sabers.

Briefly, Klamath imagined using the Magisters of earthquake to shatter the whole lower plateau. They could send tons of rock tumbling down on Rile's forces. But then he remembered the Bay of Lights. Rile also had earthquake-wielders. They could dismiss whatever Magister Astride and her comrades attempted.

And Klamath had one more concern. His Magisters lacked the stamina that Rile's sorcerers had displayed in the bay. They would have to rest as often as they struck.

"General Klamath?" insisted Captain Rowt. "They have come to fight for us. They need orders."

Still spinning with ideas, Klamath shoved the weight of snow off his shoulders, forced his stiff muscles to lift him upright. Awkwardly, as if he had forgotten words, he said, "Thank you, Captain. That is welcome news." He peered around at the falling snow. "Where are they?"

The young man gestured vaguely uphill. "I kept them together, sir. In a gully where they will not be seen."

"Good, Captain." The General felt an unfamiliar flush of confidence. "We must decide where they can serve best." After a moment, he remembered to add, "And we must contrive to feed them. I cannot predict this storm. It may endure for days."

"There is no need, sir," answered Rowt. "They brought food. And they were advised before they left. The Repository expects the skies to clear at sunrise."

Good! thought Klamath fervently. "Then it is not too soon to guide them to their places. We must be ready."

He expected a bloody defeat. Against Rile's forces? Hells, he expected to die himself. But with his own men and so many Magisters, he could make the enemy pay for the privilege of killing him.

For two days, the storm seemed endless. But the weather-wise among the theurgists sensed that it would pass before dawn. The sun would rise over the Wall Mountains into clear skies.

Summoned by Magister Avail, a crowd gathered in the librarian's workroom, where her windows looked out over the wide balcony that served as the keep's battlements. From the balcony, the lower plateau was visible beyond the edge of the Repository's porch. Beyond it, nothing was certain.

Queen Estie was there with Commander Crayn. A number of Magisters had answered Avail's call. Escorted by Fifth Daughter, Third Father had come as well. Estie saw none of the Farsighted. No doubt, they could watch as much as they dared wherever they were. But Apprentice Travail was present, looking wan. Apparently, he expected Magister Avail to need him.

The chamber was Beatrix Threnody's, but she stood apart from the gathering, making room for people who might have more to contribute than a mere librarian. Closer to the windows, the space was dominated by the clenched fuming and bared teeth of Magister Rummage.

Out on the balcony, more Magisters and apprentices had gathered. Forcing their way through drifts that reached their thighs or waists, they braced themselves among the crenellations to watch the lower plateau and the foothills.

The view from the windows was a scene of pristine loveliness, of barren stone and slopes transformed by deep cloaks of purest white. Snow covered the keep's plateau of welcome like a blanket, undisturbed from edge to edge. It softened the rough heads of boulders, crowning them with gentleness. It made soft mounds of the dead or wintering brush, lay as clean as fresh sheets on the swaths and runnels of dirt between the rocks. Where it was touched by sunlight, it blazed like promises.

It should have been appreciated.

But no one regarded the beauty of the landscape. Queen Estie hardly noticed it herself. The lower plateau compelled everyone's attention.

Defying the storm, Rile's priests and servants had been busy.

The stone there had been swept or burned free of snow, leaving a bare expanse. The cannon and their remaining loads of shot and chain were gone. In their place, a pavilion commanded the space.

It was large, an oilcloth-roofed rectangle that occupied the plateau's center. Wooden pillars supported its corners, leaving its sides open. Its length faced the Repository, as did the long trestle-table it sheltered. Behind the table, a row of empty stools waited.

The table and stools served no obvious purpose. They looked like a setting where men could sit in judgment on the Great God's enemies. But Estie ignored them. The god himself compelled her attention.

Shining like hot bronze or gold, Rile occupied an ornate chair like a throne at one end of the table.

Even seated, he was taller than any of the men hustling around the pavilion. At first glance, he seemed too perfect to be anything more than a statue. The muscles of his nude form were clearly limned, and the lines of his torso and arms were more than human. But his head moved from side to side, inspecting the work of his priests and servants. The rubies of his eyes blazed.

In his right hand, he held his staff upright, a slender shaft as tall as himself. Near its top, it had the shape of a cross, its arms extended, its crown raised proudly. There at the ends of each arm, and at the top of the cross, more rubies burned, as large as fists, and as imperious as the Great God's eyes.

By comparison, the gem in Tak Biondi's cross was trivial.

Rile's mere presence announced him as greater than the Repository's people had ever imagined. Even at this distance, his power flushed Queen Estie's face. Without seeing her, he demanded her worship. She had to force herself to look away.

When she was finally able to consider what was around him, she felt a different kind of dismay.

In an arc across the front of the pavilion ranged a large throng of priests, globes shining. Them, she had expected. Their Shields would protect the god and his intentions from the Repository's Decimates. Nothing that General Klamath could throw at him would strike.

In front of the priests crouched the fanged men of the horde. They had clambered partway up the slopes and hunkered down in the snow, poised to spring. Despite their losses to starvation and battle, they were still too many to defeat.

And they were not alone. Rile's heavy infantry guarded the back and both sides of the pavilion, a solid wall of armor and blades. And even *they* were not alone. An immense force of light infantry filled the hillsides below the armored soldiers.

Only the skirmishers were missing. When they had ascended to the lower plateau during the storm, Waysel's command must have been waiting for them. Now they were dead. Still, they had cleared the way for the Great God.

He would not miss them. Like the cavalry, they had served their purpose. Now he was done with them.

But his preparations were not complete. That was obvious. He sat with the patience of overwhelming power, yet his watchfulness showed that he was waiting. His priests and his army and his own power were not enough. He wanted more. If the Repository's sorceries were not enough to defend it, its thick walls would hold back his forces. He may have been waiting for a weapon that could shatter stone.

That weapon would not be a Decimate. It would not be any power that the keep's Magisters knew.

General Klamath had decided wisely when he had refused to retreat. From the foothills, he and his riflemen might find a way to strike before Rile's final attack was ready.

Around Queen Estie, most of the people were deep in shock, stunned by the scale of Rile's forces. Beatrix Threnody seemed to cower against the wall, as pale as a woman on the verge of fainting. Third Father's downcast gaze hid his reaction, but Fifth Daughter's fright showed. Most of the Magisters stood still, unable to move or think. Even Magister Rummage—

But Magister Avail was cursing. His sorcerous voice filled every head in the workroom with a fierce litany of obscenities and denunciations. His intensity made it difficult for Estie to concentrate on the gestures that Apprentice Travail flung at her.

—Go, Queen! Magister Rummage needs you in your place!

With Crayn's hand on her arm, she turned and ran.

The Commander had left her warmest cloak and a pair of fur-lined boots with his supplies inside the door at the end of the last corridor. Panting with haste, she stripped off her sandals, shoved her feet into the boots, hauled the cloak over her shoulders. Ahead of her, Crayn shoved the door open against the snow piled outside.

Queen Estie of Amika hurried into her covert like a woman who did not feel the biting cold and did not care how much snow clogged her steps.

She had to swipe off snow and ice to open the gaps that allowed her to see. Then she put her face to the stones and looked out at the lower plateau.

The sight hit her like a slap. Rile in his pavilion seemed too near. Surely Waysel and his siege-guns had been farther away than this? The clear light of a new day made the priests and the horde vivid. The sun shone like flames on the armor of the heavy infantry. The Great God's power shouted at the heavens. If she made any sound, the enemy would hear her.

But Rile and his forces were focused on other matters. She was too small and too well hidden to catch their attention.

Swallowing her fright, she moved to the next gap. From there, she could peer down toward the road and search the drifts for signs of Klamath's men.

Magister Avail's shout stopped her. **Queen!** he demanded. **Hear me!**

He sounded frantic.

Yes? she answered.

At once, he replied, **Magister Bleak sees King Bifalt. Riflemen. They are with the el-Algreb just below the road on your side.**

Queen Estie staggered. Bifalt!

The deaf sorcerer took a mental breath.

They will attack the infantry. They must not! They have a more urgent task.

At once, he explained, **Below the road, priests form an aisle down to the desert. To the Great God's wagons. Servants there unload more bundles.** He must have meant, More than the materials needed for Rile's seat, pavilion, table, and stools. **Magister Bleak counts ten. They each take a bundle and run. They *run*, Queen. Up the slope in the aisle of priests. The priests Shield them. What they carry must be precious to the Great God.**

Magister Rummage fears it. The King must stop them. He *must*.

Estie stumbled against the Commander, let him brace her.

Tell him, she retorted to Avail.

The Magister swore. **You tell him, Queen. He may not heed me. Do it *now*!**

His sudden silence left a hole in her mind, a blank space that should have been filled with decisions and action. She had yearned for a moment like this. A moment when she learned that Bifalt was alive. A moment when he would understand why she reached out to him. But she had also dreaded it. There was too much at stake. She was not ready for it.

He was alive!

The Repository needed him. Magister *Rummage* needed him.

"Crayn," she panted. "Watch for me."

Then she flung other concerns away, keeping only sorcery and deafness and her husband.

Bifalt, she said, groping for a point of balance between her hopes and her fears. **Beloved. Please.**

Servants are carrying something precious to Rile. They are to the north of you, protected by priests. If it can be done, you must stop them. Do not let them cross the road. If they climbed high enough, they would be safe among hundreds of infantrymen. **Try to destroy their burdens.**

Bifalt. I beg you.

Gritting her teeth, she did not allow herself to add, I hurt you when I turned my back. I know that. I know something of your pain. Do not let it sway you. You are my husband. Rile is almost ready.

She could not be sure that Bifalt heard her. She might never know. From her vantage, she could see the road. But below it, her view was blocked by white-clad boulders and bulges, by twisted gullies, and by stunted trees draped with snow. Anything that her husband did or did not do was hidden from her.

Sheltering in a deep gulch, King Bifalt and his forces had endured two days of unremitting snow as well as they could. Now he gathered his leaders around him, Jaspid and Elgart, Amandis and Suti al-Suri. He was giving his last orders for a massed assault on Rile's infantry when he heard Estie's voice.

He recognized it instantly. Its every timbre was dear to him, every inflection of yearning, argument, and resolve. Under other circumstances, the sound might have dropped him to his knees. With one cry days ago, she had broken his image of himself, of the man he wanted to be. Furious and grieving, he had tried to give her up for lost.

But under *these* circumstances—

He was already half mad with failure and frustration. When she said his name, he froze in midsentence. When she called him *Beloved*, he trembled. But after that, he listened only long enough to understand what she wanted of him. He did not need to hear her beg.

To the startled faces of his people, he said unsteadily, "No. New orders. We have a task. We may be able to thwart Rile."

An instant later, he had himself under control.

"Suti al-Suri," he snapped.

"Brother?" murmured the chief warrior, wondering.

"This is work for marksmen." Rifles were still too new to the el-Algreb. "I leave those foot soldiers to you. Do what you can. There will be worse fighting on the higher slopes. Try to get there. My men and I will do the same."

Without waiting for an acknowledgment, the King turned to the others. "Muster the riflemen, Jaspid. We need to go north as fast as we can. Elgart, bring Crawl and Brighten. Devotee, will you join us?"

Amandis studied him for a moment, no more than a heartbeat. Her eyes were the color of burnt umber, dark with threats or promises. Her answer implied consent. "There is no trail."

Bifalt dismissed that problem. "Then leave the horses." Without a path, the mounts would lame or kill themselves on this cluttered, uneven terrain. He had to *go*. If that meant running over broken ground in deep snow, he would run.

At once, he turned away to surge through the drifts.

Estie had called him *Beloved*.

Almost immediately, his bodyguards joined him, Jeck and Malder, Spliner and Boy. Prince Jaspid shouted orders. Elgart called for the two Magisters. Leaving their precious horses, the el-Algreb readied themselves to ascend toward the road.

At Bifalt's side, the devotee of Spirit moved like a woman who knew every secret hidden by the snow.

He plowed forward, pushing off from boulders and dead trees, floundering when his feet slipped. A quick glance over his shoulder found Jaspid and the riflemen following closely. Elgart, Brighten, and Crawl were in the rear.

He crossed gullies, climbed over bulges that resembled shoulders. His labored breathing and strained muscles, he ignored. He had no time to regret his failure to train.

Then the ground rose ahead of him, a ridge like a rib of the foothills. Panting, he forced his way upward. Vapor gusted past him. Amandis put out her hand to steady him when he stumbled, then withdrew it.

Before he reached the crest, he saw light beyond it. Pale in the sunlight, the shining marked the presence of priests. He unslung his rifle and bent low so that he would not expose himself past the top of the ridge. His people crowded at his back.

The priests occupied a wide, shallow valley. Facing outward, they formed an aisle along the edges of trampled ground where Rile's army had passed. Boots by the thousands had packed the snow into slick ice between patches of bare mud. Holding up their globe-topped staffs, the priests watched for threats from both sides, north and south.

Bifalt lacked sorcery himself, but their power was unmistakable. Its faint shimmering marred the air like a smudge. It would block bullets and blades, fire and lightning. None of the weapons he commanded would pierce it.

Up the center of the aisle came men clad like servants, running hard, gasping with effort and fear, afraid to fail. They each clutched a wrapped bundle as if their lives depended on it. They ascended one at a time twenty or thirty paces apart so that any man who fell would not impede the others.

Bifalt bit the inside of his cheek, spat blood, cursed uselessly. His chance was *there*, his opportunity to strike an effective blow. Those servants brought something that the enemy needed. But he did not know how to get at them.

One of the servants had already passed him. The next was a perfect target.

If he fired, he would announce himself to Rile's sorcerers and gain nothing.

Amandis gripped his shoulder, put her mouth to his ear. "A distraction, King," she commanded. "Give me a distraction."

Before he could begin to understand her, she dove over the ridgecrest, rolled into a snowdrift. Her first movement raised a flurry of white. An instant later, she was invisible. Her raiment matched the snow. He could barely discern her passage as she crept downward.

He staggered inside himself, seemed to fall. Then he became himself again, King Bifalt of Belleger, Estie's husband, a man who faced every challenge.

The priests stood at some distance from each other, extending the reach of their theurgy. One of them was directly below him. Directly below Amandis.

The second servant was already passing.

"Jaspid," hissed Bifalt over his shoulder. "Take your riflemen uphill. Pick one priest. The second or third. Fire on him. If you can break his concentration, you may be able to kill him."

Could fifty riflemen shooting at a single sorcerer do that? Bifalt did not know. For the devotee's sake, he had to try.

Without hesitation, he called for Elgart and the Magisters.

"Downhill," he demanded. "Three or four priests below me. Strike as hard as you can. Try to strike *over* their sorcery." Brighten's Decimate of lightning could do that. Crawl's fire was more direct: it did not appear out of an empty sky. "Kill the running men."

He did not know what Amandis hoped to accomplish.

She did.

The waiting seemed interminable. It may have lasted for thirty heartbeats. Then more than fifty rifles barked almost as one. A torrent of lead poured at the priest Jaspid had chosen. Bifalt saw bullets dissolve in the blur of power or skid away. But he also saw the priest's sudden consternation. The man shouted something inaudible over the clamor of guns. The priests above and below him turned to help him.

The nearest servant staggered in fear, dropped to his knees. With panic in his eyes, he jerked himself upright and ran on.

An instant later, Crawl's Decimate blazed. A wash of fire that should have incinerated a dozen men swept toward the priests. It scalded the shimmering, drove the priests back a step. But it did not burn through their barrier.

Instead, it drew their attention and their theurgy downward, lowered their defenses. At once, Brighten's fury lashed. It caught a servant near her. He felt an instant of agony, of conflagration, then collapsed to char.

She struck again—and failed. Turning, the priests on the opposite side intercepted her lightning. It became a demented web, vivid and useless. Then it was gone.

She kept trying. Without pausing, Crawl hurled flame. The riflemen fired and fired, emptied their clips, slapped in fresh ones, and went on shooting.

Distraction.

Bifalt searched for Amandis. In a flurry of white on white, she risked rolling between two priests. They had turned toward the attacks on both sides. She passed under their sorcery.

Springing upright, she flung a dagger into an eye of one priest. He was still dying as she slashed the throat of the other.

A hole marred the blur of sorcery.

Bifalt wanted to shoot then, but she was moving too fast. He feared hitting her. Helpless, he watched as she ran at the nearest servant, broke his neck with a single punch.

Unsure of their peril, priests from both sides rushed to guard the servants. They gathered around the running men, forced the servants to halt in their midst.

Other sorcerers ran at the devotee. Now Bifalt could fire. He dropped one of them. Another.

Too late, he saw a globe thrown toward her. Yelling to warn her, he jerked his aim higher, fired, missed: an impossible shot for him. Jaspid could have hit the ball, but he was concentrating on his own task.

Deaf to Bifalt's shout—deaf or oblivious—Amandis crouched to leap at the nearest clutch of priests, to hurl herself among them and try for the servant they protected. There the grenade of sorcery struck her.

The blast killed priests. At that range, it shredded the servant and his burden.

The same force transformed the most holy devotee into a cloud of blood and guts, torn limbs, pieces of bone.

Raging, Bifalt fired until he emptied his clip. He did not see where his shots went. No more priests fell.

Three servants had been killed. Only three of ten. Two of their burdens had been destroyed. A priest had already retrieved the third. Shimmering shielded the rest. Bullets melted or skidded away. Lightning and fire touched no one.

Bifalt's cursing echoed in his mind. Aloud, he ordered his people to withdraw. He did not know what else to do. He had exposed his riflemen and Magisters as well as himself. A few globes might kill them all.

In a broken run, he fled back down the ridgeside.

Estie had called him *Beloved*—and he had failed her again.

THIRTY-TWO

THE GIFTED AND THE UNGIFTED

From the balcony outside the librarian's workroom, Magister Rummage watched the Great God's preparations with Avail, Threnody, Oblique, Bleak, and every Decimate-wielding Magister and apprentice that the Repository could muster. Spread out along the parapets, they waited for the signal to strike. Even the seventh Decimate was there in the hands of two sorcerers, an older Magister and his apprentice, a young woman. Only the eighth was not represented. Despite Sirjane Marrow's ambiguous morals, the Repository had never tainted itself with the sorcery of coercion. As for Hexin Marrow's *Final Decimate*, no one studied it for the most obvious of reasons. No one except Rummage himself understood the text.

Below the balcony and the Repository's own plateau, the keep's shadow had lifted from the Great God's pavilion. The enemy himself glowed, golden with power, but now the sun shone on the forces arrayed around him: the thick mass of the horde, the host of priests, the heavy infantry guarding the god's back. Etched in sunlight, the light infantry crossed the road and climbed.

On Magister Rummage's instructions, Magister Avail commanded the Repository's theurgists and General Klamath to wait. **Do nothing.** The mute hunchback held them back because he did not know what was coming.

The Farsighted had lost sight of King Bifalt again. Had Queen Estie reached him? Had he ignored her? Had he tried to do what she asked? Magister Rummage ached for some sign that he himself would not have to face his worst fear.

Wait.

Suti al-Suri's horse-warriors had begun to engage the light infantry. Dull in the distance, the sounds of shots and screams felt trivial. On foot, the el-Algreb attacked from the south below the road. When they ran out of bullets, they would fight with throwing daggers and cutlasses. Given time, they would deplete the Great God's defenses. But they had arrived too far from the enemy's climb toward the lower plateau. If King Bifalt failed, they would not get a chance to succeed in his place.

Holding his book out of sight under his robe, Magister Rummage glared at the god's preparations. If he had bothered to notice the people around him, he could have measured their tension and fear, their eagerness to unleash their gifts, their dread of what would happen if they were not enough. But he knew their limitations. His Magisters could not extend their Decimates as far as the lower plateau. Lightning could, and perhaps fire. None of the others.

He did not count the seventh Decimate.

The sorcerers who had left during the night to rejoin General Klamath were closer to the Great God. Magister Rummage hoped that they were strong. Their long flight from the Open Hand must have required them to exert their abilities in ways that the Repository's theurgists had never attempted. They might be more effective than the men and women Magister Rummage commanded. That was possible. He swore to himself that it was possible.

But he did not give the signal to strike. Instead, he scowled at the slopes below the pavilion. At the road and the foothills farther down. There the knuckled shapes of the terrain thwarted him. They hid what he needed to see.

The Great God sat motionless. His forces looked ready. Spread up the slope toward the Repository, the fanged men of his horde quivered with eagerness. But he did not begin his onslaught. Nor did he counter the assault of the el-Algreb. *He* was not ready.

Magister Rummage knew why.

Wait.

Magister Bleak watched for signs of the servants running franti-cally upward with burdens that must be precious to the Great God. Trapped in silence, Magister Rummage prayed that King Bifalt had stopped those men somehow. If not, nothing except terror and killing would follow. Perhaps both.

Rummage knew what those servants carried, *knew* it with the cer-tainty of the doomed. Nothing else made sense. By any other standard, the Great God's attempt on the Last Repository had already failed. Despite his throng of sorcerers and his multitude of fighting men, he could not break through the keep's hard stone. It would withstand him indefinitely. Even the gates might hold as long as they were defended by the library's Magisters. And the god had brought no siege engines of any kind. He had sacrificed his cavalry and fed the horde for no discernible purpose except to secure the lower plateau. If Magister Rummage was wrong, the Great God had crossed the world to sacrifice his empire and his tyranny for nothing.

But the mute man was not wrong. He was sure.

Wait.

Finally, Magister Bleak cleared his throat. "The sorcery of Shield-ing blurs my sight." He sounded unnaturally calm. "I cannot be certain. At first, the servants approached along an aisle of priests. Now priests cluster around them. They ascend more slowly.

"There were ten. Now I count seven. Three must have been lost. I do not know what became of their burdens."

Magister Rummage ground his teeth. That whoreson King! One simple task!

But he knew that King Bifalt's task had not been simple at all. Most of the hunchback's fury was fear by another name. Privately, he under-stood that what he had asked of Belleger's King was impossible.

Wait!

The Great God turned his head to one side, to the other. His red eyes burned like curses. If he issued commands, they required nothing of the forces around him.

Soon, Magister Rummage saw the light of globes in a wide ravine below the road.

At the same moment, Magister Bleak declared, "There! Scores of priests. The servants are among them."

Turning to Magister Threnody, he bowed. "I have done what I can, librarian. I will withdraw. When the battle begins, you will see as much as I can. I do not wish to watch it."

From the back of the balcony, Beatrix Threnody accepted his departure. If she said anything, Rummage did not hear it. The fate of the Last Repository was too great a burden for her. Magister Rummage suspected that she would never speak again.

As the priests came out of the ravine onto the road, their formation made it obvious that they protected men in their midst. At that distance, the hunchback could not tell if those men were servants, or if they carried bundles. But he believed that the reason for the Great God's delay was coming closer.

The reaction of the light infantry confirmed it. Half of them ignored Suti al-Suri's attack. Instead of fighting, they adjusted their ascent to wrap themselves around the cluster of priests. No matter what the el-Algreb did, they would not get close to those priests. The rest of the foot soldiers barred their way.

Magister Rummage clutched his chest as if his heart were bursting. The people with him did not appear to understand that their doom had arrived. When those protected servants scrambled up the hillside to deliver their burdens—when the Great God's minions were forced, willing or unwilling, to take their places at the trestle-table—

Driving his fingers like spikes into his friend's hand, Rummage wrote: —Now! Strike *now*!

Magister Avail winced at the pain, but he did not falter. As loud as a rank of trumpets, he blared, **"NOW!"**

The sudden crash of sorcery and rifle-fire began the battle.

In her covert of boulders above and south of the lower plateau, Queen Estie heard Magister Avail's call. The force of his shout shocked her.

Commander Crayn shook his head as if his ears were ringing. His mouth shaped questions that she could not hear.

But he knew what the command meant as soon as she did. The clamor of rifles was unmistakable, some nearby, others faint with distance. Ungifted as he was, he felt the abrupt sizzle and slam of the Decimates. He could not sense their unleashing as Estie did. He recognized them by their effects.

Every rifleman in General Klamath's command was firing, every soldier with a clear shot at the enemy. His Magisters unleashed their Decimates. And from the high balcony of the Repository came a torrent of destruction.

Fighting her weakness, Estie forced her head into the gap that gave her a view of Rile's pavilion and the slopes below it.

The migraine theurgy of the priests protected them and their god. Lightning broke high over their heads and scattered, wasting its force. Waves of fire splashed against the Shields and sank away. But everywhere else—

Sorcery poured onto the horde. Blasts of wind tossed the fanged men despite their unnatural strength. Pestilence flowed down the slopes, spreading sickness. Drought sucked single men and packed groups dry, shriveling muscles. When the Magisters of lightning and fire turned their power on closer targets, they delivered slaughter.

General Klamath's people had not positioned themselves to fight the horde. His riflemen and Magisters struck at Rile's heavy infantry below the pavilion. But Estie could not see what they accomplished. They were on the north side of the enemy, out of her sight. Instead, she watched the horde.

Its ruin was absolute. Magisters of earthquake had joined the Repository's fury, ripping up sheets of rock, crushing fanged men in the rubble. Bolts of lightning still reduced men to scorched bones. Fire made bodies burn like torches. Everywhere, Rile's enslaved allies died, killed by sickness or thirst, or flung off their feet and broken. Warm blood raddled the snow on all sides, transforming deep white blankets to red sludge.

Deaf to the carnage, deaf even to herself, Queen Estie croaked, "Why?"

She meant, Why does Rile not Shield them? They are helpless.

Crayn could not have heard her. Nevertheless he answered:

—He no longer needs them. Like his cavalry, they have served their purpose.

In silence, Estie protested, Has he not abused them enough? But she understood.

The Great God was testing the reach of the Repository's Magisters. Exposing the positions of Klamath's men. And wearing down the defenders.

Unaccustomed to their exertions, the library's theurgists might need hours to recover.

Gods! she cried out to Avail, to Rummage, to anyone who could hear her. **This is madness! It is what Rile wants!**

Crayn heard her as well. He gestured urgently:

—There is more. Look.

Too shaken to react, she did not move. He took her by her shoulders, shifted her look downhill.

The extermination of the horde lingered in her sight. At first, she could not see what Crayn tried to show her. Rile's cruelty— He had forced the Repository to act. Its defenders had no choice except to kill the men he sent against them. If they had not dealt with the horde, they might not be able to counter his next atrocity.

But to the west below her covert, there was no sorcery. As her vision cleared, she saw muzzle flashes, hundreds of guns spitting bullets. Klamath's hidden riflemen were firing. And other men had appeared lower down, closer to the road, men clad like nomads. They carried guns and cutlasses, bandoliers of daggers. As they rushed closer, they were shooting into the mass of Rile's light infantry.

On her shoulder, the Commander tapped:

—The el-Algreb. They must be.

Then he added:

—I do not see King Bifalt.

As if that name had the power to command her, Estie concentrated.

The el-Algreb. The Farsighted had spoken of them. They came up the foothills and onto the road south of the enemy, firing as they ran. She did not know how anyone running could shoot accurately.

Apparently, the el-Algreb lacked that skill. The infantrymen responded like men who did not fear rifles. Instead of dropping to the ground or scattering until they had a chance to close with Suti al-Suri's warriors, they stood to form a wall on this side, and on the north as well. Anyone—even Estie—could have fired at that barrier and hit *some* foeman.

The el-Algreb kept running. In front of them, the wall seemed to melt as soldiers fell, wounded or dead. But more infantrymen surged forward to support the barrier. They were—

They were *what*? Estie needed an instant to answer herself.

They were protecting something. Something essential to Rile. Priests already surrounded it, yet he was not content. He sent his light infantry to stop bullets so that something he desired or needed would reach him.

A shift among the infantrymen and priests gave Estie a brief glimpse of men who looked like servants. Carrying wrapped bundles and gasping desperately, they struggled uphill.

Why was Rile waiting? Instinctively, Estie guessed that those servants were the reason. But she had no idea what their coming meant.

Making decisions in a rage of frustration, King Bifalt led his riflemen up the twisted slopes. He had implied to Suti al-Suri that he would rejoin the el-Algreb, but he did not follow them. Instead, he took a gully that cut through the foothills more directly east. It angled away from the fighting above the road. That suited him. He aimed to climb past the immediate battle, then turn to strike at Rile from an unexpected direction.

He had only a vague idea where Rile was. Apparently, the god had established himself on a flat outcropping some distance below the Repository's porch. Bifalt did not know the place. But he would be able to see it when he had drawn his riflemen and Magisters high enough.

Beyond the gully, he stumbled on a path, followed it briefly, lost it. From his left, he heard the feverish crack of rifles, the ravages of sorcery, the screams of men. With an effort, he ignored it. Every blow of his heart pounded pain into his damaged hand. He struggled for breath, and could not get enough.

Without any obvious effort, Prince Jaspid and Jeck kept up with him. Elgart, Malder, and Boy labored at his back. Spliner did what he could. The riflemen climbed at the pace of the Magisters, who had not spent years training for toughness.

When the shape of the hills gave him a chance, King Bifalt veered more to the north, closer to the tumult. He had a few moments of easier running. Then a ridge barred his way. He flung himself up its ragged slope. The clamor of fighting called to him, demanded him. He needed to see where he was. Where Rile was. What was happening.

He found answers at the ridgecrest.

The outcropping was *there*, at least a stone's throw above him and a long rifle-shot north. It formed a broad flat place large enough to hold a pavilion, the Great God himself, hundreds of priests, and a numberless mass of armored infantrymen in a cordon that guarded Rile on three sides, north, west, and south.

The horde had moved uphill to the east, but it was already finished, dying helpless under tidal waves of sorcery from the high ramparts of the Repository.

Downhill, below the pavilion and the heavy infantry, the unarmored infantrymen stood their ground. A stupid tactic. They had no defense against the gunfire and arrows of the el-Algreb, and no way to strike back. And Suti al-Suri's people were not alone. Scattered everywhere across the hillsides, riflemen were firing. In their coverts, they were safe from an enemy that did not advance.

North of them, another battle raged. Bifalt heard the distant rattle of rifle-fire. He could not gauge that conflict past the mass of the heavy infantry, the uneven rise and fall of the terrain. But whoever commanded there had Magisters with them, Bellegerin and Amikan. The King saw lightning strike, and gouts of flame. None of the other Decimates were visible.

Klamath! That brave, self-doubting man had justified Bifalt's trust. Somehow, he had brought his army here and positioned it on both sides of the enemy's advance. A lesser General might have retreated to the Repository. That would have kept his men alive, at least for a time. It would also have made them useless.

Elgart caught up with King Bifalt. He and Jaspid crouched beside Bifalt at the ridgecrest. Breathing hard, the bodyguards waited at Bifalt's back. Behind them, the riflemen brought Crawl and Brighten up the ridge.

The King sighted his rifle, confirmed that the range was too long for him. In any case, he could not support his gun with his bad hand. It gave him too much pain. He had to get closer.

With part of his attention and one ear, he tracked the firing of the el-Algreb. It had been almost constant. Now it was stuttering. Suti al-Suri's warriors were running out of bullets. Soon they would be forced to engage the enemy with their blades.

Klamath's men were more sparing in their shots. They chose their targets and fired with care. But they, too, did not have endless ammunition.

Bifalt hoped to take some of the pressure off Klamath's men, and Suti al-Suri's, if he could. While he considered his choices, he mastered his breathing, then asked his companions, "What do you see?"

He meant, What should we do?

"Rile," said Elgart. He snatched air, pointed at the pavilion. "Sitting. Waiting? For *what*? He has lost the horde. His men are dying. Waiting *costs* him."

Clearly, the Great God did not care. Only the servants bringing some necessary treasure mattered.

Prince Jaspid had a different answer. "Direct attack, Brother." After days of denial, he sounded eager. "The heavy infantry. Let us attack there. If that does not make Rile respond, nothing will."

King Bifalt nodded. "As you say, Brother."

Slipping between his bodyguards, he slid a little way back down the slope to his approaching company. "Drink," he commanded. "Empty your waterskins. Discard them and your packs. We must run in earnest now. Do not shoot until you are sure of your aim."

Quickly, he scanned the riflemen, picked ten of the weariest. "Crawl and Brighten are yours," he told them. "Bring them behind us. Come as close as you dare, but do not risk them. We need all the support that they can give."

Without another word, he returned to the crest. His men had come too far and endured too much to fail him now.

The el-Algreb had used up their ammunition. Swinging their cut-lasses, they charged. As if they were not tired and had no fear, they shouted as they ran. Their howling sounded like glee.

"They will be slaughtered," groaned Elgart.

Bifalt made a spitting sound. His only allies— "If that is their choice." Surely Suti al-Suri knew that he and his people had done more than the King had any right to ask.

Jaspid ignored the el-Algreb. "Are we ready?"

"Soon," answered King Bifalt. "When the men join us. If you want overwhelming odds, you will have them."

Grimly, he stayed where he was until Jeck tapped his shoulder. Then he rose to his feet, took one last deep breath, and started down the ridge-side toward the enemy.

With fifty riflemen and two Magisters, Belleger's King went to challenge the thousands of Rile's heavy infantry.

Jaspid led the way. Elgart and Bifalt's bodyguards accompanied their King. When he reached the foot of the slope, he broke into a run.

Ahead of him, the terrain rose into a low hillock like a clenched knuckle. He took it as fast as he could, cradling his rifle. At the top, he stretched out on the ground. His hand *hurt*, but he had no time for pain. With his elbows braced in snow and mud, he fired.

Elgart and the bodyguards dropped beside him to shoot. Prince Jaspid remained upright, encouraging the enemy to see that he was not afraid. With casual ease, he dropped infantrymen one at a time.

Moments later, the riflemen arrived. Some of them stood like Jaspid. The rest followed King Bifalt's example, used the earth to steady their straining muscles.

Bifalt emptied his first clip, slapped in a second. He aimed for faces, but most of his slugs glanced off iron breastplates. Two or three foemen staggered, fell. If their wounds were minor, they would rise again.

Jaspid was faster, and almost inhumanly accurate. His men were good shots. If the infantrymen remained where they were, holding their ground for no obvious reason, their losses would mount.

Abruptly, the armored men moved. They had received some command, or had simply exhausted their willingness to wait and die. Two or three hundred of them started toward the King.

They did not charge. Holding their broadswords ready, they marched closer. For every one who fell, two more came forward.

Bifalt no longer knew how the el-Algreb fared. He had no attention to spare for them. Despite the support of his elbows, every kick of his gun seemed to break more bones in his bad hand. He emptied another clip, replaced it. When the infantrymen were within fifty paces, he jumped to his feet.

"Keep firing!" he shouted at his company. "As long as you can!"

Shooting wildly with one hand, he used up one more clip. Then he discarded his rifle, snatched out his saber, and ran to engage the enemy.

Jaspid went ahead, still using his gun with inhuman ease. Elgart joined Bifalt, followed at once by his bodyguards. Like the Prince, Jeck and Boy kept shooting. Malder and Spliner drew their blades.

Behind them, the riflemen made a concerted effort to redouble their fire. Dozens of the enemy fell, hit in their faces, or struck by shots that pierced their armor. Others stumbled, bleeding, to their knees. Their bodies fouled the strides of the men behind them. Gaps appeared in the foemen's line.

King Bifalt aimed for one of those gaps.

Jaspid shouldered his rifle, brought out his saber and dagger. Unable to fire effectively while he ran, Elgart had already dropped his gun, readied his blades. Jeck and Boy did the same. Riflemen followed Spliner and Malder, shouting for Belleger and Amika.

Like the point of a spear, seven men flung themselves against Rile's heavy infantry.

Bifalt hardly noticed that Jaspid was already several strides ahead of him, leading the way, protecting him. The King hacked at a thigh on one side, ducked under a cut, slashed at a face on the other. After that, he seemed to lose consciousness. There was nothing left of him except fighting.

On the north side of the enemy's line, General Klamath watched the battle and considered his choices.

Covered by the fire of his men and the Decimates of his Magisters, he had worked his way high enough to glance at the Great God's pavilion between shots and commands. He had a clear view of the golden figure seated on its throne, as perfect as a sculpture, and flagrant with power.

Klamath resisted the impulse to shoot at Rile. He recognized the strange blur of the priests' sorcery. It would stop his bullets. And he would betray his position. With very little effort, half a dozen armored infantrymen would be enough to drive him back. Or they might hunt him down and kill him.

He needed a better option.

He had no idea why Rile had not already unleashed his assault on the Repository. Indeed, the General could not imagine what form that assault would take. It would require theurgy, that was certain. Mere men with swords and lances, or priests with exploding globes, would never break through the stone of the keep. But Klamath knew almost nothing about the possibilities of sorcery.

Still, he knew *waiting* when he saw it. The Great God was definitely waiting. For what? General Klamath did not try to guess. He could see that whatever Rile needed was coming closer. It would reach him soon.

This was demonstrated by the actions of the light infantry far down the hillsides. They had been standing like a human wall, letting themselves be butchered by bullets and Decimates. Now, without any audible command, they broke formation and charged. Yelling their fury, they spread out across the slopes, seeking the riflemen who had savaged them with bullets, the Magisters who had burned or sickened them, or had sucked them dry.

The General faced a bitter choice. He could commit his forces against those infantrymen. Or he could try to do something about, well, whatever it was that Rile awaited.

He had to attack the god directly.

Klamath had no time to think. He had come this far to defend the library. Killing distant infantrymen would not suffice.

More of his people would die. Or they would die faster.

He did not have a better idea.

He called new orders to Captain Rowt. "Pass word to our riflemen. Tell them to disengage. I want them here." He needed to concentrate his forces. "And bring our Magisters closer. We will strike at Rile's heavy infantry."

Rowt glanced around at the enemy, swallowed arguments. "As you say, General."

Crouching to avoid attracting the enemy's notice, he hurried downward.

An appalling amount of time seemed to pass. Then Klamath saw distant riflemen leave their shelters and sprint upward. The Magisters moved as well without ceasing their waves of sorcery, the relays that allowed some of them to rest while others struck.

Their Decimates warded them. Lightning slew whole squads of the enemy. Fire drove infantrymen back, burning. Pestilence and drought left their victims staggering until wind flattened them. But the Decimate of earthquake was more effective than the others. The earthquake-wielders lifted sheets and slabs of stone, heavy boulders, mounds of scree, and pitched them against the enemy.

With his heart beating in his throat, Klamath watched his people come. He feared a counterstrike by Rile's priests. But most of them remained concentrated around their self-appointed god. The rest moved through the center of the light infantry, ascending cautiously. Klamath's people reached him without any new losses.

Now he had another decision to make. He had no hope against the priests. How should he attack the heavy infantry defending the pavilion? His Magisters had drained much of their strength. The riflemen were running low on ammunition. Which force should he risk sacrificing first?

That decision was easier. When the Magisters exhausted themselves, they would be little better than fodder. The soldiers had spent seasons or years training with sabers as well as guns.

"Rowt!" yelled Klamath. "Tell the Magisters to keep their distance! Conserve their Decimates! They are our last chance."

As soon as the young Captain called an answer, General Klamath gathered riflemen around him.

"The heavy infantry, men. There." He pointed at the place where the throng of priests faded into the cordon of armored infantrymen. "We will fire until we have no more bullets. Then we will charge."

"Their armor, sir," panted one of the veterans.

"Breastplates," retorted Klamath. "They have no other iron. They can be killed. Their swords are heavy. Our sabers are faster." Grimacing, he added, "If those priests turn on us, our Magisters will do what they can."

He did not doubt his Magisters. He doubted their endurance.

At once, a younger voice called, "As you say, General!"

That was enough for Klamath. He nodded as if he were sure. "Find clear targets," he told his men. "Do not waste your shots."

Turning, he unslung his gun, took aim at one of the nearest infantrymen, and fired first.

Quickly, the riflemen spread out around him. One at a time as they found their positions, they started shooting. For a moment, they managed only a scattering of gunfire. Then all of their rifles began barking at once.

Their fusillade would have withered long lines of unarmored men. Most of the bullets that struck iron glanced off like flung stones. A few hit squarely, pierced the breastplates and bit flesh. But Klamath's men understood their orders. Instinctively, some of them aimed at the chests of their enemies. The rest were more effective.

A bullet that found a face killed instantly. A leg-shot infantryman was as good as a dead one. A man with a damaged arm or shoulder would have to swing his broadsword with one hand, if he could swing it at all.

If only Rile had not brought such an *abundance* of men— He had already sacrificed thousands, yet he still had more than enough, so many that he did not feel compelled to answer Klamath's assault.

Soon, the shooting staggered as riflemen emptied their last clips. The hail of bullets became sporadic bursts. It dwindled to single shots. In moments, only Klamath still had ammunition.

Ah, hells.

Had King Bifalt chosen him for this? For *this?*

Perhaps not. But the King was not there.

General Klamath dropped his gun, his satchel of clips. He unsheathed his saber and dagger.

First at a walk, then at a trot, finally running, he led his men against Rile's heavy infantry.

Sickened by the slaughter of the horde, Queen Estie clung to her view downhill as if it might offer some version of hope.

It did not.

Far below her, the unarmored infantrymen were released at last from their fatal passivity. The el-Algreb stood their ground until they had no bullets. Then Suti al-Suri's warriors advanced to engage the enemy.

At first, they seemed improbably successful. As swift as winds, they hacked and slashed with their cutlasses. With thrown daggers and ferocity, they kept the javelins and short swords of their foes at bay.

But they were too few against so many. Despite his losses, Rile could afford more. Estie saw the precise moment when the tide of fighting turned. The el-Algreb were driving their opponents back. Then they were being driven. To stay alive, they had to retreat. With every backward step, they left more of their own dead under the boots of the infantrymen.

A man who may have been Suti al-Suri went down, buried by the onslaught. An instant later, he was on his feet again, leaving a tangle of slashed throats and stabbed eyes where he had fallen.

But he had lost his cutlass in the struggle. His people were snared in confusion. Waving his arms, apparently shouting, he pulled his surviving warriors into a more orderly withdrawal. They contested every step, but now they fought to protect each other instead of to kill their foes.

If Rile had recalled his men then, the remaining el-Algreb might have escaped.

Perhaps he did. Estie did not see it. Her attention was snatched away.

A jolt shook her world when she saw King Bifalt appear on the crest of a hillock halfway down the slope from her covert.

Prince Jaspid and Elgart were with him. His bodyguards. He had a company of riflemen at his back. Behind them were two Magisters. She knew them by their bloodied, travel-grimed robes.

That was his whole force.

Bifalt!

Estie gathered herself to shout his name. Crayn's sudden clench on her arm silenced her. He must have guessed what she would do. Jerking her around, he gestured urgently.

—Do not, Majesty! Say nothing! You will distract him!

She wanted to shout, Distract him? Why not? She knew what her husband had in mind as if she had already seen it. With nothing except his paltry command, he was going to attack Rile's position. It would be suicide, a more certain death than if he had cut his own throat.

She had to stop him.

But he was more than her husband, her beloved. He was King Bifalt of Belleger. He had been preparing for this fight as long as she had known him. He would not turn from it.

And he was not alone. Jaspid would die himself before he let Bifalt fall. Elgart and the bodyguards would sacrifice themselves without hesitation. Indirectly, Klamath's riflemen spread across the slopes would support their King. Bifalt had only two Magisters, but they had proven themselves.

Estie's husband may or may not have succeeded at the task she had given him. She could not justify interfering with a task that he had chosen for himself.

Acknowledging her Commander with a nod, she turned from him to watch Bifalt fight.

Her argument with herself seemed to take no time at all, yet when she looked downhill again, Bifalt was already moving. With his companions around him and his riflemen at his back, he charged Rile's heavy infantry.

The god may have recognized the man who had cost him so many lives and thwarted his desire to use Estie's road. He may have been furious. He sent a large force to overwhelm the King's attack.

She expected to see her husband killed at any moment. Despite his paltry numbers, he had not brought all of his riflemen. A few remained behind, apparently guarding his Magisters.

But now Prince Jaspid was leading the way, the best fighter in Belleger and Amika. Elgart, Malder, and Jeck were veterans of the old wars. They covered Bifalt. And the Magisters were ready. As the King and his defenders pierced the mass of infantrymen, fire and lightning struck.

The Decimate of fire cooked foemen in their armor. The Decimate of lightning reduced men to smoking bones with every bolt. Together, they cleared a path for Bifalt's attack into the midst of his enemies. Then they directed their power elsewhere to avoid harming the King's company.

Briefly, Estie scanned the rampage of sorcery. The Decimate of fire came in unsteady gouts, fatal but sporadic. That Magister was weakening. But the other delivered lightning with a fury that seemed to have no limits.

Many of Rile's infantrymen were already down. He sent more.

When she looked for Bifalt again, he was gone. Jaspid, Elgart, the bodyguards: they were all gone.

"Crayn!" she gasped. "Oh, Bifalt. Crayn!"

The Commander snatched at her attention.

—Melee, Majesty. Speed against weight and numbers. The King and his men must be *fast*. They must duck and roll. Use their foes as shields. Slash where they are not expected. The confusion hides them.

Grimly, he added:

—They will be cut down if they are not fast *enough*.

Estie wanted to scream. It was too much to bear. The thought of Bifalt *cut down* threatened her sense of who she was. She was more than his wife, more than Amika's Queen. She was a sorceress now. She had been sent to her covert to serve the Repository's defense. She had to do *something*.

Rather than endanger Bifalt, she chose to risk General Klamath.

Klamath! she called. **Hear me! King Bifalt attacks from the south. His Magisters do not suffice. He needs you.** She had no heart to speak of the el-Algreb. But she could not stop herself from saying, **I need him.**

Then there was nothing for her to do except watch.

It was not enough.

After the destruction of the horde, the Repository's Decimate-wielders collapsed in weariness. They had never fought in battle, never killed defenseless foes. Pallid with strain and dismay, some sat on the floor of the balcony, gasping. Others leaned against the wall, hardly able to breathe.

Unaware of them, Magister Rummage stood at the parapet, Magister Avail at his side. A man and woman gifted with the seventh Decimate were there as well. Nearby, Magister Oblique watched. Only she and perhaps the librarian knew the secret of the hunchback's gift. She studied him, fear in her eyes.

Fear and woe.

Locked around himself, Magister Rummage watched the arrival of the burdens for which the Great God waited. Seven servants and one priest stumbled into the pavilion, clutching their bundles.

There were ten stools ready at the long table, spaced more than an arm's length apart. At a glance from their god, the servants went to the first seven stools. The priest took the eighth. As one, they set their burdens on the table. As one, they removed the coverings. Their hands shook, the servants' from exhaustion, the priest's for other reasons.

At once, the servants stumbled away. The priest withdrew to the back of the space. His eyes glared as if he were terrified.

Exactly as if he were terrified.

Magister Rummage understood.

"Books?" demanded Magister Oblique. "The Great God has been waiting for *books*?"

Rummage wrote feverishly on Magister Avail's forearm. For everyone who could hear him, Avail repeated:

Not books. *Book.* **Eight copies of one book.**

The hunchback was sure.

He did not react when Magister Threnody joined him. He had no room for surprise. For a moment, she peered down at the pavilion, at the table, at the books. Then she murmured unsteadily, "Magister Rummage is right. That is Hexin Marrow's *Final Decimate*." She spoke as if she were dying inside. "Or it is the Great God's version of Hexin Marrow's work."

Magister Oblique translated that announcement for Magister Avail. When he understood her, every line of his face betrayed horror.

Cries scattered along the balcony. The final Decimate? The *final*—? Magister Rummage heard none of them.

This Decimate could be countered or dismissed by another sorcerer with the same gift. Hexin Marrow had made that clear. The attempt would destroy the man or woman who made it.

Cringing, the librarian retreated to the back wall, taking the wielders of the seventh Decimate with her. She looked lost, utterly out of her depth.

As stately as the ruler of the known world, the Great God rose to his feet. He held his staff upright like a challenge, an emblem of pride and scorn. His eyes and the gems of his cross shone, as avid as triumph in the clear sunlight.

Instinctively, all of the priests flinched back a step.

Their god ignored their alarm. He glanced to the left, to the right, choosing. With a small wave of his staff, he summoned.

Compelled, seven priests answered. Leaving the other sorcerers, they came to the pavilion, entered it, joined the priest already standing at the back. Along the way, they dropped their own staffs.

They had changed. Like every other priest, they had resembled ordinary men. They had walked normally, had used their arms and eyes and expressions like anyone else. Now, coerced, they moved like men who had been hammered together out of discarded scraps of wood. Only their eyes remained of who they had once been.

They were as terrified as their waiting comrade.

Groaning, Magister Oblique said, "That is the *eighth* Decimate. The Decimate of coercion. Without it, no one would risk the final Decimate."

The shattering of the Last Repository was about to begin.

Biting his lips until they bled, Magister Rummage clutched his own book inside his robe. Other people might find hope in knowing that the Great God did not wield the final Decimate himself. Or in the fact that he had brought ten copies of the book and now had only eight. Or in the likelihood that no single blast would be enough. Magister Rummage had no hope left.

The Great God was growing impatient. With a stamp of his staff, he exerted his power to grasp the last priest in the line and force him forward. Like a derelict, the man shambled toward the table. There he dropped onto his stool as if his knees had been cut. He seemed blind with fear, but his god did not permit that. Without his eyes, he could not read the text.

Sweating and shaking, he put his hands on the book. Opened it near its middle, where its secrets were kept. Instructions and dire warnings filled the rest of the tome. Descriptions of the Decimate's effects.

Unable to refuse his god's command, the priest began to read. He appeared to read aloud, but the Repository did not hear him. The lower plateau was too far away.

The priest read the words in front of him. Turned a page. Read more.

Without warning, he became an eruption of light like a little sun.

His Decimate struck with the force of a cataclysm. A tremendous concussion hit the Repository. From end to end, the battlements lurched. Magisters staggered. Some of them screamed. Cracks webbed the stone, as delicate and complex as a spider's work. The crash and rumble of breakage pummeled the air, left everyone momentarily deaf. Magister Avail dropped to his hands and knees. Magister Oblique clutched at Rummage for balance.

When the blast ended, the iron-bound doors of the keep were gone, transformed into splinters and flung scrap. Where they had stood, the stone anchoring them had become a crude arch gaping open to the Great God. Mounds of rubble marred the Repository's porch.

The screaming did not stop. It might not stop anytime soon.

In the aftermath of the blow, even Magister Rummage was slow to notice that the priest reading the book was gone as well. He had been reduced to ash, and his book with him. Briefly, the table where the book had lain burned. Then the flames faded to smoke and charred wood.

Magister Rummage had known what to expect, but still he could not breathe. The blood had been shocked out of his muscles. His lungs refused to work. A grey haze swirled around the edges of his vision, spreading—

To catch himself, he dropped like Magister Avail, pulling Oblique with him. For a moment, his gaze met his friend's aghast stare. If he had ever had a voice, he would have wailed.

Then someone—Apprentice Travail?—thumped Rummage's back, and the jolt enabled him to snatch a frantic breath. Dust clogged the air, the powder of crushed stone. It hurt his contorted chest. Nevertheless he surged upright.

Coughing, he surveyed the debris on the porch, the appalled priests waiting in the pavilion, the Great God. Rile grinned back at him like a predator closing on its kill.

Around him, people cried that the way was open, the Great God could enter whenever he wished, he could send his priests and infantrymen storming up the slope to rush in and begin havoc.

Magister Rummage knew better. The Great God had not come to occupy the Last Repository. He intended to destroy it. And he still had seven copies of his book.

He would not risk himself against the library's surviving theurgies. Instead, he would compel his priests to Shield him until the work was done.

Bitter at the end of his life, Magister Rummage took out his book from its hiding place in his robe.

Hexin Marrow's *Final Decimate.*

That or nothing would kill the Great God.

Magister Avail had been as stunned as anyone, as profoundly shocked, scarcely able to draw breath. But seeing the book in his friend's hands brought him back to himself.

Fighting his weakness, his slack muscles, his weight, he floundered to his feet. At once, he threw himself at Rummage as if he imagined that he could outwrestle the hunchback.

"No!" His cry was pure anguish. "Do not!"

Almost casually, Magister Rummage knotted one fist in Avail's robe, held the deaf sorcerer away from him. With the other, he wrote on Avail's chest:

—Who else *is* there?

Gasping at the dust in the air, or at the force of his friend's tapping, Magister Avail demanded, "Let *me!*"

Rummage stared.

—How?

Avail could not read the book. That was not his gift.

Magister Avail controlled himself, spoke only to his friend.

My gift. Those Shields cannot silence me. I can make him *hear* me. I can hurt him. Loosen his grip on his sorcerers. Avail dragged in a deep breath. **By the Decimates, Rummage! I may be able to *kill* him.**

As Queen Estie had killed Tak Biondi.

Magister Rummage froze. Could Avail do that? Apart from Amika's Queen, no other sorcerer in living memory had shared the deaf man's talent. Books on the subject were few and vague. What were its limits? Could it affect a self-proclaimed god as powerful as the Repository's enemy?

The god seemed to gaze straight up at Magister Rummage. His eyes shone with something like glee as he required another of his priests to sit at the table, open the next book.

The hunchback embraced his friend, then shoved him away. He did not know another way to give his consent.

Magister Avail stumbled to the parapet, caught himself on one of the crenellations. Straining for air, he gathered his strength, his voice. He appeared to take a long time. Then he faced the enemy.

His shout was focused on the Great God, as direct as a rifle-shot, but he mustered more force than he could contain. Despite his concentration, everyone heard him.

BUTCHER!

The god's head jerked. Sorcery jolted his mind. He lurched, bared his teeth. The backs of his knees struck his chair. He fell into it. The red scorn of his eyes and his gems dimmed.

For an instant, confusion swept through the priests. The smudge of their Shields vanished. The priest at the table jumped away from his book. The others looked around frantically. Some of them staggered like their god. The infantrymen stumbled and stopped with their blades raised.

But only for a few heartbeats.

Then the Great God lifted his head, wrenched himself upright in his chair. His crimson glare resembled madness. With a thud of his staff, his cross, he resumed control.

At once, the priests steadied themselves. In an instant, they restored the barrier of their theurgy.

Other uses of the eighth Decimate seemed to take longer, or perhaps they demanded more of their wielder. The priest near the next book hung back, resisting his god's will. The infantrymen stood as if they had forgotten what they were doing.

Magister Rummage wheeled on his friend. If he had not been born mute, he would have shouted, Hit him again! *Again!*

But Magister Avail could not hear anyone. He had plunged to his knees. Blood streamed from his ruptured eardrums, his burst eyeballs. He carried too much weight for his untested strength to bear. In the extremity of his gift, his body failed him.

His last words were for Queen Estie.

You are alone now. I am done.

Coughing up his life, he sprawled on the stone.

The librarian tried to respond. Frantically, she cried out for shamans, physicians, servants. But there was no help anywhere that could arrive in time.

General Klamath heard Queen Estie's call. **King Bifalt attacks from the south. He needs you.** Her appeal tore at his heart. He wanted to answer it. But he had no time. He was fighting for his life.

Rile's infantrymen came at him in their iron breastplates, swinging broadswords heavy enough to crack stones. They carried the weight of their armor and blades easily, and fought with the relentlessness of fanatics. Whatever they were in their own lives, *here* they were Rile's true believers or his compelled servants. They feared nothing, flinched at nothing. When the men around them were fried by lightning or cooked by fire, they took no notice. Other Decimates did not daunt them. They had many times the General's numbers. They were going to prevail.

But they had trained to fight men who fought as they did, standing face to face and hacking until one of them fell. Klamath's soldiers relied on different tactics. No Bellegerin or Amikan in his right mind would stand and trade cuts against broadswords and heavy iron.

Despite Prince Jaspid's indifference to authority and command, he had taught the riflemen well. Klamath was not among the best of them, far from it. But he knew when to duck and parry. He understood the value of a slashed thigh, a severed hamstring. When the opportunity came, he could thrust at a throat or a face without hesitation.

And he had his dagger. It moved as if it had a life of its own, protecting him like a comrade at his side.

All around him, infantrymen fell, tripping on their own soldiers, or baffled by unfamiliar strikes. Despite their ferocity, they were thwarted by riflemen who dodged and spun, by blades that cut at unexpected angles.

The infantrymen were winning. There were too many of the bastards. If General Klamath had paused to count his own losses, he might have wept. His King needed him. But if he and his men tried to disengage, tried to turn and run, they would die. They could not defend against foes at their backs. Forced to ignore Queen Estie's summons, Klamath fought as if he had given his body to someone else. As if fighting were a kind of trance. He had no other choice.

Then he heard a concussion like a mountain shattering. The ground under him felt it. It knocked him several steps down the slope.

He had no idea what it meant. Now he was too far below the pavilion. He could not see Rile. A clenched bulge of the foothills blocked his view of the Repository. And he was not sensitive to sorcery. He could only guess that something vicious had occurred. Vicious and horrible.

But it changed nothing. Undeterred, Rile's soldiers kept coming. Desperate and grim, Klamath and his people fought back.

Without warning, a shout of pure fury shocked him. It was only in his mind, soundless amid the gasps and screams and ringing iron, yet it hit like a thunderclap.

BUTCHER!

The jolt could have cost him his life. Any number of his riflemen could have died, their concentration broken. But their foes did not take advantage of it.

Between one instant and the next, the tight throng of priests became milling confusion. The blur of their power vanished. And the infantrymen froze, locked in place by an unexpected shift in the compulsion that drove them.

General Klamath took his chance while the god's men held back.

"Strike south!" he yelled. Across the slopes below the plateau and the pavilion, through the mass of Rile's infantry. "Guard the Magisters and *go*! King Bifalt is there! He *needs* us!"

At once, the combined forces of Belleger and Amika broke away from their foes.

Some of the riflemen took four running steps, Klamath himself managed three, before Rile's soldiers remembered who they were and followed.

The priests were recovering quickly, but did nothing to support the infantrymen. Their only task was to protect their god. Waving their staffs, they renewed their shimmering.

Pursued by laboring foes, Klamath sent his men and Magisters at the crush of heavy and light infantry where it spread down the hillsides, separating the north side of the battle from the south.

Beyond that solid barrier were more of the General's riflemen. If Hegels had any sense, he had already committed his people to support King Bifalt. And if the First Captain hesitated, Hellick was there. He would know what to do.

For the moment, Klamath's sole duty was to breach the barricade of infantry.

It should have been impassable.

But fierce winds slapped foemen aside, forced a way into the throng. Drought and pestilence weakened the edges of the opening. Lightning and fire savaged Rile's men farther away. Sharp heaves of earthquake kept infantrymen off Klamath's back.

Then Klamath was in the midst of the fighting. His King needed him. With all of his waning strength, he answered Queen Estie's call.

Shielded in her covert, Estie could not see the Repository, but she witnessed the extravagant flare of power from the pavilion. It was too bright to bear. It left blind splotches across her sight. Sensations of sorcery ran along her nerves like stinging insects.

Before she could see again, she felt the concussion, the blast like the detonation of an arsenal. The stone under her shifted. The boulders concealing her tilted, came within inches of falling away. Crayn held her, ready to drag her back through the doorway if she lost her cover.

As the blots in her vision lessened, she saw fire burning on the table in the pavilion. Almost immediately, the flames faded to smoke and died.

The priest who had been at the table was gone. His book had been destroyed. Only ash remained.

"Gods!" she panted. "What was that?"

Her companion had no answer.

For a time, there was nothing that she could do except stare.

Rile grinned up at the Repository. He coerced another priest to take a seat at the table. His other sorcerers Shielded him. More infantrymen hurried down the hillsides to attack King Bifalt's command. Riflemen hidden all over the lower slopes fired and fired, doing their best to support the King. When they ran out of bullets, they left their shelters. Discarding their guns, they drew their sabers and sprinted uphill, into battle. Estie saw Hegels among them, and Hellick. No one else she knew.

Then she heard Magister Avail's mental shout: a roar of rage louder and more savage than any voice she knew. It was not for her. It was aimed at Rile. She caught only its edges. It was too fierce to be perfectly focused.

Knowing what she had done to Tak Biondi, she understood.

Avail's yell punched Rile's head, knocked him backward. He collapsed in his chair as if he had lost consciousness.

The effect on the priests was immediate. The man at the table sprang away. Panic gripped the others. They became a knot of chaos. Some of them dropped their staffs, gazed about them wildly. The sorcery that protected Rile evaporated.

And on the slopes below Estie, the infantrymen halted. Some of them froze in midswing. The others locked their knees and stood panting like men who had forgotten who they were.

She hoped for an instant counterattack from the Repository.

There was nothing. The pavilion was beyond the reach of those Magisters—or the keep had been too badly damaged.

Moments later, Rile lifted his head. He straightened himself in his seat. His eyes glared an incandescent red. With a thump of his staff, he reasserted his coercion.

But apparently he had been damaged. He needed time to recover his full control. The priest who had left the table was allowed to remain at the back of the pavilion. Instead, the god began with the sorcerers who had been Shielding him. Roughly, he jerked them back to their task. Then, as his protective haze regained its force, he freed his infantrymen from their uncertainty. At once, they wrenched themselves into motion and resumed fighting.

The pause between Rile's collapse and his recovery took almost no time at all, but it was enough for Estie. During that small window of opportunity, she grasped several things almost simultaneously.

Magister Avail's last words lingered in her mind. *You are alone now.* A sigh like a dying breath. *I am done.* Now he was dead.

The Repository depended on him.

Nevertheless he had shown her how Rile could be hurt. That was important. Astonishing. It had implications for her that she was not ready to face. But it was possible.

She had to find a way. There was no one else. Without his friend, Magister Rummage could not make himself heard. Only she had the ability to arrange an effective strike.

At a distance below her, however, King Bifalt's attack was failing. If her husband had not already been *cut down*, he had been given a brief respite. Now he had to fight again. The riflemen racing upward were not enough to save him. And General Klamath could not reach him in time. He would be overwhelmed. Everyone with him would die.

Estie had a choice to make, her husband or the Repository. She could call Rummage's Magisters down from the keep until they were near enough to hit the pavilion, the priests, the Great God. She could *demand* their power and their lives until they broke through the priests' theurgy. Or she could try to protect Bifalt with her voice. He was the heart and spirit of his men. Without him, they would be lost.

But she hesitated. Who was *she* to command the Repository's defense? What could her gift do for her husband?

Then Rile found his strength again. From his chair, he rose upright, radiating power as if gold were the hue of wrath.

At once, the consternation of the priests fell away. Scrambling to obey, they renewed their Shields.

A moment later, the infantrymen shook off their doubts and surged back into battle.

Estie had missed her chance.

She might have wept then, intolerably frustrated, disgusted with herself. But Crayn surprised her by grabbing her shoulders. She lost her view of the pavilion and King Bifalt's dying men. By plain strength, Crayn turned her to face the southward gap in her covert.

A woman in a white robe was there, squeezing her way through the space between boulders. A woman Estie knew.

The most holy devotee of Spirit Lylin.

As soon as the devotee reached the clear floor of the covert, she adjusted her robe and smiled. Her mouth moved. Unable to hear, Estie simply shook her head.

Lylin frowned. She barked a demand at Crayn. As if Estie were not present, Lylin and the Commander exchanged a flurry of questions. Crayn's answers made Lylin's face twist with chagrin. At his next words, her expression cleared. She smiled at Estie again. At first, her smile seemed tentative. Then it became a fierce grin. The Commander translated for her.

—You are needed, Majesty. Summon Prince Jaspid. The Repository will fall without him.

Estie gaped like a half-wit. The devotee's sudden appearance had driven everything out of her mind.

Lylin frowned in vexation, appeared to sigh. Crayn repeated what she said.

—Forgive me, Majesty. I have no *time*. The keep cannot endure many of those blasts. Forget what you have lost. Accept your gift. Summon the Prince.

—I would rely on Magister Avail, but I cannot reach him quickly. The Prince must come to me. Tell him to come here. When he is safe, I will guide him.

Finally, Estie managed a few words. "Why Jaspid?" she asked as if she were choking. "What do you want him to do?"

The devotee appeared to snarl. She appeared to shout.

Scowling his disapproval, Crayn signed:

—Do you not understand, Majesty? *We have no time.*

Shaken, Estie could hardly think. The woman who had once beaten

Jaspid half to death needed him now? How did that make sense? How would Bifalt survive without his brother?

How could she turn away from her husband a second time?

Nevertheless Lylin's intensity compelled her. It forced her to acknowledge that she could not save Bifalt. Her gift was simply too small to affect a host of infantrymen. She lacked Magister Avail's years of experience. She had not learned how to direct her power against large numbers.

The thought of her love's peril wrenched her heart. But she had to let him go.

"I will do it," she said in a rush. "I do not know if he is alive. But I will call to him."

The devotee snapped:

—Do it *now*. Then pray that he succeeds. He will give you your moment to strike. Wait for it.

At once, she left, pushing her way between the boulders toward the fighting.

Queen Estie watched Lylin hurry partway down the slope, then crouch to conceal herself. In the untrodden white of the snow, she resembled part of the hillside.

We have no time.

Estie swallowed her grief. **Jaspid!** she called. **Come to me.** Her voice held a sob. **I need you.** She would have preferred to face her father again. **We need you.**

With a few words, she described her location. In a few words, she told him where to look for her. She could not bear to say Lylin's name. The devotee had too much power over him. Instead, she added, **No one else can save us.**

Did he trust her enough to abandon his brother, his King?

When she was finished, she surrendered to her fears for a moment. Wheeling on the Commander, she struck his breastplate with both palms.

"Gods, Crayn! What does she expect me to do? How am I supposed to know my moment?"

She *needed* Bifalt.

Crayn's gaze was an ache of regret. Carefully, he replied:

—I hardly know the devotee, Majesty. But I have seen her fight. In your place, I would do what she asks.

Her pulse hammered in her chest, in her throat, even in her cold hands. She had to control herself. She had been afraid for a long time. She could not afford her fears.

Do what Lylin asked? What other choice did she have?

She tried to think.

In Avail's place, she could command the Repository's Magisters. She had that power. She could call them out of the keep and down the hill to hurl their Decimates against the priests and the Great God. An attack like that might turn the battle.

Or it might prove fatal if they failed. How would the Repository survive without its last defenders?

The risk was too great.

Lylin had told her to wait for her moment.

She no longer watched the fighting below her. If she had chanced to spot Bifalt in the bloody press, the sight might have wrecked her. Instead, she concentrated on the pavilion, on the Great God and his priests, trying to believe that she would be given a chance to affect the battle. And that she would be equal to the challenge.

A few moments passed before she realized that Rile had adjusted his tactics. Rather than one, he drove *two* of his priests to confront the books resting on the table.

A heavy concussion somewhere above King Bifalt staggered the hills. He felt it, but it meant nothing to him. His Magisters drew infantrymen away from him, aided his charge with fire and lightning. Following his brother, he strode into chaos, the wild crush of infantrymen, the ringing iron, the curses and gasps and cries.

Prince Jaspid cut a swath that led slightly uphill and a little to the north. He fought with fluid ease. His precision seemed prescient. His saber and dagger swept foes aside despite their broadswords, their breastplates, their strength.

Inevitably, some of the enemy got past him. Those men Bifalt crippled or killed.

The savagery of the fray crowded around him. Nevertheless his own battle should have been straightforward, easier than the task that Jaspid and his other guardians faced. Jeck guarded his right. The man's saber moved like lightning. Elgart covered Bifalt's left, where the King's damaged hand refused to grip his dagger. And at his back, he had Malder, Spliner, and Boy.

King Bifalt was safer than any of his riflemen.

But Elgart was right. Bifalt had not been training. His limbs remembered their skills, their reflexes. His heart and lungs could not match them. Too soon, every breath became a little battle. Fire filled his chest. Before long, he was reduced to a few simple movements, a few automatic sequences.

Against an overhand cut, he shifted to the side, deflected the broadsword, and used his own motion to flick his saber at his opponent's crotch. If he missed that target, there were large veins on the insides of both legs. His foe's life would pump out into the slush and mud.

Against a slash at his neck or head, he ducked, dragging his blade across the infantryman's thighs. Or if the blow came too low to duck, he took half a step backward, knocked the broadsword down with his saber, and turned his swing into a thrust at his attacker's throat.

Three elementary combinations. His men had learned dozens. Jaspid probably knew hundreds. Bifalt could only manage three. Protected on all sides, he did not need more.

Shift, deflect, flick. Duck and slash. Step back, knock down, thrust. Again and again.

Like an avalanche, the infantrymen kept coming.

Then they stopped. Suddenly, as if their hearts or their minds had failed, they seemed to freeze where they were. Between one heartbeat and the next, the force that compelled them was withdrawn. At Prince Jaspid's back, the King and his men surged ahead. They cut down every foe within reach.

The opportunity was brief. After a few moments, fresh determination restored the infantrymen. With renewed fury, they gave battle.

Every swing of Jaspid's saber flung blood. His dagger slashed wrists or throats. Jeck and Elgart tried to match him. Blow after blow, they protected their King.

Step back, knock down, thrust. Bifalt strained for air. Shift, deflect, flick. His limbs felt sluggish. His heart labored as if it were pumping mud. Duck and slash.

Again and again.

Without warning, the Prince jerked up his head. For an instant, he halted. He still defended himself, but he seemed unaware of his own movements. Then, as reckless as a madman, he turned to face King Bifalt, giving the enemy his back.

Time seemed to stop. If it had kept moving, Jaspid would have died.

Blood streamed down his arms and legs from a fretwork of small cuts. His bronze breastplate had taken a blow that dented it deeply enough to damage his ribs. With every movement, it would hurt him more.

He still had his rifle slung over his shoulder. The bulge of his satchel showed that it held a few clips.

Ruefully, he met Bifalt's stare, Bifalt's sudden anguish. Barely audible through the clamor, he appeared to say, "I am sorry, Brother. Estie needs me."

At once, he whirled on his foes.

But now he took a new heading. Faster than before, faster than anyone with him, he went directly uphill. With his saber and dagger flashing, he assailed the infantrymen as if they were wheat ripe for his scythe.

Without Elgart and his bodyguards—without Brighten and Crawl—Bifalt would have fallen. His limbs were too heavy to move. Every beat of his heart hammered panic through him.

Estie.

Needs.

Me.

Nevertheless he remained Bifalt, Belleger's King. Defying his own terror, he flung himself back into the fight.

At first, he followed Jaspid upward, dragging all of his people behind him. But his brother was too fast. He was falling behind. Whatever happened, he had already lost the Prince.

Gasping curses, he let Jaspid go. Instead, he turned toward his personal crisis, toward the pavilion and the self-appointed god, and forced his legs to support him against a rising wave of foemen.

Shift, deflect, flick. Duck and slash. Step back, knock down, thrust.

Somewhere after Jaspid's departure, Elgart had disappeared. The King did not know when or why. Malder had already taken Elgart's place.

A good man, Malder. Loyal. Strong. But he was a natural brawler, not a swordsman. Instinctively, he wanted to grapple with his foes, slam them into the earth until they broke.

Bifalt climbed more slowly despite the rage and dread that goaded him. In growing numbers, the infantrymen rushed to stop him.

He managed half a dozen steps, a dozen. If he could have looked away, he might have seen the lower plateau a little distance above him on his left. But he did not lift his gaze. Every step presented more foes. Every upward lurch left him weaker.

Jeck wielded his saber as if it were an instrument of sorcery. He kept King Bifalt safe on that side. Nevertheless the pressure compelled him to fight defensively. He had no time to dispatch the infantrymen. They crowded closer.

On Bifalt's left, Malder's instincts betrayed him. With a guttural roar, he rushed the nearest foe. With his arms and his weight, he took that man to the ground. A sword thrust through his chest ended him.

Spliner took Malder's place.

Like Malder, the teamster relied on strength more than skill. But he was a stand-up fighter, not a brawler. Gripping his saber in his left hand, he struck with his right, aiming to drive his fist into a face, or to jab his stiffened fingers at a throat. He dropped four or five infantrymen before a blade reached him. Then he, too, fell.

Boy came to the King's left, leaving the nearest riflemen to cover Bifalt's back. He lacked a veteran's years of training and his father's bulk of his muscle. He had seen his father killed. He fought with frenzy in his eyes, but his movements were cautious, hampered by desperation.

Heaving for breath, Bifalt tried to protect him. Duck and slash. Hells! Step back, knock down, thrust. Whoreson! Shift, deflect, flick. Die, you bastards!

Spliner's son did not deserve this death.

For a few steps, Boy's caution kept him alive. Then, at the edge of his sight, Bifalt saw a broadsword that Boy did not. His damaged hand screamed as he grabbed Boy's arm, jerked the younger man back.

Boy stumbled against him. Bifalt staggered for balance.

In that instant of distraction, a blade sliced open the King's left side below his ribs. Spilling blood, he fell facedown in the red slush.

He tried to rise, but he was too weak. There was no air in the world and no one to help him. Boots skidded off him as Rile's soldiers rushed to attack the remaining riflemen. Those impacts may have broken some of Bifalt's ribs. If so, he did not notice the damage. The impossibility of breathing demanded everything. He had nothing left.

Elgart had not abandoned his King. He had left Bifalt's side unprotected to answer the call of a spy's instincts, the impulse to draw sudden conclusions and trust them.

He had glimpsed signs of sorcery, fire and lightning, the hard punch of winds. They were some distance below him, and too far north of the King's struggle.

King Bifalt had left Magisters Crawl and Brighten a bit south and west of him. The Decimates in the north had to be General Klamath's sorcerers. Trusting himself, Elgart believed at once that Klamath's people were trying to reach the King.

But they were too far downhill. Even if they succeeded at breaching the barricade of infantrymen, they would not arrive where they were most needed.

Elgart turned away from his King, his friend, to warn the General.

He had to earn every step. Infantrymen crowded against him, eager to kill. As a much younger man, Elgart had trained with Belleger's army. He had ridden into hell against Amika more than once. But he was not a soldier by nature. His work as King Bifalt's Captain of Spies had been a better fit. Instinctively, he fought with a low cunning that was better suited to surprise attacks in dark alleys than to direct conflict against vast numbers. Some of his tactics—tripping and kicks, feints, blows rather than cuts—lured his foes to miss him. They won him half the distance to Klamath's army. And the terrain helped him. He made the boulders serve him, the shelves of rock, the slick swaths of mud. But he knew at every moment that his task was hopeless. Sudden evasions and luck were not enough.

When he lost his saber, he met his fate with a wolf's grin on one side of his face, a grimace of despair on the other.

Nevertheless he did not accept death. He had not given in to Makh. He did not falter now. The stakes were too high.

As he ducked under a slashing longsword, he snatched out his garrote. Leaping behind his assailant, he whipped his killing wire around the man's throat. But he did not pull hard enough to end the man quickly. Instead, he used the strangling man as a mount. With all of his strength, he forced his victim to go where he wanted.

Briefly, he crashed through other infantrymen, riding his shield. Foes were knocked aside. Blades clanged off the breastplate of Elgart's mount. But then the man stumbled. The jerk tightened Elgart's garrote. Dying, the man fell on his face.

Elgart rolled away. Stones, snow, and slush slowed his rise to his feet. As he struggled to stand, a broadsword caught him across the face. Angled downward, the blade sliced above his right eyebrow and through his left eye. The weight of the blow stunned him. Weeping blood, he toppled.

He was finished then. He knew it. He had done what he could, and he had failed.

He had no idea what was happening when the rock under him lifted, sent him tumbling away from the nearest infantrymen.

Abruptly, the hillside became a hailstorm of gravel and scree. It pelted infantrymen off their feet. Blasts of wind pummeled them. Other foemen scrambled away.

To stop the bleeding, Elgart clamped a hand hard over his streaming eye. With the other, he wiped away the blood from his brow. The impact of his wound still rang in his skull. He was too numb to feel pain. That would come later. But he could not focus his eyes.

Blinking frantically, he tried to identify the woman standing over him.

"Get up, Elgart with no title," snapped Magister Astride. "We cannot hold this position. Or carry you. You must walk.

"We have a conversation to finish."

She looked taller than he remembered, stronger. Her steps seemed to shake the ground as she turned to defend him.

Magister Astride. He had dreamed about her. Her control of her Decimate had saved him again, as it had when Belleger's Fist had collapsed. She had credited her success to desperation, but clearly she had acquired new skills since then.

Elgart did not know how to refuse her. Covering his ruined eye, he straggled to his feet and went after her.

If any infantrymen threatened him, he did not notice them. Magisters watched over him. He felt the caress of distant flames on his face, the swift kick of winds. He seemed to recognize Magister Trench.

In a blur of sorcery and feverish combat, he approached Klamath.

The sight of his old friend stopped him. The General stood gasping with exertion and pain in the center of a clear space ringed by riflemen and Magisters. For a heartbeat or two, Elgart did not understand why Klamath had stopped there. Then he saw that some blade had taken Klamath's sword-arm at the elbow. A belt hauled tight around his upper arm served as a tourniquet. The stump of his elbow dripped blood.

Swaying, Elgart stared. He could hardly keep his feet.

Klamath came closer. In a rush, he flung his good arm around his friend. "Elgart," he croaked like a sob. "Elgart."

Wrestling with himself, Elgart panted, "The King needs you."

Klamath jerked back, stared at the former spy's cleft face.

"South of the pavilion." Elgart could not find enough air for words. "He is trying to reach Rile.

"You are too far below him. Too far north."

Klamath gaped at Elgart for an instant. Then he became the General again.

"Rowt!" he roared. "A new heading! We must break through the enemy below that plateau and climb! King Bifalt is there!"

Relief took the last of Elgart's strength. He sagged to his knees. Now seemed like as good a time as any to rest.

Drifting on the edge of darkness, he seemed to hear Klamath shouting for a Magister of fire.

Fire? thought Elgart. For me? Oh, hells.

Then he went away for a while.

Watching from the balcony outside the librarian's workroom, Magister Rummage saw a man, apparently a rifleman, emerge from the fray on the south side and stride upward. Before long, a patch of clean show shifted and became a woman in white. They may have spoken to each other. He wiped his saber on his thighs, sheathed it. Together, they ascended past the lower plateau.

In the north, General Klamath's forces struggled across the slopes, perhaps trying to rejoin King Bifalt and the rest of Klamath's army. Aided by his Magisters, Bellegerin and Amikan, the General drove into the mass of the Great God's infantry.

But those were details. Magister Rummage noticed them and forgot them. His attention was fixed on the pavilion. On the table and the books. On the priests and the Great God.

The god had recovered from the effects of Magister Avail's shout. He stood away from his chair, holding his tall cross upright as if it were the emblem or instrument of his inevitable victory. In a golden nimbus, he faced the Repository. Despite his brief setback, he still seemed to look straight at Magister Rummage, daring the hunchback to respond.

Rummage met that stare without flinching. His only friend had sacrificed himself for nothing. He was more than angry. He was no longer afraid.

He had his own singular gift for sorcery. He had feared its cost for many years. But that was behind him now. In truth, Magister Avail had *not* sacrificed himself for nothing. He had spent his life in a brave attempt to spare Magister Rummage. The futility of his death did not diminish it.

The mute sorcerer intended to match his friend.

Grimly, he held his enemy's gaze. While he waited for the Great God to strike again, he imagined Rile's growing ire, the god's indignation that his antagonist did not show dread. All of his servants and slaves dreaded him. His rule rested on dread.

The Great God looked away before Rummage did. Scowling, he scanned his priests, made his selection. With a brusque gesture, a harsh word, he coerced two of them to the books on the table.

Ah! thought the hunchback. *That* is your gambit.

Now he and his enemy would learn what the final Decimate could do against itself. The Great God might care. Rummage did not. He was ready at last.

The other priests betrayed their relief. The chosen two expressed the terror that Rummage had left behind. As awkward as a child's marionettes, they entered the pavilion, lurched to seat themselves on stools. There they hesitated, resisting their god's will.

Savagely, Magister Rummage slapped Hexin Marrow's *Final Decimate* on the parapet. Then he grabbed Magister Oblique's arm. Tapping faster than speech, he told her:

—Clear the balcony! At least twenty paces on both sides! Do it *now*! The next blast will strike *here*.

His demand shocked her, appalled her, but she understood it. She knew his gift. For one brief moment, she regarded him with anguish. Then she obeyed.

"Get back!" she shouted at the crowd of Magisters and apprentices. "The Great God will target *us*! Go as far as you can! You are not *safe* here!"

Her command was enough. The Repository's people had already felt the final Decimate once. In a rush, they scrambled away from Rummage. None of them knew what a safe distance might be.

Waiting, Magister Rummage was relieved to see the librarian scurry away along the back wall. For reasons of her own, she took the two wielders of the seventh Decimate with her, the older man and the young woman.

Magister Oblique stayed.

"Please, Rummage," she urged softly. "Do not do this. We can rebuild the keep. We may be able to save some of the books. We cannot restore you."

For her sake, he tried to smile, but he had lost the use of those muscles. He had recognized the meaning of his life at last. Intending kindness, he waved her away.

She wept as she left.

At once, he turned back to his book and the Great God.

The compelled priests had placed their shaking hands on the covers of their own copies. When their god stamped his staff, they began to open the pages.

A heartbeat behind them, Magister Rummage did the same. But he was sure of himself now. He knew the passage of the text that he wanted. He caught up with the priests before they began to read.

The power was in the words. They did not need to be spoken. They simply had to be read. Even in silence, a voice was nothing more than a way to declare the reader's purpose. Magister Rummage's purpose was as vivid as sound in his mind.

Ward yourself, butcher. I mean to kill you.

As the priests read, the hunchback recited the same words to himself.

While the three of them went through the necessary portions of the text, nothing happened. The Magister's heart beat faster. He expected death.

Soon, he assured himself. Soon.

He and the priests finished together. At their last word, he felt an instant of absolute confirmation. Every particle of his identity became fire. Every yearning of his crippled body and thwarted heart found its release in an astonishing blaze of light. For a tiny sliver of time, he saw himself and was satisfied.

Then his gift claimed him, and he burned. Shedding flames, he was gone. Nothing remained except ashes until the winds swept away.

From the edges of the balcony, the librarian and her people saw that Magister Rummage had both succeeded and failed. His Decimate did not touch the Great God, but it counteracted one of the priests. That man died in fire as his power rebounded against him. His sorcery harmed only him.

Nevertheless the second priest achieved his god's purpose. With his death in conflagration, he tore down a long chunk of the balcony and destroyed Magister Threnody's workroom. During its single instant, his Decimate ripped open the keep's thick wall from the battlements down to the breach made by the first blast.

After the earlier concussion, a crowd of servants, students, and even a few scribes had come out onto the upper plateau to watch the battle. They must not have heard Magister Oblique's warning. Falling rubble crushed them. Bloody chunks of granite covered the porch as if a portion of the Wall Mountains had collapsed.

If the Great God had ever meant to enter the library, his forces would have to spend days clearing the way. But that was not the end he desired.

At a distance from her hiding place, the Queen watched Prince Jaspid and Lylin hurrying upward. She ached to call out to them, but she forbade herself. She did not truly desire to make them hear her. She wanted them to *answer*.

Where is Bifalt? Is my husband alive?

The Prince and the devotee might not know.

When they had passed out of sight, climbing toward the Repository, she looked back down at the fighting and bodies below her, searching for some sign of Bifalt.

There were so *many* bodies, infantrymen and riflemen. Their struggles had turned the snow and earth into a red muck that made the dead indistinguishable. Bifalt could be anywhere down there. Even if he still lived, still fought, he might be impossible to locate. The confusion of men and Decimates masked the conflict from edge to edge. It concealed everyone.

Nevertheless Estie tried, staring until her sore eyes felt like coals in their sockets. Crayn kept his hand on her shoulder to steady her, but his touch did not require her attention.

She had expected another blare of brilliance from the doomed priests in the pavilion, yet it took her by surprise when it came. It distorted her vision, made her head reel. The concussion that followed shook the rock under her feet. It staggered the boulders of her covert, shifted them on their foundations. One and then another of them rolled away, leaving her exposed.

She did not care. Rile's attention was focused on the keep, avid to see what his attack had accomplished. Two more of his priests were gone. Their books burned briefly, then faded to smoke and ash. He had five left—but only five. She had no idea what they did. Perhaps they would not be enough.

Too slowly, she recovered her sight. The absence of the boulders gave her a wider view of the battlefield. She could see more, search harder.

She caught her breath when she saw Magisters forming a cordon below the lower plateau and the pavilion. With the ragged remnants of their stamina, they held back the infantrymen, driving the enemy downhill, while Klamath's men scrambled to reach the shelter of the Decimates.

She could not guess how many of the General's people had survived. Among the Magisters were two men she knew.

Klamath and Elgart.

Sudden tears blurred her eyes. Both men looked hurt. But they were too far away. She could not identify their wounds. Blinking furiously, she finally saw that they were kneeling, one on either side of a man prone in the muck. They plucked at him, tugged on his arms, tried to lift him.

He did not move.

Holding her breath while her pulse pounded in her throat, Estie watched.

Klamath's and Elgart's insistence seemed to imply that the fallen soldier was still alive. They were trying to rouse him.

For no apparent reason, Crayn jerked Estie's shoulder. She glanced aside just as a bullet skidded off the Shields of the priests.

The Commander gestured urgently:

—The Prince, Majesty! He shoots at Rile. This must be your moment. *Now,* while the priests are distracted!

Her moment? Gods! The moment that Lylin had promised her. Now?

Panic and doubt threatened to overwhelm her. She fought them down so that she could concentrate.

Bifalt! she cried. **Husband! Please hear me! This cannot be the end!** Bullets could not reach Rile, but the priests might falter. **Jaspid tries to give you an opening.** The Great God had no priests at his back. **It will close soon. You must strike now.**

With her whole heart, she promised, **I love you!**

The body between Klamath and Elgart quivered. The right hand moved. Dragging through the slush, it braced itself.

By agonizing increments, King Bifalt tried to obey his wife.

At once, Klamath and Elgart raised him. With their help, he stood, tottering. His left hand clutched his side. Dark fluid leaked between his fingers. His right hand groped, empty and helpless.

Estie turned away. *We have no time.* She did not know what she was supposed to do. She knew what she *could* do.

Now Queen Estie of Amika did not resist her fears. She used them. She needed every scrap of passion to shout at Rile.

Butcher!

She did not try to match Magister Avail's force—or her own extremity when she had first screamed Bifalt's name. One blow would not be enough. She had to deliver more.

Rile's head jerked as if he had been slapped.

Tyrant!

He staggered back a step, caught himself. With one hand, he rubbed at his forehead.

Coward!

He looked around wildly. She thought that she saw a trickle of blood at the corner of his mouth. With a frantic gesture, he sent two more priests to his books.

You kill your own servants!

He tottered.

Estie gathered herself for one more shout, but she could not do more. At that instant, her world was flipped on its head. Her power left her. Without it, she could *hear*.

As timorous as prey, Beatrix Threnody clung to the inner wall near the edge where the balcony had been broken. Bits of stone still slipped from the torn rim and fell out of sight. Fright was her only enduring gift. It seemed to be the only one she had.

But she did not lose her grip on her two wielders of the seventh Decimate. On her left, she clutched the older man, Magister Able. On her right, she held the young woman, Apprentice Evensong.

She expected to cower where she was until she was killed. What else could she do? Her bond with the library and all of its knowledge was useless here. Magister Rummage had tried the final Decimate and failed. She was doomed to be the last steward of the Repository.

But then Magister Oblique called to her.

"Librarian! There is a devotee of Spirit among the rubble! Lylin, I think. She has a rifleman with her. He may be Prince Jaspid.

"He has fired at the Great God! Now he waits."

Abruptly, Magister Threnody's concern for her books and her people thrust every other fear aside. Her other Decimate-wielders could do nothing. They were too far from the enemy. But if Prince Jaspid could *shoot* the Great God? If his bullets could pierce the Shields that covered him?

If an ordinary man had so much daring?

The time had come for Magister Able and Apprentice Evensong.

They were the librarian's last, desperate gamble. They would suppress all theurgy in the Repository, and in the battle raging below the lower plateau. They would make every sorcerer powerless. But they might also clear the way for the Prince.

If the Great God was not too strong for them.

Beatrix Threnody had to try.

"Come!" she snapped at Able and Evensong as if she had become a different woman, a librarian driven by certainty. Dragging them with her, she forced her way through the crowd to the parapets.

There she waited until she saw the Great God struck by a power like Magister Avail's. By Queen Estie's voice.

At that moment, Magister Threnody became what she was meant to be, the steward of the Last Repository.

"Now!" she commanded. "The seventh Decimate! Make those priests impotent!"

Magister Able blinked at her, confused, paralyzed by alarm.

Apprentice Evensong did not hesitate. She was said to be as strong as Facile. As soon as she finished her training, she would be made a Magister. Bracing her hands on the parapet, she summoned her gift.

At first, she was not enough. Waves of weakness ran through the shimmer of Shielding. It flickered in places, faltered. The priests looked around in alarm, unsure of the threat. Quickly, they renewed their sorcery.

A moment later, Magister Able collected his wits and joined Evensong.

The haze vanished as if it had never existed. The priests wielding it staggered in confusion. They struggled to raise their power again. But they could not. It had been locked away within them.

Over the clamor of fighting, Magister Threnody heard the devotee, clarion and clear.

"Now, Prince! *Now!*"

Sure of himself, the rifleman took his time, steadied his aim.

Fired.

But not at the Great God.

Instead, one of the rubies in the god's cross shattered.

Yes! thought the librarian. The gems! The instruments of his Decimate. Magister Rummage had described them for her. Until this moment, she had not understood that they were vulnerable.

The Great God did not react. He appeared rigid with shock.

Casual and confident, the rifleman recocked his gun, aimed again.

At his next shot, another ruby burst into splinters.

Abruptly, the Great God howled. Fury contorted his perfect visage. Snatching up his staff, he whirled it around his head. The golden hue of his power grew brighter, stronger, as he forced his coercion through the remaining gem.

"Look!" someone shouted. "The infantrymen! They have stopped fighting!"

Magister Threnody did not look away from her enemy.

With an air of unconcern, the rifleman shrugged. He took more time to settle his aim.

His third bullet broke the slender shaft of the staff. Its cross fell away. Clattering, it landed on the table among the books.

The rifleman nodded to himself. His next shot destroyed the last ruby.

Like a man standing secure in the eye of a storm, he removed the clip from his rifle, dropped it in his satchel, took out another and slapped it in place. Then he began firing at the books. His bullets tore through the pages, scattered them like dead leaves.

People around the balcony cheered as if the battle had been won. Magister Threnody did not. The Great God was unharmed—and growing brighter. She could hardly bear to look at him. His howling sounded like the end of all things.

Gasping through his teeth, King Bifalt tried to recover his balance. He had lost it somewhere. He could hardly see. His surroundings swayed from side to side, and the unsteady labor of his heart seemed to beat in his eyes. He would have fallen again without Elgart's support, and Klamath's.

Moments passed before he managed to glance at his friends.

Then he wanted to weep.

They were grievously hurt. Elgart had a dirty strip of cloth tied over his left eye. The socket oozed blood. Another scar for the scarred man. The stump of Klamath's right elbow was a lump of charred meat. A belt cinched his upper arm.

Bifalt's friends—

He was hurt as well. Clamped below his ribs, his left hand seemed to grip a bundle of broken glass. It shredded his side. He had been cut there. The wound leached away his life.

But Estie had commanded him. *Jaspid tries to give you an opening. You must strike now.* He could not stop for pain, his friends' or his own.

There was no one behind him. The infantrymen had driven Klamath's riflemen and Magisters downhill. Only the King and his friends were close enough to obey his wife.

I love you!

He worked his throat until he had summoned a little moisture, enough for a hoarse whisper. "We must go up. To Rile. We have a chance."

"Up there?" Elgart groaned. "How? I can hardly see."

"I can see," muttered Klamath. "I cannot fight."

Bifalt told Elgart, "Then support me." He looked at the General. "Give me your sword."

Elgart's was gone. Without a word, Klamath reached across his body, fumbled his blade from its sheath. Trembling, he put it in Bifalt's hand.

The King hefted the saber as if he were capable of wielding it. "One last blow," he promised himself. "Take me to Rile."

After a moment, Elgart nodded. "If we come at his back, you may find an opening. He has no priests there."

Klamath attempted a shrug.

Alone while the fighting below them lashed on, the three damaged men struggled uphill.

Bifalt heard rifle-fire from somewhere above the pavilion. Slow shots, carefully spaced. For no apparent reason, the clamor of killing diminished. He forgot it.

The lower plateau was not as far away as it seemed. He feared that he would never reach it until his friends half carried him onto level stone.

The Great God stood at the front of his ruined pavilion. He radiated heat and power like the ruddy core of a forge. The trestle-table near him was burning. The pavilion's roof of oilcloth had drifted away in flames. A puddle of molten stone lay under his feet. His staff was ashes.

In gold and fury, he was too intense to regard directly. By will alone, he forced a number of his priests to shelter him with their shimmering. A wasted effort. The rifle-fire had ceased.

Brandishing his fists, he screamed up at the broken Repository.

"No, you whoresons!" His staff had been nothing more than a tool. He did not need it. "You craven pedants, *no*!" Ignoring his compulsion, some of his priests had scattered. None of the infantrymen came to his defense. "I will tear out your guts with my own hands and *feed*!"

"No," muttered Bifalt through his teeth. "You will not."

Limping, he and his friends crossed the outer rim of the plateau until they stood unsteadily behind their enemy.

He was too weak for this. But it was for Estie. *I love you.* And for all of the bloodshed that Rile had caused.

Somehow, the King shook off his friends. In his good hand, he raised Klamath's saber like a spike, not a sword. Leaning until he almost fell, he lurched into a run.

He could not look at the Great God. Instead, he watched his feet until the heat scorching his face told him that he was close. Then he hammered his blade into Rile's back.

The eruption of power from the wound tossed him away like a handful of flung gravel. If Elgart and Klamath had not caught him, he would have pitched over the rim of the plateau. But he did not feel them grab him.

His war was done.

THE LAST CHALLENGE

King Bifalt did not feel the passage of time. His absence seemed brief. In fact, he was gone for several days. The Repository's herbs and drugs kept him sleeping.

While he slept in a clean bed, the open wound in his side was stitched and bound to protect his damaged ribs. His broken hand was set in splints. Poultices and powders were smeared over the fierce burns of Rile's fury. When the physicians and shamans had done what they could, Estie spent hours every day at his bedside, mopping the sweat of occasional fevers from his face, replacing his blood-sodden bandages, lifting his head and stroking his throat to help him swallow healing elixirs. At intervals, she murmured encouragement.

When other duties called her away, or she needed rest herself, Commander Crayn or Apprentice Travail took her place. Healers visited regularly. Monks, servants, and Magisters looked in on him. The librarian herself spent an hour with him, simply keeping him company.

Later, he was moved to a different bed. There was not enough room for him in the Repository's infirmary. Soon after the battle ended, and for the next two days, swarms of people emerged from the keep to scour the foothills for survivors. Servants, scribes, students, teachers, apprentices, Magisters, all labored up and down the slopes, looking for anyone whose life might still be saved. In that task, they made no distinctions. Horse-warriors and Bellegerins, Amikans and infantry-men, even priests were carried into the Repository and delivered to the physicians and shamans. Soon the infirmary was overwhelmed. A field hospital had been set up in the great hall, and still Magister Threnody scrambled to find more beds. The healers worked themselves ragged, and yet had more to do.

To ease their efforts in one small way, Queen Estie had her husband carried to her own quarters, where he was settled in the Commander's chamber adjoining her sitting room. Crayn had lost his guardsmen when sub-Commander Waysel and the cannoneers were overrun. He had rooms and beds to spare. There Bifalt slept on, never alone. Especially at night, Estie sat near him.

At other times, the Queen was busy elsewhere, consulting with the librarian and Magister Oblique, or ensuring the comfort of riflemen, el-Algreb, and Magisters who needed nothing more than rest and good food. She also visited the infirmary and the field hospital to show her support for everyone there, whether or not they had once been her foes. And she spoke at length with General Klamath, Elgart, and Prince Jaspid. She could not hear them. Her gift had been restored. But with the aid of Crayn's signs and gestures, she pieced together their explanations of how and why they had come to be where they were needed most. Later, she addressed Chancellor Sikthorn in Maloresse, telling him what had happened—and what to expect.

But her first thoughts every day, and her last, were for Bifalt. She knew now that he would live. Still, too much between them remained unresolved. She wanted him to wake.

When he finally opened his eyes, they refused to focus. He recognized the blur of lamplight, walls at strange angles, a chamber of some kind. Nothing else. There was an emptiness in his mind, a gulf that swallowed comprehension.

His arms lay outside whatever covered him. Blankets? He was not sure. Hoping for something familiar, he lifted his arms a little, peered at his hands. But they were little more than vague shapes. They told him nothing. He closed his eyes again.

Wondering what had been done to him, he became aware that

his face felt parched. A familiar sensation. He had experienced something similar long ago, when Set Ungabwey had abandoned him in the
desert. But this was worse. His face and arms had been scalded.

He did not understand.

He imagined touching his face, exploring it. The fingers of his left
hand refused. They were trapped somehow. He used his right.

That was not *his* face. He recognized the pressure of his touch. The
dull burning lingered. His fingers increased it. Nevertheless his features were wrong. He found slick patches covered with grains like sand
scattered on oil. They had a peculiar smell. They did not fit him. And
his beard—

He remembered his beard. He had kept it cropped short, but he
knew it.

It was gone.

Trembling a little, he explored farther. Eyebrows? No. On his head?
The same dull burning, but no hair.

Who am I now? He wanted an answer, but there was no one he
could ask.

"Your hair will grow again, King," offered a familiar voice gently.
"Your flesh will heal. You may not resemble yourself for a few days. But
the gifts of the shamans are remarkable. Soon you will recognize your
reflection."

A tug of memory encouraged Bifalt to reopen his eyes. Turning his
head, he made out an indistinct shape that made him think of Third
Father.

He tried to ask, Father? No sound came. The muscles of his throat
were as useless as his left hand.

Someone he did not see slipped an arm under his shoulders, lifted
him a bit, set pillows to support him. The lip of a flagon nudged his
mouth. He tasted something ripe and soothing, tried to swallow it.
One sip enabled another. It eased his raw throat.

Panting, he leaned on the pillows.

"You will live, King," murmured the monk. "I am pleased to say it.
And more pleased to acknowledge that you have surpassed yourself
yet again. My expectations were high. You have flown higher."

None of that made sense. But since Third Father mentioned expectations, Bifalt expected himself to ask, "And you?"

The monk seemed to smile. "It is not for me to say. But as it is you who ask, King, I will confess that I believe so. For a moment, I was more than I imagined myself to be."

Bifalt may have nodded. But he had already lost the thread of Third Father's reply. He had a more compelling concern.

With an effort, he cleared his throat. "Estie?"

Third Father sighed, a comforting sound. "The Queen is well, King. More than well. Her straits have been difficult. Yet she, too, has surpassed herself.

"She has spent many hours at your side. She will be saddened that she missed this moment of awakening. But she and the lib—"

The monk stopped himself. "Forgive me, King. You may not be aware that Sirjane Marrow is dead. The librarian is now Magister Beatrix Threnody. You will not call her arrogant."

Then he resumed. "The Queen was called away. She and the librarian preside over a remembrance of the dead and a celebration of the living. It will be a lengthy ceremony. There are too many names, the dead and the living, and none should be forgotten.

"I was asked to attend. But I am near the end of my days, and my strength fades. I prefer to sit with you for a time."

Bifalt retained parts of Third Father's explanation. Other details slipped into the gulf where his recent memories should have been. But Estie was well. That was the important thing.

He went back to sleep.

When he awoke again, he had no idea how much time had passed. He lay in an unfamiliar bed. The lamplit chamber was strange to him. But he recalled a bit more of who he was. Scraps of events drifted at the edges of coherence. The same vagueness afflicted his vision.

Estie's voice drew him toward her. It seemed to give him meaning.

"Welcome, my lord King." She had lost none of her sweetness. "Third Father sent word that you have begun to rouse. I came as soon as I could."

He blinked again and again. The blurring of his sight resembled the smear of sorcery that the priests had used against him. He hated it.

Through the haze, she looked inexpressibly weary. But as soon as he managed to croak "My lady," she became radiant. Lights sparkled in her soft eyes. Her smile lifted everything around her.

"I feared for you, my lord." He could not interpret her tone. It sounded like weeping or teasing. "I should have known better. You are too great to be slain by armies or gods."

She was as bad as Third Father. Half of what she said did not make sense. But she was *here*. That was what mattered. Eventually, perhaps, Bifalt might remember why *he* was here.

At his best, he could not have matched her smile. He needed all of his strength to say, "You called me *Beloved*."

She nodded. "I did. And I said more. I told you that I love you. I should have said so long ago. I will not miss another chance. I love you, Bifalt."

He was still trying to pick up the fragments of things that he should have known. Uncomfortably, he confessed, "When I heard your voice the first time. We had escaped the Fist. I thought—"

A sudden memory plucked that thought away. Instead, he stared at her, desperate to see her clearly.

"You hear me. How can you hear me?"

The angles of her smile shifted. It became arch. With one hand, she directed his attention to the other side of his bed.

A young woman sat there. A very young woman. She held herself awkwardly, as if she were uncomfortable in the grey robe of a Magister. She had an air of concentration. Some task preoccupied her. If it involved sorcery, Bifalt could not detect it. But her eyes and her smile were kind.

"My lord," said Estie, "let me introduce Magister Evensong. A few days ago, she was an apprentice, but she has proven herself. She wields the seventh Decimate, as Magister Facile did. It quelled Rile's priests so that Prince Jaspid could destroy his staff. Her gift would be dangerous in a keep full of theurgists. But Magister Facile showed me that the seventh Decimate can be focused on a single sorcerer.

"While Magister Evensong and I are together, she can relieve me of my deafness and my other voice."

As Estie spoke, the young woman lifted a flagon to Bifalt's lips. He recognized it by its aroma, and did not want it. It would make him sleep. But he was too weak to refuse.

After a few swallows, he turned back to Estie. Fighting a wave of drowsiness, he asked, "Then how can we speak? How can I tell you I love you? If we are never alone?"

Her smile held more light than all of the lamps. "Silly man." With one hand, she rested a cool caress on his forehead, encouraging him to relax. "I will teach you. It is easier than you suppose."

He tried to say, Teach me now. But the elixir was potent. It carried him away.

The next day, King Bifalt felt stronger, a bit more alert. His vision had improved. Some of the breaks in his memories had repaired themselves. Despite his damaged side, he was able to sit more upright in his bed.

This time, he was given water to drink and a little food. A few raisins. Some bread sopped in wine. A meager meal, but he could not have eaten more. While he forced himself to finish it, he fretted.

He wanted Estie again.

She did not come. His next visitors were Elgart and Klamath.

One part of him sighed for his wife. Another was glad to see his old friends.

They brought back more memories. They carried themselves like men who had almost recovered from their separate ordeals. Clearly, more time had passed than Bifalt knew.

Yet they had been badly damaged. Elgart wore a clean band around his head covering his ruined eye. It made him look like a brigand.

Tightly wrapped in bandages, Klamath's right arm resembled a club more than a limb. Whenever he forgot that he could not use it, he grimaced.

In other ways, the General's recurring scowl suggested a grudge. At first, Bifalt suspected that Klamath resented the burdens he had been given, the decisions he had been forced to make. Then Bifalt dismissed the notion. Klamath was not a resentful man. Whatever vexed him now had a deeper cause.

Murmuring greetings, the two men came to the King's side. When they had touched his bound hand and frowned at the state of his face, they found stools for themselves and sat.

Bifalt had questions, but he did not know how to ask them. He had forgotten some of the words, or he could not decide where to begin.

Elgart spoke first. Feigning seriousness, he said, "You will inquire about my injury, Majesty." His grin mocked his tone. "I can only say that I do not recommend using the Decimate of fire to cauterize an eye. The pain was extraordinary. I still wonder whether I am alive."

Klamath snorted. "Magister Astride does not doubt it." Then he told the King, "That woman has refined her gifts, Majesty. She is capable of more than you know. She took command when she heard that Elgart was in danger. Fool that he is, he risked himself against all of those infantrymen to warn me that you needed us. Without him, I would not have known where to look. Magister Astride and Magister Trench rescued him from the full cost of his recklessness."

Bifalt remembered Astride. She had saved him and all of his people when he had destroyed Belleger's Fist. If she had become capable of more, she was truly remarkable. But he had not realized that she knew Elgart—or that she cared enough to hazard her life for him.

Privately, he sighed again, saddened by his own ignorance. Then he let it go.

"And you, Klamath?"

The General glared at his bound stump. "There is nothing to tell, Majesty. I was slow." A moment later, he betrayed a hint of belligerence. "I will have more to say when you have asked your questions."

Bifalt accepted this. "Then speak of my brother." Jaspid had rushed away from Bifalt in battle, a choice so uncharacteristic that it suggested madness. *I am sorry, Brother.* "Is he well?"

"He is, Majesty," answered Klamath gruffly. "A little bruised, no more. He looked in on you earlier, but you were asleep. Now he trains with that devotee, Lylin."

Elgart chuckled. "He calls it training. I call it courtship. I would fear for him, but she appears to be as smitten as he is." The scarred man laughed outright. "They are a perfect match, Majesty. Imagine them sharing a home filled with wrecked furniture, broken crockery, and passion."

Scowling, Klamath persisted in his report. "Much happened while we were fighting for our lives, and yours. Now we hear that this Lylin claimed Prince Jaspid for his marksmanship. She guided him to the porch of the Repository. When his chance came, he shot out the gems of Rile's staff and destroyed Rile's books.

"Those books were the final Decimate. We have seen the damage they did to this keep. It is severe. The Prince prevented them from achieving worse."

For a moment, Bifalt's attention wandered. The servants, he thought. Their bundles. Rile's books.

Estie had urged him to stop them. He had failed. Amandis had given herself in the attempt, but she was only one devotee. He had done nothing except enable her sacrifice. The memory of her death was a pang that he did not know how to ease.

But Klamath was not done. More harshly, he continued, "Yet even that would not have been possible without Queen Estie. First she called Jaspid away from the battle. Then she struck at Rile with sorcery. She *hurt* him, Majesty. That moment of distraction enabled what followed."

Speaking of Estie brought Bifalt's attention back. Carefully, as if to ward off a fresh injury, he asked, "Rile is dead?"

"Killed by your blow, Majesty," declared Elgart. "His power gushed out of him like blood. He fell and died."

Klamath confirmed it. "His fire left the imprint of his body in the stone. Nothing else remains."

King Bifalt expected to feel relief, if not vindication. Perhaps he did. But the death of his enemy raised a more important question.

"Then tell me, General," he commanded with as much severity as he could manage. "What are our losses? How many lives did this battle cost us?"

That touched on the source of Klamath's bitterness. Frowning fiercely, he answered, "Seven hundred, including First Captain Hegels. That is our best count. It may be higher, if the healers cannot save some of our injured. If they lose sub-Commander Hellick. I do not think it can be less."

While Bifalt groaned, Klamath rasped, "But almost four hundred of those were horse-warriors." He clenched his fist to keep himself from shouting. "Majesty, I must speak of this. Of all of us, only the el-Algreb fought without Magisters.

"You did not see them, our Magisters. They risked themselves again and again while we fled from the Open Hand. But in the last battle, Majesty—" He beat his fist on his thigh. "They did not fight from safety, as they did during the old wars. In the end, they refused even the shelter of the Repository. Instead, they *joined* us. Wherever we fought, their Decimates supported us. *That* is why our losses were so much less than Suti al-Suri's. It is the *only* reason.

"You call our Magisters arrogant. Unworthy of their power. But I tell you, they are Magisters *second*. *First*, they are Bellegerin and Amikan. Their loyalty to their homes and their people is as great as ours. It is as great as *yours*, Majesty. I will not—I *cannot*—countenance—"

Abruptly, he stopped. As soon as Bifalt understood the cause of the General's ire, he began to make placating gestures. At last, Klamath noticed them.

"Klamath, please," said the King hoarsely. "My old friend. I have been humbled enough." He could not forget Magister Pillion's sacrifice in the Bay of Lights, or Magister Solace's gift of healing to Matt, or Magister Astride's courage during the fall of Belleger's Fist. "I am *married* to a sorceress. And I love her. I will tell her so until she believes me. How long do you suppose that I can cling to my distrust while she is who and what she is?"

Startled out of his tirade, Klamath turned his head away. When he faced Bifalt again, he seemed chastened.

Again, Elgart laughed. "Well said, Majesty." He looked as happy as a man could with one eye ruined and scars across his face. "If you persisted in your loathing, I fear that it would cast a blot on our friendship. For myself, I am prepared to pursue Magister Astride to the ends of the earth."

"Then be at peace," said the King. "When you are inclined to doubt me, remember Queen Estie."

He was starting to fade, but he fought the impulse. He still had questions.

"Now. Tell me more of the el-Algreb. Does Suti al-Suri live? Is he here? How does he bear his losses?"

Klamath cleared his throat. "The chief warrior is well enough, Majesty. He sneers at his wounds. But I have never seen him so shaken. His bravado is gone. It may never return.

"He is not here. He has taken his surviving warriors and left for their homeland. They reclaimed many of their mounts from the foothills below the road. And they retrieved every rifle that they could find on the battlefield. Two days ago, they departed."

"They cannot carry so many guns," put in Elgart softly. "The librarian has given them wagons."

"Before he rode away," continued Klamath, "he charged me to remind you that your promise is only half fulfilled."

As if Suti al-Suri's assertion needed clarification, Elgart murmured, "The promise I made in your name, Majesty."

Klamath explained. "The el-Algreb have rifles. They do not have bullets. The Cleckin are raiders, and the horse-warriors are now too few to defend their lands. While their guns are useless, and their losses are so great, they will be ravaged."

King Bifalt tried to believe that he was strong enough to sit up longer, but his need for rest compelled him. He sagged into his pillows.

"See to it, General," he said like a sigh. "As soon as you can. When we return to the Open Hand." If Rile had not burned the entire city—

"Elgart knows where the el-Algreb live. And the library must have maps."

Considering the difficulties, Klamath answered, "As you say, Majesty. Suti al-Suri's people have given us their lives. We will do whatever we can to aid them."

Even if the smithies remained intact, the forges would be cold. The substances the alchemists needed to make gunpowder might have been scattered. And most of the Hand's people had left for Amika.

Already half asleep, Bifalt said, "Then recall Commander Forguile." Estie could do that. "Send him and his men to the el-Algreb. They can defend our allies until my promise is kept."

He wanted to say more. He had other questions. But his need to sleep outweighed them.

The next time he saw Queen Estie, he was out of bed. Wearing a simple linen shift, he was learning how to walk again.

A monk attended him, a shy woman who identified herself as Fifth Daughter. She kept one hand on his arm, but gently, encouraging him to awaken his muscles and rediscover his balance. To distract himself from his weakness, he had been asking her vague questions. Without raising her eyes, she had informed him that life in the Last Repository went on. Teachers, students, scribes, and servants, all had returned to their tasks. Efforts to repair the damage of the final Decimate had begun. At the same time, the Farsighted kept watch on the survivors of the Great God's armies. If they could be helped, the librarian did not mean to let them die in the desert. In a darker mood, Magister Threnody intended to respond if the infantrymen began forming bands to raid and kill.

Bifalt did not inquire how the librarian would respond—or who the Farsighted were. He simply wanted to hear Fifth Daughter's voice. It helped him put one bare foot in front of the other.

Estie's arrival banished everything else. Bifalt shed the monk's grasp, tottered toward his wife. He had to put his hands on her shoulders to catch his balance. He might have dared to kiss her. But she had Commander Crayn with her. He held back.

She hugged him quickly, fiercely, then withdrew to study his face. The lamplight shone in her eyes like tears.

"Majesty." The Commander produced a formal Amikan bow. He had left his weapons behind. Under one arm, he carried a book. "Accept my gratitude. You have given us a great gift. Your recovery makes it complete."

Bifalt flinched, acutely aware of his frailty. He had earned no one's gratitude. He had not earned his place as Belleger's King. He had been born to it. He had simply tried to prove worthy of his father—and perhaps of his wife.

"My lord," she said, teasing him to ease his discomfort, "you must learn to accept thanks. The whole Repository wishes to thank you. You must endure it."

More seriously, she explained, "I have brought my Commander with me because Magister Evensong has other duties. He knows how to repeat what you say with signs and gestures. I *need* that, husband. I cannot hear you.

"The book he carries is *A Complete System of Gestures for Speech with the Deaf and Dumb*. He has mastered it well enough. If you choose to study it, you will soon be able to address me directly. For the present— with your consent—he will stand where I can watch him. When you speak, he will show me what you say."

"Commander." Bifalt swallowed his unworthiness. It was deeply ingrained in him, but he seldom admitted it. He could not deny it now. "Thank you. Stand where you wish."

His legs were trembling. "And tell my lady that I must sit."

Smiling, Crayn bowed again. His hands and arms moved incomprehensibly for a moment. Then he placed the book on the bed and brought a chair closer. As Bifalt sank into it, the Commander produced a stool for his Queen. At once, he took an unobtrusive position behind Bifalt.

Adjusting her stool, Estie sat close enough to reach Bifalt and clasp his good hand with both of hers. "My lord," she began. A flush came and went on her cheeks. Her smile shifted from one emotion to another. "Your progress pleases me. Soon you will be well enough to leave your chamber. How do you feel? What is your impression of your recovery?"

His left forearm itched. So did his stubble of beard. But he could not scratch them. His left hand was still trapped in bandages. "Better for seeing you, my lady," he said hoarsely. "Always better. My worst complaint—" The lines of her face made him forget what he was saying. He frowned while he recalled it. "My only complaint is that I sleep too much. I am told that you come often when I am not awake. I wish that you would rouse me. I would heal faster."

Apparently, she was able to read Crayn's gestures without looking away from Bifalt. "I will consider it, my lord." Now her smile had an arch tilt. "But it would also please me if you came to me. You may not know that this room adjoins my quarters. The door behind me opens on my sitting room. Opposite is my bedchamber." A blush fled across her face. "Wake me as often as you wish."

For a moment, Bifalt could not speak. He understood her well enough—and did not understand her at all. Her invitation inspired a sensation of urgency that he had not felt for a long time. He had worked hard to suppress it. When she had first shouted in his mind, while he was escaping from Belleger's Fist, he had heard only rejection. Why else would she call out to him? But now he wondered at himself. Why had he been so quick to believe that she had turned her back on him?

How had she become a woman who would invite him to her bed-chamber?

He did not know how to manage his confusion.

And they were not alone. Crayn was there. Fifth Daughter had not left.

Unsure of himself—unsure of everything—he temporized. Coughing to unlock his throat, he countered, "You have been busy, my lady. You have duties. All I do is sleep. I do not know if it is day or night."

She bit her lip, a brief flicker of chagrin. "Of course, husband. I understand. This deep in the Repository, day and night are one. If Crayn did not knock on my door to announce my breakfast, I would not be aware that the sun had risen."

"Then tell me, wife," said Bifalt to cover his awkwardness. "What are your duties? How do you spend your days?"

She shrugged dismissively. "Talking. Wandering." Then she took his question more seriously. "I visit our people in their quarters, and also in the infirmary and hospital. There my task is reassurance. They have suffered and bled and lost comrades in your name. They want news of you. I have told them the tale as far as I know it, but they cling to the belief that their victory and Rile's defeat are your doing. Yours alone." A single tear slipped down her cheek, yet she kept smiling. "You underestimate your stature in their eyes, husband. They honor General Klamath, Prince Jaspid, and Elgart. Despite his moment of weakness, they respect First Captain Hegels. But they *believe* in you."

Bifalt wished devoutly that she would not tell him such things. Fortunately, she seemed able to read his reactions despite his burned visage, his habitual severity. "Most of my time, however," she continued promptly, "is spent with the librarian and her people. She and Magister Oblique—oh, and Magister Bleak—are now the chief stewards of the Repository. They have many decisions to make.

"They asked me—"

He tightened his grip on her hand. "A moment, my lady. I have been asleep. There is too much that I do not know. Amandis told me that Magister Marrow was slain. Third Father confirmed it. How was it done? Who killed him?"

He did not remember Sirjane Marrow kindly.

She betrayed a quick rush of embarrassment. Or perhaps it was shame? "Forgive me, my lord. There must be large gaps in what you know of events here. I should have begun with them."

She hesitated for a moment, then forced herself to continue.

"The former librarian was killed by gunpowder. His killer was one of Rile's servants masked as a servant of the Repository. Magister Facile warned us of a traitor here. Now he is gone."

At the King's back, Crayn whispered, "I will tell you more if you wish, Majesty."

Bifalt shook his head. He did not want to know more. Estie's manner assured him that she had played a role in dealing with the traitor. That was enough.

"So," he said to her, putting the subject aside, "that was Magister Marrow. And Magister Avail awakened your sorcery. There was a third when I was here before, the hunchback, Magister Rummage." The man who had hurt him. "What became of them?"

She frowned at painful memories. "Magister Marrow was as arrogant and ungiving as you described him, husband. I would not say the same of Magister Avail and Magister Rummage. They were churlish, unhappy men, but they were good to me after their fashion. And they gave their lives for the Repository.

"The three of them ruled here for a long time. Now many things must be made new. The Repository is no longer threatened. It must change to fit its new circumstances."

Holding her hands to steady himself, to claim her, Bifalt asked, "What does the librarian want of you, my lady?"

Mildly vexed, Estie frowned. "She wishes me to stay. To assume Magister Avail's role. And she believes that I can help her in other ways. Fortunately, Magister Oblique understands that I will not. I will not abandon my realm again. Or you.

"I have my carriage. We can leave together when you are well."

Bifalt tried to mask his relief. He may have succeeded. More easily, he inquired, "Then what will the librarian do? How will the Repository change?"

She considered her answer. After a moment, she replied, "There are many details, husband. I will not trouble you with them. One will suffice to show the nature of her intentions.

"You may recall that a man here, Apprentice Travail, was Magister Facile's lover before she joined you in Belleger. He is the one who was poisoned.

"Since my arrival, Travail has given me many hours, teaching me how to endure my deafness. But he has not fully recovered from his poisoning. And he may never recover from the loss of Magister Facile. Still, the librarian sees more value in the sorcery of *hearing* than her predecessor did. She has asked him to accept the robe of a Magister, and to assume a great burden. She hopes that he will consent to teach others who share his gift.

"I fear for him, husband. He is a good man worn down by poor health and thwarted love. Any new burden may be too great for him. But Magister Threnody will try to persuade him. She is not a woman who seeks to impose her desires. She prefers the support of people who listen and understand."

Bifalt approved. While Estie sat in front of him and held his hand and met his gaze, he might have approved of anything.

"Then she should consult with Third Father," he suggested. "Or Fifth Daughter. Or any monk. The Cult of the Many teaches them to hear more than people say."

Estie smiled. "She has, husband. She will continue. She knows now to value the Cult of the Many."

He was content. He wanted to sit with her for a while in silence, basking. But her smile faded. As if she were stiffening her spine, she said, "There is one other matter, husband. The librarian has a boon to ask of you. She hopes that I will persuade you. If I do not, she may try to insist."

Reflexively, he scowled. "What does she want?"

"When you have recovered," began Estie cautiously, "when you are well enough, she asks you to meet with the people on whom the life of the Repository depends, the Magisters and apprentices. She wants you to address them. She considers it essential that they hear your tale. They must understand what their survival cost you."

Bifalt flinched. More harshly than he intended, he said, "I do not make speeches, my lady."

"I have not forgotten, my lord."

He tried to swallow his dismay. "Do *you* ask this?"

She met his glare without faltering. "I do. You have kept yourself to yourself for too long. I think it would be well for you to speak—and well for the Repository to hear."

He sagged. Suddenly, he wanted his bed. Hells, he wanted the elixir that made him sleep.

"Then I will do it, my lady." Sighing, he added, "When I am stronger."

She surprised him by leaning closer, leaving a soft kiss on his lips. "When you are stronger," she murmured like a promise.

A moment later, she was gone, taking Crayn with her.

With Fifth Daughter's support, Bifalt returned to his bed.

He spent four days pushing his limits. The care of the physicians and shamans healed his body. Estie's frequent visits strengthened his spirit.

When she was not there, he walked.

He refused to wear anything that would distinguish him as Belleger's King. In the garb of a servant, a plain brown shirt and trousers, soft moccasins on his feet, he ventured out of his bedchamber. The long halls gave him room to test himself. Attended always by one of the monks in case he misjudged himself or lost his way, he went farther every day.

And when he was not walking, or concentrating on his wife, he studied Lamit Karsolsky's book. At first, he found its concepts and instructions impenetrable. But as he regained the use of his mind, he began to understand. Then Fifth Daughter informed him that some of the Cult's monks were also learning Karsolsky's *System*. With their help, he practiced.

During those days, however, he kept his progress from his wife. Whenever she came to him, he used only his voice. Painfully aware of his awkwardness, he was reluctant to take a more intimate risk.

On the fifth day, he decided that he was ready. Not to make a speech—hells, no!—but to pretend that he could for her sake.

As he informed her with Crayn's help that he would attempt to satisfy the librarian, her delight brought tears to her eyes. She kissed him again, a soft, lingering kiss that left him light-headed. Then she hurried away to apprise Magister Threnody.

A few hours later, the Queen returned to escort her husband to the gathering of the Repository.

During the interval, the excitement of her kiss had faded. A darker mood took its place. A speech? *Him?* What could he possibly say that would vindicate the sacrifices that Belleger and Amika had made, the suffering that their people had endured, the lives that both realms had lost? For the first time since the war's end, Estie's smile did not lift his heart.

With a glance, she took in his drab raiment, but she did not comment on it. Taking his arm, she held him tightly. As she steered him to the door, she said, "I know that this does not please you, beloved. Whatever you say, I am yours."

That assurance failed to steady him, but it helped him walk.

After some distance, he began to recognize her destination. It was etched in his memory despite the intervening years. He had first encountered Commander Forguile there. Magister Rummage had almost broken his wrists. Elgart had faced him in mortal combat.

The refectory of the Last Repository.

It was a vast hall cut deep into the keep's stone. Ordinarily, it held trestle-tables and chairs enough to accommodate several hundred hungry people at any time of the day or night. Now, as on the occasion of Bifalt's confrontation with Elgart—the moment which had transformed Bifalt into a man he hardly knew—the tables and chairs had been pushed against the walls, making room for a multitude.

Apart from a small clear space in its center, the place was full.

The sight cost Bifalt a moment of balance. His vision swam. These were the people on whom the librarian depended most, these hundreds? And they expected him to—what? *Explain* himself? Shame them for the former librarian's dishonesty and arrogance? Without Estie's clasp on his arm, he might have stumbled.

But then he began to make out familiar faces. In fact, most of the people around the inner ring of the clear space, the people who would stand nearest to him, were men and women he knew. General Klamath was there, enjoying his King's discomfiture. Holding Magister Astride's hand, Elgart grinned like a madman. Prince Jaspid stood directly behind a most holy devotee of Spirit with his arms wrapped around her. If she objected, she showed her disapproval by leaning her head on his shoulder. Captain Rowt and a number of the riflemen acknowledged King Bifalt's arrival with their best bows. The Amikans among them performed their florid salutes. Sub-Commander Hellick supported himself on a crutch. Magister Trench applauded until he noticed that no one joined him. Magister Brighten bared her teeth like a woman who would have preferred to be surrounded by men and women she could kill.

The librarian must have arranged them deliberately. Bifalt had not expected so much consideration from a woman he had never met.

"Do you see, husband?" whispered Estie. "There are many here that you do not know, but all of our people have come. You will not address an assembly of strangers."

Bifalt would have felt more sure of himself if they were strangers. He could have faced them as if they were his foes. Instead, he trembled.

He found a brief comfort in the idea that at least his wife would not be able to hear him. But then he saw Commander Crayn standing nearby, ready to repeat whatever Bifalt said for his Queen.

Ah, hells.

Fortunately, he did not have to wait long. Soon two women filtered through the crowd, crossed the open center, and approached him. Both wore the robes of Magisters. One was small, almost tiny, with a lustrous sweep of black hair and an air of painful diffidence. The other, taller and more confident, had the knowing look of a woman who understood too much.

They both bowed. "King Bifalt," said the taller, "I am Magister Oblique. Allow me to introduce Magister Beatrix Threnody, the librarian of the Last Repository."

Her companion bowed again, hiding behind her hair.

"This gathering is for you, Majesty," continued Oblique. "We are all eager to hear you. None of us have other duties. Say as much or as little as you wish. The Repository still stands because you have given it twenty years of your life. No one else could or would have done so much. We are simply grateful that you have consented to speak."

Watching Crayn out of the corner of her eye, Estie nudged Bifalt. "Go now, beloved," she breathed. "Trust yourself."

As if he were on the way to a scaffold, King Bifalt walked out into the center of the hall. With his right hand, he held his left behind his back to keep his posture upright. Perhaps his audience would not notice the unsteadiness of his steps.

For a moment, he gazed around him. He could see too many faces. Along every wall of the refectory, men and women stood on chairs and tables to watch him. Near the back, three women had a table to themselves. He recognized them by their raiment, and by their sorrow, rather than by any other sign. They were Set Ungabwey's daughters.

He had never felt so exposed. So small.

But this had to be done. Who was he, if he did not stand to meet every challenge?

Because he had seen those three women, he began with them.

"I hardly knew Master Set Ungabwey. I know that he sacrificed his living and almost his life to keep the Great God's raiders away from Belleger. And I know more. Dying, he clung to life until he had destroyed many hundreds of the Great God's men in Belleger's Fist. He told me why. He did it for his daughters."

While the women wept, Bifalt turned to the rest of his audience.

"You knew Master Ungabwey," he continued more strongly. "You also knew the most holy devotee of Spirit Amandis." Like Klamath, he could make his raw voice carry. "Before the final battle, she sacrificed herself to stop the approach of the Great God's books. She only failed because I failed her.

"I am what you see, an ordinary man with ordinary gifts. I fail as often as any man. I am wrong as often as a man can be.

"I was wrong when I came here long ago. I judged the Magisters you have lost wrongly. I interpreted their intentions wrongly. When I left, I vowed to myself that I would humble their arrogance. I was wrong.

"And in my own realm, and in Queen Estie's, I was wrong. I feared sorcery. I saw every wielder of a Decimate as dishonorable and cowardly, Belleger's as well as Amika's. In all of my dealings with them, I betrayed my scorn. I could not bear to admit that their gifts diminished me. I was wrong.

"Worse, I treated my wife wrongly, my Queen-Consort, Estie of Amika. You do not know the pain I caused her. I do. My father, King Abbator, was a good man. He would have groaned to see my treatment of her."

For a moment, the King paused, bowed his head. During their last exchange in Belleger's Fist, Third Father had encouraged him to surpass himself. He did not know how.

Nevertheless he knew what he had to say.

He raised his head, faced the gathering like a man who knew himself.

"But I was not wrong when I sought an alliance with Amika, or when I married Queen Estie to confirm it. I was not wrong when I chose Commander Forguile and Captain Flisk to defend the Bay of Lights. They were defeated, yes, but only because I asked too much of them.

"I was not wrong when I made Klamath the General of my army, and of Amika's. You know what he has done. I was not wrong when I relied on Elgart for the security of my realm and the alliance. He did more than seek out treachery. He exposed the Great God's Archpriest. And he brought Suti al-Suri and the el-Algreb to fight for us.

"I was not wrong when I trusted Queen Estie and Amika to remain faithful to our alliance despite my conduct toward her. I was not wrong when I asked my brother Lome to command the evacuation of the Open Hand. He gave his best to the task. I was not wrong when I put my life in the hands of Magister Astride and her wielders of earthquake. I was not wrong when I required my brother Jaspid to remain with me until the time came when only his unmatched skills would suffice.

"Above all, I was not wrong when I heeded Queen Estie's voice in my mind. At first, I heard it wrongly. I did not have it in me to believe that her heart remained open. But she spoke to me again, and yet again, trusting me despite my reluctance. And as she persisted, the wall that I had erected against her cracked. In the end, I *heeded* her."

King Bifalt paused again. When he continued, he spoke like shouting.

"You have gathered here to honor all those who endured suffering and bloodshed for your sake. I give you Commander Forguile and Captain Flisk. I give you General Klamath, Elgart, and the el-Algreb. I give you Prince Lome and Prince Jaspid." His voice shook. "I give you the Magisters of Belleger and Amika, who fought in every battle without regard to their own safety. I give you all of the most holy devotees, wherever they may be.

"With my whole heart, I give you Queen Estie of Amika, who provided our only chance for victory."

All around him, the people of the Last Repository were utterly still. None of them seemed to breathe.

Their silence suited him. Perhaps they expected him to say more. He did not. Instead, he turned away and left the center of the hall, heading toward his wife.

Behind him, a few people started talking. Their voices were soft, gentle. They fell into the hall like scattered raindrops. But the sound became a mild drizzle. Then it grew louder. Soon it resembled a downpour, resounding against the walls of the refectory, multiplying itself until it seemed to fill the Last Repository. It was an ovation.

King Bifalt ignored it. Queen Estie's radiance drew him like a lodestone.

When he could stand so that no one else would see his gestures, he told her:

—I want you.

In the same way, she answered:

—Then come with me, beloved.

Holding his arm with both hands, she drew him out of the storm.

Together, they went to discover who and what they had become.

ACKNOWLEDGMENTS

I want to thank BrandyEileen Alatt and Terry Mulcahy for their prompt and insightful readings of this book's various revisions. Their help improved the telling of this story.